D1078034

THE
MEMORY
CATHEDRAL

Jack Dann is the author or editor of over forty books, including the novels *Junction*, *Starhiker*, and *The Man Who Melted*. A German edition of *The Memory Cathedral* has recently been published and several more foreign language editions are due shortly. Jack Dann lives in New York and Australia. He is at work on a new novel, set during the American Civil War, entitled *The Silent*. His forthcoming anthology *Dreaming Down-Under* (edited with Janeen Webb) will be published by HarperCollins.

£6.00
fiction. (37)

THE
MEMORY
CATHEDRAL

A Secret History of Leonardo da Vinci

JACK DANN

flamingo

Flamingo
An imprint of HarperCollins *Publishers*, Australia

First published by Bantam Books 1995
First published in Australia in 1997
by HarperCollins *Publishers* Pty Limited
ACN 009 913 517
A member of the HarperCollins *Publishers* (Australia) Pty Limited Group

Copyright © Jack Dann 1995

This book is copyright.
Apart from any fair dealing for the purposes of private study, research, criticism or review, as permitted under the Copyright Act, no part may be reproduced by any process without written permission. Inquiries should be addressed to the publishers.

HarperCollins*Publishers*
25 Ryde Road, Pymble, Sydney NSW 2073, Australia
31 View Road, Glenfield, Auckland 10, New Zealand
77–85 Fulham Palace Road, London W6 8JB, United Kingdom
Hazelton Lanes, 55 Avenue Road, Suite 2900, Toronto, Ontario, M5R 3L2
and 1995 Markham Road, Scarborough, Ontario, M1B 5M8, Canada
10 East 53rd Street, New York NY 10032, United States of America

National Library of Australia Cataloguing-in-Publication data:

Dann, Jack.
The memory cathedral: a secret history of Leonardo da Vinci.
ISBN 07322 57190.
1. Leonardo, da Vinci, 1452–1519 — Fiction. I. Title.
813.54

Cover illustration © Tim Jacobus 1995
Printed in Australia by Allwest Printers, Perth

9 8 7 6 5 4 3 2 1
99 98 97

In Memory of
Joey LoBrutto, Judy Roberts Vescovi,
Becky Levy, Jean Lindsley,
and my beloved father,
Murray I. Dann

The author would like to thank the following people for their support, aid, and inspiration:

Richard Alverson, Gary Barnes, the captain and crew of the sailing ship *Bounty* out of Sydney (Australia), Susan Casper, Edith Dann, Lorne Dann, Patrick Delahunt, Gardner Dozois, Greg Feeley, Jim and Louise Feeney, Keith Ferrell, Lou and Liz Grinzo, David Harris, Merrilee Heifetz, John Kessel, Rob Killheffer, Tappan King, Trina King, Bernie and Beth Levy, Mark and Lillian Levy, Joseph Lindsley, Pat LoBrutto, Barry N. Malzberg, Beth Meacham, Howard Mittelmark, Kim Mohan, Pamela Sargent (whose help was invaluable!), my son Jody Scobie, Jeanne Van Buren Dann, Lucius Shepard, Janna Silverstein, John Spencer of the Riverow Bookshop, the staff of The Bookbridge, the staff of the Vestal Public Library and the Binghamton University Library, Norman Stillman, Michael Swanwick, Bob and Karen Van Kleeck, Fred Weiss, Sheila Williams, George Zebrowski . . . and, of course, Janeen.

And special thanks to my editor, Jennifer Hershey, and publisher, Lou Aronica, for their faith and patience.

The great bird will take its first flight
    on the back of his great swan,
      filling the universe with wonders ...
                          —Leonardo da Vinci

Slowly, slowly, he swims on through space,
    wheels and descends, but I can sense it only
    by the way the wind blows upward past my face.
                          —Dante Alighieri

People in the Story

FLORENCE AND ENVIRONS

A'isheh, whore and servant of Devatdar Dimurdash al-Kaiti
Abbaco, Benedetto d', engineer, friend of Toscanelli
Achattabrigha, Leonardo's stepfather
Agostin, gunnery officer
Antonio, Medici guard

Baccino, a tailor
Baroncelli, Bernardo de Bandini, adventurer and Pazzi sympathizer
Becchi, Gentile, bishop, friend of the Medici
Benci, Ginevra de', Leonardo's lover
Benci, Amerigo de', wealthy banker, father of Ginevra
Botticelli, Sandro, artist and friend of Leonardo, apprentice to Verrocchio
Bracciolini, Giordano, author and leading member of the Platonic Academy

Caterina, Leonardo's mother
Columbus, Christoforo, explorer, adventurer, protégé of Toscanelli
Credi, Lorenzo di, artist, apprentice to Verrocchio

Dei, Benedetto, traveler, adventurer, and friend of Leonardo
Devatdar (Dimurdash al-Kaiti), lieutenant of the Caliph Ka'it Bay

Francesco of Naples, lute player

Ginevra, see *Benci, Ginevra de'*
Grosso, Nanni, senior apprentice of Verrocchio

Il Moro, see *Sforza, Ludovico*
Il Neri, nickname for Guglielmo Onorevoli

Kuan Yin-hsi, slave and mnemonist

Leonardo, see *Vinci, Leonardo da*
Luca, servant of Simonetta

Machiavelli, Niccolò, young apprentice of Leonardo
Medici, Lorenzo de', ruler and First Citizen of Florence; known as Il Magnifico
Medici, Giuliano de', Lorenzo's brother
Medici, Clarise de', wife of Lorenzo
Melzi, Francesco, student and companion of Leonardo
Miglioretti, Atalante, lute player and singer; friend of Leonardo
Mirandola, Pico della, philosopher and theurgist; friend of the Medici

Nicolini, Luigi di Bernardo, wealthy merchant and friend of the Pazzi family
Nori, Francesco, friend of the Medici

Onorevoli, Guglielmo, young patrician; see *Il Neri*

Pasquino, Bartholomeo di, goldsmith, friend of Il Neri
Pazzi, Jacopo de', patriarch of ancient family of Florentine bankers; enemy of
    the Medici
Pazzi, Giovanni de', son of Jacopo
Pazzi, Francesco de', son of Jacopo
Pazzi, Gugliemo de', son of Jacopo
Pazzi, Bianca de', sister of Lorenzo de' Medici and wife of Gugliemo de' Pazzi
Peretola, Zoroastro da, hoaxer, conjurer, and friend of Leonardo
Perugino, Pietro, artist, senior apprentice of Verrocchio
Poliziano, Angelo Ambrogini, poet and confidant of Lorenzo de' Medici
Polo, Agnolo di, senior apprentice of Verrocchio
Pulci, Luigi, poet and satirist; friend of the Medici

Raffaello, cardinal and nephew of Pope Sixtus IV
Ridolfi, Antonio, friend of the Medici

Saltarelli, Giovanni, brother of Jacopo Saltarelli
Saltarelli, Jacopo, artists' model
Salviati, Francesco, archbishop of Florence
Sansoni-Riario, Raffaello, see *Raffaello*
Scala, Bartolomeo, humanist and friend of the Medici family
Sforza, Ludovico, brother of Galeazzo, Duke of Milan; later assumed the title
    and power himself. Also known as Il Moro.
Simone, Francesco di, Verrocchio's foreman
Smeralda, Verrocchio's servant
Stufa, Sigismondo della, friend of the Medici

Tista, apprentice to Verrocchio and Leonardo
Tornabuoni, Marco, a young Florentine patrician
Toscanelli, Paolo del Pozzo, physician, astronomer, and geographer

Ugo, apprentice of Toscanelli

Verrocchio, Andrea del, artist, goldsmith, sculptor, and Leonardo's master
Vespucci, Amerigo, explorer and protégé of Toscanelli
Vespucci, Simonetta, mistress of Lorenzo de Medici
Vinci, Leonardo da, artist, inventor, senior apprentice to Andrea del Verrocchio,
    master of engines and captain of engineers
Vinci, Piero da, Leonardo's father, a notary
Vinci, Francesco da, Leonardo's uncle
Vinci, Alessandra da, Leonardo's aunt

Zoroastro, see *Peretola, Zoroastro da*

LANDS OF THE CALIPH AND THE TURK

al-Latif, Abd, master of ordnance and Mamluk eunuch
Angiolello, Giovan Maria, ambassador from Venice to the empire of the Turks

Calul, son of Ussun Cassano
Cassano, Ussun, ruler of Persia

Fāris, eunuch, Mamluk emir

Gutne, Zoroastro's slave

Hilāl, eunuch, high ranking Mamluk emir

Ka'it Bay, Caliph of Egypt and Syria

Mehmed, ruler of Turkey
Mithqal, young Mamluk eunuch
Mustafà, son of Mehmed

Unghermaumet, son of Ussun Cassano
Ussun Cassano, see *Cassano, Ussun*

Zeinel, son of Ussun Cassano

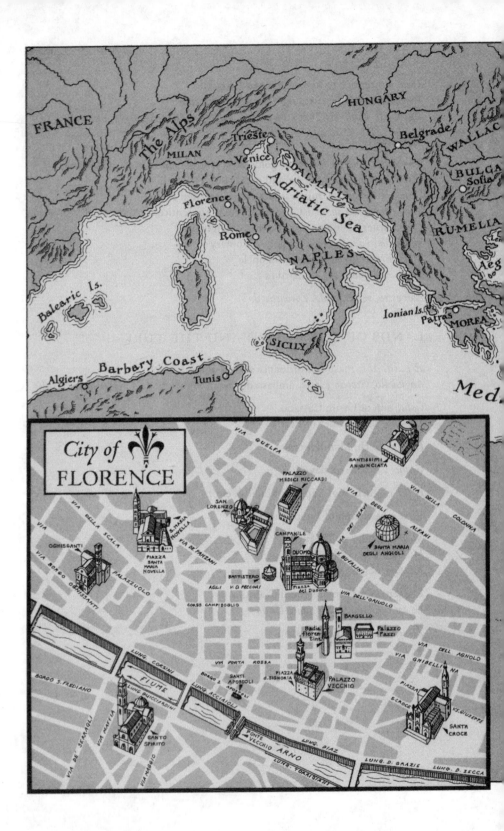

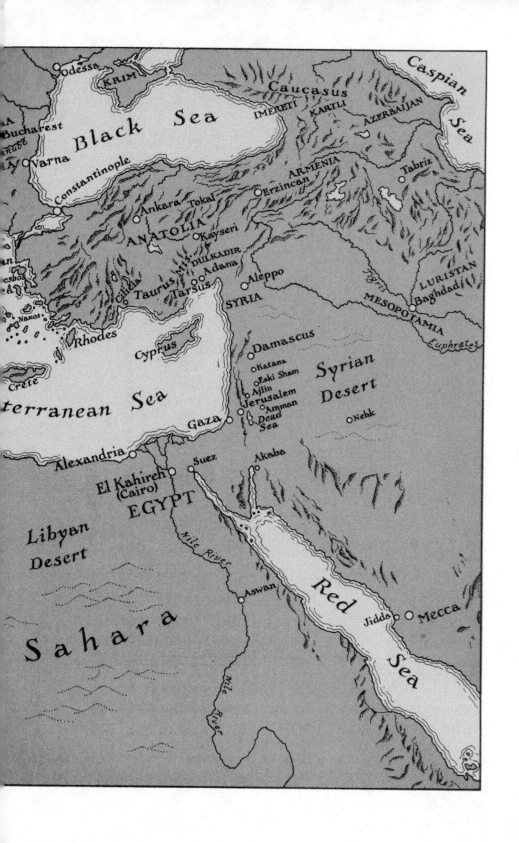

The
Memory
Cathedral

Prologue: The Memory Cathedral

In the transparent April twilight of Amboise, France, the maestro Leonardo of Vinci sat before a small fire and dropped the pages of one of his most precious folios into the orange-streaked flames. The fire sizzled as the green, unseasoned wood perspired drops that evaporated in the heat with a snap; and the pages curled like flowers closing, then blackened as they burst into flame.

Although he still had a last vestige of strength left, he could feel the nearness of death. Hadn't his right arm already died? It hung limply, resting on his knee, as if it were someone else's appendage, devoid of feeling. At least his last stroke hadn't affected his left arm; he had been able to paint a little, even though his final painting, the voluptuous and naked *St. John the Baptist,* was completed under his direction by his young student and companion, Francesco Melzi.

A wan light filtered through the high, narrow windows, refracted through the bull's-eye center panes as if they were poorly constructed prisms; in the distance, meadows and trees could be seen descending to the green glow that was the River Amase. The whitewashed walls of the large bedroom were streaked with soot from one or another of Leonardo's experiments—there had been too few of those, these days, for although Leonardo's mind was quick and still full of ideas, his body had failed him like the guy ropes of a pulley bearing too much strain. Books and papers and rolled sheets were stacked along the walls and on long desks; and scattered on the tables, and on the floor as well, were maps and papers and instruments and lenses and various gadgets of his own invention: a calorimeter to measure the expansion of steam, odd-shaped columnar flasks for his hydromechanical experiments, balances with silvery half-circular frames, a hygrometer to measure moisture in the atmosphere, cranequins, curved mirrors, and a device for demonstrating an eclipse according to ideas set forth in Joannis de Sacrobusto's *Sphera Mundi.*

All of this was concentrated in his bedroom, even though the villa of Cloux was more than spacious, with libraries, morning rooms, bedrooms, balconies, atria, living rooms, and parlors; it was a small castle assigned to Leonardo by Francis I, King of France.

Leonardo smiled as he carefully tore out page after page and fed each to the fire, but it was an ironic smile born of despair. He gazed at one of his notebook pages before consigning it to the flames. He had made this sketch during his secret sojourn in Syria, but it was done in such detail and with such care as to be a blueprint. It depicted a flying machine with long fixed wings like those of a bat; and under the skeleton of fuselage was the figure of a man in harness, his arms outstretched and hands holding devices under the wings like a Christ aloft.

He tore out the page and threw it into the fire. The one that followed was more a cartoon for a painting than a sketch; it depicted the flying machines in the air, brought to life as if seen through a glass, and above the winged craft were hot-air balloons of charcoal-black cloth: great sacs rising up toward the unknown regions of fire and the separate and successive spheres of the planets.

That, too, into the flames.

He had failed, even though he had had his terrible and glorious moment aloft when the heavens were filled with these flying machines of his own design. He remembered the chill of the air in the highest and rarest atmosphere, which was close to the sphere of elemental fire, and for one perfect instant he believed that the ancient Pythagoras was correct, that there was a music of the spheres: the impossible friction of the heavens. He had passed above the clouds, which were countries of cold breath and ice and imagination, but unlike Icarus, he did not rise too far toward the destructive sphere of fire, nor did he seek the aid of demons and receive a broken neck as his reward, as had Simon Magus.

Leonardo could remember exactly how the land had looked from the air; even now he could visualize the mountains and rivers and valleys, the fields and fortifications and villages that looked like models on a table. Below him the terror-inspiring armies of Mehmed the Conqueror—the Grand

Turk who threatened Syria and Asia Minor—were but columns of ants, and castles and fortifications were no larger than drawings.

The memories were strong and clear . . . and painful.

And he remembered . . . he remembered. . . .

He had let himself become a whore and a murderer in the employ of the Sacred Sultan of Babylon. He had killed as thoughtlessly as any brigand or thief—only he had *thousands* of tormented souls weighing upon his conscience—and all he could do now to expiate himself was burn his precious diagrams and drawings and plans so that no one else could misuse—as he had—his hard-won knowledge.

But to destroy pure and perfect knowledge was also a kind of murder.

Leonardo closed his eyes, as if that would shut out the past, but he had learned, too late in life, that memory, not sight, was the primary sense. It was memory, cold and dark and everlasting, that hung upon him like a coat of mail. Memory was all that was left of his life and endeavors, and guilt was the eye of memory, an eye that could not be closed. Leonardo's curse was that he remembered everything, for long ago his friend and teacher Paolo Toscanelli—the great physician and geographer—had taught him how to build his own memory cathedral in the great tradition of Simonides of Ceos, Quintilian, and Thomas Aquinas. A holy house of memory, from which nothing could be lost.

Leonardo tried to wrench his thoughts out of his imaginary cathedral, a place more familiar to him than the room he was sitting in, a mnemonic that had become as large and complex as a city, with various additions to house his later experience. But he could not. He could only look into the flames and see the curling pages. His work. His life. His failure.

In anger and shame and frustration, he threw what was left of the folio into the flames. This was his punishment, self-inflicted, for what he had done. Perhaps the Holy Catholic Church would forgive him . . . the same Church that he had scorned throughout his lifetime. Now, in his illness and old age, he took the Holy Sacrament from the clergy that he had once defamed as Pharisees.

"Maestro, what are you doing?" cried Francesco Melzi as he entered the room. He dropped a tray of soup and bread, ran to the fire, and tried to save the last of the pages, but it was useless.

"Let it be," Leonardo said in a calm voice. "You'll burn yourself."

"Why have you done such a thing?" Francesco asked as he knelt beside Leonardo. "We've worked so long collecting and ordering your notes."

Leonardo sighed. "Those that I destroyed were not part of the notes."

"Certainly not now," Francesco said sarcastically as he stood up. For such a seemingly placid young man, he had a temper; and as loyal as he was, there had been times when Leonardo had considered sending him back home to Milan. He was a conundrum: one moment a humble servant, almost fawning, then suddenly insolent, as if he had just remembered his privileged social position. "You made me swear to you that I would keep your folios safe, that I would not let them be sold or destroyed. And I swore because I thought they were priceless, that they would help make the world better."

Leonardo rested his head against the high back of his chair and closed his eyes. "You swore because you thought I was dying."

"And because I love you."

Leonardo nodded, accepting that. He felt a warmth in his right arm, and an itching, as if it had fallen asleep. Slowly the warmth turned to pain.

"Destroying those pages is like murder," Francesco said.

"You wouldn't talk so if you knew about murder." After a pause Leonardo said, "I promise you, though, those pages weren't part of my work. They were nothing more than divertissements, and of no consequence." As he talked, the pain worked up his arm to his shoulder like cold water flowing, impossibly, uphill, coursing through him, leaving a wake of numbness behind it. Leonardo made no outward reaction; that death would stretch out to him came as no surprise. Yet he was not ready for it, nor would he ever be, for he had not even begun to understand the stuff of the world and the heavens.

"That's a lie," Francesco said, incensed as only someone of his age could be. "Those were your notes for flight. I read them. I know that you have flown in the air, I read all the notes. And the letters."

Leonardo opened his eyes. Had Francesco searched through all his drawers and closets for notes on scraps of paper? "All fabulation," he said. "A story to entertain a king."

"For *Francis*? I have been with you when you spoke with the king and—"

"It was for Ludovico Sforza's entertainment, my young disbelieving friend, and that was some thirty years ago. I wasn't much older than you. When I discovered that His Most Illustrious Lord had no interest in my proposals for instruments of warfare, I was put in the embarrassing position of maintaining my position with the court through my facility with the lute and my talent for storytelling. He was not so much impressed with my skills of invention and architecture and painting. Ludovico Il Moro was a man without patience and of limited intellect, but he did love music and high tales. Do you remember my telling you of the lyre I had constructed of silver in the shape of a horse's skull?"

Francesco nodded, as if against all his better judgment. He was obviously frustrated with his master, who seemed to be musing to himself. Leonardo's usually sonorous voice was low, almost a whisper.

"He brought me into court on the basis of that instrument, he loved it so. And I became little more than a designer and inventor of toys for his grand masques and festivals and weddings. You've read my notes for the *Il Paradiso,* which I devised for the wedding of Duke Galeazzo? For that I invented a pulley to elevate the Sacred Nail." Leonardo warmed to the story, and the pain in his arm and shoulder subsided, as if discourse and deception were the cure; but he felt suddenly chilled.

Yet he did not feel like a dying man. Perhaps once again he had eluded the scythe.

"I've read your letters to the Devatdar of Syria. I know of the earthquake and the great Mamluk invasion and your hempen bombs and—"

Leonardo chuckled, forcing it a bit. "All bullwash. I was never in the Orient. Stories for Il Moro, entertainments, ideas I gleaned from traveling monks and explorers and slaves from Nubia and Russia and Circassia."

"But all those drawings and inventions and notes . . . ?"

"I would dress in disguise and read them to Il Moro and his friends over table every week. And I would show them the sketches and cartoons and diagrams. They loved it."

"Master, I cannot believe this. If it was true, why, then, didn't you burn the fables we collected?"

"How do you know I don't intend to do that very thing?" Leonardo asked, a hint of gentle mocking in his voice. He was wearing a white damask gown; its smoothness and plainness seemed to accentuate his pale, graven face and the strong, almost harsh, features that the gravity of years had pulled downward.

In his youth Leonardo's angelic face had been the model for some of Verrocchio's most sublime sculptures. But now age lines divided and scoured his face, as if it were a tabula rasa that had been attacked during the long night by a demon experimenting with silver point. Leonardo's once soft, almost feminine, mouth had hardened, the corners of the thin upper lip curving down, their lines extended by the growth of his long, flowing white beard. But with age his eyes had become his most arresting feature; they took friends, courtiers, and kings by surprise. They were pale blue and set deeply into his proud, worn face, giving the unsettling impression that he was a robust young man wearing a Greek mask.

But just now the face was still, the eyes somehow dim and focused on some perspective point burning in the hearth before him. After a pause he said, "No, I shan't burn any more pages." Again he chuckled, ironically, as the pain returned with greater strength than before. But he kept up the ruse. As if this were another production staged for Francis, Ludovico Sforza, or the ingrate Lorenzo de' Medici. "The work is too important. That's why I entrusted my estate to you."

"Then why?"

"I burned what was frivolous and dangerous, for the substance of my life's work must be taken seriously. The fables are legitimate art, not sleight of hand. But *you* believed I had secretly been to the Orient, didn't you? And so would others. If it were discovered that all of that was fabulation, and discovered it would be, then none of my work would be taken seriously. If a prince had one of my machines of fancy constructed, and the flyer fell to his death like Icarus, as he certainly would, I would be remembered as just another prestidigitator and charlatan, such as my old companion, Zoroastro da Peretola, may he find his way to heaven."

"You could have simply appended a note to the folio, explained what you have told to me," Francesco said.

"Would you believe such a thing?" Leonardo felt pain coursing through his arm and shoulder and chest, as if the previous tingling and numbness had been a vacuum waiting to be filled with it.

Francesco lowered his eyes. "No. I don't believe you now."

"Then there you are, Francesco, doubting your master in his last hours. *Quod erat demonstrandum.* Now, help me to bed, young friend," Leonardo said, straining, as if out of breath, "and then call our most illustrious king's physician . . . and a priest, that I may take the Holy Sacrament." The deep, familiar pain became more insistent, and he had the curious thought that his chest would burst open as had that of a lion that he had constructed of felt and metal two years ago.

Just then he saw Francesco seemingly caught in the air, as if all motion had somehow been stopped; Francesco was bending over him in a position impossible to maintain for more than an instant. But maintain it he did, and then Leonardo watched his aristocratic young friend and servant disappear, just as one often does in a dream when scenes and personages shift without causal sequence, and he found himself standing before the memory cathedral of his own making.

The cathedral was larger and more expansive than the great Duomo of Florence or Brunelleschi's Santo Spirito. It was a church of many domes rising from an octagonal base, and around the domes were cupolas reaching upward into a pure azure Florentine sky. It was as perfectly formed as a geometrical theorem, for it was, indeed, a living structure of pure mathematics. It was pure white, and smooth as dressed stone, and was the form for all of Leonardo's ideas on architecture, the perfection he had never been able to express fully outside his mind's eye.

As he had so many times before, Leonardo entered the cathedral, but this time he was not musing or searching for an obscure fact; he was walking into the structure that contained all the treasures that were his life. Maestro Toscanelli had taught him well, for now, at the end, Leonardo had the safe haven of perfect memory with which to shut out the pain and fear of death. Toscanelli had told him long ago to construct a church in his imagination, a storage place of images—hundreds of thousands of them—which would represent everything Leonardo wished to remember.

A church for all his experience and knowledge, whether holy or profane.

And so Leonardo had learned not to forget. He caught the evanescent and the ephemeral stuff of time and trapped it in this place, all the happenings of his life, everything he had seen and read and heard; all the pain and frustration and love and joy were neatly shelved and ordered inside the colonnaded courts, chapels, vestries, porches, towers, and crossings.

He passed under large reliefs and terra-cotta roundels—each figure and line an image, a cue for memory—and through the principal doorway into the north tower. The bronzen statue of a three-headed demiurge stood before him, as if to block his passage. One of the heads was his father's: the strong chin, glaring expression, and prominent, hooked nose; cheek to jowl beside his father's face was Toscanelli's: a calm, soft visage, deep, tired eyes gazing compassionately at Leonardo; and the third head was Ginevra de' Benci's: the most beautiful face Leonardo had ever seen. As a young man, Leonardo had once burned with passion for her and was, in fact, engaged to marry her. But that was before his accusation and public humiliation.

Ginevra had the same heavy-lidded, gazing eyes as Isabella d'Este—whom Leonardo had painted as the *Mona Lisa*—although her face was rounded with youth and haloed with curly hair. But it was her mouth, pouting, yet pulled tight, that gave her a quality of both earthy sensuality and the sublime. And in life her eyes had been reflections of her red hair, as if a feral goddess had descended into the Garden of Eden.

Leonardo was looking at the faces of revealed knowledge, the subjects every university student had to recite from Gregor Reisch's *Margarita Philosophica*. Although Leonardo had never gone to university, he had read the book, remembered the frontispiece, which depicted the three branches of Philosophy: *materia,* that which is natural or material; *mens,* that which pertains to the mind; and *caritas,* which stands for love. All branched from those three heads, which stared blankly at him, as they always did when he entered their quarter to retrieve this or that bit of information.

But then Ginevra's lovely sculptured head slowly came to life, the expressive face becoming motile, the high-boned cheeks reddening as her eyes turned pale and became as unnaturally colored as he had once painted them. She turned her head, focusing on him, and smiled. And in her face and eyes Leonardo saw a reflection of himself as he had once been: selfish, sensual, self-obsessed, incapable of love. She was a cruel mirror for an old penitent.

As Leonardo approached her, his father's head came to life, as did Toscanelli's.

"What do you want here?" his father asked sternly, as if he were still a notary admonishing clients even in death.

Struck by the question, Leonardo was at a loss for an answer. The statue moved toward him, blocking his passage entirely. "There's no sanctuary for you here."

"Not for a sodomist and a murderer," Ginevra said, her eyes glassy, as if with tears.

"I was *not* a sodomist," Leonardo said, his gravelly voice rising to a shout.

"It does not matter now," Toscanelli said quietly. "Memory is for the living."

"You cannot remain here," his father said. "Only hell remains for you."

"We will guide you there," Ginevra said. "Come. . . ."

And the creature reached out to embrace him, stepping through the dark mahogany portal of the entranceway as it did so.

Leonardo fell back, barely escaping its stony grasp, and then lunged past this Geryon monster that had taken the faces he had most loved and hated.

He ran through the narthex and into the nave, through aisles divided into vaulted squares and gilt-bronze doors that led into baptisteries which contained his experiences and books and all the people he had ever seen or met, past dark windows topped with pediments that promised all his ideas for paintings and sculptures and inventions. He ran through the squares and corridors and chapels and choirs that were much more than the manifold bits of information he had consigned to memory, but were the ghostly substance of his life itself: cold walls and friezes of fear; tapestries of familial and sensual love; small chapels of security and pure, lucid meditation; and dark chambers of loathing, ambition, and guilt.

He passed through his dozens of chapels and apsidals and came to a high-columned, domed room aglow with thick wax candles. An altar seemed to rise from its antependium. High mass was being read, but the only words Leonardo could hear in the empty room were, "To God our Lord and Master and Ruler, to the Glorious Virgin Mary, to Monsignor Saint Michael, and to all the blessed angels and saints in Paradise. . . ."

An entrance to his right led into a gallery, and Leonardo shivered, knowing what it was. He had designed a mausoleum more magnificent than any before conceived, and like most of his projects, it was never built. He knew all of its terraces and doorways and sepulchral halls, each hall containing five hundred funeral urns, and each vault constructed like the Etruscan *tumuli*. The passageways were as labyrinthine as those in the pyramid of Cheops or the treasury of Atreus at Mycenae.

As Leonardo hurried through a corridor, the granite floor cold on the

soles of his feet, he passed the dark room he could not pee
that he would find himself in one of the sarcophagi he had

The revelation chilled him, but did not surprise hir
which of the passageways led out of the tomb, down the ter
into the streets of Florence, into that particularly pellucid ligix of the city of
his youth. Although he moved quickly and unerringly through the cathedral
that had taken his life to construct, through its halls and mausoleum mazes,
he could not help but pause as he passed these last rooms. How could he
break free of them, even now at the moment of death? He looked into them
and saw angels dropping fire from the heights upon armies. He saw himself
making love behind a painting of his lover, and he saw the angels who
watched him from the ceiling of a torture chamber as he sacrificed his friend
for lack of a word. He looked upon his great painting of *The Last Judgment*,
rendered in oil and varnish in the Dutch manner, and saw himself swimming through the clouds of the eternal sky with a king's slave, saw himself
floating and flying and falling in contraptions of his own design; and below
on vast seas he saw his countrymen chained to oars, drowning. He saw himself breathing underwater; and on battlefields beyond the seas, he saw his
machines shooting and exploding and cutting down soldiers. And in the very
center of the painting, as if it were all a trompe l'oeil, he saw himself smashing dead men's eyes under his fists; and saw the phantasms of heaven burning in a dying woman's eyes.

Then Leonardo found and opened the bronze door that led outside;
and as he stood on the terraced steps in the soft, almost blue light which
comes just before dusk, he could feel the cool scented breezes and see Florence below and around him.

I cannot be dead, he thought as he smelled the aromas of hyacinth,
lilies, chicken, figs, fava beans, fish, and smoke, followed by the pungent
odors of horses, feces, and urine, all the familiar smells of the city he loved.
From here he could see the great copper dome of the Duomo, and next to it
the Baptistery, and the Campanile. He was home. There the greenish-yellow
Arno flowing as if it were time itself, and the ancient walls that were the
perimeters of the city, and below him spread the chockablock buildings, the
warehouses and churches and villas and tenements, the gardens and olive
trees and ponds of meadowsweet and lily, and the castles and pillared houses
of the rich. The streets crowded with merchants and littered with refuse, the
vellum-covered windows of the buildings, the festivals . . .

Then he was walking through the streets, as a youth once again, pausing at the markets and fairs and bazaars, pushing through the crowds of
street vendors, guildsmen, beggars, and merchants of silk and satin. He
watched the tall men with fair hair and long noses and the fulsome, civilized
women who bound their hair and wore gowns of fine gold brocade and pea-

cock colors of alexandrino, verde, and berettino. The vendors hawked their wares and gossiped with customers, beggars shook and danced for a denaro, children in rags scampered and shouted and frightened the veiled wives of burghers hurrying to get home before sunset curfew.

Gossip flowed around him like warm, turgid bathwater: a Bolognese youth was arrested on the Day of San Giovanni for cutting off the tassels of men's belts, a man was hanged on the gallows but did not die and had to be hanged again, a bear owned by someone in the city gored the daughter of Giovacchino Berardi (yet she lived, thank God!), the Palagio de' Signori was struck by lightning, and a monster with a horn in its forehead and a mouth split to the nose was born in Venice.

He crossed the Ponte Vecchio, a bridge lined with the reeking stalls of blood-spattered butchers and squealing pigs.

The streets began to darken . . . and empty, and Leonardo heard the wails and cries of peasants paid to walk behind the coffin of a torch-lit funeral procession. A train of sixty peasants marched through the streets, a few of them stopping by the little wickets of great houses and palaces that fronted the street to buy a flask of sour wine. Such was the Florentine custom.

Leonardo knew it was he they followed, but he escaped through the labyrinth of claustrophobically narrow streets, all shadowed by arches and overhanging walls. The buildings, which smelled of moss and dampness, were like huge twilight creations, living beings, caught between infinite breaths. Their tiles and walls of broken stucco were covered with hundreds of years of graffiti, just as the skin of the slaves brought from the Orient were covered with fantastical tattoos; but Florence's chiseled runes and crude portraits and names and crosses and markers of pubescent love would survive as long as its stone.

He walked through the now desolate arcades and tile-floored passageways of the artisans' quarters, past the stalls of furriers and blacksmiths and fruit and vegetable vendors; most of the stalls were empty of goods and produce, and the shopkeepers' windows were closed for safety, for it was about seven o'clock in the evening.

He walked through the goldsmith district, passing Botticelli's workshop, until he finally came to Andrea del Verrocchio's gray *bottega,* a house and workshop of three stories in the Via dell'Agnolo. The great cathedral of Santa Maria del Fiore loomed in the distance, the greatest work of the greatest city in the world.

Leonardo had lived and apprenticed here for ten years, and during that time Verrocchio had often assumed the roles of parent, teacher, friend, collaborator, and confessor. Leonardo could hear his master's high-pitched voice, among others, through the open windows on the second floor. They were arguing about Donatello's paradox, that something may be beautiful even if it's ugly.

Leonardo could not help smiling, but his reverie was disturbed by the criers who began shouting in the empty streets.

In a few hours curfew would be lifted, although the city gates would remain closed to all but a few. Soldiers and police would be out in strength to protect the good citizens of Florence. This was Easter Eve, and at midnight sparks would be struck from the ancient flints of the Holy Sepulcher brought from the Holy Land during the Crusades, and a fiery dove would fly out of the Duomo, the great domed cathedral. The cobbled streets would overflow with peasants and citizens come to goggle in the torchlight at the grand procession of the Pazzi; and merchants and cutpurses would be plying their respective trades.

Tonight, for a few hours, the terrible grind of daily life would be forestalled, while fantasy and gaiety and, of course, danger, reigned. Such was the magic of festival, even on Easter, which was limned with reverence.

But right now it was dark, except for the yellow glow of candles flickering and guttering through the windows of the city, which created a luminous haze that seemed to float toward the star-dimmed sky.

As he pushed open the thick oaken door, which was not yet bolted, he could hear bells sounding throughout the house and studio. Verrocchio always left the door unlocked for him, as Leonardo was always late. Even though it was dark and hot and damp smelling in the hallway, Leonardo felt safe and secure once again. He bolted the door behind him and then made his way through the darkness toward the stairs; he could already smell the delicious even if slightly stale odors of figs, sweetened fruit, and roasted pheasant. But he was caught by the sudden, potent aroma of perfume....

After a long pause, Verrocchio, hearing the bells, called his name.

Leonardo was finally home.

Where it had all begun....

Behold now the hope and desire of going back to one's own country or returning to primal chaos, like that of the moth to the light, of the man who with perpetual longing always looks forward with joy to each new spring and each new summer, and to the new months and the new years, deeming that the things he longs for are too slow in coming; and who does not perceive that he is longing for his own destruction. . . .

—Leonardo da Vinci

Detail of Sandro Botticelli from
The Adoration of the Magi

Part One
Caritas

....
....
....
....
....
....
....
....
....
....
....
....
....
....

1

Fantasia
dei Vinci

Portrait of Ginevra Benci

As thou dost to me, so shall I do to thee.
—Motto of Ludovico Sforza

*L*eonardo, wait," whispered a voice in the darkness.

There was a rustling of silk and then Ginevra de' Benci's arms were around Leonardo's neck. She was a tall, fleshy girl, just turned seventeen. Her moon-shaped face, which touched his, was slick with sweat, and she had a delicious odor of musk about her.

"What are you *doing* here?" Leonardo asked. "It's hot as an oven." He kissed her hard, as if by mere pressure they would turn into spirits and pass one into the other; then he pulled her behind the stairs, which had always been his special place of safety when he had first come here as a twelve-year-old apprentice. The cedar storage closet that was now behind him had once seemed as large as a small cottage in the town of Vinci, where he was born. He wondered if the candles he had once stolen from the Painters' Guild were still hidden in the closet, along with his early notebooks.

Excited, he deftly but anxiously pulled up her chemise and silken *gamurra* overgarment and pressed her close to him. They had practiced this dance before—once in her own bedroom at her father's palace—and never tired of it.

"Stop, Leonardo, you're crushing me," she said, but she allowed him to fondle her. "I did not wait here for you for . . . this. And your master Andrea just called for you. What, then, are you going to do about him?"

"Master Andrea," Leonardo shouted, raising his chin and looking up, even though nothing but blackness could be seen. "I shall be upstairs in a moment."

"What are you doing down there, Leonardo?" Andrea called back from the top of the stairs. "Screwing one of the cats?" There was laughter from the studio, which was also the makeshift sitting room. Andrea always had six or seven cats around his *bottega;* he claimed they were more intelligent and far better company than his widowed sister or any of his coterie of poor relatives and apprentices.

Ginevra pushed Leonardo away and struck him in mock anger.

"I'm preparing something interesting for you and your guests, and I need but a few minutes to think. Be patient, old man." Leonardo had a reputation as a hoaxer and juggler and conjurer; and even if he could speak only passable Latin, he was a sought-after party guest.

"*Old man!*" Andrea shouted. "Go find a Medici to give you your bread tonight. Perhaps he'd let you live in his gardens among the statuary you've failed to help me repair." Leonardo could hear the boards creak as Verrocchio walked away and called to his friends. "Did you hear what that young snoke-horn called me . . . ?"

Leonardo embraced Ginevra, but she pulled away from him. "Papa's upstairs with Messer Nicolini. I told everyone I was going to take a nap, and I waited for you here because I have something to tell you . . . it's important."

Leonardo drew back at the mention of Luigi di Bernardo Nicolini, a business associate of Ginevra's father, who was a silk merchant. Nicolini was an old man, soured and wrinkled and balding. And very, very rich. "Yes . . . ?"

He could hear Ginevra exhale plosively, nervously, and after a pause she said, "It's about my family's . . . troubles."

"You mean money."

"Yes, but it's much worse than I had told you. Papa cannot possibly pay what he owes without selling his estate."

"Well, perhaps that might be a wise course, he could then—"

"I won't let him bring dishonor upon our family," she snapped.

"And what has all this to do with Messer Nicolini?" Leonardo asked, feeling the hot flush of anxiety. His glands seemed to open up, unleashing a rush of emotion that burned like acid on zinc. His heart was beating so that it seemed as if it were trying to find an exit through his throat.

"Messer Nicolini has offered a thousand gold florins, as a loan, so that Papa could offer a proper dowry."

"Ah, so that's it," Leonardo said coldly. "A 'loan' which would never be paid."

Ginevra did not answer.

"You would be betrothed to his son?" Leonardo asked, testing.

"To him," she whispered.

"That's what I thought. The filthy old pig. And what about us, or is that of no consequence to you?"

"I've got a plan, Leonardo," Ginevra said quietly.

Yet it was as if Leonardo did not hear that. "But surely your father knows how we feel about each other."

"No, he thinks we are dear friends, that's all."

"But you were going to tell him, that's what we had discussed—"

"I couldn't."

"Because I'm a bastard."

"Because you're poor . . . right now. And he's in debt to the hilt."

"Surely he can borrow—he's a man of substance."

"It's gone too far. Which is why I told him we were only friends and that I would consider Messer Nicolini. Papa loves me, and he's also nervous that I'm already seventeen and unmarried."

"Then that settles it," Leonardo said, feeling himself turning cold, numb.

"It settles nothing, Leonardo. Don't you understand? It's a trick, like one of your conjurations. Once Papa receives the money, once the intermediaries are appointed, I'll tell him I love you. I'll tell him that I didn't realize it before, and that I simply cannot go through with such a marriage."

"By then it will be too late," Leonardo said, feeling relieved yet humiliated. In the vacuum left by the easing of his anxiety, his temper rose, but he couldn't turn away and give vent to his anger—not yet—for if he did, he would surely lose her altogether. "Your father would certainly have to return the dowry money to Messer Nicolini, at the very least. There would be scandal."

"By that time Papa's affairs would be in order. He could pay back the money. He just needs time." She laughed softly, but it sounded forced. "There would be no scandal, dear Leonardo, for what man would admit that he made a gift of a dowry as a 'loan' in order to procure his bride?"

"I don't like it at all," Leonardo said, swallowing bile.

"I know how you must feel, but it has to be," Ginevra said. "You can make excuses to your friends, tell them you've tired of me. With your past reputation, that would not be difficult for them to believe. But I've no choice in this matter." She was controlled; Leonardo knew he would not be able to persuade her. "I love you, but my family must be first . . . until we are married, and then you will be my entire life. I promise you that."

Leonardo could hear the sliding of silk as she raised her chemise and moved toward him. She loved excitement and danger, and as much as he loved her—and he knew that all else notwithstanding, she loved him, too—he also understood that *she* was dangerous. But she overwhelmed him. She was his first love, as he was hers. "I do love you," she said. "It tears at me every moment, wanting you. I won't marry him, I promise you." Leonardo wanted to believe her; after all, she had always prided herself on her honesty. She thought of herself as a man in that respect, for by her lights honesty was the bridle of honor. This ruse must be difficult for her. Yet he felt as if he were sinking in sand.

She pressed herself against him, fondled him, and became the aggressor; and he, for his part, touched those secret places which she had once told him most pleased her, massaging her until she finally opened herself to him as they knelt on the dusty, cobwebbed floor, and he felt as if he were water washing and flowing and pouring and crashing on flesh as smooth and hard and pure as stone.

Leonardo left Ginevra to make her way up the back stairs to Master Andrea's bedroom, where she was supposedly sleeping, while he made a grand entrance into the inner workshop. This room was almost free of the dust that permeated the outer rooms, where castings were filed and canvases gessoed. He was dressed as if he were on fire, wearing a doublet of heliotrope and crimson over a blood-red *camicia* shirt. The fabrics were rich velvets and linens. Leonardo was tall and well built; he could wear the tight-fitting garments created to delineate the Greek ideal of muscle and body shape. But he would not wear his heart on his sleeve like a peasant in mourning. He smoothed his fingers through his tangled auburn hair and theatrically stepped into the room.

Andrea had invited a robust and august company of men to what had become one of the most important salons in Florence. The many conversations were loud, and the floor was stained with wine from bottles that had been set on it for lack of a convenient table and kicked over with a misplaced step.

The aged Paolo del Pozzo Toscanelli, who had taught Leonardo mathematics and geography, sat near a huge earthenware jar and a model of the lavabo that would be installed in the old sacristy of San Lorenzo. A boy with dark, intense eyes and a tight, accusing mouth stood behind him like a shadow. Leonardo had never seen this boy before; perhaps Toscanelli had but recently taken this waif into his home.

Beside Toscanelli sat his students and protégés Amerigo Vespucci and Benedetto Dei. Vespucci, a tall, lanky, awkward-looking young man, grinned at Leonardo, for they had been students together. Leonardo's fellow apprentices stood near the walls, discreetly listening and interjecting a word here and there into conversations. Normally, Master Andrea cajoled the apprentices to work—he had long given up on Leonardo, the best of them all, who worked when he would—but tonight he had closed the shop, as it would soon be festival. Lorenzo di Credi, who always looked as if he had just awakened—nodded in greeting, as did Pietro Perugino. Perugino was senior apprentice and was about to go out and become the master of his own *bottega*.

"Come, Leonardo, you must help us out," called Verrocchio. "We've been waiting for you to astonish us with one of your 'miracles,' but first you must help us decide a philosophical disagreement." Verrocchio, who was thirty-three, portly, and could pass for a priest with his full, clean-shaven face and dark gown, was standing with Amerigo de' Benci, Ginevra's father, and his associate Nicolini.

Just outside that immediate circle stood Sandro Botticelli, a favored guest at Verrocchio's studio. Although Leonardo did not see him as often as he did the other apprentices, he considered Botticelli his closest friend . . . his only friend. Sandro in certain aspects looked like a younger version of Master Andrea, for he had the same kind of wide, fleshy face, but Botticelli's jaw was stronger, and while Verrocchio's lips were thin and tight, Sandro's were heavy and sensuous. Yet it was Botticelli who strained toward asceticism, even though his work was lush and vibrant.

Sandro squeezed Leonardo's arm; Leonardo reciprocated with a smile. But though he tried to appear confident and convivial, he found it difficult to concentrate. His breathing was also ragged, as it always was when he was upset. He greeted Master Andrea and Amerigo de' Benci, feigning the warmth he would normally have felt, and nodded to Nicolini. The older man had a strong, lined face, and ears that would have made an elephant proud, or so Leonardo thought. Although he would be considered handsome by some, Leonardo found him repellent.

"I'm not a philosopher," Leonardo said, answering Verrocchio. "I'm merely an observer. You should rather have invited Messer Ficino, or any one of the brilliant gentlemen of his academy, who have a most profound knowledge of what dead men have said."

The gibe at the humanists did not escape Toscanelli, who had a habit of feigning deafness so as not to be interrupted in his studies, but could hear well enough now. Unlike Leonardo, who was ostracized because he could not converse fluently in Latin, Toscanelli had strong ties to the Platonic Academy. He considered Marsilio Ficino's recent and popular *Theologia platonica* to be on the level of Plato's own works. Leonardo had argued that it was frivolous and a waste of ink and paper.

"You will enjoy this, Leonardo," Toscanelli said sarcastically, "for it's quite 'frivolous.' " Benedetto Dei laughed at his master's remark, Amerigo Vespucci smiled faintly, but the boy standing behind Toscanelli stared intently at Leonardo, searching. And Sandro just watched, seemingly unconcerned with everything going on around him, yet waiting . . . as if he were soon to come onstage.

Nicolini, however, turned to Toscanelli and said, "I would not consider a discussion of the very stuff of the spirit to be frivolous."

Toscanelli merely nodded at the man.

Ginevra's father smiled at Leonardo and said, "We are having but a friendly theological argument about spirits, which my friend Luigi di Bernardo Nicolini believes can be nothing else but separated souls. But Plato says nothing whatsoever about the condition of souls in a state of isolation from the body."

"But he does say that the soul is itself the principal of motion," Nicolini said. "The soul has always existed and is independent of the material world. And such isolated souls, or spirits—whether they be divine or demonic—can certainly manifest themselves in our mortal realm. They are simply not dependent upon matter, as we are. Does an angel need to drink, or to eat? No more so than a ray of light needs a pot of porridge to shine.

"We are but instruments in their conflict of good and evil. Would you believe that Satan could not make himself known to us in this very room because he is not mortal? Would you not have Christ on the Nail because—"

"But, my friend," Amerigo de' Benci said, "Christ partook of both the mortal *and* the eternal."

"Exactly! But, then, would you confine the Holy Ghost?"

"Well, Leonardo," Verrocchio asked. "Can you resolve this matter?"

"Begging everyone's pardon," Leonardo said, "but I must agree with Messer de' Benci. The spirit, by definition, must be invisible in substance, for within the elements there are no incorporate things. Where there is no body, there must be a vacuum, and no vacuum can exist in the elements because it would be immediately filled up. Thus a spirit would continuously generate a vacuum and inevitably be constantly flying toward the sky until it quitted the material world, which is why we find so few spirits hereabouts." That generated laughter and scattered applause; everyone was listening now.

"And why must the spirit be invisible in substance?" asked Nicolini, obviously over his head here. He stood tall, as if he could win the argument by posture alone. "The spirit is true substance. It can inhere in any form."

"Then it would be wrapped in mortal flesh, as we are," Leonardo said. "No one would argue that with you. But unless that is the case, the spirit would be at the mercy of the slightest wind; and even during the instant when it might appear to you, how could it talk?

"The answer is that it could not. A spirit cannot produce a voice without movement of air. And air in it there is none, nor can it emit what it has not." Leonardo bowed. Again there was applause.

Nicolini shook his head slightly and gazed at Leonardo imperiously. "I believe there is an edge of blasphemy here, young sir."

"I believe the word you're looking for is 'logic,' Messer. I think neither God nor Plato would take argument with that."

"Where's our Ginevra?" Amerigo de' Benci asked, changing to a more agreeable subject.

"Most likely still napping," Andrea said. "It's unseasonably hot for Easter Eve. I'll have one of the apprentices awaken her. Tista!" he called to a blond-haired boy who was leaning against the wall. "Go to my bedroom where Madonna Ginevra is taking her rest and knock softly, softly mind you, on the door. Tell fair Penelope that her suitors are impatient for her presence."

The boy blushed with embarrassment and quickly left the room.

Nicolini softened and said, "And like Odysseus must I fall on them hip and thigh with arrow and sword?"

"Perhaps later, but first you'd best put a ring on her finger," Amerigo de' Benci said good-naturedly.

Leonardo felt his ears burn, but angry and mortified as he was, he prayed that no color would come to his face to reveal him. Once again Sandro clasped his arm affectionately. He knows, Leonardo thought.

But no more than a minute had passed when Ginevra de' Benci, wearing a silken, crimson *gamurra* with a brocade of gold flowers and sleeves of pearls, entered the room. She wore a very narrow turquoise cape, which was no more than a scarf, and her long red hair was pulled away from her pale, soft face. Tight curls framed sleepy eyes and the high cheekbones that gave her a haughty air. She wore no rouge on her lips, nothing to detract from her eyes, which mirrored the highlights of her hair. She smiled at everyone, obviously pleased and used to being the center of attention. As she postured, her lower lip pouted affectedly—or so Leonardo thought. Everyone else was enchanted.

She met Leonardo's gaze, and for an instant there was a knowing, a sharing, and Leonardo saw into her. She was only acting; and he, if he ever hoped to master and possess her, must do the same.

"May I make the announcement?" Ginevra's father asked Andrea.

"Why, certainly," Andrea said, and called for everyone in the room to listen.

"It is my pleasure, dear friends," Amerigo de' Benci said, "to announce the engagement of my beautiful daughter Ginevra to my friend and associate Luigi di Bernardo Nicolini. You are all cordially invited when we welcome the bride to her new home, which will, of course, be Our Most Illustrious Lord's magnificent family palace. And we guarantee it will be a grand affair!

"I would also like to announce," he continued, once the applause had ebbed, "that we are going to commission a portrait of my beautiful daughter to commemorate her impending marriage." He turned to Leonardo. "I have made all the arrangements with Master Andrea for you to do the painting. Will you accept?"

Leonardo felt Sandro gently pressing against his back with two fingers and said, "Yes, of course, Messer de' Benci. I would be honored."

Again there was applause, for Leonardo already had a reputation in Florence as one of her most promising painters. It was rumored that he would soon be out of Verrocchio's *bottega* and the master of his own.

"No one else can paint like Leonardo," Ginevra said. "Except perhaps Sandro, a little bit," she hastened to add, smiling at Botticelli.

"I certainly do *not* paint like Leonardo," Sandro said with mock petulance. "He and Paolo Uccello . . . all they care about is perspective. For me, I can do such landscapes by throwing a sponge filled with pigments at the canvas and get on with the important work of the painting."

Leonardo did not take the bait. Instead, he looked at Ginevra, but she averted her eyes from his; and in that instant he was certain that she didn't love him. Yet he *knew* that wasn't true. It was only his emotions turning against him. How could he expect her to face him?

"Leonardo, you must now call me Amerigo, just as your father does," Amerigo de' Benci said as he drew his daughter close to him. "After all, you are now our family painter." Ginevra then smiled at Leonardo tentatively, but she looked suddenly pale, as if she were going to faint.

"Are you all right, Ginevra?" Leonardo asked, wishing to embrace her and stop this charade.

"Yes," she said, warning him. "I'm fine." She looked at her father and elderly fiancé. "Truly, I'm *fine*!"

Then Nicolini pulled her to him possessively and whispered in her ear. She shook her head to his question, but he held her close nevertheless. He gazed sternly at Leonardo for a few seconds, as if he were establishing that he, and only he, possessed her. Leonardo was angry and humiliated, but he looked away.

The crowd pressed in on Ginevra, her father, and Nicolini to offer congratulations. Ginevra was animated and vivacious once again. Amerigo de' Benci shook hands with friends, accepted their felicitations, and then said to Leonardo, "Your father regretted that he couldn't attend this fete, but he's out of town on business for the Signoria."

"Ah," Leonardo said, nodding, as well-wishers crowded and elbowed around him. He had no idea of his father's whereabouts these days, since Ser Piero da Vinci had taken a third wife, the young Margherita di Guglielmo, who Piero hoped would give him a legitimate heir. Although his father was always gracious and proper at family gatherings, Leonardo knew he had become unwelcome in his father's house—especially now, as Margherita was with child.

Leonardo gladly allowed Sandro to remove him to a less crowded corner of the studio. He took a draught of the heavy, tannin-pungent wine Sandro proffered. "So it seems you've let Ginevra go," Sandro said.

Leonardo nodded noncommittally.

"Better to be free," Sandro continued, smiling. "After all, you've got a reputation to uphold."

"Indeed, I do," Leonardo said, pouring himself more wine.

Then Sandro leaned toward him. "Do not fear embarrassment, my friend. Those who love you will know, and other acquaintances will either assume you've dropped her for another, or they'll assume you decided to cast her off in favor of a proper dowry."

"I appreciate your support, old friend," Leonardo said. "But one must remember that Ginevra is marrying one of the richest men in all Florence. I'm afraid that not even you could persuade our friends and acquaintances into believing that I dropped her. No more so than you could persuade them that a rooster lays eggs."

"Well, there have been rumors," Sandro said. "How could there not be? Everyone loves and respects Amerigo de' Benci, but even his friends aren't deaf and dumb to the whispers of . . . commerce."

Leonardo smiled bitterly. So the rumors have already made their way into the street.

"I know how much you care for her," Sandro continued. "But we will all play along, I can guarantee you of that. You've gudgeoned your way through unfortunate situations before on sheer bravado . . . you've never suffered a scarcity of that. And that's what you need to do now."

"Sandro," Leonardo asked, "what do *you* believe?"

"I believe she loves you, but she's trapped. That's not so unusual in these times."

"She *will* marry me," Leonardo insisted, but he regretted the words even as he said them.

Sandro seemed taken aback. Recovering, he said, "In the meantime, it might be a welcome change to have you around for a bit. You've become somewhat boring since you've been captured by Cupid. It might do you good to carouse with your friends once again . . . only to keep a proper face to the public, of course." Sandro's grin was infectious.

"Of course, you're right," Leonardo said. "And my thanks." There would be vindication enough later when he won her back.

"Posh," Sandro said, "but I would advise against consuming any more of Master Andrea's local wine, or you'll be shitting your pants."

Sandro was referring to underpants, for Leonardo's doublet was rather short and revealing. "Not to worry," Leonardo said. "I'm not wearing any."

"So that's why your bows are so shallow," Sandro said, breaking the tension. Nevertheless, Leonardo felt as if everyone was laughing and whispering about him, as if he were the cuckold. A part of his anger at what Ginevra had done had turned into an icy lump in his chest.

He resolved that as soon as festival was over, he would bury himself in his work. He had an important commission to complete for an altarpiece in the Chapel of St. Bernard, two paintings of Our Lady in various stages of completion, and he had designed his Great Bird, which needed to be made ready for its first flight.

He had more than enough with which to occupy himself.

———

There was a tinkling of bells all over the studio and the muffled pounding of the great iron door knocker. The bell system was an invention of Leonardo's, for Master Andrea could never hear the door and was always worried that he would give offense to one of his important patrons.

"Who could that be at this time?" Verrocchio asked, and sent one of the apprentices down to investigate. A moment later a breathless boy announced that a party of most illustrious lords and ladies were waiting downstairs, namely the brothers Lorenzo and Giuliano de' Medici, who ruled Florence. But even before Verrocchio could hurry downstairs to greet his most important guests, Lorenzo could be heard singing his own composition loudly off-key as he climbed the stairs:

> Come, be gay
> While we may
> Beauty's a flow'r despised in decay;
> Youth's the season made for joys,
> Love is then a duty. . . .

He and his brother Giuliano entered the room first, puffing and laughing and then starting another verse. Lorenzo, who was in reality the First Citizen since the death of his father Piero the Gouty, loved divertissements, and wherever he went, so went his circle of wits and poets and philosophers. And Lorenzo was a genius as a poet: he wrote *ballate, canzoni di ballo,* and *canzoni carnascialesche.* He influenced the entire artistic life of Florence. He also loved licentious verse and plays and masques and banquets, and the Florentines loved him, for he had so often turned the city into carnival for them.

"Aha," Lorenzo said as he entered the room. "My painter Andrea has a party, but does not invite us. And who, I ask you, could love you more than the Medici?" Lorenzo gesticulated with his arms at Andrea and then hugged him as if, indeed, Andrea was family.

Lorenzo was magnetic, captivating, charismatic, and ugly. He was dressed informally, but richly, *in zuppone* . . . in shirtsleeves. The peasants and burghers in the streets for the parade tonight would consider him one of their own. His face was coarse, overpowered by a large, flattened nose. He was also suffering one of his periodic outbreaks of eczema, and his chin and cheeks were covered with a flesh-colored paste. He had a bull neck and long, straight brown hair, yet he held himself with such grace that he appeared taller than the men around him. His eyes were perhaps his most arresting feature, for they looked at everything with such friendly intensity, as if to see through things and people alike. His brother Giuliano was, on the other hand, extremely handsome, with a slightly girlish face and brown curly hair.

Standing beside Lorenzo and Giuliano were Angelo Ambrogini Poliziano, poet and philosopher and close friend of the Medici, and the fantasist and poet Luigi Pulci. Ludovico Sforza, the brother of the Duke of Milan and a guest of the Medici, stood beside the beautiful Simonetta Vespucci. It was rumored that she was Lorenzo's mistress, but no one could be sure; Giuliano was certainly infatuated with her.

"Pray God that Simonetta is not with that pig Sforza," Sandro said. "His brother loves nothing better than corpses. Rumor has it that he nailed his latest peccadillo inside a chest while she was still alive, and then sat vigil himself until he heard her death rattle. Would you think his brother to be of different blood?"

With that, Sandro left Leonardo and rushed toward Simonetta. It was no secret that he, too, was in love with her. She had become an obsession with him, and Leonardo wondered if Sandro could paint anyone's face but hers, for she seemed to appear like a signature in all his latest work. She was a Florentine Venus, the most admired woman in the city. Women admired her as much as men, for she was gentle and ethereal, a paragon of worldly virtue and classic beauty. She did not color her eyebrows, which were all but invisible, and that gave her face an expression of constant surprise. Wearing a revealing silk slash-sleeved gown of Venetian style that showed off her pale skin and ample bosom, a gold-and-sapphire necklace, and a matching headband in her luxuriant yellow-blond hair, she was fashion itself.

She looked directly at Leonardo and smiled.

Sandro Botticelli, who was an intimate of the Medici, hugged Giuliano and did a dance with Lorenzo, showing off for Simonetta, who allowed him to embrace her.

"So, Andrea," Lorenzo said to Verrocchio, "I see you have your musician in residence."

"Ah, you mean my apprentice, Leonardo?" Andrea turned to look for Leonardo and impatiently beckoned him to join their party. "He's working with me in your gardens, repairing your statuary."

"So I understand," Lorenzo said, smiling at Leonardo. "He has an abundance of God's gifts, yet one hears that his curiosity sometimes deflects him from his commissions. I understand that the good monks of St. Bernard are getting impatient for your brilliant work to continue on their altarpiece. But, you see, dear Ludovico," Lorenzo said, patting his guest on the shoulder, "that's what happens when God is profligate with his gifts." Then he spoke directly to Leonardo. "I understand that you've constructed a lyre that is like no other. That's why we came . . . and also to see our dear friends, of course. But the lovely Simonetta wished to see this miracle and hear you play. What can we do but obey her command?"

Leonardo bowed to his patrons and was introduced to Ludovico, who was square-framed and heavy, with olive skin and dark hair that was singed so it would lie like a polished helmet on his head. Simonetta took Leonardo's hand and, while others looked on jealously, said, "Come on, Leonardo. Show us this instrument of yours."

Just then two youths appeared behind Leonardo; both were about his age. The taller one, who had thinning black hair, sallow skin, and deep-set blue eyes that seemed as hard as pebbles, held a package covered with purple velvet cloth. His name was Tomaso Masini, but he liked to call himself Zoroastro da Peretola and had made the spurious claim of being the illegitimate son of Bernardo Rucellai, who was a distant Medici. He was dressed like a dandy, albeit an incongruous one, in orange and black dags, doublet, hose, and codpiece. The other boy, who was a bit older than Leonardo, was Atalante Miglioretti. He was shy, and like Leonardo, a bastard, but also one of the finest lute players and singers in Florence.

With an exaggerated, sweeping gesture, Zoroastro da Peretola handed the package to Leonardo.

"When did you arrive?" Leonardo asked, surprised. "And how did you know to bring my—"

"One who is omniscient and omnipotent needn't answer such questions," Zoroastro said, but he would not look Leonardo in the eye, and he seemed nervous, embarrassed.

"I pray you excuse my idiotic friend," Leonardo said. Although Peretola was often the butt of Leonardo's jokes, he was a cunning weasel. He had great mechanical talent and was a brilliant goldsmith, but he fancied himself an adventurer and conjurer and hoaxer. He had learned to juggle and swindle, and although Leonardo was the master, Peretola had shown him his oft-used parlor trick of magically creating iridescent flames by pouring red wine into a saucer of prepared boiling oil. Beggars and peasants would pose for Leonardo for hours to see such a miracle.

Zoroastro *must* have hidden himself somewhere in the studio, Leonardo thought. Perhaps he had constructed some sort of listening device. . . .

"There is no need to excuse your young friend," Lorenzo said sarcastically, yet with good humor. "After all, he is a Medici, is he not?"

Zoroastro's cheek and neck reddened, but he bowed with his usual exaggerated flourish.

Leonardo glanced toward where Ginevra had been standing and

caught her jealously watching him ... while Nicolini watched her. She quickly turned to her admirers, but Nicolini gazed at Leonardo. His tight, hawkish face could not belie his anger. Feeling somehow vindicated, Leonardo pulled the lyre out of its velvet sack. It was made of silver in the shape of the skull of a horse, and it was perfectly modeled, for Leonardo had learned much from his master Verrocchio. The horse's teeth functioned as frets, which delighted Lorenzo and Simonetta especially. The dour Ludovico Sforza nodded in appreciation and said, "It is most beautiful. We always have need of such superb craftsmen in our duchy."

The import of his remark did not escape Leonardo, nor presumably Lorenzo, for whose sake the remark had been made.

"I am sure our Leonardo's sublime craft would beautify your lovely city," Lorenzo said. "But I'm afraid just now he has responsibilities and obligations here in Florence."

"And Florence is my home," Leonardo said. "It is the fount of my inspiration." That was for Lorenzo's benefit, although Sforza's invitation could do his reputation no harm in Florence. Leonardo might one day have need of a favor from this man, and he smiled at him as if Ludovico were Simonetta herself.

"Oh, please, play your lyre for us," Simonetta asked.

And so Leonardo played and sang in chorus with Atalante Miglioretti, who had a voice that was as deep and sonorous as a bell. Everyone in the room was attentive; and the song, which Leonardo had written when he was carefree and reveling in the streets every night, was especially appropriate just now:

> Let him who cannot do the thing he would
> Will to do that he can. To will is foolish
> Where there's no power to do. That man is wise
> Who, if he cannot, does not wish he could.

Simonetta clapped her hands before any of the others; and then, warming to the game, Angelo Poliziano, Florence's foremost poet, composed his own lyrics to the same tune.

> White is the maid, and white the robe around her,
> With buds and roses and thin grasses pied;
> Enwreathed folds of golden tresses crowned her,
> Shadowing her forehead fair with modest pride.

As he sang, Ginevra moved away from her party and stood beside Leonardo, who felt her anger—as if *he* had humiliated *her*. All the men bowed and made a fuss over her, as did Simonetta, who complimented her on her clothes and lovely hair. Ginevra seemed unnerved, for Simonetta seemed genuinely happy to share the attention with her. Yet although Ginevra was the more obviously beautiful, it was still Simonetta's court, Simonetta who was in control, Simonetta who could command the love of the most creative and most powerful men in Florence.

But then Leonardo, looking at Simonetta, who was blond and pale and ethereal as air, sang to her; yet he turned toward Ginevra in such a way that his words and gaze encompassed her too. For this instant Leonardo had control, as if he had wrested it from Simonetta. Just now he wasn't the cuckold, the bastard, the artist without fortune. And he sang and played his silvery equine lyre not for Simonetta, but to Ginevra:

Serene she poses, with gesture queenly mild,
And with her brow tempers the tempests wild.

When he was finished, Simonetta kissed him on the cheek; and Leonardo smelled her musky odor, not unlike Ginevra's, except Simonetta had a feral, almost male, smell about her, as if she, too, had just been making love. Then he looked at Ginevra and knew that she wanted him, that, indeed, he had nothing to fear from this chicane of hers. Ginevra's face was tight, perhaps expressing a mixture of anger and jealousy, and she touched his arm and complimented him. Her face was flushed, as it had been when they had made love in her father's house, under the very noses of the servants and family.

Just then Nicolini appeared to fetch his fiancée. Leonardo could immediately feel the tension between Nicolini and the Medici court, for Nicolini was economically and politically attached to the aristocratic Pazzi family. The Pazzi were the keenest competitors of the Medici banking business and especially hated Lorenzo, whom they blamed for closing off all political offices to them.

Introductions were made and courtesies exchanged before Nicolini could steer Ginevra out of this noble circle. He pressed her forward, a gesture that infuriated Leonardo, and whispered, "Young master, may I have a few words with you in private?"

Leonardo could only nod. He excused himself, shrugging when Sandro Botticelli asked him what was going on. Sandro followed them until Nicolini turned to him and said, "Messer Botticelli, would you do me the kindness of escorting my lovely lady to the window for a breath of air, as she complains of feeling a trifle faint? I shall certainly be in your debt, as the heat is also affecting me, and I shall have to sit here for a moment with Master Leonardo, if he will keep my company." Nicolini gestured toward two cushioned stools, and though Ginevra looked nervous, she left with Sandro. She could not afford a scene. To find a window, Sandro would have to take her out of this studio into one of the outer workshops. It seemed that Nicolini was indeed capable of dealing with Ginevra.

But Nicolini did not sit down. He stood close to Leonardo, and Leonardo could smell his fetid odor, one that not even the fine perfumed waters could conceal. He smelled ripely of sweat and decomposing food, for his teeth were decayed and unevenly spaced, although that was noticeable only upon close inspection. Yet he was not unlike most of the citizenry of Florence, patricians included; it was Leonardo who had a fetish with cleanliness and washed himself completely from a basin three times a week. "Young Master," Nicolini said, "I will speak to you of this only once. Then it shall be forgotten, as if it never happened."

"Yes," Leonardo said, a defiant tone in his voice; he moved slightly backward, away from this overpowering patrician.

"Do not fool yourself into believing I am stupid, son," Nicolini said. "I may be of mature years, but I am not deaf, dumb, and blind. Do you think that I don't know about your feelings for Ginevra, or hers for you?" After a pause he said, "Well, I know most of it." He studied Leonardo, and Leonardo, for his part, returned his unblinking stare. "I even know when you fucked her in her father's house." His voice was low and vicious. "I know you had her downstairs, not more than an hour ago, you little bastard whelp."

Leonardo could feel his face burning; Nicolini had been having him followed. His left hand moved toward the dagger on his belt.

"It would be most indecorous for you to try to kill me here," and he glanced to his right, where a burly, impeccably dressed man moved toward them, smiling. Nicolini seemed completely unruffled, as if he were used to making deals with the edge of a sword. "This is a game which you cannot possibly win. I will marry her, no matter how she might think she can scheme to favor her father and deceive me. And do you know why?"

"Are you quite finished?" Leonardo asked, controlling himself. Nicolini's henchman was standing close behind him.

"Because I love her, and I have the means to do so. You must not, nor will you, see her again, except for those times when she poses for her portrait. You can be assured I will make certain that she is properly chaperoned. If you try to see her, I will ruin you. Eliminate you, if need be. All that you *might* accomplish is to make Ginevra unhappy, a prisoner in her own home, which will be mine. Is that understood?"

"If you'll excuse me now, sir," Leonardo said loudly, ending this humiliation as best he could, "I've some matters to attend to for Master Andrea." Leonardo turned away, only to see Zoroastro watching him and smiling faintly, as if he were gloating. Yet his expression changed to concern in an instant.

"You should be more careful, Leonardo," Zoroastro said.

"What do you mean?" Leonardo asked, fighting back tears of anger and frustration.

"I could not help overhearing your conversation with Messer Nicolini."

"You mean you could not help eavesdropping," Leonardo said.

"You are my friend. I was worried. . . ."

Toscanelli interrupted the conversation by calling to Leonardo, who excused himself to greet his old teacher and the dark, thin-lipped boy who stood by his side.

"It is good to see you looking so well, and so spry," Leonardo said, but his voice sounded hollow.

"And you look as if you've seen one of those spirits Messer Nicolini was so inexpertly defending," Toscanelli said. "It is lucky for you that most of the men of the academy are better schooled in rhetoric and logic than your ancient opponent."

Leonardo smiled in spite of himself. He desperately wanted to be alone to compose himself, but he tried to concentrate on Toscanelli's small talk and forget his humiliation. After all, Toscanelli was a great man, deserving of the utmost respect. Leonardo would know little of the geography of the heavens and the world beyond Florence if it weren't for this old man.

He needed to confide in someone, but whom?

Ginevra would surely be so well guarded that she might as well be imprisoned in one of Nicolini's towers. Perhaps he could talk to Sandro, but later. And by then, with God's help, he might be sufficiently composed to handle his problems by himself.

"But I want you to meet a young man with whom you have much in common," Toscanelli continued. "His father is also a notary, like yours. He has put young Niccolò in my care. Niccolò is a child of love, also like you, and extremely talented as a poet and playwright and rhetorician. He is interested in everything, and he seems unable to finish anything! But unlike you, Leonardo, he talks very little. Isn't that right, Niccolò?"

"I am perfectly capable of talking, Ser Toscanelli," the boy said.

"What's your name?" Leonardo asked.

"Ach, forgive me my lack of manners," Toscanelli said. "Master Leonardo, this is Niccolò Machiavelli, son of Bernardo di Niccolò and Bartolomea Nelli. You may have heard of Bartolomea, a religious poetess of great talent."

Leonardo bowed and said with a touch of sarcasm, "I am honored to meet you, young sir."

"I would like you to help this young man with his education," Toscanelli said.

"But I—"

"You are too much of a lone wolf, Leonardo. You must learn to give generously of your talents. Teach him to see as you do, to play the lyre, to paint. Teach him magic and perspective, teach him about the streets, and women, and the nature of light. Show him your flying machine and your sketches of birds. And I guarantee, he will repay you."

"But he's only a boy!"

"Messer Toscanelli," said Niccolò, "I think it would be less trouble if I just stay here and try to become useful to Master Verrocchio."

"What?" Leonardo asked.

"I've taken care of it with Master Andrea that this boy remain here for the next few months. He's learned enough from me. But his talents need to be nurtured in public life; my home is too solitary a place for him."

"But you're visited by *everyone*."

"I'll take him back when you've shown him some life. He needs more than books and maps. Will you do it?"

"It might be . . . dangerous for him."

Toscanelli leaned back against Verrocchio's earthenware jar. "Good," he said, smiling. His two missing teeth could be seen only when he smiled. "But I warn you, young master, he can handle a sword as well as you. Now, talk to him," and with that Toscanelli weakly pushed Machiavelli toward Leonardo with his foot. Then he stood up, and Amerigo Vespucci and Benedetto Dei, who were standing on the other side of the room, rushed toward him. "Too much commotion here," he said to them. "Be kind enough to take me home before the streets erupt with festival."

"Perhaps we'll see you later," Benedetto said to Leonardo. "After—"

"After they've deposited this old man safely into the arms of Morpheus," Toscanelli interrupted, smiling. "Now, help me over to the Medici so that I may extend my felicitations to them and then be gone."

"We'll be meeting on the Ponte Vecchio during the procession," Benedetto said. "You must join us. Most everyone you know will be there. It will be a frolic."

Leonardo nodded, once again feeling anxious and solitary, finding himself trapped in this distinguished coterie with the boy who was put in his charge. Leonardo looked for Ginevra in the crowd, but could not see her. Nicolini was standing beside her father, Amerigo de' Benci, receiving people, as if the marriage had already taken place and would soon be consummated. Leonardo couldn't bear even to think about Nicolini inserting himself into Ginevra, yet he could not rid himself of that image flashing through his mind like bright light: Ginevra struggling while the bald, chicken-skinned Nicolini overpowered her.

As was his way, he could even visualize the room where the rape—and rape it would be—would occur: the bed would rest upon a platform of inlaid chests that served as seats and linen storage; the bedclothes would be crimson, as would be the curtains. Ginevra's hair would seem to disappear against the coverlets. Her white skin against the crimson defined; her eyes squeezed shut, as if human reality could be shut out as easily as sight. And Nicolini, his arms weak, crushing her with his weight. Nor would he need care for her comfort. He had only to bring himself to completion, as if she were some whore to be laid upon.

Finally Leonardo's head cleared. He was somehow relieved that Ginevra had left the room. Yet he had to find her. She had most likely escaped into the privacy of one of Master Andrea's bedrooms. Perhaps she was as panicked as he. Leonardo, at least, knew the house well. But the idea of searching for her evaporated as he caught Nicolini's henchman watching him.

He would have to bide his time.

Niccolò Machiavelli stood before Leonardo, staring at him expectantly, as if concerned. He was a handsome boy, tall and gangly, but his face was unnaturally severe for one so young. Yet he seemed comfortable alone in this strange place. Merely curious, Leonardo thought.

"What are you called?" Leonardo asked, taking interest.

"Niccolò," the boy said.

"And you have no nickname?"

"I am called Niccolò Machiavelli, that is my name."

"Well, I shall call you Nicco, young sir. Do you have any objections?"

After a pause he said, "No, Maestro," but the glimmer of a smile compressed his thin lips.

"So your new name pleases you somewhat," Leonardo said.

"I find it amusing that you feel it necessary to make my name smaller. Does that make you feel larger?"

Leonardo laughed. "And what is your age?"

"I am almost fifteen."

"But you are really fourteen, is that not so?"

"And you are still but an apprentice to Master Andrea, yet you are truly a master, or so Master Toscanelli has told me. Since you are closer to being a master, wouldn't you prefer men to think of you as such? Or would you rather be treated as an apprentice, such as the one there who is in charge of filling glasses with wine? Well, Master Leonardo . . . ?"

Leonardo laughed again, taking a liking to this intelligent boy who acted as if he possessed twice his years, and said, "You may call me Leonardo."

"And where will I stay . . . Leonardo?"

"That we'll have to determine," and Leonardo looked around, as if once again for Ginevra. Where was Sandro? he asked himself. Well, it *was* getting late.

Many would be leaving to gather at the Palazzo Pazzi and follow the procession led by Jacopo de' Pazzi to the Santi Apostoli, the oldest church in Florence. It was a Pazzi who had brought back the holy flints from the tomb of Christ in 1099 during the Crusades. And it would be a Pazzi who would carry them from Santi Apostoli to the Duomo for the ceremony of the Scoppio. Certainly the Medici brothers would be in no hurry to attend the procession until the holy flints were in the vicinity of the Duomo, the most magnificent church in Christendom. The church of the Medici.

The holiness of the city was dependent upon ancient and rare relics such as these flints from the Holy Sepulcher. They protected the city from disease and the ruin of war; although a church that had the Host would be called sufficient, relics and images could only help to make manifest the living presence of the Holy Spirit. *Cose sacre,* the holy things, were like magnets of holiness, and a full-bodied Florentine church housed the body of Christ, the guardian angels, and saints.

Leonardo called to Verrocchio, who hurried over to him. Andrea was delighted that the Medici had favored his *bottega* with their important and robust company this special night; his cheeks were flushed, a certain sign that he was excited. Leonardo always knew when a business transaction was going Andrea's way, for his cheeks would redden as if a handshake and verbal contract were as inebriating as wine.

"I was supposed to give you a message, but with all that's going on, I completely forgot," Andrea said. Obviously, he had no idea that Leonardo was in love with Ginevra. "Please forgive," he added.

"What was the message?" Leonardo asked.

"Sandro escorted Madonna Ginevra home. He did not want you to worry, and he wants to meet you at nine o'clock by the benches near the Palazzo Pazzi. He said not to worry because he is taking care of everything."

"That's very reassuring," Leonardo said, not without a hint of sarcasm.

"Later, perhaps tomorrow, when we are alone"—and Andrea glanced toward young Machiavelli when he said that—"we must talk. There is much I need to know and much I need to tell you. We have good news from Lorenzo."

"That could be easily guessed," Leonardo said. "But you're right, we can discuss that tomorrow. What are we to do with this young gentleman?"

"Ah, yes, Messer Toscanelli's apprentice—and how are you, young sir?"

"Very fine, Master Andrea."

"Well, firstly, I shall introduce him to Tista, our other young apprentice, who will share quarters with him."

"Did not Master Toscanelli say anything else to you about the boy?" Leonardo asked.

"Only that he is extremely bright and quick," Verrocchio said. "I'm to teach him all I can and then return him to Messer Toscanelli. He has a fine drawing skill, so perhaps his destiny is to become an artist."

"Master Toscanelli has asked me to . . . watch out for the boy."

Verrocchio laughed and said, "Isn't that a bit like putting poison in his milk?" He looked at Leonardo, who could not help grinning.

"I'll make certain he does not frequent the bagnios," Leonardo said.

"But brothels *should* be part of my education," Niccolò said earnestly. "Master Toscanelli is too old to take me, but I've gone with Messer Dei."

"Ah, so you have, have you," Verrocchio said.

"Where else can one learn about the politics of the state?"

"And who told you that?" asked Verrocchio.

"I can tell you that," Leonardo said. "It sounds like Master Toscanelli's words, but he meant them in jest."

"No, Leonardo, he did not," said Niccolò. "He said that the streets and bagnios are the best teachers, for men are vile and can always be found trying to satisfy their lusts. One need only to watch and listen to men of importance when they are in their cups. But one must also be privy to the discourse of peasants, if one is to know how the world works. And one needs protection—"

"The boy can stay in my room," Leonardo said, shaking his head yet smiling. "I'll have him ask Tista to prepare a mat for him on the floor."

"Excellent," Verrocchio said. "But I think it is time for you to perform, as it's getting late and the guests will become impatient to get into the street." He looked at Machiavelli and grinned wryly. "You did promise to do a conjuration," he said to Leonardo. "And we have important guests."

"Yes," Leonardo said. "But I'll need a few moments—"

"Everyone, listen to me," Verrocchio shouted immediately. "We have in our midst the consummate conjurer and prestidigitator: Leonardo da Vinci, who has fashioned a machine that can carry a man in the air like a bird, who can pour wine into another simple liquid and create combustion without friction or foreign fire." Then Verrocchio was, in his turn now, interrupted by Lorenzo de' Medici. Although many of the guests laughed at the idea of a flying machine, Lorenzo did not. He left his party and stood in the center of the room, nearer to Andrea del Verrocchio and Leonardo.

"My sweet friend Andrea has often told me about your inventiveness, Leonardo da Vinci," Lorenzo said, a slight sarcasm in his voice. "But how do you presume to affect this miracle of flight? Surely not by means of your cranks and pulleys. Will you conjure up the flying beast Geryon, as we read Dante did, and so descend upon its neck into the infernal regions? Or will you merely paint yourself into the sky?"

Everyone laughed at that, and Leonardo, who would not dare try to seize the stage from Lorenzo, explained, "My Most Illustrious Lord, you may see that the beating of its wings against the air supports a heavy eagle in the highest and rarest atmosphere, close to the sphere of elemental fire. Again, you may see the air in motion over the sea fill the swelling sails and drive heavily laden ships. Just so could a man with wings large enough and properly connected learn to overcome the resistance of the air and, by conquering it, succeed in subjugating it and rising above it.

"After all," Leonardo continued, "a bird is nothing more than an instrument that works according to mathematical laws, and it is within the capacity of man to reproduce it with all its movements."

"But a man is not a bird," Lorenzo said. "A bird has sinews and muscles that are incomparably more powerful than a man's. If we were constructed so as to have wings, we would have been provided with them by the Almighty."

"Then you think we are too weak to fly?"

"Indeed, I think the evidence would lead reasonable men to that conclusion," Lorenzo said.

"But surely," Leonardo said, "you have seen falcons carrying ducks, and eagles carrying hares; and there are times when these birds of prey must double their rate of speed to follow their prey. But they only need a little force to sustain themselves, and to balance themselves on their wings, and flap them in the pathway of the wind and so direct the course of their journeying. A slight movement of the wings is sufficient, and the greater the size of the bird, the slower the movement. It's the same with men, for we possess a greater amount of strength in our legs than our weight requires. In fact, we have twice the amount of strength we need to support ourselves. You can prove this by observing how far the marks of one of your men's feet will sink into the sand of the seashore. If you then order another man to climb upon his back, you can observe how much deeper the footmarks will be. But remove the man from the other's back and order the first man to jump as high as he can, and you will find that the marks of his feet will now make a deeper impression where he has jumped than in the place where he has had the other man on his back. That's double proof that a man has more than twice the strength he needs to support himself . . . more than enough to fly like a bird."

Lorenzo laughed. "Very good, Leonardo. But I would have to see with my own eyes your machine that turns men into birds. Is *that* what you've been spending your precious time doing, rather than working on *my* precious statues?"

Leonardo let his gaze drop to the floor.

"But, no," Verrocchio interrupted, "Leonardo has been with me in your gardens applying his talent to the repair of—"

"Show me this machine, painter," Lorenzo said to Leonardo. "I could use such a device to confound my enemies, especially those wearing the colors of the south." The veiled reference was to Pope Sixtus IV and the Florentine Pazzi family. "Is it ready to be used?"

"Not just yet, Magnificence," Leonardo said. "I'm still experimenting."

Everyone laughed, including Lorenzo. "Ah, experimenting is it? Well, then I'll pledge you to communicate with me when it's finished. But from your past performance, I think that none of us need worry."

Humiliated, Leonardo could only avert his eyes.

"Tell me, how long do you anticipate that your . . . experiments will take?"

"I think I could safely estimate that my contraption would be ready for flight in two weeks," Leonardo said, taking the advantage, to everyone's surprise. "I plan to launch my great bird from Swan Mountain in Fiesole."

The studio became a roar of surprised conversation.

Leonardo had no choice except to meet Lorenzo's challenge; if he did not, Lorenzo might ruin his career. As it was, His Magnificence obviously considered Leonardo to be a dilettante, a polymath genius who could not be trusted to bring his commissions to fruition. But it was more than that, for just now Leonardo felt that he had lost everything; he could afford to be reckless. Perhaps through sheer bravado might he win Ginevra from Nicolini . . . and perhaps there might be a way to perfect his flying machine for Lorenzo.

"Forgive my caustic remarks, Leonardo, for everyone in this room respects your pretty work," Lorenzo said. "But I will take you up on your promise: in two weeks we travel to Fiesole. Now, are we to see a conjuration tonight or not?"

"Indeed, you are, Magnificence," Leonardo said, and with a bow he stepped backward. "If you can be patient for but a moment, I will make manifest to you a theological argument in which I was privileged to engage our bridegroom Messer Nicolini." He raised his voice so that all might hear. "Ser Nicolini, if you will be so kind as to step forward, I shall show you . . . a soul!"

The crowd pushed Nicolini forward, seemingly against his wishes, and for the moment Leonardo had them all intrigued. No one would leave for festival yet, even though the noise filtering through walls and windows from the streets was becoming increasingly louder. Leonardo looked around the room until he saw Zoroastro da Peretola, who nodded to him and disappeared through another door.

He would need Zoroastro's help.

"May I accompany you?" Niccolò Machiavelli asked.

"Come along," Leonardo said, and they made their exit out of the studio and into one of the casting rooms. This room was used for storage. Tools and shelving and packing cases lined the walls. Sandbags were strewn about on the floor, and one had to make one's way around rough-cut pieces of stone and marble that were left near the door because the apprentices were too lazy to carry them any farther than necessary. On the far wall was a bronze statue of David with the severed head of Goliath between his feet. It was overwhelming and drew the eye away from everything else. This was perhaps Andrea's best work.

"Is that *you*?" Machiavelli asked, obviously impressed.

Indeed, it was an idealized Leonardo.

"The master was at a loss to find a decent figure for a model, so he was forced to use Leonardo," Zoroastro said, stepping into the room.

"We have no time to waste," Leonardo said impatiently as he searched through the shelving, but then he said, "At least you seem to be back to your old self."

"What do you mean?" Zoroastro asked warily.

"When you appeared before Il Magnifico, you looked nervous as a cat. What did you do, steal his ring?"

Zoroastro made a flourish with his hand, as if to produce the First Citizen's ring by magic. "What's this about a soul?" he asked, changing the subject.

"Where's that pumping device we constructed? I *know* we stored it in here."

"Ah, you're going to do the trick with the pig."

"Did you dye and sew together the intestines as I asked you?" Leonardo asked.

Zoroastro burst into a laugh. "*That's* going to be the conjured soul? Aren't we being a bit sacrilegious?" He laughed again, then said, "But yes, my friend, I did as you asked, although I never realized you'd use such a trick on such . . . valuable company."

"Just help me find what we need," Leonardo snapped.

"It's here, dear Leonardo," Zoroastro said. "I stored everything together." Then Zoroastro directed young Machiavelli to carry the pump while he lifted a brightly painted storage box. "I trust you have strong arms, young man." Then, to Leonardo, "What's the signal?"

"I'll clap my hands once." With that Leonardo left the room and made a grand entrance into the salon. The party was impatient, and Nicolini stood slightly in front of the others, a look of consternation on his face. This was obviously humiliating for the man. "And now," Leonardo said to Nicolini, "herewith a demonstration of what will inevitably happen to a spirit not protected by mortal flesh."

"Blasphemy!" Nicolini said.

Leonardo clapped his hands and threw open the door. At once an expanding milky membrane ballooned into the room. The soughing of the pump outside could not be heard over the din in the salon, for, indeed, this membrane was filling up the doorway, threatening to grow ever larger, until it fitted every nook and cranny of the room.

Leonardo stepped deftly aside, giving the expanding soul room to grow. "There, you see, it must generate a vacuum, and rise and rise. But like we mortal beings, it, too, cannot escape the confines of the physical world . . . this room!"

The party drew back, some shouting in fear, others laughing nervously. Nicolini's face drained of color as he stepped back, but it was Lorenzo who pulled a pin from his sleeve and burst the slatternly soul. There was a slight odor of paint and glue and animal fat in the air.

Lorenzo smiled and said, "Thus we dispatch this good spirit to its own realm." Nicolini pushed his way out of the room; hurrying behind him was Andrea del Verrocchio, ever the good host. But His Magnificence seemed pleased, for he had no liking for Nicolini's Pazzi connections.

"I'm looking forward to our appointment," he said to Leonardo. "A fortnight, remember."

Simonetta, who was standing beside Lorenzo and Giuliano, stepped forward and embraced Leonardo, kissing him lightly on the cheek. "You *are* a magician," she said. Then she turned to everyone in the party and said, "Isn't it time for festival? Your Magnificence?" she said to Lorenzo, indicating that he should lead the way.

And as the room emptied out around Leonardo, he felt as if a dark curtain had fallen around him, and he shivered as if he had just awakened.

2

The

Burning Dove

Lovely little bird, my martyrdom is upon me . . .
—Tullia d'Aragona

Every instrument requires to be made by experience.
—Leonardo da Vinci

The dark Arno reflected the torchlight processions that moved across the bridges. Peasants from the countryside scourged their dirt-encrusted bodies with leather and chain while their priests carried precious relics from their damp churches, guarding the bones of saints and wood chipped from a thousand Christian crosses, as they all made their way toward the wildly beating heart of Florence. So too did Florentine citizens clog the cobbled avenues and alleyways of their city, which were wildly, kaleidoscopically lit by thousands of torches.

Huge shadows leaped and crawled up the jagged surfaces of building walls and broidered doors and overhanging arches to the coffered roofs as if they were spirits and demons from the dark realms made manifest. A myriad of smells delicious and noxious permeated the air: roasting meats, honeysuckle, the odor of candle wax heavy as if with childhood memories, offal and piss, cattle and horses, the tang of wine and cider, and everywhere sweat and the sour, ripe scent of perfumes applied to unclean bodies. The shouting and laughter and stepping-rushing-soughing of the crowds were deafening, as if a human tidal wave was making itself felt across the city. The whores were out in full regalia, having left their district, which lay between Santa Giovanni and Santa Maria Maggiore; they worked their way through the crowds, as did the cutpurses and pickpockets, the children of Florenza's streets. Beggars grasped on to visiting country villeins and minor guildsmen for a denaro and saluted when the red *carroccios* with their long scarlet banners and red dressed horses passed. Merchants and bankers and wealthy guildsmen rode on great horses or were comfortable in their carriages, while their servants walked ahead to clear the way for them with threats and brutal proddings.

Rising from the torch-lit streets like minarets around a heavenly dome that had somehow been mistakenly grounded in Dante's concretions of hell, were the Duomo, the Baptistry, and the Piazza della Signoria. They were ablaze with light and festooned with flags, but their light was almost liquid, the color of warm butter. Their candles burned behind oiled vellum and clear and stained glass, a testament to the miracle of the Ascension in the Carmine; for it was Easter Eve, and Florence was not yet under papal interdict.

Leonardo made his way through the crowds toward the Pazzi Palace. The frantic, noisy streets mirrored his frenetic inner state; and he walked quickly, his hand openly resting on the hilt of his razor-sharp dagger to deter thieves and those who would slice open the belly of a passerby for amusement. Walking with him were Niccolò Machiavelli and Zoroastro da

Peretola. They walked arm in arm, with Niccolò in the middle. The boy had insisted on accompanying Leonardo. Everyone in Verrocchio's *bottega* was also heading for the Palazzo Pazzi, and left unattended, this precocious swipe would have simply taken to the streets alone in search of whores and the discourse of peasants and patricians.

They pushed their way through the crowds and finally reached the Via del Proconsolo and the Palazzo Pazzi, which was festooned with banners of blue and gold that hung below the loggia and from the balustrades. The palace, with its stylish, rusticated walls inlaid with medallions of heraldic crosses and bellicose, sharp-toothed dolphins—the Pazzi coat of arms—occupied an entire block.

The procession had already begun, for Leonardo could see the Pazzi family led by its patriarch, the shrewd and haughty gambler Jacopo de' Pazzi. He was an old, full-bodied man sitting erect on a huge, richly carapaced charger. His sons Giovanni, Francesco, and Gugliemo rode beside him. Gugliemo had been married to Lorenzo de' Medici's favorite sister, Bianca, and she rode behind in a litter of gold brocade, surrounded by a retinue of Medici retainers with the symbols of the palle and the French fleur-de-lis on their doublets; but except for these liveried attendants, the Medici were noticeably absent. All the Pazzi were richly dressed in blue and gold, and Jacopo wore a surcoat covered with dolphins worked in gold thread. Their grooms in livery wore the Pazzi colors, as did the symbolic guard of knights, which numbered sixty men in heavy armor. The procession seemed to stretch for a mile, and the entire population of Florentine clergy seemed to be part of it. Dressed in robes of black or gray, the priests and priors and monks and nuns were like sanctified spirits drifting together in the unnaturally warm night breezes. They held their tapers high, so as not to burn the citizenry crushing in on them; and the candlelight became a luminous cloud such as that which was said to have floated before the ancient Israelites to guide them through the desert.

His Great Eminence the archbishop would be waiting for Jacopo in the Santi Apostoli, which was near the Ponte Vecchio. Unlike the great Duomo, this church was no more than a parish, but it was claimed to have been founded by Charlemagne, and Giovanni della Robbia had designed its tabernacle of glazed terra-cotta. The archbishop himself held the flints from the stones of the tomb of Christ. With great pomp and ceremony, he would give these dull but sacred shards to the old man.

But they were destined for the Duomo, the church where the family Medici would be waiting. Tonight the spirit of Christ would burn within the walls of Florence, symbolized by these flints and a magical bird of fire bringing luck to the most fortunate city in the world.

"Do you see Sandro?" Leonardo shouted to Zoroastro da Peretola as he held tightly to Niccolò, lest he lose the boy in the crush. The benches were crowded, mostly with women and children, and Leonardo could not find Botticelli anywhere in the vicinity.

A middle-aged and elegant woman with finely chiseled features, who wore her dark hair twisted and wrapped in narrow veils and her sleeves folded back to her shoulder in the classical style, sat near where Leonardo was standing. She was talking angrily to a matronly woman beside her and was, obviously, a Pazzi sympathizer. All the gossip this month was focused on Lorenzo's high-handed action against the disaffected Pazzi family. Two clients of the Lorenzo family had contested the inheritance of one Beatrice Borromeo, the wife of Giovanni de' Pazzi. Her father had died intestate and she claimed the inheritance, which was a fortune. But Lorenzo had used his influence to pass through the council a retrospective law in favor of his friends. Under this new law, the estate of any intestate father passed not to the daughter, but to the nearest male relative. Giovanni's son Francesco had become so enraged over the passage of the law that he quitted Florence and was residing in Rome.

"Well, I must say that I'm surprised to see that Francesco has returned to us from Rome to be in the procession," the elegant woman said.

"You shouldn't be," said the matron. "It's his obligation to bring honor upon his family."

"Unless the Medici rescind that onerous law, there will be trouble between those families, mark my words. And don't you think that we'll all suffer, especially women."

"Ach," said the matron, sniffing and looking about. "We are made to suffer. And I think His Magnificence was peeved because his little brother lost the palio race this year to a Pazzi, that's what I think."

"Well, mark my words . . . there will be trouble."

Young Niccolò Machiavelli, who had obviously been eavesdropping on the conversation, said to Leonardo, "I don't think His Magnificence would harm an important family such as the Pazzi over a horse race, do you?"

"Come along," Leonardo said, distracted. Where could Sandro be? he asked himself. And for that matter, where was Zoroastro? He began to think the worst. Perhaps something had happened to Ginevra. Leonardo walked around the perimeter of the benches once more; the crush of people had thinned, but ever so slightly. Then he noticed that Niccolò had got away from him. He panicked, calling his name, as he pushed past a clot of twelve young men, all wearing the livery of a noble family, probably newly nominated members of a patronal confraternity: *armeggiatori*.

But these boys wore no weapons.

"I'm right here," Niccolò said, pushing his way through the young men. "I was listening to the women. They were talking about transforming their skin to eliminate their wrinkles. Do you wish to hear what they say?"

Leonardo nodded, surprised at how animated his young charge had become; but he was still distracted. Sandro was not here; he was certain of that. Now he looked for Zoroastro while Niccolò talked. Sandro should have been here.

Niccolò spoke as if all his thoughts had been pressing to pass through his mouth. His face took on the motility and expressions of a boy, rather than the tight mask of maturity that he had displayed at their first meeting. It was as if he considered Leonardo an equal, someone with whom he could feel comfortable after the long days and months of concentrated study with Master Toscanelli and his students. "These women claimed that you must take a white dove, pluck it, and remove the wings and the feet and the intestines. They must then be thrown away, after which you take equal amounts of grape juice and sweet almond oil, and however much dittany you would need for two doves, and you wash them well. Then all these things are distilled together, and the solution is used to wash the face. Although these women looked to be highborn, they could only speak such nonsense as this." He smiled disdainfully, but nevertheless it was a smile.

"Perhaps an element of what they say might be true," Leonardo said. "How can you ridicule them for ignorance until you've tested what they say?"

"But it's *nonsense,*" Niccolò insisted.

"Come along," Leonardo said, taking the boy by the elbow. "I can't wait for Zoroastro all night. Once again he's played his disappearing act. Damn his eyes!" Leonardo looked around again and thought he saw Zoroastro talking to a man who looked like Nicolini. Both men were standing near a carriage; but it was too dark and too far, and torchlight fooled the eyes.

Leonardo pressed through the crowds searching for Zoroastro and Sandro, until Niccolò shouted, "There he is," and pointed to a figure waving and calling Leonardo's name. Leonardo and Niccolò pushed toward Zoroastro.

"I saw you talking to someone who looked like Nicolini," Leonardo said to Zoroastro.

Zoroastro looked surprised. "So the stories about your marvelous eyesight aren't true, after all; you *can't* see in the dark. No, Leonardo, I could not get close to Messer Nicolini, or Madonna Ginevra. But your friend did. Look." Zoroastro gestured at the forward carriages in the procession, which were slowly moving southwest toward the Palace of the Signoria and to the ancient church of Santi Apostoli.

Leonardo searched and saw a man who might be Sandro riding in a sumptuous carriage that displayed a Pazzi banner and another of blue and white. But the flickering torchlight seemed to change the very nature of motion, as if separating cause from effect.

"It's Sandro, and the lady beside him is Ginevra," Zoroastro said. "The blue and white are colors of the Nicolini family."

"What is he doing in Nicolini's coach?"

"Nicolini himself is riding just behind the Pazzi brothers. He'll probably enter the church with them and perhaps touch the holy flints. Quite an honor."

"So you could not get close enough to speak to them," Leonardo said. Although the procession was moving at an easy pace, it was impossible in these crowds to keep up with the carriage carrying Sandro and Ginevra.

"No one can get close. The Pazzi *armeggiatori* would just as soon put a lance through my chest as spit. But Sandro saw me jumping and waving at him."

"And . . . ?"

"He shouted to me that he'll meet you at the Devil's Corner after the bird flies. I suppose he'll explain all to you there."

"What about Ginevra?" Leonardo asked impatiently.

Zoroastro shrugged.

Could it be possible that we might all be able to meet later? Leonardo thought. But surely that mutton-monger Nicolini would have a rope around Ginevra. "Did she seem well, Zoroastro? Tell me that."

"It's difficult to see, Leonardo. 'Twas a miracle that I recognized Sandro." Zoroastro paused, as if weighing what he was about to say, then said, "But she looked, I think, as if she had been crying, for her face seemed wet. But who knows? The torches create strange effects."

"I have to see her," Leonardo said, burning with rage as he stared at the procession. No one will stop me, he thought, especially Ser Nicolini; but even in his anger—which limned everything he thought and saw with the quality of nightmare—he knew he would have to bide his time.

As they made their way northward toward the great dome of the Duomo, Niccolò nattered on; his newly found freedom and the frenzy of holy festival obviously excited him. He was miraculously transformed back into a boy. "I learned more nonsense from these women," he said, craning his neck so as not to miss a single sight in the swirling, torch-lit street.

A huge horse reared up, throwing its rider onto the cobbles originally laid down by Romans; those behind him, who were part of the procession, continued on as if he were but a duffel dropped by a traveler. Although Leonardo's sketch pad hung from his hip and bumped against his leg, he did not reach for it. His thoughts passed feverishly from Ginevra to Nicolini.

"Perhaps some of it might interest you, Master Leonardo," said Niccolò, "especially their homespun formula for making a dye of any color that will tint *corni,* feathers, furs, skins, hair, and other things. You might see fit to test their superstitions." Was there a hint of sarcasm there?

Without waiting for a cue from Leonardo, he continued. "They say to take some rain, or well water, and urine from a five-year-old child, and mix them together with white vinegar, live lime, and oak ashes until the liquid is reduced by a third. Then strain the mixture through a piece of felt. After that, put some alum into the solution, add some color, which has been ground, and dip the object into the dye for as long as necessary."

Leonardo could not help listening to Niccolò, albeit halfheartedly; he stored the information in his memory cathedral as Toscanelli had taught him. He had modeled his mnemonic cathedral on the great Duomo, although his structure of imagination, when compared to Giotto's and Brunelleschi's brilliant structure that was the crown of Florence, was the Platonic ideal. It was perfection.

He stored the recipe in a niche in the baptistery, where it colored red the water of a rocaille-worked fountain that poured from the grimacing stone face of Ginevra's fiancé.

For blood was on his mind.

———

On the Via de Pecore, near the ghetto of the Jews and the tenements where whores could readily be found, and yet also close to the Baptistery and the great Cathedral of Santa Maria del Fiore, known as the Duomo, was a warning affixed to a pole. A diadem of torches illuminated the proclamation.

> The magnificent and potent Signori etc. ban and notify that since they have notice through certain Florentine citizens that a mounted *armeggeria* is to be held in the city of Florence with, as they understand, a large concourse of riders, that if any accidental case occurs in which any person, of whatever status or condition he be, is injured or killed or trampled in any way by the said *armeggiatori* with the lances and their horses on the said day or the eve of Easter in the city of Florence, no office or official of the commune of Florence will be competent, nor can form a process nor proceed against them in any way. For this has been solemnly deliberated and provided by the Signoria.

Leonardo did not pay much attention to the proclamation, other than to note it, as such signs were always affixed to poles in the streets on holy days or festivals when the brigades would ride. Yet Leonardo and his friends could barely make their way to the Duomo, even though they had left the Pazzi procession and walked directly to the church.

The crowded streets and alleys around the Via dei Servi stank of manure, and hundreds of Medicean devotees rode in *armeggeria*. The Medici procession, coming from the opposite direction as the Pazzi, slowly moved toward the cathedral. This procession was composed of brigand units of no more than twelve men each—twelve, the number of the Apostles—the law required.

The function of the *armeggeria* was to demonstrate the brigades' power. Often a clash of brigades from competing families turned festival into battle. However, more often than not, bystanders were crushed or kicked to the ground rather than the quarreling *messeres*. All the scions of the great families that supported the Medici—the Neroni, Pandolfini, Acciaiuoli, Alberti, Rucellai, Alamanni, among others—were out in force, carrying Medici colors; and Lorenzo and Giuliano, the grand signores of the collective brigands, were also on horseback. They rode identical gray horses, gifts from King Ferrante of Naples.

An advance guard of the Pazzi procession would soon be coming from the south, and their trumpets played by cordons of young pages would be heard.

"Sandro might well have put himself at risk by riding in the Pazzi procession," Leonardo said to Zoroastro as they approached the cathedral. "It compromises him, as he is a close friend to the Medici. I don't like this at all, and I worry for Ginevra especially. I hope His Magnificence can control his men, for I'm sure they would like to spill some Pazzi blood tonight."

"God forbid, on Easter Eve," Zoroastro said.

"I wasn't aware of your religious sensibility, Zoroastro," said Leonardo sarcastically.

"Few know of my profound spirituality," Zoroastro said. The hint of a smile went unnoticed in the darkness.

"I think the flints will provide sufficient insurance, for both Medici and Pazzi respect holy objects, if nothing else." Leonardo released his tight grip on Niccolò's arm. "I don't want to be looking about for you in these crowds," he said to the boy. "You must stay close to us. Is that understood?" Niccolò nodded brusquely, but his attention was fixed on the brigands and the force of feared Medici-supported Companions of the Night, the darkly dressed Dominican friars who held the informal but hated title of *inquisitore*. The brigands were sumptuously outfitted by the Medici in armor and livery of red velvet and gold. Lances and swords flashed in the ruddy torchlight. The horses were richly clad in covers of the same cloth as the riders. Over fifty torchbearers wearing blue damask and short cloaks emblazoned with the Medicean palle walked ahead of and behind the brigands, which were led by Lorenzo and Giuliano. Giuliano, ever handsome, was wrapped entirely in silver, his silk stomacher embroidered with pearls and silver, a giant ruby in his cap; while his brother Lorenzo, perhaps not handsome but certainly the overwhelming presence in the procession, wore light armor over the simple clothes he had on at the party and a large velvet cloak with the escutcheon of lilies and palle and the inscription *Le tems revient*. However, as a concession to pomp and ceremony, he carried his shield, which contained "Il Libro," the huge Medici diamond reputed to be worth twenty-five hundred ducats; it was below the Medici escutcheon of five roundels and three fleur-de-lis, the latter being a gift and honor bestowed upon Lorenzo's grandfather by Louis, King of France.

Before the Medici brothers walked a phalanx of white-robed priests, canons, chaplains, altar boys, communal trumpeters, and penitential confraternities around a float cloaked in purest white damask, upon which rested the image of a saint: a painting. Crowds of handworkers, wage laborers, petty merchants, peasants, and masters cried *"Misericordia!"* and begged forgiveness for their sins as the float passed them.

"It's Our Lady of Impruneta," Zoroastro said, referring to the sacred image carried by Dominicans on a devotional litter. "She is known for many miracles. The Medici must sorely need her benefit to have her brought from her church in the country."

The church claimed that St. Luke himself had painted her and did not deny that the image could miraculously affect the weather. The people of Florence worshiped Our Lady of Impruneta, for she was the very manifestation of God's love, a tangible miracle in their midst. They had absolute proof of the painting's supernatural power: it had never been known to rain when the Impruneta was in procession. Indeed, God would never allow His tears to fall on the holy image.

But even as Zoroastro was speaking, it began to drizzle and soon became a downpour. There was a sudden silence, followed in the next instant by a nervous buzzing as thousands of men and women whispered, as if in fear of being overheard. Then cries erupted; the crowd was beginning to panic. Spectators were running for cover under arches and roofs and doorways; the paving stones of the streets glistened like streams reflecting the sizzling torchlights. Those in the procession looked around, as if suddenly lacking authority, although Lorenzo and Giuliano were trying to reassure them and rouse them to keep stout hearts.

After taking cover under an arch with Leonardo and Niccolò, Zoroastro said breathlessly, "It's a bad omen."

"That's nonsense," Niccolò said, but he nevertheless glanced sideways for confirmation from Leonardo.

"The child is right," Leonardo said. "It is merely happenstance, albeit an unfortunate one for the Medici this night."

"I think Our Lady resists being used by the Medici for selfish ends," Zoroastro said. "This night is the Pazzis'."

"You talk of a painting as if it is the Madonna herself," Leonardo said. "Like the peasants, you believe the image is more real than life. A painting cannot see, nor feel, nor change the weather. If it could, I'd be a well-respected and well-paid thaumaturge instead of a poor painter." He caught himself, as he was being too hard on his friend.

"More blasphemy from the font," Zoroastro said sarcastically, yet he did not seem angry; he was playing another role, perhaps to cover the depth of his feelings, and he talked quietly and stood still as stone. "For a man who has turned brush and pigment into his only objects of worship, I'm not surprised that you find it difficult to make the transition to Christ's truth. I think you've spent too much time with Toscanelli and those Jews who live in the whores' district."

"Master Toscanelli goes to mass and takes the Host daily," said Niccolò. "Do you always equate original ideas with blasphemy?"

Leonardo smiled, but it passed quickly. "I maintain that the sacred books alone are the supreme truth," he said quietly. "But I must confess I don't hold seriously to the fabrications of the friars, who make their livelihood upon the remains of dead saints. They spend nothing but words, yet receive great gifts because they claim the power to bestow Paradise upon sensitive souls such as yourself."

"Remember those words on your deathbed, Leonardo." But even as Zoroastro spoke, fighting broke out in the street. Some youths had pulled one of the Medicean *armeggiatori* from his horse. Lorenzo rode into the thick of it. He circled around the toughs and his fallen signore, who was a brigade leader, and shouted to *armeggiatori* and spectators alike that misfortune would fall upon the entire city and all its populace if blood was shed in the presence of Our Lady.

As Leonardo watched, he worried about the Pazzi procession, which would be soon approaching, for there was sure to be trouble; and Ginevra and Sandro could possibly be in the thick of it. But Lorenzo and Giuliano, his brother, were distracting the crowd. They called for the floats, which were supposed to be unveiled and put before the crowds to amaze and entertain them *after* the dove flew onto the piazza.

The decorated carts appeared, as if from nowhere, but of course they had been strategically hidden; even as they were pulled into the piazza, processional laborers were dropping the black drapes to reveal the painstakingly modeled religious tableaux, some of which had been created and constructed in Verrocchio's studio. There were candle-festooned carts symbolizing all the Stations of the Cross in great larger-than-life detail, carts with religious and Florentine scenes and symbols, a *dernier cri* that was over sixty feet tall with a bleeding heart in flames atop its *trionfo,* and a raft containing three glass beakers the size of men: one was filled with a liquid the color of blood, another was half-filled, and the last one was empty. The full beaker symbolized the New Dispensation, the half-full beaker symbolized the Old Dispensation, and the empty beaker symbolized the end of the world. All this was based upon the Book of Isaiah, but for the beautiful young women standing on the float. Handsomely dressed in silks, their hair crowned with wreaths, they held torches and crossed halberds: three incarnations of the goddess Pallas. But the float that seized the crowd's attention was a huge statue of Our Lady of Impruneta, which represented her exactly as she was in the holy, magical painting.

"The float of Our Lady looks to be your work, Leonardo," Zoroastro said.

"Mine and many others."

And just then the rain turned once again to drizzle, then stopped, as if by a miracle, as if by the sacred power of the huge, unveiled Madonna.

The crowds applauded, shouting *"Miracolo . . . in nomine Patris, et Filii, et Spiritus Sancti. Amen."* Some people fell to the ground crying; they thanked God and the sacred Madonna. The tension broke immediately, leaving only the damp and pungent smell that often permeated the streets after a shower. Leonardo was relieved also, for Ginevra and Sandro would have safe passage into the cathedral.

"Well, Master Leonardo," Niccolò said, "it appears that you *are* a thau . . ." He paused, obviously trying to complete the word.

"Thaumaturge," Leonardo said. "It's from the Greek words *thauma,* which means miracle, and *ergon,* which means work. Didn't old Toscanelli teach you anything?"

"Master Toscanelli obviously taught him how to blaspheme," Zoroastro said.

"You sound much like Ser Nicolini," Niccolò said to Zoroastro.

Leonardo could not help chuckling.

"Don't you believe that Our Lady caused the rain to stop falling?" Zoroastro asked Niccolò. "You saw it with your own eyes."

"No, I don't think I do," Niccolò said.

"Why is that? Have you not had a proper religious education?" asked Zoroastro.

"My mother is very religious. She writes excellent poems. But I don't believe in God."

Not to Leonardo's complete surprise, Zoroastro said, "Neither do I, son."

And with a blaring of trumpets, the Pazzi procession announced its presence.

Leonardo looked for Ginevra's carriage.

At that moment the streets appeared to be awash with blood, for the torches of thousands of penitents, both Pazzi and Medici, glowed extraordinarily bright, as if they had caught a more potent fire from the sacred stones of Christ's own tomb.

Leonardo had seen Ginevra and Sandro, but they were too far away to hear his call. He would wait for them beside their carriage here on the edge of the crowded, flower-garlanded piazza. Leonardo kept to the cover of the crowd, for several men bearing arms and wearing the colors of the Nicolini family stood beside the carriage. His plan was to intercept Ginevra on her way back from the fireworks. Young Machiavelli wanted to go with Zoroastro, who was intent on getting as close as possible to the fireworks cart near the steps of the cathedral, but Leonardo was afraid the boy might be hurt.

The cathedral rose into the dark, clouded sky like a mountain, its marble cliffs and roofs and spires and overhangs—its chapels and cupolas and apses and tribunes—as dark and shadowed as the architecture of Leonardo's dreams. High mass was in progress, and everyone was still. The Paternoster could be heard through great open doors.

Then the Blessed Sacrament. *"Agnus Dei, qui tollis peccata mundi: miserere nobis."* The masses in the piazza prayed, some kneeling, while others watched curiously, waiting, as the great mystery and miracle of the Resurrection unfolded once again. The choir sang, and the words and melody leaked out of the windows and doors and the very stones themselves like ancient perfumes; incense was in the air: myrrh, cassia, spikenard, saffron, onycha, stacte.

Then there was a great shout that was echoed by the crowds, and fashionably dressed young men and women from the great and aristocratic families ran out of the church onto the black-outlined steps. They were followed by Florence's foremost citizens, who filed onto the stairs for the best view of the colorful pyrotechnics.

And Ginevra appeared on the steps; Nicolini to her right and Sandro to her left . . . or so Leonardo thought, for he could just make them out before they were lost in the crowd descending the steps.

"It's time," Leonardo said to Niccolò. "Now you will see it." Unseen from Leonardo's vantage, the archbishop lit the firework rocket concealed inside the large papier-mâché dove. A special guy-line wire stretched across the entire length of the cathedral; it extended through the door and into the piazza. The sparkling dove would travel its length to ignite a satin nest filled with fireworks and thus bring good fortune for another year to the thousands of fortunate and faithful spectators.

Suddenly the bird, shooting red-and-yellow fire and black smoke, soared through the door. Everyone near and under its path ducked and shouted as it passed over. It was so bright that for an instant Leonardo could not see past the red afterimages that hung like pastel clouds wherever he looked.

There was a great cheering, which turned suddenly to gasps as the wire snapped. The bird tumbled and fell far short of the nest, falling as if thrown, onto a large cart that contained all the festival's fireworks, which were piled like cannon on a bed of planks. As it burned, its wings peeled back and curled into charcoal.

In seconds the firework rockets in the cart caught fire, and there was a thunderous explosion, followed by a staccato, as cylinder upon cylinder of gunpowder ignited. The entire cart canted over, spilling hundreds of rockets, which exploded and shot out in all directions. The rockets lit the church phosphorescent white, carnelian, electric blue, viridian; and a thousand deep, cutting shadows danced like flibbertigibbets. Rockets smashed into its walls and leaded windows to burst into showers of color followed by cannonlike retorts. Sparks whirled on the floor of the piazza, bathing the screaming, frantic bystanders in exploding fire, which caught the clothes of children as their mothers screamed and tried to stamp out the flames. An obese man dressed in a rough frock caught a rocket square in the chest. An explosion of sparks and flames illuminated his dance of death. All was noise and kinetoscope brightness. Rockets landed atop the roofs of nearby buildings, which began to burn. A makeshift second-story balcony caught fire, and the festively dyed canvas awnings dropped in flames onto the crowds below. The acrid scent of pitch mixed with the sweet residue of incense in the air.

Leonardo rushed into the crowded piazza. He screamed for Ginevra; and, as if in response, others seemed to be shouting back at him as he pulled and pushed and grasped and clawed his way through the crowd toward the Duomo. He was pummeled by those who panicked like animals caught in a forest fire, but he felt numbed. It was as if he were dreaming of being caught in an ocean of dark molasses. His movements were heavy, as if time itself had slowed down, soon to come to a halt like an unwound clock.

Niccolò called to him.

But he had told the boy to stay by the carriages . . . hadn't he?

Ducking whenever another battery of rockets exploded, praying as he ran toward cover, he looked for Ginevra. He kept himself low, ready to drop to the ground for safety. He stepped around a young woman kneeling in the piazza; she was praying, seemingly oblivious to the rockets and crush of bodies around her. Gangs of pickpurses and ragamuffins were crawling about, braving the fire to pull rings and jewelry from those who had fallen and who were huddled close to the ground. They kicked and pummeled and sometimes stabbed the poor unprotected unfortunates when they resisted. A thief with a scar that seemed to extend from his lip to his cheek raised his blade toward Leonardo, but drew back when he saw that Leonardo had his drawn also.

Leonardo had to find Ginevra. Nothing else was important. He would have cut open the jackleg's belly if necessary.

Fireworks still exploded thunderously, sparks and fire shooting randomly in various directions. Frantically, Leonardo searched, and at last found her and Sandro behind the safety of a barricade of overturned vendor's carts. She was trembling and crying; Sandro held her protectively, although even in the torchlight and fluorescing explosions of the rockets, he looked ashen-faced.

"Ginevra, I've been worried sick for you," Leonardo said. He nodded to Sandro and touched him lightly on the shoulder.

"You must leave here at once," Ginevra said. She was in control once again, as if she had just defeated some private and terrible demon. She stopped shaking, and her tears mingled with the perspiration glistening on her face.

"Come. Sandro and I will take you away from here."

"No," she said, looking at him but avoiding his eyes. "Leave me be, please."

"Sandro, she can't stay here," Leonardo said.

"My fiancé will be here straightforth," Ginevra said. "Leave me be, please!"

"Your *fiancé?*" Leonardo shouted. "Damn your fiancé, that stinking *puttaniere.*"

"So now you think me a whore," she said. Then to Sandro, pleading, "He *must* leave." Sandro nervously looked to Ginevra, then to Leonardo for direction.

"I am not afraid of your . . . fiancé."

"That's not to the point," Ginevra said. "I've made my choice. I am going to marry Messer Nicolini."

"Out of fear," Leonardo said, moving closer to her. Her braid had come undone, and wisps of her long red hair clung to her resolute, shadowed face. Yet she seemed so vulnerable; and Leonardo yearned for her, for her very vulnerability, which excited him.

It was like an oven in the piazza. Bells pealed as citizens ran to douse the dangerous roof fires that could threaten all of Florence.

"A decision has been forced, it is true," Ginevra said. "But it is *my* decision; and I can assure you, it is made from logic, not fear. You humiliated Messer Nicolini . . . and me. Indeed, your selfish, self-concerned, and jealous antics humiliated my entire family and made it obvious that we were lovers."

"But we are!"

"We *were*." She drew a deep, sibilant breath and said, without looking at him, "Ironical that you should call him a whoremaster, for you, by your actions, made me look like a whore."

"You exaggerate, I—"

"You humiliated him with the bowels of a pig."

"He threatened my life," Leonardo said. "When he asked Sandro to escort you for a breath of air. He threatened also to have you locked up."

"If you loved me, you would have heeded his threats, then, and not put me in danger as well."

Leonardo put his hand upon hers. It was cold, and she didn't move away. Yet it did not quicken her; he could feel that. She was stone. "Sandro," Leonardo asked, indicating to his friend that he needed privacy.

Sandro nodded, seemingly relieved. He stood up and edged away from them.

The explosions had stopped; now there was only shouting and wailing . . . and the waggling of ten thousand tongues.

"He's had someone spying on us," Leonardo said.

"He's told me everything, Leonardo," she said as she stared straight ahead, as if blind. "He is very honest."

"Ah, so he's absolved for his honesty, is that it?"

"He told me that he knows of our making love at Master Verrocchio's. It is we who need absolution."

"*We?*" Leonardo said, furious. "He is taking you by force, Ginevra," and the image of Nicolini raping her atop scarlet sheets came to mind once again. "You can't resist him with guile. He is stronger than you. He will force you to marry him."

"I am his, Leonardo."

"But a few hours ago you were mine."

Then she looked at him levelly. "I am decided."

"I am going to tell your father what you are doing in his cause. He will never permit this."

"Leonardo," she said, her voice dropping to a whisper, "it is done, over. I am sorry. . . ."

"You must not permit this to happen. There is a way—"

"It must be *this* way," Ginevra said. There was a quaver in her voice, yet still she stared straight ahead.

"Your family can manage."

Ginevra did not respond.

"Look at me directly and tell me you don't love me," Leonardo said, taking her gently by the shoulders and turning her toward him. He had difficulty holding her at arm's length. He could smell the perfumes in her hair. But she was as distant as the Duomo's clerestory above him. Now she looked at him directly. "You do love me," he said.

"I am going to marry Messer Nicolini, and, yes, I do love you. But that is of no consequence now."

"Of no consequence . . . ?" Leonardo tried to embrace her, but she pulled back from him. She felt cold to his touch. "My mind is made up," she said quietly. "Now, please, leave us."

"I cannot. I love you." Leonardo felt ill, as if he were on a ship caught in a storm, for his stomach rolled and his throat felt as if he had swallowed lye. He heard the desperation in his voice, but could not control it. This was nightmare. It could not be true. She loved him; he had only to break through her resolve. But it was as if he were experiencing déjà vu. He knew what was coming, for he knew her; and the next few terrible moments were as determined as the planets rotating in their heavenly crystalline orbits.

"If you interfere and harm my family, I will despise you," Ginevra said. "I have given myself to Messer Nicolini. In time I will love him. If you truly feel for me as I believe you do, then please leave me be."

"I cannot," Leonardo said. His jaw ached, it was clenched so tightly.

Once again she trembled, although she looked at Leonardo directly. "I will not see my father a bankrupt, with *pitture infamanti* of him on the streets and in the Signoria." Grotesque paintings of bankrupts and traitors and perjurers often hung in public places and were desecrated with spittle and feces and all manner of graffito. "Leonardo," she whispered, "you cannot wrest me from destiny. You must leave and put me behind you, for under no circumstances would I ever marry you."

"Stop this now," Leonardo said, "and it will all be forgotten in a year. I promise you. No matter how serious the debt, your family would not be bankrupt. At worst—"

"At worst we would become as beggars. Dishonor is never forgotten. *I* could not forget. We—you and I—have caused my family dishonor. I swore on the holy grave of my mother and upon the life of my father that I shall never do so again. And that, my Leonardo, is stronger than my love for you."

"Ginevra," Leonardo said, pleading, "this was all but a ploy to keep your father solvent."

"But now it is also a matter of honor."

"And honor must take precedence over love and sensual gratification," said Nicolini, who had just now come upon them. Standing beside Sandro like an apparition dressed in Pazzi colors of blue and gold, he wore a blue damask doublet and long velvet robes broidered with escutcheons of porpoises in gold thread. He was perspiring; his hair was matted with sweat. But a man in Nicolini's delicate social position—just on the cusp of equality with the highest of patrician families—would readily take on the discomfort of such rich, heavy, emblematic clothing, no matter what the weather, if it might impress the family he was courting. He nodded to Sandro and walked past him to Ginevra. He extended his hands to her, saying, "When the ill-omened accident occurred, I was frantic for your safety. Thank God you're safe, Madonna." She clasped his hands, and he lifted her to her feet. He looked at Leonardo, seemingly without malice, for he had won Ginevra as his prize.

"But how can *you* retain honor when you know that Madonna Ginevra loves me?" Leonardo asked, purposely goading him to draw his sword. "When you know that she was making love to me even as you were upstairs?"

Ginevra turned away from him, and Nicolini put himself between her and Leonardo.

"Honor is manifested in appearances," Nicolini said coolly, not taking the bait, "for does not pretense abound in a civil society such as ours? Does not a great lord graciously conduct himself with an inferior as if both were upon an equal plane? *Humilitas seu curialitas,* if you recall your Latin, young Ser. But certainly they are not equal. So it is that a society remains civil and maintains itself."

"Thus untruths function as well as truths," Leonardo said, feeling his face burn as if scalded with steam. "And you care not which coin you hold."

"Perhaps I am also a conjurer like yourself . . . or better yet, an alchemist. For, you see, Master Leonardo," he said softly, "I shall transform Madonna Ginevra's respect and courtesy into love." He then looked at Ginevra and said, "If Madonna will open her most private self to my affections."

Ginevra lowered her gaze, humiliated.

Nicolini's innuendo was not lost on Leonardo, and he drew his sword. Nicolini's guards were not here; it would be a fair fight.

"Leonardo, *no!*" Sandro said.

But it was Ginevra who delivered the cut to Leonardo, for she made her decision felt by pulling Nicolini away, tugging his sleeve like a well-tempered child, leaving Leonardo standing alone.

Nicolini paused, turned to Leonardo, and said, "I shan't need bodyguards to protect me from your rapier, young Ser. But please do as Madonna asks, for your sake as well as ours." With that he steered Ginevra out of sight, past the barricades, and into the crowded piazza. Leonardo stood where he was, sword in hand, as if frozen.

"Come," Sandro said, "we shall go to the Devil's Corner. A drink will do us all good . . . and we can talk."

Leonardo did not respond. He looked at the thousands of people kneeling in the direction of the litter that contained the original and most sacred painting of Our Lady of Impruneta. A preacher was giving a sermon from the litter, as if it were a pulpit; and he held the painting against his chest as he spoke. Standing like a gigantic apparition behind him was the papier-mâché statue of Our Lady, the float which Leonardo had helped create. Its grandeur heightened by thousands of burning torches held aloft, the statue was transformed into the stuff of pure and holy spirit, for how could such a perfect and exemplary image be composed of ordinary wood, paint, and paper? The penitents, rich and poor alike, prayed for forgiveness. Many held crucifixes, and their coded genuflections seemed choreographed. They wailed and gestured, reaching for the *virtu* of spirit that had been lost . . . petitioning and propitiating the holy painting whose tears had rained on Florence, deluging her with misfortune.

"Leonardo," said Sandro, "you could not have beaten Nicolini." Leonardo turned to Sandro, as if he were going to slash his friend with the sword meant for Nicolini. "He is no fool," continued Sandro. "He had three men standing in shadow behind me."

Leonardo could only nod. Hiding his humiliation and frustration, he turned away from Sandro and saw Niccolò standing before him.

"Nicco," Leonardo said dazedly. "Didn't I tell you to remain by the carriages? What have you to say for yourself?"

Niccolò averted his eyes and did not answer.

"Tell me why you disobeyed me," Leonardo insisted.

"I didn't disobey you, Leonardo," said Niccolò, his dark eyes still averted as if he was afraid to look at his master. "But you ran off and left me. I only thought to help you . . . as it is dangerous here."

"Forgive me," Leonardo whispered, shamed.

Then young Machiavelli sought his hand and squeezed it tightly, as if he understood the nature of pain that lay beyond his years.

> How gentle is deception . . .
> —Niccolò Machiavelli

3

Simonetta

ome, Leonardo, we can't remain here forever," Sandro said, but Leonardo stared into the courtyard of the Duomo as if his friend had not spoken a word.

The Duomo, Baptistery, and Campanile, connected by darkness and shadow, seemed to waver in the overcast torch-lit night, as if cloaked in a misty miasma. The Duomo was now green and rose, its arcades rising above the darkness of Brunelleschi's doors, its inset windows reflecting like mirrors the bonfires of penitents who would remain to pray all night in the piazza. Although not aflame, nearby rooftops smoldered. The wounded and the dead had been blessed and carried into the church; nuns administered to the needs of the living and prayed for those who had been "carried into heaven in the arms of Our Lady."

Although Lorenzo and Giuliano were nowhere to be seen, the Medici-controlled Companions of the Night and the Medici *armeggiatori* combed the area on horseback to purge the rabble and cutpurses. Brandishing polished swords in their outstretched hands, they passed through the crowds of devotees like soldiers of heaven to restore the will of the people through terror and violence. All who weren't praying or properly genuflecting were at risk. Almost all of the citizens had fled in panic when the fireworks exploded, but there were a thousand people remaining, and their garlands of flowers and altar candles wound like a burning rosary around the cathedral. Guildsmen, wives, peasants, patricians, whores, and Magdalenes alike were praying to the *virtu* of the Madonna, praying for intervention to dispel the evil omen brought upon Florence by the falling, flaming bird. The painting of Our Lady, heavily guarded by Medici men, was still in the center of the piazza; she had been moved from her devotional litter, which had been damaged by one of the rockets, to a *carroccio* that was draped with a golden *palio* and had carved lions upon its four wheels.

She would still oversee the proceedings with her blind, painted eyes.

Carried by the thin, erratic breezes, the perfume of lilies mingled with the acrid odors of smoke.

"Master Leonardo, do you see something before us that we cannot?" asked Niccolò, who finally released the pressure on Leonardo's hand.

"Such as what, young Nicco?" Leonardo asked after a pause.

"If I knew the answer, I would have no need to ask you the question."

"I was looking into myself. Although my eyes saw all of that which is before us, I perceived only my thoughts. Do you understand that?"

"Of course. I have an aunt who sleeps with her eyes open like an owl, yet she wouldn't cease her snoring if you pissed on her foot."

Leonardo smiled, then turned his gaze toward Sandro and nodded to him in wordless apology.

"But when I look without seeing, it is because I am in . . . darkness," Machiavelli said. Leonardo looked at the boy indulgently, but Niccolò continued. "This darkness is in my soul, and I feel as if I'm about to fall from the ledge of a very smooth cliff into absolute eternal darkness. Yet sometimes I *wish* to fall off." The boy looked at Leonardo intently, as he had when Leonardo had first noticed him standing behind Toscanelli in Verrocchio's studio. "Is that what you feel just now because of this woman Ginevra?"

Leonardo stood up and said gently and with respect, "Yes, Niccolò. That is exactly how I feel." And then to Sandro: "You must tell me all you know. I cannot accept what she said to me."

"But I'm afraid that you must, Leonardo," Sandro said. As he spoke, there was a great commotion around the devotional litter. "It seems that the Virgin is, indeed, unhappy; we should leave this place before there is more trouble."

"I agree," Leonardo said, "for we must talk"—but Niccolò shouted just then that he would return in a few moments and slipped through the crowd toward the lion-wheeled litter. Leonardo called after him angrily. "I make a poor nursemaid," he muttered to Sandro. "Come, let's find him and be gone. I left him once in this crowd; I shan't do that again." For the moment, at least, Leonardo forgot himself; and his anxiety and love-anguish receded.

Leonardo and Sandro pressed through the crowd, which became a tight, impenetrable ring around the *carroccio*. The *armeggiatori* and armor-laden and crimson-robed *inquisitore* formed the innermost circle, and anyone who dared to move closer would be cut down by overanxious priests and Medici supporters yearning to gain honor: the Florentine romance with *virtu*. It was difficult to see what was happening ahead; but hearing was another matter, for gossip spread through the crowd like dye in water.

A young peasant from the neighborhood of the Sieci had hidden himself inside the church; after the rockets had misfired, he had found his way into the nave and dashed past the chancel rail, run up the stairs of the altar of Our Lady, and struck her marble image with a stonecutter's chisel. After breaking her right eye, he had exposed his genitals and urinated from the antependium. The guards, incensed, had dragged him out of the church and beaten him senseless.

"We must find Niccolò," Leonardo said anxiously. He was frightened for the child. The crowd had become vicious, and he felt as if he were caught in an angry, boiling sea. Everyone was screaming for blood and crying, "*Ebreo, Ebreo, Ebreo*," which meant "Jew."

Suddenly the crowd broke into a frenzy of screaming, and then the peasant boy was pulled up onto the now crowded *carroccio,* where Leonardo and Sandro could see him.

His right hand had been severed and was being thrown among the crowd, arcing upward and trailing blood as it fell, only to be tossed again. The boy was thin and gangly with long, matted brown hair. His face was bloody and already swelling from the pounding he had received. It was obvious that his nose had been crushed. His arm was rigidly outstretched, and his mouth was open in incomprehension. It was as if he had just awakened to find that his hand had been amputated. His face had become a death's-head grimace.

Torches surrounded him in a bright nimbus. The armored *inquisitore* and *armeggiatori* sat atop their horses and watched; they would not intercede. While a toothless woman with thinning white hair held up the painting, so that the image of Our Lady might witness what was about to take place, five men restrained the boy by his arms, legs, and hair; his head was snapped backward by a dirty-looking garroter who was probably no more than a cut-purse himself. Then another man waved the boy's chisel to the cheers of the crowd. He was obviously no peasant, for he was wearing a sideless tunic decorated with jewels and metal fringing. He genuflected to the painting, made the sign of the cross with the chisel, and then used it to gouge out the boy's eye.

Once again the crowd was in a frenzy of shouting and cheering. The boy's eye had been exchanged for the eye of the Virgin; and the hand that had desecrated her had been cut off; for this the Holy Virgin should be satisfied.

Perhaps she was. But Leonardo knew that it would not be enough for the crowd. He pushed through the rabble with Sandro beside him, frantic with worry for Niccolò, who could easily be harmed in the melee that was certain to come. His heart was beating quickly, and images passed feverishly through his mind: Ginevra, always Ginevra, now being taken by Nicolini, now being mutilated by this mob that was transformed into a thousand-headed beast with a single thought and a single rapacious purpose.

His mind's eye would not close. He saw Ginevra, exposed, in fetters, in pain.

And he was helpless.

Leonardo looked at the peasant boy who was pulled tight as a sail, blood pooling in his right eye socket and streaming down his face; and he imagined he was seeing Niccolò, as if it were Niccolò's eye that had been gouged, and Niccolò's hand that was soaring like a bird over the crowd.

But he also felt the power and ardor and lure of the crowd. Perhaps Our Lady *was* indeed in control, and the torch-lit painting the true manifestation of her holy, scouring spirit.

"There you are, Leonardo," shouted Zoroastro. "Look who we've found." He and Benedetto Dei were holding on to Niccolò, propelling him through the crowd.

Relieved to see that Niccolò was safe, Leonardo shouted back and fought his way toward them. Sandro followed.

The crowd was working itself into a frenzy. Leonardo came upon a young woman of obvious means who was crying and praying and by turns balling her fist and shouting at the boy who had desecrated the Holy Mother. Her curly hair was damp and clung to the sides of her thin, yet beautiful, face. Then she stood stock-still as if she were in a trance. Reflexively, Leonardo made a mental sketch of her and stored it in his memory cathedral. Her slack-jawed expression; her bloodless, balled fists; her necklace of pearls and *vestito* of purple cloth edged with balas rubies; the burly servants who guarded her. Suddenly she screamed *"Deo grátias!"* and prostrated herself on the ground; her retainers brandished knives and protectively closed in around her.

Niccolò broke away from Zoroastro and Benedetto Dei and scurried toward Leonardo; but he brushed too close to one of the servants guarding the young woman and was roughly thrown out of the way. Leonardo broke the boy's fall, and another woman screamed behind him. The crowd retreated, seemingly from Leonardo and Niccolò.

But it was the severed hand, which was still being thrown like a beanbag, that had caused the crowd to fall back a pace.

The bloody, severed hand had landed beside Niccolò.

The peasant who had flung Niccolò out of his path rushed toward him; and Leonardo, his face hard and blade at the ready, blocked his way. "Another step, you snoke-horn, and I'll relieve you of your middle leg."

"Excuse me, sir, but I only mean to pick up the Jew's hand. I mean no harm to you." The man was about Leonardo's size, but with red hair and a beard that was so thick it seemed to cover his face up to his dark, squinting eyes. He wore a dagged cap; a simple, but clean, doublet; tight ribboned hose; and a codpiece. He glanced at young Machiavelli and said, "Nor do I mean harm to your young friend, sir. I apologize for being a little rough when he came near me, but I was protecting my mistress, Madonna Sansoni."

"From a boy?"

The man shrugged and said, "May I pass?"

Leonardo stepped aside; and the man picked up the bloodied, but doughy-white, hand and wrapped it in a satin handkerchief.

"Why would she want such a thing?" Leonardo asked.

"If she keeps it, then the scummer's stinking soul won't even be able to reach purgatory. It'll be trapped right *here*," and he held up the package, as if to assure himself that he indeed had it. After he carried away the tainted hand of the *"Ebreo,"* the crowd poured back into the area.

"That boy's hand will get them into trouble," Leonardo said to his friends; and, indeed, Madonna Sansoni's retainers were shouting and gesturing at the curious who would take the hand by force now that it was wrapped tight as a ball. An instant later they were fighting a gang of filthy street Arabs who had been working their way through the crowd.

The peasant boy's severed hand had suddenly become valuable.

Even now the *trionfi* float of Our Lady of Impruneta which Leonardo had designed was being converted into a makeshift gallows. A gallows pin was erected between her outstretched, reinforced, papier-mâché arms, from which was tied the hempen noose; it would seem to the crowds that this larger-than-life Madonna had, indeed, ordained this execution.

Gesturing to Zoroastro and Benedetto, Leonardo dragged Niccolò away from the piazza. They stopped only when they were safely out of harm's way at the end of the narrow Via dei Servi. Shuttered, shadowed walls barricaded the street, and the cathedral and its cupola rose above the houses as if it were a natural palisade of perfect marble. But the air in these claustrophobic environs was fetid, as if heavy with the collected psychic miasma of the city.

There was little life here in the street, which was unusual for a festival holy night; but neighborhood residents, wary of being on the streets below, were hanging out windows and standing upon their balconies to glimpse whatever they could. Red and blue and yellow and green and orange shutters were splayed open like prison doors during an amnesty.

Then a shout went up, and there was sudden, deafening applause. . . .

Although the makeshift *trionfi* gallows were not visible from this end of the Via dei Servi (the lower part of the Duomo was blocked from sight by the three- and four-storied buildings), Leonardo did not need to be in the Duomo Piazza to know that the *"ebreo"* had just been hanged.

Niccolò, who was walking beside Leonardo, shivered and folded his arms across his chest, as if to protect himself.

Leonardo paused when he reached the Piazza della Santissima Annunziata. "If you have no objections," he said to Zoroastro and Benedetto Dei, "Sandro and I have some matters to discuss. We will meet up with you later . . . at your pleasure."

"I was supposed to meet—or rather *we* were supposed to meet— Francesco, Atalante, Lorenzo di Credi, and Bartholomeo di Pasquino—the goldsmith who lives in Vacchereccia—on the Ponte Vecchio after the procession; but it's very late now. I can't be certain that they'll be there," Benedetto said. He was an exceptionally tall man, and thin, with thick brownish-gold hair that puffed out from his red cap. He had wide-set sleepy eyes, high cheekbones, and a full, pouty mouth. "Your troublesome friend Il Neri said he had a surprise for us all, some fete involving Simonetta."

"And what might that be?" Sandro asked, obviously interested.

"That's all I know," Benedetto said. "He was very secretive about it all ... but we can go on," he said to Leonardo, "and discover what's afoot. Perhaps we can post your apprentice Machiavelli there to wait for you ...?"

Although Sandro was obviously impatient to find out about Simonetta, he said, "That would give Leonardo and me time to talk ... in fact, we shouldn't be there much later than all of you. We just need a bit of privacy."

"I don't want Niccolò left alone," Leonardo insisted. "Certainly not standing about on the Ponte Vecchio."

"It's safe enough," Zoroastro said.

"Nothing is safe enough tonight."

"Then we'll post Zoroastro," Benedetto said, smiling. Zoroastro in turn made a face.

But Niccolò seemed unsettled; he made no motion to go with Benedetto and Zoroastro.

"Niccolò ...?" asked Sandro.

Machiavelli drew nearer to Leonardo and asked, "Master, might I walk with you?"

Leonardo looked at him, saw the boy's distress, then nodded. Sandro said nothing, although he was plainly surprised.

Niccolò would not understand most of what would be said, Leonardo told himself, and what he did comprehend would not become gossip. He was sure of this boy, and Leonardo—whom his teacher Toscanelli had often chided for his propensities toward hubris—considered himself to be an unerring judge of character. But more than that, Leonardo discovered that he wanted Niccolò's company.

Indeed, Benedetto was right: Niccolò had become Leonardo's apprentice. Toscanelli was a shrewd man of science, who considered the human psyche as chartable as the heavens; he understood that Leonardo and Machiavelli were much alike in temperament and intellect.

Zoroastro and Benedetto went on ahead. Singing and shouting the poet Sacchetti's famous and oft-repeated lines, "Each one shouts for joy, and death to those who will not sing," they swaggered as if they were taking over the street.

"Your friend Zoroastro does not seem particularly sensitive to your problems," Sandro said.

"You should know him by now," Leonardo said. "That's his way. He has been acting odd, though ... the cutpurse is up to something. But he did do what he could to help me find you and Ginevra."

"To my mind, he's a *scagliola*."

Leonardo pursed his lips in the slightest of smiles. "But he's an authentic fraud, and he does have a flair for mechanical devices."

"Ah, so now mechanical ability has become a measure of character," Sandro said.

Niccolò walked closely beside Leonardo, but seemed lost in his own thoughts. Leonardo patted the boy's shoulder; then, with a rasp in his voice, he said to Sandro, "You know that I am sick with worry and fear over Ginevra. What is going on? How could she do such a turnabout? She loves *me*, yet . . . You spent the evening with her, you're her confidant. . . ."

"As I am yours," Botticelli said.

"Then tell me." Now that Leonardo could finally let down his guard, he felt that particular emptiness he had often experienced as a child. He thought of Caterina, his mother. How he longed to return to Vinci and see her and her good husband Achattabrigha.

"You know as much as I, my friend," Sandro said patiently. "Ginevra is lost. There is nothing you can do to extricate her from this impending marriage. She is in her own trap."

"But she doesn't have to be!"

"If she leaves Nicolini, he'll destroy her entire family to save his own honor. He would have little choice, actually."

"Nonsense!"

"Leonardo, use your reason," Sandro said, obviously frustrated. "Ginevra must marry this man."

"She will *not*."

"Nicolini has you checkmated, Leonardo. What can you do? If she goes against him, she will dishonor and ruin her family. You would not permit such a thing—her father is your friend."

"Which is why he would listen to me. There is a way, an alternative. Nicolini is not the only wealthy man in Florence."

Botticelli paused, and his eyes met Niccolò's; it was as if they understood something that was beyond Leonardo's comprehension. "Amerigo de' Benci would not, nor could he, listen to you," Sandro said to Leonardo. "Ginevra has prided herself on her honesty, and you would accuse her of deceit? You might just as well tell her father you think her a whore."

"But how does Ginevra *feel*?" Leonardo asked. "She doesn't love him. How can she go through with it?"

"She told me that these wounds will heal, whereas honor and family are eternal."

"Only the fixed stars are eternal."

"She said that you would understand . . . eventually."

"But I don't and I won't," Leonardo said.

"She asks that you talk with your mother, your real mother."

"Why?"

"Because your situations are similar. Just as your father could not marry your mother—"

"Stop it," Leonardo said. "Enough!" His face burned, and he seethed with anger. "My mother may be a peasant, and I may be a bastard, but . . ."

"I'm sorry, Leonardo."

"Did she tell you to repeat this in order to hurt me?"

"Perhaps to help you understand."

"Well, I certainly would not wish her to marry below her station," Leonardo said sarcastically. As if reality was but a reflection of his temper and anger, they came upon two burly young men fighting and calling each other names. They were playing *civettino,* the object of which was ostensibly to knock off the opponent's hat. A crowd of ruffians had gathered and were making bets on who would win. Each man had his right foot extended, and the taller man was stepping upon the foot of his opponent. Whoever moved his foot away first would lose the fight. Both men's faces were bloodied, for it was a brutal sport. One of them might even kill the other before the match was over; for, more often than not, such matches escalated into street fights. Certainly, the spectators could not be counted on to stop it.

After they rounded a corner, leaving the boxers behind them, Niccolò said, "Leonardo, I am sorry you are distressed." Leonardo patted him on the shoulder, but said nothing. His anger had frozen within him, and he felt as if he were going numb; he could almost imagine great slabs of ice separating him from the world . . . a cathedral of frory blue ice, majestic, invulnerable. He sought respite from his pain by escaping into the familiar cloisters of his memory cathedral. He took comfort in the artifacts of his childhood, but kept well away from those warm rooms that contained his memories, his feelings, his very conception of Ginevra.

"I too am distressed," Niccolò said. Then, after a beat, when Leonardo did not respond, the boy tugged at his sleeve. "Leonardo . . . ? Leonardo!"

Leonardo's reverie was broken. "I'm sorry, Nicco. Now, tell me why you are distressed. Surely, it concerns the boy who was dismembered and hanged."

Machiavelli nodded. "I can understand the violence of the crowd, for a crowd is nothing more than a beast. But that boy, why would he be so foolish?"

"Well," Sandro said, "if he was a Jew, it would make a certain sense."

"Why?" Niccolò asked.

"Because the Jews killed Christ. Out of sheer hatred and malice. To a Jew, all Christendom is the enemy. We are, to them, like Saracens. They hate the church, and you, and me. They hate every sacred painting and plaster

Madonna. That is why Pater Patriae, may he rest in peace, made them sew yellow badges upon their hats and sleeves, so as to protect their neighbors. To protect *us*."

"Then that would make him a martyr to his faith," Niccolò said to Sandro.

"I would not exactly say that. . . ."

"It makes no sense to me," Niccolò said. "Leonardo, help me."

"I have no answers for you," Leonardo said. "If there is one, we will probably never know it."

"Do *you* think he was a Jew?"

Leonardo shrugged. "Perhaps, perhaps not. But we call anyone we don't like a Jew, so what does it mean?" Seeing that Machiavelli was visibly agitated, he said, "The boy could have just been crazy, Nicco, or perhaps he felt the Madonna had broken a contract with him. Perhaps it was a matter of the heart—a young girl; young men often desire to become martyrs when spurned or cuckolded." Leonardo could not help but grimace at his self-revelation. "Do you not remember the story by Arlotto about the old man who begged a statue of Christ to his young wife who was dying of the cough?" When Niccolò shook his head, Leonardo continued: "This man had been a loyal Christian and had been devoted to this particular statue for over twenty years. You could have lit the world with the candles he placed before it. But this particular image of the Christ did not fulfill its part of the bargain, for the man's wife died horribly, prayers and devotions notwithstanding. Enraged, the man dug out the Christ's eyes and shouted, so that everyone in the Church of Santo Spirito could hear, 'You are a mockery and a disgrace.' "

"And what happened to him?" Niccolò asked.

"If you believe the story, his brethren tore him apart," Leonardo said.

"Blasphemy!" Sandro said. "God-fearing Christians do not desecrate holy images. You must not teach the child heretical lies and blasphemous fictions." Grasping Niccolò's arm to gain his attention, he said, "Arlotto was nothing more than a fabricator and a panderer." For all of Botticelli's good humor and the sensuality and vivacity of his paintings, there was a vein of priggishness that was only very occasionally exposed.

"My friend," Leonardo said, "if you continue to paint those voluptuous pictures of our lovely Simonetta, people might think you to be a libertine, and they might start calling *you* a heretic . . . or a Jew."

Machiavelli laughed at that, which broke the tension, for Sandro, at the mere mention of Simonetta, was willing to become a saint or debauch himself in the street if it would gain him her smallest affection.

And for Leonardo, the revelation had come to him quietly and sadly, in emptiness and with finality, that Ginevra would not love him.

The Ponte Vecchio, which had been completely rebuilt after the great flood of 1333, was mostly dark; but the Arno, which it crossed, reflected the city lights of festival. The river was itself like a candle flame; it rippled, as if flickering, reflecting the light of lamps, candles, and torches that burned in the adjacent streets and buildings. Most of the shops built upon the bridge were closed, as this was the butchers' quarter, and stank; but a few stalls were open, selling sweetmeats, roasted nuts, fava beans, and cheap wine. Tired-looking prostitutes worked the area, which was traveled mostly by tourists and citizens on their way to take the Sacrament or goggle at the festival doings around the Palazzo Vecchio. Many were also going to visit the Medici Palace; tonight its courtyards were open to all, and enough suckling pigs were being roasted there to feed an entire village.

"Ho, Master Leonardo, is that you?" asked a boy standing on the ancient paving stones of the Oltrarno near the entrance to the bridge.

"Yes?" answered Leonardo. He recognized the boy as Jacopo Saltarelli, who was an apprentice goldsmith and often modeled at Verrocchio's *bottega*. Leonardo had often sketched and painted Jacopo, who had a good, muscular body, but was thick-featured, with flaring nostrils and sallow, pimply skin. His beard, which would probably grow thicker as he matured, was sparse and scraggly; but his long, unkempt hair was curly and luxurious.

"Messers Dei and da Peretola asked me to wait for you and take you to their destination," Jacopo said.

"You mean they paid you to wait for us, don't you?" Sandro asked, teasing the boy.

"As you wish, sir."

"And what might our destination be?" asked Sandro.

"To the Via Grifone."

"Yes . . . ?"

"A great banquet, sir, at L'Ugolino. Master Guglielmo Onorevoli is giving a party in honor of Madonna Simonetta Vespucci."

"If Il Neri is hosting the party," Sandro said, "then we can be certain to be entertained." The wealthy scion of the Onorevoli family was called Il Neri because he always dressed in black; it was his signature, done for effect.

"It seems a strange fete to me," Jacopo said as they walked. "The entire villa is as dark as a cellar, except for the lamps at the gate."

"But why would the house be dark?" Sandro asked, and he and Leonardo, with Niccolò following suit, dropped behind Jacopo to talk. They waved Jacopo ahead and kept a good distance behind him, which was easy to do, for the streets thereabouts were not so crowded. "I'm surprised that Simonetta would attend a public gathering hosted by Il Neri," Sandro continued.

Leonardo turned toward him, questioning.

"Il Neri has dangerous political affiliations."

"Are you referring to the Pazzi?" Leonardo asked.

"Even they think him too crazy," Sandro said. "But Simonetta . . . she is so often in the company of Giuliano and Lorenzo de' Medici. It is not politically wise for her to have connections with their enemies. I worry for her."

"I think you'd best keep your worries for yourself," Leonardo said with gentle sarcasm. "Simonetta's beauty allows her to rise above morality and politics."

"She is virtue itself, its very form. But I still worry for her," Sandro said. "For her health, too."

Leonardo laughed, as if he were his old self for an instant. "Perhaps you should leave her health to her doctors?"

"I have heard her cough. It doesn't sound good to me, it's deep in the lungs."

"You should stay away from Antonio del Pollaiuolo's *bottega,*" Leonardo said. "Anyone who stands too long at his dissection table becomes deluded into thinking he's a doctor."

"I do not need to carve up a corpse to detect a cough . . . or, for that matter, to better paint the human figure," Sandro said testily.

"I apologize," Leonardo said, patting his friend on the shoulder.

"Madonna Simonetta is mistress of the brothers Medici, is that not correct?" Niccolò asked, to Sandro's and Leonardo's surprise.

"She is their friend, Niccolò," Sandro said.

"Rumors say not," Machiavelli said.

"Perhaps we should not discuss such things in front of the boy. . . . Niccolò seems to have his ear right at the door of the rumor mill."

"Well, what do you expect?" Leonardo said. "He is one of Toscanelli's brightest apprentices. That studio is a clearinghouse for information."

"For slander."

"Sometimes one and the same," Leonardo said. "And of course Simonetta is their mistress, Sandro. But perhaps she might have some small reserve of love with which to nourish you."

Sandro blushed and made a growling noise.

"You may talk as you like," said Niccolò in apology. "I will not listen," and he walked ahead to catch up with Jacopo Saltarelli.

When Leonardo and Sandro reached the Onorevoli estate, which had an uninviting approach—a narrow uphill road winding between crumbling walls, which, in turn, led to a very high, wide passageway—Jacopo and Niccolò were waiting. But before Jacopo could lead on, Leonardo said, "Nicco,

I've changed my mind. This is no place for you." Although Leonardo was concerned for the young Machiavelli, he recoiled at the prospect of making small talk and entertaining Il Neri's diverse, and probably perverse, guests. He felt suddenly ill, as if despair and lovesickness were an illness that came in waves like the nausea that follows bad food.

"Leonardo, we're already here," Niccolò said. "I'm hungry. Surely there will be food. And did not my Master Toscanelli specifically ask for you to be my mentor so I might experience life? Well, life is through that passage." Niccolò indicated the dark facade to the villa. "Please . . . ? It will do you good, too, Master. Excitement will take your thoughts away from matters of the heart."

"Out of the mouths of babes," Sandro said. "He's absolutely right. Come on. . . ."

Leonardo followed, trying to keep his anxiety at bay; but it was like a dark and rabid retriever following him. Through the passageway they came upon an immaculate lawn and garden, a true *tapis vert*. High walls were covered with climbing jasmine, a saloon widened into a terrace overlooking the city, which was a constellation of lights. A peristyle of Corinthian columns stood like ancient ruins in this modern yet eternal place. Lamps glowed in vases and urns situated around giant topiaries.

Leonardo and his friends followed Jacopo up the stairs and into the house, which was dark, except for a penny candle burning atop a small but heavy-looking table on the wall opposite the door.

"You see, it is just as I told you," Jacopo said. "Now, follow me."

"You know where you are going?" asked Sandro.

"I have been given instructions from Master Onorevoli," and the boy led them up a flight of stairs, then down a flight of stairs, across what seemed like an abyss for lack of illumination, to a black door. Niccolò kept close to Leonardo until Leonardo took his hand.

"It seems that Il Neri has turned the house into a reflection of his soul," Sandro said.

"More likely an evening of grotesquerie," Leonardo said.

"It will be worth it for an evening with Simonetta," Sandro said.

"Are you frightened, Niccolò?" Leonardo asked.

"No," Machiavelli said emphatically, but his voice sounded thin.

Suddenly the light was extinguished, and Jacopo disappeared.

Unable to see even a shadow in the darkness, which seemed to have its own density, Leonardo felt for the door that he knew to be before him. "Nicco," he called, "stay where you are. . . . Sandro . . . ?"

"We're here . . . ," said Sandro.

"If I find that Jacopo—" Niccolò said.

"He's only following his orders," Leonardo said, finding the door latch. "There," and he pushed open the door.

Niccolò screamed.

Leonardo clasped his shoulder. They were looking into a room covered with curtains of deep black. Candles in sconces upon the walls cast an eerie, wan light. Each wall had cubby indentations, and each cubbyhole contained an illuminated human skull. Full skeletons were hung in the four corners of the room, and they were also illuminated with candles to frightening effect. In the center of the room was a long table covered with a black cloth. As a centerpiece, another skull rested upon a wooden plate, and around the skull were set four wooden glasses. Dressed in the black cloth of a priest, his face powdered chalk-white and his lips painted crimson, Il Neri addressed Leonardo in an almost girlish voice. "Gentlemen, this is but the first course of an evening of delights. Please be seated, for when we are finished here, we shall move along to the next . . . station."

"Where are our friends, Neri?" Leonardo asked.

"I assure you, they are here," he said. "But they are slightly ahead of you in discovering tonight's pleasures. Leonardo, tonight I shall outdo even your prestidigitation. So now, please, sit."

Once the guests were at the table, the skulls revolved without any noticeable mechanism, and as if by magic, sausages extruded through their eyes and dressed pheasants appeared upon each plate.

"Very good, Neri, but do we dare eat this fare?" asked Sandro.

"That's entirely up to you, dear friend." Neri sat down and proceeded to pull apart his pheasant.

But the bird on Leonardo's plate smelled foul as feces. "Don't eat anything," Leonardo said, directing himself especially to Niccolò. "We'd best leave this place the way we came."

"Ah, you're a bad sport, Leonardo," Neri said. "But when it's your tricks on display, you expect everyone to show proper deference."

"But I have never put shit before your face."

"There seems to be nothing wrong with my food," Niccolò said.

"Nor mine," said Sandro.

Just then there was a sudden crashing noise above them. Everyone jumped in fright, but it was merely a distraction; for when they looked upon the table again, they noticed that great silver bowls of salad had replaced their pheasant and sausage.

Sandro made a disgusted noise and pushed himself away from the table, almost falling as he did so.

"What is it?" asked Leonardo.

"Look for yourself."

Leonardo did, and saw the maggots moving among the greens. "Neri, this is quite enough. Niccolò, Sandro, let's get out of here."

"Come now, my friends, you've no sense of humor," Neri said placatingly. "It's all meant in fun, for effect, and you must admit, the effect is quite good."

"This is not the time for such grotesque goings-on," Sandro said. "And we've a child with us."

"It's true enough that there is a young man in our midst, but isn't he here for the purpose of learning about life and its mysteries?"

"So you have spoken to Zoroastro and Benedetto," Leonardo said.

Neri nodded and smiled. "But what better night than this for what I have planned," he said to Sandro. "A holy night, the night before Resurrection. A night to remember the chill and dampness of the grave, a night to contemplate eternal sleep and the worms that consume all flesh. If the miracle of the divine Christ were mundane, if it were not itself frightening in its pure and supernatural aspect, then it would not be worthy of Our Lord. Is that not what we must teach our children?"

There was another sharp, sudden noise, this one more distant; Niccolò jumped nevertheless and sought comfort near Leonardo. "We are leaving, Neri," Leonardo said.

"Oh, come on . . . please. I shall immediately lead you to your friends . . . to less frightening surroundings."

"No, thank you."

"But, dear friends," Neri said, "you cannot find your way without a guide. Without light."

The candles suddenly went out, leaving only retinal afterimages in the blackness.

"Well," Neri continued, "will you accompany me to the main party? I promise you will enjoy yourselves."

"And what of the child?" Leonardo demanded.

"I am hardly that," Niccolò said.

"Well . . . ?"

"You have my solemn oath," Neri said, "that if anything untoward should happen, the young man shall not be privy to it. I will arrange for him to be accompanied home. If you desire, *you* can take him home, or Sandro. But I assure you both, you will not wish to leave. This banquet will still be spoken about in the years to come. And, Sandro, I assure you, it is in keeping with the holy occasion."

"I was under the impression that this fete was in honor of Simonetta," Sandro said.

"And so it is," Neri said.

"Where is she?"

"She is here, I assure you. But it is up to you to find her." A candle caught fire, again as if by magic, in Neri's hand. "Now . . . please, follow me." He opened a door and left the room.

Leonardo and Sandro had no choice but to follow; both held on to Niccolò.

"Here we are," Neri said, and he led them through a walnut door with a brass mounting into a great, vaulted hall, with huge fireplaces of *pietra serena* and high corniced windows draped with black cloth. There were so many lamps and candles in the room that Niccolò exclaimed in delight, "It's a world of stars!"

At least a hundred guests, many already drunk, milled about long tables covered with candles and food: pheasants, partridges, beef, pork, fruit, condiments, and greens. The guests were a disparate, exotic group; but, then, such had come to be considered de rigueur for a memorable party. There were several cardinals, dressed in the lusty color of their office, from the See in Rome; wealthy courtesans wearing very revealing virgin-white chemises popular in Venice and Milan; humble prostitutes, who looked greasy and self-conscious, and spoke too loudly the low Tuscan dialect of the street; and wealthy guildsmen who represented the great families of Florence. Only the Medici, it seemed, were absent. There were outlandishly garbed visitors from Famagusta, Bejaïa, Tunis, and Constantinople; agents and merchant clients from Seville, Majorca, Naples, Paris, and Bruges, here for festival. A lieutenant of the Sacred Sultan of Babylon wore a white turban with his stylish Florentine costume; he wore a red stocking on his right leg and a blue one on the left; even his shoes were of two colors: amethyst and white. But the most exotic bird of all was a tall, robust-looking Chinese man dressed in robes and slippers of purple silk. Servants, both male and female (but mostly young men), wore gowns of the sheerest gauze; in fact, they might as well have been naked. They carried trays of glasses filled with wine.

"You're hurting me," Niccolò said to Leonardo, who was holding him tightly by the arm.

"Then stop trying to break away from Sandro and me."

"Let me go. You're not my father."

"Don't test me, Nicco," Leonardo said. "Another word and I'll take you home right now."

"To Ser Toscanelli's *bottega*?"

"You made your choice to be my apprentice," Leonardo said. "And that you'll remain." Niccolò stopped wriggling about and smiled at Leonardo, as if that was all he had wanted to hear. Leonardo released the boy and turned his attention back to Neri. "Was everyone here honored to dine as intimately as we?" Leonardo asked.

"Only those very special guests whom I particularly wished to impress," Neri said.

"I am sure not the good prelates, nor the man with the tilted eyes," Leonardo said.

"Especially the good prelates," Neri said slyly. "Now, please feel free to eat and drink whatever you like. I can assure you, all the victuals will be to your liking."

There was an explosion of light in a corner of the huge ballroom, and then applause. A crowd had gathered around a man who looked like Leonardo.

In fact, he looked exactly like Leonardo.

"And who might that be?" Leonardo asked Neri.

Neri laughed. "Why, it is *you*."

"It *is* you," Sandro said, delighted. "And look, he's done the trick of creating flames by pouring red wine into boiling oil. One can understand the effect of such a magick on the rabble, but these are citizens of stature. Still . . . I suppose it *is* a good trick."

"Come, I'll introduce you," Neri said, his smile exaggerated, for his lips were clownishly streaked with paint.

"To myself?" Leonardo asked, genuinely amused.

They followed Neri to the corner of the room where Leonardo's doppelgänger was amusing the crowd with a witty story. He was the same height as Leonardo; his clothes, clean and fresh, were identical to those Leonardo was wearing: a tight-fitting doublet of heliotrope, crimson *camicia* shirt, hose with only a piece of leather attached to the underside of the *calze* to protect the soles of his feet. But it was the face that fascinated Leonardo. It was like looking into a mirror; the features were perfect, or at least seemed so in the buttery glow of the candlelight.

How did he do it? Leonardo wondered. Only the voice was off, a bit too throaty. But nevertheless . . .

"Leonardo?" asked Zoroastro, who was standing near the fake Leonardo, having assisted the conjurations. "Is that you?" Bemused, he moved toward Leonardo.

But Neri focused the guests' attention by making introductions. "Leonardo, I would like to present . . . Leonardo."

"Are they twins?" someone asked.

"Impossible, my friend, for there is but one genius called Leonardo da Vinci," Neri said.

"Then one is a fake."

"But *which* one?"

"Who are you?" asked Leonardo, admiring the man before him.

But Zoroastro, who had undoubtedly been fooled, interrupted, saying to Leonardo, "I thought this man who seemed to be no one else but you sounded strange . . . too hoarse, gravelly." He turned to Leonardo's double and said, "And you told me you had a cold."

"But I do," said the man, unruffled.

Unable to resist the joke, Leonardo said to Zoroastro, "Are you then so certain that I am the real Leonardo?"

"Niccolò and Sandro came with you," Zoroastro said, desperately trying to maintain a show of equanimity. *"Facta, non verba."*

"But *I* asked them to run an errand while I went on ahead," Leonardo's double said, taking his cue, as if he were a player on stage.

"Yes, you did, Master Leonardo," Niccolò said to Leonardo's double, his face as somber as if he were telling the truth. "You insisted on walking alone to think."

Zoroastro retorted, "As far as I'm concerned, you can both be Leonardo."

"An excellent idea," said Leonardo's double. "Master Leonardo, let us combine our considerable talents. I have just completed the construction of a flying machine. Perhaps you might consider piloting its initial flight?"

That quieted the room.

"It will be propelled," he continued, "by angels, such beings being, of course, lighter than air. They will pull my machine past the Sphere of the Moon, past the Sphere of the Fixed Stars, to the Crystalline Sphere, to the Primum Mobile itself."

"And then, of course, to the Empyrean Paradise," Leonardo said.

"Absolutely. Then you, too, are engaged in a similar adventure?"

"Indeed, but even if I weren't, could I sensibly argue with someone of such stature that he can command the sacred power of angels? I would be afraid of being accused of disbelief and heresy."

Leonardo's double laughed at that—a good-natured laugh, one that was oddly familiar to Leonardo. Yet he could not quite place it.

"If you have constructed your own machine, I could not ask you to pilot my humble assemblage."

"Au contraire," Leonardo said, smiling. "I would be honored, for it is not often one is asked to fly with the angels."

But then Neri took Leonardo by the arm and announced that this Leonardo would have to be excused from the party.

"I cannot, nor will not, leave the boy," Leonardo whispered. He gave Niccolò a sharp look, for he was standing too close to a beautiful doe-eyed girl, one of Neri's servants. The girl smiled at Niccolò, who was blushing, perhaps at her nakedness. He certainly did not notice Leonardo's disapproving gaze.

Neri said a few words to Sandro, who promised to look after Niccolò for a time, and, if necessary, to see to his safety, which meant keeping him away from beds and servant girls. "There, you see," Neri said. "*Alea iacta est.* Now, will you trust yourself to me?"

"I would not be so foolish."

"But I must show you why I invited you," Neri said.

"I would have thought it was to meet my twin."

"And now you've met him." After Leonardo exchanged a few words with Niccolò and Sandro, and was satisfied that all would be well, he permitted Neri to guide him across the room. Those curious few who tried to follow were skillfully obstructed by Neri's servants. Once out of the vaulted hall, two young male servants walked before them and illuminated their way through the house.

"It's gratifying to see you so concerned for your young apprentice," Neri said. "I didn't know you cared for anything besides your work, but come to think of it, you do have a reputation as a rogue. Why else would you be attending such a party as this?"

"I came for Sandro's sake," Leonardo said.

"Ah, yes, for Sandro's sake," Neri said with uncharacteristic sarcasm. "But I will do my best to entertain you; and before the night is over, I will introduce you to someone I believe you will find delightful."

"I trust you are not implying that it will take all night for us to return to your guests," Leonardo said.

"That, Leonardo, will be up to you," Neri said mysteriously.

"And this guest? Is he the other 'me'?"

"No, but he is a visitor from far away. You both have something in common."

"And that would be?"

"I'll not say anything more, lest it spoil everything."

"Neri, enough of this," Leonardo said. "You must tell me who my double is."

"This time *you* must follow the lead of others for answers," Neri said, smiling, as he walked behind his servants through rooms and corridors where shadowy portraits of stern merchants, ancestral ladies, and grotesque trompe l'oeil centaurs, naiads, and satyrs stared fixedly at them as they passed. They went up a flight of stairs, and then another, always ascending, until they came to a heavy, embrasured door. The servants positioned themselves on each side of the door in heraldic stance; if they had had halberds, they would have crossed them.

"Neri, I think you're taking this game too far," Leonardo said, suddenly nervous.

"I'll let you judge that . . . in a moment," and he opened the door and stepped into a well-lit but rather small, unostentatious bedroom, except for the bed, which was a large four-poster with bedposts carved into the shapes of ostrich feathers at the top; rich, draped velvet curtains embossed with red griffins hung to the rough plank floor. Candles burned in sconces in the four corners of the room, and a lamp was set upon a good-sized table; beside the lamp were glasses, a flask of wine, a white porcelain basin, soap, and a neat stack of pale-blue linen towels embossed with feathers and griffins. Neri poured Leonardo a glass of wine and held it out to him. "Sit," he said, nodding toward the bed, "and I'll be ready in a moment."

"Neri, just show me what you've brought me here to see," Leonardo said, becoming impatient.

Neri pushed back the dark hood and pulled off a tight-fitting headpiece. Long, curly golden hair fell across the dark cloth of the chasuble.

"Who are you?" Leonardo asked, shocked that he'd been fooled by this impersonator who was now removing layers of thin material—animal skin, most likely. After an application of soap and water and a scrubbing with the towels, the newly revealed face was more astonishing than any of the trompe l'oeil paintings on the corridor walls.

It was Simonetta's.

Devoid of any makeup, her complexion was ivory-white, but not in the least pallid. She looked at him intently, her face grave, not a shadow of frivolity or conceit or meanness there. Her eyes were motionless, unfathomable, and as she watched Leonardo, she unfastened her robes and let them fall around her feet. Only her breasts, which now seemed small, were rouged, a tinct of vermilion and pink against white.

"No, please don't look so anxious, Leonardo," she said in her own voice, which was quite different in register and resonance than her imitation of Neri's. She moved to the table, where she poured herself a glass of wine, and then she sat down beside him.

"I must leave," Leonardo said, shocked and embarrassed.

"Why? You are lovesick. You will not heal yourself by leaving. But perhaps by staying . . ." She smiled, but there was no slyness to it. Only sadness. She did not try to cover herself, but sat before him, seemingly comfortable.

"What do you want with me?" Leonardo asked.

"I have always wanted you, Leonardo," she said softly, matter-of-factly.

"If Lorenzo or Giuliano found us here—"

Simonetta then shook her head and laughed. Her hair appeared gauzy in the candlelight. "For me it would not much matter, but for you, Leonardo, for you it would be the end of everything."

"And for you too; now, let us leave," Leonardo insisted, the frustration evident in his voice.

"I know what has happened to you," Simonetta said, moving closer to him. Leonardo looked down at the floor, avoiding Simonetta's nakedness, although her smell and nearness aroused him.

"And just what is that?" Leonardo asked.

"I know all about you and Ginevra and that old stick Nicolini."

Surprised, he looked directly at her.

"I have talked to Sandro."

"And he told you of my private affairs?" Leonardo asked, incredulous.

"He would tell me anything . . . because he knows I can be trusted. And do you know why?"

"No," Leonardo said, angry and humiliated. "I do not."

"Because I am dying. Sandro knows it but cannot admit it, for he loves me."

"I do not believe you are dying," Leonardo said, looking at her as if she were Ginevra.

"It is true, but I shall try not to cough out my lungs before you as proof." Then she embraced him and said, "But tonight we are both of us dying."

Leonardo felt trapped, although he knew he could get up and leave. Yet he felt excited by Simonetta. She had caught him when he was most fragile. She, and not he, was the enchanter, the conjurer, the *thaumaturgus*. It was as if she had suddenly—impossibly and irresistibly—freed him of the world, as if now dreams, and nightmares, were made of the same stuff as fire and water and chairs and walls, these walls, these floors, this bed, this woman caressing him.

But what had really caught him, even distracted him from Ginevra, was her profound sadness. Indeed, she was dying; it could not be otherwise.

He watched as Simonetta swept her hands along his legs, touching him, releasing him from his codpiece. He felt he must stop her, but it was as if he had forgotten how to work the muscles necessary to move away from her. What did it matter? Indeed, he was free; but such freedom was itself a nightmare. Before he could shake loose of this dream . . . or nightmare, she knelt upon the floor and took his member into her mouth. He was still, as if caught; only his heart beat and pumped thunderously in his throat. He thought of water, of the surface of the sea, of Ginevra, always Ginevra; and Simonetta's mouth was hot upon his member, which he imagined was as hard and cold as ice. Or stone. As if he were some misbegotten Lot who could not resist looking upon Sodom and hardening into cold, implacable stone. But she sucked on him, warming him, as if she were a furnace, thawing him, until he pulled her onto the bed, kissing her, smelling her, as they began to sweat and pound, one into another, like oiled engines of flesh and bone.

As he kissed her deeply, discovering, tasting, she helped him pull off his clothes; she insisted on being close to his skin. Leonardo sought her tongue, permitting her to fill his mouth with hers; and as she lay back upon the bed, open and akimbo to him, he ran his tongue along her collarbone and sucked upon her breasts, as if he were a child trying to pull the milk through her small, erected nipples.

Leonardo pressed his face between her legs and smelled the sour dampness of the earth. Childhood memories flooded past him: a sudden bright sunlit image of the slopes of Monte Albano above Vinci, the ocherous mines in Val d'Elsa, the flowers and herbs and stratification of the dark grotto in Vinci, his grotto, where he spent so many solitary hours; even now he remembered the perfumes of sage, thyme, mint, and blackberry in the air. He remembered his mother, and his first stepmother, the young and beautiful Albiera di Giovanni Amadori. His father's wife was not much older than Leonardo, and how many interminable days had Leonardo spent in the grotto longing for her. Now Leonardo raised himself above her, to penetrate her more deeply. She exhaled sharply as he did so and looked up at him, as if shocked. She stared at him, her face taut, as if trying not to reveal a secret agony. She was, indeed, beautiful, her thick blond hair a nimbus of glory around her soft, aristocratic face. Yet her face contained all the grief and stricken appearance of a mourner.

At once she was vulnerable . . . and deadly.

A Madonna of purity.

A grieving mother torn from her family.

A cold, beautiful whore.

She grimaced, ready to come, and for an instant Leonardo saw her as Medusa. He had painted just such a face when he was a boy, and his father had sold the panel for three hundred ducats. In that instant, in that hallucinatory second before he ejaculated, he imagined her lustrous hair transformed into golden, writhing serpents; and he was frozen. One of the darting-tongued creatures wrapped itself around him as he pressed himself upon her. The suction of their wet skin was the muffled sounds of distant creatures being joined and torn apart.

Suddenly Leonardo felt Ginevra watching him, as if from some peripheral corner of his memory cathedral. As if it were *he* who was committing the sin.

But even now, especially now, as he pumped his life into the beautiful Simonetta, he felt the aching loss of Ginevra.

And in that cold, watery, and lonely moment of ecstasy, Leonardo found himself looking into Simonetta's gray eyes.

Ginevra's eyes . . .

She was crying . . . as was he.

4

The Secret

of the

Golden Flower

We have three souls, of which the one nearest to God is called by Mercurius Trismegistus and Plato *mens,* by Moses the spirit of life, by St. Augustine the higher part, by David light, when he says "In thy light shall we see light." And Mercurius says that if we join ourselves to this *mens* we may understand, through the ray from God, which is in it, all things, present, past, and future; all things, I say, which are in heaven and earth.

—Giulio Camillo

Anyone who wishes, let him be merry; there is no certainty in tomorrow.

—Lorenzo de' Medici

L eonardo stared up at the high ceiling, imagining all manner of faces and creatures and scenes in its cracked and shadowed imperfections. These various scenes and personages, which Leonardo saw in great detail, constantly shifted like clouds drifting in a dim, gray sky. There, the perfect, curved line of a shoulder leading with mathematical exactitude to the gentle slope of a breast; here, the detail of a fortification, complete with banquette, bastion, moat, covert way, and glacis: a blueprint. A scorpion was transmogrified into the curling hair of a cherub, whose face seemed to turn: a drunk, macabre Cupid. He saw Madonnas, rough-sketched, as if from his notebooks: one *caritas* resembled Albiera, his first stepmother, who had died when he was but twelve; another looked like Francesca di Ser Giuliano Lanfredini, his second stepmother, who had died five years ago. These wives of his father were little more than girls . . . and as a boy, Leonardo had guiltily yearned for them.

The room was quiet, except for Simonetta's rasping, although even, breathing. She lay on her back beside him, her arm resting over her eyes, as if to prevent them even in sleep from glimpsing the hypnotic dreamscape above. An interfusion of stale odors hung richly in the air: wine, perfume, perspiration, sex, lamp oil. Leonardo considered rising to open a window, but was afraid he would awaken Simonetta and that the miasmas of the night might harm her lungs.

She sought him now, even in her sleep. Perhaps she sensed he was awake and might leave, for she turned toward him, resting her legs upon his, grasping for his arm and his chest. As Leonardo watched her—she was so blond and pale, a ghost given flesh—he could imagine that reality had indeed been breached for a few hours.

But now Leonardo was awake; his mouth tasted sour, his head ached, and he felt completely alone. The enchantment was broken.

Simonetta suddenly began to cough, again and again, which seemed to throw her this way and that. She awakened immediately, her eyes wide, staring straight ahead as she wheezed for breath and held her arms tightly across her chest. Leonardo held her and then gave her some wine. She had another fit of coughing, which finally subsided. "I'm sorry to disturb you like this, beautiful Leonardo," she said, wiping her mouth on the damask sheet that she held around her.

"I was awake."

"Have you been for long?" she asked.

"No, not very."

"I'm sure our party is still active. Do you wish to return?" Simonetta coughed again, got up from the bed, combed her fair luxurious hair, which reached to her buttocks, then opened a chest in the wooden platform surrounding the bed and removed an indigo tight-waisted dress sans chemise. It revealed her shoulders, which appeared pale as moonlight beneath silk mesh joined with gold beads and precious jewels.

Only Ginevra could best Simonetta as a beauty.

"Haven't you questions?" she asked, smiling.

"You were going to tell me who is playing my double," Leonardo said; still feeling awkward, he followed her lead and dressed.

"Leonardo?" Simonetta asked.

"Yes?"

"You seem so . . . distant."

"I'm sorry."

Simonetta moved close to him and said, "I can be trusted. Your heart is safe with me. And perhaps I can help you."

Leonardo could feel his glands opening inside him, spilling icy adrenaline. Perhaps Nicolini could be bested and Ginevra regained. "But how could I return your gifts in kind?" he asked.

"You cannot."

"Then why—"

"Because I'm dying and wish to be generous. Because I'm afraid and cannot show myself to those in power. And I certainly cannot trust other women. But I can trust you, dear Leonardo."

"How can you be sure?" Leonardo asked tentatively, carefully.

"Because I trust Sandro, who thinks of you as a brother."

"Then would not Sandro be the better choice? He lives for you."

"Exactly. And he loves me. I could only raise his hopes and dash them. I could not permit him to become close to me. You'll have your hands full enough with him when I pass on."

"Simonetta, you must not—" But Leonardo stopped himself. There was nothing that could be said; she was well enough prepared for what Virgil had called "the supreme day and the inevitable hour." After a beat he said, "I suppose you're right about Sandro."

Simonetta drew close to Leonardo; he was tall, and she had to look up at him. "It is not only making love," she said. "That's the least of it; I am supplied with more than enough of that. But I am completely alone."

"All of Florence worships you," Leonardo said.

"Nevertheless . . ."

He held her, wishing she was Ginevra, but glad for her warmth and closeness and sweaty perfume . . . and perhaps, just perhaps, there might be balm in Gilead, after all.

Perhaps she could help him. . . .

Leonardo felt himself getting excited again, but Simonetta backed away, laughing. "Perhaps I *can't* be sure of you."

"Then tell me who it was downstairs that claimed to be me."

Simonetta sat down on the bed, sipped a bit of wine from her glass, and said, "Why, it was Neri, of course."

"I thought as much," Leonardo said, sitting down beside her. "To his credit, he did a fair job of imitation."

She laughed and said, "Well, dear Leonardo, if it is indeed true that all of Florence worships me, as you say, then I'll tell you that Neri worships *you.*"

"I didn't think he had much use for me, except as seasoning for his parties."

"He's a frustrated painter. But he has a good eye and collects well. He even has some of your work."

"What?"

"Just sketches, Leonardo. You're a difficult man to collect. Rumors have it that not even the marchioness Isabella d'Este could obtain one of your little pictures of the Madonna."

"I paint very slowly, Madonna Simonetta; but I am working very hard on several little Madonnas."

"I would not wager on having better luck than the marchioness," Simonetta said.

"Rich patrons have not exactly been beating down Andrea's doors with commissions for me."

"You've gained a bad reputation for not completing past commissions, but Lorenzo is interested in you. I will see what I can do."

"Well, I must say that both you and Neri had me fooled," Leonardo said.

"Yes?"

"If he made up your face and his own, then he is, indeed, very good. Perhaps I should apprentice with *him.*"

Simonetta laughed softly, then said, "You make the automatic assumption that Neri was the painter."

"If not Neri, then who?"

"Could you not conceive that it might be me?" she asked.

"I am astonished."

"Only because you are a man, Leonardo. I also taught Neri how to imitate your voice, for he croaked like a frog." She did a fine imitation of Neri and then continued, "Are you familiar with an artist called Gaddiano?"

"Of course," Leonardo said. "It is rumored that he is Sienese; his patrons have to contact him through his notary . . . a man by the name of Mazzei. Gaddiano sculpted a magnificent terra-cotta Cybele that stands beside the fountains in the Medici gardens at Careggi. Is that not correct?"

"You are very observant," Simonetta said. "That is indeed Gaddiano's work." Then she stood up, made an exaggerated bow, and said, "And *I* am Gaddiano."

"You?"

"That should not be difficult to believe for someone who but a few hours ago thought I was his friend Neri."

"I apologize for my surprise, Madonna, but most of us mortals have enough trouble trying to master one life; yet you have mastered *two*," Leonardo said, intrigued. "It is like . . . being in two places at once."

Simonetta laughed and said, quoting the poet Horace, "No one lives content with his condition."

"Under the guise of Gaddiano, you've established an enviable reputation as a sculptor and painter," Leonardo said. "But most of us do not have such abilities to transform ourselves. Perhaps you are Paracelsus' bird-of-fire in disguise. Turning yourself into Neri, and Neri into me, must have been child's play."

"What would you have had me do?" Simonetta asked.

"What do you mean?"

"Could *you* live without painting, without sculpting stone?" Simonetta asked. "Ah, you probably could, as long as you had your science and could indulge yourself in invention."

"As long as I can see, I could just as easily indulge my eyes in all the various things of nature, as of art," Leonardo said.

"But I could not, dear Leonardo. And I could not paint and be known as myself . . . as Simonetta."

"Such beautiful work—such painting and sculpting—could only bring honor upon you."

"As a woman I would be considered a trifler," Simonetta said. "I could not be taken seriously, nor could I gain even the most humble of commissions. But as a man . . . as a man I can compete equally. I can direct other men's hearts and minds. As a woman, I can control only for a time their hearts and their stiffened members."

"Perhaps you underestimate a woman's control over a man."

"Of all the women in Florence, I would not have thought that I could be accused of that," Simonetta said. "But whatever you think, a woman—no matter how well positioned—is but a servant. I wanted to have the opportunity to seize immortality. . . . *Carpe diem.* Unlike the rest of you, my time was limited."

"But Gaddiano has been painting for—"

"Exactly three years here in Florence," Simonetta said. "It was three years ago that I realized I was dying. Gaddiano's past was created by me; it is built on rumor, paintings dated *posteä,* and a few fabricated records. Oh, I thought of trying to use my connections with powerful friends, but like your young friend Machiavelli's mother, Bartolomea, I would never have been taken seriously."

"But she *is* respected, as a poetess."

"Yes, as a religious poet. Yet is she read in the churches? In the streets? She'd do better as a midwife." Simonetta began to pace the room like one of Lorenzo's caged lions.

Leonardo stood up and caught hold of her hands. She looked down at the floor, as if Leonardo were her father rather than one of her many lovers. "I had no idea such anger was contained inside you," Leonardo said.

Simonetta tightened her hold on Leonardo's hands and said, "Now you know all my secrets . . . just as I know yours. More than you think, Leonardo."

"Be that as it may," he said, cursing Sandro silently, "but you have no need to let your anger poison you. As Gaddiano, you are insured a place in Florence forever. I promise you that is the truth." That seemed to please her. "And as Simonetta," Leonardo continued, "you will be remembered as the face of Venus and of so many Madonnas."

"Thanks to Sandro," she said, smiling faintly. Then she broke away from him and crossed the room to the door. "I will leave you a servant as guide. It would not do for us to be seen coming down together, lest our guests imagine an inappropriate liaison." Again she smiled, slyly, and left.

Leonardo waited a few moments, then followed the remnant servant through the dark, winding, whispering halls and down the cold marble treads of what could only be imagined in the dark as secret stairways. Hours had passed since he and Simonetta had come to their room, and now the many rooms of this great house were being utilized by the guests. Every landing and hallway was filled with night noises, as if Leonardo were being guided through some magian forest. Light as wan and eerie as firedrake, St. Elmo's fire, or ignis fatuus coruscated around the cracks between door stiles and jambs.

Leonardo stopped beside a door on what he supposed was the third landing: he thought he recognized a voice. He told the servant he would find his own way and listened behind the door to a poem sung in a high, clear voice, accompanied by a lyre and the discordant gabble and susurration of several rather boisterous conversations.

Someone moaned, as if in ecstasy, and the song continued:

. . . and flowers combine
Their gayest hues, her earliest steps to share:

With smiling grace, nor less than forms divine
Three duteous nymphs receive the stranger blest,
And with a spangled robe her limbs invest....

It was Atalante Miglioretti's voice.

Leonardo opened the door and was about to join Atalante in the popular song until he saw Il Neri, still dressed and made-up as Leonardo himself.

Closing the door behind him, Leonardo said, "Neri, you should remove my features from your face."

Neri was sitting upon one of several chairs covered with green and gold velvet, and the youth Jacopo Saltarelli was kneeling before his open legs and performing fellatio upon him. Saltarelli was completely naked and painted as if he were some sort of crimson piebald creature. Many of the people in the room were also naked. A young woman wearing a black robe with a vermilion band around her head lay on the floor beside Neri and was being simultaneously penetrated front and back by two middle-aged men whom Leonardo did not recognize. Candles burned fitfully in sconces high upon the walls, creating sickly light and long shadows. Although the furnishings were sumptuous—gleaming porphyry and carvings, fine tapestries depicting the most voluptuous scenes of classical mythology: Io's transformation into a heifer, Europa and the bull, Danae and the shower of gold—this was but an ordinary orgy. Only Atalante's sweet voice and expert playing distinguished this crowd of revelers from any other gathering of decadents.

Leonardo could not help but notice the three couples engaged in various positions of penetration on the single but ornate bed under the leaded window; it did not surprise him that one of the women—a girl, actually—was the servant with whom Niccolò had been so enamored earlier in the evening.

Where were Sandro and Niccolò...? he wondered. He would have to find them.

Atalante smiled at Leonardo and offered him the lute. Leonardo declined. A young boy holding a flagon of wine asked him if he wished a drink; Leonardo politely said no and turned away. He recognized very few of the people here: Bartholomeo di Pasquino, a fair-to-middling goldsmith; Baccino, who was Neri's tailor; Giordano Bracciolini, a leading member of the Platonic Academy and author of a commentary on Petrarch's *Triumph of Fame;* the debt-ridden adventurer Bernardo de Bandini Baroncelli, who was fulsomely praising one of Neri's naked servant girls as if she were Simonetta herself; and Jacopo Saltarelli's scrubby, hard-faced brother, Giovanni, who was sitting by himself and masturbating. Seemingly oblivious to the orgy going on around them, several impeccably dressed patrician youths from the Bardi and Peruzzi families were arguing excitedly about the crookedness of the Medici-controlled Signoria, the Balia election committees, and the impotence of the Parlamento, all of which one of the young men pompously pronounced to be *"contra bonos mores."*

Atalante began singing again; he chose one of Lorenzo's Tuscan poems. "Well, has a cat got your tongue?" Leonardo asked Neri.

" 'Tis not my tongue that the cat's got," Neri said, smiling. Then he proceeded to pull away the lifelike skin coverings from his face. He ordered Jacopo to fetch him a linen, with which he wiped the remaining makeup from his face. Without apparent concern or embarrassment, Jacopo returned to his fellatio of Neri's now semiflaccid member. "There, my good guest," Neri said. "Your smallest wish is my greatest desire. Now you are indeed Leonardo and I am indeed—" He looked down at Jacopo and asked, "Who *am* I? Aha," he said, directing himself to Leonardo. "I am *mala in se* . . . inherently bad. And what have I done as the very incarnation of you, Leonardo? To quote Quintus Horatius Flaccus: *'Exegi monumentum aere perennius.'* "

Neri laughed, but Leonardo blushed in humiliation, for he could not understand the Latin, which was too quickly spoken. At least Leonardo could now read Latin fairly well, but an "educated" man could quote all the ancient poets and speak the dead language as well as Lucan or Quintilian or Claudian; in these he was sadly lacking.

"Leonardo, it's a *joke*. I only said that 'I have raised a monument more durable than bronze.' That's all it means. Please forgive me if—"

But Leonardo excused himself and left. He soon lost himself in the darkness of the house as he padded through the hallways, guided by the splinters of light around the doors. He extended his hand to touch the walls, keeping a brushing contact with the house as he walked, as if he were a blind man making his way through unfamiliar alleys. Memories seemed to come back to him at once, as if they were made of the same stuff as darkness: Ginevra, Nicolini, the garroted boy. He had lost Ginevra forever, but that was impossible . . . that simply could not have happened. Neither could he have just left the warm bed of the beautiful and beloved Simonetta. She could not be Gaddiano . . . nor could Neri be Leonardo. Yet tonight all things terrible and exquisite seemed possible; and he could not help but feel that these were all portents, that fate was leading him on.

When he reached the stairway, he saw lamps aglow in sconces in the walls. Then he heard a peal of applause, followed by shouts of *bravissimo! evviva!* and *valete ac plaudite!* He rushed forward; before him was the great, vaulted hall where he had left Sandro and Niccolò. From the candle-flickering, shadowy gloom of the corridor, the hall looked as if it were the essence of light itself, its very concentration; and Leonardo felt as if he were escaping from the fuliginous mazes of hell into the brightest sphere of Paradise.

When he entered the room, Simonetta broke away from the crush of guests, who seemed mesmerized by the present attraction: a Chinese man in damson silk who stood behind a long table with his arm held dramatically in front of his eyes. As she walked toward Leonardo, several of her would-be suitors turned to watch her. She looked the regal figure, full-bodied, soft-featured, and straight-backed; it was as if she were gliding above the floor rather than touching the miserable wood.

After Leonardo kissed her hand, she linked her arm with his and said, "Now, Leonardo, I will introduce you to the guest whom I told you about before we . . ." She smiled at him, as if to remind him that he was her lover. "I'm sure that you will both find much in common."

Leonardo felt awkward, but suddenly Niccolò ran over to him. "I didn't see you come in," Niccolò said, taking Leonardo's hand. He was obviously excited, for his face was flushed.

Sandro followed behind Niccolò. Although he greeted Leonardo warmly, he appeared agitated. It was as if he was somehow tentative, unsure of himself now in Simonetta's presence. Perhaps he was afraid that he would be seen by her as just another anxious, self-serving suitor.

Yet Leonardo sensed something else: jealousy . . . anger.

Indeed, if Sandro knew that Leonardo had occupied Simonetta this night, he would be beside himself. Leonardo felt a chill feather down his spine; perhaps Sandro could see the guilt upon his face.

"You must see what this strange-looking man can do," Niccolò said. He was obviously eager to return to the crowd at the far end of the room, for he kept looking there, as if he were missing the very words of thunder and fire that God had spoken at Sinai. "His name is Go On He Sees."

Simonetta laughed, ruffled Niccolò's hair, and said, "No, young Nicco, his name is Kuan Yin-hsi, which he told me means 'The Master of the Pass.'"

"He seems overly dramatic," Leonardo said, watching his exaggerated movements. "I do not believe most people of his race act thus."

"But he is like *you*, Leonardo," Simonetta said, turning back to him, for she had taken Niccolò's hand; and he was pulling her toward the entertainment. "He's a magician, a genius, a charmer, an actor, a bewitcher . . . an astrologer."

"I am no astrologer," Leonardo said.

She raised Niccolò's hand, laughed, and said, "You see, little Nicco, your master rebuffs me for calling him an astrologer, but he'll admit to all the rest."

Leonardo and Sandro held back.

"Are you all right, Little Bottle?" Leonardo asked Sandro in a whisper. Leonardo was one of a very small circle of friends who was permitted to call Sandro by his nickname. Sandro had been an overweight child; his father had given him the derisive nickname.

"Why shouldn't I be, except for your leaving me with this fourteen-year-old voluptuary?"

"Niccolò?"

"And who else?"

"What did he do?" Leonardo asked, then caught himself and said, "Ah, the maidservant? I saw her upstairs with her legs spread as if desiring to be treated to *a trentuno reale*."

"I don't think that little thing could survive seventy men," Sandro said, "but she certainly ate up our little Niccolò—"

"Or vice versa."

"I had to feel around in the dark outside the door before I found him," Sandro continued. "She's a noisy one."

"And ... ?"

"Well, it was obvious that he had already begun; I thought it best to let him finish."

Leonardo laughed. "Well, Nicco was in earnest about prostitutes, for he told me they should be part of his education. And that according to Toscanelli."

"I could hardly believe that!"

"Actually, neither could I, but one never can be sure of the old man."

"Leonardo?" Sandro asked.

"Yes, my friend."

"Where have you been all this time?"

"You saw me leave with Neri," Leonardo said, uncomfortable. "He had to give me the grand candlelight tour, which ended upstairs in an orgy in which I did not participate."

"I am no prude," Sandro said. "Your personal life is entirely your own. You need make no explanations to me."

"Sandro, what is it?"

"Then who was your double?"

Realizing that it would be only a matter of time before Sandro discovered that Neri had impersonated him, Leonardo said, "All right, Little Bottle, you've pulled the loose thread. My double was Neri, and he directed someone to play himself. I met up with him later."

"I spent most of the night watching for Simonetta," Sandro said pointedly.

"And from the blush in your face, my friend, I'd say you spent part of it with the thimble and thumb."

"I've had but one glass of wine," Sandro said.

Leonardo did not pursue the matter. "I saw Madonna upstairs," he said, breaking the ice. He would have to skirt the truth as best he could.

"She's like a cat, always on the move." Sandro frowned, and Leonardo said, "No insult intended. In fact, we talked about you."

"Yes?" Sandro asked, brightening.

"She believes that your paintings have given her immortality. What greater gift could any other man give her?"

"Indeed," Sandro said. "Did she say anything else to you?"

"Only that she wishes no hurt come to you."

"What does that mean?" Sandro's face became red.

"Only that she cares for you."

"If she did, she—"

"She belongs to the First Citizen, my friend," Leonardo said, albeit giving his friend false hope. But it would not make a difference, for he would yearn for her against all logic anyway.

"Was she accompanied by . . . anyone?"

"Did you see Il Magnifico Lorenzo, or any Medici, at this soiree?" Leonardo asked, misleadingly.

"No."

"Well, then, there is your answer."

Niccolò dashed back to Leonardo and, interrupting, said, "Come *on*, you'll miss everything." Simonetta turned to them, gestured subtly to Sandro by nodding her head, and then gave her attention to the man called Kuan Yin-hsi. Sandro, Leonardo, and Niccolò crossed the room to stand beside Simonetta.

Kuan Yin-hsi was tall and well-proportioned; but a thin, sensitive mouth and tilted eyes, which were wide-set, seemed cold and haughty. A welted scar ran like a tear from the corner of his left eye to disappear in the tangle of a thick and immaculately neat beard. "And might I borrow a pin or a needle from one of the adored and honored ladies?" he asked. Although his execution of the Tuscan dialect was exact, his intonation was flat and even.

Simonetta stepped smoothly through the crowd and handed the oriental a golden clasp, which cinched her velvet *mantello* cloak. "Here, Kuan, will this suffice?"

"Very nicely, Madonna Vespucci," he said, bowing as he took the pin. Then he lifted a red sack from a stack of large leather-bound books on the table before him, revealing: Boethius' *De Arithmetica,* Varro's *Res Rustica,* Donatus' *On the Eight Parts of Speech,* Euclid's *De Ponderibus,* one of Orosius' *Seven Books of Histories against the Pagans,* a thin volume by an anonymous author mysteriously entitled *The Secret of the Golden Flower,* and an ornate, jeweled Bible recently translated from the Latin into the vernacular.

Leonardo looked on now with more than a little interest. He had read all the books except for the Orosius and the anonymous title, which fascinated him. He wanted to peruse the little book and extract its eponymous "secret," but he would have to wait until this man had completed his parlor trick.

Kuan Yin-hsi pushed the Bible across the table to Simonetta. "Please, Madonna, would you do me the honor of selecting a page?"

"Do you wish something particular?" she asked.

"No, Madonna, any page will do. Just close your eyes and choose a page and a line . . . but first, I must be as if blind." He took the heavy sack that had covered the books, put it over his head, and then turned around so his back was to Simonetta. "Please take no offense, Madonna. And now . . . please select your page."

Simonetta opened the book, closed her eyes, and leafed through the heavy vellum pages. "There," she said, opening her eyes, and everyone applauded as if she had just solved a difficult riddle.

"Kindly tell me the page and the line with which your selection begins?" Kuan Yin-hsi said, and then, with as smooth a patter as any western prestidigitator, he said, "I should tell all of you who have shown me such patience, that these books—with the exception of my secret volume—have been graciously lent to us by the great master Toscanelli, who is known and appreciated far away from his own lands, in places that are perhaps unknown even to you."

While Kuan spoke, Simonetta counted the lines on the page. Then she said, "Page three hundred sixteen. Line . . . twenty-five."

"A good choice, dear lady," Kuan said. "It reads, exactly: 'Hast thou not heard? Long ago I made it. In ancient times I fashioned it. Now have I brought it to pass. Yea, it is done, that fortified cities should be laid waste into ruinous heaps. Therefore their inhabitants were of small power. They were dismayed and confounded. . . .' Shall I continue?" he asked. "I can go on quoting the Scripture as long as my voice holds out." With that he turned around, his hood disguising the outline of his head; and everyone clapped and shouted and praised him. "Not yet, gracious friends," he said. "We're not quite finished." Then he presented Simonetta with her own pin and asked her to choose a word and press the pin into it.

"I fear that might be construed as a small sacrilege, Kuan," Simonetta said. She turned to the cardinals from the Holy See and asked, "Could it not be so, Your Eminences?"

"It may . . . or may not be," said one of the cardinals, a burly young man who had the thick features of the campagna. But his skin and hair were pale, and his eyes an astonishing blue.

His companion, an older man with sleepy-looking eyes and a strong, prominent chin, asked, "Are you a Christian, good sir?"

"I believe in the holy Christ," Kuan Yin-hsi said, turning in the direction of the cardinals.

"That may indeed be true, but is it not also true that one who reads the Koran may also believe in Christ?" asked the young cardinal.

"Would you permit one who learned of Christ from the poor adherents of Nestorius, patriarch of Constantinople, to be Christian?"

"The patriarch was condemned as a heretic," said the younger cardinal.

"Yet in the land where I dwell that was how I came to know Christ."

"But knowing that you were converted by a heretical sect, you should not be averse to making a proper conversion to the true, Roman faith," continued the cardinal unctuously.

"How, then, could I reject conversion, Your Eminence? I would welcome it."

Surprised, the cardinal said, "And you would be willing to give up those beliefs that are heretical?"

"If the Holy See considers them incorrect, I would give them up."

The younger cardinal looked to his companion, who said gravely, "We will make those arrangements for you."

"I am most appreciative," Kuan Yin-hsi said. "Perhaps, then, we can continue this demonstration at a later date."

The guests were disappointed and the room buzzed with it. The cardinals conferred and the older man said, "We have decided to give you our permission to finish your demonstration."

When the noise died down—for the guests cheered the cardinals—Kuan said, "My thanks, Your Eminences. Now, then, Madonna Simonetta, please push your pin into the sacred vellum."

"There," she said.

"Push it through as many pages as you can, or as you like. Are you finished, Madonna?"

"Yes, it is done."

"Be kind enough to tell me the word through which you pushed your pin."

"*Antico.*"

"Now, Madonna, please count how many pages the pin has pierced."

"Four pages."

"If you look at the corresponding word through which the pin has pierced on that fourth page, I believe you'll find it is 'Gerusalemme.' "

"That's correct," Simonetta said, clapping her hands together.

Kuan pulled the sack off his head and without looking down toward the Bible recited, " 'And the high places that were before Jerusalem, which were on the right hand of the mount of corruption, which Solomon the king of Israel had builded for Ashtoreth the detestation of the Zidonians, and for...' " Kuan Yin-hsi's eyes seemed hard as black porcelain as he stared into the crowd, but it was as if he were staring through those who attended him.

Guests pressed around Simonetta to see the words pierced by the pin, but they made way for the cardinals, who carefully examined the pages and nodded in affirmation, thus giving Kuan's fantastical trick—and Kuan himself—their imprimatur.

Kuan bowed generously.

The spectators looked awestruck; it was as if they were in the presence of a holy, living talisman. Courtesans and guildsmen and gentlewomen alike did obeisance by folding their hands, making the eightfold sign of the cross, and murmuring Paternosters.

Indeed, two miracles had taken place: one of memory and another of imminent conversion.

Then everyone crowded around Kuan, questioning and praising him until Simonetta deftly extracted him from his admirers; but not before he put the books, which were precious, in the red sack.

There was a stir in the room as musicians appeared with cornets, violas, lutes, and even a bagpipe, while servants bustled back and forth with trays of delicately formed cakes and candies, which were laid upon the tables along with eating utensils of spun sugar that appeared to be made of glass. Although the musicians were "beardless youths," they played and sang with subtlety and humor; two of the singers were not boys at all, but castrati, and their voices were as pure as the ringing of bells. They cried, *"Danzare,"* and guests soon began to dance as the music became louder and more frenzied, and the lyrics became more suggestive, for they were the songs of the whores and courtesans.

> *Cosi dolce e gustevole divento,*
> *quando mi trovo in letto,*
> *da cui amata e gradita me sento*
> *che quel mio piacer vince ogni diletto . . .*

> *I become so very sweet and pleasing*
> *when I happen to be in bed*
> *with one who loves and welcomes me*
> *so that my pleasure surpasses all delight . . .*

And the air seemed to change with the music, as if warmer, charged with body heat.

Leonardo, Simonetta, Niccolò, and Kuan Yin-hsi stood in the shadowy penumbra between two lamps flickering in sconces on the wall. Sandro kept an uncomfortable distance, as if he were intruding upon a private conversation.

"Come, Sandro," Leonardo said. "Are you too famous now to stand neck by neck beside your humble apprentice?"

"Niccolò is not my apprentice," Sandro said, coming into the circle.

"I meant myself," Leonardo said.

"Leonardo, do you not believe I have any capacity for irony?" Sandro said, smiling. Simonetta took his arm, and he seemed to relax.

"I was most impressed with your mnemonic feats, sir," Leonardo said to Kuan, who bowed and smiled in response. "Do you have a system such as that described in *Ad Herennium*?"

"Indeed I do, sir," Kuan said. "In the manner of your revered Cicero, we place our first thoughts in an imaginary forecourt, and then we imagine a room, which in time becomes filled with memory images; but just as you construct great cathedrals of memory, we create temples, mosques . . . entire cities. Do you use your memory cathedral to gain insight into the three times?"

"I'm not sure I understand what you ask."

"Santo Augustine wrote that there are three times: the present of things past, the present of things present, and the present of things future. My system of learning permits the adept to remember before his time, to remember the unlived past . . . and future."

Leonardo felt himself become impatient, as he always did when confronted with religious superstition. "And might that system be enumerated in the book that was before you?"

"*The Secret of the Golden Flower*," Kuan said. "It is but an outline." He fumbled in the sack and handed the book to Leonardo. "Would you care to borrow it? It concerns memory and the circulation of light, which Master Toscanelli tells me is of interest to you."

"I have some interest in optics," Leonardo said, examining the book. "But this is far too valuable—"

"If I've quitted Florence when you've finished the book, you may return it to Messer Toscanelli. I have been the recipient of his generous hospitality these last few days."

"As you wish," Leonardo said. "And thank you. I will make sure it is returned."

Kuan smiled, as if he sensed Leonardo's incredulity, and said, "It was through just such a system that Ludolfus of Saxony determined that the wounds of our Savior were five thousand four hundred ninety in number. Have you not read the *Rhetorica Divina*?"

"I must confess I have not," Leonardo said, smarting.

"It seems to be more difficult to obtain books in Christendom," Kuan said, looking to Simonetta and smiling. "I mention the book only because it exemplifies a system similar to my own. The *Rhetorica Divina* enables one to be present at and to experience the Crucifixion."

"But one should be most careful, for such texts are held in dispute by the Church," interrupted the young cardinal, who stepped into the circle. He seemed especially interested in Simonetta and stood beside her. Sandro politely stepped back, but one could see a blush come into his cheeks. "Many of our most learned theologues believe that such supposed insights into realms divine are false, mere fantasies, and that these spiritual exercises, as they are called, are no better than mystery mongering. If these brothers are correct, then your entertainment would be heresy itself."

Kuan Yin-hsi bowed to the cardinal. "That would be most distressing, for those who have preceded me would also become known as heretics: the angelic Thomas Aquinas and Augustine, the doctor of grace." The taunting hint of the mischievous, which crossed Kuan's stony face, was not lost on Leonardo . . . or the cardinal.

"It is blasphemy even to make such comparisons," the cardinal said. "You have a sinful, unregenerate soul, Signore, and I shall do my best to see to it that in future you will not be so free to poison our Christian wells."

Simonetta took hold of the cardinal's arm. "Your Eminence, certainly you misunderstand Kuan. He is a good man, an advocate of Christ and deserving of praise." She pulled him away and said, "Now, will you be so kind as to keep me company for a little while?"

The cardinal tapped the book Leonardo was holding and said, "I fear for your soul, *signore artista,* if exposed to such exsufflation." Then he left with Simonetta.

Across the room, several sections of a dance platform decorated with tapestries, forms, and benches to seat those of high estate were being pushed together by well-muscled servants. Then, with a blaring of horns, a company of male and female dancers suggestively dressed in cloth the color of peach blossom began to dance.

Guests made way for Simonetta and the cardinal, who took their seats as the company bowed to them. "Come, let us watch," Niccolò said to Sandro, who, looking upset, excused himself from Leonardo and Kuan.

"Your companion seems to be much taken with the beautiful lady," Kuan said to Leonardo.

"It is the cross he must bear," Leonardo said.

"Speaking of bearing crosses . . . ," Kuan said. "Perhaps it would be best for you to return the little book I gave you now, rather than risk the ire of the priest."

"He's hardly a priest," Leonardo said, smiling in spite of himself. "But why did you anger him?"

"That certainly was not my intention," Kuan said. "He had more than his share of anger and pomposity before he fixed his eyes on me."

"He could be a powerful enemy," Leonardo said.

Kuan laughed and said, "I have no need of enemies."

"It seems you've created one."

"But I shall not linger long here in your beautiful country, Master Leonardo. Soon I shall be back in places where your fair tongue has never been heard."

"And where would that be?"

"Have you not talked to Master Toscanelli?" Kuan said, looking surprised.

"About what?"

"Ah," Kuan said, as if that were an answer.

"How do you know the maestro?" Leonardo asked.

"Master Toscanelli and I have been corresponding for some time now. We trade books and useful information. I have visited your land with some regularity; and I must say I've found much reward in trading with your many principalities, although that is not my true vocation."

"And what might that be?"

"I am a traveler, a seeker of knowledge, like your famous Marco Polo. And like you, Master Leonardo, I am an engineer. Maestro pagholo Medicho has spoken of you to me."

Leonardo was impressed that Kuan knew Toscanelli so intimately, for only intimates called him "pagholo Medicho."

"It was destined that we would eventually meet," Kuan continued.

"Ah . . . and have you learned of this destiny by 'remembering' our future?" Leonardo asked.

Kuan bowed his head slightly and smiled.

"What is your destination, then? Back to your land?"

"That depends on the maestro and a certain lieutenant of the Sultan of Babylon. He's the Devatdar of Syria. He's also here, at this party," and Kuan pointed out a man wearing a turban and stylish Florentine clothes; Leonardo had seen him earlier. In fact, Simonetta was in the process of introducing him to her young cardinal. Kuan laughed. "His Eminence and the Devatdar make unlikely companions."

"Indeed," Leonardo said.

Kuan smiled, bowed, and headed toward the cardinal and Simonetta; Leonardo was curious to follow, but as he had not been invited, he hung back.

When Kuan reached the platform where Niccolò, Simonetta, and the cardinal were seated, Niccolò left them and dashed across the room to Leonardo. "Come, you must see the dancers. They are so light and beautiful as to be like sylphs that can float in the very air."

"From what Sandro tells me, you have indulged in enough beauty for one night."

Niccolò averted his eyes. "Are you going to stand by yourself, Maestro?"

"Perhaps for a while, Nicco."

"Are you still sad, Master?"

Leonardo smiled at the boy and squeezed his shoulder. "And you . . . are you still frightened?"

Niccolò said, "I will have nightmares of the boy who was scourged. But right now I need not think of it."

"A practical philosophy."

"Just so. And so you should not think about your—"

But Simonetta suddenly appeared and said, "Come, Leonardo, it's time to be gone. Will you and your young friend do me the favor of escorting me home?"

"And what about the dance?" Leonardo asked.

"Our friend from the East will be doing his own dance with His Eminence and the lieutenant." She laughed. "I think His Eminence will have his hands full with our visiting dignitaries. Our Holy Mother be thanked, at least he is presently too occupied to direct his no doubt ecclesiastical affections toward me."

"Where is Sandro?" Leonardo asked. "I'm sure he—"

"He's relieving himself," Simonetta said, "and I think it's best we leave now before he returns."

"His feelings might be hurt," Leonardo said.

"They have already been hurt," Simonetta said. Then she turned to Niccolò and asked him if he would bring her a handful of sugar candies from one of the tables. Once he left, she said, "Sandro's jealousy has got the best of him tonight. He drank a bit too much wine, and he's been questioning me like a husband. Tomorrow, I trust, he'll recover and be contrite. But tonight he's not himself."

"Does he think that—"

Simonetta looked at him. "Yes, he thinks you and I had a liaison."

"But how?"

"Perhaps Neri made up a story, as he so loves to do."

Niccolò returned with the candy.

"Shall we?" Simonetta asked, and they left the room. Servants carrying candles led the way through the halls; but in the echoing darkness they could hear Sandro calling.

"Simonetta! Simonetta . . ."

A voice as faint as sweet memory.

5

The Dream
of the
Great Bird

When man conceives of a material thing
through imagination, this thing acquires an
actual existence (*spiritus ymaginarius*).

—al-madjriti

By concentrating the thoughts, one can fly; by
concentrating the desires, one falls.

—*The Secret of the Golden Flower*

You will see yourself fall from great heights . . .

—Leonardo da Vinci

One could almost imagine that the Great Bird was already in flight, hovering in the gauzy morning light like a great, impossible hummingbird. It was a chimerical thing that hung from the high attic ceiling of Leonardo's workshop in Verrocchio's *bottega*: a tapered plank fitted with hand-operated cranks, hoops of well-tanned leather, pedals, windlass, oars, and saddle. Great ribbed batlike wings made of cane and fustian and starched taffeta were connected to the broader end of the plank. They were dyed bright red and gold, the colors of the Medici, for it was the Medici who would attend its first flight.

As Leonardo had written in his notebook: *Remember that your bird must imitate none other than the bat because her web forms a framework that gives strength to the wings. If you imitate the wings of feathered birds, you will discover the feathers to be disunited and permeable to the air. But the bat is aided by the membrane which binds the whole and is not pervious.* He had written the notes backward from right to left in a "mirror" script of his own invention— he did not want others stealing his ideas.

Although he sat before a canvas he was painting, his eyes smarting from the miasmas of varnish and linseed oil and first-grade turpentine, Leonardo nervously gazed up at his invention. It filled the upper area of the large room, for its wingspan was over twenty-five ells—more than fifty feet.

For the past few days Leonardo had been certain that something was not quite right with his Great Bird, yet he could not divine what it might be. Nor could he sleep well, for he had been having nightmares, a consequence of his apprehensions over his flying machine, which was due to be flown from the top of a mountain in just ten days. His dream was always the same: he would be falling from a great height . . . without wings, without harness . . . into a barely luminescent void, while above him the familiar sunlit hills and mountains that overlooked Vinci turned vertiginously.

He had torn himself away from his machine to spend the first hours of the morning painting a little Madonna for Lorenzo, which the First Citizen had commissioned from Leonardo as a gift for Simonetta. They would certainly want to view the painting's progress, especially Simonetta. Leonardo had told her the *caritas* was near to being complete: a lie, of course, for he had been too preoccupied with the Great Bird to complete any of his commissions.

There was a characteristic knock on the door: two light taps followed by a loud thump.

"Enter, Andrea, lest the dead wake," Leonardo said without getting up.

Verrocchio stormed in with his foreman, Francesco di Simone, a burly, full-faced, middle-aged man whose muscular body was just beginning to go to seed. Francesco carried a silver tray, upon which were placed cold meats, fruit, and two cruses of milk; he laid it on the table beside Leonardo. Both Verrocchio and Francesco had been at work for hours, as was attested by the lime and marble dust that streaked their faces and shook from their clothes. They were unshaven and wore work gowns, although Verrocchio's was more a frock. Leonardo had often wondered if Verrocchio envisioned himself as a priest to art.

"Well, at least *you're* awake," Andrea said to Leonardo as he looked appreciatively at the painting-in-progress. Then he clapped his hands, making such a loud noise that Niccolò, who was fast asleep on his pallet beside Leonardo's, awakened with a cry. Andrea chuckled and said, "Well, good morning, young Messer. Perhaps I could have one of the other apprentices find enough work for you to keep you busy during the spine of the morning."

"I apologize, Maestro Andrea, but Maestro Leonardo and I worked late into the night." Niccolò removed his red woolen sleeping cap and hurriedly put on a gown that lay on the floor beside his pallet.

"Ah, so now it's Maestro Leonardo, is it?" Andrea said good-naturedly. "Perhaps you should go along with my good friend Francesco. I'm sure he can find another errand for you to do." Andrea winked at Francesco, who chuckled. Niccolò, however, did not seem amused; and a deep blush worked across his face.

"What is it, Niccolò?" Leonardo asked.

"We sent your young apprentice on an errand yesterday while you were going about town," Andrea said. "When you were a new apprentice, we sent you on the same errand."

Leonardo smiled, remembering; he knew the errand to which they referred. When he had first come to Verrocchio's *bottega,* he had been told to go to the Via Tornabuoni to the studio of a certain colorman and bring back a particular paint that had the unique—and impossible—quality of being striped.

"They did that to *you,* too, Leonardo?" Niccolò asked, but he still stood beside his pallet, as if ashamed to come forward.

"But your master succeeded in collecting exactly what we'd sent him for," Francesco said, "while you, young Ser, came back empty-handed."

"How is that possible?" Niccolò asked Leonardo.

"Go ahead, Leonardo, tell him," Andrea said. "And eat your breakfast, both of you. Today I'm a happy man—I have news."

"Well . . . what is it?" Leonardo asked Andrea.

"First tell Nicco your story."

"I, for one, have work to do," Francesco said. "I've had enough celebrating for one day. There's a studio to be run, and fifteen apprentices sitting about downstairs with their fingers up their respective arses."

"You must learn to rest when your master so orders," Verrocchio said.

"I like to see the faces of my family at least once a day, Andrea. But you—you'll be working late tonight, if I know you." With that Francesco bowed curtly and left.

Andrea took an apple, and with his mouth full said, "If I had ten more like him, I'd be rich. Unlike you, Leonardo, who—even though you're technically *my* apprentice—work only when it suits you."

"You and my father have well gained from my labors and ideas," Leonardo said. "And you even sell my mechanical inventions for a fair price."

"Your father and I don't get as much as you'd like to think. Certainly my share isn't enough to feed my house for a week."

"If you'd been blessed with fewer relatives . . ."

"Take some fruit and tell Nicco of your inspired errand," Andrea said, beaming. "The boy should know his limitations."

Leonardo turned to Niccolò. "When I was a young apprentice, I too was taken in by all this nonsense. Like you, I went to the shop of the colorman; and when I explained the purpose of my errand to him, he became sick with laughter. Then he told me that I was the butt of one of Maestro Verrocchio's jokes. I didn't believe him because I was afraid that if I didn't return with Andrea's striped paint, I'd be sent back to my father to become a notary. Certainly being an apprentice—even to someone as vile and despicable as Andrea—was more desirable than being chained to a notary's desk."

Andrea made a humphing noise and sat down at the table beside Leonardo.

"I asked the colorman to give me the base materials out of which such striped paint might be manufactured, and right there on the floor of his shop I mixed oil of linseed with hansa primrose, chrome oxide, rose madder, indigo, and cobalt. I thus had the primary hues. It was nothing to carefully pour these colors side by side, fusing them into a rainbow, but making sure that one did not mix with another. Then I simply poured eggwhite over these pigments and carefully carried them back to my master."

"I almost popped my eyes out of my head when I saw that mélange," Andrea said. "So you see, Nicco, I had hopes that you would follow in your master's footsteps, for no other apprentice since Leonardo has ever provided such a creative solution."

Niccolò looked crestfallen.

"Come and eat," Leonardo said to him. "I've told you before, your temperament is too rigid. You can't solve problems if your thoughts are so tightly wound. You must let them fly like birds, and only then might you catch them. Now, if you directed yourself to science and painting and poetry as you do toward women, you'd be more successful."

"What's this?" asked Andrea.

"Our Nicco is quite the *amoroso*. It seems he learned the art of seducing servant girls from Master Toscanelli."

Andrea laughed and said, "Not from Toscanelli would he learn such tricks. But perhaps the old maestro was right to put this boy in your care, Leonardo. *Pares cum paribus* . . . birds of a feather, as they say. But as our beloved Vergil wrote, *'Amantes amentes.'* It is true, my dear Leonardo: 'Lovers *are* lunatics.' " He laughed and made a mock-nasty face at Leonardo. Then to Niccolò he said, "Now, get to the table, young sir, and eat your breakfast!"

Niccolò did as he was told and ate like a trencherman, spilling milk on his lap.

"One would never guess he came from a good family," Andrea said, watching Niccolò stuff his mouth.

"He has loosened up a bit," Leonardo said. "Remember how dour and formal he was when Maestro Toscanelli dragged him to us?"

"Indeed."

"Now, tell me your news," Leonardo said.

"Il Magnifico has informed me that my 'David' will stand prominently in the Palazzo Vecchio over the great staircase." Andrea could not repress a grin.

Leonardo nodded. "But, certainly, you knew Lorenzo would find a place of especial honor for such a work of genius."

"I don't know if you compliment me or yourself, Leonardo," Andrea said. "After all, you are the model."

"You took great liberties," Leonardo said. "You may have begun with my features, but you have created something sublime out of the ordinary. You deserve the compliment."

"I fear this pleasing talk will cost me either money or time," Andrea said.

Leonardo laughed. "Indeed, today I must be out of the city."

Andrea gazed up at Leonardo's flying machine. "No one would blame you if you backed out of this project, or at least allowed someone else to fly your contraption. You need not prove yourself to Lorenzo."

Niccolò gave him an earnest look and said, "I'll fly your mechanical bird, Leonardo."

"No, it must be me."

"You are not satisfied it will work?" Andrea asked.

"I am worried," Leonardo confessed. "Something is indeed wrong with my Great Bird, yet I cannot quite put my finger on it. It is most frustrating."

"Then you must not fly it!"

"It will fly, Andrea. I promise you that."

"You have my blessing to take the day off," Verrocchio said.

"I am most grateful," Leonardo said; and they both laughed, knowing that Leonardo would have left for the country with or without Andrea's permission. "Now," Leonardo said, "tell me your news."

"This very morning Il Magnifico visited our studio," Andrea said.

"He was *here?*" Leonardo asked, vexed. "And you did not call me?"

"I sent Tista to fetch you, but Lorenzo ordered him not to disturb you if you were at work painting his little Madonna."

Leonardo groaned.

"Although Lorenzo claims he can't afford it," Andrea continued, "he's buying the Villa Castello and needs to furnish it. So he and Angelo Poliziano and a strange boy named Pico della Mirandola swept through this humble *bottega* like locusts, commissioning everything you could imagine: fountains, forks, goblets, tapestries, garden benches, and *cassone*. After all was said and done, it was decided that Pietro Perugino will fashion all the chests, and our dear Sandro will do a large painting. Some of the work will also be done by Filippino Lippi. Still, there is more than enough work, most of it for us."

"For you, not for me," Leonardo said, chagrined that Lorenzo had not commissioned anything from him.

"For God's sake, Leonardo, don't look so glum," Andrea said. "Il Magnifico did not forget you. In fact, I have wonderful news, but I must confess to being guilty of baiting you. So you must forgive me."

"Yes . . . ?" Leonardo said, his curiosity piqued.

"Lorenzo asked me if I would be willing to let you go," Andrea said, pausing dramatically. "He wishes to have you live and work in the Medici gardens; and he is most anxious to have his ancient statue of the satyr Marsyas repaired. To do that, you will have to create it completely from old stone."

"But you are working on—"

"I'll have more than enough to do," Andrea said. "But *you*—my fine ex-apprentice and future ambassador to the First Citizen—will become part of the Medici household. Like your friend Sandro—you will become one of the family."

"And what about me?" interrupted Niccolò. "Do I go with you, Leonardo, or stay here with Master Andrea?"

"What do you wish?" asked Andrea.

Niccolò looked down at the tray of food and said, "I think it would be best if I go with Master Leonardo, as that was the wish of Maestro Toscanelli."

"Then it's settled," Leonardo said, pleased.

"You mean you prefer Leonardo's company to ours?" Andrea asked. Niccolò did not look up, but stared at the table with such intensity as if to scorch its surface. "That's fine," Andrea said, laughing. "You now have our permission to raise your head from your plate."

"Did Sandro accompany Lorenzo?" Leonardo asked guiltily; he had not talked to his friend since he had left Neri's party with Simonetta and Niccolò.

"No," Andrea said, sighing. "Lorenzo told me that he stopped at Sandro's house, but the lovesick fool refused to get out of bed. He's in another one of his lachrymals over Simonetta. Perhaps you might cheer him up and be the bearer of this good news."

"I'll make certain I do."

"How are you faring?" Andrea asked.

"Fine," Leonardo lied, for Andrea was referring to his feelings for Ginevra.

"I trust that's so," and Andrea handed Leonardo a letter. "It was delivered by one of Messer Nicolini's servants this morning. Are its contents a secret?"

"Nicolini wishes me to begin the portrait of Ginevra," Leonardo said. "He wishes to receive me next week." He felt a flash of anger, followed by a warm wash of anticipation. He would, at last, see his beloved Ginevra; but Ginevra's father should have extended the invitation, not Nicolini. Indeed, Nicolini had taken over the de' Benci household; the family name, honor, and estates had become his dowry. However many florins it had cost the old man to purchase Ginevra, she was a *bon marché*. But there was hope, he told himself, thanks to Simonetta, who was already working her wiles upon Lorenzo in Leonardo's behalf. Surely something could be done. After all, Nicolini's association with the Pazzi family would not endear him to the Medici. Nicolini might be experienced in affairs of money and state, but perhaps he could still be outwitted in affairs of the heart....

Andrea nodded, then said, "It's important that you be here early tonight, for Lorenzo wishes to bring Simonetta to see the progress of your little Madonna. Don't wander too far, lest you be late." Then he looked at the painting again, as if transfixed by the glaze of saffron, which gave a luminous golden effect to the Madonna, who had the appearance of a very young Simonetta.

"Well, we must be off," Leonardo said, for Andrea looked as if he might gaze at the painting all morning.

"Remember what I told you," Andrea said. "It would show poor judgment, indeed, if you were not here to greet Lorenzo and his friends when they arrive." Then he left, as if he were musing over the painting, neglecting to say good-bye to Niccolò.

"Come on, Nicco," Leonardo said, suddenly full of energy. "Get dressed." As Niccolò did so, Leonardo put a few finishing touches on his painting, then quickly cleaned his brushes, hooked his sketchbook onto his belt, and once again craned his neck to stare at the invention that hung from the ceiling. He needed an answer, yet he had not yet formulated the question.

When they were out the door, Leonardo felt that he had forgotten something. "Nicco, fetch me the book Master Kuan lent to me. I might want to read in the country."

"The country?" Niccolò asked, carefully putting the book in a sack, which he carried under his arm.

"Do you object to nature?" Leonardo asked sarcastically. "*Usus est optimum magister* . . . and in that I agree wholeheartedly with the ancients. Nature herself is the mother of all experience; and experience must be your teacher, for I've discovered that even Aristotle can be mistaken on certain subjects." As they left the *bottega,* he continued: "But those of Maestro Ficino's school, they go about all puffed and pompous, mouthing the eternal aphorisms of Plato and Aristotle like parrots. They despise me because I'm an inventor, but how much more are they to blame for not being inventors, these trumpeters and reciters of the works of others? They considered my enlarging lens a conjuring trick, and do you know why?" Before Niccolò could respond, Leonardo said, "Because they consider sight to be the most untrustworthy of senses, when, in fact, it is the supreme organ. Yet that doesn't prevent them from wearing spectacles in secret. Hypocrites!"

"You seem very angry, Maestro," Niccolò said.

Embarrassed at having launched into this diatribe, Leonardo laughed at himself and said, "Perhaps I am, but don't worry about it, my young friend."

"Maestro Toscanelli seems to respect Messer Ficino," Niccolò said.

"He respects Plato and Aristotle, as well he should. But he doesn't teach at the academy, does he? No, instead he lectures at the school at Santo Spirito for the Augustinian brothers. That should tell you something."

"I think it tells me that you have an ax to grind, Master . . . and that's also what Maestro Toscanelli told me."

"What else did he tell you, Nicco?" Leonardo asked.

"That I should learn from your strengths and weaknesses, and also that you're smarter than everyone in the academy."

Leonardo laughed at that and said, "You lie very convincingly."

"That, Maestro, comes naturally."

The streets were busy and noisy, and the sky, which seemed pierced by the tiled mass of the Duomo and the Palace of the Signoria, was cloudless and sapphire-blue. There was the sweet smell of sausage in the air, and young merchants—practically children—stood behind stalls and shouted at every passerby. This market was called Il Baccano, the place of uproar. Leonardo bought some cooked meat, beans, fruit, and a bottle of cheap local wine for Niccolò and himself. They continued on into different neighborhoods and markets. They passed Spanish Moors with their slave retinues from the Ivory Coast; Mamluks in swathed robes and flat turbans; Muscovy Tartars and Mongols from Cathay; and merchants from England and Flanders, who had sold their woolen cloth and were on their way to the Ponte Vecchio to purchase trinkets and baubles. Niccolò was all eye and motion as they passed elegant and beautiful "butterflies of the night" standing beside their merchant masters under the shade of guild awnings; these whores and mistresses modeled jeweled garlands, and expensive garments of violet, crimson, and peach. Leonardo and Niccolò passed stall after stall—brushing off young hawkers and old, disease-ravaged beggars—and flowed with the crowds of peddlers, citizens, and visitors as if they were flotsam in the sea. Young men of means dressed in short doublets wiggled and swayed like young girls through the streets; they roistered and swashbuckled, laughed and sang and bullied, these favored ones. Niccolò could not help but laugh at the scholars and student wanderers from England and Scotland and Bohemia, for although their lingua franca was Latin, their accents were extravagant and overwrought.

"Ho, Leonardo," cried one vendor, then another, as Leonardo and Niccolò turned a corner. Then the shrieks and cries of birds sounded, for the bird sellers were shaking the small wooden cages packed with wood pigeons, owls, mousebirds, bee-eaters, hummingbirds, crows, blue rockthrushes, warblers, flycatchers, wagtails, kites, falcons, eagles, and all manner of swans, ducks, chickens, and geese. As Leonardo approached, the birds were making more commotion than the vendors and buyers on the street. "Come here, Master," shouted a red-haired man wearing a stained brown doublet with torn sleeves. He shook two cages, each containing kites; one bird was brown with a forked chestnut tail, and the other was smaller and black with a notched tail. They banged against the wooden bars and snapped dangerously. "Buy these, Maestro Artista, please . . . they are just what you need, are they not? And look how many doves I have, do they not interest you, good Master?"

"Indeed, the kites are fine specimens," Leonardo said, drawing closer, while the other vendors called and shouted to him, as if he were carrying the grail itself. "How much?"

"Ten denarii."

"Three."

"Eight."

"Four, and if that isn't enough, I can easily talk to your neighbor, who's flapping his arms as if he himself could fly."

"Agreed," said the vendor, resigned.

"And the doves?"

"For how many, Maestro?"

"For the lot."

Leonardo was well-known in this market, and a small crowd of hecklers and the merely curious began to form around him. The hucksters made much of it, trying to sell to whomever they could.

"He's as mad as Ajax," said an old man who had just sold a few chickens and doves and was as animated as the street thugs and young beggars standing around him. "He'll let all those birds go. Watch, you'll see."

"I've heard he won't eat meat," said one matronly woman to another. "He lets the birds go free because he feels sorry for the poor creatures."

"Well, to be safe, don't look straight at him," said the other woman as she made the sign of the cross. "He might be a sorcerer. He could put evil in your eye, and enter right into your soul!"

Her companion shivered and crossed herself.

"Nicco," Leonardo shouted at his apprentice, who had wandered off into the crowd. "Come here and help me." When Niccolò appeared, Leonardo said, "If you could stop looking around for whores, you might learn something about observation and the ways of science." He thrust his hand into the cage filled with doves and grasped one. The tiny bird made a frightened noise; as Leonardo took it from its cage, he could feel its heart beating in his palm. Then he opened his hand and watched the dove fly away. The crowd laughed and jeered and applauded and shouted for more. He took another bird out of its cage and released it. His eyes squinted almost shut; and as he gazed at the dove beating its wings so hard that, but for the crowd, one could have heard them clap, he seemed lost in thought. "Now, Nicco, I want you to let the birds free, one by one."

"Why me?" Niccolò asked, somehow loath to seize the birds.

"Because I wish to draw," Leonardo said. "Is this chore too difficult for you?"

"I beg your pardon, Maestro," Niccolò said as he reached into the cage. He had a difficult time catching a bird. Leonardo seemed impatient and completely oblivious to the shouts and taunts of the crowd around him. Niccolò let go of one bird, and then another, while Leonardo sketched. He stood very still, entranced; only his hand moved like a ferret over the bleached folio, as if it had a life and will of its own.

As Niccolò let fly another bird, Leonardo said, "Do you see, Nicco, the bird in its haste to climb strikes its outstretched wings together above its body. Now look how it uses its wings and tail in the same way that a swimmer uses his arms and legs in the water; it's the very same principle. It seeks the air currents, which, invisible, roil around the buildings of our city. And there, its speed is checked by the opening and spreading out of the tail. . . . Let fly another one. Can you see how the wing separates to let the air pass?" and he wrote a note in his mirror script below one of his sketches: *Make device so that when the wing rises, it remains pierced through, and when it falls, it is all united.* "Another," he called to Niccolò. And after the bird disappeared, he smiled as if his soul had just escaped into the air, as if he had finally gained his freedom from his troubles. He made another note: *The speed is checked by the opening and spreading out of the tail. Also, the opening and lowering of the tail, and the simultaneous spreading of the wings to their full extent, arrest their swift movement.*

"That's the end of it," Niccolò said, indicating the empty cages. "Do you wish to free the kites?"

"No," Leonardo said, distracted. "We'll take them with us," and Leonardo and Niccolò made their way through the crowd, which now began to disperse. As if a reflection of Leonardo's change of mood, clouds darkened the sky; and the bleak, refuse-strewn streets took on a more dangerous aspect. The other bird vendors called to Leonardo, but he ignored them, as he did Niccolò. He stared intensely into his notebook as he walked, as if he were trying to decipher ancient runes.

"Leonardo?" Niccolò asked. "Leonardo . . . ?"

"Yes," Leonardo said, letting his notebook drop to his hip, for it was connected to his belt with a piece of leather.

"You seem . . . angry again," Niccolò said. "Are you angry?"

"No, Nicco, I'm not angry. I'm just thinking."

"About the flying machine?"

"Yes," Leonardo said.

"And Sandro?"

That took Leonardo aback. "Why, yes, Nicco, I was thinking about Sandro."

"Then are we going to visit him?"

"Yes, but later."

"Don't you wish to see him now? It's on our way."

Leonardo hesitated. He could not go; he was not ready to face his friend yet. "I haven't yet worked out the best way to help Sandro," he said to Niccolò.

They passed the wheel of the bankrupts. Defeated men sat around a marble inlay that was worked into the piazza in the design of a cartwheel. A crowd had formed, momentarily, to watch a debtor who had been stripped naked being pulled to the roof of the market by a rope, only to be dropped onto the smooth, cold, marble floor. A sign attached to one of the market posts read:

> Give good heed to the small sums thou spendest out of the house, for it is they which empty the purse and consume wealth; and they go on continually. And do not buy all the good victuals which thou seest, for the house is like a wolf: the more thou givest it, the more doth it devour.

The man dropped by the rope was dead.

Leonardo put his arm around Niccolò's shoulders, as if to shield him from death. But he was suddenly afraid—afraid that his own "inevitable hour" might not be far away; and he remembered his recurring dream of falling into the abyss. He shivered, for on some deep level he believed that the poisonous phantasms of dreams were real. If they took hold of the soul of the dreamer, they could affect his entire world.

Leonardo saw his Great Bird falling and breaking apart.

"Leonardo? *Leonardo!*"

"Don't worry. I'm fine, my young friend," Leonardo said.

They talked very little until they were in the country, in the high, hilly land north of Florence. Here were meadows and grassy fields, valleys and secret grottoes, small roads traversed by oxcarts and pack trains, vineyards and cane thickets, dark copses of pine and chestnut and cypress, and olive trees that shimmered like silver hangings each time the wind breathed past their leaves. The deep-red tiles of farmstead roofs and the brownish-pink colonnaded villas seemed to be part of the line and tone of the natural countryside. The clouds that had darkened the streets of Florence had disappeared; and the sun was high, bathing the countryside in that golden light particular to Tuscany, a light that purified and clarified as if it were itself the manifestation of desire and spirit.

And before them, pale gray-blue in the distance, was Swan Mountain. It rose thirteen hundred feet to its crest.

Leonardo and Niccolò stopped in a meadow perfumed with flowers and gazed at the mountain. Leonardo felt his worries weaken, as they always did when he was in the country. He took a deep breath of the heady air and felt his soul awaken and quicken to the world of nature and the *oculus spiritalis:* the world of angels.

"That would be a good mountain from which to test your Great Bird," Niccolò said.

"I thought that, too, for it's very close to Florence. But I've since changed my mind. Vinci is not so far away; and there are good mountains there, too." Then, after a pause, Leonardo said, "And I don't wish to die here. If death should be my fate, I wish it to be in familiar surroundings."

Niccolò nodded, and he looked as severe and serious as he had when Leonardo had first met him. An old man once again seemed to inhabit the boy.

"Come now, Nicco," Leonardo said, resting the cage on the ground and sitting down beside it, "let's enjoy this time, for who knows what awaits us later? Let's eat." With that Leonardo spread out a cloth and set the food upon it as if it were a table. The kite-hawks flapped their wings and slammed against the wooden bars of the cages. Leonardo tossed them each a small piece of sausage.

"I heard gossip in the piazza of the bird vendors that you refuse to eat meat," Niccolò said.

"Ah, did you, now. And what do you think of that?"

Niccolò shrugged. "Well, I've never seen you eat meat."

Leonardo ate a piece of bread and sausage, which he washed down with wine. "Now you have."

"But, then, why would people say that—"

"Because I don't usually eat meat. They're correct, for I believe that eating too much meat causes to collect what Aristotle defined as cold black bile. That, in turn, afflicts the soul with melancholia. Maestro Toscanelli's friend Ficino believes the same, but for all the wrong reasons. For him magick and astrology take precedence over reason and experience. But be that as it may, I must be very careful that people don't think of me as a follower of the Cathars, lest I be branded a heretic."

"I have but heard of them."

"They follow the teaching of the pope Bogomil, who believed that our entire visible world was created by the adversary rather than God. Thus to avoid imbibing the essence of Satan, they forfeit meat. Yet they eat vegetables and fish." Leonardo laughed and pulled a face to indicate they were crazy. "They could at least be consistent."

He ate quickly, which was his habit, for he could never seem to enjoy savoring food as others did. He felt that eating, like sleeping, was simply a necessity that took him away from his work.

And there was a whole world pulsing in the sunlight around him. Like a child, he wanted to investigate its secrets. *That* was his work, his life's passion.

"Now . . . watch," he said to Niccolò, who was still eating; and he let loose one of the kites. As it flew away, Leonardo made notes, scribbling with his left hand, and said, "You see, Nicco, it searches now for a current of the wind." He loosed the other one. "These birds beat their wings only until they reach the wind, which must be blowing at a great elevation, for look how high they soar. Then they are almost motionless."

Leonardo watched the birds circle overhead, then glide toward the mountains. He felt transported, as if he too were gliding in the empyrean heights. "They're hardly moving their wings now. They repose in the air as we do on a pallet."

"Perhaps you should follow their example."

"What do you mean?" Leonardo asked.

"Fix your wings on the Great Bird. Instead of beating the air, they would remain stationary."

"And by what mode would the machine be propelled?" Leonardo asked; but he answered his own question, for immediately the idea of the Archimedian screw came to mind. He remembered seeing children playing with toy whirlybirds: by pulling a string, a propeller would be made to rise freely into the air. His hand sketched, as if thinking on its own. He drew a series of sketches of leaves gliding back and forth, falling to the ground. He drew various screws and propellers. There might be something useful. . . .

"Perhaps if you could just catch the current, you would not have need of human power," Niccolò said. "You could fix your bird to soar . . . somehow."

Leonardo patted Niccolò on the shoulder, for, indeed, the child was bright. But it was all wrong; it *felt* wrong. "No, my young friend," he said doggedly, as if he had come upon a wall that blocked his thought, "the wings must be able to row through the air like a bird's. That is nature's method, the most efficient way."

Restlessly, almost hurriedly, Leonardo wandered the hills. Niccolò finally complained of being tired and stayed behind, comfortably situated in a shady copse of mossy-smelling cypresses.

Leonardo walked on alone.

Everything was perfect: the air, the warmth, the smells and sounds of the country. He could almost apprehend the pure forms of everything around him, the phantasms reflected in the proton organon: the mirrors of his soul. But not quite. . . .

Indeed, something was wrong, for instead of the bliss which Leonardo had so often experienced in the country, he felt thwarted . . . lost.

Thinking of the falling leaf, which he had sketched in his notebook, he wrote: *If a man has a tent roof of caulked linen twelve ells broad and twelve ells high, he will be able to let himself fall from any great height without danger to himself.* He imagined a pyramidal parachute, yet considered it too large and bulky and heavy to carry on the Great Bird. He wrote another hasty note: *Use leather bags, so a man falling from a height of six brachia will not injure himself, falling either into water or upon land.*

He continued walking, aimlessly. He sketched constantly, as if without conscious thought: grotesque figures and caricatured faces, animals, impossible mechanisms, studies of various Madonnas with children, imaginary landscapes, and all manner of actual flora and fauna. He drew a three-dimensional diagram of a toothed gearing and pulley system and an apparatus for making lead. He made a note to locate Albertus Magnus' *On Heaven and Earth*—perhaps Toscanelli had a copy. His thoughts seemed to flow like the Arno, from one subject to another, and yet he could not position himself in that psychic place of languor and bliss which he imagined to be the perfect realm of Platonic forms.

As birds flew overhead, he studied them and sketched feverishly. Leonardo had an extraordinarily quick eye, and he could discern movements that others could not see. He wrote in tiny letters beside his sketches: *Just as we may see a small imperceptible movement of the rudder turn a ship of marvelous size loaded with very heavy cargo—and also amid such weight of water pressing upon its every beam and in the teeth of impetuous winds that envelop its mighty sails—so, too, do birds support themselves above the course of the winds without beating their wings. Just a slight movement of wing or tail, serving them to enter either below or above the wind, suffices to prevent their fall.* Then he added, *When, without the assistance of the wind and without beating its wings, the bird remains in the air in the position of equilibrium, this shows that the center of gravity is coincident with the center of resistance.*

"Ho, Leonardo," shouted Niccolò, who was running after him. The boy was out of breath; he carried the brown sack, which contained some leftover food, most likely, and Kuan's book. "You've been gone over three hours!"

"And is that such a long time?" Leonardo asked.

"It is for me. What are you doing?"

"Just walking . . . and thinking." After a beat Leonardo said, "But you have a book, why didn't you read it?"

Niccolò smiled. "I tried, but then I fell asleep."

"So now we have the truth," Leonardo said. "Nicco, why don't you return to the *bottega*? I must remain here . . . to think. And you are obviously bored."

"That's all right, Maestro," Niccolò said anxiously. "If I can stay with you, I won't be bored. I promise."

Leonardo smiled in spite of himself and said, "Tell me what you've gleaned from the little yellow book."

"I can't make it out . . . yet. It seems to be all about light."

"Indeed," Leonardo said, and he settled down in a grove of olive trees and read; it took him less than an hour, for the book was short. Niccolò ate some fruit and then fell asleep again, seemingly without any trouble.

Most of the text seemed to be magical gibberish, yet suddenly these words seemed to open him up:

There are a thousand spaces, and the light-flower of heaven and earth fills them all. Just so does the light-flower of the individual pass through heaven and cover the earth. And when the light begins to circulate, all of heaven and the earth, all the mountains and rivers—everything—begins to circulate with light. The key is to concentrate your own seed-flower in the eyes. But be careful, children, for if one day you do not practice meditation, this light will stream out, to be lost who knows where . . . ?

Perhaps he fell asleep, for he imagined himself staring at the walls of his great and perfect construct: the memory cathedral. He longed to be inside, to return to sweet, comforting memory; he would dismiss the ghosts of fear that haunted its dark catacombs.

But now he was seeing the cathedral from a distant height, from the summit of Swan Mountain, and it was as if his cathedral had somehow become a small part of what his memory held and his eyes saw. It was as if his soul could expand to fill heaven and earth, the past and the future. Leonardo experienced a sudden, vertiginous sensation of freedom; indeed, heaven and earth seemed to be filled with a thousand spaces. It was just as he had read in the ancient book: everything was circulating with pure light . . . blinding, cleansing light that coruscated down the hills and mountains like rainwater, that floated in the air like mist, that heated the grass and meadows to radiance.

He felt bliss.

Everything was preternaturally clear; it was as if he was seeing into the essence of things.

And then with a shock he felt himself slipping, falling from the mountain.

This was his recurring dream, his nightmare: to fall without wings and harness into the void. Yet every detail registered: the face of the mountain, the mossy crevasses, the smells of wood and stone and decomposition, the screeching of a hawk, the glint of a stream below, the roofs of farmhouses, the geometrical demarcations of fields, and the spiraling wisps of cloud that seemed to be woven into the sky. But then he tumbled and descended into darkness, into a frightful abyss that showed no feature and no bottom.

Leonardo screamed to awaken back into daylight, for he knew this blind place, which the immortal Dante had explored and described. But now he felt the horrid bulk of the flying monster Geryon beneath him, supporting him . . . this, the same beast that had carried Dante into Malebolge: the

Eighth Circle of Hell. The monster was slippery with filth and smelled of death and putrefaction; the air itself was foul, and Leonardo could hear behind him the thrashing of the creature's scorpion tail. Yet it also seemed that he could hear Dante's divine voice whispering to him, drawing him through the very walls of Hades into blinding light.

But now he was held aloft by the Great Bird, his own invention. Leonardo soared over the trees and hills and meadows of Fiesole, and then south, to fly over the roofs and balconies and spires of Florence herself.

He moved his arms easily, working the great wings that beat against the calm spring air. But rather than resting upon his apparatus, he now hung below it. He operated a windlass with his hands to raise one set of wings and kicked a pedal with his heels to lower the other set of wings. Around his neck was a collar, which controlled a rudder that was effectively the tail of this bird.

This was certainly not the machine that hung in Verrocchio's *bottega*. Yet with its double set of wings, it seemed more like a great insect than a bird, and—

Leonardo awakened with a jolt to find himself staring at a horsefly feeding upon his hand.

Could he have been sleeping with his eyes open, or had this been a waking dream? He shivered, for his sweat was cold on his arms and chest.

He shouted, awakening Niccolò, and immediately began sketching and writing in his notebook. "I have it!" he said to Niccolò. "Double wings like a fly will provide the power I need. You see, it's just as I told you: nature provides. Art and invention are merely imitation." He drew a man hanging beneath an apparatus with hand-operated cranks and pedals to work the wings. Then he studied the fly, which still buzzed around him, and wrote: *The lower wings are more slanting than those above, both as to length and as to breadth. The fly when it hovers in the air upon its wings beats its wings with great speed and din, raising them from the horizontal position up as high as the wing is long. And as it raises them, it brings them forward in a slanting position in such a way as almost to strike the air edgewise.* Then he drew a design for the rudder assembly. "How could I not have seen that just as a ship needs a rudder, so, too, would my machine? It will act as the tail of a bird. And by hanging the operator below the wings, equilibrium will be more easily maintained. There!" He stood up and pulled Niccolò to his feet. "Perfection!"

He sang one of Lorenzo de' Medici's bawdy inventions and danced around Niccolò, who seemed confused by his master's strange behavior, then grabbed the boy's arms and swung him around in a circle.

"Leonardo, what's wrong?" Niccolò asked, drawing away at the first opportunity.

"Nothing is wrong, everything is perfect." Then suddenly Leonardo's mood passed; and he saw himself as he imagined Niccolò saw him: as the fool. Could invention dissolve his pain? Could it harden his heart to Ginevra?

Perhaps it could . . . for a few moments. But it was an infidelity, just like his tryst with Simonetta.

"Perhaps the women watching you free the birds were right," Niccolò said. "Perhaps you are as mad as Ajax."

"Perhaps I am," Leonardo said, "but I have a lot of work to do, for the Great Bird must be changed if it is to fly for Il Magnifico next week." It was already late afternoon. He placed the book of the Golden Flower in the sack, handed it to Niccolò, and began walking in the direction of the city.

"I'll help you with your machine," Niccolò said.

"Thank you, I'll need you for many errands."

That seemed to satisfy the boy. "Why did you shout and then dance as you did, Maestro?" Niccolò asked, concerned.

Leonardo laughed and slowed his stride until Niccolò was beside him. "It's difficult to explain. Suffice it to say that solving the riddle of my Great Bird made me happy."

"But how did you do it? I thought you had fallen asleep."

"I had a dream," Leonardo said. "It was a gift from the poet Dante Alighieri."

"*He* gave you the answer?" Niccolò asked, incredulous.

"That he did, Nicco."

"Then you *do* believe in spirits."

"No, Nicco, just dreams."

They walked almost the entire way in silence, for Leonardo was lost in concentration. He stopped every so often to scribble a note in his sketchbook or to sketch whatever caught his fancy.

When they were back in the city, Niccolò asked, "Maestro, do you believe in the evil eye?"

"Why do you ask?"

"A woman at the market today said that you might be a sorcerer, that you could enter people's souls right through their eyes. Can you do that, Leonardo?"

"No, Nicco," Leonardo said gently. "That the eye is the gateway to the soul, I'll not argue. But no spiritual force can emanate from it."

"I saw one of Messer Vespucci's servants become sick and die from the evil eye," Niccolò said matter-of-factly.

"You were probably mistaken."

"I saw it." Then Niccolò said, "Have you forgotten that we must stop at Maestro Botticelli's?"

"No, Niccolò, I have not forgotten. But I must try to complete the little Madonna painting before Il Magnifico and Simonetta visit our *bottega*. After they leave us, I shall visit Sandro."

"I think you are afraid, Master," Niccolò said without looking up from the street.

"Afraid of *what*?"

"—That you have made Maestro Botticelli sick." Niccolò made the sign of the eye. "You . . . and the beautiful woman Simonetta."

6

Vapors

Fascination is a force which, emanating from the spirit of the fascinator, enters the eyes of the fascinated person as a phantasm and penetrates his heart. Spirit is therefore the instrument of fascination. It emits from the eyes rays resembling itself, bearing with them spiritual quality. Hence rays emanating from eyes that are bloodshot and bleary, on meeting the eyes of the beholder, carry with them the vapor of the spirit and of tainted blood, thus spreading the contagion to the beholder's eyes.

—Agrippa of Nettesheim

So confused was I that I lay near death, whether imagining or dreaming or having a vision or daydream, it seemed to me that, truly, Cupid had removed my heart from my body.

—René of Anjou

When Leonardo returned to Verrocchio's *bottega*, Simonetta was waiting for him in his studio. She was sitting before the little Madonna and staring closely at it, as if deciphering runes. The late afternoon had become overcast, and the light in the high-ceilinged studio seemed dead . . . gray. As Leonardo and Niccolò entered, Simonetta pulled away from the painting. "Ah, sweet Leonardo, you've caught me," she said. "I was memorizing every stroke of your brush. I think you must be a follower of the Pythagoreans."

"And why would you think that?" Leonardo was surprised to see her so early—and in his room. Where could Andrea be? Certainly Simonetta was an especially important guest and deserved proper attention. He kissed her hand, which she held out to him. Something was amiss, but Leonardo could not skirt the obligatory tittle-tattle that introduced serious conversation.

"Well, the Madonna and child and cat seem to be composed upon the form of a triangle," Simonetta said. "Does not Plato himself in the *Timaeus* represent the immortal soul as a triangle?"

"I'm sorry to disappoint you, Madonna Simonetta, but I'm not a Pythagorean . . . not that I know of." Simonetta laughed and Leonardo went on, "But the triangle seemed to be the proper form for this painting. Perhaps, in this case, the immortal Pythagoras was correct. It could not be otherwise that I painted you to represent the beauty and purity of the Virgin soul."

"And it was in no small measure because Lorenzo had commissioned the piece?"

Leonardo could not help but laugh, for she was goading him in a most endearing manner. "I trust you have not been inconvenienced, but I did not expect to meet you until duskingtide. But where is Il Magnifico? I had thought that he was to accompany you?"

"He's with—" Simonetta caught herself and then said, "Niccolò, would you be so kind as to fetch me some wine? I do have a thirst."

Niccolò bowed politely and said, "Yes, Madonna." But in a hole-and-corner way he cast a nasty look at Leonardo before leaving the room; Nicco could not stand to be left out of anything.

After he had left, Simonetta opened her arms to Leonardo—like a mother to a child—and he knelt before her. She kissed him, and he saw how tired and worried she looked. "What is it, Madonna?" Leonardo asked.

"Lorenzo is with Sandro, as is your master Andrea."

"But why? What has happened?" Leonardo asked, fearing the worst.

"Lorenzo and Giuliano and I had planned a happy afternoon. They awakened me at daybreak to go to Careggi, and on the way we were to pull Sandro out of his bedcovers, so I would have companionship while they discussed Plato with Joannes Argyropoulos and Marsilio Ficino. But when we arrived at Sandro's, we knew immediately that *everything* was wrong. His *bottega* was in complete disarray. He had draped all the windows so that only the faintest light could get in. We found him in bed. He could not have been eating, for he was skin and bone. And we could *smell* that he was sick." She pressed her face against Leonardo's. He could feel her trembling. Then she pulled away from him and said, "But his eyes . . . they were luminous. When he first saw me, he turned away and said, 'You are too late, I already have you.' He sounded most rational."

"What could that mean?" Leonardo asked.

"I fear he has infected himself with a phantasm . . . of me. I don't need a physician to tell me that he has the lovesickness. One could determine that from his eyes alone."

"It's probably *melancholia illa heroica*," Niccolò said as he entered the room. He looked flushed and seemed excited; he had obviously been listening outside the door. "That is a disease of melancholia that is indeed caused by love. It wastes away body and spirit. Only the eyes are lively, for therein resides the soul's 'internal fire.' Maestro Toscanelli taught me about such things. He's learned in medicine, and magick, too."

"Nicco, this is a private matter," Leonardo said sharply.

"But I care for Sandro, too," Niccolò said. "And I can help. I've read the *Lilium medicinale*. Have you?"

"You are being impertinent," Leonardo said, but without anger in his voice.

"Please, let him stay," Simonetta said, moving away from Leonardo, who stood up and poured her a glass of the wine Niccolò had brought.

"I *can* keep a confidence," Niccolò said earnestly.

Simonetta took Niccolò's hand for an instant, then removed herself to the window. "I'm at fault. Sandro was in love with *me*."

"You can't blame yourself, Madonna," Leonardo said.

"I heard him call that night when we left Il Neri's party, and I hurried on."

"You did that for his own good. I'm to blame, for I haven't seen him for a week. I could have prevented him from getting so lost in his imagination."

"I should have given myself to him," Simonetta said in barely a whisper, as if she were talking to herself. "I have given myself to others." After a pause she said, "Lorenzo had his physician brought to Sandro's *bottega*. He is still there, leeching him. But even he suggested that we bring a theurgist to the bedside."

Leonardo nodded, although he had little use for the theurgists' magick.

"Lorenzo attended to that, too," Simonetta said.

"Then Sandro is under their care."

"Yes, and Lorenzo sent me to wait for you."

"But surely Sandro would wish to see you above all others," Leonardo said.

"After he told me that I was too late, he became anguished whenever I approached him," Simonetta said. "In fact, I was kept from his room, for he thrashed about uncontrollably in my presence. He tried to get out of his bed and reach for me. The physician feared he might do me harm. But he kept calling my name, even when I was in another room, just as he did when we left the party. It is a nightmare, Leonardo. But I must confess to feeling relieved when Lorenzo asked me to fetch you."

"Of course you would," Leonardo said.

"You must not go back to Sandro's *bottega* with us," Niccolò said. "It's dangerous."

"How is that?" Leonardo asked. "She would be protected."

"If Sandro is infected with his own phantasm of Madonna Simonetta, he will try to draw out her spirit through her eyes."

"It may well be that Simonetta should not return to Sandro's, but that is superstitious nonsense."

"Madonna, did Sandro close his eyes when he spoke to you?" Niccolò asked.

"Why, yes, he did."

"And were they open when he was not in his senses?"

"Yes," Simonetta said. "He stared as if to devour me."

"And you said that he was frenzied and tried to get out of his bed. Dr. Bernard of Gordon calls that symptom 'ambulatory mania.' And I would also guess Maestro Sandro's pulse to be irregular."

"The physician indicated that, yes," Simonetta said.

"The symptoms of melancholia are lack of sleep, food, and drink," Niccolò said, unable to conceal his youthful, vainglorious enthusiasm. "The whole body weakens, except for the eyes. If Maestro Sandro isn't treated, he'll become maniacal and die. Il Magnifico was correct to call for a theurgist. But, Madonna Simonetta, he closed his eyes when he first saw you, in his rational moment, so as not to infect *you* with his 'internal fire.' "

"Nicco, that is—"

"Please, Maestro, permit me to finish. I know you don't believe in internal fire or the igneous rays which project through the eyes. But I'm simply applying the training I learned from Master Toscanelli. May I continue?"

Leonardo nodded and sat down beside Simonetta, who took his hand. One had to respect the boy. In a situation of lesser gravity, Leonardo would have been delighted with Nicco's exposition.

"Your image has passed through his eyes and into his heart; it's as real as his thoughts and has become part of his pneuma, his very soul. The image, the phantasm, is a reflection of *you;* but it is poisoned, and poisonous."

"What can be done to help him?" Simonetta asked.

"If more gentle methods do not work, then whipping, and perhaps sensual pleasures, such as coitus with several women. If none of that proves helpful, then . . ."

Simonetta turned her head away.

"Well, I'm going to see what can be done," Leonardo said, directing himself to Simonetta. "I do believe, though, that Nicco might be correct concerning your safety. You are distraught, why not rest here for a time? Niccolò will look after you."

"But—" said Niccolò, obviously disappointed that he might miss the performance of the theurgist . . . and perhaps he was also truly concerned about Sandro.

"No, Leonardo, I simply must do what I can to help him," Simonetta said. "I would feel nothing but guilt if I remained here. I am sick with worry over him, now more than ever."

Leonardo looked sternly at Niccolò for upsetting Simonetta. "You will wait here for us, then."

"But I *must* go," Niccolò said. "At least I know something about this disease; and I, too, care for Maestro Sandro. What have you to lose by permitting me to accompany you?"

"I worry about the dangerous notions you might pick up . . . and what you might see that is untoward," Leonardo said.

Niccolò voiced his impatience and displeasure by making a sound that was something of a growl and a cough, and said, "But wouldn't Maestro Toscanelli tell you that I must be exposed to—"

"Nicco . . . enough! You may come only upon the condition that you do not make a pest of yourself."

"I promise."

Distraught as she was, Simonetta smiled faintly; but Leonardo had become distant, lost in thought. As they walked through the crowded streets to Sandro's *bottega,* the weakened rays of the afternoon sun seemed to expose and excoriate him.

Simonetta had been right, the *bottega* smelled of sickness. Leonardo noticed the cloying, pungent odor as soon as he stepped into the atelier. All the rooms were dark, for the interior shutters had been closed over high and narrow lozenge-shaped windows. Only the door of the *salle* that overlooked a small postern courtyard was opened wide. Thus might some of the poison-ous effluence pass out of the house.

Yet it was considered too dangerous to open the rooms to light, lest Sandro's leaching soul be attracted and escape.

As they passed the courtyard, they glimpsed a hag in a torn *gamurra;* her hair was filthy and most likely lice ridden. Like an apparition she ap-peared, then removed herself from sight. They took the staircase to the sec-ond floor, which divided into four rooms: two studios, a bedroom, and a toilet chamber. The floors were polished tiles; the rooms themselves, each containing a fireplace, were high-ceilinged but small.

Verrocchio, who was standing outside the door, greeted them with a nod and a tight smile. "Should you be coming into this room, Madonna?" he asked Simonetta.

"I shall be careful, Andrea," she said. "If there's the slightest commo-tion, I'll leave. I promise. . . ."

Although Andrea seemed to be at odds with himself, he led them into the darkened bedroom, which also served as a kitchen; the tarry smell of herbs and medicine was pungent and cloying. It was hot as an oven, and close. A roaring fire cast an eerie light and shivering shadows upon Lorenzo, his brother Giuliano, and their small retinue that stood near Sandro's bed. Sandro lay naked, his head propped upon a bolster. He stared fixedly at the ceiling while two whores tried to excite him—to no avail. Every few seconds he trembled, as if to a blood-rhythm of his own.

Leonardo took a sharp breath upon seeing his friend, for Sandro looked to be in a death-coma: his face was slick with oil and the perspiration of heat and fever; his eyes were glazed and looked sunken, for he had lost too much weight; and his breathing was thready. He was bleeding from recent wounds and bloodlettings: large welts stood in relief against his pale flesh like arteries on old, pallid skin.

Horrified, unable to help himself, Leonardo pushed away the whores and covered his friend's nakedness. "Little Bottle, it's me, Leonardo." But Sandro didn't seem to hear him. He was murmuring something, and Leonardo leaned close to his friend to hear him whispering over and over, "Simonetta . . . Simonettaettaettaetta . . . Simonetta . . ."

Leonardo put his palm upon Sandro's forehead, which was hot to the touch, and said, "Do not worry, my friend, the Madonna is here, as I am."

Lorenzo de' Medici gently pulled Leonardo away from his friend. He embraced Leonardo and shook his head, despairing over Sandro.

"It's no use," said one of the whores. "He's in no way to be fuckish. There's no blood in that soft worm of his." She had a large frame and pen-dulous rouged breasts; her hair seemed as dirty as the hag Leonardo had glimpsed on the courtyard; but she did have a certain coarse beauty. "If you think it right, we could whip him again, Conte," she said, directing herself to a youth hardly older than Niccolò, who stood beside Lorenzo and Giuliano de' Medici near the cloth-covered step that led to the high bed.

This was Count Pico della Mirandola, the darling of Lorenzo's court, the young magician and scholar who had unlocked the secrets of the Jews' Cabala and had written the brilliant *Platonick Discourse upon Love* as a commentary on the poem by his friend Girolamo di Paolo Benivieni. He was certainly a comely boy, actually extraordinary looking. He had very pale skin; penetrating gray eyes; white, even teeth; a large, muscular frame; and elaborately coifed, reddish-blond hair. He wore the traditional garb of the theurgist: a crown of laurel and an immaculately clean white wool gown. He was sweating profusely from the heat; the other men, including Verrocchio and Lorenzo, were dressed in shirtsleeves, *in zuppone,* while the servants were bare-chested.

"Leave him, you've done your best," Mirandola said; and the whore left the bed, as did her companion, who was flat-chested and could have been easily mistaken for a boy.

"Il Magnifico," said the large-framed woman, "do you wish us to remain to . . . help any of your other citizens?" She cast a glance at Niccolò and then at Mirandola. Her skin was slick and shiny in the firelight. "Your magician certainly looks to be in need of some firkytoodle, is that not true, *mio Illustrissimo Signore?*"

Mirandola coolly ignored her, although color came to his cheeks. "Thank you, no . . . on all counts," Lorenzo said, smiling; and he placed a florin in each woman's hand.

After the whores left, Simonetta came forward; but she was cautious. She took Leonardo's and Lorenzo's hands and asked, almost pleading, "What can we do? This is so . . . degrading." She was in tears and could not take her eyes from Sandro, who must have heard her or sensed her presence, for he suddenly snapped into alertness.

He sat up in the bed, looking frightened, as if he had just awakened from a nightmare. Before he could be restrained, he jumped to the floor. Repeating her name over and over, he lunged for Simonetta.

Giuliano brought Sandro down; but, like the others, he had been caught off guard. Leonardo, Lorenzo, and Verrocchio held him, although it was difficult, for he was thrashing and kicking; then, as if this had been some erotic seizure, Sandro seemed to fall back into his coma of shallow breathing and periodic tremors.

As the men lifted him with difficulty back to his bed, Mirandola took Simonetta by the elbow and led her firmly to the door. "Madonna Simonetta, did I not tell you to keep *out* of this room? It is absolutely too dangerous for you to be in here . . . dangerous for you *and* Messer Botticelli."

"Don't be angry with me, Pico. What harm can I do now? I only wish to help. It seems that he is wasting away . . . that he is inhabited by demons, please God protect him. I fear he is going to die."

"Perhaps not. I am going to try another exorcism, Madonna. If that fails, I will come to you."

"Yes?"

"And then you will have to make a decision that might well endanger *your* life."

Simonetta nodded; but to look at her, it seemed as if she had been relieved of a great burden.

Then she slipped out of the fire-stoked room.

———

When one of the servants asked Lorenzo if the fire could now be put out, lest someone faint, Mirandola answered for Il Magnifico. "The fire must be stoked *up*, but first fetch the hag to us immediately."

"What use is the fire?" Leonardo asked.

"Perhaps we should damp it out," Lorenzo said, wiping the perspiration from his face with a cloth. "This heat has not seemed to help Sandro one whit."

"I beg a bit more of your patience, Magnifico," Mirandola said. "The fire is not for Maestro Sandro, but for us. The heat is to protect *us* from the dangerous influence of Sandro's phantasm of Eros."

"And why would heat give us this protection?" Leonardo asked, curious about this superstition.

"Are you not familiar with Aristotle's differentiation of cold melancholic vapors and pure, or hot, spirits?"

"I must confess I am not," Leonardo said.

"Well, suffice it to say that heat prevents the infection of dreams and phantasms from 'cold' and hence impure melancholy."

Leonardo thought better than to continue questioning Mirandola further, lest he humiliate this insolent and pompous young aristocrat, especially in the presence of Lorenzo.

"If the shrew can't break these bonds," Mirandola said to Lorenzo and Giuliano, who came over from Sandro's bedside, "then only Simonetta can help him."

"How is that?" asked Lorenzo.

"Sandro's diseased spirit might be cleansed if it could reestablish contact with the object of its obsession: Simonetta. But to do that, Simonetta would have to absorb the phantasm that is poisoning Sandro." After a pause he said, "We can only hope that his soul isn't dead inside him. If that is the case, then he lives only through the object of his obsession. If that is so, then he is lost to us."

"And what of Simonetta?" Leonardo asked, believing this to be superstition, but dangerous nevertheless.

"She would, in effect, be taking herself—her own phantasm—back. But this spirit that was generated in Sandro's soul out of melancholy anguish is tainted. It's not a true reflection of Simonetta. It would be as if she had imbibed poison."

"Then that cannot be permitted," Lorenzo said.

"But . . . ," Mirandola continued, "there's a very strong chance that she can then be cured, exorcised, if such cure is undertaken immediately. It's very risky; but there is, so to speak, an antidote.

"You should also realize," he continued, "that if our Sandro's soul has already languished, he will die—as surely as if a knife pierced his heart—when she accepts the phantasm he has created."

At that moment the hag entered the room; and Leonardo almost gagged at the smell of her. But her odor was not merely that of filth, but of decay, such as rotting meat. She now wore a black *mantello* of cheap material draped over her head and shoulders. She bowed her head to Lorenzo and Mirandola and said, "I make you no promises, Lords."

But Mirandola, ignoring her, walked over to the bedside. He fixed his eyes upon Sandro's—or upon the phantasm reflected in his eyes—and said: "O supreme master of hallowed name, O Master Saturn, you who are frigid and sterile, and bleak and baleful of countenance; you who are wise and impenetrable, who knows neither pleasure nor joy, who knows every ruse and art of the divine deceiver, who carries prosperity or ruin, and who brings men pleasure or misery! O Magnificent Father, through your goodness and benevolence, please permit your servants to cure this man's weakened, contaminated soul of its phantasmic sickness."

Sandro closed his eyes tightly and shivered. Then he shook his head from side to side, as if he were about to have an episode.

"Bind his hands and legs to the bed," ordered the hag. "And be soon, before he slips back to his swoon!"

Leonardo protested, but Mirandola nodded at the servants, who did as the old woman asked. As Sandro was being tied, Lorenzo said, "Leonardo, this is difficult for all of us; but we have no other choice, unless we wish to let our friend die."

Leonardo held his tongue, for it would be impossible to convince Lorenzo, or anyone else present, that this sorcery would not work; and it would be especially dangerous to oppose young Count Mirandola, Il Magnifico's favorite.

When this humiliation was over, Leonardo would attend to Sandro.

But the hag lost no time. She threw small bags tied with twine into the fire. Their contents crackled as they burned, discharging vapors that smelled of sweet grass, perfumes, formaldehyde, and resin. They burned the eyes and caused various shapes and colors to form in the consuming flames.

Leonardo felt dizzy, as if he had had too much to drink. Afterimages seemed to be exploding along the edges of his vision. He was certain the hag's vapors were meant to addle all who inhaled them, so he stepped back from the fire and covered his mouth with his sleeve until the vapors dissipated, ordering Niccolò to do the same.

The hag walked around Sandro's bed and began swearing at him in her raspy voice. She humiliated him, calling him a Jew and a work-back sodomite; she maligned Simonetta, the object of his desires, as a putain and a whore-bitch. She leaned over him, pulling back her *mantello,* so her dugs hung over him in a grotesquerie of sensuality. Then she became louder, shouting as she shook him by the shoulders. "Your woman is a scrub, a skrunt, a fuckstress." She crawled upon the bed—straddling Sandro's head with her spindled, slap-sided legs—and said, "Look up my snatch, shit-poke." And in a girlishly sweet voice, she asked, "Is your woman's love-flesh as pretty as mine?" She pulled back her clothes, exposing her genitals, and pulled away a rag soaked in menstrual blood—certainly not her own—that was tied around her waist.

"Take down the curtains from the windows," she shouted at Mirandola.

"That's to help free Maestro Sandro's phantasm," Niccolò said.

Leonardo shook his head in disgust and said, "I don't think you need to see any more of this." But Niccolò behaved as if nothing had been said and edged away to the other side of the room.

Mirandola pulled down the makeshift curtains; and each time he did so, he invoked *"Deus lux summa luminum"*: the invisible light of God. Faint light of the dying afternoon suffused the room, as transparent and diaphanous as the light of Sandro's paintings, one of which Leonardo now noticed standing against the wall. It was the Primavera; and the dancing group of graces, depicted as described in a passage in Apuleius, seemed to be created out of light. But these figures did not seem to have any physical existence. They were luminous spirits, angelic, ineffable visions, phantasms of Simonetta wrested from Sandro's mind.

And, indeed, the faces and figures of this *tabula picta* were Simonetta's.

Perhaps it was the vapors from the fire that witch-struck his vision, but Leonardo imagined that the graces were all in subtle movement; they were alive and tortured, caught in that timeless, two-dimensional space of the painting.

Waving the blood-stinking rag above Sandro's face, the hag made sexual noises and sat upon his chest. She brushed the rag against his face, held it under his nose, and uttered the *malleus maleficarum:* "Your swinish woman, your slut, she is like this . . . *like* this. A bane of nature she is."

Then she crawled backward on her knees and manipulated Sandro's penis inside herself.

Sandro eyes were open, and they seemed focused upon her.

Indeed, only his eyes seemed alive. . . .

After gyrating upon him in a grotesque parody of coitus, the shrew finally gave up. Still crouching over him like a four-legged spider, she turned to Mirandola and Lorenzo and said, "This is not a man, but a devil. Nothing can help him!" Dismounting Sandro, she climbed down from the bed. She pulled her *gamurra* around her and walked stiffly out of the room with the mien of a woman of high birth who had just been insulted.

To Leonardo's horror and disgust, Sandro—who was still trembling and mumbling Simonetta's name—had an erection.

———

When Mirandola returned to the room with Simonetta, Leonardo dared not protest too much, lest Lorenzo guess his involvement with her; surely that would be more dangerous for Simonetta than any of this magical hugger-mugger. But at the sight of Simonetta, Lorenzo moaned; then he stood as stiffly as one of his guards, as if he had to be an example for the others. Giuliano stood quietly beside his brother.

"Do you wish to clear the room?" Mirandola asked Lorenzo.

"Would it have a disruptive effect upon Sandro's . . . cure?"

"I don't think so, but it could be dangerous for others."

"Then anyone who wishes to leave should do so now," Lorenzo said so that all could hear. The physician, looking tired and unkempt, bowed to Lorenzo as he left the room with his urceus of leeches.

Verrocchio gave Lorenzo a bear hug and said, "As much as I love Sandro, I think it best if I give Madonna and you, Magnifico, your privacy. If I am needed, I will be but a call away."

"You'd better take Nicco along," Leonardo said.

Andrea nodded, smiled grimly, and called Niccolò. "Come along," he said, pushing Niccolò and a young servant before him.

"Are you certain you wish to take this risk?" Lorenzo asked Simonetta; there was an edge of desperation in his voice. Simonetta nodded and kissed him on the cheek. Lorenzo embraced her and said, "There *must* be other alternatives."

Mirandola said, "I'm sorry, Magnifico, but we have exhausted all of the established remedies."

"Then we must study the matter further," Lorenzo said. His hands rested upon Simonetta's shoulders. "I cannot permit you to do this, Madonna. I care for you too much." As he pulled her to him, Leonardo and Giuliano politely backed away.

"And what of poor Sandro?" Simonetta asked. "He might die without our help. Don't you care for him?"

"Of course I do, he's like my own brother. But I cannot lose you, my darling."

"Magnificence, if I don't help him, he will surely die. I could not live with that. I love you, but I must do this thing. You must permit me to re-deem myself."

"Redeem?" Lorenzo asked.

"Don't ask me to explain, for I would tell you the truth, as always. But remember your promise? We shall ask no questions of each other." Then she whispered, "We shall only give of ourselves. Is that not true?"

Lorenzo hung his great, ugly head, and Leonardo felt a sudden, deep sympathy for this man.

"Now's my chance to test my faith," Simonetta said. Lorenzo nodded and managed a smile. "Now you must all leave. I am mindful of your safety, for I love you all." She smiled at Leonardo, as if sharing their secrets.

"I shall remain," Lorenzo said.

"And I shall keep you company," Leonardo said.

"And I, too," said Giuliano.

"Giuliano . . . ," Lorenzo said, but then he caught himself. He gave his brother a great hug, and then espied Niccolò, who had slipped back into the room and was standing in shadow behind the door. "But *you,* precocious young man, must leave. Or would you disobey me, too?"

Niccolò stepped into the light, bowed, and apologized. His ears were burning red, but he had enough composure to say to Simonetta, "I wish you God's mercy on your endeavor, dear lady."

After he left, Mirandola said to Simonetta, "There is not much time, lest Sandro become agitated. You must draw his spirit into yourself, but do not let it infest you. When it passes into you, you must confine it behind your eyes, lest it reach your heart and circulate. As I explained to you, dear lady, you must visualize a vast and bright space—such as a cathedral flooded with sunlight—behind your eyes."

"Yes, Pico, I remember."

"Then go to him."

"Be careful," Lorenzo whispered, and then uttered a prayer.

As Simonetta walked directly to his bed, Mirandola went to the hearth and placed another log on the fire. The wood crackled and steamed, for it was not yet completely seasoned. Then he dropped a small bag into the flames, and a pungent, sulfurous vapor filled the room as if it were light it-self. Once again Leonardo felt dizzy . . . and expansive. Although it was im-possible to avoid the smoky effluvium, he pressed his sleeve against his face. Just now Leonardo could imagine that bodies and space and physical exis-tence could be ignored, that everything was indeed spirit: image detached from matter.

Such was Sandro's belief. . . .

Simonetta stood beside the bed and took Sandro's hand, which was still roped to a headpost. "Little Bottle," she whispered, "it's Simonetta, I have come to you to take your pain. To free you. . . ."

"Simonetta . . . Simonettaetta," Sandro mumbled in a singsong. An in-stant later his brows furrowed, and his face seemed to come alive. But he closed his eyes so tightly that his lips were drawn upward by the strain, as if Simonetta were the sun itself, too bright to be looked at directly.

Sandro strained at the ropes and shook his head. Then, as if suddenly lucid, he said, "Go away, please leave me! I do not wish you harm. My lovely Simonetta, Simonetta . . ."

"I will not leave," Simonetta said, taking his face firmly in her hands. "Look upon me, I am here."

But Sandro refused to open his eyes. He thrashed about in the bed; it was as if Simonetta's softest touch was a brand searing his flesh. But she would not be thrown from the bed. She held on to Sandro until he stopped bucking and flailing himself about.

And suddenly she caught him.

He opened his eyes for an instant, saw her, and turned his head away, pressing the side of his head against the bed, as if hoping to bury himself in-side it; but then—shaking with strain, fighting the muscles that would obey his spirit, but not his mind—he turned to her.

Looking upon her, wide-eyed, transfixed, he suddenly became quies-cent.

It was dusk. The fire was low, and piles of embers glowed redly in the hearth. Candles flickered in wall sconces, casting pale, wavering shadows; and lamps burned on table and bench. Although the fumes from the potions thrown upon the fire had disappeared into the suffocating air, Leonardo saw—or, rather, glimpsed—something vaporous pass between Sandro and Simonetta.

It passed from his beclouded eyes to hers, which were clear and lus-trous.

This vapor was sanguineous, pure, and hot: it was a flicker, a swiftly passing glory as pale and subtle as the aura that surrounds the moon on a misty, stormy night.

Gazing one upon the other, locked in an embrace that was not physical, they kissed. Their eyes remained open, watching each other as if in wonderment, as tongue prodded tongue.

They acted as if there were no one else present.

Lorenzo shifted his weight nervously from one foot to the other.

"I pray this is not their *binsica*," Mirandola said.

Leonardo thought that the idea of the ecstatic kiss of death was superstitious nonsense; but he felt a chill feather down his spine, which was certainly the result of the hag's vapors.

"*Multiplex semen, multiplex Venus, multiplex amor, multiplex vinculum,*" Mirandola intoned, as if a description of principles would bind them to life.

"Untie him," Simonetta said as she pulled the vair-lined bedding from his erect penis.

As Mirandola walked toward the bed to comply with her wish, Lorenzo started after him. Then he stopped, shook his head, and sighed. Leonardo squeezed his arm, and Lorenzo nodded in appreciation. "She will not be harmed, Leonardo," Lorenzo said, as if trying to convince himself.

But Leonardo understood that the First Citizen was also feeling the shock of jealousy, for he could feel his own rising to the surface.

Mirandola untied Sandro; and Simonetta, as if dream-born, climbed onto his bed. Sandro embraced her; and then with an abrupt movement, he pulled her down upon the mattress. He rolled on top of her, kissing her, while he urgently raised her undergarments. She screamed as he entered her; and they coupled savagely, each staring into the other's eyes.

Consumed by their souls' internal fires, they became one flesh.

"I can't stand to watch this," Lorenzo cried; and he turned away. But then, as if a certain fascination of the abominable had taken hold of him, he turned back. Giuliano took his arm, and Leonardo, who was standing on the other side of Lorenzo, grasped his hand tightly. Lorenzo recoiled, but Giuliano and Leonardo held on to him until he regained his composure.

But even as Lorenzo watched, the *vinculum vinculorum,* the chain of chains, was broken.

Sandro lifted himself away from Simonetta, who lay upon the bed. She seemed lifeless, drained of blood and color, her eyes open and staring upward. But she was breathing slowly, as if she were asleep or in a trance. Sandro rubbed his eyes and, uncomprehending, stared directly at Leonardo. "What has happened?" he asked in a whisper; and then he turned to Simonetta. As he looked at her, he began to cry. He touched her face and said, "Jesù, what have I done?"

Leonardo and Lorenzo reached the bedside. While Leonardo calmed Sandro, Lorenzo tried to rouse Simonetta.

"Magnifico, wait," Mirandola said to Lorenzo, as he gently pulled him away from the bed. "You must allow me to awaken her. There is little time, and her soul is full of the poison of Sandro's phantasm. Look, you can see it filling her eyes." Lorenzo nodded and stood back. Then Mirandola turned his attention momentarily to Botticelli. "Truly, this woman cares for you, Sandro. She has healed you. Now, with God's help, you will begin to gain back your strength."

But Sandro—who was perspiring heavily, as if, indeed, all the poisons were pouring out of him—fell back into Leonardo's arms in a dead faint.

"Leave him," Mirandola said. "There is little time. The Madonna must be moved away from Sandro."

As Leonardo and Giuliano removed her to an ornately carved bench situated near the far corner, Mirandola hurried everyone out of the room. Then to Leonardo and Giuliano he said, "If you must remain, then stay near Sandro. Even while he is in a swoon, you must block his view of the Madonna. Cover his eyes, if you must. It's not impossible that this phantasm could reestablish itself in Sandro's heart. Then both he and the Madonna would weaken and die. Now please, Magnifico, leave us."

Leonardo and Lorenzo watched Mirandola from the bedside, where they sat in positions so to obstruct Sandro's view of Simonetta, should he awaken. Mirandola held on to Simonetta, lest she fall forward from her seat. The room was dark, although dusty moonlight passed through the window and the candles guttered, casting yellowish, flickering light. A lamp cast its own wan aura from its place on the end of the bench opposite to where Simonetta sat. Mirandola pulled the lamp toward him and reached inside his robes for a small mirror, which he placed on the bench within easy reach. Then he took out a leather pouch, from which he removed balsam, a square of sugar, a gold amulet, myrobalan, a thin vial of sweet perfume, and a scattering of precious stones. He placed these things beside the mirror and said, "May these gifts of the animate world—these *homines phlebotomici*—become the recipients of the poisonous pneuma. May they become divine enticements and, through their affinities to the higher world, gain you the support of angels ethereal."

He held the vial near Simonetta's nostrils. Her head jerked backward as if she had just smelled ammonia water; but before he covered the vial, he inhaled its contents, closing his eyes for a beat, as if he were transported. Then, putting down the vial, he clapped his hands loudly before Simonetta's face. "Awaken," he said, holding the mirror before her.

Her eyes were dilated. She took the mirror from him and smiled as she stared into it. "It's lovely," she whispered, looking at her eyes as reflected in the mirror.

She seemed to be in a state of bliss.

"What do you see?" asked Mirandola anxiously.

"Sandro's pneuma . . . his creation. It flatters me, for his phantasm is an angel. How could I live up to such a perfect image?"

"Madonna, do not let the image bewitch you," Mirandola said. "You must expel it. Do you understand?"

"I can look directly into the higher world. . . ."

"Madonna. Madonna! Can you hear me?"

She nodded.

"If you wish to imbue yourself with the qualities of the higher world, then you must allow these things I have placed before you to become your affinities. Let them be the recipients of the pneuma you have taken from Sandro; and if the qualities of that phantasm are polluted, they will reject it . . . and you will be safe. But to do that, you must let Sandro's phantasm pass into the mirror."

"I see it there," Simonetta said.

"Very good. Now close your eyes and look into yourself, into the bright space behind your eyes. That's where you trapped the phantasm, is it not?"

Simonetta nodded.

He pressed the jewels, amulet, and sugar into Simonetta's hand, which rested on her lap. "Now tell me, Signora Vespucci, does some of the image still remain in the cathedral you created in your thoughts?"

Again she nodded.

"Then you must force it into the mirror. Let the objects in your hand give you the strength of the higher presences. Open your eyes now. Give the phantasm to the mirror."

"It's dark. The mirror is dark."

"Has the phantasm left you?"

Simonetta nodded.

Mirandola took the mirror from her and threw it to the ground, then crushed it underfoot. He made her open her hand and drop the jewels and amulet, then wiped the sugar from her palm. "It is done," he announced. "The servants must now take the jewels, shards of glass, and other affinities, which are now poisonous, and bury them. And the physician must let the blood of both Maestro Botticelli and Madonna Vespucci with his leeches. I give you back your friends," he said to Lorenzo. He smiled warmly at his benefactor.

As he spoke, Simonetta looked directly at Leonardo.

And she, too, smiled.

But it was a smile of dissimulation.

Suddenly Sandro awakened. He gasped for breath, as if he were a drowning man breaking the surface of the sea. Looking directly at Simonetta, he asked, "Leonardo, where is she? Where is Simonetta . . . ?"

"Be quiet and rest now," Leonardo said as he wiped the perspiration from Sandro's face with a corner of the bedcloth. "All is well."

"And Simonetta, what of Simonetta?"

"Like you, Little Bottle, she will soon be in high feather," Leonardo said, even as a chill worried its way up his spine.

"Do you promise that's the truth, Leonardo?"

"Yes, my friend," he lied.

7

The Cave
of Daedalus

Now, destroyed by time, you lie patiently in
this confined space, your bones stripped and
bare....

—Leonardo da Vinci

*I*t was as if the black miasmas of Sandro's exorcism had leaked into the world, poisoning it, for the next day, a Thursday, one of the small bells of Santa Maria del Fiore broke loose and fell, breaking the skull of a stonemason passing below. By a miracle, he lived, although a bone had to be removed from his skull.

And on Friday a boy of twelve fell from the large bell of the Palagio and landed on the gallery. He died several hours later.

By week's end four families in the city and eight in the Borgo di Ricorboli were stricken with fever and buboes, the characteristic swellings of what had come to be called "the honest plague." There were more reports of fever and death every day thereafter, for the Black Reaper was back upon the streets, wending his way through homes and hospitals, cathedrals and taverns, and whorehouses and nunneries alike. It was said that he had a companion, the hag Lachesis, who followed after him while she wove an ever-lengthening tapestry of death; hers was an accounting of "the debt we must all pay," created from her never-ending skein of black thread.

One hundred twenty people had died in the churches and hospitals by *nella quidtadecima:* the full moon. There were twenty-five deaths alone at Santa Maria Nuova. The "Eight" of the Signoria duly issued a notice of health procedures to be followed by all Florentines, and the price of foodstuffs rose drastically.

Lorenzo and his retinue—which included his wife, Clarise, and their children; his sister Bianca, who had married into the Pazzi family; Giuliano; Angelo Poliziano; Pico della Mirandola; the humanist Bartolomeo Scala; and even Sandro Botticelli—fled to Villa Careggi or thereabouts. But rather than follow suit and leave the city for the safety of the country, Verrocchio elected to remain in his *bottega.* He gave permission to his apprentices to quit the city until the plague abated, if they had the resources; but most, in fact, stayed with him.

The *bottega* seemed to be in a fervor.

One would think that the deadline for every commission was tomorrow. Verrocchio's foreman, Francesco, kept a tight and sure rein on the apprentices, pressing them into a twelve- to fourteen-hour schedule; and they worked as they had when they'd constructed the bronze *palla* that topped the dome of Santa Maria del Fiore, as if quick hands and minds were the only weapons against the ennui upon which the Black Fever might feed. Francesco had become invaluable to Leonardo, for he was quicker with things mechanical than Verrocchio himself; and Francesco helped him design an ingenious plan by which the flying machine could be collapsed and dismantled and camouflaged for easy transportation to Vinci. The flying machine, at least, was complete; again, thanks to Francesco, who made certain that Leonardo had a constant supply of strong-backed apprentices and material.

Leonardo's studio was a mess, a labyrinth of footpaths that wound past bolts of cloth, machinery, stacks of wood and leather, jars of paint, sawhorses, and various gearing devices; the actual flying machine took up the center of the great room. Surrounding it were drawings, insects mounted on boards, a table covered with birds and bats in various stages of vivisection, and constructions of the various parts of the redesigned flying machine—artificial wings, rudders, and flap valves.

The noxious odors of turpentine mixed with the various perfumes of decay; these smells disturbed Leonardo not at all, for they reminded him of his childhood, when he'd kept all manner of dead animals in his room to study and paint. All other work—the paintings and terra-cotta sculptures—were piled in one corner. Leonardo and Niccolò could no longer sleep in the crowded, foul-smelling studio; they had laid their pallets down in the young apprentice Tista's room.

But Leonardo's sleep was fitful, and only a few hours a night. He was fretting over Ginevra, who had left Florence with her father and Nicolini without word; Leonardo had arrived at an empty house on the day when he was to paint her portrait. Only an elderly servant remained. So like Verrocchio, but for different reasons, Leonardo lost himself in his work. The Black Death had given him a reprieve—just enough time to complete and test his machine—for not only did Il Magnifico agree to rendezvous in Vinci rather than Pistoia, he himself set the date forward another fortnight.

———

It was unbearably warm in the studio as Niccolò helped Leonardo remove the windlass mechanism and twin "oars" from the machine, which were to be packed into a numbered wooden container. "It's getting close," Niccolò said, after the parts were fitted securely into the box. "Tista tells me that he heard a family living near the Porta alla Croce caught fever."

"Well, we shall be on our way at dawn," Leonardo said. "You shall have the responsibility of making certain that everything is properly loaded and in its proper place."

Niccolò seemed very pleased with that; he had, in fact, proved himself to be a capable worker. "But I still believe we should wait until the dark effluvia have evaporated from the air. At least until after the *becchini* have carried the corpses to their graves."

"Then we will leave after first light," Leonardo said.

"Good."

"You might be right about the possible contagion of corpses and *bec-chini*. But as to your effluvia . . ."

"Best not to take chances," Verrocchio said; he had been standing in the doorway and peering into the room like a boy who had not yet been caught sneaking through the house. He held the door partially closed so that it framed him, as if he were posing for his own portrait; and the particular glow of the late-afternoon sun seemed to transform and subdue his rather heavy features.

"I think it is as the astrologers say: a conjunction of planets," Verrocchio continued. "It was so during the great blight of 1345. But that was a conjunction of *three* planets. Very unusual. It will not be like that now, for the conjunction is not nearly so perfect."

"You'd be better to come to the country with us than listen to astrologers," Leonardo said.

"I cannot leave my family. I've told you."

"Then bring them along. My father is already in Vinci preparing the main house for Lorenzo and his retinue. You could think of it as a business holiday; think of the commissions that might fall your way."

"I think I have enough of those for the present," Andrea said.

"That does not sound like Andrea del Verrocchio," Leonardo said, teasing.

"My sisters and cousins refuse to leave," Andrea said. "And who would feed the cats?" he said, smiling, then sighing. He seemed resigned and almost relieved. "My fate is in the lap of the gods . . . as it has always been. And so is yours, my young friend. But I promise to pray for your safety; and in your honor I will also paint a portrait of St. Nicholas of Tolentine for the monastery of the Badia. The holy saint is venerated for many miracles, and he is reported to be especially helpful to mariners, of which you are one of a sort."

"I thank you for your love, kind Andrea." Then Leonardo asked, "Now, will my noble master at least enter the room, or does he fear that he might become contaminated in the presence of his poor apprentices?"

"As you wish," Andrea said, taking off his black cap, which was discolored by lime dust. Then, looking suddenly mischievous, he pushed the door open wide to reveal Sandro Botticelli and let him enter first.

"Little Bottle, I thought you were at Careggi," Leonardo said, shocked to see his friend, who had gained back some of the weight he had lost. Sandro's characteristic flush had returned to his full, sensual face; his light-brown curly hair was overly long and unkempt; but his eyes seemed heavy, as if he were still under the influence of drugs or magick. He was dressed in robes of the Medici colors rather than the shorter *vestini* tunics that younger men usually wore. Leonardo felt awkward, but Sandro immediately stepped forward and embraced him.

"And so I was," Sandro said, wiping his sweaty forehead with his silk sleeve. "I was worried you might have already left. There isn't much time, for Lorenzo is on his way, too. But I left early to be with you, my friend. Do you find that so difficult to believe?"

"Of course not," Leonardo said, lying.

"I will explain everything later," Sandro said. "But I could not help but worry for your safety in that contraption, lest you break your neck trying to imitate the angels."

"I'm very happy you're here, Sandro. The Great Bird is all ready to fly, and there is absolutely no need for you to worry . . . after all, I built it."

Sandro chuckled and shook his head; Andrea rolled his eyes. Leonardo grinned at them; but it was all bravado, for he had been having his recurrent dream of falling again. Then he said, "If nothing goes awry, we will leave for Vinci early tomorrow. Certainly you will join us."

"That was my intention. I thought you might have need of another strong back."

Niccolò stood beside Sandro, obviously excited to see him. "I have been a great help to Maestro Leonardo," he said.

"I can imagine you would be."

"He has learned much, Little Bottle," Leonardo said. "I fear I have become dependent on him."

"And has he been cured of the whores?"

"I did not think they were a disease," Niccolò said, smiling nervously when everyone laughed. "And you, Maestro, have you been cured of your melancholia?"

"Yes, my young friend. As well as anyone can be cured of it."

"And what of Madonna Simonetta? Is she well, too?"

"Nicco!" Leonardo said, looking sharply at the boy.

"It's all right, Leonardo," Sandro said. "A perfectly legitimate question." Then he turned to Niccolò and said, "Yes, she is well."

But when Sandro turned back to Leonardo, the guilt and anxiety could be read in his eyes, as if they truly were reflections of his soul.

⎯⎯⎯

They left the city just after first light, keeping a good distance from the few filthy *becchini* straggling back from the mass graves where they had unceremoniously buried the latest victims of the Death. Although a mist hung heavily in the air, it promised to be a clear, transparent day, a perfect day for a journey. A group of about twenty criers and trumpeters, returning from a grave site, walked beside the choppy, oily waters of the Arno on the Lungarno Acciaituoli. Only a very worthy—or wealthy—man would be accorded such honors during these times when Death had enforced its own curfew.

Niccolò and Sandro crossed themselves as the cortege passed, as did Zoroastro da Peretola and Lorenzo di Credi, who had a face as beautiful and innocent as one of Verrocchio's altarpiece angels. Besides Sandro, Niccolò, and Atalante Miglioretti, there were several of Andrea's apprentices in Leonardo's company; they all rode on the two horse-drawn wagons, which contained under canvas the component parts of Leonardo's Great Bird. Leonardo and Sandro walked beside the first wagon, and Niccolò and Tista seemed to be excited to have it for themselves; they shared holding the reins.

"I usually make this journey to my home in Vinci in a day," Leonardo said to Sandro, who had become uncomfortably distant. "I know a shortcut through Vitolini, Carmignano, and Poggio a Caiano. It's an old, deserted mountain road that runs right up Monte Albano; but you have to be willing to climb. And we wouldn't have a chance with the wagons. So we are obliged to follow the Arno and put up with Il Magnifico's soldiers questioning us in every little town we pass through. We do, however, have a pass with Lorenzo's seal upon it."

Sandro seemed to be lost in thought, but Leonardo pressed on nevertheless: "Whenever my father struck an important deal in Florence, he'd send me home in a hurry with a message for Francesco, who still manages his estates. I think I would be winded if I tried to do that now." Then, after a beat, "Sandro, I'm worried about you."

"Don't be, my friend," Sandro said, suddenly coming back to life. "Everyone tells me I disconcert them with my musings. I think the vapors of my soul are not yet clear."

"Do you still fear for—?"

"Yes, I still fear for Madonna Simonetta," Sandro said. "And for myself. After the physicians had done with me and I was feeling stronger, I insisted on accompanying Lorenzo and Pico della Mirandola to the Vespucci villa to see her. I knew something was not right with her, I could *feel* it. Lorenzo, of course, was justly apprehensive, but I pleaded with him; and the young count Mirandola said he would mind both the lady and myself."

"Yes . . . ?" Leonardo said, when Sandro did not continue.

"I told them that the passion had evaporated, that only guilt remained."

"Is that true?"

"Yes, Leonardo, I am afraid it is."

"You should be grateful to be well and whole again."

"That's just it, Leonardo; I am not whole. More like the opposite. I fear that when the count cleansed my soul, he also, unwittingly, dissolved its capacity for natural love, for ecstasy."

"Of course you feel enervated and emptied of natural emotions," Leonardo said. "But you must put your mind to rest and give yourself time. You have not yet recovered."

"Nevertheless, I had to prove to myself that I was empty . . . a eunuch."

"Be gentle with yourself, Sandro," Leonardo scolded.

"I felt a great sadness when I saw her," Sandro said, musing. "She was very ill. It was my fault, of that I am convinced."

"Couldn't Count Mirandola help her?" Leonardo asked.

"That's just it, he would not believe there was anything wrong."

"Then perhaps you are—"

"I could tell she was ill, you must believe me," Sandro said.

"Was she coughing?"

"No, she did not cough," Sandro said. "She looked frail, but that is part of her beauty. She is like an angel; her flesh looks as if it is spirit itself. But I had a moment alone with her, for everyone by then could see that there was no danger for me; and they were not afraid for her. I knew then, I knew . . ."

"What did you know, Little Bottle?"

"That Simonetta had absorbed my poisonous phantasm into herself and would not reject it. Mirandola had exorcised her, but it was a sham; she fooled the physicians and kept the phantasm."

Although Leonardo could not consider seriously the business of the exorcism and the keeping of phantasms, he tried to reach out to his friend and humor him; for Sandro had obviously not yet recovered from his dangerous infatuation with Simonetta. "How do you know that she did not reject it?"

"Because she would not deny it. She smiled and kissed me and begged me not to pursue the matter with Lorenzo."

"I hardly think that—"

"She told me she was going to die. Then she said that my love was a perfect and exquisite treasure, a balm which soothed the aching of her heart. But by 'love' she meant the phantasm I had created of her. She called it a . . .'doorway into the higher world.' " After a pause Sandro said, "And I could see it then. I could see the phantasm directly in her eyes."

"I think you have been through a difficult time, my friend," Leonardo said . . . and he suddenly remembered how Simonetta had smiled after Mirandola had exorcised the phantasm from her. He felt the hair rise on the back of his neck.

"I thought, when I was in the throes of my lust and need for Simonetta, that I could not stand it, that it would be preferable to be an empty gourd devoid of emotion."

Leonardo smiled sadly. "I think every lover believes that."

"But now that I am empty, I desire only to be full."

Leonardo clapped his friend on the back and walked with his arm around him. "You will be well soon, I promise. Not a country maid will be safe from you."

"Do not lie to me again, Leonardo," Sandro said, seemingly without malice. "And you did lie to me."

Leonardo pulled away from him.

"I know that your friendship for Simonetta is not innocent. But you need not fret, for I would never harm either one of you." When Leonardo began to speak, Sandro interrupted him and said, "Please, do not make excuses or apologies. None are needed now. I have felt the distance between us of late, and I have worried . . . for you, my friend. Let us not permit our friendship to turn cold." Then Sandro smiled—it was both an expression of intimacy and an assent, for he nodded and said, "Without each other, who would we have to turn to?"

Leonardo agreed. He felt awkward and humiliated and angry with himself, for Sandro had been Leonardo's only confidant; and Leonardo, who had more facility with machines and canvas than people, had come precariously close to losing his friend's love.

They walked in silence and then he said, "I do not care to admit it, Little Bottle, but I am afraid. I have once again been having dreams of falling."

"Perhaps you should ask Lorenzo to—"

"No, my Great Bird *shall* fly," Leonardo said. "Be assured."

"It is Lorenzo's fault. He goaded you. Sometimes he forgets that he is not an emperor. He can sometimes be as hard as those tyrants he hates. But it is not worth your very life, dear friend."

"I should not even have mentioned it, Little Bottle. Please, do not worry. My invention is sound; I will not come to any harm. I am merely experiencing a small heartquake, such as every orator does before speaking to a crowd."

"Of course," Sandro said softly, as if to calm his friend.

But Leonardo had regained his composure—and his humor. "And soon I shall be the subject of poetry." He turned and shouted, "Ho, Atalante. You must compose a song to be played as I drift through the clouds." Atalante Miglioretti—who was sitting beside Zoroastro da Peretola in the last cart—waved his hand in acknowledgment and began playing a soothing, rather haunting melody on his lyre. Then Leonardo lapsed into a thoughtful silence. After a time he said, "I will succeed, for I am not ready to be the gazingstock of all Florence. And lose Ginevra."

"Then I have a message for you," Sandro said.

"Yes?"

"Simonetta told me to tell you that she will talk to Il Magnifico."

It was Leonardo's turn not to respond.

"I believe she refers to Ginevra," Sandro said. "*Audaces fortuna juvat.* You are the proof of the saying."

Fortune favors the bold.

———

The town of Vinci was a fortified keep dominated by a medieval castle and its campanile, surrounded by fifty brownish-pink brick houses. Their red-tiled roofs were covered with a foliage of chestnut and pine and cypress, and vines of grape and cane thickets brought the delights of earth and shade to the very walls and windows. The town with its crumbling walls and single arcaded alley was situated on the elevated spur of a mountain; it overlooked a valley blanketed with olive trees that turned silver when stirred by the wind. Beyond was the valley of Lucca, green and purple-shadowed and ribboned with mountain streams; and Leonardo remembered that when the rain had cleansed the air, the crags and peaks of the Apuan Alps near Massa and Cozzile could be clearly seen.

Now that Leonardo was here, he realized how homesick he had been. The sky was clear and the air pellucid; but the poignancy of his memories clouded his vision, as he imagined himself being swept back to his childhood days, once again riding with his Uncle Francesco, whom they called *lazzarone* because he did not choose to restrict his zealous enjoyment of life with a profession. But Leonardo and the much older Francesco had been like two privileged boys—princes, riding from farmstead to mill and all around the valley collecting rents for Leonardo's grandfather, the patriarch of the family: the gentle and punctilious Antonio da Vinci.

And with a thrill of remembered fear and joy, he thought of the monster he had found in the chill, dark, high-ceilinged cave on the slippery slope of Mount Albano. He had been thirteen years old; that same year he became an apprentice to Verrocchio.

Leonardo led his retinue of friends and junior apprentices down a cobbled road and past a rotating dovecote on a long pole to a cluster of houses surrounded by gardens, barns, peasant huts, tilled acreage, and the uniform copses of mulberry trees, which his Uncle Francesco had planted. Francesco, "the lazy one," had been experimenting with sericulture, which could prove to be very lucrative indeed, for the richest and most powerful guild in Florence was the Arte della Seta: the silk weavers.

"Leonardo, ho!" shouted Francesco from the courtyard of the large, neatly kept main house, which had belonged to Ser Antonio. It was stone and roofed with red tile, and looked like the ancient longhouses of the French; but certainly no animals would be kept in the home of Piero da Vinci: Leonardo's father.

Like his brother, Francesco had dark curly hair that was graying at the temples and thinning at the crown. His face was intense, perhaps due to his downturned lips and large, aquiline nose; deep wrinkles made arbitrary demarcations below his eyes and on his jowly cheeks. Francesco embraced Leonardo, nearly knocking the wind out of him, and said, "You have caused substantial havoc in this house, my good nephew. Congratulations. I have not had such a good time since I did a grouse with the peasant girl who—"

"Francesco! That's quite enough of your... *tauri excretio,*" said Francesco's wife, Alessandra, who appeared in the doorway. Her glory was her hair, which was long and golden.

"Can't you just say 'shit,' my pride?"

"No, I certainly cannot, for although I've pledged to live with a bear who can only sleep and eat—"

"And shit," Francesco corrected.

"And defecate," Alessandra said, "... I shall remain a lady," and with that she kissed Leonardo and invited his friends into the house.

"Your father is quite anxious," Francesco said.

"I'm sure of that," Leonardo said as he walked into the hall. "It's wonderful to see you, Uncle."

Beyond this expansive, lofted room were several sleeping chambers, two fireplaces, a kitchen and pantry, and workrooms, which sometimes housed the peasants who worked the various da Vinci farmholds; there was a level above with three more rooms and a fireplace; and ten steps below was the cellar where Leonardo used to hide the dead animals he had found. The house was immaculate: how Leonardo's father must have oppressed the less than tidy Francesco and Alessandra to make it ready for Lorenzo and his guests.

This room was newly fitted out with covered beds, chests, benches, and a closet cabinet to accommodate several of the lesser luminaries in Il Magnifico's entourage. Without a doubt, Leonardo's father would give the First Citizen his own bedroom.

"Lest you become too comfortable, nephew, you'll have to explain yourself to your father," Francesco said; then he pulled a face.

Leonardo sighed, feeling the uneasiness he always felt around his father, as if Leonardo were his apprentice rather than his son.

Piero came down the stairs from his chamber above to meet Leonardo. He wore his magisterial robes and a brimless, silk *berretta* cap, as if he were expecting Lorenzo and his entourage at any moment. "Greetings, my son; and to you too, Sandro Botticelli."

"Greetings to you, Ser Piero," Sandro said, bowing.

Leonardo and his father embraced.

"Francesco, would you be so kind as to attend to my son's friends?"

Piero asked, and then, tightly grasping Leonardo's elbow, he said, "May I take you away from your company for a few moments?"

"Of course, Father," Leonardo said politely, allowing himself to be led upstairs.

They entered a writing room, which contained a long, narrow clerical desk, a master's chair, and a sitting bench decorated with two octagonally shaped pillows; the floor was tiled like a chessboard. A clerk sat upon a stool behind the desk and made a great show of writing in a large leather-bound ledger. Austere though the room appeared, it revealed a parvenu's taste for comfort; for Piero was eager to be addressed as Messer, rather than Ser, and to carry a sword, which was the prerogative of a knight. "Will you excuse us, Vittore?" Piero said to the clerk. The young man rose, bowed, and left the room.

"Yes, Father?" Leonardo asked, expecting the worst.

"I don't know whether to scold you or congratulate you."

"The latter would be preferable."

Piero smiled and said, "Andrea has apprised me that Il Magnifico has asked for you to work in his gardens."

"Yes."

"I am very proud."

"Thank you, Father."

"So, you see, I was correct in keeping you to the grindstone."

Leonardo felt his neck and face grow warm. "You mean by taking everything I earned so I could not save enough to pay for my master's matriculation fee in the Painters' Guild?"

"That money went to support the family . . . your family."

"And now you—or rather the family—will lose that income."

"My concern is not, nor was it ever, the money," Piero said. "It was properly forming your character, of which I am still in some doubt."

"Thank you."

"I'm sorry, but as your father, it is my duty—" He paused. Then, as if trying to be more conciliatory, he said, "You could hardly do better than to have Lorenzo for a patron. But he would never have noticed you if I had not made it possible for you to remain with Andrea."

"You left neither Andrea nor me any choice."

"Be that as it may, Master Andrea made certain that you produced and completed the projects he assigned to you. At least he tried to prevent you from running off and cavorting with your limp-wristed, degenerate friends."

"Do you, then, consider Sandro Botticelli to be a degenerate?" Leonardo asked, unable to keep the anger out of his voice.

Piero shook his head impatiently. "Sandro is acceptable. But I see you've also brought young Miglioretti into my home. There's evil talk circulating about him; he is no better than your friend Onorevoli, the one who is called Il Neri."

"Ah, you mean those who are not in Il Magnifico's retinue."

"Don't you dare to be insolent."

"I apologize, Father," Leonardo said, chafing.

"The Onorevoli are no friends of the Medici; they're thick with the Pazzi. You would be well advised to stay away from them and their ilk. Mark my words, the Pazzi will come to a bad end."

"Yes, Father," Leonardo said, but he had become sullen.

"You're making that face again."

"I'm sorry if I offend you."

"You don't offend me, you—" He paused, then said, "You've put our family in an impossible position."

"What do you mean?"

"Your business here with the Medici."

"It does not please you to host the First Citizen?" Leonardo asked.

"You have made a foolish bet with him and will certainly become the monkey. Our name—"

"Ah, yes, that is, of course, all that worries you. But I shall not fail, Father. You can then take full credit for any honor I might bring to our good name."

"Only birds and insects can fly."

"And those who bear the name da Vinci." But Piero would not be mollified. Leonardo sighed. "Father, I shall try not to disappoint you." He bowed respectfully and turned toward the door.

"Leonardo!" his father said, as if he were speaking to a child. "I have not excused you."

"May I be excused, then?"

"Yes, you may." But then Piero called him back.

"Yes, Father?" Leonardo asked, pausing at the door.

"I forbid you to attempt this . . . experiment."

"I am sorry, Father; but I cannot turn tail now."

"I will explain to Il Magnifico that you are my firstborn."

"Thank you, but—"

"Your safety is my responsibility," Piero said, and then he said, "I worry for you!"

After a pause Leonardo asked, "Will you do me the honor of watching me fly upon the wind?" He ventured a smile. "It will be a da Vinci, not a Medici or a Pazzi, who will be soaring in the heavens closest to God."

"I suppose I shall have to keep up appearances," Piero said, then raised an eyebrow, as if questioning his place in the scheme of these events. He looked at his son and smiled sadly.

Though once again Leonardo experienced the unbridgeable distance between himself and his father, the tension between them dissolved.

"You are welcome to remain here," Piero said.

"You will have little enough room when Lorenzo and his congregation arrive," Leonardo said. "And I shall need quiet in which to work and prepare; it's been fixed for us to lodge with Achattabrigha di Piero del Vacca."

"When are you expected?"

"We should leave now. Uncle Francesco said he would accompany us."

Piero nodded. "Please give my warmest regards to your mother."

"I shall be happy to do so."

"Are you at all curious to see your new brother?" Piero asked, as if it were an afterthought.

"Of course I am, Father."

Piero took his son's arm, and they walked to Margherita's bedroom.

Leonardo could feel his father trembling.

And for those few seconds, he actually felt that he was his father's son.

———————

Although Leonardo was awakened every night by his recurring dream of falling, he felt refreshed in his mother's earthen-floored, thatched-roofed cottage where he had spent his early childhood. Caterina doted on him. It was from her that he had inherited his crooked finger; and it was for her that he painted their little deformity into all of his "little Madonnas." She had a wonderfully strong, frank face; a longish nose with a tiny hump in the bridge; and sad, pensive lips. She was tall, fleshy, of sallow complexion, and rather homely; so markedly different from the three young girls Leonardo's father had wedded. But for the crook in her finger, one would be hard put to find any resemblance between mother and son.

And unlike Leonardo's father, she was generous and physical with her love.

"Leonardo!" she shouted as she waved her arms at him from the doorway of the cottage. Her barrel-chested husband, Achattabrigha, who was a *fornaciaio,* a builder of kilns, stood in the yard between the carts that contained the disassembled flying machine. It was ready to be taken to the cliff where it would fly. Achattabrigha, too, was shouting, calling Leonardo back.

Leonardo had spent these last few days by himself, shunning even the company of Sandro and Niccolò; they seemed to understand, for he often acted this way when he was working. He catnapped during the day and slept little during the night. He sketched and wrote in his notebook by the light of a water-filled lamp of his own invention, and spent endless hours under his flying machine, which was supported by a sturdy framework of wood cut from the forest nearby. The Great Bird was a brightly colored chimera. Its twin dragonfly wings were shaped and ridged like a bat's and were made of fustian lashed with thin strips of fir. Beneath the great blue-and-gold wings were the pilot's harness, twin "oars," hand-operated cranks, a collar connected to the rudder, which was like a bird's tail, and a windlass and foot pedals.

Leonardo was to fly his Great Bird tomorrow for Il Magnifico; he knew he was ready, for he suddenly longed for noise and companionship. But there was one last thing he wanted to do, and he wished to take Niccolò with him.

He left Sandro to watch over the apprentices.

"We will be back in a few hours, Mother," Leonardo called, for he and Niccolò were already a good distance away from the house.

Caterina waved her hands and shouted, "You must come back now! You—"

Before Leonardo could answer her, he saw Lorenzo de' Medici step out from beside the house, where he had tethered his oversize horse. In deference, Leonardo and Niccolò immediately walked down the hill toward him; but Lorenzo rushed to meet them. He wore a short doublet cut in the latest fashion, hose, and a black silk hunting hat. His square, smiling face was flushed and clear of eczema; his dark eyes, which gave his face the appearance of such intensity, were narrowed in the sunlight; and wisps of his thick brown hair clung to his forehead. He had probably spent the morning hunting and exercising with his friends.

"Ho, Leonardo, I must apologize for intruding upon your march, but I wished to talk to you . . . alone, before tomorrow."

Niccolò bowed to Lorenzo, who greeted him warmly, and said, "I will wait for you there." He pointed to a hillock surrounded by olive trees.

"Thank you, Nicco," Leonardo said. As Niccolò walked away, Leonardo felt awkward in Lorenzo's presence. They stood for a time and listened to the cicadas.

"I spoke to Sandro for but a moment," Lorenzo said. "He looks much better than when he left our house."

"The country agrees with him."

"Indeed. But I think it is you who deserves credit; your friendship has restored him. He tells me that you're taking young Niccolò on a grand tour of your childhood places."

Leonardo laughed; he felt self-conscious. "I asked Sandro to join us, but he wasn't up to it."

"So he told me."

"Magnificence, you are, of course, welcome to join us."

Lorenzo smiled and said, "If you wouldn't mind such an imposition, I would like that very much. This is a good time for us to become acquainted, for you will soon be part of my family." He put his arm around Leonardo's shoulders and said, "When we are alone together, such as we are now, we must pledge to have nothing formal between us. I have long been jealous of Sandro's friendship with you. But now we have the occasion to forge our own."

Leonardo felt his face become warm.

"And now that we have contracted to be friends, I must apologize to you."

"Apologize? For what?"

"I was not fair with you when we made our bet at Andrea del Verrocchio's party. I pressed you to wager your life to save your honor. We both acted without thought." After a beat Lorenzo continued. "I could not permit you to risk your life."

"Magnificence—"

"You are too valuable. . . ."

"Did my father speak to you of this?"

"No, Leonardo," Lorenzo said. "Ser Piero has been very gracious, but we've hardly passed a word. It was Simonetta who enlightened me. She worries for both of us."

"Sandro worries that she is not well," Leonardo said, thinking to divert him.

Lorenzo nodded. "She is very frail. It is as if a fire burns inside her, consuming her." Then he said, "I have decided to commission someone else to pilot your flying device . . . but the honor will be yours alone."

"I appreciate your concern, but only I can fly the Great Bird," Leonardo insisted. "Unless one has made a careful study of the winds and understands the science of flight, such an endeavor would be extremely dangerous."

"There is no hurry, Leonardo; we need not rendezvous tomorrow. Certainly with time you could train someone to use your machine."

"Magnificence, if you were me, would *you* permit someone else to take your place?"

"But I am *not* you, Leonardo. I am—"

"The First Citizen."

Lorenzo shook his head and laughed. But then he became pensive and said, "Leonardo, I fear for your life. And if I were to allow you to risk your neck on my account, I would also fear for the condition of my soul."

"You need not fear for either, Lorenzo. But you must let me prove my invention to you. If someone were to replace me, it would reveal to all of Florence your lack of trust and my cowardice. Please . . ."

After a long pause Lorenzo said, "All right, Leonardo, you shall have the honor. Madonna Simonetta also told me of your ... situation with Messer Nicolini. I don't know exactly what might be done; however, I shall look into it. But it will all be for naught if you fall from the sky tomorrow. It would be wise to reconsider. ..." Then he started toward the hillock where Niccolò waited; Leonardo walked beside him.

Lorenzo seemed burdened, as if Leonardo's imminent danger was emblematic of the First Citizen's other concerns. *"O tempora! O mores!"* Lorenzo intoned, using the ancient words of Cicero to decry these unsettling times. "My friend Pico della Mirandola assures me that the plague is abating in Florence. It did not seem so, however, when I left. As if the plague were not evil enough, I must contend with His Holiness, who continues his campaigns in the Romagna and Umbria."

Leonardo was surprised that Lorenzo would so openly condemn the Pope. Lorenzo was, of course, correct in his estimation: Francesco della Rovere, who had assumed the title of Sixtus IV, was educated and able; but he was consumed with ambition to provide positions of wealth and power for his family, and he thereby threatened Florentine interests and security.

"But enough," Lorenzo said as they approached Niccolò, who picked up the sack he had been carrying. "As the immortal Boccaccio relates, 'Let us be happy, for it was, after all, unhappiness that chased us from our beloved city.' That is, alas, a loose translation."

"Are you coming with us?" Niccolò asked Lorenzo; the boy was obviously excited.

"Indeed, I am, young Ser. What do you carry in the sack?"

"Food ... and torches."

"Torches?" Lorenzo asked.

Niccolò shrugged and said, "Master Leonardo told me to bring them, and flints, too."

"Were you planning on remaining in the woods overnight?" Lorenzo asked Leonardo.

"No, Magnificence."

"Well?" Lorenzo asked.

Leonardo smiled and said, "Would you have me spoil the surprise for the boy?"

Lorenzo laughed agreeably, and they walked at a hard pace through woods of pine, cedar, and juniper, and past fast-running mountain streams that carried away the sharp stones that would slowly be ground into the pebbles that rest in riverbeds. "I can almost feel the ancient gods and their nymphs and dryads watching us from the wood," Lorenzo said; and he composed a song, which he sang off-key:

Come to my sweet nest, I await you.
Vulcan is gone; he cannot disturb our love.
Come, for I am deliciously naked in my soft bed.
Delay not even a moment, for time is flying.
My breasts are wreathed with flowers of crimson.
So come, come to me, Mars, for I am alone.

When they came to the craggy slopes of Monte Albano, the bright noontime sunshine cast sharp shadows on the rock faces and grotesquely shaped cliffs. Then, with Leonardo leading the way, they worked their way up the mountain.

"I didn't expect such a strenuous climb," Lorenzo said, wiping his perspiring forehead with a cloth when they stopped to rest on a ridge. An overhang loomed high above them. It was a hot summer afternoon, the sky completely clear and hazy blue.

"We are almost there," Leonardo said, and he guided Lorenzo and Niccolò to a notch in the rock face that rose like a canyon wall above them. Leonardo took the sack from Niccolò, who duly protested, but only as a show for Lorenzo. Then Leonardo carefully worked his way onto a nearby ledge, using the same handholds and footholds he had used as a boy.

There he found the hole to his secret cavern.

Steam blew out in a soft exhalation, like smoke from a pipe; and it was noticeably damp hereabouts. Strong gusts of wind swirled around the opening, and the ledge itself was slippery and wet. Leonardo went back to help Niccolò onto the ledge, and Lorenzo followed. "Now, Nicco," Leonardo said, as they stood around the dark hole and rested. "Do you wish to be the second person to enter my secret place?"

"Who will be the first?" Niccolò asked.

Leonardo laughed. "I already was the first!"

"I can hardly believe that such a place exists," Niccolò said as he knelt and looked into the entrance. He held on to the rocks outside, lest he somehow be sucked into the cavern. "It is completely dark, and so narrow. One would have to crawl in like an animal. And it feels wet. I've never seen anything such as this."

"Are you afraid to go in, Nicco?"

"Certainly not! When you've lit the torches, I shall be the first inside."

"Are you afraid of the dark, then?" Leonardo smiled at the boy, who had no choice but to feel his way into the cave.

"There's no room," Niccolò complained.

"It becomes larger. Keep going and have patience."

"Are you coming?" Niccolò asked, his voice sounding hollow. "With the torch?"

"Tell me what you see."

"Only vague shapes," Niccolò said. "And I am drenched."

"It is humid, indeed," Leonardo said, "for the fire generated deep within the body of the earth warms the waters trapped inside this cavern. The heat makes the water boil and changes it to vapor."

"Have you ignited the torches yet?" Niccolò asked, sounding anxious.

"When I found this place, I was a few years younger than you are now. I remember feeling two emotions: fear and desire. What do you feel?"

"What did you desire?" Niccolò asked.

"To see what marvelous things might be found inside."

"And what did you fear?"

Leonardo struck the flint to stone to ignite the torches. "I was afraid of the dark, just as you are."

"I most certainly am *not*."

Leonardo grinned and winked at Lorenzo, handed him a torch, and then hunkered down to crawl into the cave. Niccolò looked relieved to see the two. "You haven't gone in very far," Leonardo said. "Come on and push ahead, or we will all be asphyxiated by our own torches."

Niccolò crawled ahead until the narrow corridor opened into a huge cavern. Leonardo stood up and held the torch high, illuminating the vast room and its grotesque, crystalline rock formations: ledges, curtains, columns, helictites, recesses, dripping stalactites, and stalagmites. This place seemed alive with dancing shadows; the torches cast a nervous light, and the room seemed even larger and more cavernous than it probably was. Lorenzo and Niccolò were silent, awed; all that could be heard were sibilant breathing and the echoing drip of water into pools that were limned with concentric ripples. Incongruously, the smell of the street was in here, the smell of stone after a rain: a robust, damp, yet chalky odor.

"Would you like to explore?" Leonardo asked Niccolò, offering the boy his torch. His voice sounded resonant in the echoing darkness.

"If we are . . . together," Niccolò said.

"We will allow no harm to come to you. Perhaps you can discover a new chamber."

"I fear I might become lost."

"For a young man who has no fear of the streets, of ruffians and bagnios, you seem suddenly reticent," Leonardo said; and he walked through the cavern, winding his way under a bridge of the rimstone, past a crystal pool, to the piled concretions and stone curtains of the far wall. The roof curved upward there, meeting the wall at a sharp angle. Leonardo illuminated an outcropping; and Niccolò, frightened, made a yelping noise before he caught himself. Even Lorenzo jumped backward.

A creature as tall as a house loomed above them.

A serpent . . . a gigantic beast caught in the stone.

Here was Leviathan herself watching them through the stone veils of eternity: a sea creature with a long, bony skull and huge, sharklike jaws. Its bleached bones protruded from the stone wall like a relief.

"Leonardo, is this yet another of your conjurations?" Lorenzo asked. He seemed angry, as if he had been duped.

"This is no trick of mine, I swear to you. The creature is just as I found it as a boy, Magnificence. But imagine how many kings and peoples and events have passed since this wondrous creature met its end in the dark recess of this cavern." He gazed up at the creature and said in little more than a whisper, "You are destroyed by time, yet your very bones are the frame and support for this mountain." Once again he experienced the awe and excitement and featherings of fear that he had felt as a child when he had found this eyeless monster whose bones were as ancient as the dripstone tusks that hung from the ceiling. He touched Niccolò's shoulder; and Niccolò, in turn, patted Leonardo's arm—as if the boy understood why his master had brought him here, as if he had indeed understood the unspoken lesson.

Here was death wreathed in awe and mystery and eternity.

And here were the dark springs of Leonardo's curiosity, creativity, and genius.

His first discovery.

In the familiar coolness of this stone womb, Leonardo shed his fears. He looked up at these skeletal remains and realized that he would never return to this place again.

Meanwhile, torch in hand, Lorenzo examined the bones; and as he studied the creature, he found the fossil remains of seashells. "Look at these, Leonardo," he said. "How could these exist so far from the sea? It's impossible."

"It seems obvious, Magnificence," Leonardo said, shaking off a feeling of sadness . . . as though he had lost something in here. "At some time before history, this mountain and cave were covered by the sea."

"Of course," Lorenzo said, suddenly excited. "The Great Deluge!"

"May I speak freely, Magnificence?"

"It should not be otherwise."

"I have a doubt that the flood which came in the time of Noah was universal." Leonardo paused, then said, "If you do not fear what might be considered blasphemy, I shall continue. Otherwise . . ."

"Do so, Leonardo. We are in private."

"Well, Magnificence, as you know, the Bible records forty days and forty nights of continuous rain, and this rain rose until it was ten cubits higher than the tallest mountain in the world. But if that were the case, that the rain was universal, it would have formed a covering around the world in a spherical shape, for is it not a truth that a sphere has every part of its circumference equidistant from its center?"

"Yes . . . ?" Lorenzo said.

"Therefore," Leonardo continued, "it would be impossible for the water on the surface to move, for water cannot move of its own accord, except to descend. Now, if the waters of this greatest of all floods had no power of motion, how then could they depart from the earth? And if they did depart, in what direction would be their movement unless the waters went upward? So natural causes fail us. We can only call upon a miracle or say that this flood of water was evaporated by the heat of the sun."

Lorenzo turned a seashell in his hand.

"Magnificence?" Leonardo asked.

"What you say makes sense in here, but perhaps only in here, in the dark. I only hope that once we step outside into the light, true reason will once again be revealed."

"Sandro often chides me for speaking loosely," Leonardo said in apology.

"What you say is fascinating," Lorenzo said. "You can certainly be assured that your words are safe with me." Lorenzo laughed, but his face, illuminated by the flickering torchlight, looked worn and cynical. "His Beatitude would like nothing better than to create another disturbance in our beloved Florence. I would caution you to be careful to whom you speak, Leonardo . . . and you, too, Ser Niccolò, for many will soon consider you to be Medici, albeit without the privileges and responsibilities. Perhaps that's not such a good bargain for you." Lorenzo squeezed Leonardo's shoulder and said, "You will soon have legions of enemies, most of whom you do not even know." Lorenzo laughed again. "You might best reevaluate even your friends . . . such as Il Neri, who has ties to families that don't have our best interests in their hearts. And you, too, Niccolò. Take heed."

Leonardo could only nod; but Niccolò, seemingly caught up by the mysteries of the rocks and fossils, said, "Magnificence, I was taught that shells such as these are created under the influence of the stars."

"That is one such belief encouraged by the Church," Lorenzo said, looking hopefully at Leonardo. "But do go on, Leonardo. Edify us with your no doubt dangerous thoughts on this subject."

Leonardo examined his torch, which was burning low, and then said, hesitating at first, "If the Holy Church is correct, and the eternal stars in their heavens somehow produce these shells deep in the caverns of the earth, then how do you explain the shells that vary in size, in age, and in kind? I think the Church was closer to the truth with their explanation of the Deluge. But nature usually produces her effects gradually, not cataclysmically. Nature's violence is a rare occurrence. No, these shells were once living creatures that were covered over by successive layers of mud, their flesh and organs worn away, leaving only these . . . signatures. And each layer, each inundation of mud and silt, entombs the remains of yet another generation of God's creatures."

"I think perhaps we'd better leave," Lorenzo said, "lest we be entombed here as a punishment for our impiety," and he led the way. Niccolò motioned for Leonardo to follow, then waited for his master. But Leonardo waved him ahead and stood in the cavern for those few seconds alone, the illumination of his torchlight casting ruddy coruscations over the slippery walls of bone and stone. He dropped the torch, took a last look at the ancient creature, the fabulous creature of his youth, and left the chill of the cavern.

Ahead, Lorenzo was speaking to Niccolò; and Leonardo heard him say *"lusus naturae"*: freak of nature.

And as Leonardo crawled through the dim, hazy twilight zone of the cavern into the blinding afternoon sunlight, he felt completely alone: as isolated from his ken as the monster he had left behind.

He stood on the ledge and looked down at Vinci in the distance.

Indeed, he was ready to cast himself into the sky.

8

The Kite

An instrument may be made to fly withal, if one sit in the midst of the instrument, and turn an engine, by which the wings, being artificially composed, may beat the air after the manner of the flying bird.

—Sir Roger Bacon

And as a hare whom horns and hounds pursue,
Points to that place from which at first it flew.

—Anonymous monk

. . . among my earliest recollections of infancy, when I was in the cradle, is of a kite which came to me and opened my mouth with its tail and then with its tail struck my lips many times.

—Leonardo da Vinci

The Great Bird was perched on the edge of a ridge at the summit of a hill near Vinci that Leonardo had selected. It looked like a gigantic dragonfly, its fabric of fustian and silk sighing as the expansive double wings shifted slightly in the wind. Niccolò, Tista, and Leonardo's stepfather, Achattabrigha, knelt under the wings and held fast to the pilot's harness. Zoroastro da Peretola and Lorenzo di Credi stood fifty feet apart and steadied the wingtips; it almost seemed that their arms were filled with outsize jousting pennons of blue and gold. These two could be taken as caricatures of Il Magnifico and his brother, Giuliano, for Zoroastro was swarthy, rough-skinned, and ugly looking beside the sweetly handsome Lorenzo di Credi. Such was the contrast between Lorenzo and Giuliano de' Medici, who stood with Leonardo and Sandro a few feet away from the Great Bird. Giuliano looked as radiant in the morning sun as Simonetta would have, while Lorenzo seemed to be glowering.

Zoroastro, ever impatient, looked toward Leonardo and shouted, "We're ready for you, Maestro."

Leonardo nodded, but Lorenzo caught him and said, "There is no need for this. I will love you as I do Giuliano, no matter whether you choose to fly . . . or let wisdom win out."

Leonardo smiled and said, "I will fly *fide et amore.*"

By faith and love.

"You shall have both," Lorenzo said; and he walked beside Leonardo to the edge of the ridge and waved to the crowd standing far below on the edge of a natural clearing where Leonardo was to land triumphant. But the clearing was surrounded by a forest of pine and cypress, which from his vantage looked like a multitude of roughhewn lances and halberds. A great shout went up, honoring the First Citizen: the entire village was there— from peasant to squire, invited for the occasion by Il Magnifico, who had erected a great multicolored tent; his attendants and footmen had been cooking and preparing for a feast since dawn. His sister Bianca, Angelo Poliziano, Pico della Mirandola, and Bartolomeo Scala were down there, too, hosting the festivities.

Leonardo waited until Lorenzo had received his due; but then, not to be outdone, he, too, bowed and waved his arms theatrically. The crowd below cheered their favorite son, and Leonardo turned away to position himself in the harness of his flying machine. But he had not seen his mother Caterina, a tiny figure nervously looking upward, whispering devotions, her hand cupped above her eyes to cut the glare of the sun. His father, Piero, stood beside Giuliano de' Medici; both men were dressed as if for a hunt. Piero did not speak to Leonardo. His already formidable face was drawn and tight, just as if he were standing before a magistrate awaiting a decision on a case.

Lying down in a prone position on the foreshortened plank pallet below the wings and windlass mechanism, Leonardo adjusted the loop around his head, which controlled the rudder section of the Great Bird, and he tested the hand cranks and foot stirrups, which raised and lowered the wings.

"Be careful," shouted Zoroastro, who had stepped back from the moving wings. "Are you trying to kill us?".

There was nervous laughter; but Leonardo was quiet. Achattabrigha tied the straps that would hold Leonardo fast to his machine and said, "I shall pray for your success, Leonardo, my son. I love you."

Leonardo turned to his stepfather, smelled the good odors of Caterina's herbs—garlic and sweet onion—on his breath and clothes, and looked into the old man's squinting pale-blue eyes; and it came to him then that he loved this man who had spent his life sweating by kiln fires and thinking with his great yellow-nailed hands. "I love you, too . . . Father. And I feel safe in your prayers."

That seemed to please Achattabrigha, for he checked the straps one last time, kissed Leonardo, and patted his shoulder; then he stepped away, as reverently as if he were backing away from an icon in a cathedral.

"Good luck, Leonardo," Lorenzo said.

The others wished him luck. His father nodded and smiled; and Leonardo, taking the weight of the Great Bird upon his back, lifted himself. Niccolò, Zoroastro, and Lorenzo di Credi helped him to the very edge of the ridge.

A cheer went up from below.

"Maestro, I wish it were me," Niccolò said.

"Just watch this time, Nicco," Leonardo said. "Pretend it is you who are flying in the heavens, for this machine is also yours. And you will be with me."

"Thank you, Leonardo."

"Now step away . . . for we must fly," Leonardo said; and he looked down, as if for the first time, as if every tree and upturned face were magnified, every smell, every sound and motion, clear and distinct. In some way the world had separated into its component elements, all in an instant; and in the distance the swells and juttings of land were like that of a green sea with long, trailing shadows of brown; and upon those motionless waters were all the various constructions of human habitations: church and campanile, shacks and barns and cottages and furrowed fields.

Leonardo's heart was pounding in his chest; and he wished for the security and safety of his memory cathedral, where the past was tangible, and neither cause nor effect were open to question. A breeze blew out of the northwest, and Leonardo felt it flow around him like a breath. The treetops rustled, whispering, as warm air drifted skyward. Thermal updrafts flowing invisibly to heaven, pulling at him. His wings shuddered in the gusts; and Leonardo knew that it must be now, lest he be carried off the cliff unprepared.

He launched himself, pushing off the precipice as if he were diving from a cliff into the sea. For an instant, as he swooped downward, he felt a dizzying elation, followed by heart-pounding, nauseating fear. Although he strained at the windlass and foot stirrups, which caused his great fustian wings to flap, he could not keep himself aloft. His pushings and kickings had become almost reflexive from hours of practice: one leg thrust backward to lower one pair of wings while he furiously worked the windlass with his hands to raise the other, turning his hands first to the left, then to the right. He worked the mechanism with every bit of his calculated two-hundred-pound force, and his muscles ached from the strain. Although the Great Bird might function as a glider, there was too much friction in the gears to effect enough propulsive power; and the wind resistance was too strong. He could barely raise the wings.

He fell.

The chilling, cutting wind became a constant sighing in his ears. His clothes flapped against his skin like the fabric of his failing wings, while hills, sky, forest, and cliffs spiraled around him, then fell away; and he felt the damp shock of his recurring dream, his nightmare of falling into the void.

But he was falling through soft light, itself as tangible as butter. Below him was the familiar land of his youth, rising against all logic, rushing skyward to claim him. He could see his father's house and there in the distance the Apuan Alps and the ancient cobbled road built before Rome was an empire. His sensations took on the textures of dream; and he prayed, surprising himself even then as he looked into the purple shadows of the impaling trees below. Still, he doggedly pedaled and turned the windlass mechanism.

Then he felt a subtle bursting of warm air around him, and suddenly, impossibly, vertiginously, he was ascending.

His wings were locked straight out. They were not flapping. Yet still he rose. It was as if God's hand were lifting Leonardo to heaven; and he, Leonardo, remembered loosing his kite-hawks into the air and watching them search for the currents of wind, which they used to soar into the highest of elevations, their wings motionless.

Thus did Leonardo rise in the warm air current—his mouth open to relieve the pressure constantly building in his ears—until he could see the top of the mountain a thousand feet below him. The country of hills and streams and farmland and forest had diminished, had become a neatly patterned board of swirls and rectangles: proof of man's work on earth. The sun seemed brighter at this elevation, as if the air itself was less dense in these attenuated regions. Leonardo feared now that he might be drawing too close to the region where air turned to fire.

He turned his head, pulling the loop that connected to the rudder, and found that he could, within bounds, control his direction. But then he stopped soaring; it was as if the warm bubble of air that had contained him had suddenly burst. He felt a chill.

The air became cold . . . and still.

He worked furiously at the windlass, thinking that he would beat his wings as birds do until they reach the wind; but he could not gain enough forward motion.

Once again, he fell like an arcing arrow.

Although the wind resistance was so great that he couldn't pull the wings below a horizontal position, he had developed enough speed to attain lift. He rose for a few beats, but, again, could not push his mechanism hard enough to maintain it, and another gust struck him, pummeling the Great Bird with phantomic fists.

His only hope was to gain another warm thermal.

Instead, he became caught in a riptide of air that was like a blast, pushing the flying machine backward. He had all he could do to keep the wings locked in a horizontal position. He feared they might be torn away by the wind; and, indeed, the erratic gusts seemed to be conspiring to press him back down upon the stone face of the mountain.

Time seemed to slow for Leonardo; and in one long second he glimpsed the clearing surrounded by forest, as if forming a bull's-eye. He saw the tents and the townspeople who craned their necks to goggle up at him; and in this wind-wheezing moment, he suddenly gained a new, unfettered perspective. As if it were not he who was falling to his death.

Were his neighbors cheering? he wondered. Or were they horrified and dumbfounded at the sight of one of their own falling from the sky? More likely they were secretly wishing him to fall, their deepest desires not unlike the crowd that had recently cajoled a poor, lovesick peasant boy to jump from a rooftop onto the stone pavement of the Via Calimala.

To his right, Leonardo caught sight of a kite-hawk. He wondered if it was a vision and remembered his dream of the great bird: the kite swooping toward him when he was a child and slapping his face with the smooth, oily feathers of its tail.

The ground was now only three hundred feet below.

The kite was caught in the same trap of wind as Leonardo; and as he watched, the bird veered away, banking, and flew downwind. Leonardo shifted his weight, manipulated the rudder, and changed the angle of the wings. Thus he managed to follow the bird. His arms and legs felt like leaden weights, but he held on to his small measure of control.

Still he fell.

He could hear the crowd shouting below him, part of the muffled rushing of wind. It scattered, as people ran to get out of the way. He thought of his mother, Caterina.

And he followed the kite, as if it were his inspiration, his own Beatrice.

Caterina.

Ginevra.

And the ground swelled upward.

Then Leonardo felt as if he was suspended over the deep, green canopy of forest, but only for an instant. He felt a warm swell of wind; and the Great Bird rose, riding the thermal. Leonardo looked for the kite-hawk, but it had disappeared as if it had been a spirit, rising without weight through the various spheres toward the Primum Mobile. He tried to control his flight, his thoughts toward landing in one of the fields beyond the trees.

The thermal carried him up; then, just as quickly, as if teasing him, burst. Leonardo tried to keep his wings fixed and glided upwind for a few seconds. But a gust caught him, once again pushing him backward, and he fell—

Slapped back to earth.

Hubris.

I have come home to die.

And he imagined that he was standing before the bronzen statue that guarded the entrance to his memory cathedral. It was a three-headed demiurge. The faces of his father, Toscanelli, and Ginevra stared at him; but it was Ginevra who spoke the words that would banish him from the world, the words of Luke: *"nunc dimittis servum tuum, Domine."*

Lord, now permit thy servant to depart.

No, Ginevra, I cannot leave you. I love you. I have not yet finished my work, my—

His father's face scowled at him.

Leonardo had failed.

Trees wheeled below him, twisting, as if pulled from their roots; and once again the natural sequence of ordered time failed him. He saw familiar faces; stones embedded like jewels in the coarse black soil; wisps of cirrus clouds flying, flashing, across the sun; the scrumble of the mountainside; long-leafed plants spiderwebbed with thin, perfect veins.

Thus was time stretched . . . and compressed.

As the darkness behind his closed eyelids turned to dusk.

Perhaps I am dead.

nunc dimittis . . .

Yet in the comforting darkness, Leonardo could secrete himself inside his memory cathedral, his church of many domes and rooms not yet filled. He was safe inside the confines of his soul; and so he flew from portal to tower, from nave to chapel, through perfect and reclaimed memory, chasing after the kite-hawk.

The very one that had appeared to Leonardo.

Long ago.

As if in a dream.

Those routed souls scattered across the scene, their
faces once again turned toward the mountain where
Reason spurs and Justice picks us clean. . . .
                                        —Dante Alighieri

Savage he is who saves himself.
                                        —Leonardo da Vinci

Portrait of Lorenzo the Magnificent

Part Two
María

9

Memento

Mori

Portrait of Simonetta Vespucci

Every day I die.
> —Petrarch, a letter to
> Philippe de Cabassoles

Like sunlight in a glass, the twofold creature
shone from the deep reflection of her eyes, now
in the one, now in the other nature.
> —Dante Alighieri

ven after three weeks, the headaches remained.

Leonardo had suffered several broken ribs and a concussion when he fell into the forest, swooping between the thick purple cypress trees, tearing like tissue the wood and fustaneum of the Great Bird's wings. His face was already turning black when Lorenzo's footmen found him. He recuperated at his father's home; but Lorenzo insisted on taking him to Villa Careggi, where Pico della Mirandola could have his physicians attend to him. With the exception of Lorenzo's personal dentator, who soaked a sponge in opium, morel juice, and hyoscyamus and extracted his broken tooth as Leonardo slept and dreamed of falling; they did little more than change his bandages, bleed him with leeches, and cast his horoscope.

But Leonardo cemented his relationship with Lorenzo at Careggi. He, Sandro, and Lorenzo swore to be as brothers: a gentle deception, for the First Citizen could at best claim to be what the notary Lapo Mazzei had called "a friend and not a friend." It could not be otherwise, for Lorenzo could not slip the collar of the *padrone*. The First Citizen trusted no one but Giuliano and his mother, Lucrezia Tornabuoni.

It was also said that he confided in Simonetta.

Leonardo forged other important friendships at court, namely with Mirandola himself, who had influence with the Medici family. Leonardo found, to his surprise, that he had much in common with the son of Cosimo de' Medici's physician. They had both secretly dissected human corpses in the studios of Antonio Pollaiuolo and Luca Signorelli, who were reputed to rob graves to maintain their artistic and pedagogical activities; and Leonardo was shocked to find out that Mirandola had also been an apprentice, of sorts, to Toscanelli.

Nevertheless, Leonardo was more than relieved when the plague finally abated enough so that he could return to Florence. He was hailed as a hero, for Lorenzo had made a public announcement from the *ringhiera* of the Palazzo Vecchio that the artist from Vinci had, indeed, flown in the air like a bird. But the gossip among the educated was that, indeed, Leonardo had fallen like Icarus, whom it was said he resembled in hubris. He received an anonymous note that seemed to say it all: *victus honor.*

Honor to the vanquished.

Leonardo would accept none of the countless invitations to attend various masques and dinners and parties. He was caught up in a frenzy of work. He filled up three folios with his sketches and mirror-script notes. Niccolò brought him his meals, and Andrea Verrocchio came upstairs a few times a day to look in at his now famous apprentice.

"Haven't you yet had your bellyful of flying machines?" Andrea impatiently asked Leonardo. It was dusk, and dinner had already been served to the apprentices downstairs. Niccolò hurried to clear a place on the table so Andrea could put down the two bowls of boiled meat he had brought. Leonardo's studio was in its usual state of disarray, but the old flying machine, the insects mounted on boards, the vivisected birds and bats, the variously designed wings, rudders, and valves for the Great Bird were gone, replaced by new drawings, new mechanisms for testing wing designs (for now the wings would remain fixed), and various large-scale models of free-flying whirlybird toys, which had been in use since the 1300's. He was experimenting with inverted cones—Archimedian screws—to cheat gravity, and he studied the geometry of children's tops to calculate the principle of the flywheel. Just as a ruler whirled rapidly in the air will guide the arm by the line of the edge of the flat surface, so did Leonardo envision a machine powered by a flying propeller. Yet he could not help thinking that such mechanisms were against nature, for air was a fluid, like water. And nature, the protoplast of all man's creation, had not invented rotary motion.

Leonardo pulled the string of a toy whirlybird, and the tiny four-bladed propeller spun into the air, as if in defiance of all natural laws. "No, Andrea, I have not lost my interest in this most sublime of inventions. Il Magnifico has listened to my ideas, and he is enthusiastic that my next machine will remain aloft."

Verrocchio watched the red propeller glide sideways into a stack of books. "And Lorenzo has offered to recompense you for these . . . experiments?"

"Such an invention would revolutionize the very nature of warfare," Leonardo insisted. "I've also been experimenting with improvements on the arquebus, and I have a design for a giant *ballista,* a crossbow of a kind never before imagined, and I've developed a cannon with many racks of barrels that—"

"Indeed," Verrocchio said. "But I have advised you that it is unwise to put your trust in Lorenzo's momentary enthusiasms."

"Certainly the First Citizen has more than a passing interest in armaments."

"Is that why he ignored your previous memorandum wherein you proposed the very same ideas?"

"That was before, and this is now," Leonardo said. "If Florence goes to war, Lorenzo will need my inventions. He told me so."

"Ah, certainly," Andrea said, nodding his head. Then, after a pause, he said, "Stop this foolishness, Leonardo. You're a painter, and a painter should paint. Why have you been unwilling to work on any of the commissions I have offered you? And you've refused many other good offers. You have no money, and you've gained yourself a bad reputation. You have not even finished your *caritas* for Madonna Simonetta."

"I will have more than enough money after the world watches my flying machine soar into the heavens."

"You are lucky to be alive, Leonardo. Have you not looked at yourself in a mirror? And you nearly broke your spine. Are you so intent upon doing so again? Or will killing yourself suffice?" He shook his head, as if angry at himself, and then said softly, "Perhaps you do need a strong hand. I blame myself. I should have never allowed you to proceed with all this in the first place." He waved his hand at Leonardo's machines. "But your honor was at stake, and Lorenzo promised me that you would not go through with it. He was, indeed, taken with you."

"Are you saying, then, that now he is not?" Leonardo asked.

"I am describing his nature, Leonardo."

"I am to blame for his change of mind. But perhaps I should put him to the test . . . it was you who told me of Lorenzo's offer of accommodations in his gardens."

"He would not refuse you," Andrea said. "But neither will he have patience for you, nor for any of us, for that matter."

"What are you saying?"

"Galeazzo Sforza has been assassinated. He was stabbed in the doorway of the Church of Santo Stefano. In a *church*. . . ." Verrocchio shook his head. "I only just found out."

"That augurs ill for Florence," Niccolò said. Obviously hungry, he had been standing and furtively eating the boiled meat Verrocchio had brought.

"Indeed, it does, lad," Andrea said. "With Milan in turmoil, the league is dead. Florence has only Venice now, and she is a most capricious ally. Lorenzo has sent envoys to Galeazzo's widow in Milan, but she will not be able to control her brothers-in-law. And once Milan is under the Pope's influence—"

"The peace of Italy will be dead," Leonardo said.

"I think that may be too strong," Andrea said. "But it will be difficult to turn the advantage to Florence."

"Il Magnifico is an able negotiator," Niccolò said.

Andrea nodded. "The babe is correct."

Young Machiavelli scowled at Andrea, but said nothing.

"I fear that I am correct about the peace of Italy," Leonardo insisted. "It shall soon be dead. Have we not already lost Federigo of Urbino, our finest condottiere, to the Holy See? Now more than ever Lorenzo will need a military engineer."

Andrea shrugged. "I am but a painter," he said, the sarcasm in his voice revealing his frustration with Leonardo. "But I do know, as do you, that Lorenzo already has an engineer. Giuliano da Sangallo is in his employ."

"Sangallo is a poor artist and a terrible engineer," Leonardo said.

"He has distinguished himself in several campaigns, and he is Lorenzo's choice."

"You're wrong. Lorenzo will not forget my inventions."

Andrea made a *tss*ing sound by tapping the roof of his mouth with his tongue. "I bid thee good night. Leonardo, eat your food before it gets cold." Then he walked toward the door. "Oh, yes," he said, pausing in the doorway. "Madonna Vespucci requests an audience with you."

"When?" asked Leonardo, ignoring his master's sarcasm.

"Tomorrow, at one o'clock in the afternoon."

"Andrea?"

"Yes?"

"What has turned you against me?"

"My love for you. . . . Forget invention and munitions and flying toys. You are a painter. Paint."

———

Leonardo took his master's advice and spent the night painting. But he had been too long away from the fumes of acetic acid, varnish, linseed oil, and turpentine. His eyes burned and teared, and his head ached; yet he was painting as well as he ever had. He suffered from a raw tingling in his sinuses and over his eyes, and he had trouble breathing through his nose; but Pico della Mirandola's surgeons had assured Leonardo that these aggravations would disappear when the "internal swellings" were naturally cleansed by the blood. While he worked, Niccolò applied one of Pico's prescriptions to his forehead: linen soaked with a mixture of oil of roses and root of peony.

Atalante Miglioretti came to look in on Leonardo and brought a friend to cheer him: Francesco of Naples, reputed to be the finest of lute players. Leonardo asked them to stay and keep him company while he painted; and he wished for news and gossip, for he had to be prepared to visit Simonetta tomorrow. Francesco, who was small, delicately built, and clean-shaven, demonstrated his skill playing the lute; Leonardo asked Niccolò to give Atalante a lyre formed in the shape of a goat, which was similar to the instrument he had given to Il Magnifico.

"My intention was to cast this lyre out of silver, as I did the other," Leonardo said to Atalante. "But I did not have enough silver."

"Metal changes the tone of the instrument," Atalante said.

"For the better?" Leonardo asked.

After a pause Atalante said, "I must confess a preference for wood . . . such as this."

Musing, Leonardo said, "Perhaps Lorenzo will wish to purchase the goat as a mate for his silver horse. If he would supply the metal, the remainder would be my payment."

"Perhaps he might," Atalante said. "And you'd still have the original." He paused. "But if there is a war, none of us will have any silver. . . .

"Do you know that Galeazzo Maria Sforza was assassinated? Already the talk is in the streets."

"Yes," Leonardo said.

"His widow is already begging the Pope to give the duke posthumous absolution of his sins."

"That, too, is gossip in the streets?" Leonardo asked.

Atalante shrugged. "They say she will go over to the Pope, and that will cause war."

"We do not even know if she will hold the reins of power," Niccolò said. "Perhaps Milan will become a republic . . . like Florence."

The men smiled, for Florence was a republic in name only; but Atalante was not in the least bit condescending to Niccolò when he said, "The conspirators were indeed republicans, my young friend. But the Milanese people loved their tyrant and regret his death. The leader, Lampugnani, was killed on the spot and dragged through the town. The others were found shortly thereafter and tortured hideously. No, you'll not have a republic there. And even if Milan became a republic, who is to say she would remain our ally?"

"What do you think, Francesco?" Atalante asked.

The lutenist shrugged, as if he were impatient with politics and wished only to proceed with making music. "I think you Florentines find forebodings of war and scandal under every rock. You spend all your precious time worrying about your enemies' grand designs . . . and then you are soon dead from old age."

Leonardo laughed; he could not help but feel drawn to this cynical little musician who looked scarcely older than Niccolò.

"Come, now," said Atalante.

"No one, least of all Sixtus, wants a war," Francesco said.

"He is ambitious," Atalante said.

"But cautious," replied Francesco. "If it be anything, the murder is a bad omen. It sets an evil precedent, for now not even the holy sanctuaries of God are safe. *Now* might we play for Messer Leonardo?"

"Indeed," said Atalante. "I'm afraid we have not accomplished our task—just the opposite."

"And what might that be?" Niccolò asked.

"To lift your master's spirits."

"A nigh impossible task," said Sandro Botticelli as he entered the room. "But even the Lord Paramount Leonardo might yet be overcome."

"Will Andrea allow anyone to enter his *bottega*?" Leonardo said with good humor. "Have none of you any fear of Il Magnifico's guards, that you walk about after curfew?"

"I cannot remember a time when that worried you, Leonardo," Atalante said.

"Alas, even I have been known to act young and foolish," Leonardo said. Then, to Sandro, "What did you mean?"

"By what, Leonardo?"

"That I could be overcome."

"Victus honor."

"Then it was *you* who sent that note."

"What note?" Sandro asked, a merry look on his face.

"Well, I can see that you are feeling better," Leonardo said.

"At least I am no longer an empty bottle," he said; yet all the same, there was an underlying sadness, as if he was indeed what he professed not to be: empty and lonely and anguished. "Atalante, let us hear you and your friend play; and perhaps Leonardo and I shall sing."

"I think that is a threat," Leonardo said.

"God's Hooks! Then I *won't* sing."

"I have created a melody for a poem by Catullus," Atalante said, "for he is your favorite, Leonardo, is he not?"

"Indeed, he is," Leonardo said. "Although it may be considered blasphemy, I am partial to some of Marcus Tullius Cicero and Titus Lucretius Carus; but I must confess impatience with the work of our most honored Virgil, and Horace and Livy the same. I am sick of poetry about poetry. Let our friends at court quote Cicero. But Catullus . . . now he is a man whose words will sound through eternity. Tell me the poem, and I shall accompany you."

" '*Lesbia me dicit,*' " Atalante said; he nodded to Francesco, and they began to play and sing. Atalante wove his sweet, rather thin voice around Leonardo's, which was more resonant, but limited in range.

Forever Lesbia rails
She speaks of me
To pierce my heart

> *Yet I have pushed aside*
> *Her deception and her art*
> *'Tis I who've pierced her heart*

The tune was played and sung slowly, although the words were light-hearted; and they passed from one song to another, to more of Atalante's Catullian inventions:

> *Odi et amo....*
> I hate and love.
> You ask me "How?"
> I lack an answer.
> You have me on the rack.
> *Odi et amo....*

Sandro poured wine, and Leonardo allowed himself to get a little drunk. He permitted Niccolò to take his share. By the time Atalante and his Venetian friend left, Niccolò was fast asleep on his pallet with a large folio of Roman poems in his arms. He looked like a reposing Bacchus as if conceived and sculpted after Praxiteles, for his hair was thick and unkempt and curled over his forehead.

"It is late; I, too, should leave," Sandro said to Leonardo. He whispered, so as not to awaken Niccolò, and lifted the drape from Leonardo's portrait of Simonetta. Smiling, he said, "You portray the flesh and show the spirit. I paint the spirit and show the flesh."

"You are drunk," Leonardo said.

"Indeed I am. And so are you, my friend. I see that you have put Simonetta in Vinci." He was referring to Leonardo's painting of the Madonna with the cat. "No matter what you paint and what you depict, always the mountains and streams of Vinci are there, are they not? But you are still infatuated with the Flemish technique. I think you have become more proficient than your competitor Van der Goes."

"Is that all you see in my painting, Little Bottle? Proficiency?"

"No, Leonardo, I see Simonetta in the flesh. I can almost read her thoughts, for you have given her life. I cannot deny that."

"Thank you," Leonardo said. "We have our differences, but—"

"Perhaps not so many."

"I meant as painters."

"Ah...," Sandro said. Yet as he stared at Leonardo's painting, he looked witch-held. As he had when his eyes had caught Leonardo's during the exorcism.

"Little Bottle, is there something you know that you're not telling me?"

Sandro smiled and pulled the drape carefully over the painting. "You must be careful when you carry it. It will be wet."

"Sandro?" Leonardo said, getting worried.

"Tomorrow," Sandro said as he stared intently at the canvas, as if he could still see the portrait hidden beneath.

———

Leonardo arrived at Simonetta's in the afternoon; he was precisely on time, which was unusual for him. Although most artists were punctilious as merchants, doctors, and other men of affairs concerning appointments, Leonardo could not manage even this fundamental trait of the bourgeois. Tardiness had come to be one of his unfortunate trademarks. But today his thoughts were not distracted by machines of flight and war; nor was he distracted by natural science, nor even painting and the play of light and shadow, although he carefully held his painting of Simonetta, making sure that the silken cover cloth did not press against the still gaumy glazes of linseed oil and varnish.

His thoughts were directed toward Simonetta, and what she wished of him. He felt a guilty shiver as he remembered their tryst at Il Neri's perverse party; yet he thought of her as a friend, a true friend, as absolute and guileless as she promised him she would be. He felt a confusing mélange of guilt and attraction—and worry, too, for Sandro had been insistent that she had absorbed his poisonous phantasm in spite of Pico della Mirandola's ministrations.

Indeed, what more was Sandro keeping from him?

And was Sandro, God forbid, himself still suffering from certain manifestations of the cold black bile: *melaina cholos* . . . the deadly melancholy?

He passed through a wrought-iron gate and then down a narrow lane—which was no more than an alleyway, but nevertheless guarded by marble griffins, satyrs, naiads, warriors of perfect physique, and the huntress Diana herself—before he reached the courtyard and open loggia of the two-story Vespucci home. He knocked on a heavy glazed door; and a servant led him through frescoed, airy rooms, through grotesque-adorned chambers, studies, and ocher-walled halls, to a rear open court where peacocks roamed free. It was there that Simonetta sat, a faint smile upon her pale, freckled face, as she looked down over a vine-covered wall at the streets and lanes below. Her eyebrows were plucked into thin lines, and her mouth was pursed, pushing her bottom lip slightly forward. She seemed to be in the deepest contemplation. There was just a faint breeze, which nevertheless disturbed the baby-fine wisps of her long, blond, and intricately braided hair. She wore a *gamurra* of crimson satin with puffed silk sleeves, which was cut low upon the bodice, and a pendant upon a chain around her neck; mounted in the center of the golden, nielloed disk was a bit of unicorn's horn: the universal antidote for poison.

She was indeed an ethereal figure; and for an instant Leonardo felt as if he were looking into one of Sandro's allegorical paintings. Simonetta was Botticelli's Venus-Humanitas come to life.

"Leonardo, you are staring. Have I grown a wart on my chin perhaps?"

"No, Madonna, you are quite lovely."

"And I'm very happy to see that you, dear Leonardo, have but the shadow of a bruise on your face," Simonetta said. "Sandro exaggerated the extent of your injuries. But you must promise me that you will never again put yourself at such risk."

Leonardo bowed, acknowledging her kindness. "I must tell you that Sandro has captured the essence of your perfect beauty in a painting that he has shown to me."

A slight flush came to her cheeks. "And this painting?"

"He calls it 'Allegory of Spring' and tells me that it was inspired in small part by a passage found in one of Marsilio Ficino's works."

"Do you know this work?"

"I am ashamed to say I do not," Leonardo said.

"Do you give so little credit to his academy?"

"It seems that their intellectual pursuits are quite beyond me," Leonardo said ironically. "But *you* are the idée fixe upon which he molds every figure in the painting. His depiction of the Three Fates is nothing else but your different expressions. No man could look upon that painting and not fall completely in love with you."

"Then I fear this might be a dangerous painting."

Leonardo laughed.

"Sandro has only spoken of it to me. But he is too timid to let me see it," she said.

"Only because he has not finished it, Madonna. You know, in actuality, he dawdles more with his paintings that I do with mine; yet *I've* acquired the bad reputation."

It was Simonetta's turn to laugh, but Leonardo sensed that she was gently and perhaps even with love treating him as the fool. After a pause she said, "Are you afraid to draw close to me? And what do you hide under the cover? Could it be the painting I've been waiting for?"

Leonardo bowed and said, "But in comparison with Sandro's diaphanous depiction of you, my gift is a somber one, indeed."

Again she laughed and opened her arms. "Well, bring it to me; I'll be its judge."

Leonardo leaned the canvas against the wall before Simonetta and then lifted its linen covering.

She leaned toward it, as if she were nearsighted, and said, "Leonardo, it's beautiful. You've changed everything since I last saw it. Is it truly possible that I could look so fragile and virginal? I feel as if I'm looking at the woman I would wish to be. It is like the double-faced mirror of Synesius that reflects both the world above and our own. And there"—she pointed to the almost geometrical rendering of trees and hills in the painting—"I can look upon the landscape of heaven. And it is lit with heaven's light."

She smiled, and Leonardo was caught by that melancholy, yet self-possessed and altogether enigmatic, smile. He memorized it even as he felt that he was violating her, for one day he would paint that smile rather than Simonetta. "It is merely the country of my childhood, Madonna."

She turned her face to his and said, "Thank you, Leonardo."

"The glazes are not yet dry."

"I will be careful. I cannot help but fear that only now am I being allowed to see myself thus, in heaven as it were; yet I would not have your magical mirror go dark, as in the nursery rhyme."

"What do you mean?" Leonardo asked.

She ignored the question and rang a bell for her footman, a boy of no more than twelve years. "You are to carry this painting into the house, and you must take the utmost care with it," she said to the boy as she draped the painting. Then to Leonardo she said, "I fear the dust in the air, lest it cling to your perfect painting."

After the boy had left, Leonardo questioned her again; but she shook her head and said, "Sit beside me and hold me."

Leonardo looked down beyond the wall at the streets below.

"Do not worry," Simonetta said. "We cannot be seen."

She held Leonardo tightly, pressing his head against her bosom; and he felt her smooth, slightly damp skin and the heavy texture of brocade velvet; he smelled her odor mingled with perfume of violet. Her breathing sounded shallow and raspy, the noise magnified, like waves shoaling upon rocks, as it was conducted from her flesh to his ear. Then she lifted his face to hers; and Leonardo once again felt passion for her; but she suddenly was taken by spasms of coughing. She pulled away from him, as if from mortification; but Leonardo caught her and held her. She coughed and wheezed and then, choking, tried to catch her breath. She trembled and exhausted herself, straining with each racking cough, her body taut as a bowstring; and Leonardo imagined that something delicate was breaking inside her; and he felt her spittle soaking his shirt.

Then discovered it was mixed with blood.

When the coughing subsided, she did draw away from him. Her eyes were pinched shut, as if she were concentrating, as if by sheer will she could transform herself into a phantasm of health; and that, Leonardo thought, was exactly what she was doing. She wiped her face, which was white as dead flesh, and daubed her mouth with a crimson handkerchief that would not reveal the bloodstains.

She looked directly at Leonardo. Her eyes were shiny, as if she were on the verge of tears; and Leonardo knew that, indeed, Sandro had been right. Her eyes, although clear and ocean-blue, were haunted. He imagined that he was staring past transparent veils, that she was lost to him, lost to the world.

An instant later she was herself: poised, yet embarrassed. She held his hands tightly; her palms were dry, though his were sweaty. "Do not ask me, Leonardo, for now you know."

"Madonna, I—"

"And I have ruined your *gonnellino,* but at least it is dark, like my hand cloth, and won't show the blood too badly."

"That hardly matters," Leonardo said. "Can I get you something to drink?"

"Sandro has told you everything, hasn't he?" Simonetta said, although she phrased it as a question. "No, perhaps not everything, sweet Leonardo."

"I do not wish to play such a game," Leonardo said.

"But that is the nature of all intercourse, is it not?" she said, smiling. Her color had returned to her face, which, at best, was pale. Her eyes, though, seemed to be burning with pale-blue internal fire, a phantasmal overflowing: a *miracolo gentil.*

"What, then, has Sandro told you?"

"Nothing, Madonna, except that he worries about you."

"I shall be gone soon," and she laughed; it chilled Leonardo. "In a sense, my dear friend, I have left."

"You need rest and perhaps a change of location." Leonardo felt uncomfortable, out of his element. "You should be back in the country and not breathing the noxious miasmas of the city."

"And did Sandro tell you that I have not released his perfect vision of me? I have taken it as my own, as solace."

"I don't understand," Leonardo said.

"Of course you do," Simonetta said, resting her head on his shoulder. "What difference if love suffocates me, as I am to die soon? My soul is eternal, is it not? I shall soon enough be in *morte di bacio.* In my heavenly rapture I shall pray for you, Leonardo. And Sandro. But, Leonardo, are you not afraid that I will steal something from you, as I have from Sandro?"

"Simonetta . . ."

"Can't you smile, my friend?" she asked, looking up at him. "Your soul and ideas are perfectly safe from me."

"I don't find this amusing," Leonardo said, pulling away from her.

"Poor Leonardo," she said softly. "I have upset you more than a little. I am afraid to die. I am afraid to be alone."

"You shall not die; at least, not until your natural age. And you have no need to be alone."

"On both counts you are wrong, Leonardo."

"How do you know?"

She smiled sadly. "Perhaps I have had a vision."

"And Il Magnifico, what of him?"

"He knows nothing, not even that I cough. That is why I have not been able to see him very much lately, and I fear that he and Giuliano are becoming upset."

"Then you should let them care for you."

"I will not. They shall remember me as beautiful, if that is what I still am, and not what I shall become. I love, and have loved, both of them, as I love Sandro." After a pause she said, "I have let him into my bed."

Leonardo was shocked. "Then he knows . . . everything."

"About us and about my health, of course. But I made him promise not to dwell on my illness and impending death." She laughed. "I told him that my spies are everywhere, that he cannot trust anyone . . . not even you, dear Leonardo; and that if I hear tell that he has fallen prey to the influence of Saturn, I shall lock my doors to him."

"Are you not afraid that this will make him sick again?" Leonardo asked.

"I shall not allow him to be harmed. He loves me as no one else does; I can at least give him this time. No matter, he will grieve. And you, sweet Leonardo, will be left with him . . . to take care of him. You will do that."

"Of course."

"It should not strike you as perverse that I wish to put my life in order, pay back debts, and perhaps do a bit of penance before I die. That is as natural as intercourse."

"Is that why you have summoned me?" Leonardo asked.

"Perhaps," Simonetta said. "But you seem angry, Leonardo. Are you angry with me?"

"No," Leonardo said, "of course not. I am just—"

"Shocked?" she interrupted.

"I don't know," Leonardo said, embarrassed. "I feel so helpless . . . and impotent."

"I usually do not affect men in that way."

She smiled at him playfully, and Leonardo at last smiled back. The tension broken, they embraced and stared together at the street below, neither one speaking for some time. Leonardo marveled at her luxurious mass of golden hair. She was so close to him; indeed, he could fall in love with her, as did most men who were privileged to know her. Yet he could not help but think of Ginevra, even now; and no matter how much he wanted Simonetta, he ached for Ginevra.

"Now, Leonardo," Simonetta said in almost a whisper, "you must tell me of your flight into the heavens, for I know only what others have told me. . . ."

But their reverie was disturbed by a knocking, as if from far away.

"It must be important, or Luca would not disturb us," Simonetta said. She motioned for her servant to enter: the same boy who had taken Leonardo's painting into the house.

"Do you wish me to whisper, Madonna?" he asked, glancing at Leonardo—the intruder—then lowering his gaze. He was holding a small package wrapped in gold-brocaded velvet and was obviously nervous.

"Certainly not. I have taught you better manners than that, Luca. What have you got?"

He handed the package to Simonetta and said, "You told me that you were to be told immediately if Il Magnifico—"

"Is he *here*?"

Leonardo felt a rush of fear, for if the First Citizen was barred from these private chambers, what excuse could he, Leonardo, have for being here?

"No, Madonna, his footman brought the package. Was I wrong to disturb you?"

"No, Luca, I am very pleased with you. And has our other guest arrived?"

"Yes, Madonna."

Simonetta nodded and said, "Now leave us." Then she proceeded to read a note enclosed in the package.

"Madonna, is everything all right?" Leonardo asked. He would not presume to ask about Simonetta's guest. He imagined an impatient and heart-smitten Sandro waiting for her in her bedchamber.

"Yes, of course," and Simonetta opened the package, which contained three interlaced rings of gold wreathed with diamonds: Lorenzo's personal heraldic device, which symbolized strength and eternity.

"They are beautiful," Leonardo said.

"Yes," she whispered, "and they are from Lorenzo's own finger. His wife will certainly notice their absence."

"Madonna, I fear that you have, indeed, put Sandro in danger."

"And you, too," Simonetta said.

"That was not my thought."

"I know, but you are correct, Leonardo. Lorenzo has eyes and ears everywhere, and I fear too many might be inclined toward this house." She laughed softly. "But I cannot hold him at bay; it would be to no avail, for according to his note, he plans to lay siege upon my fortress tomorrow afternoon. In truth, I miss him. I love him above all men. And so I shall tell him, lest I die before I can explain."

"You shall live," Leonardo insisted.

"That would take a miracle." But Simonetta looked at Leonardo sidelong and said, "Not that I disbelieve in them, for I have realized one for you."

"What do you mean?" Leonardo asked, but Simonetta pressed her finger against his lips.

"A miracle should be savored, not devoured like meat by the likes of starving men." She brought her face very close to his and asked, "What do you want most in the world?"

Leonardo blushed.

"It is Ginevra, is it not?"

"Yes," Leonardo said.

"She is here, Leonardo."

10

Veils

of the Soul

Those born under the same star are so disposed that the image of the most beautiful among them, entering through the eyes into the soul of the other, conforms absolutely to a certain preexisting image, impressed at the beginning of procreation onto the celestial veil of the soul, as well as on the soul itself.

—Marsilio Ficino

Do you not know that your plans are disclosed?

—Cicero

Y ou must let me see her now."

"You must first compose yourself," Simonetta said. "And know what you are about."

"Upon what pretext did you bring her here? Is she with her retainers?"

Simonetta smiled and said, "Certainly. They are presently with her, but I shall soon entertain them, for Gaddiano, unlike some of the court painters, insists on working alone with his model."

"Gaddiano?" Leonardo exclaimed, for he knew that Simonetta was Gaddiano.

She smiled and said, "Indeed. Lorenzo himself commissioned the artist to paint Ginevra as a wedding gift. And I offered up my quarters to the artist."

"Does Lorenzo know?"

"That I am Gaddiano?" Simonetta asked. "No. But he wishes to help you. He especially liked the idea of deceiving Nicolini, for whom he bears no love; the old man is a Pazzi sycophant."

"And Ginevra, does she know about you?" Leonardo asked.

"No one knows but you, dear Leonardo."

"And what will you have me do?" Leonardo asked. He was excited and felt as if he had been running and could not quite catch his breath.

Simonetta smiled indulgently at him. "I would not presume to instruct you in matters of such inviolate delicacy." She rose. "But I will go in now and escort Nicolini's footmen out of the house—they seem to be more than happy to spend their afternoons at the Inn of the Bad Kitchen. And when they return, they will find Gaddiano himself in the flesh painting the lovely Ginevra; and poor Simonetta, alas, will be in her quarters taking her rest. But in the meanwhile, you will have her to yourself."

"I am forever in your debt," Leonardo said, standing, but a distance away from her.

"Well, then, perhaps if I live long enough, I can make even your obligation by calling upon you for a delicate favor." Simonetta came to him, brushed her fingers over the fading bruise on his cheekbone, kissed him, and said, "I told your beautiful Ginevra that you and Gaddiano were very dear friends, and that he agreed that this painting shall be a collaboration of sorts. So you must not spend all of your precious time in each other's arms. You must make progress on the painting, lest you arouse the suspicions of Nicolini's men."

"Has Ginevra asked your part in all this?"

"She knows we are friends, that's all. So you need not fear her jealousy. But do not worry, Leonardo. I assure you, she will be too preoccupied to question you in detail. Luca will be here for you in a few minutes." With that, Simonetta left.

———

Luca closed the door of Simonetta's studio behind Leonardo, who, upon seeing Ginevra, was transfixed. The vaulted room, with its huge *pietra serena* fireplace and high windows and ceilings, was a perfect studio; and the afternoon sun lit the room, turning all surfaces into golden patina and bleaching the shadows, which were as unobtrusive as cats in hiding. Ginevra sat stiffly on a *cassone,* upon which several cushions had been placed for her comfort. She looked at Leonardo, her lips tight and eyes direct; those beautiful heavy-lidded eyes that always appeared to be sleepy were now piercing. "Will you not come in, Leonardo?" she asked, her round face seemingly impassive.

Leonardo walked to the easel where a painting of Ginevra was mounted, but did not even glance at it. He felt himself shaking, and his heart beat quickly. Yet for that instant, he felt numbed. It was as if, like Sandro, he had suddenly been exorcised of all emotion, as if his love for Ginevra had burned away. He was cleansed. But then why was he shaking? Why was his heart filling his throat?

"You are looking well," he said awkwardly.

"And you, too," she said without moving from her place; it was as if she were confined to her *cassone,* as if she had to retain her pose for the artist. "I was worried that—" But then she stopped herself and averted her eyes. She looked lovely in her simple red-sleeved dress, which she wore over a sheer chemise. A black scarf was draped over the bare portions of her heavily freckled shoulders, and a net of black lace covered the back of her head. Her curly red hair was disheveled, breaking the almost too-perfect symmetry of her delicate oval face.

"Do you like the painting that your friend Gaddiano has begun?"

Only then did Leonardo look at Simonetta's painting. She had captured Ginevra's special charm admirably; in fact, the painting was light itself. It was rich with precise layerings of glazes in Leonardo's own style, and as deep and serene as a summer's Sunday afternoon. "It is indeed a fine portrait," Leonardo said, impressed. Then, after a pause, Leonardo said—and even as he spoke, his face began to redden—"Ginevra, why . . . are you here?"

"I was under the impression you wished it."

Leonardo kept a distance. "I have wished to be with you since—"

"And I with you, too," Ginevra said, her face coloring. She looked down at her hands, which were shaking; and she clasped them tightly together. But for her hands, she seemed very still, and posed; it was as if Leonardo were speaking to her image, not Ginevra herself, who was youth and flesh and passion.

"I could not see you before," she continued "for I have been a virtual prisoner. Surely you guessed that." She stared fixedly at her hands, which she opened, as if to release something precious she had trapped. "Leonardo, I love you. Why else would I be here?"

Shaken, Leonardo could only nod. But like a dry twig, he caught fire, kindled by an emotion that could not be distinguished from anger. Yet he felt himself stiffen, desiring her again with a familiar immediacy. She had opened herself to him . . . and his body responded to her words as it had to her caresses. Yet he could not release himself to her; some overweening, disbelieving part of himself had surfaced and grasped for control. "If that is true, then why did you speak as you did after the dove ignited the fireworks by the Duomo?"

She looked stricken. "Because I knew that Messer Nicolini had spies everywhere. Did he not appear like an apparition just after we talked? Do you forget, Leonardo? And do you not think that he earnestly wished to hear what I had to say to you?"

"You could have let me know . . . somehow. Instead of torturing me."

"I could not jeopardize my family." Ginevra's voice was quavering, yet defiant; and Leonardo imagined that she had been suffering for him as he had been for her. "And when I first tried to get word to you," she continued, "it was simply impossible. If it weren't for your friend, Madonna Simonetta, I don't know what I would have done."

"I love you, too," Leonardo said.

"I am to be presented with Luigi di Bernardo's ring," she said, which meant that her "contract" with Nicolini would soon be consummated in the old man's bed. She still looked at him directly—only now, it seemed, with expectation.

"What do you propose to do about it?" Leonardo asked. He too was trembling. He wished to embrace her, but it was as if he were rooted in place; and the words of this hollow conversation seemed to echo, as if they were spoken in a great, empty hall.

"I cannot marry him," she said, meaning Nicolini, "if you . . . still want me. I thought I could, for the honor of my family."

Leonardo nodded.

"I told Papa of the possibility that I might not take my vows to Messer Nicolini."

"And . . . what did he say?"

"He cried, Leonardo." She spoke slowly, as if she were merely reciting facts. Her eyes appeared luminous, filled with tears, which did not wash over onto her cheeks. "But . . ."

"Yes?"

"He understands that he would not be disgraced publicly. He has already received the . . . dowry, which could not possibly be called back, for then it would be Messer Nicolini's disgrace. Now we owe nothing, and the family is not in jeopardy; although, in fact, we might be able to repay him in two, perhaps three, years. But I have disgraced my father nevertheless. I have failed him and turned him into a cheat and a liar." Tears leaked from her eyes. "I just couldn't go through with it. I am too selfish. I could not be with him." She shuddered. "He would suffocate me, I would die, I would—"

"Then you meant to go through with it?" Leonardo asked.

"I don't know, Leonardo. For a time I didn't, and then I did. I thought I had to do it for Papa. Why do you torture me?" she asked, anger evident in her voice and her narrowed eyes.

"Because I am afraid," he confessed.

"Of what?"

"Of losing you again, for I would become like Sandro."

She smiled, a worried smile. "I think, perhaps, I already am. I thought that if I would die from the melancholy of love, then I would at least have the reflection of your soul inside me forever."

"You speak foolishness," Leonardo said.

"But we are images of each other, Leonardo," Ginevra insisted. "When I dreamed of you making love to me, I would see the face of the angel Raphael above our heads. He would whisper to me that he would heal us, that at our creation we were formed in each other's image, and that this image is his own."

"But he is the patron of the blind, my sweet Ginevra," Leonardo said with an ironic smile.

"I vowed to light a candle every day before Santo Raphael if—"

"If . . . ?" Leonardo asked, finding himself standing before her while she looked up at him nervously.

"If we could be together," she whispered; and he knelt before her, as if he were presenting his own *ex voto* upon the altar. She bent over him and then bore her weight upon him as he kissed her. But their lips hardly touched; it was as if they were holding themselves back from even this mildest of all ecstasies, lest it be lost in progression. They continued to stare into each other's eyes, as if searching for the reflections of their souls; but although both explored with their hands, only the quickness of their breath and the rustling of silk broke their silence. Then by some mutual decision of loins and hearts, they suddenly tore at each other's clothes. Too impatient to provide for their own bedding, they rocked and slid and clutched each other upon the cold and uncomfortable tiles of the floor. They took care not to leave marks upon each other as they tried to slip one into the other, kissing and biting and sucking, as if suddenly uncomfortable within the confines of their own blood and bone.

"Cosa bellissima," Ginevra said as she pulled away Leonardo's codpiece and maneuvered herself so that she could take his penis into her mouth and thus give him the ultimate and most intimate of pleasures. She had never done this before; and the warmth of her mouth reduced him until he was only that part between his legs, growing hot as a coal; but he fought against his own sensations and watched his lover's work, which was as pure and holy and beautiful as heaven's voice. She was worshiping him with love distanced from lust, that most perfect form dreamed by Plato . . . or perhaps Raphael, the most holy of angels.

And Leonardo reciprocated, kissing her, tasting her salty secretions, then crawling upon and over her, his erect penis an anchor seeking its rest; and they watched each other's expressions as Leonardo pressed himself into her as deeply as he had bone to give. They brought themselves to completion quickly, for their emotions were too high to be hindered, especially Leonardo's; he could not hold back his ejaculation. But he continued to press himself upon her, for although he was, for the time being, sated and his penis now numb and insensitive, he was determined to give her the full measure of pleasure he had received. He worked at her, as if she were stone to be chiseled and shaped; and she finally gave herself up, whispering over and over that she loved him, straining and arching her back against the floor that was limned with their sweat. She appeared to be completely unaware of herself as she dissolved for the instant into the purest and most liquid of love and pleasure.

Leonardo rested, not quite asleep, but in some region between dreaming and waking; he held Ginevra tightly. She was awake and watching him. "Leonardo . . . Leonardo . . . ?"

"Yes," Leonardo said, the word muffled, as his face was pressed against her breast. He pulled away from her and rested his weight on his elbow so he could look directly into her face.

"Did you ever make love to Madonna Simonetta?" Ginevra asked. She appeared suddenly serious and also childlike; but her eyes, for an instant, seemed to be mere reflections of her red hair.

"No," Leonardo said, caught off guard. He forced a laugh and sat up. "Of course not. Why would you think that?"

Ginevra shrugged, as if she had already forgotten that she had asked him such a question, and pulled him to her; but Leonardo felt caught nevertheless. "How many women have bowed before you, as I did?" she asked, referring to her gentle fellatio.

"Ginevra!" Leonardo said. "Such questions."

"Ah, so many that you cannot answer it?" she asked mischievously.

"Indeed, uncountable numbers," he said, relaxing; and he began to fondle her, touching her face, neck, and shoulder, then her breast, as she touched him. He was ready, as was she; and although the passion was dulled, it was only slightly so. He had regained her, thanks to the miracle of Simonetta; but as Ginevra and Leonardo made love, as if they were praying noisily, a phantasm shadowed his thoughts: Simonetta. He could not help but imagine her, as if it were she and not his true Ginevra beneath him, as if Simonetta's blond hair were brushing against him . . . Simonetta's pale skin sweating and seizing against his own, as if she were present to torment him by sucking him into her own ancient, watery vortex of ecstasy.

Leonardo pinched closed his eyes, trying to dispel Simonetta's ghostly presence; but he had reached orgasm and his guilt converged into pleasure. Such was the perversity of even the most ardent lover.

11

The

Lion's Head

More are killed by word of mouth than by the sword.

—Leonardo da Vinci

Whom will you love now? And by whose name will you be called?
Whom will you kiss? Whose lips will you in fondness bite?
Catullus, you must be resolute and stern.

—Gaius Valerius Catullus

And laying aside all fear, [the unicorn] will go up to the seated maiden and go to sleep in her lap, and thus the hunters take it.

—Leonardo da Vinci

The days that followed were as pleasant and languorous as those of deep summer, yet without summer's heat and humidity. For a time Leonardo was as happy as he had ever been. Although he constantly invented and drew machines, work had ceased to be his great passion. But just as he dreamed of Ginevra, so did ideas form naturally and unwilled in his mind and hands; his machines of destruction had the same valence as his paintings of Madonnas, as if his powers to create—and love—were as blind as fate.

He lived from day to day, waiting for Lorenzo to summon him to work in the Medici gardens and repair his statue of the satyr Marsyas. In the meantime, he worked for Andrea; took easily completed commissions as they came (such as decorating a clock face for the gentle monks of San Donato); walked the environs around Florence with Niccolò, sketching and jotting notes onto his leather-bound pad; and visited Sandro and even Pico della Mirandola, with whom his friendship had deepened.

It was carnival season, and Florentines took a particular, almost ferocious joy in attending these chthonic rites of spring: the jousts, feasts, football games, and endless parades that filled the *viales* with oversize floats and armies of *armeggeria* dressed in spectacular costumes.

The First Citizen was no exception. Although Lorenzo steadfastly ignored Leonardo's earnest and insistent memoranda on flying machines, weapons of war, and military techniques, he lost no time in inviting Leonardo, who had gained quite a reputation for his strength and agility, to play on his football team. This was quite an honor, for the players were from the noblest of Florentine families, and the games were charged with as much pomp and ceremony as any joust.

Along with drummers, referees, trumpeters, standard-bearers, and a ball thrower, there were twenty-seven men on each team. Leonardo enjoyed wearing the Medici colors of red and gold: the light shoes, costume of silk and velvet, long hose, and doublet and cap. He would bide his time until he could convince Lorenzo of his merits as a military engineer. Meanwhile, he was in the First Citizen's society; he was a *sconciatori*, a spoiler; and he and Lorenzo's brother Giuliano were charged with attacking the opposing runners, one of whom carried the ball.

It was indeed a rough-and-tumble game: arms and legs were often sprained or broken, and skulls were easily cracked. It was not unknown for players to die on the field as if in battle, which did in fact happen when Lorenzo's team played the Pazzi. An unfortunate incident, for a young *corridori*, a runner, from the important Nerli family, died of a broken spine. He was wearing Pazzi colors. The blow was inflicted, accidentally, of course, by Giuliano himself; and the Pazzi made much of it, for they were capitalizing lately on their hatred for the Medici. Lorenzo paid the Nerli family and by dint of his personality secured their loyalty.

But although Leonardo seemed to be living every moment as if time were a meal placed before a starving man, he was living for Ginevra, for those blissful days when Simonetta's footman would arrive at Verrocchio's *bottega* to take Leonardo to the Cattaneo-Vespucci residence. There he would spend an hour with Simonetta alone, as brother and sister, before she would transform herself into Gaddiano . . . into a man; and Leonardo had come to think of her in this guise as a male, just as he would Sandro or Andrea or Zoroastro or even Nicco.

And she would give him Ginevra, as if it were in her power to bestow both life and love.

Leonardo would paint and make love during those hours. He had made the painting of Ginevra his own; and some might say that it spoke of Leonardo even as it represented Ginevra, for he had transformed Simonetta's oil and varnish into the very stuff of his dreams, yet every detail was in service of the coherent whole. Simonetta had painted expertly and luminously; but Leonardo turned her painting into a poem of light, a vision, an ode given flesh. Behind the golden face of Ginevra, which seemed now to radiate its own numinal light as if she were the Virgin herself, Leonardo painted juniper trees, which seemed to contain, as if in a frame, Ginevra's fleshy, yet spiritual, glory. He chose the juniper as a play on her name, for in French the tree was called *genievre;* and in her long and slender hands he placed St. Vyvyan's *brachino* flute: it was said that with this instrument the holy saint could melt the meanest and hardest of hearts. But except for Ginevra, the rest of the painting seemed lost in a roseate haze; and in this haze, in the dimness of the distant hills, Leonardo had painted his own memory cathedral.

For, indeed, he had dreamed about it.

Yet the dream's contents eluded him.

"When will your father speak to Nicolini?" Leonardo asked Ginevra, who sat poised upon her *cassone*. "If he waits much longer, the painting will be finished!" He was painting in exquisite detail the juniper pine needles that formed her dark halo. Ginevra smoothed her hair into place; even though they had made love over an hour ago, her face still held a slight blush and seemed puffy, as if her skin had been pressed hard but not bruised.

"He does not tell me of such things," Ginevra said.

"Have you implored him?"

"Would you put me in such a position? It is difficult enough for him.

Can't you have a little patience, Leonardo? We will have our whole lives together."

"But now we must meet like thieves."

"Which is what we are," Ginevra said, as if to herself.

"I'm sorry," Leonardo said. "I'm sure your father will do what is best at his own time."

"He wants us to be happy. You know how he feels about you, but this whole matter, it is beyond him. He is not double-handed or double-hearted. He is a good-living, simple man. A good man of business—nay, a brilliant man of business. It was evil fortune that almost ruined him, but I can promise you, he'll never be caught by poverty again." She had raised her voice as she spoke to Leonardo, as if he were the offender; and then she caught herself. She turned her face away from Leonardo, for she began to cry; and he left his painting and knelt before her.

"I can wait," he whispered, caressing her. "I'll not question you again."

"I am sorry," she said, wiping her eyes and nose with her tufted sleeve. But when Leonardo's caresses became more sexual, she gently pulled away from him. "No, Leonardo, there is no time. Messer Gaddiano will be here shortly to replace you."

Leonardo nodded; but he was worried, for Simonetta had not been available to see him before he met with Ginevra. Might something be wrong? Turning out such thoughts, he asked, "Did I hear you to say that Gaddiano would *replace* me?" He pressed himself upon her with exaggerated ardor.

She giggled. "Surely, you have had enough. You can't be still—"

"Would you care to measure the stick behind my codpiece?"

"I dare not, lest I break the thing." She playfully pushed him away. "Please, Leonardo."

"But you are always asking me for proof."

"Proof? Of what?"

"Of my fidelity," Leonardo said. "Could I be so hungry for you if I had other mistresses in my bed?"

"From the stories I've heard about you, I would not be surprised."

"Do you mean that?" he asked, pulling a hurt expression.

"No," Ginevra said. Then she stood up, took Leonardo's hand, and led him across the room to the painting. "I want to see what you have done today."

"I have ravaged a beautiful maid."

"Indeed," she said, staring intently at the painting. "What is that, there?" she asked, pointing toward the indistinct outline of the memory cathedral that Leonardo had set in the blue-green haze of the hills.

"A cathedral," Leonardo said.

"So am I now your shrine?" Ginevra asked, looking at him sidewise and smiling.

"You are all of that." But as Leonardo gazed at the portrait, at the work he had done today, he felt a chill crawl up his spine. The vague remembrance of a dream.

She clapped her hands. "Then we shall get married right in there," she said. "In our very own cathedral."

Leonardo forced a smile; but just now, as he stood beside Ginevra, as he smelled the perfume of her hair, which barely masked the sweet, pungent odor of sweat that clung to her after making love, the dream came back to him with the terrible clarity of hallucination.

He was inside his memory cathedral, trying to pass through a doorway, which was guarded by a three-headed bronzen statue. One of the heads was that of his father; another was Toscanelli's; but it was the third head that frightened him the most, for it was Ginevra's. As her heavy-lidded eyes gazed into his, he saw that they were devoid of passion . . . or of love.

He had lost her.

Her eyes accused him. But of what?

"There's no sanctuary for you here," said his father as the statue moved toward him, as it reached out to embrace him, to squeeze the life out of him.

Leonardo shut his eyes for an instant, then picked up a brush and painted over the cathedral, creating an ugly smear of burnt umber on the upper right corner of the canvas.

"Leonardo, why would you do that?" Ginevra asked, obviously upset.

"I'm sorry, Ginevra, I just remembered a bad dream."

"But why—" she asked, breaking off her question. "Was this dream about me, Leonardo?"

Leonardo did not answer her.

"Leonardo?"

"I dreamed you no longer loved me, that you accused me. . . ."

"Of what?"

Leonardo shrugged and turned away from the painting, but he did not look at Ginevra. "I don't know."

"Well, I *do* love you, and—"

But she was interrupted by a knocking at the door. It was just about time for Gaddiano to make an entrance. Ginevra looked sadly at Leonardo, as if to transmit an unspoken message. Then she pressed her curls into place and walked back to her *cassone*. "Come in."

And Simonetta, disguised as Gaddiano, entered the room.

This Gaddiano of studied poise and carefully applied makeup resembled Leonardo somewhat: in the finely defined, almost sweet face that Andrea del Verrocchio had modeled as his *David*. The chin was similar, the lips full yet pursed, the nose thin, almost aristocratic. But Simonetta could not be kept out of Gaddiano's face: her haunted eyes gave her away; in contrast to Leonardo's, they were much softer and less piercing, for Leonardo had an earnest, almost angry look about him.

But just now, the eyes of Gaddiano the artist looked tired.

"Hello, sweet lovebirds," Simonetta said in a voice indistinguishable from a man's. She smiled at Ginevra, bowed perfunctorily, and stepped over to the painting.

Leonardo sensed immediately that something was wrong. Even in disguise, she looked weak and unsteady.

"Well, I can see that our collaboration is coming along," she said to Leonardo. "But what is this blotch?"

"A change of heart," Leonardo said.

Simonetta looked at him quizzically, then sat down upon the stool before the portrait. She picked up a brush and began scrumbling paint over the smudge. "Leonardo, my friend, should you not be leaving before Nicolini's men arrive?"

"Yes, of course," Leonardo said. "Good-bye, Gaddiano, and thank you." He bowed to Ginevra and kissed her as if they were alone. "Please, do not doubt me. I love you more than—"

A bell rang outside the door: Luca warning them that Nicolini's men had arrived to reclaim Ginevra.

As Leonardo was about to step out of the door, Simonetta coughed; in an instant she was doubled over with spasms. The intake of her breath was a wheezing, a whistling, as if her throat had closed itself.

Turning, Leonardo rushed to her side, and Ginevra followed. Leonardo reached out to steady Simonetta, but she pulled away from him. As if by an act of will, she stopped herself from coughing, but her breath was gravelly and phlegmy.

"Messer Gaddiano, you are too ill to be here," Ginevra said, concerned. "I shall fetch Madonna Simonetta—"

"No, no, Madonna, she is indisposed. I will be fine, it is merely some infection of the lung I contracted from the night air last week. Her servant will provide for me; but you, Leonardo, you *must* remove yourself from here, lest both of us suffer the points of Messer Nicolini's lances."

"Certainly his servants don't know who I—"

"They are the very same men who accompanied Messer Nicolini during the Celebration of the Burning Dove at the Duomo," Ginevra said earnestly. "They saw your face."

"You are not quite unknown in Florence," Simonetta said, still in the character of Gaddiano, and even now able to summon sarcasm. "Are you so intent to put us all at risk?" Simonetta had another fit of coughing, but quelled it, as if by will. She wiped her mouth with a vermilion hand-kerchief now wet and darkened with her blood. Her face had drained of color.

"He's right, Leonardo," Ginevra said. "Please, you must leave right now."

Leonardo did so; and just in time, too, for as he slipped out of the door and turned down a hallway, he could hear Nicolini's footmen. Well oiled af-ter an afternoon at the tavern, they were laughing at Simonetta's young ser-vant Luca.

But then Ginevra shouted, and Leonardo stopped, as if a portcullis had dropped before him.

"Help . . . someone!"

She was answered by Luca and Nicolini's footmen, who ran through the hallway to the studio; Leonardo also ran back as far as he dared. Frus-trated, he swore under his breath, then listened: it sounded as if Simonetta was coughing up her lungs, and then there was silence.

"Just lift him up," Luca said, and one of the footmen grunted. "Follow me, we'll take Messer Gaddiano to a bed; and you . . . go to the Medici Palace and fetch Messer Pico della Mirandola."

"For an artist?" one of the men said.

"He's a friend of the First Citizen—now, hurry!" Ginevra said impa-tiently, imperiously. As if indeed she, and not Nicolini, controlled her des-tiny.

Then—suddenly, it seemed—the voices and footfalls were swallowed into the rich darkness of this great house; and Leonardo was left alone, standing in a windowless hallway, the only sounds his rapid breathing and the fearful thumping of his heart.

Simonetta, you must not die.

You cannot.

He thought of Ginevra.

He thought of his tenuous relationship with his patron, Il Magnifico. Of the machines of war he wished to build for him.

Simonetta, you have eased my way through the machinery of Florence to the Medici . . . to Ginevra. I need you.

You must live.

I love you, my sister.

He felt a stirring for Simonetta, for the long whiteness of her. He craved the healing passion and melancholia they shared unspoken.

She was both tool and refuge.

But he had used her and was no better than a thief; for even now, if only in his thoughts, he sinned against her and his beloved Ginevra.

It was but a few days later that the dark Companions, the Ufficiali di Notte, burst into the workshop where Leonardo was working on a terra-cotta statue of a virgin and a unicorn for Verrocchio.

Surprised and shaken, Leonardo faced them; he held a hammer in one hand and a chisel in the other, as if they were weapons with which he might fend off the black-robed priests. These soldiers—the Police of Public Morals, the Officers of the Night and of the Monasteries—wore the vestments of the Medici-supported Dominicans; they were the wolves of the church: *inquisitores,* henchmen, executioners, and messengers. The great irony was that these were Lorenzo's own henchmen. It would seem that they were turned against their own by a hand subtler than theirs.

"Leonardo, we are here," said Pico della Mirandola anxiously, waving from behind the crush of clerically clad soldiers, trying to gain his friend's attention. "Do nothing rash. Sandro and I are here to help you." Then he turned to the captain, an old soldier whose face was pocked and scarred and who was taller than the other men, and asked, "Illustrissimo Signore Capitano, might I have a moment with Messer Leonardo da Vinci?"

"I have received my orders to bring him directly to San Marco," the captain said. A certain deference could be detected in his voice. "You may, however, if you wish, accompany Signore da Vinci in the carriage, but I am afraid that your friend—" He nodded toward Sandro.

"Do not worry, I shall follow in one of the other carriages," Sandro said. "If that is all right with the captain."

The captain nodded curtly.

"Might I know what this is all about?" Leonardo asked, unable to conceal his anger. He was being discussed as if he were furniture simply to be moved.

"You have been accused of a crime, Signore."

"And what crime would that be?" Leonardo asked, sarcasm edging his voice.

"Leonardo," Pico said in warning.

"*Sodomia,*" said the captain, his voice lowered, as if in discretion, although everyone in the room could hear.

"*What?*" Leonardo shouted, his voice husky with fury. "And who makes this accusation?"

"Signore Leonardo, you will please accompany us," the captain said, his voice calm; he was certainly used to situations such as this. "Or would you prefer to endure the bite of our irons upon your legs?" A few of the Companions unsheathed their swords and menaced Leonardo by pointing them toward him. "Now, will you please put down your tools, kind sir, lest I finally lose my Christian patience with you?"

Leonardo was still holding the hammer and chisel as weapons, for in his rage, he appeared to be without fear or concern for consequences.

"I must know who has made this malicious accusation."

"All will be clarified soon enough." The captain nodded to the men closest to him and then backed away.

"I must know now!"

"Leonardo," Pico said imploringly, "put up your tools. There is nothing to be done but to endure the order. I shall ride with you, attend to your business, and talk with the authorities."

Leonardo was about to speak but, thinking better of it, nodded, then gave Pico the hammer and chisel.

"Come along," said one of the Companions, slapping the side of his sword blade against Leonardo's thigh.

"So you and Sandro knew of this . . . accusation?" Leonardo asked Pico.

"We were warned, but . . . obviously, it seems, too late. It was found in the *bocca di leone* this morning."

"Ah," Leonardo said, his eyes narrowing. His heart pounded; tears veiled his sight for an instant.

It was not unusual for anonymous informers to drop letters of accusation into the lion's-head receptacle outside the Palazzo Vecchio. Such invidious *delatores* were rampant in these times of conspiracies, rivalries, and petty hatreds. Lorenzo, who lived in fear of conspiracies against his own house, allowed the infamous *tamburos,* the denunciation boxes—for might not important, even vital, information be found within?

"I have an idea who would consider such a perfidious trick," Leonardo said to Pico as he left the room and allowed himself to be led down the several flights of stairs to the waiting funereal-black carriages.

The banners of the *carroccios* hung listlessly, for there was hardly any wind on this hot, dry afternoon. Pico was, indeed, allowed to ride with Leonardo in the closed black carriage, although the quarters were cramped, for two soldiers rode with them, both young men with ruddy, pimply faces. They were watchful as ferrets, their rapiers resting in glinting, angled readiness upon their knees.

"I shall act as your lawyer," Pico said; and even though he was young, he looked formidable in his white theurgist gown. Pico was the quintessential dandy, and his reddish-blond hair was now dyed as black as Francesco Sforza's; it framed his pale, handsome face and piercing gray eyes. "You shall have to undergo some indignity, my friend, but that cannot be helped."

"Tell me what you know," Leonardo asked.

"Only that this ugly accusation has been made against you and others."

"By *whom*?" Leonardo asked, exasperated.

"The *tamburos* are the receptacles of cowards," Pico said, "and I have never seen a name attached to any accusation found inside them. Nor would I expect to find one now." He shrugged and said, "But Lorenzo will not disallow them."

"Who else is involved?"

Pico shook his head. "I am sorry, but that is all I know."

"And what of Si—"

Pico pressed Leonardo's leg with his own, warning him. "Lorenzo could stop this," Leonardo said nevertheless.

Pico looked at the soldiers, another gesture directed at Leonardo, lest he be too open before these strangers. "Not even the First Citizen can frustrate the civic processes." But after a beat he said, "However, I'm certain that he is aware of your predicament. . . ."

Leonardo consciously tried to control his trembling. Who could be his accuser? he asked himself. And of sodomy, the basest of accusations? Whom had Nicolini paid to do this? That Nicolini was involved, Leonardo had no doubt.

He was numb. He had surely lost Ginevra.

Irrevocably. . . .

Nay, not lost, he thought. Stolen.

But he forced those anguished, angry thoughts from his mind. He must not think of consequences. He must especially not think of Ginevra. He would soon be defending himself from Nicolini's calumny. God help me, he thought.

"How is Madonna?" he asked Pico, veiling his reference.

Pico nodded, clearly understanding that Leonardo meant Simonetta.

"She is ill and plans to leave the city, for its miasmas weaken her."

"Have you seen her?" Leonardo asked, feeling as if he were working through some very lucid and sharply defined nightmare; nevertheless, he felt removed from himself, as if he were watching from a distance. He could try to break out of the carriage; but without a weapon, he would not succeed; and, in fact, might get his friend hurt in the process. "Well?" Leonardo asked when Pico did not respond.

"She has refused visitors, but that means nothing," Pico quickly added. "She has been known to turn away Lorenzo."

"I can hardly believe that," Leonardo said, now catching sight of the Monastery of San Marco. He felt his heart racing and wished only that he could make a good accounting of himself, retain a modicum of pride. He thought of Piero, his father, and burned with shame. But the loss of Ginevra, that was unbearable.

He had finally lost everything.

He shielded his face from Pico.

"Leonardo . . ."

"Yes."

"You *will* be exonerated."

He laughed bitterly. "You mean because I am innocent. Do you believe that makes any difference? And even so, the damage has already been done. Can my father stand before Franciscan or Dominican now and serve either as notary? Can he do the same for the Mercatanzia. I think not. Can I still . . ." He was going to say, "marry Ginevra," but he swallowed his words, as if they were ratsbane.

He was, indeed, already poisoned.

Even before he was accused.

As they debouched from the carriage, the guards blocking Leonardo's way and keeping their swords lowered but pointed in his direction, Pico quickly said, "Leonardo, if the magistrate should order you incarcerated, do not fear. Lorenzo promised Simonetta that he would see to your release."

Jail . . .

Leonardo felt as if Pico had struck him in the chest, and at the same time felt foolish. Of course, jail. . . . And he heard himself say, as if he were hardly worried about his situation, "Then you *did* speak to our Madonna. . . ."

———

Leonardo was escorted through the shaded and timeless-looking loggias into the dungeon-stone monastery founded by the Silverstrines in 1299. Now it was a center of Medici activity, and the surrounding gardens had been compared with Eden's own.

How ironic that here should Leonardo be taken. As if the Medici were powerless to stay their own hands.

Leonardo did not fail to notice Fra Angelico's fresco of the Crucifixion, which faced the entrance from the piazza, nor that same good artist's painting of St. Peter Martyr, a dagger buried deep in his shoulder and his forefinger raised to his mouth, conveying silence and secrecy.

But there was no silence, nor secrecy, where Leonardo was being taken. As he was hurried down the stark, polished halls, he could hear the angry buzzing of voices, as if a crowd had gathered in the streets. He halted, but the captain pressed him on. They passed a number of evenly spaced rounded doorways, one of which the captain opened. Leonardo was told to go into what was effectively a cell and wait.

"How long will I remain here?" he asked, feeling a claustrophobic constriction.

"I will see what I can do now," Pico said. "Do not worry, you are safe. Nothing will happen without my being with you, my friend."

That was scant consolation.

Sandro stood beside Pico, looking pale, as if it were he who was to be interred. "Can I remain with him?" Sandro asked the captain.

"You may wait in the chapter room, Signore, with the others," the captain said.

Then Leonardo found himself alone, locked in the small monk's cell, a shaft of light cutting across the floor like a fallen pillar. He sat upon the stool provided and gazed upon the only decoration on the walls: a large crucifix, the Christ figure carved in realistic, even lurid, detail.

The hours passed, the room filling with the misty light of late afternoon; and then the door was unlocked and three Companions escorted him down the hall toward the chapter room, which had been converted into a courtroom.

From behind, someone called, "Ho, Leonardo." It was Il Neri, dressed in black and also escorted by guards. He looked pale and frightened.

Leonardo turned and nodded, feeling the flush of humiliation. He glimpsed someone behind Il Neri who looked familiar, but he was being pulled along by the guards; and then he was in the close, fetid-smelling chapter room.

To his humiliation, he had to pass makeshift galleries filled with the good citizens of Florence: the beggars, the curious, the idle, and an assorted collection of gentry, shopkeepers, and patrician wives collecting gossip first-hand. Leonardo kept his gaze ahead, as focused and rigid as if he were himself a soldier.

The crowd was noisy, and one of several court officers, wearing Dominican robes, walked along the gallery and simply raised his hand. All talking and whispering ceased.

Leonardo stood before the magistrate, who was seated high on a dais and protected by wooden scaffolding. He wore white robes and had a longish, jowly face that seemed to droop as if the soft, wrinkled flesh were weighted. He looked bored, and, obviously nearsighted, he held a paper stamped with the Medici seal very close to his face.

Then Il Neri arrived; he stood to Leonardo's right, looking nervous. He began to speak, but one of the guards said, "Quiet! Know before whom you stand, criminal." The guard referred to the magistrate, of course. Il Neri nodded, then looked down at his feet.

Guards brought in Bartholomeo the goldsmith and Baccino, the tailor; Leonardo had a passing acquaintance with them, for they were friends of Il Neri. But he was surprised and somehow relieved to see Marco Tornabuoni walk into the room, flanked by Companions, as if, indeed, he was their captain and not their captive. Tornabuoni, a young swell who had befriended Leonardo, bore one of the finest names in Florence. His family had business connections with the Medici. Perhaps his presence in this collection would act as a balm.

Their gazes met for an instant of recognition, but that was all. But why were they all summoned here together? Leonardo asked himself. Then he felt the reassuring touch of Pico della Mirandola. But he dared not question him. Two other men arrived with Pico, obviously as counsel for Il Neri and Marco Tornabuoni. Neri's was a small man with close-set eyes and large ears that were exaggerated by the formal but overly large cap that he wore; and Leonardo recognized the other man, for he was an acquaintance of his father's.

Leonardo nodded to the man, then turned away on the pretext of perusing the galleries. There was Sandro standing in the rear of the gallery, looking embarrassed, as if somehow it was his own fault that Leonardo had been caught in this net. Leonardo was glad to see him there.

"Are these, then, all the accused?" the magistrate asked the captain who stood between the judicial dais and the gallery.

"Yes, Most Reverent Lord."

The magistrate nodded and, looking down at Leonardo and the others, said, "I shall now read you the text of your accusation found on the eighth of April by our prelates in the drum outside the Palazzo Vecchio.

" 'Be informed, father Officers, that it is a true thing that Jacopo Saltarelli, blood brother of Giovanni Saltarelli (he lives with him in the house of the goldsmith in Vaccbereccia opposite the Buco, and his age is about seventeen), the said Jacopo having suffered many misfortunes, he consents to comply with those persons who exact of him certain evil pleasures. *Sodomia* being one of them. In this way he has had occasion to do many things, that is to say, to serve several dozen people about whom I know a good deal. To mention only some of them, there are Bartholomeo di Pasquino, the goldsmith, who lives in Vaccbereccia; Leonardo di Ser Piero da Vinci, who lives with Andrea del Verrocchio; Baccino, the tailor, who lives in Orto San Michele; Marco Tornabuoni' "—and the magistrate looked down over his paper at the young man after he mentioned his name; and, shaking his head, continued— " 'and Guglielmo Onorevoli, called Il Neri, who dresses always in black.' "

Jacopo Saltarelli, Leonardo thought. He had led Leonardo and his friends to Il Neri's on Easter Eve; indeed, it was he who had been painted that night like a crimson piebald creature, he who whose mouth had been upon Il Neri's member when Il Neri was impersonating Leonardo. But Saltarelli knew he wasn't performing fellatio on Leonardo, for Neri had revealed himself by removing the coverings and makeup from his face.

Leonardo understood that he was not standing here by chance.

"So, young criminals," the justice said as he turned the paper in his hands, "I have it on the best information that you have no respect for our city's curfews; that you run through the streets brandishing swords and shouting, 'Death to those in our way'; that you are debauched with drink, free living, and licentiousness with both men and women alike. Were you not all gathered together on Easter Eve to blaspheme Christ at an orgy where the young boy Jacopo Saltarelli was sodomized by you? Did you not worship Satan on that very night in the house of Onorevoli, which is turned into a fuckery?" The justice raised his voice, as if becoming more excited by his own harangue. "And you, young Onorevoli, did you not crack his butt, child that he was? You who fancies himself an apprentice of Satan even by your black dress. You shall soon find that your only privilege will be a square of cloth with which to wipe yourself."

The gallery roared at that.

Then he gazed down at Marco and Leonardo. "For shame, Marco Tornabuoni and Leonardo di Ser Piero da Vinci; Marco, you of an ancient and patrician family; and you, Leonardo, whose father is a notary of established reputation and well-known to me. To be lecherous of children, the shame of pederasty upon you."

"I am not a pederast," Leonardo shouted, unable to control himself any longer. "I am no sodomite."

The guards were upon him at once, but Pico intervened smoothly, apologized to the judge for him, and whispered, "You must not make an outburst; an arrangement will be agreed upon, but if you provoke the judge, there will be nothing I can do."

"But this humiliation . . ."

"It cannot be helped. You must endure it."

"Quiet," the magistrate said, and he continued his accounting of sin and perversion attributed to those standing frozen below him. Leonardo used his entire will to put the judge's voice and the snipping of the gallery beyond him; once again he dreamed of his memory cathedral, counted the foci of names, places, and events, and had a quick, vertiginous sense of déjà vu: of burning papers and Levantine aridness . . . of earthquakes and heartquakes, of blood and murder and cataclysmic destruction. And thus he daydreamed, as if his reverie were a closet, and he was a child hiding inside it while he watched through a crack the smoke and flame of a consuming fire.

He felt warm, as if there were a hot spot on the left side of his face, upon his cheek and neck, as if light were being focused through a lens upon him. He had the sense that someone's gaze was boring into his flesh, which should not have surprised him, for the gallery was full. But he could not help but look again at his accusers, those who thought him guilty whether or not it be true; and he saw his father standing near the door, his face as pale as one who is ill.

Ser Piero da Vinci stood erect in his notarial robes, directing from his narrowed eyes concentrated emanations of internal fire at his son.

Such was not ordinary vision; it was raw hatred.

And in that instant when their eyes met, Leonardo felt as if he were being burned alive.

"But you have no defense, Leonardo," Pico said during a recess ordered by the judge. It was late, and the sun was low in the sky. Leonardo was exhausted, for there had been no respite to his humiliation.

"It was Neri who impersonated me, not—"

"I understand what you told me, and I am certain that it is so. But no one will believe you. And I know this judge; he would not look kindly upon your blaming another."

"But that is what happened!"

Pico looked up at Leonardo and shrugged.

"Then what are we to do?" Leonardo asked.

"I have already made arrangements."

"Yes . . . ?"

"We will try to buy your freedom. Il Magnifico has made some money available."

"But that will not clear my name," Leonardo said sourly. "Lorenzo could have stopped this."

"We've been over that," Pico said, irritated. "If he could have saved you from the *tamburo,* he would have. But he is the First Citizen, not a tyrant. Whatever you might think, he cannot just act as he pleases."

"You're right, I'm sure, Pico," Leonardo said. "I apologize; and you have been more than kind."

"I can make you no guarantees. You may, in fact, have to spend a month or two in prison. But surely no more than that. . . ."

"You told me that Lorenzo would see to my release."

"And so I did. But it will still take time."

Leonardo closed his eyes, then nodded, as if the decision had already been rendered.

Leonardo stood in the courtroom before the jowly-faced magistrate who was ready to render his decision. Once again he could feel his father's baleful stare on the back of his neck. He clasped his trembling hands together and endured the jeers of the gallery.

Pico pleaded with the judge on Leonardo's behalf: "... The cult of the beauty of ephebus is entirely Platonic ... in the best sense. What is it if not an exultation in the beauty of comradeship and friendship ... ?"

The judge nodded, impatient. But he seemed to relish going on to discuss Ficino's brilliant and controversial "Apologia de moribus Platonis" and Pomponio Leto's defense of Socrates. Like any paid actor or foil, the judge played to the gallery.

And he did so very well indeed.

Finally Pico found it appropriate to ask, "Perhaps a proper bailment could be arranged. We have raised two hundred florins...." There was noise in the gallery, guffawing and whistles, for that was a large sum of money.

Leonardo took a deep breath. If it was to be prison, he thought, then so be it. His will regained, his thoughts drifted; and in those long beats before the judge decided his fate, Leonardo remembered a game of childhood. He had been taught by a holy father in Vinci how to visualize Christ in the flesh, how to see through time ... how to see as the Carthusian monk Ludolfus had seen: "And you must proceed with devout curiosity. You must feel your way. You must touch each wound of your Savior."

Leonardo had counted 662 wounds.

But Ludolfus had counted 5,490.

Once again Leonardo counted the wounds in the Savior's flesh and felt the agony washing over his soul.

12

The

Olive Branch

A man who is in despair you should make turning his knife against himself, and rending his garments with his hands, and one of his hands should be in the act of tearing open his wound. Make him with his feet apart, his legs somewhat bent, and the whole body likewise bending to the ground, and with his hair torn and streaming.

—Leonardo da Vinci

The eye, which is called the window of the soul . . .

—Leonardo da Vinci

Could this all have been a bad dream, a febrile nightmare, a phantasm?

Although Lorenzo's bailment had been accepted by the court and Leonardo had escaped being imprisoned, he still stood publicly accused and humiliated. Surely this was the stuff of Mirandola's *Ars notoria:* the demonic magick of hopelessness, of *melaina cholos.* Events had lost their familiar reality; they had become portents, forms, symbols, occult purposes. Even time had lost its balance: hours passed in excruciatingly slow rhythm while days quickly disappeared, one dropping away after another, as if they were coals being thrown into a dark pit. Time and events had become limned with the aura of nightmare, and although Leonardo was raging and howling to wake up, he could not.

Had the world really changed?

Had he *really* been arrested and accused . . . ?

He sat before a table in his studio. The room was dim but for a water lamp, which was also on the table: a contrivance of Leonardo's that magnified the oil-soaked wick and radiated a constant light. It was not nearly evening, but the day had been overcast and gray; the available light seemed to darken and oppress the usually bright, airy studio.

Anatomical drawings were scattered on the table and floor, most of them stained and brown, spattered with gore and blood. Beakers and jars and flasks and dissecting equipment took up most of the space: steel and fork and bistoury, thongs, pipe clay and wax, a saw for bones with fine teeth, a chisel, inkstand, penknife.

He had turned the studio into a laboratory, a dissection chamber.

Several burners were heating a half-filled bowl of viscous liquid to a boil: egg whites; and boiling in this mess were the eyeballs of slaughtered oxen and pigs. Leonardo had been to the slaughterhouse only this morning, had watched the squealing animals thrown onto the blood-soaked floor by a butcher's assistant and then deftly stabbed through the heart with a stiletto by the butcher. They knew him there and had allowed Leonardo to gouge out the eyes and take them without charge.

As the eyeballs danced and percolated—rising and falling—in the metal bowl, they themselves looked like eggs: white and spongy.

Although Leonardo's hands were unclean, he composed a letter. He wrote upon the folio paper at hand beside notes for a camera obscura and sketches depicting cross sections of the eyes of various birds and animals. He wrote quickly in his mirror script, writing in code, as he did all his first drafts. He would petition Bernardo di Simone Cortigiani, who had been a friend of his father's. He was *gonfalonieri* of the Weavers' Guild, an important man who liked Leonardo and his work and was sympathetic to his plight.

Perhaps Piero da Vinci had not yet poisoned him against Leonardo.

Piero had turned away from his son in anger and humiliation. Leonardo had written to his father, to no avail; he had even presented himself at his father's house, only to be turned away by the servants.

. . . You know, sir, Leonardo wrote, *I have said this to you before, that there is no one who takes my side. And I cannot help but think that if there is no such thing as love, then what is left of life?—Friend!* Leonardo stopped, then, as an afterthought, surrounded the last word with flourishes. He swore, tore what he had written from the page, and crumpled it in his fist.

He had written everyone who might be able to help him. He had even written to his uncle in Pistoia, in hopes that he might be able to soften his father.

Francesco could do nothing.

Leonardo might as well be dead, or a ghost without effect. Indeed, he felt like a ghost, for the studio was all but empty: Andrea had taken his apprentices and family to the country, finally persuaded of danger when a family was found dead of the plague down the street. Sandro and Mirandola had left with Lorenzo to wait out the heat and plague in Careggi; and Leonardo had sent Niccolò back to Toscanelli, for how could an accused pederast remain the master of a young apprentice?

"Ginevra," Leonardo said. It was a plaint, yet spoken barely above a whisper. He rested his elbows on the table and covered his face with his large, crooked, almost feminine hands.

She had left with her father for their country home the day after Leonardo's accusation. He prayed for her, that she would hold fast to him, that she would not allow Nicolini—

Surely, she loved him. He could depend on that. He should instead be scolding himself for doubting her.

But he had lost her, irrevocably. He knew it, felt it as an emptiness, a cold, dark vacuum growing inside him.

Just now he would not have been surprised if this sickness of soul suddenly manifested itself as the plague. That would be most fitting. He imagined the pressure of buboes under his arms and visualized his own death. An image floated into his mind: the plague virgin, the hideous twin of the gentle goddess Flora. Instead of garlands, she sprinkled poison on the streets and in the fields.

Leonardo made a sketch of her and wrote a note beneath it for future reference.

Then he stood up, leaned across the table, and removed the eyeballs from the bowl of boiling egg white with a kitchen skimmer. He pinched out the flame of the burners and laid the eyes before him. They were as solid as hard-boiled eggs. He chose a scalpel from his ordered array of dissecting tools; and then, pushing his notepaper aside, he began cutting the eyes transversely so that no portion of the middle could leak out. As if in a frenzy, he would dissect, and then make notes and anatomical sketches upon the bloody leaves of paper near to hand.

It is impossible that the eye should project from itself, by visual rays, the visual power . . . , he wrote; and as he did so, he felt his face grow warm as he remembered the fiery emanation of his father's hateful, baleful gaze upon his neck.

Then he scribbled along the side of a diagram he had copied from Roger Bacon's *Opus Maius: And even if the eye was made up of a million worlds, it could not prevent itself from being consumed in the projection of its power; and if this power, this emanation, traveled through the air as perfumes do, then the winds would bend it and carry it away to another place.*

Surely Plato and Euclid and Vitruvius, and even John Peckham and Roger Bacon, were wrong.

The eye could emit no ray.

His father could not burn him with his gaze. . . .

And so Leonardo dissected the eyes, one after another, his anger dissipating as the table became slippery with blood and ichor. He talked to himself as he worked, as he committed his thoughts to paper. He was especially interested in the "lentil" of the eye itself: *Nature has made the surface of the pupil convex in shape so that objects may imprint their images at greater angles than would be possible if the eye were flat.*

But when he was spent and the pigs' and bulls' eyes ruined and run to paste upon the table, his thoughts turned to philosophy, or, rather, to himself, for he wrote: *He who loses his eyes condemns his soul to a dark prison where there is no hope of ever again seeing the sun, the light of the world.*

Ginevra . . .

Then there was a loud knocking at the door.

"Master Leonardo," shouted the gravelly, masculine voice of Smeralda, Andrea's oldest servant, who had refused to leave the *bottega* with her master.

"I told you not to disturb me, Smeralda. I am *not* hungry."

"I didn't ask if you were," she said insolently, opening the door. "And I wouldn't care if you were, so!"

She was stout in her coarse dress and apron and seemed weighted down by a wreath of amulets and pomanders. She wore the bone from the head of a toad, a hazelnut shell filled with mercury, the tongue of a venomous snake, and she smelled of resin and amber and cloves and tobacco: all these were certain remedies and protections against plague and other misfortunes. She also daily wrote certain prayers upon paper, which she folded seven times, and then ate on an empty stomach. Thus she had no reason to fear the plague or Leonardo's inconstant temper. But when she saw that Leonardo had been dissecting again at his table, she crossed herself seven times quickly. She pulled a face, mumbled a formulary, and said, "It stinks in here. I believe you *want* to let in the dark dancer."

"Smeralda, what is it?"

She raised a pomander to her mouth. "There's someone at the door for you."

"Who?" Leonardo asked.

Smeralda shrugged.

"A lady?"

Again she shrugged.

"Surely, you know who it is."

"Will you receive a visitor?"

"Is it Sandro . . . ? Pico della Mirandola?"

She stared at him, blinking.

Leonardo swore impatiently.

"And I'll be back to bring you something to eat, too!" she said, leaving the pomander behind to clear the air.

———

"It is even worse than I had expected," Sandro said, entering Leonardo's studio. "You look terrible!" He glanced around the room in disgust; then, staring incredulously at the mess on the table, he asked, *"Autophaneia?"*

Leonardo smiled wanly, but it was the first time he had smiled in days, perhaps weeks. "You'll not find any demons hereabouts today. I invoke them only on the Sabbath."

"Then what *is* all this?" He walked over to the table, then backed away.

"Those are the remains of the most perfect organs: they are, or rather were, the windows of the soul. Have you not eyes to see them?" Leonardo had not meant the sarcasm, but he could not help himself. Yet he did not wish to be alone; he was happy to see his friend; and that in itself surprised him.

"This must all be cleaned up," Sandro said. "And you must have fresh air."

"Indeed," Leonardo said in barely a whisper.

Sandro opened the windows, methodically working himself around the room, and then asked, "Why have you not answered my letters? Did you receive them? You were invited to be Lorenzo's guest."

"If I could leave Florence, do you not think I would have followed Ginevra?" Leonardo asked. "I cannot prevail in society until this . . . is over." He was still under bailment and could not leave the environs of Florence. Were he to be seen outside the city limits, whosoever was in his company could be charged as his accomplice; he was a pariah, both under the law and in fact.

"You needn't have worried about that, for Lorenzo would not have refused you. You would have had the protection of the First Citizen."

"Neither did he invite me. If memory serves, it was you who proffered the invitation."

"Well, it is moot now. We have all returned home. It seems that Florence is safe again, except, perhaps, for this place of effluvium."

"And Ginevra?" Leonardo asked, looking intently at his friend, as if the answer could be read on his face. "You said nothing of Ginevra."

"I did not see her," Sandro said. "We were not long enough in Careggi before Madonna Clarise had a dream that the plague virgin was stalking her. As she was very frightened, we moved to Cafaggiolo. The distance was too great."

Leonardo nodded at the mention of Lorenzo's wife, Clarise. "Have you no news of Ginevra at all?"

Sandro looked uncomfortable. "I wrote her, as I did you."

"And . . . ?"

"She responded with the usual felicities. She is well, but she reported that her father had to be bled for his gout. I take it that you have not heard from her?"

"Not one word," Leonardo said, the bitterness evident in his voice. He had tried to excuse her, but he could not deny the truth: she had fled from him as if he were the plague itself.

Sandro squeezed Leonardo's arm, then reached into the sleeve of his *gonnella* tunic and pulled out a letter sealed with wax. He handed it to Leonardo. "This is a gift from the man you berate."

"And whom would that be?" Leonardo asked.

"Il Magnifico."

"I have never—"

"Open your letter," Sandro said in a chiding tone. But his expression, which was normally placid, could not hide his state of excitement.

Leonardo opened the letter. On a sheet of Lorenzo's gold-edged paper appeared only the words *absoluti cum conditione ne retamburentur.*

The charges against Leonardo had been dropped.

Leonardo shouted and crushed Sandro in a bear hug.

"Enough," Sandro said, laughing. "I am only the messenger." When he was released, he continued: "Lorenzo only just found out himself, and I asked him if I could carry the glad tidings to you."

"I'm glad you did," Leonardo said. "I must see Ginevra." He looked for his cap and cloak, as if he were about to leave.

"Please, Leonardo," Sandro said. "Accord me *some* little courtesy, for I have yet another surprise. But you must have just this much patience." Sandro curled his index finger over his thumb, leaving an inch between them. "Well . . . ?"

Leonardo agreed to wait, but paced about as if he might lose everything if he tarried but a second. Presently, there was a knocking at the door; and Smeralda entered the room with a large tray of food and wine.

Niccolò followed her. "What is *that*?" he asked as he dropped his sack of clothes and bedding to the floor and pointed at the table.

"An experiment," Leonardo said. He smiled at the boy, who in the next instant was in his master's arms. Although he had not realized it until this moment, Leonardo had sorely missed his company. Niccolò was indeed his charge.

"May I stay with you, Leonardo?" Niccolò asked, straightening himself to appear taller than he was. He was, indeed, almost a man. "I have Master Toscanelli's permission."

"I don't know if that would be the best thing for you."

"But it might be the best thing for *you*, Leonardo," Sandro said.

"That is not relevant."

"Toscanelli thought it was. He imagined, correctly, that you'd be all caught up in yourself."

Leonardo made a growling noise.

"I wrote you from the Romagna," Niccolò said. "But you never answered."

"I was ill, Nicco. I was like a *sonnambulo*. Remember when Sandro was ill? It was a little like that."

"I am not a child, Leonardo. You can address me as you would Sandro." But he nevertheless seemed satisfied with that explanation. He looked again at the matter hardening on the table and said, as if stating an incontrovertible fact, "Melancholy. But impure."

"No, Niccolò," Sandro said, "it's not as you think. He was not inducing demons. But he is ill, even now."

"I am as fit as you," Leonardo said, smarting.

Sandro nodded noncommittally and then asked Niccolò to call Smeralda, who, it turned out, was nearby, for she had been eavesdropping behind the door. "This room needs to be cleaned," Sandro said to her. "Immediately."

Smeralda crossed herself and said, "Not by the likes of me." Then she left in a huff.

As Leonardo watched Niccolò picking at pieces of the meat and boiled cabbage that Smeralda had brought, he found himself suddenly hungry. But like a carouser just recovering from the effects of his dissipation, his head and limbs ached and his mouth tasted dry and cottony. Nevertheless, he began to eat the boiled cabbage and even a little bit of the meat, until Sandro cautioned him to slow down lest he become ill. He took some wine and then said, "I must find Ginevra and tell her the news. And until I do that—"

"Let me go with you," Niccolò said, insistent.

"As happy as I am to see you, I'm not yet up to the responsibility of—"

"We'll both of us go with you," Sandro said, indulging Leonardo. "But not today, not tonight. Tomorrow, when you are stronger."

Feeling suddenly tired and light-headed and relieved that he was finally free of the charges, Leonardo acquiesced; and Sandro and Niccolò disposed of the organic remains of Leonardo's dissections while he slept. Only then would Smeralda return to the room to mop the floors, change the linen, and return the studio to good order.

But when Leonardo awakened, and after he had soaked in a hot bath—he had not bathed himself properly in weeks—he insisted on going out into the narrow, crowded streets. Sandro and Niccolò had no choice but to follow, for Leonardo was now full of energy; it was as if he had been hoarding it during the past two months, and now it was bursting forth all at once.

"Where are you going?" Niccolò asked him, hurrying to keep up with his master, who was wearing fresh clothes in the best style of the dandy: a *veste togata* with a *cappuccio* draped over his shoulder, red-and-blue shoes, and a matching two-colored beretta cap.

"Nowhere . . . everywhere," Leonardo said, slapping Niccolò on the shoulder and urging him and Sandro to keep up. "I am free!" He took a deep breath; but the odors of the streets were noxious, for during the latest panic over the plague that might have carried away a good portion of the good citizens of Florence, garbage and rubbish had piled up; there was more than the dogs could eat. In some areas the filth had made the streets impassable; and everywhere Leonardo and his friends walked, the streets were slippery with organic residues: a thick blue-black sludge that seemed to stain everything, from building walls to vendors' stands.

Craftsmen and tradesmen were out in force. There was a holiday atmosphere on the crowded streets. It was warm, if unusually hazy; and there was still an hour of daylight left. Everywhere were noise and color: banners hung from windows, bright tent cloth was raised over balconies, and wealthy and poor alike were like schools of bright fish swimming in dull, still waters. The crowds seemed to be galvanized, for curfew would soon be in effect. It was as if all the shouting, buying, selling, loving, talking, and walking had to be concentrated into this dusky period before twilight and darkness. Soon, in the poorer neighborhoods and the Jewish ghetto, all but a few would have no choice but to go to sleep or sit in darkness, for tallow and even the cheaper, foul-smelling candle dips soaked in fat were more expensive than meat.

Niccolò held his nose as they passed the smashed remains of a fishmonger's stall. Sandro put a handkerchief to his face. A crowd was jeering at a thin blond-haired man pilloried beside his stall; he wore a necklace of rotting fish and a sign painted with the word *Ladro:* thief. That was the traditional punishment for dishonest tradesmen. His arms and legs confined in crude shackles, the man sat and stared downward into the street; he cried out only when he was struck on his head by a stone thrown by a young tough.

Leonardo led the way through the crowded streets. The streets of princes looked little different from other alleyways of trade. The great houses with their flat facades and *sporti* of brick and stone rose from the same curbs as their poorer cousins, for great families took over streets and neighborhoods as if they were kingdoms. They passed the palace of the wool guild, walked down the Via Cacciajoli—the Street of the Cheesemonger, down the Via dei Pittori, where artists, weavers, furniture carvers, and potters lived and worked together.

Excited and unaware of where Leonardo was taking them, Niccolò nattered away happily. "Sandro, tell Leonardo about the Marzocco festival."

"Lorenzo wishes you to join him during the festival," Sandro said. He seemed uncomfortable with the pace that Leonardo set, perhaps because he knew that they were walking to the Vespucci castle. Yet nothing was spoken of it. "I will, of course, notify Il Magnifico that you require your invitation to be delivered by himself personally."

"Stop it, Little Bottle," Leonardo said.

"There will be animals all over the streets," Niccolò said. "Wild boars and bears and lions, all set one against the other."

"Why is there to be such a festival?" Leonardo asked, although his manner was still distant, as if he were somehow removed from everything but his intention.

"You certainly have been on retreat," Sandro said. "All of Florence is celebrating because two of the lionesses in the menagerie bore cubs."

The heraldic lion, the Marzocco, was the emblem of Florence. For hundreds of years, lions had been kept by the Signoria in the dungeons of the Palazzo. They were protected by the state, and their deaths were mourned, as their births were celebrated. Their birth prefigured prosperity; their death—war, plague, and all manner of evil times and catastrophe.

"Indeed, it makes perfect sense to celebrate the miracle of birth by savaging and killing," Leonardo said. "How many animals died in the arena during the last festival? And how many men?"

But Niccolò's enthusiasm was not to be diminished. "Can we go, Leonardo? Please . . ."

Leonardo ignored him.

"You know, in all that carnage you so detest," Sandro said, "you might be able to obtain several specimens to dissect: panthers, pards, ounces, tigers . . ."

"Perhaps," Leonardo said. He wished to study the lion's receptacles for the sense of smell; and he wished to study and compare their optic nerves with other animals he had dissected. "Perhaps," he said again, distractedly.

Niccolò winked at Sandro, but that engendered no response, for Sandro said to Leonardo, "Simonetta is not well."

Leonardo slowed his pace, almost coming to a halt. "Has her coughing worsened?"

"Yes," Sandro said. "She has returned to Florence, but I worry about her so."

"I am sorry, Little Bottle," Leonardo said, feeling a sudden pang of guilt; he had not even thought of her these past weeks. "I will see her as soon as possible."

"She is not accepting visitors . . . but I am sure she will want to see you."

"There is Ginevra's home," Leonardo said, as if he had not heard what Sandro had just said. Looking through the archway before them, he could see the rusticated walls and the arched windows of the de' Benci *palazzo.* But then Leonardo swore and rushed toward the balustraded palace.

"Leonardo, what is it?" shouted Niccolò, chasing after him. But Sandro remained behind for the moment, as if he could not bear what lay ahead.

Displayed in every window were a candle and an olive branch surrounded by a wreath of gladiolus. The gladiolus symbolized the holy tranquillity of the Virgin as described in the apocryphal *Book of Jane;* the olive branch was the symbol of terrestrial felicity. Together, they announced to the world that a marriage had been consummated.

Ginevra had married Nicolini. Leonardo was beside himself with anger and grief.

He pounded on the door; but the door was not opened. As had become the custom during these times, a servant peered through a hole in the door and asked who was calling.

"Inform Messer Amerigo de' Benci and his daughter, Madonna Ginevra, that their friend Leonardo wishes to be received."

An uncomfortable period of time passed, and the servant, who had left his post at the door and now just returned, said, "I am sorry, Maestro Leonardo, but they are indisposed just now. The master extends his felicitations and regrets, for he wishes to see you as—"

"Indisposed?" Leonardo said, his face reddening with rage and humiliation. "*Indisposed?* Open this door, you catch-fart!" and he pounded on the inlaid, paneled door, then crashed into it, using his shoulder as a battering ram.

"Leonardo, enough!" shouted Sandro; but when he tried to restrain his friend, Leonardo swung at him wildly. "It's no use," Sandro continued. "You can no more break through that door than I could. Now, come along, come *on*. There is no one in there to hear you."

But Leonardo could not be moved.

He shouted for Ginevra, bellowing, and felt that he had fallen back into the nightmare of the past few months. He felt the chill of a cold sweat break out under his arms and around his torso, even though his face felt hot; but he was mercifully removed, removed from the street, the noise, his own shouting . . . indeed, removed from himself. This was a dream and he the dreamer.

"Ginevra. *Ginevra!*"

Sandro tried once again to restrain Leonardo, but Leonardo shook him off.

As if pulled together by some alchemical process, a crowd had formed on the street. The rabble, dangerous and easily entertained, catcalled and whistled.

"Let him alone," someone said.

"Aye," said another.

"Open the door, citizen, or by God's body we'll help 'im break in."

Surrendering to grief and the oblivion of his fury, Leonardo raged and railed and threatened. "*Quo iure?*" he cried out.

Why have you done this?

He was past dignity and humiliation now. His pride and composure had been swept away with his reason. How could it be that Ginevra and Nicolini had cut him down with nothing but a few dried olive branches?

But Leonardo was a spectacle. He was magnificent, he was possessed and enchained. His soul was poisoned, but not by the phantasm of *morte di bacio* that had poisoned Sandro, not by any vision of love perfected.

He was possessed by the beast. By his own furies. By loss. For he had lost everyone he loved—his father, his mother. And now, finally, Ginevra. It was almost a relief.

The door opened, and the crowd cheered.

Ginevra's father stood in the doorway. He was a tall man and had once been husky, but now he looked emaciated and ill. Leonardo hardly recognized him. Amerigo de' Benci smiled at his friend and said, "Come in, Leonardo. I have missed you." He nodded to Sandro and Niccolò, but did not invite them to accompany their friend.

The crowd cheered and then began to disperse as Leonardo entered the palace.

Leonardo bowed to Ginevra's father and apologized; but Amerigo de' Benci took his arm and led him through a colonnaded courtyard, through brass-mounted walnut doors, into a vaulted sitting room.

"Sit down, Leonardo," Amerigo said, indicating a chair beside a gaming table. But Leonardo was caught by the portrait that hung above a mahogany desk: the very one that he and Simonetta had painted of Ginevra. Yet it struck him just now that he had rendered her coldly, as if her warm flesh were, in fact, stone. She looked across the room at him from within her frame, her eyes cool as seawater—a radiant angel, haloed in juniper black. "Yes, you and Ser Gaddiano rendered her beautifully," Amerigo continued. "Ginevra has told me everything." The old man looked sad, and also rather nervous. He sat down beside Leonardo. A servant entered the room and poured wine for both of them.

Leonardo looked at the chessboard beside him, at the array of red and black carved figures: knights, bishops, rooks, pawns, and the king and queen, and said, "I have been acquitted of all charges, Amerigo."

"I had no doubt you would be."

"Then why are there branches in the windows?" Leonardo asked, now looking at Ginevra's father. "You said Ginevra told you everything. Did she not tell you of her feelings for me . . . that *we* were to be wed?"

"Yes, she did, Leonardo."

"Then what happened?"

"Leonardo, for the love of God, you were accused of sodomy," Amerigo said.

"You are a hypocrite."

"And you are also a bastard, Leonardo," Amerigo said softly, without rancor. "Your father is my friend, as you are. But my daughter . . . we are of a very ancient family. There are certain areas of life that would be closed to you."

"So you have done this because I could not be admitted to university?"

"Leonardo . . ."

"I must see Ginevra. I cannot believe she would freely place her neck into such a yolk."

"That is impossible," Amerigo said. "It is done. She is a married woman."

"It could be annulled," Leonardo said. "It *will* be annulled."

"It could not and certainly will not," Nicolini said, standing at the foot of a double stairway that led into the room behind Leonardo. "It has been properly consummated, good sir."

Leonardo stood up and faced him. He trembled, remembering a dream, an image that had so often flashed through his mind: Ginevra struggling, but no match for Nicolini, who crushed her with his weight as he entered her. "Please," Nicolini said, "I have no wish to fight with you; and even if you killed me, Ginevra would not have you, for you would only bring more humiliation to her family."

"I think Ginevra should be the one to tell me that."

"That's impossible!" Amerigo said.

"I think not," Nicolini said. "Perhaps it's time to test her mettle," and he told a servant boy to fetch Ginevra.

"What do you mean?" Amerigo asked Nicolini, obviously upset. He turned to follow the servant, but Nicolini stayed his hand.

When the servant finally returned, he said, "Madonna Ginevra begs your forgiveness, Messer Nicolini, but she is unable to come down at this time."

"Does she know that I am here?" Leonardo asked.

"Yes, Master Leonardo, I told her."

"And she said she would not come down?"

The servant nodded nervously, then took a step backward and turned on his heel.

"Then I think you have your answer," Nicolini said to Leonardo. But his expression, though stern, gave no hint of triumph or gloating.

"That's no answer at all. I must hear that she does not love me from her own lips."

"Leonardo, it is over," Amerigo said. "She is a married woman now. She agreed without coercion: *spontanea, non coacta.*"

"I cannot believe that," Leonardo said.

Nicolini's face colored. "I think this is quite enough. You've been extended more courtesy than you deserve, and that only because of my father-in-law's relationship to your family."

"I did consider him a friend," Leonardo said pointedly.

"I am your friend, Leonardo," Amerigo said. "Circumstances dictated the action. I am so sorry for you . . . but I could do nothing, I assure you."

"I think you've given him his due," Nicolini said.

"I must see Ginevra."

"She doesn't want to see you, Leonardo," Amerigo said.

"Then let her tell me that."

"I think we've had enough," Nicolini said, turning to the side and motioning with his arm. At his command, two burly servants stepped into the room. They had obviously been waiting for his signal and were armed and ready.

"Luigi," Amerigo said to Nicolini, "I don't think it's necessary to—"

But Leonardo drew his rapier, as did Nicolini's guards.

"No!" Amerigo shouted.

"It doesn't matter," Leonardo whispered, talking to himself, feeling the cleansing liquids spurting from his glands into his chest, giving him strength. He no longer felt vulnerable. Even though there were three men to his sword, he no longer cared about death. Grief had lifted him up, resurrected him; and as if this were to be his last breath, he screamed for Ginevra. One of the servants stepped back in surprise, then advanced with the other.

"Leonardo, please sheathe your sword," Amerigo said. "This has gone too far."

"Leonardo, that is quite enough!" It was Ginevra's voice, for she now entered the room. Nicolini and the servants allowed her to pass. She looked haggard and small in the richly worked Moorish-style chemise she wore.

Leonardo embraced her; but she stood stiffly, as if held captive. Nicolini did not interfere.

After a beat Leonardo let her go. "So that is all there is to it?"

She looked down at the parquet floor.

"Why didn't you answer my letters?" Leonardo asked.

Ginevra turned to her father, then said, "I never received them." Her anger was manifest only in the way she looked at her father, and then it passed, as if she had removed only for an instant her calm disguise. Amerigo averted his eyes from his daughter. Turning back to Leonardo, she said, "Nevertheless, Leonardo, it could have made no difference. *La messa del congiuonto* was already said by a priest. I belong to Messer Nicolini. Your letters were sent to a married woman."

"And that was why I withheld them," Amerigo said.

"You believed me guilty?" Leonardo asked.

"No," she said softly. "Never for a moment."

"You could not wait . . . could not give me a chance?"

"No, Leonardo, there were circumstances."

"Ah, yes, circumstances. And you can face me now and tell me that you do not love me?"

"No, I cannot, Leonardo. I do love you," she said stiffly. "But that does not matter."

"Not matter?" Leonardo said. "Not *matter?* That is everything."

"That is nothing," Ginevra said. "You deserve better than what you have been given." She was speaking now for Nicolini's benefit, for she seemed cold, dead, emotionless. "But I made a decision for my family, and I will live up to my obligation." She was resolute. Leonardo had lost her, as surely as if she were in love with Nicolini.

He turned to Nicolini and said, "You stuffed the *tamburo.*"

Nicolini gazed steadily at Leonardo, not denying the accusation.

"Ginevra?" Leonardo asked, taking her arm. "Come with me."

"Now you must leave," Ginevra said, pulling away from him. "Even though your humiliation is my own, I cannot bring more disgrace upon my family. Our wounds will heal, and one day you will understand."

"But you can marry the man who accused me?"

"Leave, Leonardo. I shall never go back on my word to God."

At that, Leonardo lunged at Nicolini with his sword. Nicolini was at the ready and stepped backward, drawing his own. One of his guards slashed at Leonardo from behind; then the other struck him soundly on the side of his head with the corrugated knuckle bow of his rapier.

Leonardo reeled. He felt a thrumming, as if a string on a lute had snapped; and even as he fell, he saw Ginevra's face.

It was stone.

Indeed, everything in his field of vision had become a frieze. And then, as if he had turned his focus and thoughts upon something else, upon another matter, everything disappeared—

Into the darkness that precedes memory.

13

Marzocco

When the lioness defends her young from the hand of the hunter, in order not to be frightened by the spears, she keeps her eyes on the ground, to the end that she may not by her flight leave her young ones prisoners.
—Leonardo da Vinci

On parting from you, I leave you my heart.
—Guillaume de Machaut

By week's end Leonardo's face was still a swollen yellow-and-purple bruise. The skin had been torn by the blow, and the physician who attended Leonardo told him that he would carry a scar from the ordeal: it would be as if some mysterious and profane seal had been stamped upon his face.

After cleansing the wound with wine, the physician sewed the edges together and bandaged it. He did not subscribe to the idea then in fashion that nature would itself close the wound by producing a viscous fluid. He insisted that windows remain closed and warned Amerigo de' Benci's servants that they must not eat leeks or onions, lest they contaminate the air. He prescribed a heavy-smelling poultice of linen soaked with root of peony mixed with oil of roses for Leonardo's headaches; and he returned periodically to inspect and change the bandages. Although the blade of Nicolini's servant had cut deep, it had not injured any vital organs.

And so Leonardo recuperated in the Palazzo de' Benci.

But Ginevra had left to live in Nicolini's castle as his wife.

Leonardo caught fever, and his back burned as if he were lying upon pokers readied in the fire. He dreamed of Sandro and Niccolò, but curiously, not of Ginevra. She was absent from his thoughts; it was as if she had left his dream cathedral for Nicolini's castle. It was as if Leonardo was scourged, not unlike the flagellants who followed the Death in procession, who were claimed from the dead and then resurrected, who spoke with the Virgin and drank with Christ . . . who were emptied of the world, of sickness, of disease, of love and caring and their burning hearts. Indeed, he also dreamed that he was walking through the various rooms of his memory cathedral, but they were dark and empty, each and every one of them, except for one room, a domed room aglow with candles that contained a sarcophagus—his own sarcophagus. There he lay dead, decomposed into wet ashes; but he had a chilling revelation that he had risen as Christ, yet was as empty as a gourd in winter. He dreamed he was floating in a white sea, the waves undulating linen sheets, the buoyant mass of the ocean a feather mattress.

He awakened with a start, choking, his arms flailing, as if he were a man drowning. It was dark. A lamp glowed like a feral eye and gave off an oily odor that mixed with Leonardo's own feverish stink; a single candle burned in a sconce on the wall facing the heavy, hanging tapestries.

Amerigo de' Benci stood before the massive four-poster bed, looking cadaverous, like a wraith. His soft yet strained face revealed the noble features that were brought to perfection in Ginevra: the lidded eyes, full mouth, and curly hair; the elongated and rather flat nose. He sighed in relief and said, "Thank you, blessed Christ." Then he crossed himself.

"I'm thirsty," Leonardo said, his voice muffled.

Amerigo poured him some water from a tumbler on a stand beside the washing tub. "You will be fine, now that you have broken a sweat. The doctors told me so."

Leonardo drank the water and asked, "How long have I been here?"

"More than a fortnight," Amerigo said, taking the glass from him. "I will call your friend Botticelli and young Machiavelli, they are downstairs in the kitchen taking their dinner. They have been at your bedside throughout your fever."

"I would thank you to call them, for I do not wish to stay here," Leonardo whispered. He strained to get up, but became immediately faint and dizzy.

"You were very ill.... We were very worried, Leonardo," Amerigo said, still standing over him, as if eager to talk and reticent to move. "Your father has asked for you."

"Has he been here?" Leonardo asked, surprised.

"No . . . but he was called to Pisa on business for the *podesta*. He is expected to return soon."

Leonardo did not answer.

"Leonardo, it was my fault alone," Amerigo said.

"Enough, Amerigo. It is never anyone's fault . . . alone."

"But I don't want you to blame Ginevra. She begged me to give her to you instead of Nicolini."

"She could have refused," Leonardo said.

"I am her father."

Exhausted, Leonardo turned away from him. Only then did Amerigo say, "No, Leonardo. I am afraid she had no choice."

Leonardo gazed into a basin of water beside his bed: the scar on his face was still a red weal, a stigmata of his folly. He could hear the muffled thudding of hammer and chisel, for Verrocchio's *bottega* was astir with work. The foreman Francesco was working his apprentices in shifts, and Andrea himself rushed about at all hours, never seeming to sleep. There was too much work to do; Andrea's many commissions were as overdue as his unpaid bills. Overtired and covered with dust, he lately looked more like a quarryman than the master of a great *bottega*.

And the days and weeks that were to follow promised even more tumult, for Andrea had taken on three new apprentices and yet another commission from Lorenzo for a terra-cotta relief of the Resurrection.

Niccolò, of course, pronounced the apprentices to be without talent. "Not even the cats are safe from them," he said to Leonardo. "They caught Bianca—the little gray malkin—and dropped her down the stairwell."

"Was the cat harmed?"

"No, but that's not to the point."

Leonardo stirred the water and then ran wet hands through his hair; he could not bear to look at himself. Raising his arms was still painful, straining his back where he was wounded. "Nicco, why are you so upset? They are only young boys, and I'm sure that Signore Francesco will put their idle hands to work soon enough."

Niccolò shrugged.

"Are you worried that you will be sent back because they are here?" Leonardo asked.

"There are three more mouths to feed," Niccolò said.

"Maestro Toscanelli sends Andrea more than enough money to pay for your food and board. I assure you . . . you are safe."

"You have suffered more this time than when you fell from the sky," Niccolò said.

"Since I fell from grace?" Leonardo mumbled; but the irony seemed lost on Niccolò.

"Your face can be repaired. I have made inquiries about the matter."

"You have, indeed," Leonardo said rather caustically.

"Yes," Niccolò said, "and there is a surgeon, a Jew who lives near San Jacopo oltr'Arno, who can remove all manner of deformities. He can work miracles. He can reform flesh as if it were clay."

"And how does he work these miracles?"

Niccolò shrugged. "His apprentice told me that a boy was brought to the surgeon because part of his nose was missing. He was born with this deformity, it seemed; and everyone pitied him because he looked like a monster."

"Niccolò—"

"He effected the shaping of a new nose by cutting open the upper arm and pressing the boy's face against it so that the nose was inserted directly into the wound. He bound the boy so tightly that he could not even move his head; and it remained just so for twenty days. But when he cut the boy's nose away from his arm, some bit of flesh adhered to the nose. He then sculpted the boy's nostrils so skillfully that no one could detect where it had been joined. Now, compared with that, Leonardo, removing your scar would be child's play."

"How do you know of this surgeon?" Leonardo asked, interested. He had never before heard of such a technique.

"Maestro Toscanelli sent me to him on an errand. His name is Isaac Brancas. I remember where he lives, I can—"

"You will do nothing," Leonardo said sharply. "My face will heal as it will."

"But, Leonardo—"

"And if there is a scar, then so be it. It will remind me not to be a stupid ass in the future." Leonardo rubbed at his forehead reflexively: the flesh felt numb and foreign and cold. Just so had his pneuma, his spirit, become as cold as the cloudy, evil-smelling water in his basin. If the chill in his heart and arteries was no cure for his sickness of soul, at least it effectively stopped the pain.

Thus he closed himself to memory.

"Well, Nicco," Leonardo continued, "didn't Sandro say that if he did not arrive by now, then we were to go on without him?" The Marzocco festival had begun; the market would be seething with people. "But his first duty today is to Il Magnifico, who probably had need of him."

Niccolò studied Leonardo for a few seconds and said, "Do you mean that? Would you go without him?"

"You mean would I go with you alone? Of course I would, Nicco. You are as dear a friend to me as Sandro. You are like a son. Have I behaved that badly toward you these past days?"

"No," Niccolò said quickly, looking embarrassed.

"Indeed, I have," Leonardo said, "but that is in the past. I promise you that today you will be the center of my attention. We will charge at the most ferocious of beasts and take our very lives in our hands."

Niccolò nodded. "Have so many men died at Marzocco?"

"Enough," Leonardo said. "If you wish to change your mind, I certainly—"

"No, I wish to go."

"Then I will take you. But, as I know from experience, protecting you from wild animals of every description can be quite a responsibility." Leonardo could not help smiling at his veiled reference to Niccolò's penchant for serving wenches, whores, and scullery maids.

Niccolò laughed, and then his face tightened. "You have frightened all your friends, Leonardo. We worry about you."

"I will be fine," Leonardo said.

"Sandro thinks that you have . . ."

"Have what, Nicco?"

"Poisoned yourself, just as he did with Simonetta."

"And you, Nicco, do you think that, too?"

"No, I think not," Niccolò said.

"Why?"

"Because you seem too . . . angry."

Leonardo thought of Simonetta as he walked with Niccolò to the marketplace, skirting the edges of the Jewish ghetto, passing the *palazzo* of the archbishop. Although he had tried to visit her as soon as his strength returned, he had been politely turned away; her young servant Luca told him that she was sleeping and was in any case too weak to take company. Yet Leonardo knew that she had seen Sandro. Her illness was sapping Sandro's strength, which Leonardo had found, to his surprise, to be considerable.

But he would soon see his friend; and Leonardo bound himself to offer whatever aid he could.

Yet that only masked his anxiety about Simonetta. She was his mirror; he had completely revealed himself only to her. And even though they had seen little of each other, he could not bear to lose her.

Not now, not after Ginevra. . . .

They were nearing the Mercato Vecchio, and the streets became so crowded that they had to detour through alleys. Even today, peddlers stood behind their portable booths and hawked meat and fowl and fruits and vegetables. Their signs were decorated with crudely painted crosses. One vendor was plucking live chickens. Beside him, a heavy, balding woman roasted the fowls on spits over a grease-spluttering fire and sold them over her makeshift counter, along with sweetbreads, fava beans, and honeyed dough. Bouquets of parsley, rosemary, basil, and fennel perfumed the offal-strewn streets. There were live birds and cats and rabbits for sale in cages; one merchant displayed several wolves, for which he was asking an exorbitant price; but he could look forward to selling them, for there would be those who wished to ape the First Citizen and gain public *virtu* by setting their own animals up against each other. On another street were displayed various holy items and all manner of carved animals, especially heraldic lions; these figures were cut from stone, carved out of wood, or made from gold or silver. The ever-prudent goldsmiths were here and had paid soldiers to guard them and their wares.

Leonardo and Niccolò wended their way through labyrinths of piazzas and alleys; houses built from the remains of old towers that had once belonged to noble warlords rose upward like prison walls, all but blotting out the sun. They heard the cries of citizens and the wails of animals before they ever reached the central marketplace. Leonardo took Niccolò's hand so they would not be separated from each other, and they fought their way through the crowds.

They finally reached the perimeter of the Mercato Vecchio. Bordered by four churches at each corner, it had been converted into an arena. The vendors' booths had been hastily boarded up, and huge grandstands erected;

they rose as high as some of the old buildings. Pennons with emblems of the Marzocco and the colors and palle of the Medici flew from the highest points of the constructions, as they did from roofs and towers.

"Look there," Niccolò said, shouting, his face flushed with excitement and fear.

Suddenly, the crowds parted, shrieking. People ran toward Leonardo and Niccolò. The largest wild boars that Leonardo had ever seen charged down the street behind them. The animals had escaped from the arena; they were in the charge of one of the *armeggiatori,* the patronal confraternities. About fifteen liveried youths ran after the boars, chasing them down; by killing them swiftly, they might mitigate the shame they had brought upon themselves and their sponsors.

But the boars were in a dangerous frenzy: half-starved, frightened, foaming at the mouth.

Leonardo kept a firm hold on Niccolò, and they pushed and jostled their way to the side of the street. Someone tried to cuff Niccolò's ears, but Leonardo deflected the blow. "Be calm, Nicco," he said; and then they were pushed backward, as if struck by the crest of a storm wave. Leonardo managed to remain standing and kept his arms around Niccolò, lest the boy be crushed underfoot.

"Leonardo, I can manage," Niccolò said, trying to see over the heads of those before him.

The crowd pushed at them again, and they stayed with it. A boar had gored a child of about ten before one of the *armeggiatori* youths could mortally wound the beast. The beast kept charging into the crowd, even with a spear protruding from its neck. Leonardo caught a glimpse of it, its mouth open, teeth red with its own blood. It swung its great head in one direction and then another, while the boy in livery slashed at it. The beast's grunting sounded so human as to be sinister. Then it went down, cracking its tusk as its snout struck the set stones of the Roman-built street. Another boar fell; a youth with sallow skin slit its throat, then jumped back in revulsion as the beast urinated upon him and defecated in its death-spasm. The other boars, one of them bloodied, charged past. The *armeggiatori* were in pursuit.

Then both boars and *armeggiatori* disappeared, as if swallowed by the streets, and the immediate danger was over.

The news radiated through the crowd. There were shouts of delight. After the gored child was lifted away by two liveried boys and her father, whose face was a hard, sweat-shiny mask of grief, the crowd surged back toward the blood-orgy of death and sacrifice in the Mercato Vecchio.

Niccolò held tightly to Leonardo, and they allowed themselves to be swept toward the arena and the grandstands above. Men armed with lances, and protected inside the movable wooden shells of "tortoises," baited bears while tigers and leopards were loosed and goaded into fighting one another. Disemboweled carcasses stank in the heat of the arena. Indeed, the marketplace had been turned into a charnel house, into a terrible festival reminiscent of Roman times. There were seventy or eighty animals roaming about the arena, watching the crowds, sniffing the intoxicating perfumes of blood, stalking and killing one another. There were fences erected before approaching streets and alleys, and the opening through which the boars had escaped was being repaired by two frightened-looking workers wearing the blue and gold colors of the Pazzi.

"It was Pazzi *armeggiatori* who loosed the boars," Niccolò said. "Do you think it was an accident?"

Leonardo shrugged. "If they had planned to hunt in the street, they would have positioned some men ahead of the boars. And you saw where the fence was broken."

"They might have just decided to board it up. It could have been a barway before it was broken. But I'm sure Sandro will be pleased."

"Why do you say that?" Leonardo asked.

"Because the dishonor falls upon the Pazzi," Niccolò said. "Have you not heard what has been going on?"

"I'm afraid I haven't."

"Pazzi and Medici have been fighting in the streets. The trouble has got worse."

Indeed, Leonardo had been lost to the world. "How so?" he asked uneasily.

"The Holy Church is on the side of the Pazzi. But Sandro says that Lorenzo is blind to it all." Niccolò looked so suddenly crestfallen that Leonardo put his arm around him. Indeed, he was a boy, although he could at times feign perfectly the behavior of a man. Now he seemed fascinated by a large, shaggy animal that stood its ground, waving its head menacingly at all that approached it.

"What is that?" Niccolò asked.

"A buffalo," Leonardo said as he stared sadly at the slaughtered animals that littered the arena like garbage strewn carelessly about. If he could obtain several of those carcasses to dissect and study, it would not be such a waste. But it was dangerous to tarry, for the crowd was screaming for another spectacle, another demonstration; and it was more than likely that they would release boars or tigers and hunt them down through the streets. Thus would the populace be sufficiently thrilled for the moment. Leonardo looked around the makeshift stadium: there were perhaps thirty thousand people here to witness the blood-orgies. Directly ahead, across the open grounds, was the grandstand reserved for the Medici. It was constructed in the form of a castle, complete with waterless moats, bartizans, and mock embattled parapets. Dozens of pennons—red palles and fleurs-de-lis on a gold background—hung limply from the battlements. The air was still and heavy, allowing no escape for the fetid odors of sweat and death.

"Come, Nicco," Leonardo said. "And quickly. It will not be safe here."

Together they had to make their way around the arena. Pushing and occasionally fighting, Leonardo held on to Niccolò. "Look, there," Niccolò said, pointing to a far corner of the arena. An officer of the *podesta* had just given the signal for the lions to be released from a large shuttered cage; and several females padded suspiciously about, protecting the cubs, which still retained the spots they bore at birth. The males followed, their luxuriant manes almost black in contrast to the rest of their lean, tawny bodies. Several men in "tortoises" kept their distances, guarding rather than goading, lest any of the cubs be harmed.

The crowds cheered.

"Keep moving," Leonardo said.

"Did you see the cubs?" Niccolò asked.

"Yes," Leonardo said, "but if any harm comes to them, there will be hell to pay."

"Then you *do* believe in omens, Leonardo."

"No, Nicco, but I do believe in superstitious people; and if they believe that an evil will befall them, they will not rest until they have it."

"I think that is the same thing," Niccolò said.

Leonardo laughed, in spite of himself. But his laughter sounded foreign to him, hollow. Yet he felt vital, as if his flesh and sinew could barely contain the storm breaking inside him. He could hear its soft thunder in his ears, the same thunder he had heard as a child after crying.

"There," Niccolò said, as if inordinately proud of himself. "You see, Leonardo, it is possible to laugh."

"Indeed, it is," Leonardo said, forcing himself to smile at Niccolò and putting his arm around the boy's shoulders. He felt suddenly light-headed, and somehow relieved; yet he was also aware of the tension in his limbs, of the butterflies beating their gossamer wings against the walls of his stomach, for it was that very tension that protected him from his own grief.

"You must try to be your old self," Niccolò said. "That is the Leonardo everyone loves."

"And you?" asked Leonardo.

"What do you mean?"

"Do you love only the old Leonardo and not the one I am now?" Seeing that Niccolò was genuinely flustered, Leonardo said, "I am sorry, Nicco. But the old Leonardo is gone forever."

"Then you will have to learn how to laugh all over again."

"The old Niccolò is also gone," Leonardo said.

Niccolò turned to him, questioning. He stopped amid the crowd, but Leonardo pulled him along.

"Since I have been . . . ill, it seems you have become a man. Would you prefer now to become a child?"

"No, Leonardo," Niccolò said. "But I cannot help it, I miss you."

"I am right here, with you."

But Niccolò did not answer. He pulled forward toward the makeshift Medici castle that was now before them. Soldiers wearing Medici colors and plumed helmets guarded the only access to the ascending benches, which would give a view of the entire marketplace.

"There you are," shouted Zoroastro da Peretola, leaning over the embrasure of a wooden turret. "Antonio," he shouted at one of the guards below, "Maestro Leonardo and his friend are here. Bring them inside without delay. I shall be right down." A guard blinked and then, seeming to recognize Leonardo, led him and the boy into the mock castle. Above them were the galleries, filled to capacity with Medici friends and retainers and hangers-on. The noise was like the roaring of the sea; and Leonardo and Niccolò had to jump out of the way of a stream of urine.

"Is there no place better protected from them?" Leonardo asked the guard, looking upward through the bleachers. He could see a thousand legs and feet; bits of paper and food fell like manna from some unholy heaven.

"One just has'ta keep an eye peeled," he said.

"I want to go up," Niccolò said, a whine in his voice.

From this vantage, Leonardo could see a portion of the arena. A wolf seemed to be staring directly at him, but an instant later it disappeared. The field of vision was narrow, and the roiling dust seemed to scratch the eyes. "We'll just wait a moment for Zoroastro."

"He could have had us brought up to the turret," Niccolò said. "There we could see something of what's going on."

A female lion roared, but could hardly be heard over the crowd. Then she came into view, dragging a struggling wolf by the neck, perhaps the one Leonardo had seen before. She was joined by a full-maned male and two cubs that fed upon the carcass. "There, Niccolò, can you see that?"

But Niccolò looked away, his face pale.

"Leonardo," said Zoroastro, approaching them. He was dressed in dags and doublet, the uniform of the dandy; his face was sallow and seemed shiny with grease or perspiration.

"How did you manage an invitation?" Leonardo asked, making a quick gesture to indicate the castle.

"I *am* a Medici," Zoroastro said, as if put off.

"I would not deny you your birthright," Leonardo said. Could it be that someone in the Medici family actually believed that Zoroastro was a relative through the Rucellai family?

"Thank you. But—"

"Where is Sandro?" Leonardo asked. "Is he above with Lorenzo?"

"No, Leonardo, Il Magnifico asked me to wait for you and deliver a message."

"Il Magnifico?"

"Sandro, then. But I was asked to accompany you to Madonna Simonetta's *palazzo*. She is ill."

Leonardo was heartsick, but maintained his composure. "Niccolò, you may remain here with Zoroastro if you wish."

"But I am to accompany you," Zoroastro said, insisting.

"I wish to go with you, Leonardo," Niccolò said, stepping closer to his master.

Leonardo nodded, then said to Zoroastro, "I would ask you a favor."

"Yes?"

"Sandro had thought that I might obtain a few animal carcasses." Leonardo motioned toward the arena.

"Ah, Niccolò told me about your practice of *autophaneia*—"

Leonardo gave Niccolò a quick and nasty look and said, "I need the carcasses only for dissection, Zoroastro. To study. Science, not magic."

Zoroastro seemed disappointed, but said, "I will see to it that some specimens are collected for you."

"It will not get done unless you oversee it yourself," Leonardo said.

"I am to come with you," Zoroastro insisted.

"Your presence might embarrass Il Magnifico. It is not a good idea, especially as it seems that he is disposed toward you."

"That he is, of course," Zoroastro said pompously.

"Then you will do me this favor?" Leonardo asked.

"It seems I have no choice. But how is it that the presence of your apprentice will not disturb the First Citizen?"

Leonardo did not answer; he saluted his friend and, taking Niccolò by the arm, left the Medici galleries. Once they were well away from the Mercato Vecchio, the litter-strewn streets and twisted alleyways seemed deserted.

"Are you ill, Leonardo?" Niccolò asked. "You look so pale."

"I am fine, Nicco," Leonardo said.

"We can stop and rest." Niccolò pointed out an *archi da bottega* that connected two tall towers; there were two stone benches cut into the narrow, shady passageway below the arch.

"No . . . thank you."

Leonardo sensed that they could lose no time.

Suddenly there was a roar behind them, as if the Arno had been lifted up and then dropped upon Florence, a tidal wave of human cries.

Niccolò started and turned around, but Leonardo only shook his head.

"What is it?" Niccolò asked.

"Perhaps Zoroastro will find me a lion, after all," Leonardo murmured. After a beat he continued, "I would guess that one or more of the marzoccos have been killed."

"That would be a very bad omen."

"Yes, Nicco, a very bad omen. . . ."

"I thought you didn't believe in such things."

But Leonardo did not answer, for his thoughts were focused on Simonetta.

Il Magnifico and his entourage stood nervously outside Simonetta's bedroom, as if they were at the ready to block the way of a deadly, implacable visitor: death. Dim light leaked into the open hall, which was a sort of chambre des galeries, through a series of high, glazed windows; and the very air dancing with dust was but a reflection of the agitation of Simonetta's grieving lovers and admirers. Here were Pico della Mirandola, Angelo Poliziano, Giuliano, Sandro, and the poet and satirist Luigi Pulci, one of Lorenzo's favorites. Other groups of sycophants, friends, and family spoke in hushed tones; some cried; and courtesans, philosophers, poets, and matrons mingled in the stuffy, overheated hall.

A sumptuously dressed priest guarded the door to Simonetta's chamber like a robed Cerberus: one of Lorenzo's own Companions of the Night. He prayed and nervously fingered the black and ruddle beads of his rosary. His lips moved and his gray eyes gazed outward, seemingly unfocused; perhaps he was counting the wounds of Christ, or pondering the favors he might expect from Il Magnifico. Yet he looked directly, and with recognition, at Leonardo when he entered the hall.

Leonardo saw the priest and turned away in humiliation: he had been the captain of the company of Companions of the Night that had arrested him.

Leonardo then bowed to Lorenzo, but the First Citizen turned away from him, as if in anger; and Leonardo became even more anxious and uneasy. He felt awkward, exposed.

Mercifully, Sandro came forward. He patted Niccolò on the shoulder and, embracing Leonardo, whispered, "It seems very bad, my friend." There was a marked quaver in Sandro's voice, and he looked fragile, as if death had grasped him along with Simonetta. "Simonetta is—" But Sandro could not continue.

Leonardo could only nod, as if Sandro had told him everything. When he regained his composure, he led Leonardo away from the others so they could speak privately.

But Niccolò stayed close to his master.

"The physician is with her now," Sandro said. "He won't allow more than one person to be with her at any time. He is administering *Agnus Scythicus*. That is our last hope. Its medicinal virtues are said to be miraculous."

"Like the tusk of the unicorn . . . and as dear," Niccolò said.

"Verily," Sandro said.

"Sandro, why did Il Magnifico turn away from me?" Leonardo asked, trying to mask his anxiety.

"I saw it, too. But I don't know. Perhaps Simonetta has said something to him."

"Perhaps," Leonardo said. "But you, my friend, are you holding up?"

"I am stronger than you give me credit for."

"On the contrary, Sandro, I think you have great reserves."

"You think that because I was infected with Simonetta's *vita nova* . . . because I had to be exorcised—"

"Little Bottle . . ."

"But her spirit flowed from her eyes, from her mouth, like liquid pearls, like smoke from the most fragrant tinder."

"Get hold of yourself, Sandro!" Leonardo said, taking his hand and clasping it, as if to steady his friend. Tears leaked from Sandro's eyes; he wiped them impatiently and grinned at Leonardo. "I am a poor argument."

"But a good friend."

"It is more important that I be her lover," Sandro whispered.

"But that you are."

"I think she was the good friend, Leonardo, who gave herself to me as a doctor gives himself to a patient."

"One might indeed consider himself fortunate to have such a doctor," Leonardo said.

Sandro nodded and smiled. "Enough, perhaps I am too hard on myself. But I cannot stand for her to die, Leonardo. I just cannot—" Then he put his hands to his face, pressing hard, as if to crush his very bones. Leonardo embraced him, drew him toward the wall so that others could not watch, and held him like a child until he could stop sobbing and begin to breathe regularly.

Once composed, Sandro broke away from Leonardo.

The door to Simonetta's bedroom opened, and the physician stepped into the hall; Lorenzo and Pico della Mirandola, who was dressed in the white robe of the theurgist, stepped toward him. They conferred, and then

Lorenzo went to Simonetta. In a moment he returned and motioned for Sandro to go in. Once again Il Magnifico turned away from Leonardo.

After Sandro left, Niccolò said, "Perhaps we should extend our condolences to His Magnificence."

Shaken, Leonardo snapped, "Madonna is not dead yet. Are you in such a hurry, even for death?"

"I'm sorry, Leonardo, I meant no harm. I just thought that perhaps if you talked to him, he would stop scowling at you so."

But Leonardo was gazing toward her chamber door. He thought of Sandro—Sandro, who would collapse without Simonetta.

Indeed, how will we live without you, Simonetta?

Who will love us?

Who will listen to our secrets?

Who now will bring the world to us?

I love you, my sister.

———

When Sandro returned, it was as if he had looked upon the face of Mary herself. He seemed enraptured, even in his ruin, as if grief could be the handmaiden of ecstasy. He walked directly to Leonardo and told him that Simonetta wished to see him.

"Sandro, what happened?" Leonardo asked.

But Sandro did not answer. His eyes welled with tears.

Leonardo entered the sickroom and was met with the cloying, sickly-sweet smell of death. But he found Simonetta sitting up in her large four-poster bed. Her pillows were wet with perspiration, as was her coverlet; and she held a rosary and a crimson linen sudarium in her folded hands. She had been coughing. Although the color of the sudarium masked the moist bloodstains, there was a small spattering of red spittle upon one of her fingers. She smiled at Leonardo and motioned for him to close the door, which he did.

"Come, Leonardo, and sit beside me," she said. "Lorenzo insisted that the physicians administer this . . . fern from Araby. As if any medicine or charm could keep me from eternity." She pointed to a potion in a goblet that rested on the platform of her bed beside a discolored mortar and pestle. "Now I shall be sick to death, even while the angels call me." She smiled, closed her eyes, and shuddered.

Leonardo started.

"Do not worry, sweet friend," she said, once again looking at him, "I am not yet ready."

Leonardo sat down upon the platform, but Simonetta reached out to him and insisted that he lie beside her on the mattress. She wore only a nightdress of white damask brocaded in gold; and her long blond hair was combed and curled and woven with pearls. Her lovely face was emaciated, ravaged by the illness that was taking her life; and the healthy blush upon her cheeks was counterfeit, for she was running a fever.

But it was her eyes that frightened him. Their intensity was that of fire itself; they were reflections of the burning soul that animated her.

"But they are here," Simonetta said as she brushed her fingers over the scar on his forehead.

"Who?" Leonardo asked.

"Why . . . angels. Higher presences. Can't you see them?"

"No, Madonna."

"A pity, for they are beautiful . . . like you, Leonardo. Poor Leonardo." She looked at him, still caressing his face. "Sandro told me everything, as did Ginevra."

"Yes?" Leonardo asked, shocked. "What did she say?"

"I tried to help her, but there was nothing that could be done. Messer Nicolini won. He is a smart and dangerous man. He would have destroyed the Benci family as a matter of honor. Even if he dishonored himself. I discussed him with Lorenzo."

"And what did Lorenzo say?"

"Lorenzo does not wish to disturb the Pazzi, and Nicolini is thick with them." She sighed. "But, then, so is my father-in-law." She stopped talking and stared straight ahead, as if transported. After a time she said, as if speaking to herself, "I have warned Lorenzo that there is danger. From the Pazzi. I have kept their company, and I fear for him. But Lorenzo believes everyone loves him. He is like a child. Leonardo?"

"Yes?"

"Come closer to me." She pulled herself down into the bed, turning toward him as she did so.

"Madonna, what if someone should enter?" Leonardo asked.

"Do not worry. Even the First Citizen respects the dying."

He obeyed her request and lay beside her on the bed. She pressed herself against him, raising and resting her leg over his.

"Madonna . . ."

"Leonardo, do you care for me?" She watched him, and he could feel her trembling in his arms.

"You are my sister."

"And nothing more?"

"I love you, Madonna."

"As I love you, Leonardo. Would you caress me, even in death? For love?" She kissed him.

Her breath was sour, and she smelled of roses.

She opened her gown, revealing herself, and clung to him, pulling him against her until he thought he would suffocate. She cried softly; and then, releasing him, gazed intently at his face, as if she had to memorize his every feature.

Thus would she carry his image with her into the Higher World.

And Leonardo held her as she coughed, then wiped the blood from her lips and chin, from her hand and Lorenzo's ring.

"Leonardo," she whispered, as if too weak to speak, "you must take care of Sandro."

"You need not worry, Madonna," Leonardo said.

"He will do better than you imagine," she said.

"What did you tell him? He seemed so . . . different when he left you."

She smiled. "Perhaps he saw the angels you cannot see." She glanced away from him then, as if, indeed, an angel had alighted beside her.

"Perhaps he did."

"And Leonardo—" she said anxiously.

"Yes, Madonna."

"Promise me that you will also protect Lorenzo, as if he were your own flesh."

Taken aback, Leonardo said, "Madonna, he will not even speak to me. I am afraid I have offended him."

"No, Leonardo, you have not offended him. I did."

"Surely not."

"I told him you were my lover," she said matter-of-factly as she gazed past Leonardo. "He asked me, and I could not refuse him the truth. We agreed never to lie to each other."

Leonardo took a deep breath, then said, "That explains his behavior. He'll never forgive me, for I've betrayed him."

"He will soften to you, Leonardo, I promise. I told him that the seduction was on my part." She laughed softly. "I blamed it on him."

"What?"

"I told him that I was grieving, for he was not paying me enough attention. I told him that I knew he had made love to Bartolomea de' Nasi. He thinks that I have used you to hurt him."

"And he is not angry with you?" Leonardo asked.

"Such is the divine power of love, Leonardo," she said coyly; and just now, looking into her animated face, Leonardo could not imagine that she was near death. For an instant, he dared hope that she would get well.

"But you said that you and Lorenzo agreed never to lie."

"It was not a lie," she said.

Leonardo drew back reflexively.

Simonetta touched his hand and said, "But that does not affect my love for you, Leonardo. I also told Ginevra about us."

"Why would you do that?" Leonardo asked. He was shocked and angry.

"No, Leonardo, do not look at me so. I did it to help her let go of you, for Nicolini set a trap that could not be undone. I did it purely out of love, Leonardo. It would have been impossible for both of you. I . . ."

Then Simonetta's face suddenly became . . . empty.

"Simonetta!" Leonardo called, frightened.

"Yes, Leonardo. I am sorry, but it is difficult to keep my thoughts from wandering. . . ."

"You must get well. I cannot bear to lose you."

She looked at him sadly. "It is Ginevra you could not bear to lose, sweet Leonardo. I am, as you said, your sister."

"I love you."

"But not as I do you," she said.

"Then why did you refuse to see me, even when you allowed Sandro to enter your home?"

"If I saw you, then perhaps I would wish to live."

"I am here now, Madonna."

She smiled. "I have already glimpsed the Empyrean and the Primum Mobile. Truly, Leonardo. I have looked upon the petals of the celestial rose. I have seen the river of light and the saints in heaven. And even now I see the angels and the thrones. Even if you loved me as you do Ginevra, you could not hold me here." She caressed his face, then combed back his curly hair with her fingers. "If you look into my eyes, perhaps you will see the angels too. There, can you see them?"

Leonardo nodded, to accommodate her.

She turned away from him and began to cough; but when Leonardo tried to hold her, she pushed him away. When the coughing subsided, she wiped her mouth; there was blood smeared upon her chin and hand. "I could not ask you to profane yourself," she said. "But when I am soon free of the world, will it be you who takes me to the heaven of Venus, perfect angel?"

"Simonetta—" Leonardo said anxiously.

"Ah, I am mistaken," Simonetta said, touching his face. "You are not an angel." She watched him as if he were a study for a painting. "You are Leonardo . . . and you must leave now."

When Leonardo tried to draw close to her, she shook her head. "Perhaps you are the angel," she said. "Will you promise to do as I asked?"

"Yes, Madonna," Leonardo whispered.

———

Simonetta was carried to the Church of Ognissanti on an open bier. She was dressed in a white, full-sleeved gown. Her hair was braided, yet otherwise unadorned. Her face was powdered and white as ivory. She rested upon a bed of flowers; they formed a heavenly shadow around her. And, indeed, flowers filled the very air like soft confetti. Weeping mourners leaned out their windows and threw torn flower petals as the procession passed below.

Simonetta was a saint being carried by Lorenzo's own *armeggeria,* the sons of the most prominent of Florence's citizens. The handsome youths wore the colors prescribed for mourning: shades of mulberry, green, and brown. As the long procession wound its way through the quiet yet crowded streets, Florence mourned her queen of beauty. Her citizens wailed and rent their garments as if their own daughters or sisters had died.

Leonardo and Niccolò walked beside Sandro and followed Lorenzo's loyal friend Gentile Becchi, Bishop of Arezzo.

But Lorenzo waited inside the dark confines of the church, in deference to his wife, Clarise. He stood before the altar and looked out toward the nave and chancel, past the Corinthian columns and semicircular arches formed out of blue-gray *pietra serena,* the stone of Florence. He wore a dark belted tunic of coarse material; a rash of eczema had broken out on his face, but he had not applied any creams to conceal it.

Leonardo watched the service, yet he felt removed from every voice and prayer and shuffling and whispering. He could hear the constant roar of his own thunder, the sound of his private grief. But there would be no tears. He felt as cold and dead as the blue stones of the church. Like Simonetta, he had found his own release.

Hers was a Primum Mobile of pure, everlasting light.

His was a shadowland of death where love and pain and grief were but observable phenomena, ideas as distant and cold as Plato's perfect forms.

Purgatory.

And as he watched Simonetta, who had been transformed from flesh into marble, he prayed for her and for himself. He prayed that she would indeed ascend. He prayed that her notions of angels and higher beings were true. He prayed that she might miraculously become his Beatrice and lead him away from the dead places of his heart.

For his heart was distant agony. It was Simonetta's, and Ginevra's, but not his own.

Sandro and Niccolò each grasped him by the hand, for, impossibly, he was crying. His chest heaving, his breath choking. Tasting the salt of tears.

And then, the service over, Lorenzo was standing before him. He embraced Sandro and finally looked upon Leonardo.

"She was a good friend to you, Messer *Artista,*" Lorenzo said, his lips pulled back into a slight but cruel smile of irony. "And I am a man of my word. I shall keep my promise to our Madonna, although just now I cannot stand to look upon your face."

Leonardo could only nod; this was not the time to try to bridge the distance between them.

Lorenzo left, taking a crowd of courtiers, friends, and family with him. They were replaced by new admirers come to see the Madonna. The procession of mourners would flow all night like the Arno itself, leaving a shoaling residue of paper and food and crushed flowers upon the marble floor.

Unmindful of the crush of people around him, Leonardo gazed upon Simonetta.

Florence's dream of love.

Now a *pietra serena* of cold flesh.

"Did Simonetta show you her angels?" Leonardo asked Sandro.

"Yes," Sandro said.

"And did you see them?"

"Come, Leonardo. We must leave."

"Did you see them?" Leonardo insisted.

"Yes . . ." Sandro said. "Did you?"

Leonardo shook his head, then finally allowed Sandro and Niccolò to pull him away from the church.

14

Private
Matters

I know one who, having promised me much,
less than my due, being disappointed of his
presumptuous desires, has tried to deprive me of
all my friends; and as he has found them wise
and not pliable to his will, he has menaced me
that, having found means of denouncing me, he
would deprive me of my benefactors . . .

—Leonardo da Vinci

When Simonetta was buried, flames were seen leaping across the clear springtide sky.

Leonardo was a witness to the storm that had suddenly roiled across the heavens, accompanied by blazings of sheet lightning and a sharp, distinctive odor that saturated the air. He was standing at the grave site with Niccolò and Sandro and Pico della Mirandola when drops of rain and hail fell upon the mourners, most of whom were clapping their breasts and invoking the holy presence. Sparkling with the fire of diamonds, the hail lay upon the wet grass and in the tended bushes. It was said that inside each hailstone was trapped the repulsive image of the demons that inhabited the world of nature: salamanders, sylphs, undines, gnomes, beetles, batrachian slugs, vipers, bats, armored saurians, and avian reptiles.

Thus was this squall interpreted by scholars, theurgists, and philosophers alike as a baleful and pernicious omen, a gift from the realms of demons and the living stars. Did not St. Thomas Aquinas himself claim as a dogma of faith that demons can produce wind, storms, and rain of fire from heaven?

Even Pico della Mirandola suggested that malevolent influences were in control of the destinies of men and countries. Had not Il Magnifico been politically compromised by the condottiere Carlo da Montone, who attacked Perugia and threatened the peace of Italy? Was not the First Citizen's relationship with the ambitious Pope Sixtus IV at a breaking point, especially as he steadfastly refused to allow Sixtus' chosen archbishop, Francesco Salviati, to take possession of his see in Florence? Now all of Florence lived in fear of excommunication and war; and the rumor was that the grief-stricken Lorenzo had left the duties of state to his cabinet, to his confidants Giovanni Lanfredini, Bartolomeo Scala, Luigi Pulci, and his wise and politically experienced mother, Lucrezia.

———

Leonardo kept his promises to Simonetta. He looked after Sandro as he did Niccolò, and he tried to make amends with Lorenzo. But the First Citizen would not receive him, would not answer his letters or accept his gifts: his astonishing inventions and contraptions and toys, and a luminous painting that was as perfect a depiction of heaven as mortals could hope to glimpse. Lorenzo would not even allow Sandro to speak his name.

"He will soften," Sandro insisted. "It is his pain that speaks, not he."

But Lorenzo's pain, it seemed, was sharp.

Leonardo lost himself in a frenzy of work; that was his only escape from the terrors within and the dangers without. But he could no longer stand the idea of putting paint to canvas, of reproducing with pigment and turpentine and technique the sweet fleshiness of all that he had lost.

He would not be reminded of Simonetta . . . of Ginevra.

Instead he became obsessed with mathematics and invention and anatomy; when he drew, it was only to render clearly his mechanical ideas or to record the layerings of eviscerated flesh and sinew, for bones and mechanical devices could not trouble him with emotion or influence.

He had fashioned a cold, hollow place for himself. Yet he was outwardly as curious and gregarious as ever. His studio had expanded into hallways and adjoining rooms, to the dismay of the young apprentices who had occupied them. Leonardo's various devices and machines made for dangerous passage, for they were strewn about everywhere, as if a storm had raged indoors. The studio now resembled more a millwright's shop than an artist's *bottega;* here were winches and winding mechanisms, hooked weights hanging from specially designed releasing mechanisms, compasses and other tools of his own invention, cranes, grinders, polishers, treadle-operated lathes and mechanical saws, mechanisms for polishing lenses, and roller-bearing bell mountings. He was fascinated with the transmission of mechanical power, with all manner of gearing mechanisms and pulley systems; and his notes and sketches of valves and springs, flywheels, levers and connecting rods, screws and keys and pins and shafts, were everywhere. Although he had his own de facto apprentices fashioning his machines and models, he would not allow any of Verrocchio's household to clean these rooms, fearing that someone would steal his ideas.

But above his machines, models, tools, books, and scattered notebooks hung a new, albeit incomplete, flying machine. It seemed so light and fragile, as if *fustaneum* and silk and wood and leather could be the stuff of love and happiness.

"Leonardo, come to table," Andrea del Verrocchio shouted impatiently from downstairs.

The sun was low and golden in the sky; the makeshift dining room, which normally functioned as a workshop, seemed dreamlike and hazy, for the slanting rays of light illuminated the dust that floated in the air. A long worktable had been covered with linen and set with knives, plates, cups, and narrow-lipped flasks which held strong wine. The aromas of roast meat, fritters, and open jars of sweetmeats blended with the faint, constant odor of turpentine and the indefinable smell of the quarry, for even now the soft stone of Volterra and Siena was being worked in the outer studios. The noise was felt as well as heard.

"Are you in such a rush to complete your commissions that you work your apprentices without dinner?" Leonardo asked as he entered the room. Only Andrea, his usual retinue of sisters and cousins and nieces and nephews, Lorenzo di Credi, Niccolò, the foreman Francesco, Agnolo di Polo, and Nanni Grosso sat at the table tonight. Agnolo and Nanni were senior apprentices, favorites of Andrea.

"I thought we might have a family dinner," Andrea said, looking uncomfortable. "And yes, Leonardo, I am in a hurry to complete our commissions . . . especially the altarpiece for the good monks of Vallombrosa."

That elicited a nervous laugh from Agnolo di Polo, who was no friend to Leonardo. Although they were alike in temperament, Leonardo was more talented; and Agnolo could not mask his jealousy.

"But that project is going very well," said Lorenzo di Credi, who had been painting the panel of "San Donato and the Tax Collector" for Leonardo.

"Leonardo, have *you* been working on the altarpiece?" Andrea asked. There was an edge to his voice, as if he were angry with Leonardo . . . as if he were goading him.

Leonardo blushed. "I have completed the *predella* of San Donato, except for the head of Eustatius. Our dear Lorenzo di Credi was kind enough to lend his considerable talents to the project while I was preoccupied with my . . . inventions."

"Your responsibility is to the *predella*," Andrea said with uncharacteristic hauteur.

"My responsibility is to our *bottega,* and to you," Leonardo said, reacting and turning the tables.

"What?"

"These inventions are bringing a considerable amount of money into your lap, Maestro. Why would you have me paint, when Lorenzo can do the job as well as I?"

"Because it is not Lorenzo's job," Andrea said. "It is yours. You are senior apprentice."

"And how did you spend today, if not by painting or sculpting?" Agnolo asked Leonardo.

But Leonardo answered him, seemingly without sarcasm. "I was pursuing my studies in anatomy at the hospital, Signore Agnolo. Do you know that if a man is standing with his arm outstretched, it is a little shorter when the palm of the hand is turned downward than when it is turned up? I dissected an arm and counted thirty bones, three in the arm and twenty-seven in the hand. There are two bones between the hand and the elbow. When you turn the hand downward like this"—he gestured with his left hand— "the two bones cross in such a way that the one which is on the outside of the forearm lies obliquely over the inside bone. Now, shouldn't one who works with paint or marble know such things?"

Agnolo frowned and shook his head. He had long, oily black hair and a high forehead. "For what purpose?"

"To paint . . . or sculpt well."

Agnolo reddened and said, "I think *your* purpose is to escape the labor of painting altogether."

Everyone at the table laughed at that.

"I spoke with an old man at the hospital," Leonardo said, directing himself to Andrea. "His skin was hard as parchment, and he complained of weakness and cold. He died a few hours after we had talked; and when I dissected him, I discovered the cause of his cold and weakness and why his voice was so shrill and high-pitched. His trachea, his colon, and all his intestines were shrunken; and there were stones as large as chestnuts in the veins that pass below the collar bone. And a substance resembling dross hung from the veins."

"Uncle Andrea, I think if Maestro Leonardo continues, I shall get sick," said one of Verrocchio's nieces, who was only twelve.

"Well, then you had better fill your plate and take it to another room," Andrea said, his voice gentle. He smiled at her and then signaled Leonardo to continue.

"The arteries were thick and some were closed completely," Leonardo said, as if there had not been an interruption.

"Yes?" Andrea said.

"I believe that elderly people feel cold and weak because the blood can no longer flow freely through the blocked passages. The physicians insist that this is because the blood thickens with age. But they are wrong. They believe they can understand everything by reading *De Medicina* and *De Utilita*."

Andrea nodded, obviously interested; but he said, "Leonardo, I sympathize with such endeavors, but I am afraid you have once again become the object of much talk around the city."

"I am not the only artist studying anatomy in Florence," Leonardo said.

"But it is you who they say does not fear God."

"Who says these things?" Leonardo asked.

"I, for one," said Agnolo.

Leonardo turned to him sharply; but Andrea said, "Agnolo, you will leave the table now."

"But—"

"*Now.*" After Agnolo left, Andrea said, "When we are finished, I would like to have a few words with Leonardo." That was the signal to bring supper to an end; but before anyone could take leave of Andrea, he waved his hand for them to remain seated. "But first I have an announcement. As you are all part of my family"—and he glanced at Leonardo and his foreman, Francesco, as he spoke—"I wanted you to be the first to hear this news."

Francesco leaned forward nervously.

"You all know of my troubles with the Venetians," Andrea continued.

He referred to the equestrian statue of the Venetian condottiere Bartolommeo Colleoni. Verrocchio had been awarded the commission and had already begun work on the armature to cast it in bronze when the Venetians changed their minds and commissioned Vallano da Padova to make the figure. Verrocchio would cast only the horse. When he heard this news, he broke his model, smashing the finely wrought head of the horse to pieces, and left Venice. The Venetians, learning of this, made it known that if he ever returned to Venice, they would cut off his head.

"Well, it now seems that the Venetians have agreed to double my salary if I would return to their city and cast their statue," Andrea said, smiling.

Everyone at the table was surprised, especially Francesco, who asked, "How could this come about? They put you under sentence of death, did they not?"

"Indeed, they did, foreman," Andrea said. "And I responded to their threat. I told them that I would take great care never to return to their foul city, for it could not be doubted that once they cut off a man's head, they would not have the skill to put it back again—certainly not a head as grand and unique as mine!"

Even Francesco smiled at that.

"Furthermore, I told them that *I* would have been able to replace the head of a horse, and with one that was even more beautiful." Andrea shrugged and said, "It seems my answer did not displease them."

"When will you leave?" asked his sister, looking distraught.

"Not for a month, at the least," Andrea said.

"Then we must take time to put in order our various commissions," Francesco said. "We will need to work closely with Leonardo . . . who I presume will be master in your absence."

Andrea looked uncomfortable, as he had before, and said, "Pietro Perugino will be master."

Everyone was caught unaware, dumbstruck.

For a few seconds not a word was spoken, until Francesco broke the spell. "I thought Pietro was in Perugia," Francesco said.

"He will return in this month," Andrea said. "And now if you will excuse Leonardo and me. We have some matters to discuss."

Everyone left but Niccolò, who remained seated beside Leonardo. "Please let me stay, Maestro," he said.

"I think this is a private matter," Andrea said.

"About as private as a hanging," Leonardo said, finally giving vent to his frustration. "Let the boy stay."

"As you wish." Then, after a beat, he said, "Leonardo, I am sorry, but you gave me no choice."

"No choice?"

Andrea leaned back in his chair and looked upward, as if uttering a prayer. "Perhaps if you hadn't been accused of sodomy, if you painted and sculpted according to your rank and training instead of conceiving inventions and machines that people believe to be unholy, perhaps if you stayed away from the booksellers in the Via dei Librai, then I might have a choice. But you cannot even be bothered to be observant of the Christian Church. You have money to buy horses, yet you cannot pay your membership in the painters' confraternity or contribute five soldi on the feast of St. Luke." Andrea's voice became louder as he spoke.

"So you are telling me that you have put Perugino before me because I have not said my five Paters and five Aves every day?"

"I have put him before you because the monks of Vallombrosa will not continue to pay us while you are associated with their altarpiece. They have even asked that all your work be repainted, cleansed, as it were."

"What?"

"And there are other patrons who are displeased with you."

"It is Lorenzo who is behind this," Leonardo said matter-of-factly.

"It does not matter."

"Tell me."

"Everyone in Florence knows of his hatred for you," Andrea said. "What did you do to him, Leonardo? He favored you."

Leonardo just shook his head.

"You have been too busy with your machines to notice what's happening around you," Andrea said.

"My machines sell," Leonardo said. "That would not be possible if Lorenzo had closed his fist . . . completely."

"Indeed they sell. But to whom? To the enemies of the Medici?" After a pause he said, "You are blind, Leonardo."

Leonardo looked down at his hands, which appeared to him then like the hands of the old man he had dissected. They were cold, dead masses connected to his wrists. They felt numb, tingly, as if his heart had ceased pumping blood to his extremities.

"Why did you humiliate me?" he asked Andrea.

"What do you mean?"

"Before you announced that Perugino would replace me, why did you humiliate me with all that bullwash about my not working on the monks' precious *predella*?"

"I was angry. I did not wish to ask Perugino."

"Ah, I should have understood," Leonardo said sarcastically. "That makes complete sense now."

"I was not angry with you, Leonardo. I was angry with myself. But I directed it toward you."

Leonardo did not speak.

"Because I am a coward. I should have stood up to all those who maligned you."

"To Il Magnifico?" Leonardo asked, his manner softening. "No, you are no coward, Maestro. You have a family and other apprentices to consider. Were I in your shoes, I would have to do the same thing."

"Thank you," Andrea said. "You are like a son, and I . . . I am as bad as your father." He blushed. "I'm sorry, forgive me. I didn't mean to say such a thing. Ser Piero da Vinci is my friend. I can't imagine—"

But their eyes met, and they both began to laugh. Bemused, Niccolò smiled.

"What will you do, Leonardo?" Andrea asked.

"I shall look for a house."

"Perhaps it is time. You should have your own *bottega*."

"A painter who cannot gain commissions has no need for his own *bottega*."

"Your fortune will change. You are too good a painter to be long without commissions. In the meantime, sell your clattering machines."

"To Pazzi sympathizers?"

Andrea shrugged. "Perhaps I can interest the Venetians in your talents."

"Perhaps," Leonardo said.

They lapsed into silence and regret.

"Leonardo, what about me?" Niccolò asked, impatient with the awkward moment.

"Andrea?" asked Leonardo.

"That decision is Maestro Toscanelli's alone," Verrocchio said.

Niccolò nodded, then stared at the floor as if he were trying to burn a hole between his feet.

15

The Magic
Mirror

He who understands the relationship of the
parts of the universe is truly wise; he can derive
profit from the higher beings by capturing, by
means of sounds *(phonas)*, substances *(hylas)*,
and forms *(schemata)*, the presence of those who
are far away.

—Synesius, *De Somniis*

—that is, "Do you not see the brilliant light
which comes out of the sepulchre of the
Prophet?"

—Ludovico di Varthema, *Travels*

L eonardo moved into the narrow, run-down house that Zoroastro had found for him. Its ancient red bricks were soft and crumbly and had probably been removed from the rubble of a demolished tower that had been torn down "for the greater public security" when the people took control of the Signoria and the state in 1250. The old, fortified private towers had once been the focus of the deadly feuds between the Guelf and Ghibelline parties.

The rent was extraordinarily cheap, as well it should be, given the condition of the house. But as if in consolation, the high-ceilinged rooms kept the light well; and there was a view, albeit a restricted one, of the Arno. This was to be the *bottega* da Vinci, the new workshop where Leonardo was to create the mechanical miracles of which he had boasted.

Coincidentally, it was located near the Ponte Vecchio.

Leonardo's old master would be his neighbor.

Niccolò had been visiting Maestro Paolo del Pozzo Toscanelli every day with Zoroastro, who relished making influential connections. Indeed, Toscanelli's *bottega* was a salon for artists, travelers, eminent scholars, and the new generation of intellectuals, who were in rebellion against the old-line scholastics.

"You have been summoned," Zoroastro said as he entered Leonardo's private third-story studio without knocking. Niccolò was behind him, but would not pass beyond the threshold of the door. Leonardo had been sitting before a canvas and painting, as if in reverie. Caught by surprise, he started; and his brush skipped, blurring the details of the taut, agonized face of St. Jerome. Here, given flesh, as it were, in the form of a painting, Leonardo expressed his revulsion and bitterness at life. He modeled the saint on the old man he had dissected at the hospital: here the sunken chest, the muscled shoulder, the thin neck and fleshless cheeks. A roaring lion lay at the feet of the suffering saint. All was agony and immolation.

It was a self-portrait . . . a manifestation of his own grief.

"Well, so you have finally decided to take up the brush again," Zoroastro said, looking disdainfully at the painting. "But after all your lovely Madonnas, this is hardly what I would have expected. Is it a commission?" Zoroastro was dressed like a peacock in particolored silks.

Leonardo blushed with embarrassment, feeling unmasked. "Why have you broken into my room without even a knock?" he asked coldly. "And who has summoned me?"

"It is not exactly a summons, Leonardo," Niccolò said. "But Maestro pagholo Medicho has asked for you." Toscanelli allowed only his favorites to call him by this personal title. "After all, you have neglected him all these weeks."

"It is impossible to neglect the maestro," Leonardo said. "He is in constant company."

"Nevertheless, he requires yours," Zoroastro said.

"I am not yet ready for society. If I were, I would not need your services to sell my inventions. And you would not be stealing me blind and wearing rich and tasteless clothes."

Zoroastro did not seem irked. He bowed and said, "But if it were not for my services, which you so handily disparage, you would not have this fine house in which to work, your own apprentices, money, nor a woman to cook your meals."

Leonardo smiled and shook his head.

"There, you see?" Zoroastro said. "I am right. So please remove your smock and get dressed, for Maestro Toscanelli has guests who wish to meet you." It was plain that he was excited with anticipation.

"Nicco, please extend my apologies."

"He told me to tell you that the man who lent you the book about the secret of the flower is here," Niccolò said. "The one called Go On He Sees."

"Ah, Kuan Yin-hsi," Leonardo said. "So he has returned."

"We're wasting time," Zoroastro said. "We do not honor Maestro pagholo by being late."

"Zoroastro, were you invited to the maestro's party?" Leonardo asked.

"We are *all* invited," Zoroastro said testily.

Leonardo chuckled. "So he won't let you in without me, is that it, Zoroastro? Maestro pagholo would have made a fine shopkeeper."

"What do you mean?" Niccolò asked.

"He knows his customers. He knows full well that our friend and associate will not rest unless he is admitted to the maestro's inner sanctum. Neither will he give me any rest."

Zoroastro seemed to radiate cold anger; he walked to the door. "Don't be so sure of yourself, Maestro *Artista*," he said. There was a quaver in his voice, which was barely more than a whisper. "It will not always be so easy for you to demean me, or to take the credit for inventions that are as much mine as yours."

Surprised, Leonardo looked at Zoroastro. Surely he could not take himself so seriously.

"Maestro pagholo also told me to tell you that a sultan has traveled the distance of a world to see you," Niccolò said to Leonardo.

"He told *you* that?" Zoroastro asked Niccolò. "If Maestro Toscanelli needs to confide in a child, then he can do without my presence altogether." With that he left the room.

Leonardo gazed at the agonized figure of St. Jerome in the painted darkness before him, as if Zoroastro and Niccolò had been only temporary distractions; and he smiled at the painting, as if it were an intimate joke. In the background were the stratified rocks of the grotto behind his mother's house in the valley of the Bonchio. For an instant he could actually smell the mustiness of damp soil and the sweet medicines of blackberries and sage and thyme and mint. He had been happy there as a child in that cool, sweating stone haven.

"Come, Niccolò," he said, finally breaking his reverie. "I'm sure Zoroastro has suffered enough privation."

"Maestro pagholo also requested that we bring Tista," Niccolò said. Although Tista was just a boy, Verrocchio had allowed him to go with Leonardo as an apprentice.

"Whatever for?"

Niccolò could only shrug.

"Did *you* have something to do with this?"

"No, Leonardo. Upon my word."

———

Leonardo, Niccolò, Tista, and Zoroastro arrived at Toscanelli's with only moments to spare.

It was not yet dark, yet Il Magnifico's curfew was already in effect. Although no swords were drawn, nor cannons fired, Florence was under siege.

It was as if *fortuna* had turned away from the city of fortune. Convinced that Lorenzo was in league with Carlo Fortebraccio—the condottiere who had attacked papal territories in Perugia—Pope Sixtus IV now openly conspired against Florence. There were also rumors circulating that King Ferrante of Naples had given his blessing to Florentine exiles in Ferrara to assassinate Lorenzo. The same kind of rumors came from Milan, or so reported Lorenzo's trusted adviser, Giovanni Tornabuoni. And now that the Pazzi had allied themselves with the Pope, intrigue was near.

"Come in, Leonardo, you're late," Amerigo Vespucci said nervously as he swung open the front door of Toscanelli's *bottega*. At that instant, three black-robed Companions of the Night came around the corner.

"Stop, there," shouted one of the armed priests.

"They have been called here by Maestro Toscanelli himself, Venerable Eminences," Amerigo said to the priest-soldiers. The older of the soldiers nodded and took his hand from his sword's hilt. By then all of Leonardo's party was inside the house. They stood in a small courtyard; in the dim light the regularity of round-arched windows and thin columns gave the effect of height.

Leonardo embraced Amerigo. "Why did *you* wait for us?" Leonardo asked. "Certainly this is a job for a servant."

"Not when you choose to arrive after curfew," Amerigo said.

"Ah, any one of us could have talked to the Companions," Leonardo said. "Even Zoroastro here." For all of Leonardo's reticence at venturing outside his *bottega,* he felt comfortable now, even reckless. What did anything matter? Perhaps this would be a good night to get drunk. He could be sick in the morning and get back to work in the afternoon. He laughed at himself; and Niccolò, looking worried, frowned at him.

"I think I've been the butt of Leonardo's humor long enough," Zoroastro said to Amerigo, and turned to venture back into the streets alone.

Leonardo grabbed Zoroastro by the arm, pulling him back. He realized that he should never have ridiculed Zoroastro before Amerigo, whom Zoroastro desperately wished to impress. "I'm sorry, Zoroastro," Leonardo said. "I've behaved badly . . . please forgive me. It's entirely the fault of my bad humor. Come, we'll go up together." Leonardo nodded to Amerigo to lead the way.

"The Companions arrested and beat the nephew of Sigismondo della Stufa last night," Amerigo said, as if to delay their going upstairs. "They found him this morning, still unconscious. It seems that no one is safe on the streets now, not even those under Medici protection."

"We're all safe here," Leonardo said. "Now, come on, Amerigo, and introduce us to Maestro pagholo's guests."

"Just go on up," Amerigo said. "I will follow in a few minutes."

"So you are still the shy one," Leonardo said. "Come with us, keep us company. You have always been the smartest of Maestro pagholo's apprentices."

Amerigo smiled wanly. "But still uncomfortable with my betters." Nevertheless, he led the way, and Leonardo allowed the sulking Zoroastro to walk ahead of him.

When they entered the salon on the second floor, Toscanelli was standing and holding forth to his company. His back was to Leonardo, who stood on the top step of the narrow staircase. Toscanelli displayed an energy that was seldom seen outside his *bottega.* His audience, rapt with attention, was seated on cushioned chairs. Benedetto Dei and Pico della Mirandola smiled at Leonardo; and Kuan Yin-hsi, dressed in sumptuous robes and a cylindrical cap of the Chinese fashion, nodded. Benedetto and Pico were smoking wooden pipes that looked to be five feet long and were wrapped in colored silk and tied with golden thread. Attendants wearing caftans and turbans knelt beside them, damping and fussing with the pipes.

Seated in the place of honor was the man whom Simonetta had once pointed out as the lieutenant of the sacred Caliph of Babylon: the Devatdar of Syria. Armed attendants stood beside him, as did several women of light and dark complexions wearing rose-colored gowns, silk headdresses, and ornamented veils that only accentuated the beauty of their almond-shaped eyes. The Devatdar fixed Leonardo with his own piercing gaze, as if evaluating him.

There were others seated there, wealthy, venerable-looking Italians; but they paled beside the sumptuously dressed Devatdar and his attendants.

"Leonardo," Toscanelli said, turning around. "Greetings." He then proceeded to introduce Leonardo to the Devatdar Dimurdash al-Kaitì, who bowed his head slightly and said, "So you are Leonardo da Vinci." He spoke Italian very well, without accent. Smiling, revealing beautifully even teeth, he said, "I think I've come to know you quite well, Maestro Leonardo. Yes, quite well. . . ."

"I'm afraid you have the advantage of me," Leonardo said.

"Indeed, I do," the Devatdar said, standing up, as if to give up his own chair to Leonardo. He was a formidable figure with deep-set eyes, full lips, shaved cheeks, and a black mustache and beard. Those of the Devatdar's entourage of turbaned officers and veiled ladies who were seated beside and around him stood up, as if every chair needed to be relinquished for Leonardo, Niccolò, and Tista.

Toscanelli took advantage of the awkward moment to introduce Leonardo and Niccolò to his other guests; he seemed particularly anxious for Leonardo to make the acquaintance of his Genoese protégé, Christoforo Columbus, and Benedetto d'Abbaco, the engineer who was called Aritmetico.

When Leonardo, Toscanelli, and the Devatdar finally sat down together, Toscanelli sighed; it was as if his performance for the Devatdar had exhausted him. He wiped his large nose and gazed at Leonardo, his eyes soft, in direct contrast to the Devatdar's.

"Leonardo, I took the liberty of showing His Excellency certain of your inventions . . . and your letter to Il Magnifico."

"I found it most interesting, Maestro Leonardo," the Devatdar said.

"What are you talking about, Maestro pagholo?" Leonardo asked.

"Your secrets of warfare, your armored cars and exploding arrows; your machines that can fly and drop bombards upon the enemy to kill and induce stupor," said the Devatdar. "Ah, yes, Maestro Leonardo. It is a most interesting letter. And if, indeed, you could actually do such things, it would be even more interesting."

"But how did it come into *your* hands?" Leonardo anxiously asked Toscanelli, ignoring the Devatdar's remark.

"You must blame me, Leonardo," Pico della Mirandola said. His voice was slightly slurred; and Leonardo noticed that his usually pale face was flushed. "I knew of your letter and told Maestro pagholo about it. The Maestro asked to look at it."

"And Lorenzo?" Leonardo asked.

"He thinks of you as a painter, Leonardo. He cannot conceive of you as an engineer."

"But he knows of my inventions."

Pico laughed. "He is Lorenzo. He chooses whatever he wishes to know and to see. And since the death of Madonna Simonetta . . ."

"Leonardo . . . Pico," Toscanelli said. "You are being rude to our honored guests."

"Not at all," said the Devatdar. "I can see that Maestro Leonardo is displeased, and I apologize for any discomfort caused on my account. A'isheh!"

A veiled woman whispered over to him. She wore a long vest cut so as to leave half her ample bosom uncovered. Three bluish circles were tattooed between her breasts; and her fingers, long and graceful, were stained red with henna. She wore a headdress and her eyes were outlined with kohl. Although her face could not be seen—only her dark, luminous eyes—Leonardo imagined her as being beautiful.

The Devatdar spoke to her in Arabic and nodded toward Leonardo. "Maestro Toscanelli was kind enough to permit me to entertain him and his guests," the Devatdar said. "I insisted on being allowed to return some of the favor which he bestows upon me and my retinue every time we visit your lovely city. So you must taste some of our coffee from El-Ladikeeyeh flavored with ambergris, and drink in the smoke from our pipes."

"It is intoxicating," Pico said. Leonardo realized that his friend was drunk. The man sitting beside Mirandola, who had been introduced as Christoforo Columbus, also seemed bousy; his cheeks were flushed.

"We call it hasheesh," said the Devatdar. "I have often seen Jinn out of the corners of my eyes when the smoke has filled my lungs. Can you see them?"

"Not yet," Christoforo said, his head bobbing slightly. "But it is just dusk. Perhaps they need some shadows in which to dwell." Although he was Genoese by birth, Columbus spoke Italian with a Spanish accent. He seemed about the same age as Leonardo, and was short and muscular and thick-featured. "And you, Maestro Leonardo, have you ever seen Jinn?"

Leonardo reluctantly accepted the pipe and coffee from the woman A'isheh, who stepped between him and Columbus. She pressed a warm cup of coffee into his hand and held a taper to the bowl of his pipe; only then did she step aside.

Leonardo inhaled the resinous smoke, which made him gag. Out of politeness, he pulled again on the amber and enameled gold mouthpiece of the pipe. He did not feel his senses change, but felt suddenly warm; and the warm spot in his chest seemed to be expanding. . . .

As if *he* were expanding.

"Well, Maestro Leonardo?" asked Christoforo, insisting.

"If I have, I would not know," Leonardo said. "Pray tell me what they are."

"Have you not read the *Murooj al-Dhahah,* Maestro?" Christoforo asked.

"He refers to a book that contains a thousand and one stories, Maestro Leonardo," the Devatdar said. "The tales are very ancient. You'll find Jinn described there. But Messer Christoforo should have pointed you toward the holy Kur-án." That was spoken in such a way as to be obviously a gibe directed at Columbus. "The Prophet teaches us that Jinn are created from fire. They are a separate species, as are men, angels, and devils. They assume different shapes, human shapes"—and at that he looked at Christoforo, as if, indeed, he were one of them—"and they can appear . . . and disappear."

"Maestro Toscanelli led me to believe that your understanding knows no bounds," Christoforo said. "I am surprised that you could be ignorant of—"

"Christoforo!" Toscanelli said. "Now it is you who is being rude." Then to Leonardo he said, "My young friend is used to the banter of seamen. He has just returned a hero. His ship caught fire in a pitched battle off Cape St. Vincent, and he swam to safety in Portugal."

"But a hero to whom?" asked Kuan Yin-hsi. "He fought on the side of the Portuguese against his own country of Genoa."

"Does that trouble you?" Christoforo asked Kuan Yin-hsi; but Kuan merely gazed directly at him, as if he were watching an interesting yet nevertheless natural phenomenon, such as an eclipse of the sun. "I have been selected by God for a divine mission that transcends governments and politics."

"And what might that be?" Kuan asked.

"To discover the ends of the world; and neither reason, nor mathematics, nor maps will be of any use to me."

"What *is* of use to you, then?" asked Kuan, who seemed genuinely amused.

"Prophecy," Christoforo said matter-of-factly. "If you need proof of my destiny, you can find it in Isaiah and the first book of Esdras."

Niccolò leaned over to Leonardo and said, "This man is crazy."

"Hush," Leonardo said.

"A'isheh," Niccolò called in a low voice to the woman who had prepared Leonardo's pipe. She turned to him, and he asked for a pipe.

"No, Niccolò, absolutely not," Leonardo said.

"Will you still treat me as a child?"

"I'm not treating you as a child," Leonardo said. "But ..." He felt empty, hollowed out, and his thoughts felt thick, resinous. The hasheesh was coursing through him, coating and slowing his pneuma and blood, dissolving them into smoke.

A'isheh said something to the Devatdar in Arabic, and he, in turn, spoke directly to Niccolò. "Yes, son, of course you may drink up as much smoke and as much coffee as you like. But your young friend Tista may not taste anything but food, for we have a special use for him."

As the Devatdar's servant prepared the pipe for Niccolò, Leonardo looked at the Devatdar. "Maestro pagholo," Leonardo said as he rose to address Toscanelli.

But the Devatdar leaned toward Leonardo and said, "Do not worry about your young charge, Maestro. He will inhale nothing but strong tobacco."

Just then Niccolò began coughing on the smoke. A few of the turbaned men laughed and called to each other in Arabic; Niccolò's face burned red with humiliation. He stared at the floor, and Leonardo sat down beside him and patted his shoulder. "It made me gag, too," he said softly. "Terrible stuff, isn't it?" Leonardo felt as if his insides were sliding together, yet his vision seemed unusually acute.

"Is your young friend ready?" asked the Devatdar.

"Niccolò, he's talking to you," Leonardo said.

Niccolò turned to Tista, who nodded. "Yes. But what should he be ready for, Shaykh Devatdar?"

"Aha, young man, that you shall find out soon enough." He stood up, as did all his retainers, then drew Tista into the next room, where a stand was prepared with a chafing dish filled with coals and aromatic substances. The Devatdar nodded to A'isheh, who lit the coals. Meanwhile he scribbled with a pen upon a sheet of paper, which he then tore into strips.

In a few moments the room was filled with smoke and the thick scents of frankincense and coriander seed.

Leonardo was having difficulty breathing, and he wondered what other herbs and potions he might be inhaling. He felt constricted. All his senses seemed heightened; he listened to every whisper and breath, smelled every strain of perfume and perspiration, and watched the shadows assume human shapes.

Jinn ...

Tista began coughing, for he was standing beside the chafing dish. When his spasm was over, the Devatdar said, "My dear friend Maestro Toscanelli has informed me that several important items have been stolen from his studio, including a precious brass astrolabe. I promised to provide a demonstration of true magick to discover the identity of the thief. After all, it is the least I can do for my host." He looked at Toscanelli, smiled, and bowed. "Maestro pagholo is *not* a believer . . . yet."

Leonardo glanced around the room. Toscanelli's many servants and apprentices were standing about.

"For what purpose do you need Maestro Andrea's apprentice?" asked Pico della Mirandola.

"I am the apprentice of Leonardo da Vinci," said Tista.

"My mistake," Pico said, bowing to the child.

"In order for the experiment to be successful," the Devatdar said, "I need a boy not yet arrived at puberty, or a virgin, or a pregnant woman. Are there any virgins or pregnant women here?" he asked. "I thought not. Master Niccolò was kind enough to bring his young friend . . . Tista! Now, if anyone has an objection . . ."

"Go ahead," Toscanelli said. "Any objections can be easily raised after your demonstration."

The Devatdar told Tista to sit down in the chair that had been prepared for him. As A'isheh stirred up the coals in the chafing dish and added more incense, he took the boy's hand and drew a square upon his palm. In the center of the square he poured enough ink to form a tiny pool. Still holding his hand, the Devatdar asked, "Tista, can you see your face reflected in the mirror of ink?"

"Yes, Magnificence." Tista was shaking.

"You must not raise your head, you must not cough, you must look into the mirror. Is that clear?"

"Yes. . . ."

The Devatdar then began dropping the strips of paper he had prepared onto the coals in the chafing dish. They burst into flame and gave off a noxious odor. He mumbled an incantation over and over. Leonardo could make out only the words "Tarshun" and "Taryooshun." Then the Devatdar threw all the strips of paper upon the coals and waved his hand over the pouring smoke, which wafted directly into Tista's face.

Leonardo gagged, for the smoke seemed to fill the room anew. He drew breath cautiously, slowly. The perfumes of incense had vanished. Now the odors were evil, foul, unmasked. He felt as if he were dreaming. Indeed, now the shadows might well dance and shift and transform themselves into spirits clean and unclean.

"Do not fret, Leonardo," whispered a voice behind him. "Your head will soon clear. I have seen the Devatdar perform this magick before. He's encouraging his Jinn to aid him. He professes that they are clean spirits, but sometimes admits they are not."

Leonardo turned to find Kuan Yin-hsi.

"Did you read the book I left you?" Kuan asked.

"Yes," Leonardo said.

"And do you remember our conversation about the present of things future and Santo Augustine?"

"Yes. . . ."

"Then watch the Devatdar's trick. It is but a demonstration of memory."

"Do you see your face now in the mirror of ink?" asked the Devatdar.

"No," Tista said, trembling.

"Tell us, then, what you do see."

"I see light. Very bright."

"And where does it come from?"

"From a tomb," said Tista.

"And where is this tomb?"

"In a building. Far away."

"Is it the tomb of the Prophet?" asked the Devatdar.

"Yes."

"What is this tomb made of?"

"I don't know."

"Does it float?"

"No," said Tista, his head nodding slightly as he looked into his palm, which was still held tightly by the Devatdar.

"He's testing the boy," whispered Kuan to Leonardo, "for many believe that the coffin of the Prophet is constructed of metal and hangs suspended in the air."

"How—"

"By virtue of magnets."

"He's leading Tista," Leonardo said.

"What else do you see?" the Devatdar asked Tista.

"I see a man, an old man. He is dressed like you. In green."

The Devatdar was wearing a striped silk vest, caftan, and a green turban, which signified that he was a descendant of the Prophet, Mohammed.

"Is he a holy man?"

Tista nodded.

"What does he tell you?"

Tista jerked away, but the Devatdar held his hand still.

"I think this is enough," Leonardo said.

"He is in no danger," Kuan said. "Give the shaykh a bit more time."

Niccolò was now standing beside Leonardo; he grasped for his hand and held it tightly.

"Tista . . . answer me," the Devatdar said.

Tista began mumbling, then in a kind of singsong ululation, he said, "Lalalailalalla illala lala illala. . . ."

"Are you saying, *La ilah illa Allah*?"

The boy nodded.

"Do you know what you say?"

"No, Shaykh."

The Devatdar spoke to everyone in the room. "The boy recites the first article of faith of El-Islám. *La ilah illa Allah*. There is no God but God."

Everyone began to talk at once. The Devatdar raised his arm, and the room was silent.

"Now, Tista, sit down before the holy man," the Devatdar said. "Are you sitting?"

Tista nodded. Although his head was bowed, as if he were staring into the pool of ink in his hand, his eyes were closed.

"He will know who stole the astrolabe from Maestro Toscanelli. He will also know what else was taken from the maestro. Ask him." After a pause the Devatdar said, "Well?"

"A florin and other coins have been stolen . . . silver *fiorini*. I don't know how many. Also a magnification glass."

"I was looking for that," Toscanelli said. "I thought I had misplaced it."

"Now tell us who took these things," the Devatdar said.

Again Tista did not respond. Slumped over in his chair, he seemed asleep.

"Tista, answer me directly."

"I don't know."

"Can you still see the holy man?"

"Yes."

"Ask him. He will help you." After a pause the Devatdar said, "Well?"

Tista then haltingly gave a general description that could have fit any one of the apprentices nervously standing about.

Leonardo shook his head, but Kuan touched him lightly on the shoulder and said, "Patience, my friend. Although perhaps this time you will be right. Sometimes these magicks do not work."

"What else do you see?" asked the Devatdar.

"I see only the man. I told you what he said, that is all."

"Ask him again, it is not enough. Well? Tista, ask!"

"He says the boy has a black tooth. The boy carries a jug and a rope."

Tista opened his eyes then, and the Devatdar said, "Keep looking into the mirror. Do not move your head, not yet." Then he asked Toscanelli, "Does the boy's description fit any of your apprentices?"

"No," Toscanelli said. "But I know who it is."

"Well?" asked the Devatdar.

"He is not in this room. He is an apprentice of Matteo Michiel and often brings me tools and instruments."

"How could you know that from what Tista has told you?" Leonardo asked, an edge to his voice.

"All jug and well-rope makers are under Matteo's jurisdiction, and Tista described the boy as carrying a jug and a rope." Toscanelli shrugged. "And the boy has a black tooth." Turning to an apprentice who stood near the door, he asked, "Ugo, isn't he a friend of yours?"

"Yes, Maestro," the young apprentice said.

"Well, do you know anything about this?"

"No, Maestro . . . except that he has run away from his master. That is all I know, upon the blood of Christ that is the truth." His breathing was ragged; he was in a panic. "I would not steal from you, Maestro. Please believe that."

"Yes, I believe you," Toscanelli said. "Do not fret."

"Does anyone wish news of any person, living or dead?" asked the Devatdar.

Benedetto d'Abbaco asked about his father. Tista described in detail a man in a curious posture: hands pressed against his head; one foot raised and the other on the ground, as if he were getting up from a chair.

"Yes," Benedetto said excitedly. "He has headaches and holds his head exactly so. And he has a stiff knee. He fell from a horse when he was a child."

The Devatdar asked Toscanelli if he had a question for Tista.

"I think the boy has had enough," Toscanelli said.

"Yes, of course," the Devatdar said. "But before his vision dims, perhaps Maestro Leonardo has a question to put to the boy." He looked at Leonardo, challenging him.

Simonetta, Leonardo thought.

"Ser, did you hear me?" asked the Devatdar.

"I have no questions for my apprentice, who seems to be asleep."

"I assure you that is not the case," the Devatdar said. "Tista, can you hear me?"

"Yes."

"Think about Leonardo, your maestro. What do you see in the mirror?"

Tista jolted, his eyes widened as he stared into his palm held steady by the Devatdar. Once again the boy seemed frightened.

"What do you see?" the Devatdar asked.

"It is dim."

"Soon enough, it will dim. But it is not dim yet. What do you see?"

"Fire. It is all around you, Leonardo." He was shouting. "And someone else. Someone else is there." Then Tista pulled himself away from the

Devatdar, shaking his hand loose. He stood up, his eyes wide, and stepped backward. "I'm falling!" he screamed, flailing his arms. "Help me!"

Leonardo rushed toward the boy and held him until he quieted down. After a few seconds Tista looked around, as if he had just awakened. He seemed puzzled.

"What did you see?" the Devatdar asked. "Why were you falling . . . ? From where—"

"I think that is quite enough," Leonardo said angrily, pulling the boy away from the Devatdar. "You should never have allowed this, Maestro pagholo," he said to Toscanelli.

The Devatdar bowed his head and apologized to Leonardo, yet nevertheless pressed Tista to describe what he saw. "Surely you remember the mirror," the Devatdar said. "You must concentrate." He seemed genuinely concerned.

Tista looked dazedly at Leonardo.

"Leonardo, I know of no mirror."

———◆———

The Devatdar had been waiting for Leonardo in Toscanelli's private quarters upstairs. He sat at a long table covered with maps and charts.

"Please accept my sincere apologies, Maestro Leonardo," he said, putting down a map decorated with strange animals and monsters. "I did not mean to upset your apprentice. But I've never seen anyone react so to the mirror. Although he claims that he cannot remember, the boy saw something. I would watch him carefully, lest he come to harm. . . ."

Leonardo stood in the doorway, feeling uncomfortable. "What do you think he saw?"

The Devatdar shrugged. "The future, no doubt."

Leonardo nodded respectfully.

"But that is not why we meet here," the Devatdar continued. He gestured for Leonardo to sit beside him, which he did. "I have a proposition for you."

"Yes?" Leonardo asked.

"Can you do all you say in your letter to Il Magnifico? Can you build such machines of warfare? Or was that mere boasting?"

"It is all true."

"Then I might have work for you, if you are willing to travel and can stomach adventure." He paused, then said, "I need a military engineer. Maestro Toscanelli tells me you would be interested in such a position."

"No," Leonardo said. "He is mistaken. My work and my life are here. I could not leave, not now."

The Devatdar shrugged. "We are waging war with a renegade who has invaded our frontier provinces. We are able to pay well . . . and provide you with all the money, men, and tools necessary to build your bombards and flying machines."

"And who is this invader?" Leonardo asked.

"One of the sons of the Grand Turk Mehmed, who is the common enemy of Christian and Arab alike. His son's name is Mustafà. Surely you know of *him*."

Leonardo shook his head slightly; he was sure that the Devatdar was mocking him. "And where is this war?"

"In what you call Cilicia. But it might more aptly be called a skirmish. You might consider this to be a test, of sorts."

"And if I pass?"

"You might come to command more men and power than your own prince Lorenzo," the Devatdar said. "But first you would have to make a decision." Leonardo didn't take the bait; he gazed steadily at the Devatdar. "You would have to quit this place where you have tasted humiliation. . . ."

16

The

Conspiracies

of Fate

Men will walk and not stir, they will speak to those who are not present, and hear those who do not speak.

—Leonardo da Vinci

We are all in arrears to death.

—Simonides

I t was an extraordinary cold winter. The Arno froze into glass, and bonfires could be seen down its length every night, as if it were a Roman roadway. It was also a lean time for Leonardo, for Zoroastro could not sell Leonardo's machines; and there were no commissions forthcoming. What little income he had came from the hand of his friend Domenico del Ghirlandaio, who was painting the chapel of Santa Maria Novella. Leonardo had been reduced to being his helper.

Indeed, Il Magnifico was an unforgiving enemy; and Leonardo had also come to learn that Ginevra's husband, Nicolini, had more influence than he had expected.

Leonardo had managed to become persona non grata to both Pazzi and Medici supporters. He should have taken the Devatdar's offer to leave Florence. His heart was dead, or so he thought, yet he could not bring himself to leave Christendom.

But the Devatdar was returning and would seek Leonardo; at the very least, he would take back his gift. He had left Leonardo a tutor to prepare him for the Islamic world and teach him Arabic: his whore A'isheh.

On a cold night late in February, when freezing rain made icicles upon the trees, turned the woods into crystal, and roofed the cornfields with glass, A'isheh allowed an insistent boy to enter Leonardo's quarters.

Leonardo recognized him immediately: he had been Simonetta's footman.

"I have a letter for you, Maestro."

"A letter from whom?"

But the boy put the letter in Leonardo's hand and then ran out of the room like a thief. A'isheh looked after him, then gazed at Leonardo, as if he would describe to her the contents of the letter.

The letter bore a seal, but was not stamped.

Dearest Leonardo,

I write you with trepidation, lest this letter be intercepted. That is why I have instructed my servant Luca to put this into your hand directly. He is accompanying my husband to Florence on business. Surely, you will remember him from our afternoons at Madonna Simonetta's palazzo when you both painted my portrait. Yes, Leonardo, I knew she was Gaddiano. I knew, too, that she was your lover; or, rather, that you were one of her many inamoratos. She told me everything, but by what right could I be jealous?

Nevertheless, I hated her for telling me, God rest her soul and forgive me for impugning her now that she is in her eternal bliss.

I no longer worry for myself—I have been more than generous with self-pity—but I am impelled now by fear for your life and for that of my father. There is something evil afoot, conspiracy, and my husband is privy to it. Beware the Pazzi's hatred for the Medici. I have heard your name mentioned, and Sandro's, too.

I wish so to return to Florence. After a time, I will send Luca back to you. I pray you will not ignore me. I could not help what I did and said. My husband holds the whip hand over my father. We were no match for him. Forgive me, I was a fool.

But my heart has always been yours. If we could only be together, I would not care about anything else. As it is now, my grief and weeping have transformed me into a river. I love you and cannot help myself.

Ginevra

Torn by conflicting emotions, Leonardo folded the letter and slipped it into his tunic.

He wished he could ignore it and never think of her again. But he could not do so. She had buried him, and now, perhaps on a whim, wished to exhume him. Nevertheless, the empty, dead rage that he felt was now mixed with an awakening hope. If she really loved him, and if she was as desperate as he, then they could still bend fate to their wills. They could escape Florence, for, indeed, Leonardo was not wedded to this place. They could go to Milan; surely they would be welcome in the palace of Ludovico Sforza, who had expressed interest in Leonardo's work.

Leonardo sat down on his bed, feeling anger and hope and humiliation. He daydreamed as a child does when allowed to walk as far as he likes alone.

"Maestro, will you tell me what is wrong?" A'isheh asked in Arabic. She stood before him, unveiled, her black hair in a long braid. Her eyes were lined heavily with kohl.

"Nothing," Leonardo said in Italian. He gestured her to come closer, and she sat down on the bed beside him. He opened her vest to expose her large, tattooed breasts, which he gently fondled. For an instant she seemed surprised, for he had been unresponsive to all her seductions and had allowed her to sleep in his room only to save her embarrassment.

Then she smiled, as if she understood . . . as if she had read Ginevra's letter. She whispered to him in Arabic as Leonardo wrestled with her, as he kissed and bit her roughly, as if in anger. She fought with him, scratching him, biting him, and clasping his member firmly with her henna-stained fingers, for there she controlled him. And he gave in to her, watched her as she worked him and peeled away her clothes, watched her as she mounted him, as if he were the victim, the pursued; and he stared into her large, dark eyes while she held herself above him. He moved inside her until she screamed, reaching orgasm, and her body shook uncontrollably. Then he rolled her to the side and mounted her, as if he had led her into a trap, and pinning her arms, he lifted himself up and took her violently. He would not relinquish his position, even though she fought him; and again she screamed. She pushed herself up to him, and they slid into and against each other, pulling and pushing, straining until he brought himself to completion; and in that twisting, fluid instant he saw Ginevra.

She was the Impruneta, the Madonna. She smiled and forgave him everything.

"Maestro," A'isheh said softly.

"Yes...."

"You are hurting me."

"Stop it, that hurts!" Tista said to Niccolò, who had pulled him away from Leonardo's newest flying machine and held his arm behind him, as if to break it.

"Do you promise to stay away from the Maestro's machine?" Niccolò asked.

"Yes, I promise."

Niccolò let go of the boy, who backed nervously away from him. Leonardo stood a few paces away, oblivious to them, and stared down the mountainside to the valley below. Mist flowed dreamlike down its grassy slopes; in the distance, surrounded by grayish-green hills was Florence, its Duomo, and the high tower of the Palazzo Vecchio golden in the early sunlight. It was a brisk morning in early March, but it would be a warm day.

Leonardo had come here to test his glider, which now lay nearby, its large, arched wings lashed to the ground. He had taken Niccolò's advice. This flying machine had fixed wings and no motor. It was a glider. His plan was to master flight; when he developed a suitable engine to power his craft, he would then know how to control it. And this machine was more in keeping with Leonardo's ideas of nature, for he would wear the wings, as if he were, indeed, a bird; he would hang from the wings, legs below, head and shoulders above, and control them by swinging his legs and shifting his weight. He would be like a bird soaring, sailing, gliding.

But he was afraid of it. He had put off flying the contraption for the last two days that they had camped here. He had lost his nerve, even though he was certain that its design was correct. He could feel Niccolò and Tista and A'isheh—who was peering out of the tent—watching him.

Niccolò shouted. Startled, Leonardo turned to see Tista tear loose the rope that anchored the glider to the ground and pull himself through the opening between the wings. Leonardo rushed toward him, but Tista threw himself over the crest before either Leonardo or Niccolò could stop him.

Tista's cry carried through the chill, thin air, but it was a cry of joy as the boy soared through the empty sky. He circled the mountain, catching the warmer columns of air, and then descended.

"Come back," Leonardo shouted through cupped hands, yet he could not help but feel an exhilaration, a thrill. The machine worked! A'isheh stood beside him now, silent, watching, calculating.

"Maestro, I tried to stop him," Niccolò said.

But Leonardo ignored him, for the weather suddenly changed, and buffeting wind began to whip around the mountain. "Stay away from the slope," Leonardo called. But he could not be heard; and he watched help-lessly as the glider pitched upward, caught by a gust. It stalled in the chilly air, and then fell like a leaf. "Swing your hips forward!" Leonardo shouted. The glider could be brought under control. If the boy was practiced, it would not be difficult at all. But he wasn't, and the glider slid sideways, crashing into the mountain. Tista was tossed out of the harness. Grabbing at brush and rocks, he fell about fifty feet.

By the time Leonardo reached him, the boy was almost unconscious. He lay between two jagged rocks, his head thrown back, his back twisted, arms and legs akimbo.

"Where do you feel pain?" Leonardo asked. Niccolò knelt beside Tista; his face was white, as if drained of blood.

"I feel no pain, Maestro. Please do not be angry with me." Niccolò took his hand.

"I am not angry, Tista. But why did you do it?"

"I dreamed every night that I was flying. In your contraption, Leonardo. The very one. I could not help myself. I planned how I would do it." He smiled wanly. "And I did it."

"That you did," whispered Leonardo.

Tista shuddered. "Niccolò . . . ?"

"I am here."

"I cannot see very well. I see the sky, I think."

Niccolò looked to Leonardo, who averted his eyes.

"Leonardo?"

"Yes, Tista, I am right here."

"When I started to fall, I knew what it was."

"What did you know?" Leonardo allowed Niccolò to try to make his friend comfortable, but there was not much that could be done. Tista's back was broken, and a broken rib had pierced the skin.

"I had seen it in the mirror of ink when the shaykh used me to help him with his trick. I saw myself falling. And I saw you." Tista tried to sit up, and his face contorted in pain. For an instant, he seemed surprised; but then he looked past Leonardo, as if blind, and said barely in a whisper, "Get away from there. Niccolò, get him away from there. Do you wish to burn?"

The flooding of the Arno had been particularly destructive this year and was universally considered to be a bad omen. Yet fortune's door seemed to be opening for Leonardo. After all, here he was in the great cathedral of Santa Maria del Fiore at the express invitation of Giuliano, brother of Lorenzo de Medici, to discuss a commission for a bronze statue of Il Magnifico's wife, Clarise. And he was carrying a billet-doux from Ginevra, who had returned to Florence.

Indeed, she did love him, through it all.

If it was true that bad luck ran in threes, which Leonardo secretly believed, then perhaps the death of poor Tista had ended a terrible cycle.

He and Sandro Botticelli stood near the high altar beside other Medici friends and relations. It was a warm Easter morning, and high mass was about to begin.

"Stop fidgeting," Sandro said.

"I did not realize I was," Leonardo said, looking around at the huge crowd in the cathedral. "I fear that Giuliano will be late or will not come at all. He complained to me that his back was hurting him again."

"Do not worry, and it is not Giuliano whom you are here to see. It's Lorenzo."

Leonardo nodded. "But I feel more comfortable with Giuliano."

"All will be fine, I know. The past is over, as if forgotten; Lorenzo cannot harbor a grudge for very long. Would he invite you to the church if he were not sincere?"

"Did you tell him about—?"

"About your letter?" Sandro asked. "Yes, but he shrugged it off. He is always getting such reports."

"Then he must be careful."

"Would you have him imprison himself in his *palazzo*?"

As the organ sounded a Gregorian paean, Lorenzo appeared with Cardinal Raffaello. The cardinal was visiting from Rome. He was no more than a boy, a grandnephew of the Pope.

Lorenzo and the cardinal were met by the Archbishop of Florence and his canons, who escorted them to the high altar. Sweet incense filled the cathedral. Everyone was whispering and gossiping and making sarcastic remarks about the young cardinal while waiting for the service to begin. Leonardo looked around; he had never seen so many people in the cathedral. The crowd was enormous, even for an Easter Sunday.

"He could at least guard himself," Leonardo said.

"What?" asked Sandro.

"Lorenzo. Where are his guards?"

"They're there, you can be sure. I feel sorry for your boy Niccolò. You should have forced him to attend mass."

"I could not do that," Leonardo said, remembering how the boy had cried at Tista's funeral. "He will get over his pain in his own way. He believes himself responsible." He paused. "*I* am responsible."

"Neither of you is responsible," Sandro said. "And there is Giuliano. Who is with him?" But he answered his own question. "It looks like Francesco de' Pazzi." He shook his head. "I will never understand politics."

Someone from behind hushed Sandro as the young, freckle-faced cardinal intoned, "*In nomine Patris, et Fílii, et Spíritus Sancti. Amen.*" In his high hat and heavy, brocaded cape and ceremonial robes, the cardinal looked no more than twelve, although he was, in fact, seventeen. But his voice was deep and sonorous.

"*Introíbo ad altáre Dei . . .*"

Lorenzo had moved toward the company of friends, which included the young and brilliant philosopher Poliziano, Antonio Ridolfi, Sigismondo della Stufa, and Francesco Nori, one of his favorites; they were all being groomed for political office. He stood near the old sacristy and the altar of St. Zenobius, which was not far from Sandro and Leonardo. Lorenzo noticed Sandro and smiled, then nodded to Leonardo.

"There, you see," Sandro said. "I told you so."

The prayers continued, hypnotic, magnificent, as if every note carried the weight of eternity, every holy word a direct utterance of the divine. The antiphon, the recitation of the Paternoster, the Blessed Sacrament. The congregation kneeling.

Leonardo saw Nicolini in the crowd, looking rich and grand and self-satisfied. He was kneeling beside various representatives of Pope Sixtus and members of the Pazzi, Vespucci, and Tornabuoni families: all enemies of the Medici.

Ginevra was not with him. But, then, she had written Leonardo that she would not display her private humiliation in public. Tonight Nicolini had secret business dealings and would be out . . . tonight, finally tonight, Leonardo and Ginevra would have their assignation.

"*Agnus Dei, qui tollis peccáta mundi: miserére nobis.*"

Bells tinkled, signaling the elevation of the Host.

Leonardo looked around and noticed that the archbishop was hurriedly working his way through the crowd to the door; Nicolini was following him. "Little Bottle, look at that," Leonardo whispered to Sandro; but his friend was deep in prayer.

"*Ite, missa est . . .*"

Then Leonardo saw Il Magnifico bow his head and cross himself. Two priests were approaching him from behind. One of them drew a dagger from the black sleeve of his robe and reached toward the First Citizen, as if to turn him around and expose his throat and chest.

There was a sudden shouting and commotion on the opposite side of the choir. Shouting turned to panic, panic into a stampede. "The dome is collapsing," someone screamed, yet Brunelleschi's magnificent dome was intact.

Leonardo was already running to Lorenzo, but Lorenzo was quick, and a superior swordsman. He pulled backward, and in one movement drew his sword and swung his cloak around his left arm for protection. The priest's dagger glanced across Lorenzo's neck, drawing blood. Lorenzo stabbed his sword directly into the priest's heart; blood sprayed everywhere. Lorenzo turned to run, but another priest intercepted him, and then Francesco Nori stepped between Lorenzo and his attacker. He caught the priest's dagger in the stomach; and it was then that Leonardo reached them.

Enraged that Lorenzo had escaped him, the priest lunged at Leonardo. But Leonardo fell back, deflected the blow, and thrust his dagger into the priest's thick neck. Lorenzo looked wild-eyed; Leonardo pushed him aside and rushed forward to intercept a Pazzi bravo stealing behind Lorenzo, but Lorenzo cut the boy down himself. Lorenzo's gaze met Leonardo's; in that instant their friendship was repaired.

Fighting boiled all around them. Leonardo and the rest of Lorenzo's friends formed a circle around him to protect him from the Pazzi hirelings and the Spaniards of the cardinal's suite. They retreated to the northern sacristy; the others fell behind, fighting the pursuing conspirators.

"Quickly," Lorenzo shouted to Ridolfi and Sigismundo della Stufa, who hurriedly backed through the heavy bronze doorway. Then they all pushed against it, staving off Pazzi men at arms shouting for blood. They managed to close it long enough for Poliziano to turn the lock. An enemy's sword blade broke as the door slammed shut; they heard cries of frustration from the other side.

Lorenzo collapsed onto the floor. Lest the priest's dagger had been tipped with poison, Ridolfi sucked the blood from the wound on his patron's neck.

"Giuliano . . . ," Lorenzo said, a frightened whine in his voice. "Is Giuliano all right? I saw him come into the cathedral, I—"

"Hush," Poliziano said. "I'm sure he is well. It was you they were after."

"No, they would have had to kill us both."

"I saw Giuliano," Leonardo said.

"Yes?"

"He seemed fine." Leonardo tried to comfort Lorenzo; he could not bear to tell him that his brother had been in the company of the Pazzi.

Lorenzo turned to Poliziano and said, "Nori is dead. I loved him." It was as if he had just come to that realization.

Poliziano nodded, his long, ugly face as stricken as Lorenzo's. Then Lorenzo suddenly leaped up, pushing Ridolfi aside, and tried to open the door. Sigismundo della Stufa stopped him. "I must find out . . . I must see my brother . . . I must be certain he is not . . ." Lorenzo's voice trailed off, as if he could not say the word: *dead.*

The bell in the tower of the Palazzo della Signoria began to toll; it was so loud that Leonardo could feel its vibration in the very walls around him.

Then there was silence.

They listened. They heard the young cardinal's muted wailing: "I didn't know, I swear I didn't know. . . ."

Perhaps it was safe, perhaps the cardinal was alone.

Leonardo offered to climb into the organ loft to see who, if anyone, was in control of the building. The ladder creaked as he climbed, and dust swirled in the gauzy light as he crawled onto the marble balcony.

Below, only a few people remained. But the cardinal knelt, alone, crying and shaking with fear. He had vomited beside the altar. Giuliano was lying on the pink and green and white mosaic floor, priests and canons of the cathedral kneeling beside him and praying and weeping. Blood pooled around him like a dark shadow. His skull was crushed, his hair wet and matted, and his arm was outstretched in an awkward position, as if he were reaching up to God. Leonardo felt ill as he looked down: whoever had murdered Giuliano de' Medici must have truly hated him, for his chest was a mass of stab wounds. His torn white silk blouse was stained completely red; guiltily, Leonardo could not help but note its color. He was an artist before being a man: indeed, he told himself, I am damned.

Still he looked down at Giuliano, as if hypnotized.

And where is Sandro? he thought. Is he all right? Where are the others? What has happened . . . ?

"Leonardo, what do you see?" shouted Lorenzo. "Is Giuliano safe?"

Leonardo could not answer.

"Are you all right?" asked Sigismundo, who quickly came up the ladder. Kneeling beside Leonardo and looking down into the cathedral at the mangled corpses, he whispered, "My sweet Jesus, Giuliano. . . . Lorenzo must not know. We must get him out without seeing his brother."

Leonardo nodded.

"I'm coming up!" shouted Lorenzo.

"No, we're coming down now," Sigismundo said. "Leonardo became a bit dizzy, that's all."

"And Giuliano?"

"We did not see him," Sigismundo said.

"Thank God."

"Amen," said Poliziano. But when they reached Lorenzo and the others, Sigismundo caught Poliziano's attention and shook his head. Poliziano understood and turned away; the young philosopher had lost two of his best friends in this last hour. And just then Leonardo thought of Sandro and wondered where he was . . . if he was safe.

They threw open the sacristy doors and rushed Lorenzo across the bloodied tile floor of the Duomo, Leonardo and Sigismundo shielding Lorenzo so he would not see Giuliano's bloody corpse. The cardinal begged his attention, pleading innocence; but Lorenzo stared straight ahead, deaf to the boy's hoarse cries. The priests and priors looked up in surprise. Poliziano signaled them to be quiet and remain where they were.

When they came to the door, Lorenzo stopped as if he suddenly felt the dead presence of his brother, as if Giuliano's anguished spirit had called to him. He pulled himself away from Leonardo and Sigismundo; and when he saw his brother, he threw himself upon him. It took the strength of all his friends to pull him away. "Whoever did this will pay, I promise you that, I will have every last one of them killed, I swear on your very soul, Giuliano," and then he seemed suddenly, unnaturally calm. He led the way out of the cathedral and into the streets.

Corpses were everywhere. Mercenaries wearing Pazzi colors had been overwhelmed by Florentine guards and the bloodthirsty mob of citizens. Ragged children were busily robbing and disemboweling the dead. They squeezed out eyeballs and broke away teeth for mementos. And still the citizens screamed for blood: Pazzi blood. When Lorenzo stepped onto the street, a cry went up, as if he had risen from the dead. Some fell to their knees, others made the sign of the cross; then there was a sudden crush of people shouting his name, rushing toward him, reaching out to touch him.

Lorenzo stood tall, stretched out his arms, and commanded their attention. "My friends, I commend myself to your good actions. We must allow justice to take its course, but we must also control ourselves. We must not harm the innocent."

"We will avenge you," someone shouted from the crowd.

"My wounds are not serious, please. . . ."

But there would be no calming Florence. Lorenzo had done his duty. Now he was surrounded by guards and friends, who protected him from his worshiping subjects.

"Pico," Lorenzo shouted, embracing his friend Pico della Mirandola, who had rushed to him.

"Everyone has been frantic with worry," Pico said. "We didn't know if you were murdered, or had escaped, or—"

"We hid in the Duomo," Lorenzo said.

"We had better get you to a safe place," Pico said. "Your mother is home. She has been sending messengers all over the city looking for you."

"Does she know about Giuliano?"

"We thought it best to keep it from her . . . for the moment," Pico said. "Giuliano is being avenged this very moment, my friend. The traitors are being crushed. The citizens of Florence stoned old Jacopo de' Pazzi and his army until they retreated. Even now they are hanging traitors from the Palace of the Signoria."

"What?" asked Lorenzo.

"The archbishop tried to storm the Signoria with his own accomplices—traitors and Perugian exiles."

"I saw the archbishop leave the Duomo early," Leonardo said, and he remembered that Nicolini had followed him.

"We must go and see what we can do," Lorenzo said.

"You must go home and allay your mother's fears," Pico said. "Florence needs you safe."

"Florence has never needed me safe." Lorenzo called to his guards and they marched to the Signoria. Before they reached the Palazzo della Signoria, Leonardo asked Pico if he had seen Sandro.

"Yes. He is at the Medici Palace being treated for a wound he received. But he will be all right, a flesh wound."

"How?"

Pico smiled. "He said that he received it defending you from an attacker."

"I didn't even see him."

"Or the attacker, I presume."

By the time they reached the Signoria, it was too late. The orgy of mutilation and murder and revenge was too far along. The huge crowds cheered Lorenzo's arrival. They could not believe that he was alive. It was a miracle. They shouted thanks to the Virgin, but could not be quieted or stopped. Lorenzo's own voice was drowned out by the cries of "Down with the traitors, palle, palle." The palle were the heraldic arms of the Medici. He could do nothing but watch as the Perugians who had been trapped in the

Signoria were thrown naked from the windows into the square. Then Franceschino de' Pazzi was found, and, kicking and screaming and bleeding, he was stripped before the crowds and hanged from a window of the city palace.

"*Magnifico,* it is said that he was one of the murderers," Pico said. Lorenzo stared at the man dangling from the rope, jerking in his last death-spasms, as the crowd shouted and laughed at his erection. When they hanged the archbishop beside him, Lorenzo could not control himself; he, too, cheered.

As the archbishop fell, in his anger and frustration, he bit Franceschino de' Pazzi on the neck, and they dangled together. Guilty and innocent were dragged through the streets. All over the piazza, eyes were gouged out, ears hacked off, heads paraded on pikes. And while all this was going on, a proper hanging platform was being erected in front of the doors of the Signoria.

The order of the day was violence. It would most certainly also be the order of the days to follow.

After the archbishop was cold and turning purple, they brought Nicolini out onto the ledge. He stood stiffly as his clothes were torn from him, and he stared straight ahead, even when they dropped him to hang beside the archbishop.

Leonardo watched transfixed. Since Nicolini had been caught with the archbishop, then Ginevra, too, could be in danger. He felt fear . . . and a terrible, bestial joy. He had to get away, had to find Ginevra and secure her safety.

"Was he not a friend of yours?" Lorenzo asked Leonardo, meaning Nicolini.

Leonardo could only look at him in surprise. Surely he knew that Nicolini had been his mortal enemy. But Lorenzo was beside himself. The corners of his mouth were flecked with foam. "No, Magnifico, I hated him."

"Ah," Lorenzo said, and then turned away from Leonardo, as if distracted, for the crowd was calling to him insistently.

"Death to the traitors" became the rallying cry; it could be heard from the Medici Palace to the Ponte Vecchio. Leonardo hurried to Nicolini's *palazzo.* He kept to alleys and side streets, which were not crowded. The stench of urine and blood and smoke was in the air. Entire blocks were on fire. Children screamed in the streets. A woman holding her baby jumped from a second-story apartment, her clothes on fire.

"Are you Pazzi scum?" shouted a stocky street Arab, obviously the leader of the small gang around him. He brandished a sword at Leonardo, who fled down a cross street. There was no time. He had to get to Ginevra.

More corpses. A woman screaming in an alley. Leonardo caught only the image of a bare torso. There would be more rape and murder; it was late afternoon. What would the night bring? There was a frenzy in the streets, even those that were not crowded; it was inebriating. But Leonardo was possessed only by fear for Ginevra.

The great oaken door of Nicolini's *palazzo* was smashed.

Leonardo drew his sword, which he held in his left hand. In his right he grasped his dagger; and he slipped into the colonnaded courtyard. A peacock skittered across the stone floor. By the main doors, which were ajar, stood a servant. At first glance, it seemed that he was leaning against the doorway; he was in fact impaled upon a lance that was driven through the door stile.

Quickly, quietly, he slipped into the house, through the great rooms and halls decorated with paintings and filled with musical instruments, gaming tables, and furniture, searching for Ginevra. In the counting room he found a servant who had been beaten to death. In the sitting room he came upon two men raping a serving maid and her son.

There was a peal of laughter upstairs.

His heart pounding, Leonardo rushed toward the bedrooms.

And found Ginevra upon her bed, her face bruised and swollen, her arm broken, her clothes torn from her. A man was raping her. Another man, whom Leonardo recognized as an apprentice to the goldsmith Pasquino, sat naked upon the bed.

Leonardo felt as if he were enveloped in a haze of blood. Surprised, Pasquino's apprentice looked up at Leonardo; but it was too late, for he was already thrusting his dagger through the youth's neck. Then, dropping knife and sword, he pulled the other man away from Ginevra. He recognized him, too. He was the brother of Jacopo Saltarelli, who had accused Leonardo of sodomy, who had been employed by Nicolini to do so. But the terrible irony escaped Leonardo. With a strength inflamed by insane rage, he threw the hard-faced, stocky man against the wall and smashed his skull. The man slid to the floor, leaving a thick trail of blood upon the wall. Then Leonardo turned to Ginevra. And saw that her throat had been cut, her breasts were bruised and bloodied, and blood oozed from between her legs.

Leonardo could not speak, could not pray, could not beg for Jesus or Mary or the plenitude of holy saints to intercede, to correct reality, transform it, undo it. He took her in his arms and held her. She smelled of feces and sperm. The blood from her wounds stained his blouse, was wet against his face, which had become a mask. He stared at a goose feather that rested upon her red coverlet, as if by concentrating on that tiny piece of down, by closing his focus to exclude everything else, he could deny all existence and memory.

And then, as reason left him, he methodically, expertly, eviscerated the corpses of Ginevra's murderers. As he chopped, sliced, and rended, he remembered a time when he had sat before a table in his studio. There had been the smell of lamp oil and alcohol; and before him, in a bowl of heated egg white, the eyes of butchered cows danced like eggs in boiling water. Leonardo in a frenzy of grief and depression cut through the eyes, through those spherical windows of the soul, working, working, dissecting, carefully, repetitiously.

Just so did he now chop and slice and rend; and he seemed hardly to breathe. Ginevra, he thought, but the word no longer seemed to be connected with the woman he loved; in fact, all connections had been transformed into fire and smoke, scourging, cleansing, choking, rising smoke.

And indeed smoke was leaking into Ginevra's bedroom.

It seeped through the cracks in the blistering wood of the doorway. The drunken brigands downstairs had set Nicolini's palace on fire, and now wood and wool and horsehair snapped and blazed; and still Leonardo moved inside his dream, his knife-edged, eviscerating nightmare; and louder and louder became a whispering voice inside his head. "Leonardo, Leonardo, are you there?"

Leonardo thought the idea amusing. Here. Where was here? He smashed the remains of Giovanni Saltarelli's blue eyes against the floor, his turgid, filthy soul now empty as the clear blue sky.

"Leonardo? Leonardo!"

And Leonardo found himself at the window, suddenly conscious, his hands covered with blood and gore. It was blisteringly hot. His clothes were like needles against his skin. He couldn't breathe. Below him was . . . Niccolò? Sandro? And Tista? Impossible. Tista was dead. Yet the boy looked blindly up at Leonardo. "Get away from there," he shouted. "Niccolò, get him away from there. Do you wish to burn?"

"Yes," Leonardo cried, but he was already climbing out the window, the stone jamb warm against his blood-crusted arms and face, and then falling, ever so slowly, like a leaf, gliding, like Tista in the flying machine; and the air was cool and moist and welcoming as the bready soil around an empty grave.

••
••
••
••
••
••
••
••
••
••
••
••
••
••

Greeks! I doubt that my exploits can be written down.
Surely you know of them, even though I completed
them without witnesses, except for the shades of night,
who were my accomplice.

—Leonardo da Vinci

Undertake this journey, therefore, for the remission of
your sins, with the assurance of "glory which cannot
fade" in the kingdom of heaven.

—Pope Urban II

All the while I thought I was learning how to live, I
was learning how to die.

—Leonardo da Vinci

Portrait of Pico della Mirandola

Part Three
Mens

....
....
....
....
....
....
....
....
....
....
....
....

17

Committed
to the Wind

Bust of Giuliano de' Medici

One glass is gone
and now the second floweth . . .
—Gromet's ditty

He turns not back who is bound to a star.
—Leonardo da Vinci

*I*t was a week for blood and anger.

Leonardo watched the mobs milling on the street below his studio; saw the morning and afternoon murders and robberies; and listened to the night, which was as quiet as a burned forest. But his eyes were as dead as those he had once boiled in egg white, and he remembered nothing. When a child was trampled underfoot on the street, he saw Ginevra. When her mother screamed, he turned away, as if he could not hear it. After all, Ginevra had not screamed. Could not scream.

When Sandro and Pico della Mirandola visited Leonardo to see to his health, they found him alert yet calm, almost serene; he was still sore from his fall, which had been broken by a canopy. God's grace had been with him. But Leonardo was living the same eviscerating nightmare that had begun when he'd found Ginevra being attacked, even in death.

Time, conversation, events were fragmented:

The obsequies of Giuliano de' Medici were performed in San Lorenzo. A new Signoria entered into office. Family members of conspirators were murdered or imprisoned, their homes and goods confiscated. Lorenzo's own brother-in-law had to seek refuge in the Medici Palazzo. And the executions continued, three hundred and more. The Pope excommunicated Lorenzo. All of Florence would soon be barred from the rights of the Holy Church. War was soon to begin.

But for Leonardo, Florence would end with a song.

Leonardo came awake to the voices of children and a knocking at the door. He could not see them from the window, and went downstairs. Niccolò and A'isheh had already opened the door. While Niccolò swore at the children, A'isheh pressed her black veil against her nose and mouth. An overwhelming putrescent scent combined with dampness to pervade the room. It had been raining steadily for the entire week. Niccolò slammed the door.

"Wait, Nicco," Leonardo said. A'isheh stepped away. He pulled the door open with difficulty, for a rope was tied to the doorbell. At the other end of the rope was the disinterred corpse of Jacopo de' Pazzi, who had been the ruler of his ill-fated family.

"Knock at the traitor's door, Messer Jacopo," shouted one of the children to the corpse they had obviously dragged through the streets. The boy was soaked; his face glistened from the rain. Then to Leonardo: "Soon you'll be just like him."

"Jacopo has a letter for you," said another, a dimpled ragamuffin wearing a red sleeping cap. Then the children ran off, leaving the corpse tied to Leonardo's door, which he pushed shut.

"Are you going to leave it there?" Niccolò asked.

"Do you mean the letter or Messer Jacopo?"

"Either one."

"What would you have me do? The corpse is full of maggots and probably plague. Touching the letter could be like touching a leper. They probably took it away from Maestro Toscanelli's messenger."

"Maestro Toscanelli?"

"Although the ink has run, that's his seal. And it isn't broken," Leonardo said. "The brats couldn't read anyway. But come on, now, we're leaving."

"Leaving?"

"Help me gather my notes, and we must pack our clothes and load the horses. Quickly."

"Why do those . . . brats think you are a traitor?" Niccolò asked. "Did Lorenzo send them because he hates you? Because you were Simonetta's lover?"

"You have been listening to gossip, Nicco," Leonardo said. Nevertheless, the boy deserved an answer. "Lorenzo has forgiven me, but I think I have enemies at his court. And they are deciding who will be Lorenzo's friends."

"Then we should fear everyone," Niccolò said.

Leonardo smiled grimly. "Yes, Niccolò, we would do well to fear everyone."

A'isheh helped them pack. She was methodical and calm, as if content at last.

They were not alone at Toscanelli's, for the old man's *palazzo* had become a way station for those in political trouble, especially members of the Franciscan order; the Franciscans had sided with the Church. But Toscanelli was managing to effect escape for these clerics and other "enemies of the Florentine state."

Leonardo and Niccolò were hurried through the gate by Toscanelli himself, who bowed to A'isheh and then scolded Leonardo for openly approaching the *palazzo*. The old man's apprentices attended the horses and wagon, which were loaded with all the possessions Leonardo considered important: mostly books and instruments and, of course, clothes. In the wagon was A'isheh's huge *cassone,* locked, as it always was.

"You must have received my letter?" Toscanelli said, agitated. "Why, then, didn't you obey my instructions? You could place us all in danger. My apprentice *did* give you my letter, didn't he . . . ?" Then, as if musing to himself, he said, "The boy should have returned long ago."

Leonardo explained that Toscanelli's sealed letter was attached to Jacopo de' Pazzi's corpse.

Toscanelli seemed agitated. "You were wise not to come into contact with the dead," he agreed as they walked through the courtyard and into the house. "The rabble has been making great sport with poor old Jacopo. They have already buried him twice, yet still he stirs as if alive."

"They should not have tried to bury him in consecrated ground," said Amerigo Vespucci as he greeted them. "The farmers are superstitious. They blame Jacopo for the rain, which is ruining their crops. And they complain that they can hear the voices of demons in their fields at night. That, too, is the old man's fault."

Chilled, Leonardo was glad to be out of the drizzle. "Perhaps they can," he said, embracing Amerigo.

"So you have heeded Maestro pagholo's summons," Amerigo said.

"Was it a summons, then?" Leonardo asked Toscanelli.

"The illustrious Devatdar wishes the company of his lovely servant." Toscanelli bowed and smiled at A'isheh. "He has sent for you."

"That's what I thought when I saw the letter," Leonardo said. "We will be on our way shortly."

A'isheh looked anxious, surprised, as if she hadn't expected to be parted from Leonardo.

"Your destination?" Toscanelli asked, yet Leonardo had the sense that his old master was baiting him, manipulating him.

"Vinci, perhaps. My mother and stepfather live there."

Toscanelli shook his head. "You will not be safe in Vinci." He spoke softly; Leonardo could barely hear him.

"What, then, do you know?" Leonardo asked.

"I have heard rumors."

"What kind of rumors?"

"Some of Lorenzo's friends, who are certainly not *your* friends, are still talking of the . . . accusation, that you were apprehended with a certain Tornabuoni, whose family was implicated in the conspiracy," Toscanelli said. "And the Franciscans are about to accuse you of killing a priest . . . or so I have been told. It seems, dear Leonardo, that you have considerable enemies on both sides of the fence."

"And my friend Sandro? What does he think? Does he know of these rumors? I have not seen him these last few days."

"No one has," Toscanelli said. "There are rumors that Il Magnifico has sent him on a mission to the East."

"What?"

"That is all I know."

"He would have said something to me," Leonardo said.

Toscanelli shrugged. "Leonardo, you must leave Florence. Until your enemies lose their appetite for revenge. Until Lorenzo stops grieving and restores order."

Leonardo laughed at that. Let them all take their revenge, he thought. Just now, he feared death least of all. How could those close to Lorenzo think Leonardo a traitor . . . after he had just saved Lorenzo's life? But he knew when he had closed the door against the corpse of Jacopo de' Pazzi that he and his household were in danger.

And where *was* Sandro? Surely, he would not have left without saying good-bye.

"You have developed an odd sense of humor," Toscanelli said.

"I suppose I have. You know that Ginevra is dead." Leonardo was matter-of-fact about it, as if she were someone he did not know.

"Yes, Leonardo, I heard the sad news. I am so very sorry. Do you—"

"And you?" Leonardo asked Amerigo. "Did my maestro summon you, too?"

"I did not need to be called. I asked for refuge." Amerigo's voice was strained and he looked uncomfortable; nevertheless, he continued. "My uncle Piero—you remember him—has been imprisoned. I can only pray they will not execute him, as they have the others."

"Your uncle?" Leonardo asked, bemused. "I would think that Il Magnifico would protect your family."

It was Amerigo's turn to laugh. "Things change very quickly now in Florence. I'm told that Lorenzo believes that the attempt on his life and the death of his brother were revenge for Simonetta's death."

"What do you mean?"

"Her death was mysterious. Francesco de' Pazzi tried to convince my family that Simonetta was murdered by Lorenzo. Or by Giuliano. Jealousy."

"That's absurd," Leonardo said.

"That's why my family rejected the idea," Amerigo said. "But that matters little to Lorenzo, it seems, because his brother was murdered on Easter Day."

"Ah," Leonardo said. Simonetta had died on Easter. If the Vespucci were going to avenge one of their own, they would choose an auspicious day, an anniversary. "So the Pazzi have made it look bad for you."

Amerigo nodded.

"And what will you do?"

"I shall go with you, dear friend," Amerigo said sadly. "What else?"

They entered Toscanelli's library, which was a rather small room; but a blazing fire kept the dampness out and provided a rosy light. Seated before the fire was Kuan Yin-hsi, the Devatdar's emissary. He stood up, bowed to A'isheh, and said to Leonardo, "I am happy you accepted the Devatdar's offer."

"I did not know that I had," Leonardo said.

Kuan seemed surprised. "What other choice do you have?" Toscanelli asked.

"Indeed," Leonardo said in a low voice. "Indeed." But he had no heart for adventure. He wanted to see his mother and her husband, Achattabrigha. He wanted to go home. And if Lorenzo's men caught him, or if the Franciscans found him, what would it matter? What could they do to him? Kill him? Leonardo would embrace death. He imagined it as a dream, and he dreamed of finding Ginevra in its cold, eternal realms.

"So you have accepted the Devatdar's offer," Leonardo said to Amerigo.

"Yes, as did Benedetto Dei, who will guide us, for he has experience traveling in the East."

"That may well be, but I have business to finish here."

"It is over, Leonardo," Toscanelli said. "Only more agony, and perhaps death, await you here."

"And in the East, what would await me there?" Leonardo asked Kuan, sarcasm evident in his voice.

"Perhaps death, Leonardo, but at least death for a cause. You would carry the sword of Christianity against the Ottoman. The Turk is not only the enemy of all Italy; he is also the Devatdar's enemy. If the Grand Turk and his armies are not checked, then all of Italy and all Christendom will be conquered. It will certainly fall, as surely as Constantinople. No place will be secure, no matter how remote." Then Kuan smiled. "But that would never tempt you, would it? What *do* you care for?"

"Nothing," Leonardo said. But he squeezed Niccolò's shoulder, as if to indicate that he did not mean what he said.

"I saw your sketches for your machineries of death, and I almost felt at . . . at peace. They were purely exercises of the mind, weren't they? Now, would you really pass up this chance to bring your dreams to reality . . . to give them flesh?"

"I do not need to travel to the East to do that," Leonardo said.

"Ah," Kuan said, "then you have already gained employment as a military engineer?"

"I have had some communication with Ludovico il Moro of Milan on the subject."

"Leonardo," Toscanelli said impatiently, "Ludovico is worse than Lorenzo. If he took you into his court, it might threaten his peace with Florence. And do you think he would take you seriously as an engineer? The artist of Il Magnifico?"

"I don't know," Leonardo said. "And furthermore, I don't care. I did not come here to—"

"Have an adventure?" Kuan said. "But what else is left for you?"

Leonardo did not answer; and, indeed, he could not help himself, could not help imagining flying machines and projectiles filled with gunpowder exploding in the midst of huge armies, routing them. He saw choreographies of death and destruction; and indeed his images of metal and torn limbs were as neutral and natural as green hills and olive trees. The sacred, perfect mechanical world of nature.

But an insistent knocking at the door ended his reverie.

Toscanelli called to one of his young apprentices. "Yes, Filippino, what is it?"

"There is a commotion outside. Soldiers all over, but they are—"

"Well?" Toscanelli asked.

"Turks, Maestro." The boy looked frightened. "They are burning the city, can you not smell the smoke?"

Everyone rushed toward the courtyard. The smell of smoke was strong, and through narrow windows soldiers could be seen.

There was a loud pounding on the door.

"Open it," Toscanelli said, peering outside. "It is Benedetto and Zoroastro."

"Zoroastro?" Leonardo asked, surprised.

Toscanelli's apprentices opened the door for Benedetto Dei and Zoroastro da Peretola. A turbaned officer accompanied them into the courtyard. He carried a finely inlaid scimitar by his side and wore a kite-shaped shield on his back. Twenty or thirty Mamluk soldiers, and at least that many cavalrymen, waited outside. Toscanelli's apprentice had mistaken these slave soldiers of the Caliph of Babylon for Turkish janissaries. They appeared to be part of a trading caravan, for many of the huge Arabian horses were laden with great sacks, probably filled with damask and velvet and silks woven with gold thread: the jewels of Florence.

"What is happening?" Toscanelli asked Benedetto.

"Leonardo," Benedetto said, seeing his friend, "it is *your* house that is afire."

As the caravan passed the Rubiconte Bridge, Leonardo once again saw Jacopo de' Pazzi, for young street toughs had dropped the bloated corpse into the Arno; and they ran along beside it, shouting and singing:

Messer Jacopo is dead and floating
Down the Arno past the boating . . .

Miraculously, the corpse floated on the surface of the water, as if it were trying to keep up with the caravan. Crowds flocked to see it.

And the ditty seemed to repeat itself in Leonardo's mind.

———

It took a fortnight to reach Venice; yet once they were past the borders of Florence, the rain stopped and the cold, gray clouds disappeared. There were a few Christians in the caravan, and to a man they felt that the rain had been a sign from God. Florence was being punished; after all, the city was already under interdiction. And soon the Florentine countryside would be ravaged by the papal troops, which the caravan had come upon outside the town of Forlì.

But Florence was behind them.

This was Venice, the city that had married the sea; and Leonardo felt, for those few first moments upon entering the city, as if he were free. The air was clearer, the light brighter than in Florence. He could paint and think and write in this pellucid place where water merged with sky, as if one and the other were the same; and Leonardo felt that he had only to spread his arms to fly through the airy blue sea of clouds.

But Leonardo would not stay in Venice. Even now a small part of him was pulsing with the excitement of losing himself in adventure, invention, and new lands.

The caravan moved quickly through this city of tall posts and lovely, yet stinking, canals, to the *rivas,* the quays.

The Devatdar, flanked by Christoforo Columbus and his officers, warmly greeted Kuan and his party. He seemed especially pleased to see Leonardo and Benedetto Dei. With the assurance of a king, he immediately took possession of A'isheh, who had moved quietly away from Leonardo. Leonardo felt a sudden and surprising sense of loss. It was as if A'isheh had disappeared, as if a tall, beautiful stranger in silks and long veils had taken her place.

Before him floated the Devatdar's ships, gently rolling and pitching: his great flagship—a three-masted, Venetian-built *galleassa* bristling with oars and batteries of guns—and two sturdy Venetian caravels with their raised poops and large fore and aft lateen sails. On the decks stood sailors and soldiers with crossbows, *espingardas,* and falconets; above them, colorful banners as long as the ship snapped in the wind. But for the banners, all sails were furled. The odors of new paint, hemp, caulking tar, sun on newly adzed timber, tallow, pitch, whale oil, and the overwhelming stink from the bilges simultaneously fouled and sweetened the air.

Leonardo felt a thrill as he looked at the ships, which seemed to be locked into the sea by the banks of oars manned by sailors at the ready.

"Well, Maestro Leonardo, it is good that you have joined us," Columbus said; the sun had freckled his face and lent blond highlights to his long red hair.

Leonardo lowered his gaze from the ships. "I thank you," he said, rather formally: he remembered his last encounter with this man. Niccolò was probably correct in his assessment: Comandante Christoforo Columbus was crazy.

"I have ulterior motives, my friend," Columbus said. "You see, we have lost one of our pilots, and as you have studied with Maestro Toscanelli, and as you understand mathematics and navigation and can read the ephemerides—"

"I am no mariner," Leonardo said. "Surely Benedetto Dei is more qualified."

"Then you shall both stand on the ship," Columbus said. "It is the *Devota,* there." He pointed to the smallest of the ships, a square-rigger that seemed to sit well in the water.

A'isheh whispered something to the Devatdar, who shook his head angrily.

"Do not be alarmed," Benedetto said to Leonardo. "The ship's master will guide us." Benedetto shook his head quickly, a signal to Leonardo not to argue.

"Then it is decided," the Devatdar said. "We will be under way by third watch." A ragged lot of landsmen, some of them very old, milled about the quays, carrying long, tapering hogsheads of wine to the ships, while sailors carried away the caravan's stores and the passengers' personal possessions.

"Come along," said an officer to Leonardo and Benedetto.

Leonardo waved good-bye to Zoroastro and Amerigo Vespucci, who would be guests of the Devatdar. Although A'isheh stood beside the Devatdar, her eyes revealed her feelings for Leonardo. But when Niccolò followed Leonardo, Columbus called to him. "Young man, you're walking toward the wrong ship." The officers and sailors laughed at that. Furious, Niccolò turned toward Columbus, his face red with embarrassment. "There will be no cabin space for you aboard the *Devota,"* Columbus continued, "unless you wish to sleep with the sailors on deck or in the hold with the rats and roaches." That provoked another laugh.

"We will find room for him, Comandante," Leonardo said to Columbus.

"Where, Maestro, in your bed?" Columbus said, provoking more laughter.

Leonardo stepped forward, reaching for his sword, but Benedetto pulled him back. "Enough, Leonardo."

The Devatdar spoke to Columbus, and it was Columbus's turn to blush. Obviously, he did not know of Leonardo's accusation. "I beg your forgiveness, Maestro," Columbus said. "It was a joke, nothing more."

Then the Devatdar said, "Nevertheless, the boy will travel with us."

Leonardo argued, but to no avail. Then he stepped forward—Niccolò *would* stay with him. But before he could reach the boy, several of the Devatdar's guards stepped in front of him. They grabbed Leonardo by both wrists, and he felt blades pressing insistently against his groin and ribs. The Devatdar was in control here—not only of his ships, but of everyone's life, including Leonardo's.

And as the song of Jacopo once again repeated in his mind, Leonardo had a sudden and terrible presentiment, which he buried in his memory cathedral.

> *Messer Jacopo is dead and floating*
> *Down the Arno past the boating . . .*

> Dead and floating, past the boating . . .

18

Greek Fire

The weather was like April in Andalusia ... the only thing wanting was the sounds of nightingales.

—Christopher Columbus

Both the living and the dead will be happy tonight.

—Don John of Austria

Away with you who walk the wind ...

—Homer's *Iliad*

The ships sailed south through the Adriatic Sea, flanked by the papal states and the kingdoms of the Italies on one side and the Ottoman and Mamluk shores on the other. It was a straightforward voyage, for this was a well-traveled sea route, which branched in the Mediterranean: west to Barbary, east to Cyprus, for copper; but to the south was Babylon, or El-Kahireh, the great Bazaar. It was said that a single street in Cairo contained more people than all of Florence. It was said to be the place from which all knowledge was derived, for there had lived Hermes Trismegistos, also called Idris, before the Deluge.

South was their destination, and south they went, as if the days at sea were prayers, formulas fixed by the constant rituals of sun and stars. In clear weather, the hours were defined and punctuated by the turning of the glasses, the sand clocks, eight glasses to a watch; but time was also counted as in a church, by the offices of tierce, vespers, and compline. The captain and his sailors were deeply religious; and the sounds of prayer could always be heard, if not by the Muslim soldiers, then by Christian sailors and the young gromets who turned the clocks as they sang the traditional Paternoster or Ave Maria.

It was midnight, and Leonardo and Benedetto Dei were already at their place when the gromets turned the glasses for the new watch and sang, *"Qui habitat in adiutorio Altissimi, in protectione Dei caeli commorabitur,"* in their sweet, high voices.

Everyone stood a watch, including the captain; and Leonardo and Benedetto were allowed to take theirs together, as they preferred the unpopular dog watch from midnight to four. Dei had had experience as a pilot, and Leonardo, of course, stood in as navigator. At this time of night, navigation involved little more than sighting the Guards of the North Star with the nocturnal, an instrument with a sight and a movable arm, and following the glow of the brazier, which hung over the stern of the Devatdar's flagship *Apollonia.*

The night was clear, moonless, and filled with stars, as if the million lights of Babylon itself were twinkling overhead; and as if in reflection, the sea was luminescent.

"Leonardo . . . ?" asked Benedetto.

"Yes?"

"I depend upon your conversation to keep me awake, but a glass has been turned over, and still you have not spoken. Were you asleep?"

Leonardo laughed. "No, my friend."

"Well?"

"I was simply watching the sea, and the *Apollonia*'s brazier for instructions." The flagship was but a glowing coal ahead.

"We've received none in four days," Benedetto said, and then he called to the helmsman below, who could not see the sails and steered by compass and feel and pilot's orders. "Up helm."

"Aye," spoke a voice from below.

"Do you miss Niccolò?" Benedetto asked. "Is that it? Or perhaps it is the Devatdar's woman. . . ."

Leonardo felt a sudden, momentary longing for A'isheh, which led to a wrenching sensation of emptiness, for he also thought of Ginevra, Ginevra as she had looked to him when they made love, and Ginevra murdered in her room; his memories were reduced to these larger-than-life images in his mind's eye, superimpositions, one bleeding into the other. And they passed over him like a great wave, leaving him alone and vulnerable in the quiet spaces of sea and stars and gently rolling ship.

"I miss Nicco," he said after a time. "But he is a responsibility."

"Then you are glad to be rid of the responsibility?"

"It is here, whether he be on our ship or another," and Leonardo tapped his chest with two fingers.

"Why did you consent to Maestro pagholo's demand?" asked Benedetto. "You could have left him with the old man. He would have been safe. For that matter, Niccolò could have returned home to his own parents."

"I fear I acted out of selfishness," Leonardo said, turning away from Benedetto as he spoke and gazing out at the fluorescing wake of the ship. The dark, eternally deep water frightened and fascinated him, and somehow comforted him. It seemed to swallow pain and memory and take those who gazed upon it out of time.

A boy turned the glass, sang *"Deo Patri sit gloria,"* and then appeared on the poop with a small sack for Leonardo and Benedetto; it contained some ship's biscuit, garlic cloves, cheese, and a few pieces of pickled sardine, which smelled rancid. Leonardo thanked the boy, who then bowed and returned to his duties.

When he had finished eating, Benedetto asked, "What did you mean about acting out of selfishness?" Often during watches, conversations were taken up and dropped, as if time itself was being pulled and then compressed. The ship creaked, rocked, the sails billowed in the thin wind; they were like great sacks, never tight in the wind. Seamen, gromets, and soldiers snored and grunted. When the weather was fair, they slept on the decks rather than in the stink of forecastle or steerage. Everyone fell to sleep exhausted; no one slept for more than four hours at a time.

"I need the responsibility," Leonardo said. "Somehow Niccolò is the only unbroken thread."

When it became evident that Leonardo would say nothing more, Benedetto said, "Niccolò is on the Devatdar's ship because of the woman."

"What do you mean?"

"One of the able seamen is hard of hearing, and he's learned to read lips. He saw the woman speak to the Devatdar and plead for the boy."

"Why would she do that?" Leonardo said, musing.

"Perhaps she wanted him."

"You're a pig, Benedetto. Like Zoroastro."

Benedetto laughed and said, "Leonardo, do you know what they call this ship? They call it the *Flying Pig*. So I'm in good company, hey?" He laughed again, loudly, and someone in the dark shouted, "Shut up!"

But Leonardo, who had been leaning against the rail, suddenly stood straight and stared eastward into the foaming dark. "Benedetto, look, in the distance, do you see them? Lights."

Benedetto turned to look, but the dim glowing lights had disappeared. "Leonardo, perhaps you saw a reflection."

"I saw something," Leonardo said. Then, after a beat, "Look, there." He pointed toward the Devatdar's flagship, which was signaling with its brazier and, for emphasis, with a pitch pine torch. On, off, on, on . . .

"Up forward," Benedetto shouted; and when the angry sailors came aft on the run, he posted one to the roundtop. "And keep a watch in that direction for anything strange . . . especially for any lights or flickerings." Then to a petty officer: "Call the captain. And the master."

"We shall know by morning if they are ships," Leonardo said. "If they are unfriendly. . . ."

"The sea often produces strange apparitions," Benedetto insisted. His hand shook slightly; Leonardo knew that he was anxious.

"We will know tomorrow if they are Turks," Leonardo said, then cursed A'isheh for taking Niccolò.

He spent the remaining hours making preparations for battle. Dawn was but a few glasses away; yet now he was content, for he was lost in the familiar pleasure of work.

———

False dawn, followed by the gray, dirty light that washed away the stars. Then the clouds were tinged red with fire, and daybreak was a transformation; it was if every morning the world followed exactly the text of Genesis, as if the early prayers and sweet songs of the young gromets actually brought the world into being, creating it anew. Sails snapped in the ocean wind, and there was a keen smell of wood, of green, fragrant forest, as the dew evaporated from the decks.

But there was no calm this morning, no contentment that God was in His heaven.

Men were working feverishly, yet without talk or even much noise. It was an eerie thing to watch, as if the ship was being worked by ghosts, by the dead who no longer needed friendship and conversation and the pleasures of the flesh. The men looked exhausted and somehow small against the bright-blue backdrop of sea and sky; and, sweating, they were hurrying to bring their ship to the ready before the Turkish pirates closed in for a kill. Only the men at arms were still. They had polished and checked their weapons. They stood out of the way, moved their lips silently in prayer, and gazed out at their enemy, as if they could burn the Turk's ships with the emanations from their squinting eyes.

Five ships, all flying the crimson banners of stars and crescent, were swinging diagonally toward them, coming in slowly, inexorably; a huge Turkish carrack, bristling with batteries of guns, looked like a castle floating in the rolling water. It was obviously their flagship, and it advanced ahead, as if pulling the smaller, oared galleys in a wide arc toward the Devatdar's ships.

Leonardo stood on the poop with his friend Benedetto, the captain, the ship's master, and several officers, one of whom was the captain of the De-vatdar's Mamluk soldiers. He wore a green turban and carried a large scim-itar in his sash. Like Leonardo, he seemed agitated, nervous as a she-lion. He gazed down at the soldiers amidships, an army dressed in white, sunlight glinting on armor and arquebusiers. Some stood with raised lances and hal-berds, others cradled crossbows and held spiked maces and double-bladed axes, while the rest had knives and scimitars drawn.

"Maestro Leonardo, you must stop fidgeting," said the ship's captain. He was a small, stocky man, who, despite his size, carried an air of absolute authority. He must have been handsome in his youth, but his sleepy eyes and full mouth now gave him a bloated, decadent cast.

"There is still much left to do," Leonardo said.

The captain smiled. "'Tis done, young sir. Time has run out for all but blood and victory."

"He talks of blood and victory only because we can't outrun them," Benedetto said.

"Hush," Leonardo said, for the captain had heard.

The captain turned to the artillery officer. "Agostin, are you, too, ner-vous?"

The officer, who was younger than Leonardo, blushed and said, "We are ready, Captain. Maestro Leonardo has been a great help. He checked every ring of the bombards and found—"

"Very good." The captain turned to Leonardo to address him; but as he spoke, he gazed out at the small armada in the distance. "I understand that you thought our stock of Greek fire to be insufficient . . . and inferior. So you have made your own. I cannot stand the smell of camphor."

"My apologies, Ser. I have also compounded other substances."

"But you will not use any deadly smoke without my order. I have seen too many good men killed by their own poison . . . virtually by a gust of wind."

Leonardo nodded.

The captain looked around at his officers, then down at his sailors and gunners and the soldiers on the decks. He nodded to one of the able seamen, who blew a whistle. Then the captain harangued his men; and when he was finished, the Devatdar's captain spoke to his Mamluks in Arabic. They shouted back and lifted their weapons.

After the captain dismissed his officers, Agostin, the gunnery officer, grasped Leonardo's arm and said, "You will go below and coordinate the oarsmen. I will signal you when to fire the bombards." Cannons and oars had to be coordinated, lest the bombards, which were fastened below deck, destroy the long oar poles.

"I can do that," Benedetto said.

"I *must* be on deck," Leonardo insisted.

"And I can't afford to lose my gunnery master," said the captain. "So you have your wish, Maestro Leonardo."

The sun slowly moved toward noon, and the Devatdar made his wishes known by signaling the other ships with flag and sail in a special, private code. The Turks furled and unfurled different flags for the same effect. Stalemate.

But the wind . . . if only it would fill the sails. Then they could escape, for the galleys could not pace sailing vessels at full tilt. Mediterranean winds, though, were capricious; and for these long hours, it was like a great lake brushed only by thin breezes. Tempers were high, and every man was anxious and nervous when the Turkish galleon made its move. Oars sweeping, it closed within range and fired upon the Devatdar's ship, which returned cannon.

As did all the other ships.

A gunnery officer shouted the captain's orders to Agostin, who, in turn, shouted back. It was a chantey, of sorts, for the orders were sung, then followed with the explosion of the bombards.

Clouds of smoke rose into the air, releasing the pungent odor of gunpowder and the hot smell of iron. The ocean exploded and hissed as the handmade stone balls arced and fell, missing their intended targets. The Devatdar's ships maneuvered into battle positions, the flagship in the center.

"Furl the sails and lower the yards," ordered the captain of Leonardo's ship.

But Leonardo had little to do now. The sailors manning the few medium bombards and falconets on the quarterdeck, poop, and forecastle knew what they were doing; and he would only get in the way. One would put a lighted match to the cannon's touchhole that was filled with gunpowder; another would aim it and pray that chamber and barrel would not explode upon discharge.

Everything was at ready. Baskets of nailed fireballs that stank of turpentine—Leonardo's Greek fire; the same bombs affixed to lances, and set to be discharged from the short wooden tubes called *trombe;* earthen pots filled with pitch swayed over fires upon all the decks, and within easy reach of every soldier and sailor were piles of stones and jars of quicklime to blind their Turkish counterparts; there were also jars of oil and liquid soap to make slippery the decks of the enemy's ship, and in the high-angled sun, piles of star-shaped, razor-edged caltrops shone like quicksilver. And Leonardo had also seen to it that there were enough tubs of water to put out fires.

A gunnery officer stood on the ship's waist near Leonardo and shouted. Oars rose and eight cannons fired; and as if in echo, volley after volley was exchanged by the two flagships. At first it seemed as if this were only a game creating smoke and shock. But that was to change in a heartbeat.

Two Turkish galleys were rowing hard toward the caravels flanking the Devatdar's flagship. Head-on they came, oars biting into the water. These were themselves large ships, sleek and stripped to the bone, with thirty oar benches on each side. Built for speed, their purpose was to carry soldiers to the enemy for hand-to-hand combat; and to that end they carried very few guns.

"Aim for the oars," shouted one of the gunnery officers on the deck, but the galleys were a difficult target to hit.

The cannons fired, arquebusiers fired, the water boiled around the galleys; and as they neared, Leonardo could see the soldiers in colored robes and turbans, could hear their huzzahs and the death-knell pounding of the drums. The men there, just across the water, were frenzied to kill, to do battle, and the sea carried their cries, magnified them.

"Can you smell the stink?" Benedetto asked Leonardo. "Aye, you will in a minute, you'll smell the oarsmen, slaves they are, probably Italians, the poor fuckers. They're chained to their oars and they shit where they sit." Benedetto was talking as if he were out of breath. "Let's get near cover, Leonardo, it's almost time." Then he smiled; and Leonardo tried to make out what his friend was thinking, for Benedetto seemed both frightened and elated.

They remained amidships, on the edge, protected by the raised rail; and, indeed, Leonardo could smell the slaves, could smell sweat and excrement; and somehow he imagined that he could already smell blood.

Below decks, Agostin gave the command to fire; and Leonardo shouted to his men to raise their oars.

An instant later the *Devota*'s cannons fired.

One of the stone balls splintered the galley's hull. Another struck the side, and oars shot into the air as if propelled by rockets. There was a terrible shrieking as blood and bone exploded, as limbs were torn from bodies and thrown into the sea, which swallowed them, as if its turquoise surface was merely the manifestation of a hungry god. Leonardo felt the gorge rise in his throat, bitter as bile. And he felt a prescience, as if one thing were but a reflection of another; he turned toward the Devatdar's ship to see a volley of cannons explode into the gallery, setting the port quarter afire. The flagship replied with a volley that shattered the Turk's mainmast, which crashed forward, breaking the fore course. Two sleek galleys also fired their cannons on the *Apollonia*, but their mission was to take and board the great three-masted *galleassa* when—and if—the time came.

Leonardo was frantic for Niccolò and A'isheh; he imagined A'isheh to be in her quarters, which would be located just where the bombard had struck. And Niccolò would be on deck and ready to fight, thinking himself a man.

Arrows rained from the sky. "Get *down*, Leonardo," Benedetto shouted.

The bombards roared, the galley was hit; and it fired back with its own cannons. All about, soldiers screamed and shrieked. Many were wounded; others let go with their crossbows, but these were no match for the Turk's longbows, which had greater range. The galley came in close, even as it took hits from the bombards of Leonardo's ship *Devota;* the bombards would surely sink the galley.

An arquebusier roared, but the *Devota*'s bombards were suddenly silent, her gunners pierced through eyes, foreheads, and hearts by the Turk's accurate arrows.

Fireballs were thrown onto the deck, and Greek fire sprayed through wooden tubes. Flames licked and raced across planks; the smoke was so thick that it was like night. But it was the hail of arrows that was impossible. The only sounds seemed to be the screams of wounded and dying men and the slapslot of arrows being released from bow and crossbow.

The bowmen around Leonardo were falling. One fell right upon him;

an arrow had pierced the man's chest above the nipple, and he was bleeding and wheezing, and blood was bubbling from his mouth. He was no more than a boy. Now all was movement, quick, yet subjectively slow, as if Leonardo had suddenly lapsed into a dream without the intermediary of sleep. And he forgot everything but the beat of time, which was like the rataplan of a drum; yet his arms and legs knew what to do. He put out fires on the deck and, igniting a spiked fireball on a pole, pushed it into the chest of a Turk who had flung a grapnel onto the deck of the *Devota*. The man screamed and was enveloped in flames, which spread; and Leonardo and others were throwing fireballs, spraying Greek fire onto the enemy and the decks of the galley. In some soft, quiet place, Leonardo heard himself, and he was shouting and throwing glass vessels filled with pitch, which ignited on the burning deck of the galley.

Men fell all around him, but Leonardo was quick; and God was breathing onto his neck, for no arrows or fire could overtake him.

Now the deck, like the sea, was boiling—but with men. The Turks were boarding everywhere; and still there was the *thut-thut* of arrows whispering from above, as if there were no end to them, as if every inch of planking was bristling with them. Leonardo caught a glimpse of the Mamluk captain; he was with his men, fighting in the thick of it, hacking off limbs and bellowing like an animal, while the ship's captain remained safe on the poop, surrounded by guards who deflected enemy arrows with large, overlapping shields.

And Leonardo heard the captain shouting, but it was a distant voice, an intrusion into this dream of blood and slicing, for, indeed, Leonardo grasped sword and knife, and he swung, swung, taking off the arm of a gray-eyed Turk: another boy, who could not yet grow his beard full . . . who now never would. He turned, looking, as if he were in the eye of a storm, charmed, protected. He hacked down another Turk, and another. And now, in the din of shouting and clanking armor and snapping fire, in the slippery gore and the snorting, farting, wheezing of battle, in the throes of parry and thrust, Leonardo remembered . . .

Remembered what he had done to Ginevra's murderers. Saw himself, as if he had passed through time, for in the heat of battle, time had lost its meaning and was being squeezed and distended with every swing of the sword. He saw himself in Ginevra's bedroom, once again eviscerating her murderers, as if they were pigs and he was studying their muscle structure, the patterns of their arteries, the layerings of their flesh. And snapping out their eyes, crushing them into paste, closing the windows of their souls by tormenting their dead bodies.

Leonardo became sick, revolted by himself, and wished to close once again the doors of his memory cathedral, wished to bury the entire edifice of pain in the Lethe darkness of forgetfulness. Here he stood again, awash in blood, sticky with it, for it was like a paste that covered him.

He was awakened from this terrible reverie when Benedetto Dei took an arrow in the chest. "No! Benedetto," he shouted, and ran to his friend, whose face was bleeding from the slice of a blade, a torn section of skin on his cheek flapping as he spoke.

"Just pull out the arrow, Leonardo," Benedetto said, his face draining of color. "Please...."

"It did not pierce a lung," Leonardo said to comfort him; and he worked the arrow, removing it with as little damage as possible. Benedetto began to scream, but made only a gagging sound before he fainted, his face pale as a corpse. Then Leonardo purged and bandaged the wound deftly, for he was used to working with bone and blood and flesh. For an instant there was stillness, and Leonardo heard the *phut* of arrows being loosed, and several struck the deck beside him, just missing him. The Turks were firing longbows from the top of their foremast, upon which they had rigged a bowl-shaped platform wrapped with a mattress to prevent it from being damaged by bombs. From that vantage, the Turkish archers were invulnerable because of the height of the mast. Leonardo pulled Benedetto to better cover; and as he did, an idea came to him.

He made his way aft to the poop to speak with the captain; and on his way he slipped on the blood-greasy deck and fell upon a sharp piece of twisted metal, which tore the flesh on his leg. He felt no pain, but pulled and tied a piece of cloth around his leg above it to quell the blood.

The captain listened to his plan; and, desperate, he accompanied him, shouting orders to his men. The Mamluk captain also joined them, and they picked up enough sailors and soldiers out of the melee to effect some semblance of order. The ship's captain shouted to his men that they were to move to the starboard side upon his command. Leonardo wondered if anyone could hear the man above the din of battle; but while Leonardo worked on turning the linen and rope into a makeshift hammock, the sailors circulated the captain's orders.

The ship was on fire and black smoke swirled everywhere. The hand-to-hand combat was fierce, but the Turks were being pushed back. Their cries were high-pitched, alien, and chilling; and as they were fighting for their god, they would sooner skewer a twelve-year-old Christian gromet than attack a fellow Arab. But attack they did.

Arrows flew and men took cover.

It had to be done now.

"This could overturn the ship," Leonardo warned the captain, who nodded and gave the command to begin.

Two men, protected by large shields, climbed the ratlines to the top of the rear mast. One carried a crossbow and the hammock Leonardo had made; the other a special tube to spray deadly Greek fire.

"Let's hope the Turks do not catch them in time," Leonardo said. He knelt by the bulky rope-winch capstan; five sailors had hold of the ropes and were at the ready. The Mamluk soldiers who had climbed the mast attached the hammock to the end of the yardarm spar that projected toward the Turkish galley.

The Turkish archers on the platform saw them and began firing.

"Now," shouted Leonardo; and the sailors hauled the ropes to pull down one side of the yardarm. The other side of the spar, the end facing the enemy galley, was swept upward, lifting the men in the hammock above the archers firing from their platform. But then Leonardo's ship rocked, and the yard began to dip dangerously over the Turkish galley.

"Move to starboard," the captain shouted, and sailors and soldiers ran to the starboard side, righting the ship and raising the yardarm above the masts of the enemy.

Now the Turkish archers were vulnerable, for they were below the two Mamluk soldiers in the hammock. But one of the Mamluks nevertheless caught an arrow, which pierced his eye, and he fell, breaking his back on the deck of the galley.

An instant later there was a burst of flame from the hammock, which struck the mast of the Turkish ship. The Turkish archers screamed as Greek fire enveloped their platform and ran down the mast, raining fire on the decks of both ships.

The archers fell into the water, their clothes and hair burning.

The Turks mounted another ferocious attack on the *Devota,* and the decks listed dangerously as Christian sailors and Mamluk solders rushed to meet them. Many fell into the water, Christian and Mamluk and Turk alike. The water itself seemed to be on fire. As sailors worked furiously at the capstan to balance the ship, the captain quickly nodded at Leonardo, then left with his Mamluk counterpart, enjoining the soldiers and sailors to take the offensive.

The battle turned. This was the chance to take revenge and slaughter the Turks. Rather than release the grapnels and get away, for the wind was strong and the linkage of the two ships was in itself dangerous, the *Devota*'s men swarmed aboard the galley. There would be nothing less than wholesale slaughter.

But the *Apollonia,* the flagship, was in trouble and signaling.

The captain tried in vain to call back his men, but they were at the height of bloodlust, deaf and blind to reason; and only after the galley began to sink did the men rush back to their ship and hurl the Turk's grapnels into the sea. Turks desperately tried to fight their way onto the *Devota,* but they were pushed into the sea. The hot, smoke-choked air was filled with screaming and pleading—Arabic and Italian—for the galley slaves had not been released; and, chained to their benches, they went down with the ship.

Leonardo had seen what the exchange of bombards had done to both flagships, and was even more frantic with worry for Niccolò and A'isheh. Although the Turkish galleon was severely wounded, the Devatdar's flagship was crippled; and even now it was being boarded by soldiers from one of the Turkish galleys. The *Apollonia*'s cannons had destroyed the galley's *corsier* on the port side, killing the oarsmen. But the galley's soldiers had nevertheless managed to throw their iron claws onto the *Apollonia* and board her.

Before Leonardo could hoist his own ship's heavy yawl into the sea, the captain was giving orders to well the clew lines, and oarsmen were working, positioning the ship to fire on the galley, for the starboard bombards were still in working order. But it was the Turk's flagship that responded, firing upon the *Devota,* and hitting her. The flagship fired again, and another projectile struck home: that could have been only blind luck.

The projectiles shook the ship and silenced her guns.

Leonardo went below to inspect the damage. A gaping hole exposed the damp hold to sun and sea. Cockroaches were thick as maggots, crawling everywhere, crawling over the scattered bodies and limbs. They swarmed around Leonardo, who was suddenly terrified. As he turned to flee, he recognized Agostin, the gunnery officer. His head was cleanly severed, and Leonardo imagined that Agostin's mouth was still moving.

Leonardo shouted up to the captain, who ordered his pilot to steer to the port side of the Devatdar's flagship, out of the way of the Turks' cannons.

Even if the ship's guns were crippled, the men could still fight.

When the *Devota* was close enough to the Devatdar's ship, the Mamluks threw their five-pointed hooks against the deck. They were answered by hails of Turkish arrows and the death-splashing of burning pitch, but Leonardo was one of the first across, running and slashing, slipping on the decks that were greasy with blood and soap and littered with corpses, weapons, and razor-edged caltrops. The Devatdar's Mamluks shouted with joy when they saw their reinforcements scrambling onto the decks; and, as if drawing their second wind, they hacked away at the Turks with renewed strength. Smoke choked the air and burned the eyes. Leonardo stumbled forward, as if a shadow among shadows, swinging his sword wildly as if to cut the throats and limbs of the very air; and, indeed, he fought and felt numb and wet with his own blood.

"Nicco," he called, his voice drowned in the cries and shouts and screams of battle raging around him. He made his way aft to the cabins, and then inside, looking for A'isheh, for Niccolò. But Niccolò would be fighting on deck, if he was alive.

Inside, in the damp, shadowy darkness, he searched; and down here he found Turks, two turbaned boys raping a woman whose limbs they had lopped off as if she were a pig to be butchered. Leonardo killed them quickly, and suddenly he felt a familiar numbness radiate through him like strong liquor; he felt neither anger nor revulsion, only fatigue and an overwhelming sorrow.

He completed his task; he searched every cabin and then had to get out, for he was suffocating. The decks were afire, and he had to push himself past the flames to get above; and once on deck he ran forward to escape the flames; the heat was like nails scratching his face and arms. The wind had come up; the gods of the elements were capricious.

And his ship, the *Devota,* was pulling away.

There was a great creaking and then a cracking above him; a mast fell, and sail billowed over him, covering him like the burning shroud of a Titan. He cut himself free as seawater washed over him, quenching the flames. There was a creaking and a cracking below him as the ship began to sink. And all around him men were running and shouting and crying, Christian and Mamluk and Turk alike. The flagship listed, and Leonardo slid along the deck. He caught hold of the netting, but the ropes tore loose and an instant later he felt the shock of cold water.

———•———

When he was finally pulled aboard the *Devota,* it was dusk; and the sea seemed to be swallowing both sun and sky. Its relentlessly rolling surface was stained blood-red and purple from the sun, and pink fingers reached through the fleece of clouds above. Debris floated everywhere, rising on the foam-flecked swells and falling into the dark troughs. And upon the bleeding, darkling horizon were set three Turkish ships like cutout silhouettes. Their huge flagship would one day fight again.

Leonardo had seen those ships, had peered over the heads of waves to catch a glimpse when he was in the water; and now, safe and exhausted and wrapped in blankets, he dreamed of them still.

And he dreamed that Niccolò and A'isheh were beside him.

And Simonetta.

And, of course, Ginevra. . . .

19

The

Red Sultan

How many there are who wander distraught on the land, despoiled of their goods!

How many who spend their nights on the sea bewailing captivity and perdition!

—Abu 'Abdallah Muhammad
b. Abi Tamim

Red king of kings, you king of Jinns
Recall your spirits, that all may attend.
—Supplication

R eeking of death and human sweat and crowded as a slave ship, the *Devota* sailed toward the protective crescent of Alexandria's harbor in the dead of night. Like a wounded beast she quietly sought shelter. The pumps had to be worked constantly, for the ship was dangerously low in the water; a squall had almost sunk her. The *Devota*'s officers gave up their quarters to the Devatdar; only the captain retained a cabin, and that not his own.

It had rained steadily; nevertheless, Leonardo slept on deck rather than endure the stink and closeness and cockroaches below.

Now Leonardo stood by the rail beside the Devatdar and gazed out at a red light shining in the distance. It was like a fireball hanging impossibly over the city; and the city itself was like a thousand fires, the campsite of a vast army. As Leonardo looked south at the city, all was light, even on this moonless night. It was clear and humid; sailors and soldiers slept or rested on every inch of deck. Songs and accompanying instruments sounded thin in the fragrant air, as did the foul chatter that was an undertone, like the buzzing of flies. Yet Leonardo felt isolated, as if he and his oriental master were in a pocket of privacy; and, indeed, they were, for no one would disturb the Devatdar.

He had the power of life and death over these men, as over Leonardo. According to Benedetto, he had cut off a man's hand for saluting improperly; it was said that he would periodically punish one of his soldiers as a warning. Benedetto was below, still too weak from his wound to come above. But Leonardo could hear Amerigo Vespucci and Zoroastro da Peretola whispering behind them. His friends had been saved, as had Columbus. But why had Comandante Columbus survived while Niccolò and A'isheh were lost?

Foolish thoughts. Imaginings.

The long moments passed without conversation, as if the blazing starry sky and the whispering sea were too deep above and below to allow for words. They would be swallowed up . . . like A'isheh and Niccolò.

Standing well apart from them was Kuan Yin-hsi, watching, ever vigilant. He was in constant attendance on the Devatdar, as if he were his bodyguard—which he might well be.

"What is that light ahead?" Leonardo asked.

"I thought that might intrigue you, Maestro Leonardo," said the Devatdar. "Surely you have heard of the Pharos Lighthouse. It was considered to be one of the seven wonders of the world."

"Is that it, then?"

"The lighthouse was destroyed, first by intrigue and then by earthquake. It contained three hundred rooms on its lower story alone and was topped by a huge statue of a false god. And because of the lighthouse, Alexandria was virtually impregnable by sea. It was said that the secret of the lighthouse was lost when it was wrecked."

Leonardo waited for the Devatdar to continue. Conversation had hushed all around them.

"But that is not true," the Devatdar continued. "Alexandria is still virtually impregnable, thanks be to Allah and my master. And the secret is not lost."

"The secret?"

"The ancients claimed to be able to see ships before they appeared."

"How was this done?" Leonardo asked, curious.

The Devatdar didn't answer, but stared toward the shore. After a time he turned and motioned his guards to clear the deck for privacy. The sailors and soldiers fell back; Zoroastro and Amerigo Vespucci were among them. Then the Devatdar said matter-of-factly, "If the Caliph does not have you executed, I am sure he will show you his secrets himself."

"Why would he execute me?" Leonardo asked.

"If you fail to make good on your promises. He has your letter to Il Magnifico in his possession. Do you remember what you had written?"

Leonardo nodded.

"I will pray that was not braggadocio, but that you can truly construct miracles that can fly and swim beneath the sea."

"I can," Leonardo said.

"The peasants call him the Red King of Kings. Do you know what that means?"

Again Leonardo waited for the Devatdar to continue. Was the man goading him? And why? Leonardo wished to be done with it, wished to be alone, to think, to sketch in his notebook, which even now hung from his belt, enclosed in a leather pouch to protect ink and paper from the elements.

"They think he is a Jinn, the Red Jinn, the most violent and powerful of spirits. When he kills or punishes, he turns it into a spectacle, a feast. The poor love it, of course, for he feeds them."

"Why do you tell me all of this?"

"Only to prepare you, Maestro. The Caliph is gracious, generous, and charming. He will bestow all manner of honor upon you."

"Yes?" Leonardo asked.

"Don't be deceived." The Devatdar stared at the shore for a moment, then said matter-of-factly, "A'isheh loves you."

Caught off guard, Leonardo said, "I don't think we need to—"

"I gave her to you, did I not?"

"But I had no idea that you loved her."

The Devatdar laughed softly. "And I had no idea that she could love you."

Leonardo did not answer. He felt himself in danger.

"Your young apprentice, do you love him?" the Devatdar asked.

"I am responsible. He is dead, or a slave, because of me."

"That's not what I asked."

"If you're asking if I love Niccolò the way a man loves a woman, the answer is no." Leonardo's voice was strained. "Why did A'isheh ask for him?"

"Ah, so you know of that. Do you read minds as well as lips?"

Leonardo didn't answer.

"If you read minds, young thaumaturge, then you should know that she wanted to hurt you. She knew you loved the boy and not her. That *is* true, is it not?"

"Illustrious Lord, I don't know how to answer such questions," Leonardo said. Be careful, he told himself.

"You have just done so."

"Yes?"

But the Devatdar touched the thumb and tips of his fingers together, a gesture that Leonardo understood: go slowly, patience. A'isheh had taught him well; Arabs speak with their hands as well as their lips.

"You will leave for El-Kahireh tomorrow with your friends," the Devatdar said.

"I thought you were to accompany us."

The Devatdar gave Leonardo a sharp look, then relaxed. "That was before we were overwhelmed by pirates."

"And Comandante Columbus?" Leonardo asked.

"He will see that this ship is repaired and return to Venice. I also have some business to attend to. Then I will join you, perhaps." With that the Devatdar left.

Leonardo stood by the rail and nervously turned the ring he wore on his right index finger. It was made of fine gold, and the Medici shield was worked in green and yellow gems: one of Lorenzo's gifts to the "finest artist in Florence." If he were only back in Florence now. How he wished for her now. . . .

Alexandria was all shifting light and shadow. As malignant and insubstantial as a Jinn.

Even as Zoroastro and Amerigo Vespucci stood beside him, asking questions about his conversation with the Devatdar, Leonardo felt bereft. He looked down at the reflective surface of the sea, seemingly into its infinite depths, and found himself in his memory cathedral.

Once again he walked through intimately familiar rooms, down the wide corridors, past the mementos and landmarks of his life; and there, perfect as a straightedge and narrowing in the distance, was the work of the future. Those rooms empty . . . or perhaps already filled and merely undiscovered.

Try as he might, he could not reach them. He found no answers to his questions, only the past, the multiple rooms and corridors arranged in exquisite mnemonic detail. And there he wrote his letter. The letter to the Duke of Milan. The letter that now belonged to Ka'it Bay, al-Malik al-Ashraf Abu 'l-Nasr Sauf al-din al-Mahmudi al-Zahiri, Caliph of Egypt and Syria.

———

Al Mio Illustrissimo Signore Ludovico, Duke of Bari,

Most Illustrious Lord, having now sufficiently seen and considered the proofs of all those who count themselves masters and inventors of the instruments of war, and finding that their invention and use of the said instruments does not differ in any respect from those in common practice, I am emboldened without prejudice to anyone else to put myself in communication with Your Excellency, in order to acquaint you with my secrets, thereafter offering myself at your pleasure effectually to demonstrate at any convenient time all those matters which are in part briefly recorded below.

1. I have plans for bridges, which are very light and strong and suitable for carrying very easily, with which to pursue and at times defeat the enemy; and others solid and indestructible by fire or assault, easy and convenient to carry away and place in position. And plans for burning and destroying those of the enemy.

2. When a place is besieged, I know how to cut off water from the trenches and how to construct an infinite number of bridges, mantelets, scaling ladders, and other instruments, which have to do with the same enterprise.

3. Also, if a place cannot be reduced by the method of bombardment, either through the height of its glacis or the strength of its position, I have plans for destroying every fortress or other stronghold unless it has been founded upon rock.

4. I also have methods of making bombards, which are very conveniently transported and can hurl small stones in the manner almost of hail, causing great terror to the enemy from their smoke and great loss and confusion.

5. Also, I have ways of arriving at a certain fixed spot by caverns and secret winding passages, made without any noise even though it may be necessary to pass underneath trenches or a river.

6. Also, I can make armored cars, safe and unassailable, which will enter the serried ranks of the enemy with their artillery, and there is no company of men at arms so great that they will not break it. And behind these the infantry will be able to follow quite unharmed and without any opposition.

7. Also, if need shall arise, I can make bombards, mortars, and catapults, of very beautiful and useful shapes, quite different from those in common use.

8. Where it is not possible to employ bombards, I can supply catapults, mangonels, trabocchi, and other engines of wonderful efficacy, unknown to customary practice. In short, as the variety of circumstances shall necessitate, I can supply an infinite number of different engines of attack and defense.

9. And if it should happen that the engagement take place at sea, I have plans for constructing many engines most suitable either for attack or defense, and ships which can resist the fire of all the heaviest cannon, and powder and smoke. Also, I have plans for ships that can travel even under the surface of the sea itself to ensure surprise and success.

10. Also, I have plans for explosive shells, which themselves contain projectiles, which will burst and explode within a period of time no longer than an Ave Maria; and these shells can be dropped from ships, which rest upon the airy winds like ships floating upon the sea.

Also I can execute sculpture in marble, bronze, or clay; and also painting, in which my work will stand comparison with that of anyone else, whoever he may be.

Moreover, I would undertake the work of a bronze horse, which shall endure with immortal glory and eternal honor the auspicious memory of the prince your father and of the illustrious house of Sforza.

And if any of the aforementioned items should seem impossible or impracticable to anyone, I offer myself as ready to put them to the test in your park or in whatever place shall please Your Excellency, to whom I commend myself with all possible humility.

S.^{tor} Humil.
Leonardus Vincius
Fiorentino

Like one of the Jinn which he had spoken of, the Devatdar disappeared after the *Devota* moored in Alexandria.

But Kuan Yin-hsi ordered Leonardo, Zoroastro, and Amerigo Vespucci to debouch from the ship at first light with several Mamluk officers and about fifteen of the Devatdar's crack soldiers. Strangely, Kuan was dressed like an Arab, one of high rank; and he wore the same robes and turban as had the Devatdar. Two of the soldiers carried a feverish and moaning Benedetto Dei on a pallet. Leonardo was afraid that his friend would not last the night.

"Where are we going?" Leonardo asked Kuan.

"Didn't the Devatdar explain?"

"Yes, he said we are to be presented to the Caliph. But to be rushed out at dawn, as if—"

Kuan smiled and said, "Are you complaining of lack of sleep, then?"

Leonardo felt his face become warm, but Kuan said, "It is necessary. I will explain everything in due time."

"My friend needs medication."

"I have applied unguents, but they must be allowed time to work."

Zoroastro made a disgusted face and said, "It looks like mold, and it smells like a woman's crotch."

"It is, indeed, mold," Kuan said. "But its salutary effects are miraculous. You'll see."

Leonardo was interested, but he did not question Kuan. His attention was suddenly focused elsewhere. Although he could not pinpoint it, he sensed something wrong about the quays and streets. Storage buildings formed a high gray wall to the east, and they were part of a system of covered streets: a huge caravansary that spiderwebbed into the heart of the city, the city that was a great maze, and as alien as the interior of a beehive. Yet the streets adjoining the quays were busy with commerce: slaves were loading and unloading ships, while merchants and overseers looked on. Beggars and holy mendicants dressed in rags held out their hands for alms, while tradesmen in turbans and coarse cotton gowns hawked their wares. But the city seemed to be made up of the stuff of shadows; only the strong light of day could give flesh to the ghosts of men, dogs, camels, donkeys, and urchins playing hide-and-seek games in the narrow roofed streets.

The heavy odors of basil and cumin and turmeric mixed with those of feces and urine, both human and animal; and Leonardo could not dispel the sense that something ominous was about to fall.

Because of the quiet. . . .

The street noise became muffled as Kuan's caravan of soldiers approached, as if trouble was afoot. Every shadow was a presentiment of danger, palpable, quick, alive. Even Kuan looked around nervously, then shrugged visibly and said, "Don't worry about your friend, Leonardo." But he had waited so long that his words seemed out of context.

They walked through narrow streets, the morning bazaars; the smells of tobacco and roasted nuts and coffee were thick, confined.

"Where are we going?" Leonardo asked.

"To the Caliph's castle," Kuan said.

"Will we meet the Devatdar there?"

"No, Maestro. When you see your friend Niccolò and the woman A'isheh, then you will see the Devatdar."

"What do you mean?"

"Before he can present himself to the Caliph, the Devatdar is obligated to ransom those taken as slaves by the Turkish pirates. These followers of Islam are in some ways very much like my own people." Kuan smiled at that, as if pleased with himself.

"So where is he now?" Leonardo asked, excited. Did he dare hope that he might see Niccolò again, and A'isheh? Like a phantasm, she floated in his memory; and he felt a quick, stabbing yearning for her, as if she were a living embodiment of Ginevra and Simonetta, their pneuma, their mutual souls.

"Most likely sailing out of the harbor, even as we speak."

"With Messer Columbus?"

"Comandante Columbus," Kuan said, correcting Leonardo's slur. "No, Columbus returns home, by the grace of God, for the Caliph will blame him for losing the battle and Muslim soldiers. There is no future for him here."

The wide, cobbled Roman street that they were walking upon was empty. Suddenly Kuan motioned the soldiers to move and keep close to the walls for protection, but it was too late.

Leonardo heard the *phutt* of an arrow.

Kuan was struck in the chest. He recoiled from the impact but was unhurt. There was armor under those robes.

A barrage of arrows followed. The soldiers took cover, but they were ready for the inevitable, which appeared as a shouting mass of turbaned men wielding scimitars. Leonardo drew his sword and hacked through flesh; he could not even tell if those he killed or maimed were enemy soldiers, for, indeed, he was fighting shadows—shadows of blood and bone and flesh. He fought for his life, slashing at whoever moved before him; and in the blood-haze of the battle, Leonardo imagined that the clanking of sword and armor was like cathedral bells ringing matins and compline, bells bursting with blood.

After a few seconds, or minutes, Leonardo remembered Benedetto.

Where was he? Leonardo looked about for his friend on the pallet, but in the crush of bodies and legs could not immediately find him.

He swung his sword, felt it bite into flesh and bone; and before him a boy who could not be more than fourteen screamed as his entrails fell, filling and staining his gown of virgin linen. An instant before, he had been a blur, a shadow menacing Leonardo with a blood-smeared scimitar.

Leonardo heard himself murmur a prayer, even though he did not believe in God or gods. Only now, this instant, as the man-child slumped onto the street before him, he did. But there was no time, for he was engaged again, and then—

It was over, as if the enemy had evaporated, disappeared like roaches into the smallest crack and hole in the walls and streets. Silence, but for breathing, a rasping chorus of men trying to catch their breath as hearts beat wildly, as if trying to punch their way through throats. Corpses were scattered all over the street, their pooling blood adding color to the almost monochromatic scene, for it would remain twilight throughout the day in the walled and ceilinged suks of Alexandria.

Leonardo found Benedetto, who was awake and lucid; the soldiers who had carried him had also protected him. Although he was a stranger, it was a matter of honor. Zoroastro and Amerigo had some minor flesh wounds but were unhurt.

Leonardo turned to Kuan; anger could be heard in his voice. "You knowingly put us in danger."

Kuan looked at him directly. "The Devatdar is always in danger," he said softly. "If he were traveling with us, it would have been no different."

"But he *isn't* traveling with us," Leonardo said. "Although his enemies wouldn't know that because you wore his clothes."

"No, Leonardo. I'm wearing my own clothes."

"And now you will tell me you're a follower of Mohammed."

Kuan nodded.

"We were foils," Leonardo said. "You knew we might be attacked, isn't that correct?"

"There are always such rumors. But the safety of the Devatdar is of a higher importance than our own."

"Our lives are not yours to pledge."

Kuan shrugged. "Now we must attend to your wound. You're bleeding."

Leonardo wondered if it was a strange effect of the dawn, for everything seemed to be bathed in a melancholy red haze; it could not be the sun, for there was a stone ceiling above them. Then suddenly, as if by Kuan's suggestion, he felt a pounding ache on the left side of his head . . . and he only now remembered that although he had warded off the blade of a Saracen's ax, he had been struck a glancing blow by its haft.

And as if in a dream he saw Kuan's face looming before him, as large and smooth as the sky itself.

They sailed a hundred miles on the Nile to Cairo in a caravan of broad-sail feluccas. The Nile was a brown ocean of a river; and there was no need to take provisions, for the distance between Alexandria and Cairo was a series of bazaars. The ships anchored often to permit the men to pray on the banks, purchase supplies, and dally with the whores.

They sailed past pyramids swathed in mist, past al-Rawda, the pleasure park of gardens and promenades, and into Cairo itself, the city of a thousand minarets and mosques, of mausoleums and monasteries. Cairo, known to its inhabitants as Misr, the mother of cities, the daughter of the Nile. A hundred thousand people camped outside the city every night because there were not enough houses to accommodate them. This was a city that made Florence look like a village; it seemed to extend forever. And at its edge was the Citadel, the great fortress built by Salah ad-Din as a defense against the infidels.

The Citadel was itself a city, and Leonardo, Zoroastro, Benedetto Dei, and Amerigo Vespucci were installed in lofty, luxurious apartments. Great latticed windows worked with colored glass filtered the searing sunlight into pastel shades. Walls were painted geometries of colors and pattern, peacocks roamed at will, flowers perfumed the air, fountains played a subtle music, and in the splashing water voices could sometimes be heard.

And every door was locked and guarded by silent, sullen soldiers wearing red sashes that held large, broad scimitars.

They were prisoners.

Weeks passed for Leonardo and his friends, weeks of talking and eating and drinking; and during the night, they were visited in their separate rooms by veiled beauties who spoke only Arabic and would disappear by dawn like smoke. Leonardo enjoyed them as vehicles for his fantasies. He would cry out Ginevra's name still and would dream of Simonetta; but A'isheh seemed always present, and it was as if Leonardo had been poisoned by her phantasm, just as Sandro had once been poisoned by Simonetta's.

But he practiced his Arabic with them, as he did with his guards and servants. And he fell back into his habit of working at night and sleeping but a few hours during the day. He studied. He sketched and wrote in his notebooks. Here were page after page of new inventions: an apparatus for breathing underwater; a diving suit; projectiles with pointed noses and fins, which he called horns; a long-range, water-cooled gun barrel; and he sketched the trajectories of cannonballs, and drew various artillery pieces with multiple barrels, so cannoneers could load one set of barrels while another set was being fired. He drew a huge mortar and wrote under it, "The most deadly machine that exists," even though it existed only in his mind . . . and on paper.

Then his notes disappeared.

"Do you think they will kill us, Leonardo?" Zoroastro asked as he looked out through a window at the City of the Dead, which was a great mausoleum, hazy in the distance. Muezzins called the faithful to prayer as the sky turned to turquoise and the setting sun became a flaming orange disk; sunset turned the city of fantastical towers and domes into a phantasm, a dream that might disappear upon waking.

"You ask him that every day," Benedetto said, shaking his head. He showed no ill effects from his wound; Kuan's unguent was a miraculous cure.

"It is in all our thoughts," Leonardo said. "The Caliph has a reputation for violence."

"Then why would he keep us here?" Benedetto asked. "And give us food, and women?"

"Because he is generous to his guests," said Kuan Yin-hsi, bowing as he entered the room; he was dressed in green silks and turban and flanked by Mamluk guards. *"Salaam aleikum,"* he said in greeting. He looked at Leonardo.

"Aleikum salaam," Leonardo said. "Where is my notebook?"

Kuan smiled. "Your notebook is quite safe. It is in the hands of the Caliph. You may be as discourteous to him as you are to me . . . and ask him to return it."

"Why have we been kept here as prisoners?"

"In this land a prisoner is considered to be a honored guest."

"Then, as guests, when may we be allowed to leave?" asked Benedetto.

"We shall leave right now," Kuan said. "And you shall have your audience with the Caliph."

Zoroastro looked nervous, as if he were going to his own beheading. Leonardo walked beside Kuan, flanked by guards; it seemed that they had walked miles through a labyrinth of wide halls, corridors, and apartments.

"Where were you all these weeks?" Leonardo asked.

But Kuan politely ignored him and explained to all of them the courtesies and ceremonies of the court.

The Caliph's quarters were heavily guarded. Kuan led them into a high-ceilinged room paved in white-and-black marble; in its center were a huge fountain and a shallow pool inlaid with precious stones. They passed through a series of arches; and before them, in an elevated portion of the room, reclined the Caliph and his court on rugs and cushions. Lanterns gave off a warm, buttery glow.

The Caliph was sumptuously dressed in silk shot through with silver, for the Prophet disapproved of gold. He was thin, fortyish, weathered-looking, and somehow out of place, as if he were a bedouin chieftain itching to get back to his white camels, horses, and free nomadic life. His gaze was direct and steady, and Leonardo knew better than to underestimate this man. But sitting on the mat beside the Caliph was the Devatdar; could that mean that A'isheh and Niccolò were safe? Leonardo dared not ask . . . not now.

Introductions were made, and although the Devatdar and others sat around the Caliph, Kuan stood, as did Leonardo, Benedetto, Amerigo, and Zoroastro. The Caliph nodded and spoke in Arabic to the Devatdar. He spoke quickly, and Leonardo could not understand much of what he said. He did, however, understand that the Caliph was asking about him, and was also being sarcastic.

"So these are my Christian engineers," the Caliph said. "Which is the artist and which is the clever impostor?"

"The impostor can do almost as many tricks as the artist," the Devatdar said to the Caliph. His gaze rested on Zoroastro and then upon Leonardo. "The Caliph asks me to bid you welcome."

The Caliph motioned them to sit down near him, and a servant whose arms were the size of Leonardo's legs brought in a huge tray of brass pots, a ladle, a mortar and pestle, and tiny silver cups without handles. The servant then proceeded to make coffee while everyone watched. Dropping to one knee, he offered the first cup to the Caliph, who motioned toward Leonardo; the servant obeyed and proffered the cup to Leonardo. But Leonardo refused it, and the Caliph seemed pleased. Etiquette demanded that the Caliph have precedence. The Caliph then served Leonardo with his own hand and said in Arabic, "I have stolen your notebooks."

"So I understand."

The Caliph corrected Leonardo's Arabic, but with good humor. Then he leaned toward Leonardo, and his mood shifted dramatically. His face was tight, he seemed suddenly angry; and Leonardo could not help but think that there was something of the actor about him—or, perhaps, that he was insane.

"My Devatdar has reported that you were attacked," the Caliph said. "And my cousin enslaved."

"Your cousin?" Leonardo asked.

"A'isheh, slut that she may be," the Caliph said, but he leaned toward Leonardo so that only his intimates heard him. Leonardo was thunderstruck, for how could a woman of royal blood become the slave of a functionary, albeit a highly placed one? But perhaps that should not have shocked him. The Caliph had once been a slave.

The Devatdar's face was red; he sat beside the Caliph and stared straight ahead, as if concentrating on some distant point.

"And I understand that your young friend was killed," the Caliph continued; he watched Leonardo, as if to gauge his response.

Leonardo felt as if he had been struck a blow. "You know for certain that Niccolò is dead?"

The Devatdar seemed shocked that Leonardo would even dare to ask. "I went to the Guarded Dominions and presented the Grand Vizier himself with a letter from my Caliph to sue for their return." He would not make eye contact with Leonardo, who felt the familiar encompassing numbness of grief, as if it were a shield, a drug.

Niccolò . . .

Understanding enough to know that Niccolò was dead, Benedetto Dei reached for his hand; but Leonardo pulled it back reflexively.

"Do you doubt my word?" the Caliph asked Leonardo. That was a threat, for his Mamluk guards came to the alert, ready to execute Leonardo upon command.

Coming to his senses, Leonardo said, "No, Master, I would not doubt you, forgive me." And then he stood up and bowed, before kneeling before the Caliph.

The Caliph nodded, obviously pleased, and motioned for him to take his seat beside Benedetto.

A servant entered the room, bowed before the Caliph, gave him a message, then quickly left. "A delegation of the Turkish emperor is here," the Caliph said to Leonardo in Arabic, favoring him. "I will give you the honor of meeting them."

"I already have," Leonardo said with bitter irony.

"So we agree that all Turks are pirates," the Caliph said. "But *these* are pirates whom you are going to drown, or at least some of them."

"What do you mean?" Leonardo asked.

"And here they are," the Caliph said as three Ottoman ambassadors flanked by a retinue of janissary slave soldiers were brought before him. The ambassadors were dressed in richly colored patterned gowns, and they wore large white turbans that were topped by what looked to be red horns. The long-robed janissaries brought gifts in inlaid chests and carried a slave on a golden litter. She was covered in white silk but for a black transparent veil, which revealed a most beautiful face. The ambassadors bowed, touched the ground before the Caliph, and the leader, who was stout yet muscular and looked to be about fifty, said, "Greetings to the Commander of the Faithful, the Defender of the Faith, the Warrior in the cause of the Lord of the Worlds, may God prolong thy majesty."

The gifts were presented, the slave knelt before the Caliph, who accepted her; and the Caliph and ambassador, who was not asked to be seated, spoke. But Leonardo could not make out all they said, for the Arabic was spoken too fast. He looked to Kuan, who ignored him, as did the Devatdar.

All that Leonardo could make out was that the ambassador was offering to repair water conduits on the pilgrims' path to Mecca. The Caliph refused their offer impolitely. He seemed enraged, but before he turned away from them, he politely asked after their monarch, Mehmed the Conqueror, ruler of Turks, who had smashed Constantinople and brought it to Allah. The Caliph called him Padishah, the Prince of Liberality and Commander of the High State, but as they and their soldiers left, slaves passed them with huge brass chargers of food for the Caliph.

Thus were they humiliated by not being invited to break bread, a basic courtesy in these lands.

One tray alone held two roasted sheep atop a mountain of rice and gravy encircled by bread flaps. Two severed goat heads lay on top of the meat as proof of its freshness; and, indeed, the platter looked like some fantastical two-headed beast. Everyone ate together, after the Caliph began, all dipping hands up to elbows into the rice and gravy and meat. Leonardo wished to question the Caliph and speak with the Devatdar, but neither was possible. He would carefully measure what he said . . . and when he said it.

When the Caliph was finished, he said to Leonardo, "Your drawings are very pretty."

"Thank you, Master to whom all men are obedient."

A slave brought the Caliph water and towel while another brought him Leonardo's notebook. "Yes, and what are these drawings?" He pointed to sketches of an apparatus for swimming underwater: a bag to be fixed over the mouth of the diver with intake and exhaust tubes leading to a floating turret. Leonardo had also devised various mechanisms for pulling off planking, and thereby sinking ships from under the surface of the water.

Leonardo explained his inventions to the Caliph, who said, "Yes, Maestro Leonardo, that's what I made of them. How long would it take you to build such devices?"

"I don't know, Illustrious Lord. I would need tools, access to a foundry, metalsmiths, and—"

The Caliph made a sweeping gesture with his hand. "How long?"

"I would then have to test the device."

The Caliph smiled. "You will have your chance to do that, Maestro, for you will test it on the ambassadors' ships. There are four of them. Is a week long enough?"

"Master—" Leonardo said.

"You must sink their ships, and it will appear to be as if by magic. Only one shall be left to float, so they may tell their king what they saw." The Caliph motioned to his retinue to leave, and everyone stood up. He spoke in Italian again. "And if you fail, Maestro, then you and your friends had best remain . . . under the sea. Is that not fair?"

"Can you build the devices in a week?" asked Kuan as they left the Caliph's chambers.

"It is possible with the proper help and tools."

"You shall have everything you need."

"Then I will begin immediately," Leonardo said. "But tell me . . ."

"Yes," Kuan said, motioning Zoroastro and the others to stay behind. The Mamluk guards hesitated, then did what he asked.

"Is Niccolò really dead?"

"If the Caliph tells you he is dead, then he is dead. If it were not true, he would see that it were. Never question him, not even in your thoughts."

"I considered you an independent thinker," Leonardo said angrily.

Kuan smiled and nodded. "Ah, yes, Leonardo, that would be very important to you."

"And A'isheh? Is she all right? Has she been ransomed—"

Kuan shook his head. "Those are matters of state, Maestro. I do not think that the Caliph has yet taken you into his deepest confidence."

"But how could the servant of the Devatdar be—"

"She is what you would call an independent thinker," Kuan said; the irony was not lost on Leonardo. Even though it was difficult for anyone else to hear him, he lowered his voice. "The beautiful A'isheh has always done as she pleases, but in this world, as in your own, that is difficult for a woman. So she used the Devatdar to gain access to . . . experience."

"And the Devatdar?" Leonardo took his cue and spoke softly.

"What about him?"

"He is in love with her."

"She is what all men desire," Kuan said. "Only you seem to have escaped her charms."

"And the Caliph?"

Ignoring Leonardo's question, Kuan stopped before the huge inlaid doors to Leonardo's apartments and waited for the others to catch up. "Tell the guards what you require, and everything will be made available to you. You will lack for nothing."

"Please remain a moment, I still have questions."

"I'm sure you do, Maestro; and perhaps they will be answered in time. But right now I would advise you to begin on the Caliph's project."

"I need a studio, tools—"

"Tell the guards, they speak perfect Latin." Kuan bowed and disappeared around a corner. Leonardo and his companions were herded into the apartment. Leonardo immediately presented his demands to his gray-haired Mamluk guard, who, indeed, was fluent in Latin, more fluent than Leonardo.

When he was finished, Leonardo shut himself away from the others and sat upon his pallet, his head cradled in his hands, his tears sticky as sweat, as he tried to lose himself in empty mechanical and mathematical thoughts. There was numbing solace in cold thought, a sort of unearthly joy, the joy of the released spirit, the joy of the dead and the damned.

There would be no revenge for Niccolò.

Only smooth machineries and endless emptiness.

20

Litany
of the Nile

It is said that in Cairo there are twelve thousand water-carriers who transport water on camels, and thirty thousand hirers of mules and donkeys, and that on its Nile there are thirty-six thousand vessels belonging to the sultan and his subjects, which sail upstream to Upper Egypt and downstream to Alexandria and Damietta, laden with goods and commodities of all kinds.

—Ibn Battuta

Subject to us every sea that is Thine on earth and in heaven, in the world of sense and in the invisible world, the sea of this life and the sea of the life to come... *Kaf-Ha-Ya-'Ain-Sad.*

—Attributed to al-Shadhili

How and why I do not describe my method of remaining underwater for as long a time as I can remain without food; and this I do not publish or divulge on account of the evil nature of men who would practice assassinations at the bottoms of the seas...

—Leonardo da Vinci

*I*n the middle of the night, long after Leonardo's slaves and companions had gone to sleep (Leonardo had been given as many slaves as he needed and a *bottega* in which to work), Kuan came alone to visit. Leonardo had instructed his metalsmiths and glassblowers to make the large water lamps of his own invention, and the huge, mosquelike *bottega* was awash in bright, steady lamplight.

"I see you've been using your allotted time well," Kuan said.

Leonardo had, indeed, been working furiously, and equipment was strewn everywhere. In the middle of the room he had laid out long tubes, which connected to a turret with openings for air ducts on one end; on the other end was a wineskin that could be fixed over the mouth of a diver. A long table beside the apparatus was covered with sketches, an empty flask of wine, some half-eaten fruit that had turned brown, and a leather mask with protruding glass lenses.

Kuan picked up the mask. "And this?"

"It allows one to see underwater."

"I can do that now."

"But you can't see clearly," Leonardo said. He spoke softly, for Zoroastro was asleep on a pallet. For all his pretensions, he was a good worker and far more talented than Leonardo's other companions. After a pause Leonardo asked, "Would you like to try them?"

That seemed to take Kuan by surprise, for he laughed and then said, "At night?"

Leonardo shrugged, as if to dare him.

"Certainly," Kuan said. "And what is that?" He pointed to the apparatus on the floor.

"That will allow you to breathe underwater," and Leonardo explained the valves in the mouthpiece, which connected to intake and exhaust tubes.

As Leonardo gathered his equipment, including a lamp, Kuan asked, "We can summon slaves to help."

"That won't be necessary," Leonardo said, looping the tubes over his shoulder. But once they were out of the room and in the dark corridors, once Kuan had ordered the Mamluk soldiers who had been guarding Leonardo to remain in the *bottega,* Leonardo felt his grief over Niccolò return.

"It seems to me that you take well to being 'imprisoned,' " Kuan said, as if to goad Leonardo.

"What do you mean by that?"

"You seem to be working night and day, or so I understand."

"The Caliph asked for the impossible."

"That may well be," Kuan said. "But that is your regular schedule, is it not?"

"Not exactly."

"Well, you seemed to be in your element, there in the *bottega,* under guard. And you didn't seem anxious until we left it."

Leonardo could not argue. Kuan was uncomfortably perceptive. Leonardo could indeed lose himself in his work, close himself away from his memory cathedral, live in the absolute present.

As they walked past the mosque of Al Nasir Mohammed, which was near their destination, Leonardo asked Kuan, "Where were you these past weeks?" It was a cool night, lit by a crescent moon; and the graceful domes and minarets of the fortress looked vaporous, insubstantial, as if the legendary Salah ad-Din had molded it out of the stuff of clouds. Nevertheless, escape from this place would be impossible. "Did the Devatdar ransom Niccolò and A'isheh?"

"You mean why did I not visit you?"

Leonardo nodded.

"Because I was with the Devatdar in the Guarded Dominions."

Turkey.

Leonardo was taken aback. "But the Devatdar left before, and we were attacked—"

"You think only in straight lines, Leonardo," Kuan said, gently mocking him. "Must two travelers leave at the same time to arrive at the same destination?"

"No, of course not. But tell me what you know, please."

"What I know . . . ?" Kuan said playfully.

"Of A'isheh . . . and what happened to Niccolò. I must know."

"I was in the company of the Devatdar and other ambassadors. We tried to ransom A'isheh and others who had been captured."

"Yes?"

"But they knew that A'isheh was related to the Caliph and wished to send their ambassadors here to bargain."

"How could they have known she was related to the Caliph . . . unless she told them?" Leonardo asked.

"Her *cassone* was taken as booty. She keeps her clothes, her diaries, her past life in that chest, or so I am told."

Leonardo felt his glands open up, his heart quicken. What could she have written in her diaries?

"We were given no choice but to return to Cairo aboard Turkish ships. Our own ships are being held by the emperor, to be ransomed, too." He spoke slowly, carefully, and his voice quavered. "It was an exercise in humiliation. And it's a wonder that our Caliph did not have us all put to the sword. I would have done so. . . ."

"You are too hard on yourself," Leonardo said.

"Don't condescend to me," Kuan said coldly. "I expect such swill from slaves."

Stung, Leonardo was silent for a time. Then he asked again about Niccolò. "Did you see him?"

"We saw no one but A'isheh," Kuan said.

"Then you're not absolutely certain that Niccolò is dead, are you?"

"You are not ready to give him up, Maestro," Kuan said. "Remember what I told you about the word of the Caliph?"

Ignoring Kuan's question, Leonardo said, "It's not a question of my readiness, it's—" But he stopped himself. "No, I am not ready. . . ."

They came to a tower on the south side of the mosque. Beside the tower was a well, the Well of the Snail, which had been built by Crusaders imprisoned by Salah ad-Din. A spiral staircase wound vertiginously down its shaft to the level of the Nile.

"I had an idea you would bring me here," Kuan said. "Can I trust you not to kill me?"

"Look into your memory cathedral. Or your city of memory, as I think you called it. Can you not see the 'present of things future'?"

Kuan did not retort, but undressed to his cotton drawers and led the way down the well. "And of what use will your goggles be when I am breathing under the surface of the water?" he asked. "It will be dark."

"You will be able to see the lamp," Leonardo said. "You need only look upward." Their voices sounded hollow and echoed, as Leonardo explained exactly how the apparatus worked, how the turret with air-duct openings would float on the surface, how to affix the mask and goggles and breathe properly. Weighted with a belt from which hung several stones, Kuan lowered himself into the cool water.

It was difficult for Leonardo to see him, for the light reflected on the water. The turret bobbed on the surface, which gradually calmed; after a few moments Kuan surfaced, splashing water as he climbed onto the stairs. He pulled off the goggles and removed the breathing apparatus; he seemed out of breath. "It works," he said excitedly. "I could breathe, and see you watching me, although I could see my hands more clearly underwater than I could see you. It was like looking up at . . . heaven. Not you, Leonardo, but the light." He was shivering. "I will tell the Caliph."

Although he was pleased, Leonardo said, "Perhaps it would be best to wait."

"The Caliph is becoming impatient coddling the Turks."

"What do you mean?"

Kuan spoke softly as they climbed up the stairs of the well. "He intends on war, Maestro."

"Do you mean that he will not ransom A'isheh?"

Kuan spoke as he climbed and as he dressed. "The prince of the Turks will not accept any amount of money. Did you not understand the demand presented by his ambassador to the Caliph?"

"I thought he was offering to repair water conduits to benefit the pilgrims."

"Indeed, you heard correctly. But that is the privilege of the Caliph, for he, and he alone, controls and maintains Mecca and Medina, the most holy of places. Ka'it Bay is the Ruler of Worlds and Protector of the Faith. Not Mehmed, no matter how powerful he may believe himself to be."

"But the Caliph would still rule over his own territories, would he not?" Leonardo asked as they walked back to the workshop.

"Yes, but Mehmed would be legitimized as the protector of all Islam."

Leonardo shook his head.

"Is it any different from the Pope attempting to gain control of Florentine land by threatening to excommunicate all of Florence?" Kuan asked.

"So the Caliph will sacrifice A'isheh and the others."

"It will not be as you think, Maestro."

"What do you mean?"

When Kuan did not answer, Leonardo asked, "Another look into the present of the future?"

But Kuan did not take the bait. He bid Leonardo good night and left. Alone, Leonardo suddenly felt very homesick for Florence. It was as if the very air were made of the stuff of nostalgia and regret. He wished to be sitting at Verrocchio's table with Niccolò by his side. He wished to see Sandro and Simonetta—Simonetta, blond and frail, who had brought him together with Ginevra again. But the memory of Ginevra was invaded by his memory of her death.

He started, as if plunging out of a nightmare.

For the phantoms that seemed to materialize before him were his guards. They had been searching for him. When they saw him with the diving apparatus, one of them grinned and said, *"Mun shan ayoon A'isheh."*

Leonardo understood the words, but not the substance.

"For the eyes of A'isheh."

Tomorrow he would learn the meaning.

———◆———

The Caliph ordered the destruction of the Turkish ambassadorial vessels to take place in daylight, whether the ships be anchored or with sails unfurled. The ambassadors were ordered out of the Citadel and onto their ships by dawn; they had sailed to Cairo in five modern galley fighters, sleek and narrow and bristling with oars and cannons. The ships were stationary in the quiet dawn-pink water of the Nile, as still as stone in the seasonally deep water.

Leonardo, Zoroastro, and Kuan sailed toward the Turkish vessels on a felucca with rotting timber and sail; three families had lived on the boat before it was commandeered by Kuan Yin-hsi. Kuan's sailors were dressed in rags, and their weapons were hidden. They anchored the felucca in sight of the galleys. Leonardo's boat was surrounded by other feluccas, for the Nile was itself a village. Along the shores, *fellaheen* peasant women and children shouted *"Mun shan ayoon A'isheh,"* and were answered with the same words by those on feluccas. But their words were muffled by wind and chatter and the calling of birds: red swallows, pintails, teals, kites, warblers, and spur-winged plovers. As if calling the day into being, they sang and screaked from trees, masts, and from the air above.

Leonardo's submarine devices were laid out on the deck and covered with sail: three buoys connected to breathing tubes and long bars; awls and large borers of Leonardo's own design hung from the bars and moved freely on swivels. The Caliph's smith had delivered the borers, awls, and the ringed tubes only an hour ago, and Leonardo was not even sure they would work.

"I should do this alone," Leonardo insisted, as he pulled the linen away from the mechanisms. "Neither of you has any experience."

"I have as much as you," Zoroastro said. His face was flushed; he was plainly excited.

"And I have even more," Kuan said. Leonardo looked at him with surprise. "I have killed more men, Maestro. That outweighs your bit of technical expertise. You have killed only in defense. Can you stand to kill innocents?"

"The riverbanks are nearby," Leonardo said, wondering even as he said it why he was defending himself.

"Nevertheless, many will drown," Kuan said, "or be killed by crocodiles. And those who swim to shore will be put to the sword . . . or enslaved."

"What?" asked Zoroastro. "Surely there are no crocodiles in these waters."

"Do not fear, little magician," Kuan said. "I shall give you a salve; the reptiles will not come near you. And you will be safe *under* the water, for they will attack only on the surface." He turned to Leonardo. "Now, do you still wish all the glory for yourself?"

"I wish only to be done with it," Leonardo said. He gazed ahead at the Turkish ships. "I will do this alone."

"Why?" Kuan asked.

"Because it is my invention."

"Like your flying mechanism that killed the young man?"

"Exactly."

"Ah, so you would spare us," Kuan said. "And how many of their ships do you think you could sink without alerting them? Do you think they will remain at anchor until you are finished?"

Leonardo ignored the sarcasm. "I can move quickly, from one to the other, before they realize anything is amiss." He spoke in a quiet voice, as if he were thinking aloud, working out his strategy. He wondered when the Turks would set sail; once their ships were under way, it would be difficult to cling to their planking and open the holds to the water.

But Leonardo could not sink these ships alone. He knew that.

What did the Devatdar call the Caliph? The Red Jinn, who turns killing into a feast.

Now Leonardo would become the Red Jinn.

He turned to Zoroastro. "Do you remember everything I told you about the mechanism?"

"Yes, Leonardo."

"And the borer?"

"Yes."

"And you remember how to use the mechanism to pull off the boards of planking?"

"Yes, of course I remember," Zoroastro said angrily.

"This is important," Leonardo continued. "You must remember to make several openings in the hull, but you must be careful, for the water will rush in with terrible force. And you must remember to keep the breathing lines clear; it is easy to tangle—and break—them." He turned to Kuan. "And you, do you understand all of this?"

"Yes, Maestro," Kuan said with good humor and slight condescension, as if he were charmed that Leonardo was worried more about his friend than about himself.

"Good. I will go first . . . I will sink the galleys that are nearest to Gezirah Island." He looked out at the ships in the distance. It was a perfectly clear, luminous morning, and the colors of leaf, sky, and river seemed almost artificially bright. "You and Zoroastro take the others."

"We will take care of them," Kuan said, giving up command to Leonardo. "But the large galley, the ambassadors' flagship, must be untouched. Let them sail back to their emperor full weight and humiliated." Then he gave Leonardo his salve to protect him from crocodiles.

After rubbing himself down with the foul-smelling ointment, Leonardo pulled the breathing bag over his mouth. He put the goggles over his eyes, tested the lines, strapped on a weighted belt, and—holding the awl connected to the buoy—jumped into the water. He glimpsed sunlit trees on distant banks, a swath of vegetation, and then there was a shock of cold. He gasped, took in air, and exhaled: the valves that connected his mouth to the intake and exhaust tubes were working. He tasted the acrid leather against his lips. Visibility was very poor; he could barely see six feet ahead. Yet as he looked up to see the surface, which was now like a liquid mirror, shimmering and milky, he felt suddenly alive and vital. His invention worked. He *could* gain some little control over nature, if not fate. He headed toward the Turks' ships; it was like swimming through a luminescent fog. Soil swirled below him like sand stirred by the wind. He held on to the awl and kicked hard, propelling himself forward. The underwater world seemed silent, but only for a moment; as he acclimated himself, he could hear muffled creaking, sighing: the voices of the river. His buoy, which was connected to his air lines, dragged above him; it was painted as a trompe l'oeil to be virtually invisible on the water.

It was not so easy to find the ships, for the many hulls of Egyptian vessels were like shadows in the paleness above; he worried that his breathing tubes might become snagged. Detritus floated in the water, as if the bits and pieces of garbage and offal had found their levels and would float there forever, never sinking to the bottom. Having lost his sense of direction, Leonardo took the chance of swimming to the surface to get his bearings. The galleys were not far off, but he would have missed them if he had not changed direction.

Then one of the galley hulls was before him, a curving wall of barnacle-encrusted wood. Kicking hard, he dived as deep as he could, then pressed the borer point into the hull; and with both arms working in rotary motion, he drilled between the planks. Using the awl, he then struggled to pull the planking away. There was no rot in this wood, but it did give way to the wracking and tearing of his tools. He pulled off plank after plank, and the water rushed in like a torrent; he had to anchor himself, lest he be sucked into the hold. He swam aft and began the procedure again, boring and breaking the planking with the awl, until the ship groaned and creaked and rolled. It would soon begin to sink.

He swam to the next ship, another barnacled cliff. He constantly looked up toward the surface, lest he foul his breathing tubes. Again he drilled between the planks with the borer, then pulled them apart with the awl. All was repetition, until the water was surging into the hull from several holes. He could feel suction against him, and he heard the distant groaning of timber: the other galley was finally sinking.

Suddenly he couldn't breathe. Momentarily panicked, he pulled on his breathing tubes to release them in case they had caught on something, to no avail. They had been cut, or torn. He let go of awl and borer and swam upward, then broke the surface and took a deep breath. Something brushed beside him, rough as gravel, and an arrow cut into the water beside him. The water was bloody, boiling with Turks, who were easy targets for those on feluccas wielding knives or loosing arrows. Obviously, they thought he was a Turk.

Between the ships swam crocodiles, as long as the feluccas themselves, snapping and feasting, like ancient Egyptian gods at a sacrifice, unappeased. And he heard shouting, and what sounded like chanting.

He dived, back into silence, and swam furiously in the direction of his own felucca until he thought his lungs would burst. What if he was swimming in the wrong direction? He imagined that great crocodiles were above him, waiting for him to surface. It was as if he were swimming through a dreamscape, that his nightmares had been given form. He came to the surface, drew breath, looked around, and heard his name shouted. He swam toward the voice, to his felucca, and was pulled aboard. It had been pure luck that he had navigated himself to the ship, which was itself moving.

The voice was Kuan's. "I thought better than to try to look for you. I sank my ship and returned, as did Zoroastro."

Zoroastro embraced Leonardo, then turned to watch the Turkish flagship; its crew threw lines to those in the water as it sailed away on a thin wind to the curses and jeers of the crowd. The great river, the mother of Cairo, was swollen and bloody.

Everywhere were broad-sailed, gaily painted feluccas crowded with *fellaheen*—well-armed *fellaheen;* and they took great sport in killing Turks and crocodiles alike. They sang and chanted, as did a great crowd that had formed on the riverbanks: white turbaned men; veiled women dressed completely in black, as if in mourning; and children with their voices as high-pitched as a chorus of castrati. Together, theirs was a distant chorus.

"*Mun shan ayoon A'isheh.*"

For the eyes of A'isheh.

"What are they chanting?" Leonardo asked.

"The glorious song of war and romance," Kuan said. He smiled, but it was an expression of sadness and cynicism, the smile of a man who had seen it all before. "The Caliph instructed his troubadours to sing to the people. They sang about A'isheh and the power of magic. It was pure prophecy, for the Caliph told them he would sink the enemy's ships, by magick, as a sign. And we have just fulfilled his prophecy. We have made A'isheh immortal. *Fellaheen* and warrior alike will clamor to fight and die for her. For beauty. For perfection. It's all very Platonic."

"It's crazy," Leonardo said.

"As crazy as your friend Sandro? Did he not almost die for Lorenzo's woman?"

"Do not speak of her that way," Leonardo snapped.

Kuan bowed slightly. "My apologies, Maestro."

"I don't understand what's in it for these people. Do they even know of A'isheh?"

"Does not matter," Kuan said. "They will create her. She will become a living martyr, and the tale will grow with the telling. The troubadours will spread the word; they call her Hormat Dima and Hormat Hamra."

Woman of Blood. Red Woman.

"Her name will become a rallying cry," continued Kuan reflectively. "She will become Egypt itself, and for her all men will rise to destroy the Turks. Blood will flow. The Turks will swim in it, as they are doing now."

"And they will kill her," Leonardo said.

"No, she is quite safe. More safe than you are right now. If they give her up, war will end. She will be used for bargaining."

"And if they harm her . . . ?"

"Then, truly, the people of this land will go crazy. They will give themselves up to bloodlust. Those holding her captive have quite a responsibility." After a pause Kuan said, "What happened here should worry Mehmed. He is a religious . . . and superstitious man."

Leonardo looked at Kuan, but could detect no humor or irony in that calm, scared face. "Then perhaps he'll give up A'isheh."

"Not likely," Kuan said. "Both Mehmed and our Caliph must taste blood. You'll see, Maestro."

"And you?" Leonardo asked, curious. "How do you feel?"

Kuan shrugged. "Killing does not please or displease me."

"And what . . . pleases you?"

"I will show you. One day. Soon." And then Kuan turned away from Leonardo. They both watched the slaughter in silence.

And Leonardo thought he saw Niccolò floating dead just below the surface of the green, sun-flecked water.

As if all the young dead faces were Niccolò's.

21

Reflection
in the Desert

I first studied the fortifications which enable one to resist a powerful enemy and then applied them to aerial spheres.
—Francesco Zambeccari

I told the peasants, "My friends, back away all at the same time from the edge of the car at the first sign I give, and I shall fly away." At one beat of my hand they withdrew and I flew away like a bird. In the space of ten minutes I had reached a height of 1500 fathoms, and I could no longer make out the objects on the ground, seeing no more than the immense shapes of nature.
—Jacques Alexandre Charles

There he was shown a flying camel.
—Petachia of Ratisbon

Now climbs the rooster to the heavens.
—Aerostat motto

Even after the miracle of sinking the Turks' ships in the Nile, Leonardo was still a prisoner in his rooms and workshop, which were filled with machines and weapons forged and constructed to his specifications. But now he was truly a prisoner, for his friends had been taken from him. Kuan had come to visit only once to tell him that more inventions must be forthcoming. The Caliph wanted an invention each day. The Caliph was very pleased with Leonardo; that was Leonardo's reward. Leonardo railed at Kuan that he had been tricked, that he was not some Sheherazade of a thousand and one inventions. "Life is a test," Kuan had said, after complimenting him on his good taste in books. "Remember, Leonardo, that your friends depend on you . . . and wait for you."

"Where are they?" Leonardo had asked.

But Kuan told Leonardo only enough to keep him in suspense, that the Caliph had secretly left the luxury of Cairo to ride with his bedouins in the desert and had taken Amerigo Vespucci with him—Vespucci, who had been the shy one, who feared both crowds and women. Now he was with the Red Jinn, the Caliph who would kill him on a whim. Of Zoroastro and Benedetto, he was left to wonder.

Leonardo saw no one else but his guards and the whores who visited him like dreams in the night; but even the whores were strangers: every night a different woman appeared. He let them stay, for he desperately needed company; and he dreamed that they were Ginevra, or Simonetta, or A'isheh. Some nights he made love to them, inhaling their musk and perfume as if it were the choking smoke from the fire that had consumed Ginevra in her bedroom.

Ginevra, betrothed to death.

A'isheh. She entered his thoughts, his dreams, his fantasies again and again; and Leonardo reflected on the time he spent with her; he remembered the mundane moments, the harsh lovemaking, and wondered how and when she had insinuated herself into his thoughts. He had not been interested in her, much less in love with her. Yet she had stolen Niccolò from him out of jealousy. He remembered how she had screamed out in pain, as he entered her . . . in anger. As if she were not the object of his desire, nor sweet balm, but simply a beautiful, fleshy tool.

And always he remembered Niccolò, his charge, his responsibility and failure.

After a thin, pimply whore left his bed, Leonardo composed a letter by the light of his water lamp. The mullah would soon call the faithful to prayer, and dawn would tint the minarets pink and gold. He wrote slowly, in Latin.

Dearest Maestro pagholo,

It is with great sadness and pain that I write you this letter, but I have already hesitated, nay, procrastinated for far too long. I am reasonably certain that Niccolò Machiavelli is dead. The circumstances which led to—

Leonardo tore the paper from his notebook and crumpled it in his hands, spilling the ink across the table. He dipped the quill in a puddle of ink and was about to begin again when Kuan, who had come into his apartment as quietly as a spirit and was standing a few feet behind him, said, "So, Leonardo, I see that you're finally ready to give up your friend." Kuan was sumptuously dressed in the Caliph's clothes.

"Welcome, Kuan," Leonardo said coldly, looking toward the door to see if they were alone. "The hour is late, or should I say early? What is the occasion?"

"Wouldn't a visit on the grounds of friendship be enough?" Kuan asked.

"You make a well-suited warden."

"Very good," Kuan said, smiling at the pun. "You have learned Arabic well; I expect you will soon be writing poetry in the holy tongue."

"Perhaps I already am," Leonardo said. He gestured toward the divan and asked, "Would you care for a pipe?"

"Ah, so you've become addicted to the pleasures of hasheesh?" Kuan asked.

"I find that your tobacco stimulates my thoughts. Isn't it called 'the prisoner's friend'?"

"But I was under the impression that you were very particular about your habits. In fact, I thought you had few if any vices."

"Is this the purpose of your visit? To interrogate me about my habits?"

"No, Leonardo, I've come to take you out of here."

"And what about—?"

"Your friends?"

"Yes, my friends."

"They're safe and well away from here."

"Where?"

"The one whose life I saved and Zoroastro, the prestidigitator, are with the Devatdar."

"Yes, and where, then, is the Devatdar?"

"I will take you there, Leonardo. That is less dangerous than telling you." He motioned to the walls, as if they were lined with spies. "Were you impressed with my tricks of memory at Messer Neri's party?"

"Yes, I suppose I was, but—"

"Well, I have something else that might impress you, Leonardo, for perhaps you are not the only man who can fly. Let us play a masquerade, as we did in Florence."

"I'm sure I don't understand what you're talking about," Leonardo said, impatient.

"Are you tired, friend?" asked Kuan.

"No."

"Then let us be off."

"Now?"

"Yes, and we haven't much time."

"I must pack, I have my inventions at the *bottega,* and my notes."

Kuan opened up a satchel. "Here are the notes that were in the workshop. Take what notes are here and let us go."

"I'll need clothes."

"You're still a dandy, Leonardo. But where we're going, you'll have no need for your clothes. And don't worry about your machines. They'll be delivered to you."

With that Kuan left the room, and the guards waited at the door for Leonardo to follow.

———

"You once asked what pleases me," Kuan said to Leonardo as they stood on the wide, flat roof of one of the Citadel's eastern walls. "*That* does." There was no need for him to point at the huge billowing mass of linen and paper that ballooned and undulated above a rectangular brick furnace that was shaped somewhat like a pyramid. Even at this distance—over twenty feet away—Leonardo could smell the thick, acrid smoke that poured into the sewed linen-and-paper envelope. A meshwork of rope twined around the upper hemisphere; a wicker base was connected to the ropes.

"What is it?" Leonardo asked. It must have taken three hundred ells of linen to make the sphere, which swelled now to its fullest extent; twelve slaves pulled all their weight on ropes to keep the balloon from floating away in the air. Dawn turned the carved mountain of the Citadel gray with touches of pink, as if long fingers of light were combing over the very stone; and Leonardo stared up at the sphere, which could be seen clearly now: it was decorated with a red-and-gold camel, a trompe l'oeil, for the camel was created out of tape sewn in diamond shapes over the exterior.

Kuan ran toward the balloon and shouted at the men, "Damp the fire. The camel is filled with enough smoke. It will catch fire." Tips of flames could be seen jumping from the furnace. Slaves covered the fire hole with an iron curfew and upon Kuan's orders threw buckets of water onto the linen sleeve and wicker base of the balloon. "Come, Leonardo," Kuan shouted. "It's time. *Now!*"

Fascinated, Leonardo climbed onto the wicker base after Kuan as the balloon swayed and pulled in the air. The base in which they stood was about twenty feet in diameter on the outside and about seventeen feet on the inside. A brazier hung just above the base within easy reach.

"How does this work?" Leonardo asked excitedly. This was obviously a flying machine, and unlike anything Leonardo had ever conceived, although perhaps, in a sense, it was not so different from his idea of a para-chute—a linen tent with all the apertures sewn. He could see crowds shouting below, clamoring against the walls of the Citadel.

Kuan shouted to the slaves to let go of the guide ropes and release the balloon, which they did. "Pull the ropes up," Kuan told Leonardo.

"Why were they not cut?" Leonardo asked.

"They'll be of use later," he said impatiently; and then, as if speaking to himself, he said, "The wind is just right."

Suddenly they were lifted upward. For an instant Leonardo imagined that the buildings and people below had miraculously become smaller, for there was hardly any sense of movement, only the swaying of the basket back and forth like a hammock strung between tresses in the hold of a ship. It was as if the balloon had remained stationary, and the world was pulling away from it, that Cairo itself was receding, falling away; and for one vertiginous moment Leonardo felt that he would fall upward into the sky. But that fear faded in an instant, replaced by fascination, for Leonardo could see—and hear—everyone below, as if their conversations were magnified. He could hear dogs barking, children shouting in high voices, men arguing, fighting; and every word, slap, and thump was distinct, as if Leonardo were omni-scient, in every place at once, beside the merchants, itinerant dealers, black-veiled women, children, beggars, dervishes, dignitaries, slaves, snake charmers, and the sea of rabble, the eyes and ears and soul and mind of Cairo; and as the balloon rose higher, they genuflected and began to pray.

Seemingly satisfied that all was well, Kuan leaned over the lip of the basket and shouted down to the rabble, shouted the call to war: *"Mun shan ayoon A'isheh."* Although his face was covered, his clothes told everyone in the crowd who he was; and they looked up in terror and dismay, for *they* saw the red-robed Caliph floating through the air, the Red Jinn, the demon made flesh whose very look could kill, who destroyed at will, and yet protected the true faith, defended the faithful. He was the soul of the warrior made man-ifest.

Falling to their knees, these thousands of slaves and citizens shouted back, as if with one bellowing voice, obeying, caught by the miracle above them. Here, now, they saw with their own eyes the promise of Paradise—for wasn't the king, the Caliph, the Commander of the Faithful and Defender of the Faith ascending by his own magical power to heaven? Who else could do so in the flesh and return?

"So once again we pretend to be who we are not," Leonardo said.

"I promised you a masquerade." Suddenly the wicker began to swing dangerously, and Kuan shouted, "Leonardo, step over to the other side. Quickly."

The crowd screamed in dismay, but the basket righted itself; and then the Citadel was far below. It was transformed into a child's sand castle of miniature domes, towers, bulwarks, casements, parapets, and minarets; and still the world became smaller: the streets turned into thready map lines; the bazaars and suks became anthills the size of a thumbnail. Cairo—the greatest city in the world, the largest, the most crowded, the most civilized—became a swath of brick and mortar that could be described with thumb and forefinger, a gray geometrical form that was but an erection on the land, which extended infinitely, dwarfing all men's works, even the blue-gray pyramids of Giza to the west. The Nile, the great blue artery of Egypt, was dotted with wide-sailed feluccas, and fertile fields that were wide, tilthed umber swaths extended from its banks. Leonardo could see palm and sycamore groves and sharp-cut rocks, islands and painted temples, villages and mountain walls. And still the balloon rose, until the horizon became a perfect circle and the desert overwhelmed even the sky, whose edge to the north was the Mediterranean.

To the east were hills and mountains and desert: the geometry of sand.

That was the direction the wind carried the balloon.

Kuan added more fuel to the brazier, which was already glowing an ugly red. The fuel stank as it burned.

Leonardo was overwhelmed; for he was indeed soaring, floating into the wet cotton of the clouds themselves; but into air cut with a chill, rather than the region of fire that he feared and expected to enter. "It's so fast," Leonardo said, enraptured.

"What is so fast?" Kuan asked as he carefully attached sails, which were more like great oars, to the side of the basket and the rope mesh that encircled the balloon envelope.

"It's as if we've suddenly left the earth and passed into the clouds. Without movement. Just—" After Leonardo came to his senses, he said, "So you can sail this machine like a ship?"

"No," Kuan said, "the sail and the oar are really of little use. But better than nothing, perhaps. The machine is at the mercies of the wind, which is why we left when we did."

Leonardo looked at him, as if to question.

"We must travel east," he said matter-of-factly. "The winds were right."

"Where are we going?"

"To meet the Caliph, as I told you."

"No," Leonardo said, "you didn't tell me. You said we were going to meet the Devatdar."

"I told you the truth, Maestro. You shall, of course, meet both."

"And why in this machine?"

"To impress the rabble . . . to fight. Believe me, word of the Caliph's navigation of the heavens will travel much faster than we." He laughed softly.

"But the truth is that the Caliph remains in the Citadel."

"No, Leonardo, I did not lie to you. He is waiting for us."

"Where?"

"Down there, in the desert," Kuan said.

"How will we find him if, as you say, we are at the mercy of the winds?"

"We will have assistance, I assure you. Would you have preferred to go by caravan?" Below them and in the distance, a long bedouin caravan made its way over shingle and sandy rock ridges toward an ocean of sculptured sand.

"No," Leonardo whispered. "But why must *you* pretend to be the Caliph?"

Kuan laughed. "Because, Maestro, the Caliph is afraid. He is nervous even in the towers of the palace. He could no more have ascended with us than he could fly by flapping his wings." After a beat Kuan went on. "You look so surprised, Maestro. Don't be. We are in the heavens. Why should the rules and conduct of the earth apply here? This is the region of truth. There is no formality here. Here we are truly brothers; perhaps more than that. Here we are the same. One and the same." His expression changed. "But when we return to the world, Maestro, all will be as before. And I would kill you as easily as I feed this fire."

Leonardo did not respond. He simply gazed ahead, stared into the cobalt-blue ether, and Kuan said, "I thought, perhaps, you would have some ideas for improving my invention."

"*Your* invention?"

"Well, such things are not unknown in my lands. But they were nothing more than toys for children to play with by the fire. As you can see, I have perfected it."

"Not quite," Leonardo said.

Kuan raised his eyebrows.

"It is, as you said yourself, at the mercy of the winds," Leonardo explained.

"Nevertheless, can you imagine what a weapon this might be?"

Indeed, Leonardo could. But this was not a flying machine as he had envisioned it. There were no wings above his arms. The machine seemed to be in control rather than the man . . . or rather both seemed to be at the mercy of the elements. But perhaps if his—Leonardo's—machine was married to this one, then the beating wings and directional rudder would wrest control from the elements.

As the balloon began to descend, Kuan put more fuel in the brazier. Smoke rose into the cloth-and-paper envelope. Then, when they were high enough, he said to Leonardo, "Throw down the ropes."

"Why?"

"For ballast. I had you pull them up when we first took to the air, lest someone grab on to one of them and topple us from our basket. When we are near the ground, they will reduce the amount of ballast and save us from crashing into the earth. And at night, when you cannot see, you can feel the rope, which will tell you when the land becomes higher."

"Ingenious," Leonardo said; and they threw the ropes over the side of the platform. He wondered how long he had been aloft. It felt like a few minutes, yet he knew that it must be longer than that, for Cairo had disappeared, had been swallowed by the desert; and although he searched, he could not see the great rope of the Nile. Haze clouded his vision; the world was swathed in fog. "How does this flying globe work?" he asked.

"It is granted lift by the action of the black smoke, I think," Kuan said. "That's why we used chopped wool and straw in the great furnace that filled the envelope."

"Could it not be the heat that effects the lift?"

Kuan shrugged. "Logic would favor smoke rather than heat."

Leonardo scribbled in his notebook. It was, he was sure, the heat. But he would find out later . . . if he lived to touch the earth again. He felt dampness all around him, as they and the machine were enveloped by an even thicker fog.

Kuan extended his arms and clenched his fists, as if clutching at the mist. "It's rather disappointing to discover that clouds are"—he shrugged—"made of nothing. As a child, I thought that if I could be somehow raised to their level, I could walk about on their soft surface. I imagined that they were countries of their own, and I wished for nothing else than to explore them."

Leonardo did not know what to say to Kuan. He always felt embarrassed when others revealed themselves to him. He would never have expected such romantic notions from Kuan, but they had left the world of rules and remorse. There was no wind, and Leonardo imagined that this was more like a dream than actual experience. Hours seemed to drift by below, as if time were geological and architectural, yet for Leonardo it was all but a reverie; and he had no sense of time passing, just the endless desert, which was so white that it hurt to look upon it for too long . . . and the sky, which was a world in itself—pellucid for one moment or hour, misty and clouded the next. But out of the mist appeared an apparition, yet it was as clear as a reflection in a mirror.

There was another balloon floating in the distance.

"Look," Leonardo said to Kuan. "There."

Kuan looked where Leonardo pointed and nodded.

"It seems someone else has invented your invention. I think we'd best try to get away from them," and Leonardo was about to adjust the oars when Kuan said, "No, Maestro, you need not fear. It is but a mirage."

"What?"

"An optical illusion. You will find such in the desert, too. If I were a superstitious man, I would think it a bad omen."

Leonardo stared at the balloon in the distance.

"Go ahead, wave at the figure you see in the machine," Kuan said. "It will wave as you do, for it is, indeed, you!"

Leonardo did so, and the figure mimicked his every motion.

"You see," Kuan said. But then the balloon was buffeted by a strong gust of wind, which came from the west. The apparition dissolved, as if literally blown away by the wind. The platform swung wildly, and Kuan shouted for Leonardo to move to the other side of the basket for balance. But the wind kept pounding the balloon violently, causing the cloth of the upper hemisphere to tear, splitting apart the painted head of the camel. The balloon began to descend immediately. Kuan and Leonardo threw fuel onto the brazier, which glowed red as the flames leaping from its chamber. They were jarred and pitched by sudden windblasts, and falling too rapidly. Yet it seemed even now to Leonardo that the basket was stationary; it was the desert that seemed to be moving, rising to meet them in one great, soft deathfall.

"Throw everything out but the water," Kuan shouted; yet it seemed too late, for the ropes that held the platform to the balloon caught fire. Kuan doused what he could, and as he did so, Leonardo climbed up the network of ropes, as if up the rigging on a ship, to put out the flames; but his climbing pulled the balloon seriously off balance, and he had to come down.

The balloon, wreathed in flames, fell; and Leonardo smelled hot iron and incense: the perfume of brazier and cloth. Yet if this was falling, it was as in a dream, in slow motion. And Leonardo remembered Ginevra's room, remembered the flames and heat, and just now he imagined he could hear

Tista's ghost once again calling him through the fire and smoke. *"Leonardo?
Leonardo . . . do you wish to burn?"*

As the desert rose blinding white, Leonardo saw movement in the
east . . . dark shadows slipping through the glare.

Moving toward where the balloon would land . . . or crash.

———

The wind drew its trails in the sand, pulling the swirling white stuff
upward and letting it fall as if it were hard rain. The damaged, flaming balloon touched ground, its canvas envelope billowing, only to be dragged forward through drift sand, which covered rock ridges. Kuan was pitched from
the basket, but Leonardo was thrown against the meshwork of ropes, which
caught his leg as the balloon lifted into the air again, dragging the brazier
and basket. The brazier left a trail of sparks and fire before it finally tore
loose, and the basket bumped along a bit farther before it was smashed to
pieces on the rocky ground. Finally, the balloon came to a stop. Billowing
fabric fell upon Leonardo, who frantically pulled himself free of the ropes
and tunneled through the mountain of cloth for only a second before he
came to his senses and cut through it with his dagger. Sections were on fire;
the colorful geometrical camel upon which he stood was charred.

He stepped away from the cloth as bedouins on horseback—those
shadows he had glimpsed as the balloon had fallen—charged toward him,
toward what was left of the balloon. There were ten or twelve of them, all
dressed in coiled headcloths and black camel's-hair cloaks, their faces dark,
their clothes filthy and ragged, as if they were outcasts of one of the desert
tribes such as the Beni Sakhr, Sirdieh, or the Howeitat. There was no place
to run and Leonardo feared for his life; but he held his dagger before him
and waited like an Arab to go down to death fighting. What more was there
for him? To be butchered like Ginevra? He was flooded with memory, like
a drowning man, and he felt his glands open up in anger. It was as if he were
surrounded by Ginevra's killers, murderers, and rapists to a man; and
Leonardo would take them with him to death, would hack them to pieces
before darkness fell over him. He was trembling now, but not with fear, or
not with fear as he knew it, but with hungry anticipation, as if here, in this
godforsaken place in the bowels of the world, and on this day, which was
brighter and sharper than the air could ever be in Christian lands . . . that
here and now would be the best of all places and times to die.

After all, had he not died with Ginevra in her flaming house?

Was there not a funeral chamber for him in his memory cathedral . . .
and could he not almost remember the means and moment of his death?

The bedouins shouted *"Thibhahum bism er rassoul!"* as they rode
around him, slicing the air with their scimitars. Yet they gave him a wide

berth. Leonardo understood what they were saying: it was the cry of battle, of holy Jihad—"Kill in the name of the Prophet!"

But they seemed as frightened of him as he had been of them. They would come near the edge of the smoking fabric of the balloon, swing low out of their high-pommeled saddles to strike at the cloth fluttering and swelling in the wind with their swords, as if the balloon were itself alive, a billowy monster that had to be killed lest it kill.

Then what was Leonardo? Merely a servant of the smoking monster?

When the wind died and the cloth settled, the men became even more menacing. Although they remained on their horses, they came closer, until hooves were on the fabric. When no immediate harm came to them, they rode about on the cloth, circling Leonardo, directing themselves to him.

"Are you a Jinn that you can transform ordinary muslin into a monster that flies through the air?" asked the tallest of the bedouins, obviously the leader. Unlike the others, he wore his beard trimmed to a point in Arab fashion and sat straight in his saddle. He had a deep scar that cut across his cheek, ending at the jawline.

Leonardo was in a quandary. If he said no to the question he had been asked, would the bedouins kill him?

Or if he said yes, would they kill him . . . ?

Then let them try. "No, I am a man," he said.

"You are not dressed as a man," the leader said.

"And would you try to kill a Jinn?" shouted Kuan. He stood outside the circle of horsemen, seemingly without fear, his hands on his hips.

The leader looked at Kuan, obviously taken aback by the richness of his clothes, and said, "No man can kill a Jinn, so if I kill this one"—he shrugged toward Leonardo—"then I will know he's not a Jinn."

"But if he is a Jinn, then surely you'll bring death and dishonor to all of you and your families and tribe." Kuan came closer. "If you have family . . . and honor."

The horsemen all turned at that and seemed about to try to run him through with their scimitars when he said, "I am under the protection of Ka'it Bay al-Mahmudi al-Zahiri, Caliph of Caliphs. And so is this . . . Jinn. He is a guest of the Caliph and protected by the laws of sanctuary. If you even touch him, there will be blood feud."

The leader seemed uncertain. "You may keep your water skins and enough clothing to hide your nakedness, but all else is ours, including the monster that flies."

"But you yourself said it was mere cloth," Kuan said.

"And we will take it," said the leader, motioning to his men to begin rolling up the fabric. Bedouins were a romantic people, but practical as a carpenter's ax.

"Do you not wish to know about the monster that flies?" Kuan asked.

"Disrobe and lay your jewelry before you. My men will turn away from you." The leader seemed nervous, obviously realizing that Kuan was playing for time. He shouted at his men to take the fabric of the balloon envelope, but they refused to get down from their horses. "Are you women?" he shouted at them, and he slid from his horse and began pulling on the cloth himself. Seeing that no harm came to him, the men got off their horses and began gathering the material. They were obviously humiliated. Taking a chance, Leonardo walked across the fabric to Kuan to get out of their way.

Once the men were at work, the leader said, "Now disrobe or I will kill you myself."

Kuan shrugged and reached into his muslin underrobe for a letter that bore the stamp of the Caliph. "Would you violate those who carry this?" He held out the letter to the leader, who took it grudgingly. "Can you read it?" Kuan asked.

The man's face reddened. He read the letter, handed it back to Kuan. A look passed between them, almost as if they had once been comrades, and then he nodded and called his men to mount their horses. "Leave the spoils," he shouted, and getting on his horse, he rode off without looking back; the others followed, disappearing over a hill.

Kuan hid his letter again and smiled.

"Would they have killed us?" Leonardo asked.

"It depends whether they were on *ghrazzu* or outcasts."

"*Ghrazzu?*"

"It is a game of stealing the property of another tribe," Kuan said. "But it is a game where men die as easily as in battle." He paused, obviously musing to himself. "Well, perhaps . . ."

"Kuan?"

"If they are outcasts, then they would have certainly played with us and then killed us. What would they have to lose? If they are riding on *ghrazzu,* then they would obey bedouin law."

"They obviously obeyed *someone's* law, for we are alive."

Again Kuan smiled. "I think we are alive because their leader sensed that others would soon arrive. Or—" He paused, looking in the direction of the bedouins and then nodded toward the east, where the sun was poised.

Leonardo saw riders in the distance.

"No, Leonardo, we need not fear *them*. They are the Caliph's troops. Let's take what we can from here." He nodded in the direction of the balloon. "The cloth would make a desert tribe wealthy."

"But we can't carry it," Leonardo said.

"Don't worry, Maestro, I don't believe we'll have to. But we'd best weight it down, lest the wind carry it."

When they were finished, Kuan asked, "Did you notice the scar on the tall one's face?"

"Yes," Leonardo said.

"I once met a man with a scar like that in Akaba, near the Red Sea. He was eating with one of the Caliph's chiefs. In the desert, not in the town." Kuan spoke as if there were some disgrace to eating in town, as if, indeed, he had become a true bedouin. Yet this was a man who had seemed completely at ease in Florence, in the company of civilized men. "The man choked on a piece of sheep, and rather than insult his host by not speaking, he sliced his cheek and pulled it open to show that he had meat stuck behind his teeth."

"Was that the man?" asked Leonardo.

"The man I knew had a terrible tragedy. He left his own people, and no other tribe would give him sanctuary. Or so the story goes," Kuan added, as if to emphasize that he knew more than he told.

"What was his tragedy?"

"Forbidden love."

"Another man?" Leonardo asked.

"His sister. They were cousins of the Caliph . . . and of A'isheh."

"Were?"

He waved his hand. "They might as well be dead."

As they spoke, the Caliph Ka'it Bay rode toward them on a huge white camel. He was dressed in white *abba* and *gumbaz*—the bedouin cotton underrobe and cloak—as if he were a tribesman without rank. With him were about twenty tribesmen, all on white racing camels, the Caliph's prized possessions. These rough-looking men were the Caliph's bodyguards. Kuan had once told Leonardo that they could ride and fight longer and harder than anyone else—except, of course, the Caliph; and Leonardo had also learned that Kuan was the master of the Caliph's bodyguards, was, in fact, a slave. But that was no dishonor in this world, for Ka'it Bay himself had been a slave. The Mamluk kingdom had been ruled by slaves for generations.

Ka'it Bay was in the lead, and Leonardo was surprised to see that the Caliph looked even leaner than he remembered, as if he had been honed by sun and desert and battle. It seemed to Leonardo, beyond a doubt, that this manifestation was the authentic one. Indeed, the Caliph had been forming an army and skirmishing with Mehmed's Turks. His pale-blue eyes seemed like reflections in a cave, for his face was shadowed by his headcloth. But Leonardo was even more surprised to see his longtime friend Amerigo Vespucci. His thin, delicate face was dark and chapped; the sun had bleached his eyebrows white, and his hair, too, had turned light. He was dressed like an Arab, and it seemed to become him. He looked robust, wiry; surely, this was not the same dandy he had known in Florence.

But neither was the bedouin seated sidesaddle on the great camel beside him.

Sandro Botticelli had lost his fat and had grown a beard. He looked black as a Nubian.

Leonardo recognized him immediately. He shouted "Little Bottle!" and rushed toward him. Sandro tapped his camel with a bamboo stick and said *"Ikh,"* which meant "kneel." As the camel folded its front legs and hunkered forward, Sandro slid from the saddle and, without regard to formality—to the king who was watching him with amusement—gave Leonardo a crushing bear hug and whispered in his ear: "I have news."

22
The
White Sheep

But it is to be regretted that some Eastern kings, great in power and intellect, have not had historians to celebrate their deeds, since among the Sultans of Egypt and among the Kings of Persia, there have been men most excellent in war, and worthy not only of being compared with ancient barbarian kings famous in arms, but even with the great Greek and Roman commanders.

—Ramusio's Preface to Caterino

Slay, slay! If you conquer, you will receive great rewards from our ruler.

—Sinan Bassà

*A*ll of Cairo has seen the machine that floats in the sky, as have those in the groves and on the river and in the desert," Kuan said to the Caliph. "And they have seen the King of the Age stand upon its platform and gaze down upon them like a fiery angel."

"Or a Jinn," interrupted the Caliph, amused. His great white camel knelt beside him, as if even beasts knew to bow before him.

"The word will spread as fast as any ship can sail and any horse can ride that Ka'it Bay, ruler of worlds, can indeed . . . fly like a Jinn," Kuan continued. "I'm sure that Mehmed and all other Turks will hear of it soon enough." He spoke in an artificial voice, as if he were reciting poetry in an epic style; but the Caliph seemed pleased and was obviously happy to see his servant and friend.

"Have they not already heard—and seen—your weapons that multiply corpses?"

Ka'it Bay laughed at that and nodded. "And for that we can thank Maestro Leonardo. Let's hope his work impresses our enemies and allies alike."

Leonardo looked to Kuan for an explanation, but the Caliph said, "Do not look so bemused, Maestro. Did you think that we would do nothing with your sketches? You'll see the fruit of your creations soon enough." The Caliph turned away.

"What does he mean?" Leonardo asked.

Sandro was about to answer, but Kuan said, "Be patient and hold your questions."

A stocky guard, a Kurd with a wide, freckled face, braided hair and painted eyelids, brought Kuan one of the white racing camels, a huge animal with gauzy brown markings. Only the Caliph's camel was taller. The guard grinned at Kuan, who nodded back, but it was obvious that Kuan was pleased, and that he recognized the beast as his own. The Caliph himself brought Leonardo a camel, a gift which Leonardo accepted graciously; but when he tried to stroke its chin, the young animal jumped shyly away.

"Make friends with her," the Caliph said. "She's yours."

Kuan handed Leonardo a bread flap, which he held out to the camel. The camel took it gently with its teeth; there was something uniquely human about this animal, and Leonardo realized that it had eyelashes on its upper and lower lids. Its hair was like the best wool.

"Do you know about camels?" the Caliph asked, baiting Leonardo. "They're stupid and treacherous and ugly and they hate like no other animal. They'll repay your kindness by spitting green vomit in your face, and they'll drag themselves for miles to die in a spring so they may poison the water with their remains. They're all creatures of Shaitan. Except these, which are as white as God's eyes and as gentle as a mother." With that he got up onto his camel, talked to Kuan and a few of his guards, and then waved his arm; the guards followed, except those who stayed to roll the fabric of the balloon, as if indeed the balloon was a great beast to be butchered and carried away. Amerigo rode with the Caliph, but he turned and nodded to Leonardo, as if to tell him that they would, indeed, talk later.

"Come on," Sandro said.

"I've never ridden one of these animals before," Leonardo said.

"You'd best learn. The Caliph rides very hard, sometimes as far as two hundred miles without pause, as if he needs neither food nor drink. He's like his camels. Here, I'll show you what to do."

"Little Bottle," Leonardo said, "how do you come to be *here*?"

"First let me help you up on your beast."

"What news do you have? I must know, I cannot wait. To see you here, it's like a . . . miracle."

"Not such a miracle," Sandro said, "but it would be if you were to get to your destination without knowing how to ride this beast. Now, pay attention, and I promise, I shall tell you everything." He looked toward the men who had cut the fabric of the balloon and were now loading it upon their camels. "They're ready to leave, and we can't afford to lose sight of the caravan—we wouldn't survive long alone in these lands."

"Caravan?"

"You'll see," and Sandro showed him how to get the camel to kneel. Leonardo climbed onto the saddle—which was a wooden frame covered with a rug—and hooked his leg over the front pommel as Sandro suggested. Upon the back pommel were tied a water bag, clothes, and a scimitar that hung in a makeshift cloth: another gift of the Caliph? Leonardo felt dizzy upon the camel, which had raised itself to full and considerable height, first its front part, and then its back, almost pitching Leonardo from the saddle in the process. He had felt more secure and less fearful in the balloon.

Then Sandro climbed onto his camel, which gave out a soulful groan that sounded almost human, and guided it beside Leonardo. "It's not my weight, as you might think," he said. "Often he cries when I dismount."

"What am I to do now?" Leonardo asked, feeling the beast beneath him as if he were atop a mountain that breathed and swayed and smelled like soured milk. But he followed one question with another, for he could not contain his patience any longer. "Now *tell* me, what is your news?"

"Niccolò Machiavelli is alive," Sandro said. "That should ease the burden, my dear friend."

"Thank God!" Leonardo cried. He was overcome with joy and relief, which turned to longing sadness; and indeed he began to cry, as if he were a child, as if he could not catch his breath. And he also felt suddenly tired, as if the news had exhausted him.

"Leonardo, are you all right?"

Leonardo brought himself under control and asked, "Where . . . where did you see him? And how? You must tell me everything you know." As he spoke, the last of the Caliph's guards rode off, their camels burdened with the great bulk of linen.

"I saw him in Constantinople," Sandro said.

"Is he all right, is he—"

"He is safe, Leonardo," Sandro said as he gestured toward the departing guards. "Now we must get moving." He told Leonardo how to tap the side of the camel's neck with the stick to indicate direction, and how to regulate the gait with his heels. The camels walked, and Leonardo felt as if he were back on the *Devota,* for the backward and forward motion was like the rolling of a ship.

Leonardo was certainly not comfortable, although he did not feel that he had to hang on to the pommel for support. "Sandro . . ."

"You're riding well, Leonardo. The Caliph will find it amusing."

"Amusing?"

"Yes, he finds you very amusing, Leonardo. Perhaps he sees through your overly serious, vainglorious demeanor." Sandro smiled at his friend, feigning innocence, then said, "You know that Lorenzo—"

"It's not Lorenzo I'm interested in," Leonardo said. "Stop playing with me and tell me everything you know. Now!"

Sandro looked straight ahead, as if speaking would be painful. "The Caliph's cousin, your former concubine, is being treated by the Sublime Porte as an honored guest. She received me as if *she* were a Turkish queen." He paused, then said, "But Niccolò's in the Porte's prison, as if he were a murderer or common thief. A'isheh can do nothing to help him." Sandro sighed, as if relieved of a burden.

"I wonder how hard she tried."

"I believe she did everything she could, Leonardo. Why wouldn't she? Ah, you think because you spurned her that—"

"No, of course not."

"She told Mehmed that Niccolò was a favorite of the Caliph, that he would command a handsome ransom."

"Did he believe her?" Leonardo asked.

"Perhaps, perhaps not. But who can understand the motives of kings?"

They kept the Caliph's Mamluk guards just in sight, although sometimes they would disappear down an incline. They were riding through a wasteland of sand and sandstone slabs. There were no telltale tracks of life here—no gazelles, lizards, birds, or rats—just the grotesque molded shapes of sand and the huge, empty sky, which was as dry as the broken shell of a robin's egg.

"Tell me, how does Nicco look? Is he being fed? Is he sick or hurt?"

"Leonardo, he is alive. That's all I know. Let that be enough for you. It's futile to torture yourself."

Sandro was right; and Leonardo tried not to dwell on Niccolò's circumstances, but terrible images of Niccolò kept coming to mind, as if the boy were suffering all the agonies of Christ.

"I talked to the king myself," Sandro continued, "and tried to ransom Niccolò on Lorenzo's behalf."

"Lorenzo gave you permission?"

"No . . . he knew nothing of Niccolò's internment until I did. But he certainly would have made any reasonable ransom."

"And what was the response of the Turkish king?"

"He warned me not to press my good fortune."

"Your good fortune?"

"Yes, for he gave me Bernardo de Bandini Baroncelli."

Leonardo shook his head; for he was not familiar with the name.

"It was Baroncelli's hand that killed Giuliano in the chapel. He was hired by the Pazzi to do the killing. Lorenzo would not rest until he was found. Baroncelli will be hanged like the others." After a pause Sandro continued. "Lorenzo is not the same man he was. He's become an angel of death. He wears only black now." With that Sandro made the sign of the cross.

"Baroncelli managed to escape to . . . Turkey?"

"Indeed, but Lorenzo has long arms. He found out through his spies that Baroncelli was in Constantinople and sent a delegation of ambassadors led by his cousin Antonio to ransom him. The king, however, would not accept any ransom. He gave Baroncelli to us as a gift to cement Florence to the Sublime Porte. Although Mehmed is his enemy, Lorenzo has never stopped trading with the Turks. The profits are too great. A godless covenant."

"You should have been a priest, Little Bottle," Leonardo said. "But why did Lorenzo send *you* to ransom Baroncelli? Surely, he—"

"The Gran Turco invited me personally."

"Indeed."

"It seems that he knew of my work. Although it is, I'm told, against his religion, he has a great collection of statuary and paintings. So Lorenzo sent me with a painting for him as a gesture of goodwill."

"And what painting did you take him?" Leonardo asked.

"I call it 'Pallas Subduing the Centaur,'" Sandro said, smiling. "I promised Lorenzo I would do another for him."

"Ah," Leonardo said. "And the Gran Turco is, then, the centaur."

"If you will. . . . Come, Leonardo, we must ride faster, or we'll be lost," and they nudged the camels into a trot, which almost shook Leonardo off the saddle; but once the beasts settled into stride, into the gait of a long trot, it was not unlike riding a horse. Before them lay a plain of scrub and yellowish sand dotted with green bushes. They could not speak easily for a while, but then the guards ahead of them slowed, and Leonardo and Sandro followed suit.

"They do not ride like the Caliph," Sandro said. "He rides everywhere as if he were on the attack."

"I think he might be crazy," Leonardo said.

"No," Sandro said. "Anything but crazy."

Leonardo nodded. "How did you come to be here? Shouldn't you be accompanying your prisoner, Baroncelli?"

"I make a poor guard, Leonardo, and Antonio de' Medici had fifty men of his own to guard Baroncelli. He gave me leave and one of his best bodyguards to guide me through Persia and Arabia to find you. And the king gave me a letter stamped with his seal to ensure my safe passage. So you see, I, too, have become an adventurer."

"So I see," Leonardo said. "But why would the Grand Turk give you safe passage to visit his enemy?"

"He is a man of honor," Sandro said. "I must give him that, even if he might well be the incarnation of Satan. Certainly he wished me to convey to the Caliph his military strength. He's no fool. Leonardo, you cannot imagine it. He has more men than . . . than there are grains of sand. Surely, he is invincible. I fear that the Christian kingdoms will have no choice but to make accommodations with him, or we'll all have to take Mohammed as our Prophet."

"It seems that you've already done so."

"Don't blaspheme," Sandro said.

"And I would be careful about lauding the Turk in front of the Caliph."

Sandro nodded, as if he were receptive to good advice. "However, the Kur-án respects Christ and in some ways is most interesting. I have strengthened my own faith, Leonardo. These people—both the Turk and the Arab—embrace their God as we do not. I fear the Last Days may be upon us. There will be no escape, no reprieve, no—"

"What are the weapons that multiply corpses?" Leonardo asked.

"What?"

"Kuan was telling the Caliph of such things, and the Caliph referred to my sketches. You were about to tell me, but Kuan stopped you."

"They are fitting out an army with your inventions, Leonardo," Sandro said. "Most impressive. I congratulate you. Lorenzo made a mistake by ignoring your talents as a military engineer."

"And who better than I could produce my own inventions?" Leonardo asked.

"Your apprentice Zoroastro, it seems."

"He's not my apprentice! Why would the Caliph put *him* to such a task? He's—"

"Very talented," Sandro said. "You've told me so yourself."

"What has he made?"

"The Caliph was especially taken with your repeating cannon and serpent arquebus."

"I have an idea for something better than the serpent," Leonardo said. The serpent was a matchlock mechanism that gripped the match, which was struck when the trigger was pulled; Leonardo had been making sketches for a handgun fired by a wheel lock. "Where is he?"

"Zoroastro?" Sandro shrugged.

Leonardo smiled as he thought of Zoroastro bringing the sketches to life, but when Sandro questioned him, he didn't answer. He had purposely made mistakes in every diagram by adding extra gears and ratchets and cylinders. That should have given Zoroastro some little frustration. "And what about my flying machines?"

Again Sandro shrugged, then said, "Why would you need a machine with wings when you can build a machine that floats like a cloud?"

"Because wings are the mechanism of nature."

"And clouds aren't?"

Frustrated, Leonardo said, "Tell me about Florence. What has happened there?"

"You mean you don't know?"

"I've been kept in a bottle," Leonardo said, nodding to his friend and lifting his eyebrows, as if to question whether Sandro understood his double pun. Certainly Sandro knew about Jinn, if he had read the Kur-án. "I've heard no news of home."

"It's very bad . . . very bad," Sandro said. "Florence is at war with the Pope, who excommunicated all of Tuscany. To make matters worse, our bishops gathered in the Duomo and *excommunicated* the Pope."

"What? How is that possible?"

"They claim that the *Donation of Constantine* and the *Donation of Pépin* are forgeries." Sandro made the sign of the cross. "The bishops have repudiated the legitimacy of the papacy, God forgive us all, and they've published it and distributed it everywhere."

"And the war with Sixtus?"

After a pause Sandro said, "We're losing it."

"Tell me about A'isheh," Leonardo said.

But Sandro said, "Lorenzo sends his regards, Leonardo. He asked me to apologize for him."

"Why?"

"Because he did not honor Simonetta's request. He was hurt and angry. He wants you to know that you are welcome in Florence, and that he will make a place for you."

"If that were true, Little Bottle, he would have written me directly," Leonardo said. "I'm sure you have no letter."

"My word should be enough . . . as should his."

"What about A'isheh?" Leonardo asked.

"What do you wish to know?"

"Did she ask for me?"

"Do you love her, Leonardo?" Sandro asked.

Leonardo gave him a cold look, but didn't answer.

"Do you care for her, then?" he asked.

"Yes, Little Bottle, I do."

"She told me to tell you that she loves you, although she's certain that you must despise her for taking Niccolò. She humbles herself before you."

"That's not what I want," Leonardo said.

"What do you want?"

But Leonardo didn't answer. In the distance he could see hundreds of black tents. Horses and camels grazed on desert grass, a few palms grew in tufts like weeds in a dead winter garden. There seemed to be a commotion.

Sandro swore.

"What is it?" Leonardo asked.

"They're taking down the tents. I thought we could at least have one night's rest."

"Where are they going?"

"It's where are *we* going, Leonardo. And that I don't know."

They rode all night until they reached a village outside Akaba, which was on the northeast arm of the Red Sea. The guards on horses and camels, a thousand strong, rode through the village as if they were attacking it. A legion of the Caliph's bodyguards was encamped there, and their thorn-wood fires crackled in the dry air.

It was just after dawn, and the sky was gray and pink; this was flat country, although a low range of hills could be seen in the distance, as vague as mist, only slightly more gray than the sky. However, the sun would soon burn the vagaries of dawn into definition, and the sky would become clear and transparent and blue.

Leonardo could smell the pungent odor of coffee and the sweetmeat smell of roasted lamb and rice, which was like faint perfume. Camels roared and spat and tried to pull away from the posts where they were tied, but the soldiers had not been caught off guard. They rose to meet their Caliph with drawn swords. They were upon their camels and horses in a trice, and everyone was shouting and swinging scimitars in the air, which sounded like the *thut-thut* of arrows flying. Veiled women peered out of black tents, watching the men play; and the henna-handed whores—those who wore no veils—ran into the open, ready to sacrifice their sleep-bloated bodies to business, even though they were still sticky from earlier transactions, for there were important visitors in the Mamluk camp: three thousand Gholaums, soldiers of the Persian king Ussun Cassano, master of all of Persia, chief of the Ak-koinlu—the tribe of the White Sheep.

They too had their share of livestock, servants, and women. However, Persian wives were said to fight beside their husbands like ancient Amazons and, if the tales could be believed, were even more ferocious.

So the whores were careful.

There were ten thousand men camped in the valley of date palms, including Parthians, Georgians, and Tartars, who owed fealty to Ussun Cassano.

A man of fair complexion stood in the center of the melee. He looked around, hands resting upon his hips, as if he was enjoying hugely the riders screaming and swinging their swords just inches away from his head. A silver carnelian ring glinted on the little finger of his right hand, reflecting the light from a nearby bonfire.

He was the tallest man Leonardo had ever seen: seven feet tall, at least, and his tilted gray eyes seemed to be squinting; he looked more like a huge Mongol than the king of the Persians. He was dressed in fine red silk, and his doublet was so thickly quilted that an arrow could not pierce it. He wore a green turban, for he, too, claimed to be a *shereef,* or descendant of the Prophet, and he carried a scimitar and a brace of pistols. His own cavalry were all around him, their saddles lighter and smaller than any Leonardo had seen before, just as their stirrups were shorter than those used by Egyptians. But these men could ride as none other, except, perhaps, the Mongols. They could stop their horses in an instant . . . and so they played around Ussun Cassano. Could Goliath have been as tall? Leonardo asked himself.

Mounted on their camels, Leonardo and Sandro watched from a distance. Sandro said that he had heard rumors about the Persian king, and that this giant could be no other. "Mehmed himself told me about Ussun Cassano. He and his sons routed the Persians, and I saw with my own eyes the head of Ussun Cassano's son Zeinel, who was killed by a foot soldier in battle. The

Grand Turk keeps it in a glass flagon. It must be somehow embalmed, for it looks healthy, as if alive. The eyes are painted glass, most realistic."

Leonardo shook his head. "I wouldn't tell the giant that."

"I've told the Caliph. I'm sure he'll know best how to utilize such information. Yet the Grand Turk can be most civilized," Sandro insisted. "I've seen him spare his enemies. He did not win over the Persians handily. They won several battles, and slaughtered the Turks as they crossed the river Euphrates. But Ussun Cassano wished to humiliate the Turks. He pursued them into the mountains." Sandro shrugged, one of his characteristic gestures. "But Mehmed and his sons regrouped their armies and put the Persians to flight. To hear Mehmed tell the story, it was more than a slaughter; it was a humiliation for Ussun Cassano, who rode from the battle like a coward." Sandro spoke in a low voice, and in Italian, lest he be heard. "Mehmed claims he lost only a thousand men, but I hear that it's closer to fourteen thousand."

"And the Persians, what of their losses?"

"The same, I think," Sandro said. "This is why we rode all night, Leonardo. I'm sure of that, and I fear we are still far away from a few hours' sleep."

"It seems more clear to you, Little Bottle, than to me."

"Niccolò would comprehend, were he here," Sandro said. "Egyptian and Persian have a common enemy. It makes sense to fight together."

"But as Ussun Cassano journeyed *here,* it would seem that the Caliph is in the more powerful position."

"So you, too, have learned something from our heathen hosts. You see, we've gained from our experience." Sandro giggled nervously, as if suddenly embarrassed by his platitude. But Leonardo didn't hear him; he was exhausted and lost in thought, remembering, dreaming of Ginevra and Simonetta, Niccolò and A'isheh. Sandro looked embarrassed.

The shouting and saber rattling were finished; the camels and horses were being tied to their posts; the whores had found clients; everything was motion: slaves fed wood to the fires, soldiers pitched tents and talked and motioned and argued, sheep bleated before their throats were slashed, and within the hour a feast would be laid out to feed ten thousand.

—————

The Caliph Ka'it Bay and his guests seemed to swim through the morning meal of mutton and rice and gravy. Two steaming-hot sheep carcasses were laid upon a huge platter of gravy and steaming rice—a typical bedouin meal. Leonardo was famished; kneeling, he dipped his hand into the hot gravy, scooping up rice and meat and allowing the excess gravy to drip through his fingers over the platter. The Caliph picked out tasty morsels of liver for Ussun Cassano, who sat between Leonardo and the Caliph, and then did the same for Leonardo, as if Leonardo were the equal of a king. No one spoke during the meal in the Caliph's great black tent, which was customary, yet it was the very antithesis of Florentine custom, and Leonardo felt awkward squatting here before this aromatic oniony mass of gravy and meat. The food was delicious, albeit heavy, and Leonardo felt as if he had just drunk a bottle of good, earthy red wine; but surely all of this could not be for Leonardo, Ussun Cassano, Kuan, and the Caliph. The Caliph's officers and other guests would no doubt have their turn.

From time to time the Persian giant would gaze at Leonardo and then look away. At first Leonardo nodded to him, but the man's gaze made his flesh crawl. It was pure hatred. In those instants when their eyes met, Leonardo could well imagine that he was being burned; he felt the same kind of probing pressure, which was almost a visceral invasion, as he had when his father had watched him being charged with *sodomia* in open court.

When Leonardo was finished, he bowed his head and asked his leave from the Caliph, who said in Arabic, "Will you not share a coffee and a pipe with us?"

Leonardo was eager to visit with Amerigo and Sandro, for he could not get enough of them. Just seeing his friends made him long for home, long for the very sights and smells and sounds of Florence: the hills and winding ways, the river and the bridges, the soft and staccato sounds of Tuscan words, and the flavor of familiar food and wine. But he could not refuse the invitation. He followed the Caliph to the west side of the tent, where the goat's-hair curtains were open: to the east, the wall curtains were drawn to keep out the heat of the sun; the long, spacious tent was like a shaded pavilion.

The Caliph scrubbed his hands in the sand, and Ussun Cassano, Kuan, and Leonardo followed. However, the Persian king had wiped his hands in his hair, and so made only a perfunctory show of scrubbing with the sand. Everyone was silent while a slave prepared coffee. Only the Caliph's wives could be heard talking and laughing softly behind the rugs and tapestries that divided the *hareem* from the rest of the tent. When coffee was served, the Caliph waved the slave away and told him to close the open curtain.

They sat in a circle, smoked pipes, and sipped the coffee that was as strong as spirits. "So do you trust this kâfir to kill my son?" Ussun Cassano bluntly asked the Caliph as he looked at Leonardo.

Leonardo was so shocked by the question that he flinched; Kuan squeezed his shoulder, but Leonardo could not be silent. "What is he saying?"

Ka'it Bay shrugged and asked, "Can you no longer understand our tongue?"

"Why would you wish me to kill your son?" Leonardo asked the king directly.

"Because it does not matter if you burn in hell, Maestro," the Caliph said, as if Ussun Cassano had lost his tongue. "And because it is politically prudent. For us . . . and for you."

"For me?"

"I would think that the death of Maestro Botticelli would have certain political ramifications. Is he not Il Magnifico's ambassador to the Sublime Porte?"

Leonardo felt a chill feather up his spine, but he kept his calm. "Maestro Botticelli? But he is a friend of the Medici and a craftsman, nothing more. Why would we speak of his death?"

The Caliph raised his hand, indicating patience, then nodded to Kuan, who left the tent, only to return a moment later with Sandro, who obviously did not perceive that he was in danger. He bowed to the Caliph and Ussun Cassano and glanced at the food, which was still hot and aromatic.

"Kuan, cut Maestro Botticelli's throat," the Caliph said.

Kuan had already drawn his scimitar, and he pressed its razor-sharp blade against Sandro's throat, drawing blood as he did so. Sandro froze in surprise and horror.

"Wait!" Leonardo said, standing up. "Please! Why would you kill Sandro? What could he possibly—"

"Maestro, one would think that you had been brought up in a *hareem*. Yet I'm advised that you kill very effectively."

"I cannot imagine who would have advised you of such a thing, but what has all this to do with Sandro? Please, Illustrious Lord, do not harm him."

Kuan's blade was still across Botticelli's throat.

"I would kill Maestro Botticelli simply as a demonstration," the Caliph said matter-of-factly. He switched to Italian. "To give you, Maestro, an incentive to obey my commands." He smiled at Leonardo, then turned to Sandro. "Or shall I simply cut off your ears and nose? Isn't that the way Grand Turk sends back ambassadors from other lands?"

"I wouldn't know," Sandro said.

"But you hold Mehmed in high esteem . . . you believe his army to be invulnerable. Isn't that what you said to my slave and counselor?"

Kuan nodded, letting Sandro know he was that very person.

"You are Mehmed's very own ambassador, it seems," the Caliph continued.

"I am . . ."

"What, Maestro?" asked the Caliph. "Pray tell me what you are."

"I am a citizen of Florence. Nothing more."

"For that alone I might kill you," Ka'it Bay said; a slight smile crossed his face, as if he had made a small joke or a play on words. "For your magnificent friend Lorenzo trades with his enemies and sends spies such as you to foment trouble with his allies." He then turned to Leonardo.

"Let him go, Great Sovereign. . . . I will do as you ask."

But Ka'it Bay raised his hand; if he lowered it, Kuan would certainly cut Sandro's throat.

"I will do *anything* you ask, Master of Worlds," Leonardo said, pleading.

At that the Caliph smiled and said to Kuan, "I think our guest Maestro Botticelli is hungry."

Kuan withdrew his sword, but Sandro did not move. He looked at Leonardo, who nodded back to calm him.

"Would you call in my generals," the Caliph continued, "and ask them if they would do me the favor to partake of the rest of our repast?"

Kuan did as he was asked.

"When they have finished," the Caliph said to Ussun Cassano, "I have games prepared in your honor. And a surprise. . . ."

But the Persian king hardly seemed to hear. He pulled hard on the amber stem of a four-foot gilt silver pipe and looked ahead, as if at a point only he could see. "If you fail in any way, I shall kill you myself," he said to Leonardo. "Slowly and painfully." His voice was low and hard, and his wide-spaced eyes—the eyes of a dreamer—revealed no emotion. They were like fires that had consumed all their fuel; they were ashen gray and dead. "You must kill my son quickly, and mercifully."

The Persian looked at Ka'it Bay, who nodded, as if confirming their agreement to fight the Turk together, and said, *"Bi-smi-llah."*

Which meant "In the name of God."

———

Leonardo found Kuan near a dry riverbed preparing a large roan mare for the *furusiyya,* the games of battle. Hundreds of men, mostly Ussun Cassano's guards, were practicing lance exercises nearby. Kuan was fitting his horse with Persian accoutrements: a light saddle, snaffle, and a short iron stirrup, which would give him better command over the horse than any of the Egyptian gear.

"I've been searching for you," Leonardo said in Tuscan.

Kuan ignored him; then, as if thinking better of it, said, "Do not speak wildly here, even in your own tongue," and led Leonardo to a grove of date palms where they could be alone.

"Please explain why the Caliph has ordered *me* to kill the giant's son," Leonardo said.

"If the Caliph asks you to kill someone, there can be no hesitation. You cannot question. You certainly cannot question his order. It's a wonder he didn't have me kill you there and then."

"And you would have done so," Leonardo said.

"Absolutely," Kuan said. "And if he had asked you to kill me, you should have done so without a thought."

"Perhaps that's what separates our manner of thinking. I would not kill without a thought."

"Well, you'd better learn to do so. It's not only your own life you're responsible for. I would have blamed *you* if I had had to kill Maestro Botticelli, although I must admit I don't care much for him or his paintings." After a beat he continued. "Do you think he would hesitate for a minute to kill all your friends to make his point? But, no, Leonardo, perhaps you are correct."

"Yes . . . ?"

"He would not have killed them immediately. He would have disfigured them horribly and would not have allowed you to murder the Persian's son to save their lives, no matter how much you begged."

"And he would have let me live?"

Kuan shrugged. "That you are alive after questioning him before the Persian is proof that he loves you, Maestro."

"Why choose me? Anyone could kill the Persian prince."

"But the Caliph wants *you* to do it, Leonardo."

"As a test? To prove my loyalty?"

"He told you, but you didn't listen."

"Because I would not burn in hell. That's what he said."

Kuan nodded. "Because you do not believe in the true faith. It would be a sin for a believer to kill a prince of the faith. 'He that kills a believer by design shall burn in hell forever. He shall incur the wrath of God, who will lay His curse on him and prepare for him a woeful scourge.' "

"Yes, I've read the Kur-án," Leonardo said impatiently. "But as I understand it, it's done every day."

Kuan shrugged. "But the Persian gave the responsibility to kill his son to the Caliph. Ussun Cassano could be a powerful ally in our war with the Turk; and he has given this most delicate task to the Caliph, who has shown his resourcefulness by giving it to you."

"There are others here who—"

"He loves you. And he knows what men can do. He has seen that you kill easily."

"What?"

"He has seen the sketches for your inventions of war. Even you would have to agree that they are . . . Platonic. You depict soldiers being cut to pieces as if you were drawing flowers."

He had caught Leonardo, who, confronted with himself, felt sickened. "That is not true," he said, almost in a whisper. "They're only sketches."

"Our captain on the *Devota* gave the Caliph a good accounting of your prowess in battle, and I have certainly seen your skill with my own eyes. I think you are very different from your friends, especially Maestro Botticelli, who would be wise to remain in his *bottega*." He paused, then said, "The Persian knows your value, Leonardo."

"What do you mean?"

"Did you not notice that he wore a pistol in his sash?"

"Yes, but—"

"You did not notice that it was of your own design, Leonardo? Shame."

"I cannot murder," Leonardo said softly, as if his inventions were of no interest to him. "I have killed only in self-defense." Leonardo was speaking to himself, although ostensibly to Kuan, but something nagged at him, a memory associated with Ginevra's death. Something to do with mirrors of the soul. Going dark. Ground into . . . The image faded, banished.

"I will help you, Maestro. Or I will kill you and your friends." Then he patted Leonardo on the shoulder and said, "Do you really believe we think so differently?"

"Yes, I do," Leonardo said, musing, trying to sort out what had happened.

"Perhaps not so much as you think, for you didn't even ask why the Persian wishes to kill his own son. You imagined you knew! Babylon or Florence, the differences are slight. Slight between you and me . . . between Lorenzo and the Caliph . . . or between you and the Caliph, for that matter."

Shaken, Leonardo asked why Ussun Cassano wished to kill his son.

He would not be surprised when he learned the answer.

The games were rough, although only three men were killed, two of whom were Persian subjects. The Tartars who rode with Ussun Cassano were the fiercest fighters and could turn their horses with their legs, while Mamluks and Persians alike were at the mercy of their opponents at the end of each dusty run. It was a ragged joust, without the pomp staging of Lorenzo's ostentatious competitions; but this was preparation for battle, not civic display. Neither Ussun Cassano nor Ka'it Bay showed off their skill, although it was said that no man could match them with lance or sword. The women watched the exercises in the open and from behind brashly colored tapestries hung as barricades. The Egyptian wives and daughters, sequestered away from the men, wore veils and long rusty-black robes; the Persian women, however, flaunted crimson silks, bracelets, and braided gold coins in their hair. They were as loud and natural as the whores who spat and shouted and stirred up the men.

Sandro and Amerigo had been looking for Leonardo and found him standing behind the crowd where the games were taking place. He was working out what would have to be done. Ideas and images and memories seemed to swirl through his mind, as they often did just before he fell asleep. But Leonardo was past sleep and fatigue; the borders between waking and nightmare had collapsed; and he watched, watched the soldiers flying toward each other, crashing into each other, flinging each other to the ground. Dust rose up like steam. It was hot and dry. Boys—dressed as soldiers in iron cuirasses covered with colored silk—stood upon the saddles of their galloping horses and twirled lances. A young Mamluk slave balanced on a wooden horseshoe that rested upon the blades of two swords held by guards as they rode.

"Leonardo," Sandro said. "Are you all right?"

"Yes, Little Bottle. Just tired." Leonardo smiled and nodded at Amerigo.

"Thank you . . . for saving my life," Sandro said, but he did not meet Leonardo's eyes as he spoke. "I imagined the Caliph was a seeker of truth. A humanist like our own Lorenzo. I counseled him, as I do Lorenzo, and told him of all I had seen. I expected at the least to be under his protection."

Leonardo looked at him sharply.

"I know . . . there are ears everywhere," Sandro said. "I'll be careful."

"It is your openness and trust that always brings you into trouble," Amerigo told Sandro, who smiled, as if embarrassed.

"You make a unique ambassador," Leonardo said to Sandro wryly.

Sandro tried to laugh. "Indeed. But my work is done. I'm going back to Florence."

Surprised, Leonardo asked, "Have you spoken to anyone of this?" Certainly the Caliph would hold him until he, Leonardo, murdered Ussun Cassano's son.

"The Caliph's slave, Kuan, has made all the preparations. He tells me that you are leaving tonight."

Leonardo nodded; he could only play along. Perhaps there was a chance he would not be held to murdering the prince.

"I'm going with him, Leonardo," Amerigo said. "Lorenzo has promised his protection; I will be safe at home." He sighed; no doubt Sandro had told him how his family had fared in the aftermath of the Pazzi conspiracy. The Vespucci family had connections to the Pazzi. "And you, you will be all right?"

Again Leonardo nodded. It was as if there was a sword between them. Sandro and Amerigo dared not go further than small talk. What they knew,

Leonardo could only guess. And so they spent a melancholy hour together, watching the last game, the *kabak*. Tall poles were erected on the field, each topped with a gold or silver gourd—the gourds were really cages, and inside each one was a pigeon. One at a time, horsemen would ride hard toward the target and would let fly their arrows just when they passed the pole. When a marksman struck a target, the frightened bird would escape the cage and fly away. Ka'it Bay presented the winners with the linen from his "machine-that-floats" and the gold and silver gourds.

The spectators applauded and shouted, but then the festivities threatened to turn into a brawl; Ka'it Bay's personal guards appeared, and the crowd pulled back in terror.

The soughing sound of blades cut the air.

"There, Leonardo," Amerigo said. "There are your inventions brought out to impress the Persians."

"Brought out to impress the Caliph's own soldiers, too," Sandro said; and Amerigo cast him a nasty look, for indeed there were ears everywhere, and who could know which of these soldiers, whores, and tent followers might speak and understand the Tuscan tongue?

Unlikely—but, then, so had been the sword at Sandro's throat.

Leonardo pressed forward for a better view.

It was true. Zoroastro had brought his sketches to life. Mamluks dressed in black silk rode horses that pulled scythed assault cars; they charged through the field, the riders leaning forward upon their mares like specters. Fitted to the cars were four huge sickles powered by screws and connected to cogwheels by bent rods. The sickles were all polished curves and grace—simultaneously ugly and beautiful and terrifying, for these machines were not built to scythe wheat, but men, taking arms, legs, and heads as if they were fruit of the soil.

Leonardo could not conceal his excitement, but he turned away in disgust when the Caliph demonstrated the murderous precision of the cars by throwing a dog in their path.

The assault cars were followed by two more horses pulling a light cannon on wheels that was designed like a set of organ pipes. These riders halted, dismounted, turned the artillery piece toward a large copse of date palms, and put fire to the powder. Eleven guns fired, blowing away the tops of the palms. The crowd cheered. One artillerist turned a jack handle to lower the trajectory, while the other readied the next rack of guns. Eleven guns fired again . . . and again.

The soldiers became unnaturally quiet.

The palms exploded into burning bits and pieces of spiny bark and spur.

Again the multiple-barreled gun fired.

Another grove of palms burned and smoked and exploded.

Then Leonardo turned and like a sleepwalker moved away from the noise toward the tents. Certainly it seemed that this could only be a dream. He heard, as if from a great distance, Sandro's voice calling him.

Murderer....

It was all a dream....

Leonardo could not be here in these lands of the Saracen. Ginevra could not be dead. Niccolò could not be in prison. His sketches could not come to life, could not take life. And how could he agree to murder the son of a king?

Exhausted, Leonardo slept in the shadows of the tents; and in his fever dreams, he floated in Kuan's machine above all sound and motion and death.

23

The

Prerogative

of Kings

Son against father, father against son . . .
—Dante Alighieri

Were those my crimes already done, or mere
training for greater deeds; for what could hands
untrained in crime accomplish?
—Seneca

Does not that snake called lamia attract to itself
with fixed gaze, as the magnet attracts iron, the
nightingale, which hastens on mournful song to
its death?
—Leonardo da Vinci

The caravans of Mamluks and Persians rode northeast for three days, through hills, black basalt plateaus, valleys of grotesque sandstone pillars as high as mosques, and the desert that was called The Desolation. Families and tribes of Mamluks, Persians, Parthians, Georgians, and Tartars rode side by side, shouting across to each other, advancing like a small army. Their flanks were wide, and the columns of horse and camel were short. Taken together, Ussun Cassano's Gholaums and Ka'it Bay's guards were more like a slow, never-cresting wave than a traditional caravan.

Their destination was Nebk, for there they could graze their animals, and water was plentiful. But along the way they camped around brackish wells in barren, sun-withered oases of palm and brush. There would not be a hot meal until they reached their destination, although each night the aromas of coffee and tobacco were thick in the paper-dry desert air.

Leonardo, who accompanied the Caliph and Kuan, felt as if he were riding to his own death. Yet his dreams and thoughts were of munitions: bombards and giant crossbows, exploding finned missiles that looked like darts, catapults and ballistas, and above all, of refinements to Kuan's balloon. The hours passed quickly, and more than once he thought about his mother Caterina and his rough-handed stepfather Achattabrigha. During these days and nights in the desert, he longed for their rough embraces. Indeed, it was as if he were preparing once again to jump from a mountain, as he had done in Vinci to prove himself to Lorenzo.

When Leonardo asked about Sandro and Amerigo, Kuan had only laughed at him. Yes, they would be allowed to go home . . . as soon as the Caliph was satisfied with Leonardo. In the meantime, they would ride with the women.

They had all, after all, been kept under guard since the *furusiyya* games.

———

Nebk was plagued with snakes.

The guards pronounced it a bad omen; and the village deputies, who brought gifts of ostrich eggs, pastries, camels, and emaciated-looking horses, said that the snakes had simply appeared, like maggots on a corpse. The village had lost forty people to horned vipers, puff adders, black snakes, and cobras. All that could be done for the victims was to bind the flesh with a snakeskin plaster, recite passages from the Kur-án, and wait for Allah to manifest His decision.

That was, in fact, essentially true.

Fifteen Persians and seven or eight Mamluks died in great pain from bites received the first night of encampment. Kuan saved a few by cutting off affected limbs, but most of the victims refused his ministrations, choosing instead to put themselves in the lap of their god.

Leonardo did what he could to help Kuan.

As he was deathly afraid of snakes, Leonardo took to staying up all night and sleeping a few hours during the day; he would not be surprised in the dark by an adder or a viper. But he was shocked out of a dreamless, sweaty sleep by shrieking cries. Women were uttering the most piercing noises he had ever heard; at first he thought he was hearing something unearthly, something from beyond the grave. Men could be heard crying "Oh, my master" over and over.

Leonardo rushed out of his tent to find out what the commotion was about and learned that Ussun Cassano had been bitten by an adder.

He had just died.

Riders had already left to summon his sons.

Leonardo was relieved, for certainly he would not now have to kill Unghermaumet, the king's favorite son; and he worked his way through the camp, past Ussun Cassano's loyal guards beating their breasts and tearing their fine muslin *gumbaz* robes, past the shrieking veiled women, looking for Sandro and Amerigo.

But they were not to be found.

———

Leonardo was invited to pay his respects to the king the next day in the late afternoon. Holy men stood before the black funeral tent; they struck themselves on their chests and faces and prayed. Concubines and female domestics beat tambourines and cried "Alas for him." The holy men had been praying and the women crying all day and night. Although custom dictated that the king be buried the following day, there was no funeral procession, no chanting of the profession of faith and the "Soorat el An'ám"—the sixth chapter of the Kur-án—for the camp was waiting for Ussun Cassano's sons to claim him and bury him in his own soil.

Following Kuan, Leonardo passed through the tent flap, and, indeed, a bier—actually a long makeshift bench—had been set up; the seven-foot corpse was covered in a red Kashmir shawl. There was a faint smell of camphor and rose water and decomposition in the large, shadowy tent.

There was also a faint smell of coffee and tobacco.

Kuan led Leonardo forward, and they passed from the men's quarters through a heavy curtain of Persian tapestries into the *hareem*—Ussun Cassano had not traveled with any of his wives, only his concubines, and they had all been taken to Ka'it Bay's tent.

There they came upon Ka'it Bay, who was sitting with his back to the Persian tapestries. He was smoking a pipe and sipping coffee, as if nothing was awry.

Beside him sat Ussun Cassano, very much alive.

The Caliph watched Leonardo intently, presumably for his reaction. Surprised as he was, Leonardo bowed and said to Ussun Cassano, "I'm pleased to see you've been resurrected, Great King."

Ka'it Bay smiled, ever so slightly, approvingly.

"You will await my son here," Ussun Cassano said. "We will arrange for you to be properly hidden."

"When will he arrive, Illustrious Lord?" Leonardo asked.

"He is on his way and should be here by the night after tomorrow."

"How could you know this?"

"A little bird told him," the Caliph said, alluding to carrier pigeons; but he did not couple his joke with a smile. Both he and Ussun Cassano stared intently at Leonardo, as if expecting him to answer an unasked question. The wailing outside was a wall of noise, covering all conversation, so constant that it seemed to dissolve into a rushing susurration, like an ocean pounding upon rocks in a storm.

"The prince would have been notified earlier than anyone in the camp, then. Will that not cause suspicion?"

The Caliph nodded, obviously pleased; Leonardo was making a good show for him. "We would wish the appearance of propriety, as our belief does not allow us to keep the dead from the earth," he said. "The prince will believe this little ruse, for if my dear friend the Lord of all Persia had in reality passed into heaven, Allah would grant a small dispensation so that he might be buried in his own sacred soil." He made a motion in the air and mumbled a prayer, as if that might prevent such a blessing from befalling Ussun Cassano for a very long time.

"You will remain here until my son arrives," Ussun Cassano told Leonardo, who could do nothing but nod. "I will be here with you."

Leonardo felt a chill feather down his spine, for he had the sudden thought that the king would kill him once he had murdered his son.

Kuan and the Caliph bowed and left them alone.

He could smell the musty odor of the king, who smoked and drank his coffee as if he were alone; and Leonardo knew better than to try to initiate conversation.

"I will lie on the bier myself, for my son will wish to see my face." The king smiled wanly, then continued. "I will explain how it is to be done later."

"What of the body that is lying there now?" Leonardo asked.

The king shook his head sharply, as if he would have no congress with stupidity. "It is for those who wish to pay their respects. They would not know the difference. It smells of death, that is enough, is it not? But my son, he will wish to see my face," he repeated. "He will stay here with me. He will wish to be alone, and you will kill him as he sleeps. You will hear a young boy sing a sweet song outside the tent. That will be the signal for his guards to be put to the sword. My son must not rise from his pallet."

"How will I see?" Leonardo asked.

"You will see." After long minutes had passed, the king said, "I love my son."

Leonardo looked directly at him and nodded. He felt trapped, as if with a madman who could not discern murder from a good night's sleep; and he felt himself begin to shake. He was acting like a coward, he told himself.

And he was going to murder like a coward.

He put those thoughts from his mind and rationalized that he had Sandro and Amerigo to consider, which was true. He was not afraid for his own life just now, this minute, but it was the idea of murder, of planning such a terrifying thing so bloodlessly . . . and something seemed to be crawling about in his memory cathedral, something better left buried; and as he watched the king before him, as if through a long, narrow tunnel, he thought, *The eyes are the windows of the soul.*

And that led to another thought, which was closed to him. He could not enter his memory cathedral just now.

"He is very brave in battle," Ussun Cassano said, meaning his son. "My people still call him The Valiant One. He is better than his brothers."

Leonardo kept silent.

"We could use his courage and strategy in battle, for the war is raging from Erzurum down to the Euphrates, and in your Caliph's lands it is even worse. Do you know of these things?"

Leonardo confessed that he did not.

"Do you know why you must kill my son?"

Leonardo nodded, for Kuan had told him the story.

Nevertheless Ussun Cassano recounted the tale, as if by the telling he might expiate himself.

It was the Kurds, those who lived in the mountains, who had caused Unghermaumet to humiliate his father, Ussun Cassano.

They hated Ussun Cassano. They were envious of his might and his tribe, which ruled all of Persia. The previous year they had promulgated the rumor that the king was dead, and Unghermaumet, who had always been too credulous of what others said, rushed to take the throne before his brothers. He took his army, which was guarding Baghdad and all of Diarbekr, and conquered the walled city of Shiraz, the most important city in Persia. When the Kurds heard that, they joined him in even greater numbers, plundering as they went.

But then he, Unghermaumet, discovered that the Kurds had tricked him, and that his father had taken his standing army and was on the march to regain Shiraz. Although several chiefs tried to intercede with Ussun Cassano for him, Unghermaumet was afraid that they would betray him, as the Kurds had; and he fled to the enemy—to the Grand Turk Mehmed, who called him son, gave him unprecedented access to his seraglio, and provided him with troops to rout his father's armies.

Even now, those armies were ravaging the land.

Thus the Turks could concentrate on Mamluk territory and consolidate their Persian conquests.

"I have sent cavalry and infantry to those frontiers," Ussun Cassano told Leonardo, "but I cannot be victorious if I address my son's strengths. His weaknesses are pride, gullibility, and impatience. He will fall for the same ruse as he did with the Kurds. And I daresay he will arrive here with Kurdish men. I will make sure that they do not die as easily as my lovely son," and he then intoned, "Thanks and praise be to Him who dieth not." After a pause he said, "I would be surprised if my other sons beat him to this place. Either way, it will be a good lesson for them. But until we're finished here, you'll not leave me, even if it means watching me fuck." He laughed at that. "You fear I will kill you, don't you, Maestro? It is good not to be certain . . . and if it came to that, perhaps you would be the one to kill me."

Leonardo smiled, and oddly, for an instant, he felt an easiness and kinship with this man.

———

Two days had passed; but except for taking meager meals by the light of funeral candles after the camp was bedded down, the king had sat by himself day and night and prayed with complete concentration. He didn't seem to need sleep.

Tonight Unghermaumet and his guards were expected. The corpse on the bier—one of Ussun Cassano's guards who had been bitten by a snake—had been quietly removed, as if by ghosts or shadows.

"Great King, how can you sit so still for so long?" Leonardo asked when the king had finally stopped praying. He could not bear to sit in silence any longer.

Ussun Cassano surprised Leonardo by speaking to him as a priest would to a small child. "Devotional exercises, Maestro. The Litany of the Sea. It is the prayer that makes us safe upon the ocean's waves." He laughed softly, yet not derisively. "This life is an ocean, Maestro. I pray for my son. I pray he shall cross it into heaven"; and he recited, *"We shall blot out their sight, and they shall hasten one with another to the Bridge over Hell."*

"Who is 'we'?" asked Leonardo, gaining courage.

"God."

"And whose sight is to be blighted?"

"The enemies of God," Ussun Cassano said enigmatically. *"And God will suffice thee against them, for He is the Hearing, the Knowing. The curtain of the Throne is extended over us . . . the eye of God is watching us."*

He would have certainly continued his recitation, speaking directly to God, unmindful of the infidel eavesdropping on his prayers, if one of his concubines had not made herself known. She wore a long black veil and was decorously dressed so that little of her flesh was revealed. She bowed and waited. When he acknowledged her, she withdrew a jeweled purse from her gown; it contained pigments and a small mirror. She knelt before him and applied potions to his face and chest until his skin appeared as pallid as that of a corpse. Then she applied a shadow of kohl around his eyes. When she was done, his face had the characteristic sheen and stony appearance of a corpse. Before she disappeared, as quietly and secretly as she had appeared, he told her to leave him the kohl. He gave the vial to Leonardo and instructed him to apply the inky ointment to his face. "Now I am dead, Maestro, and you are but a shadow. . . ."

They waited.

Leonardo went back to his notebook, which he had filled with sketches and agonized notes. After wiping his hands in the sand to remove as much of the kohl residue as he could, he leafed through the pages, through diagram after diagram of gears and guns and artillery.

And as Leonardo looked at his work, it came to him that rationality was like hate and grief, as perfect, as focused, and as dead. He still felt that he had died with Ginevra; that he had jumped through fire to his death.

Jumped into hell to Niccolò's cries.

A hell that mimicked life, as a chameleon mimics color.

But when he came to his sketches of balloon airships, he was flooded with pleasure as he remembered floating with Kuan. He had filled pages with inventions, and as detailed as they were, they were also dreamlike, sublime, for to stand weightlessly in the clouds and peer down like God upon the miniature features of the earth could happen only in a dream. One of his airships—he called them *galleggiante,* or floating rafts—had the shape of a bird; his idea was that the car would be made out of light wood, with windows, and would hang below the balloon. Inside were controls to work six wings and a rudder tail with the hands and feet. He had carefully drawn a spring mechanism, which would cause the ten-foot wings to spread out quickly. His drawings, practical and impractical, were all at the least beautiful. He designed a rigid ribbed framework that would give the balloon an elliptical shape; he designed balloons powered by propellers; he drew sailed rudders and with every section of every page, the process of ideas feeding upon ideas could be seen. He had drawn gliders, which were very simple to control; the pilot would hang beneath the wings like an artist on a trapeze. And he had developed his ideas for parachutes. All the drawings were, however, machineries of war; and his sidebar notes were mostly concerned with tactics and advice: *The horns that protrude from the explosive missiles will aid striking the target and should contain powder that ignites on impact. Missiles can be fired from a catapult or dropped from a floating raft. To confound and kill the enemy by means of missiles dropped from floating rafts, make a flotilla of five gal-*leggiante *connected with hempen rope, and send them out when the wind is favorable. Be careful of your height, lest you be shot to the ground. Linen tents should be carried by the pilots, so these pilots may float to the ground unharmed before the wind carries them too far.*

But several pages on, his notes became more like ravings and ragings, reflecting his true feelings.

Many dead things will move furiously, and take and bind the living and ensnare them for the enemies who seek their death and destruction.... Men will come out of their graves and turn into flying creatures and will attack other men, taking their food like flies from their very hands or tables.

Leonardo was looking at those notes when a cry went up in the camp signaling that Unghermaumet would soon arrive.

Only then did the business of murder seem mechanical; it was as if it were already done, as if Unghermaumet were already dead.

Leonardo waited behind a false curtain in the tent, which, in turn, was behind a great *cassone* filled with the clothes and personal objects of a king. The king, however, was wrapped in his grave linen and lying motionless upon his bier, his eyes closed, hands upon his breast, cotton stuffed in his nose and ears as was customary, and his ankles bound—but the knot could be easily undone with a tug of the leg.

Through a tiny tear in the fabric of the tent, which defined within narrow limits what Leonardo could see of the outside, he watched Unghermaumet's scouts ride into camp. Torches and campfires burned, but it was a dark night, without a sliver of moon, the kind of deep darkness that seemed palpable, that seemed to swallow the world into phantasm; and it was late, closer to dawn than midnight. Then he watched a few of the guards ride off to report to their chiefs; and later the *porta*—Unghermaumet's personal guards of five hundred—rode into the camp like an assaulting army, but to great shouting and jubilation; their banners were half-furled, in deference to Ussun Cassano. Unghermaumet, however, kept himself separate from them. Accompanied by holy men chanting the Profession of the Faith, he walked into camp like a beggar; but he was dressed like a king and as tall as his father.

A few minutes later, five guards entered the tent. They talked loudly, as if frightened that they might discover a Jinn or a specter. Leonardo held his breath and was still as the blade he held tightly against his lap. He looked about his hiding space, reflexively checking for poisonous snakes; there was just enough light to discern movement. But as long as he had been in here, he had not seen a single snake; perhaps the perfumes of death did not attract them.

The guard's search was cursory, and they didn't touch the grave linen of the king, for that was the prerogative of Unghermaumet.

The king's son then entered with two holy men and a muezzin, who Leonardo later learned was blind; thus, he could not look upon the prince's concubines and wives in *hareem*. The muezzin chanted in a low, beautifully sonorous voice while Unghermaumet pulled the linen away from his father's face.

The prince cried out, wailing, and Leonardo could hear a scuffle; he watched as the holy men tried to pull Unghermaumet away from his father. Unghermaumet regained himself and ordered the others out of the tent. Then he paced around the bier, speaking to what he thought was his dead father, begging his forgiveness, praying for him. One of the holy men came to take him back to his own tent, but Unghermaumet would not leave his father.

Ussun Cassano certainly knew his son.

And so Unghermaumet paced back and forth throughout the length of the black tent. He spoke to his father, asking questions, and making promises, as if he thought that he could bring back the dead by sheer will alone. Every few minutes he would cover his face and cry and rock back and forth on his heels. An instant later he would begin pacing again; and thus it went on hour after hour, until Leonardo began to fear that the prince would not come to bed.

But how long could Ussun Cassano lie motionless?

It was only a matter of time before Unghermaumet would come to his full senses and discover the ruse; yet Leonardo could feel the young man's grief and pain radiating like heat from an exercised animal. If he touched his father again, would he notice that the flesh was warm? But, no, he would not remove the winding cloth. He would not show disrespect, for right now, right here in this tent, the realms of life and death were one and the same. Just as the living could be blind, so could the dead see.

Leonardo felt stiff. His leg was asleep, and he could not rub away the needles that seemed to vibrate in the bone and under the skin. If the prince did not come to bed, Leonardo would have to kill him face-to-face.

He shivered at the thought, yet was consoled. He smiled without mirth, for his thoughts wandered, just as they did before the darkness of sleep, and he wondered exactly where the divine Dante would locate him in his inferno, in what circle? The fourth and last water? Fixed in ice with . . .

Outside the tent, a boy began to sing in a high, thin voice.

"His perfection, how bountiful is he.

"His perfection, how clement is he.

"His perfection, how great is he."

Unghermaumet was standing near his father, listening.

It had to be done now.

Leonardo stood up, tentatively putting his weight on his numbed leg, then calculated how he would take down the prince.

If he could wait just another beat, perhaps Unghermaumet would begin to pace . . . perhaps he would come to Leonardo. But there wasn't time. There would soon be tumult and bloodletting outside. If Leonardo failed—

He would cut Unghermaumet's windpipe; he would come upon him from behind and drag him backward, away from his father; and then, like thought itself, Leonardo was in motion, counting the few steps to Unghermaumet, as if he, Leonardo, were sitting on the edge of the tent and directing someone else to murder.

As if from far away, he heard a rushing, a rumbling; a soughing: the sounds of steel cutting into meat and bone, of life gurgling from throats, and then the clang of steel and shouting, as Unghermaumet's army came awake to their own slaughter.

Or was Leonardo hearing the sounds of blood rushing in his head?

Leonardo stopped before the bier, his arm raised, knife clenched in hand.

Ussun Cassano had risen from the dead, had opened his eyes to look into the candlelight-reflecting eyes of his son. Perhaps he saw himself. But his great hands were locked around Unghermaumet's neck and face; and then Leonardo heard a terrible, nauseating cracking sound followed by a moan.

Ussun Cassano held his son through his death-spasms.

Both men were on the bier: Ussun Cassano sitting, leaning his weight on his elbow as he embraced Unghermaumet around the waist with his right arm; and Unghermaumet in death kneeling across the bier, as if to profess his eternal sorrow.

Ussun Cassano was moaning; Leonardo recognized this hollow song of utter despair, and in that terrible corridor of a moment—a sliver of time as frozen as the lake which held Satan himself—Leonardo met Ussun Cassano's gaze. Outside, the fighting continued, but that was a world away. It was the past, or the future. But the present was locked between Leonardo and the Persian king.

And the king looked at Leonardo, who remembered finding Ginevra.

Remembered killing her murderers, remembered eviscerating them, pounding them against the floor, cutting them with dead dispassion, until he was left with the eyes, which he pounded into glassy puddles.

The eyes are the windows of the soul.

But Leonardo had not lost himself in memory. He felt the full weight of Ussun Cassano's deed . . . his own deed. In the guttering candlelight, Leonardo looked like some blackened icon, for he stood as still as Verrocchio's statue of David, his face marked by his tears, which drew fleshy lines down his kohl-painted face.

"It was for me to do, Maestro," Ussun Cassano said, breaking the spell.

Still Leonardo stood where he was.

"You'll not die by my hand, nor will your friends." Then he got off the bier and hoisted his dead son over his shoulder. "One last humiliation," he said; and although he looked at Leonardo, he was speaking to Unghermaumet.

With that the king walked out of the tent and into the carnage outside.

———

Fires raged; and it was as if the entire camp was aflame, although it was only Unghermaumet's tents. The acrid chicken-smells of burning flesh and goat-hair tents were thick in the air, like grease in a kitchen. Many men were mercifully killed in one fell swoop by Ussun Cassano's guards; it was as if a thousand heads had rolled at once on a thousand chopping blocks. Others surrendered immediately; but even so the clanging of swords, the bellowing-begging of men, and the shushing of arrows could be heard. Slaughter had its own momentum, its own mind.

The high-pitched screech of Ussun Cassano's ram's horn cut through the din, as he positioned himself dramatically in the firelight so that he could be easily seen; his guards displayed the dead Unghermaumet. Astonished, his men fell to their knees upon seeing their king's apparent resurrection. He gently pulled his son's head upward by his hair, paused to allow everyone to absorb who it was, and shouted that this was the reward of treachery, no matter how high-born the perpetrator. He recited the profession of faith— "There is no deity but God, Mohammed is His Apostle, May God favor and preserve Him." His guards responded in same. He, in turn, demanded mercy for Unghermaumet's guards and then disappeared to be with the *mughassil*—the washers of the dead—who would prepare his son for burial tomorrow.

But no mercy was shown to the Kurds.

They had been dragged from their tents to die in agony; and to Leonardo's horror, horses drawing the scythed assault cars of his invention were charging into what was left of their ranks. The cars were fitted with torches, illuminating drivers and horses and flying limbs, as if these draconian guards were death itself, the four horsemen of the apocalypse. The cars cut through bodies as if they were wheat; and the drivers chased down those who would escape, even cutting down tents along with guards, women, and children inside, for the sickles were heavy-bladed and well balanced. Screams seemed muffled, as if swallowed by the night, which was beginning to change, to lighten almost imperceptibly in the east, the direction of prayer.

Soon, indeed, the first call to prayer would be sounded, for those who drove the cars and those who followed, an army of croppers, walking through the fields of death, cutting off heads, chopping off fingers for rings. It was not unlike a torch-lit procession, and Leonardo could not help but follow, as if pulled like a nail toward a magnet. In disgust, in horror and terror, he walked in the darkness like a shadow. And he looked like a specter, a demon or Jinn without a face, without a head: the kohl still covered his face, hiding it. He could not close his ears to the wounded and mutilated Kurds, who nevertheless begged for life, for just one reprieve, as the soldiers cleaned up behind the cars by lopping off heads and throwing them into sacks even as the lips were still moving. Seemingly unmindful of the human agony boiling about them, the soldiers chatted with each other as they hammered and cut and picked through bloody gobbets. Thus their shouts of delight each time they came upon something of worth . . . their shouts that mixed with their victims' prayers and death-cries.

And as Leonardo walked through the carnage in the wake of his machines, through the body parts and flapping wings of broken tents, his feet squelching in the blood and gore that fertilized the parched ground, he tried to pray, to call God to attention.

But he knew there would be no reply, for just now, *he* was God.

What he beheld was his own, the products of his thought.

Lacrimae Christi.

24

The Castle
of the Eagle

No bird that does not wish to die should
approach its nest.

—Leonardo da Vinci

Like a whirling wind that rushes down a sandy
and hollow valley and, in its hasty course, drives
to its center everything that opposes its furious
course.

—Leonardo da Vinci

There would be no sleep, for it was almost dawn.

Although the camp was in an uproar, everyone spoke in whispers. The sky was a panoply of stars, and starlight and firelight gave this early-morning scene an unearthly appearance. Leonardo had searched for his friends; numbed, he wandered through the camp. He absorbed every grotesque part of the battlefield: everyone who was in movement or stopped dead with grief or fatigue . . . everyone and everything became a continuing tableau for Leonardo, a painting that lived and changed, that grew and became corrupted and even died through time, but only as the leaves of plants wither and die, leaving the whole alive, if enervated. He saw this living painting as one finished in the Flemish mode: varnished, layered with oily pigments, as shiny and deep as the Antichrist's frozen prison.

Over and over he came back to that, as if Dante were instructing him, preying on him, punishing him for all this, for his machines of destruction, for these fields of beautiful bone and ebony death. The stars were the varnish; light itself seemed to emanate from the corpses scattered and caught on the battlefield. Leonardo wished to put them all right, to straighten out their contorted limbs, to press closed their wondering, starfilled eyes, to cover their nakedness, for, indeed, they seemed naked, caught in some painful, unnatural act. Leonardo had seen death before, but not in its manifold guises; he was never overwhelmed with it in the *bottegas* where he would cut through flesh and sinew to investigate nature. So here was death, as it was: torn, dismembered, a robber; just so had those who had fallen been picked over like garbage scraps. Many lay half-dressed, for it was a mark of honor for a bedouin to take the clothes of a vanquished enemy.

But these men were all brothers, Ak-koinlu, members of the tribe of the White Sheep. . . .

Leonardo's thoughts had a life of their own, it seemed, for he thought of a great feast: scalding fat, craters of gravy-glistening rice, the mouth-watering aroma of roasting flesh, the boiled sheep's heads topping the mountains of gravy and rice and meat, their jaws gaping, their blackened steaming tongues lolling over teeth as white as the moon.

Repelled, he turned away, but he was surrounded by death . . . and he had not even ventured into the mass of Kurds butchered with his machines . . . and he remembered the Ponte Vecchio in Florence, the bridge of the butchers where one stepped through puddles of congealing blood and looked past the newly cut corpses that would be tonight's suppers.

"Leonardo, don't you ever sleep?" asked Kuan, startling Leonardo, who reflexively reached for his dagger; this seemed to amuse Kuan.

"I am not alone," Leonardo said. "And no one else is asleep, except for the dead." He gazed ahead at the corpses.

"You'll regret it when we ride. You'll wish for blessed sleep then."

"Perhaps, then, you should take your own medicine."

Kuan ignored him and watched the grave diggers begin their work making shallow graves. Leonardo, for his part, was reminded of the plague, and shuddered.

"Have you found your friends?" Kuan asked.

"I searched the camp," Leonardo said. "They are nowhere to be found. Have they been sent home?"

"You should have visited my tent. They are in my charge, as they will remain."

"Then *you're* taking them back?" Leonardo asked. He desperately wished to go with them, to return home, but the Caliph was his best chance to find Niccolò and A'isheh. He could not go home without Niccolò; and although he would not admit it to himself, he could not leave without seeing what Zoroastro had made of his inventions.

"No, the Ruler of Worlds is not quite ready to let them go, especially your friend Sandro. They've been invited to accompany us."

"Where?" Leonardo asked, surprised.

Kuan shrugged and said, "To war."

"Why? Neither one is a warrior . . . quite the opposite."

"Because Ka'it Bay might need someone to act as ambassador, someone whom the enemy knows, someone who sympathizes with the Grand Turk." Kuan laughed softly. "And he has chosen your artist, the most undiplomatic of diplomats."

"And Amerigo?"

"We've retained him to keep both of you company, but he is free to leave." Kuan smiled slightly. "However, he is safer here, under our protection."

"I fear for them."

"You would do well to fear for yourself and let fate take care of your friends."

"What do you mean?"

"Ussun Cassano would never have allowed himself to be caught like this," Kuan said, waving his hand to encompass the dead. "The whores knew. They have their own . . . lines of communication."

"Knew what?"

"That Unghermaumet's troops would be massacred. Unghermaumet should have noticed that the whores weren't all over his men like maggots on meat, but he was too sentimental, too busy wailing like a woman over his father."

Muezzins sounded the call to prayer, and for the next few moments everything seemed to stop, as if even nature—the small scurrying and scuttling creatures, the heavy sea of atmosphere, the stones and sand and distant veiled hills—were waiting for the rejuvenation of prayer; for if words could create the universe, they could certainly rekindle another day. As if in response, the stars dimmed in the east, as gray light poured into that corner of the night, dissolving the darkness like a solvent.

Unghermaumet was buried with the pomp and ceremony of a prince who had fallen in battle.

Mass graves were closed.

Ka'it Bay and Ussun Cassano met.

And their armies rode off separately in the morning heat, through monotonies of hot, sparkling sand and mud flats as smooth as polished stone.

Leonardo was allowed to ride with Sandro and Amerigo, but they knew as little as he did of their destination as they rode northwest.

To Jerusalem?

But Leonardo had expected to go to Damascus, to see Zoroastro and Benedetto, and the *bottega* that was producing his inventions.

The desert was a punishment for all the killing and maiming, for the robbing and desecration of the freshly dead.

A choking wind blew like a gale across the dunes and brush. It began in fits and starts, gusts and eddies like an Egyptian *khamsin,* constantly gaining strength until it seemed that the Caliph's troops were walking face-on into the steady blast of a furnace. Leonardo felt his sweat like ice on his cheeks; he tested the salty wetness with his tongue, as if to counteract the granular dryness of chapped lips and face and hands. Even though his mouth and nose were covered by his headcloth in the Arab fashion, his eyes were raw. The sand burned like acid.

All was white haze. There was little visibility. It was like floating in a dream, a painful dream of buffeting waves. The camels trudged on, slowly working their way through the smoky atmosphere that seemed to be solidifying around them; and every so often Leonardo would start, as he often did when in a deep sleep. He could barely swallow, and it panicked him, for his throat seemed to close so tightly that he imagined he would choke to death. Although he had learned the bedouin trick of drinking like a camel at every well—indeed, he had drunk until he thought he would burst before he left—he was already thirsty. He tasted only metal.

They had stopped for only an hour to huddle under the protection of blankets, and then Ka'it Bay resumed his forced march. His troops did not even try to speak into the wind, to cry "For the eyes of A'isheh," as they had done countless times. A'isheh was a desert presence. Men spoke of her as if they knew her, as if she were the pearl beyond price, the grail; as if she were the very incarnation of the beauties they would find in Paradise, their reward for dying for God. She was philosophy and purpose and destiny. She was idea, flag, and country.

And that was Ka'it Bay's magic.

Through his troubadours and holy men and the miracle of word of mouth, he had transformed her from flesh to spirit, from whore to goddess.

Just as Florentines spoke of their saints as if intimate acquaintances, as if they were rich—if distant—relatives, so did these men talk of A'isheh.

But to Leonardo's mind, it was unfathomable that these people who constantly fought among themselves, who could not agree on the most tangible of issues, could accept and sacrifice themselves for the idea of love.

The wind blew through the day and into the night.

Leonardo's face burned and bled, and he shivered with fever as he curled under his blanket in a fetal position for a few hours of rest before Ka'it Bay called his guards to ride again. It was well before dawn, and Leonardo rode behind Kuan in a darkness of swirling sand that looked like smoke in a dark room; the moon was barely a smudge overhead in the sandstorm's distortion of space. After two hours the storm suddenly gained new strength and blew hot sand so hard, it drew blood. The camels had to be prodded, for they turned away from the column, as if they could turn away from the fury of the wind.

To one side of Leonardo was Amerigo; to the other was Sandro. They could not speak in the storm, so they rode as they had the day before: eyes half-closed, faces covered, rocking atop the camels in something akin to sleep, thinking empty thoughts, dreaming; and Leonardo slipped in and out of his memory cathedral, spinning back and forth through time like an old man looking into the past while thinking it the present, slipping into the grottoes near Caterina's house, the place of his birth and youth, the background of so many of his paintings; in those paintings his memories were seen through windows, as if pigment and linseed oil could refresh tired eyes to see into the perfections of childhood.

Leonardo's eyes burned and ached; it was as if he were seeing the white storm through blinders, looking at blinding light through long, dark corridors. The men around him appeared and disappeared, as the storm breathed them in and out of reality. Leonardo wondered if it was fever or sand.

"Sandro," Leonardo shouted into the gale. "Sandro, where is

Amerigo?" Amerigo had disappeared, yet Leonardo could not tell whether it had been minutes or hours.

"I don't know," Sandro shouted back. "I—" But the wind took his words, and it was impossible to discern any expression, as his mouth and nose were covered with his headcloth.

Leonardo searched the ranks, riding forward, then dropping back, at last finding Amerigo's riderless camel tied with the baggage camels. He felt a chill draw up his back. If Amerigo was lost in this storm, in this desert, then he was as good as dead. "Where is the man who rode this camel?" he asked a shrouded bedouin leading the pack animals.

The bedouin shrugged, but Leonardo was insistent. "I must know." If a man from his tribe were lost, he would certainly not appear so unperturbed.

"I have not taken anything," the bedouin said. "You can see for yourself." He gestured at the loaded camel.

"I would not accuse one of Ka'it Bay's chosen of being a thief," Leonardo said. "I merely wish to learn what happened." Sandro had followed and was riding beside him, but not so close that the bedouin might become nervous.

Seemingly appeased by Leonardo's polite language, the bedouin said, "This camel joined the others as if it had been lost. I reigned in the beast, to keep it safe."

"And for that you shall be rewarded," Leonardo said.

The man nodded, but then the wind ended conversation. When it had abated, he said, "The rider, he could have fallen off."

"Fallen off?"

"I have seen this happen, one falls asleep and . . . falls off. I have also seen it happen when a man rides a woman too long." He laughed at that. "In this storm, it would be easy to lose the way." The man was right; visibility was barely ten feet.

Leonardo rode forward to tell Kuan; surely he would mount a search party. Kuan immediately checked Amerigo's camel himself and talked to the bedouin overseeing the pack camels in a desert dialect that Leonardo could barely understand. The bedouin seemed very animated, but the conversation was short. Leonardo himself could barely stay saddled upon his camel; waves of burning fever washed over him, as if carried by the wind, and with the fever had come boils.

The wind died, as if catching its breath for the next exhalation of dust, sand, and hot, putrid air; and Kuan said, "I'm sorry."

Leonardo was astonished. "Sorry?"

"I can do nothing."

"But the storm has abated; you can see that," Sandro said.

"I would not even presume to ask the Caliph for a party to go back after your friend," Kuan said. "I know the answer. And he is not in good humor."

"Surely, his guards would not get lost," Leonardo said.

"Don't presume to know when you do not," Kuan said. "Unlike your friend"—and he meant Sandro—"he is not important." Then he rode forward, leaving Leonardo and Sandro riding beside the bedouin who tracked the pack animals.

Leonardo had felt Kuan's cold anger, his fury, and he realized that Kuan hated Sandro.

It was the fever . . . or a fever-dream.

One moment Leonardo was riding with Sandro; then he was alone, lost, caught in a dream of swirling wind and sand, a cocoon of grayness, of flowing heat and dry fire; and when the wind calmed, the camel could be heard moaning, as if in despair. Leonardo felt simultaneous pain and relief, relief from thought and memory, for now there was only motion . . . wind and motion and aching, grinding pain.

Minutes—or hours—later the wind died, revealing a smooth, dead, sculptured world. The storm was over. The seemingly sudden intensity of the sun hurt Leonardo's eyes, for the glittering sand reflected light and heat. Images seemed to appear and disappear wherever Leonardo looked: plains and valleys as smooth as stone, as motile as water; and with every movement of the camel beneath him, Leonardo felt the pangs of thirst growing more intense.

If in earlier delirium he had thought to find Amerigo by himself, now he wondered about the very nature of direction. It was all one direction: ahead. He saw shapes, black shimmerings that might be Kuan and a party of guards, or perhaps he was seeing a city—no, it was a castle . . . or a cathedral that seemed to be floating in the distant air; and now he remembered. The heat and emptiness had become the very canvas of memory, and objects from the past appeared as easily as the wind eddies that swirled handfuls of sand into live things. The desert had imagined and reproduced the cathedral Leonardo had painted in the upper corner of his portrait of Ginevra, the castle he had painted and then scrumbled out.

Even now he could hear Ginevra's voice and see her face, as bright as the sun. Her voice as silvery as water, her tongue as quick and as slippery as mercury, reflecting, reflecting. . . .

"Leonardo. *Leonardo!* You'll be all right. Hush, don't speak now, try to sit up and take this water purse."

Kuan resolved out of a hazy blur of sunlight, and Leonardo could see as if he were looking through a magnification lens: Kuan's scar was a red weal cutting across his unshaven cheek, but not even his light growth of beard could conceal it; his skin was dark and chapped, and a crack in his lip seemed to be perfectly straight, as if deliberately cut with an edge; but it was his eyes that looked cool and dark, as cold and shocking as the water that he was squeezing from the skin into Leonardo's mouth.

Cold as the air in the upper climes, beneath the clouds.

"Give the floating raft an elliptical shape and—"

"Hush, Leonardo," Kuan said, smiling. "I have seen your notes."

"Amerigo?"

"We found him before we found you."

"Is he well?"

"We found him before his brains began to boil like yours," Kuan said. "He had fallen from his camel; he has quite a lump on his head. He struck something when he fell and was unconscious. He would not have needed to be unconscious very long to be lost in that storm."

Leonardo's fever seemed to ebb, as the winds had before the gale began again. "I must confess, I do not know how I got here."

Kuan shrugged. "It was a stupid and yet brilliant ploy, Maestro. You must love your friend very much."

"What do you mean?"

"Well, you knew that Amerigo was dispensable. Now, if your compatriot Sandro had fallen off his horse, the Caliph would certainly have sent a party after him . . . just as he did when Sandro reported that *you* were missing. So although you took a risk that we might not find you, you knew we would come after you."

"What does your looking for me have to do with finding Amerigo?" Leonardo asked. "It does not follow that you would look for him because you were ordered to look for me."

"Perhaps not," Kuan said, "although I would have thought that my affection for Amerigo was obvious."

"Not as obvious as your dislike for Sandro," Leonardo said, surprised at Kuan's confession.

Kuan nodded in acknowledgment.

"I'm flattered that you would credit me with such a strategy." Leonardo would have guessed Kuan too cold to grow close to others. After all, Amerigo had never spoken of him. Had this affection flowered during their time in the desert? Could they have taken each other for lovers? "If you cared for Amerigo, how could you be so . . . calm when I told you he was missing?"

"Perhaps you are not perceptive," Kuan said. "I was most certainly not calm."

"But you would have left him to die."

With that Kuan smiled, a smile that chilled Leonardo, for it reminded him of Ginevra's.

The fever kindled inside him, his eyes burned, rolled upward into the darkness of his flesh, and Leonardo passed out.

He awoke to find himself riding through hill country. The air smelled of salt and moisture. With great care for the camels, whose delicate feet were cracked and blistered, Ka'it Bay's phalanx of Mamluk guards was riding through a natural stone amphitheater; around them were cliffs that looked like blocks cut out of the rock and hastily piled one atop another. Beyond were more hills, which to Leonardo's dry, burning eyes resembled the forms of reclining women, heavy in the breasts and stomachs, defined by valley and rise, by grass and trees.

There was the faint, distant aroma of wormwood, the smells and shapes of life, of moisture and decay.

Sandro made a fuss over Leonardo; Amerigo was still unconscious or sleeping, tied to his camel in what looked to be a very uncomfortable position. Even as Leonardo looked at his friend, he could feel the dull ache in the small of his back, which seemed to radiate into his thighs, legs, and upward through his chest and neck, culminating in a wedge of pain over his eyes.

"Where are we?" Leonardo asked.

"Near the Dead Sea," Sandro said.

"Do you know our destination?"

"I have heard the Pool of Ziza, but everything I hear is rumor."

Leonardo looked at Amerigo and asked, "Are you certain he will be all right?"

"You sound like a child, Leonardo. Perhaps Kuan was right . . . perhaps your brains did boil." When Leonardo did not respond, could not even smile, Sandro said, "Kuan assured me that he will be fine. He comes back to check on him whenever he can. Kuan is not the person you think."

"And what do I think, Little Bottle?"

"You think he is without feelings. His ministrations saved Amerigo's life once before, do you remember?"

Leonardo thought to say, "Feelings are not skills nor talents," but instead he merely nodded as he felt the weight of sleep folding over him again, collapsing, until all light and being became narrowed to the camel and rider ahead, as if all of Leonardo's studies of perspective were confused, for space and vision had been transformed into time; and the day slid past him, liquid and distant; until the sun's rays became long and tinted the shadows of the hills purple.

Ahead was Al-Karak: the Castle of the Eagle.

Huge squarish towers with conical tops rose one from inside another, or so they appeared from a distance. Its only entrance was hewn from solid stone; a river encircled it completely; and cliffs surrounded it.

Leonardo recognized it immediately; he had seen it before, as a mirage in the desert, which in his delirium he had mistaken for his memory cathedral.

Kuan—and St. Augustine—had been right: there was a present of things future; and one could glimpse it, as if in remembrance. But this illumination was quickly swallowed by Leonardo's fever, a boiling Lethe, which still coursed through him.

25

The

Iron Tongue

At last, an answer to our prayers, time has
brought help even to us . . .

A god's help.

—Virgil

By *quastio* is to be understood the torment and
suffering inflicted upon the body to gain the
truth.

—Domitius Ulpianus

This know also, that in the last days perilous
times shall come.

—II Timothy 3:1

The torture chamber was beautiful.

It was situated in the western ward of the castle, near the kitchen, and it looked more like the vaulted hall of an Italian prince than an instrument of repentance. The far wall, divided by pilasters, contained frescoes depicting great battles painted in European fashion—indeed, Leonardo recognized the hand of Filippo Lippi and Marco Zoppo, and Petrus Christus—and in the dusty light, the figures seemed to move slightly, as if the din of war had been stilled and death stopped for but an instant. All the other walls contained paintings, both religious and secular, which would have been worthy of Lorenzo himself; the portraits and depictions of Crucifixion and Annunciation were luminous. The floor was painted majolica tiles; and the carved wooden wainscoting that decorated the walls jutted out into benches.

Leonardo took in the room at a glance, but his attention was focused on the instruments of torture: a rack to pull apart bone from joint, a scavenger's daughter to crush the body to paste. There was a cradle; its inside contained rows of spikes; and there was a machine to lift the cradle into the air. There were gallows and pillories and tables covered with tongs and irons and all manner of knives and saws and axes and harrows and devices to burn and crush and hack and garrote. All of this furniture of death was situated around a small, blazing furnace, which had a lip, upon which were placed several glowing red tools. Various iron contraptions were neatly hung on the wall; some looked like masks, others like grapnels and headbands and spiked cages. Heavy tapestries divided the wall of torture, hiding one victim from another . . . hiding victims from spectators. The smells of rancid sweat, roasted flesh, fear, feces, and sickness were overwhelming, and Leonardo and Sandro covered their mouths.

Their host, Ka'it Bay, seemed amused by this, and turned to Sandro. "Take heed, Maestro, lest you, too, forget who my enemies are."

Leonardo thought the phrasing of the warning curious. Was this a veiled threat addressed to him? He had not yet recovered from his fever, which had broken two days ago, although the painful boils that had covered his arms and chest and buttocks had disappeared.

Then the Caliph ordered one of the torturers to pull back a curtain, which revealed a man who appeared to be standing, but was actually lying upon a blood-stained rack. His emaciated body was filthy and purple with bruises. He looked as if he might have once been handsome and muscular. He was tall, mustached, and his hollow eyes were deep-set. His teeth had been broken and his hands were bandaged in bloody rags. It was obvious that his fingers had been cut off.

"This man was one of the Grand Turk's officers, a diplomat, an ambassador like you, Maestro." Once again Ka'it Bay addressed himself to Sandro, who was visibly shaken.

"Why have you brought us here, Ruler of Worlds?" Leonardo asked. Kuan touched him lightly on the shoulder, signaling him to take care what he said.

"Surely, you cannot chide me for being impatient, Leonardo. I waited until you and your friend were fit and hearty to show you my precious objects." He waved his arm to indicate the paintings and frescoes. "Surely this is proof that I honor you and your art, so much so that I will suffer in the world to come for possessing such images."

Leonardo kept silent.

"Do you approve?" Ka'it Bay continued. He gestured to a cleric who stood quietly beside him. "My imam here certainly does not approve."

Leonardo said, "It is difficult to appreciate the beauty of your art, when—"

"Do you imagine I brought you here without reason?"

"Surely, not, Master," Leonardo said, sickened at the poor soul bound before him.

"I have news that will lighten your hearts," Ka'it Bay said, "but you must accept my blessing in its true frame," and with that he spoke directly to the prisoner in a soft voice. "Are you ready to die?"

The man on the rack nodded.

"Then tell your story once more, and I shall allow you to die with honor."

The prisoner just seemed to babble on in several tongues, which Leonardo could not make out, until he whispered, "A'isheh."

She was being held in a mountain fortress near Erzingan, which was only a few days' ride from here . . . but why would the Grand Turk bring her to Persia?

"And what of Niccolò?" Leonardo asked, forgetting himself.

The janissary ambassador just stared at him, and Ka'it Bay nodded.

The torturer, who was soft and fleshy and might easily be mistaken for a clerk or a cleric, directed two men to remove the man from the rack; and with a strength and ferocity that surprised Leonardo, he beheaded the janissary with a wide-bladed ax. Then he placed the severed head in a basket, even while its lips were moving.

Sandro became pale and could not help himself: he turned away from the Caliph and vomited. Leonardo reflexively looked away, and in that instant his eye was caught by the ornamental stucco ceiling: the fresco insets were all angels and pagan gods smiling and looking down upon the proceedings from the pure-white heights of heaven.

The Caliph would keep his word: the jannisary's head would not be displayed on a post for all to see and for vultures to eat. He would be buried in an unmarked grave. Cold solace for him, Leonardo thought.

Thank Christ that A'isheh was still alive, and so close . . . for Niccolò might be with her.

He could only pray that was so.

But this business was far from finished. The Caliph had staged this exhibition as if it were an indoor theatrical, and with a wave of his hand, another curtain was drawn to reveal another victim. He was carefully balanced on his haunches and his hands inside a spiked metal cradle that hung from a beam by a chain that could be worked from a pulley. His head was covered with an iron mask that muzzled his face like a dog's and gagged him with an iron tongue; his eyes—startlingly blue—looked glazed and dead.

The cradle was a duplicate of the one that Leonardo had seen when he had first entered the room.

The Caliph ordered it to be lowered.

The prisoner could make only a choking sound as it lurched, pressing him against the spikes.

The cradle hovered a few feet from the ground. While one of the torturers locked the pulley mechanism, another opened the swaying cage and removed the iron mask from the prisoner's head. The metal tongue, which had been plunged into his mouth, was wet and bloody; and Leonardo could also see that the man's teeth had been broken, probably when the "crown" had been forced over his head.

The cradle was then closed and locked.

It took Leonardo an instant to realize, to his horror, that the prisoner was Zoroastro. He was black with dried blood and bruises; his hair was shiny with filth and sweat. He moaned, as if breathing itself was torture.

Leonardo ran to the cradle, but two torturers blocked his way. "Let him pass," Ka'it Bay said.

At first it seemed that Zoroastro didn't recognize Leonardo; it was as if he were in a trance, but then he became alert and said in amazement, "Leonardo, can it be you?" He could barely whisper.

"Yes, my friend, and Sandro's here, too." Sandro had followed Leonardo; he reached into the cage and grasped Zoroastro's hand.

Leonardo turned to the Caliph in fury. "Open this cage and let him out!"

"After he speaks, I will allow you to judge him," Ka'it Bay said. "If that is not satisfactory, I have another cradle and valets enough to rock both you and your friend."

"*This* is why they call you the Red Jinn," Leonardo said, lifting his head in anger and defiance to indicate that he meant all the instruments of torture around him.

Kuan tried to intercede for Leonardo, but the Caliph brushed him away. "Zoroastro da Peretola, tell your friend Leonardo how you betrayed me," Ka'it Bay said in Italian.

Zoroastro tried to speak. Finally he whispered, "I accepted an offer. . . ."

"And what was the offer you accepted?" the Caliph asked.

"To . . ."

Ka'it Bay waited patiently, and when Zoroastro did not continue, he asked him, "Who made you an offer?"

"The Grand Turk."

"Ah, our enemy, the very one who holds my cousin and your friend Niccolò Machiavelli prisoner, is that not true?"

Zoroastro did not acknowledge the question; it was as if something more important had caught his attention: he was staring blankly at the ceiling, at the angels. Perhaps he imagined that they had suddenly come alive . . . perhaps they were beckoning him to join them in the frescoed heights.

"Now tell your friends what the Grand Turk's emissary offered you."

After a pause, and without even looking at the Caliph, Zoroastro said, "A position as . . . captain of engineers."

"And did you show the Turkish spy Leonardo's sketches?"

"Yes."

"And did you tell him they were your own?"

"Yes."

"Then you are a traitor, are you not?"

"I am a Florentine," Zoroastro said.

"We are almost finished," the Caliph said. "But a few more questions. Tell your master Leonardo about Ginevra."

"Ginevra?" Leonardo asked. "She is dead." He sighed and said, "That is all—blood under the bridge."

"Tell them," the Caliph ordered Zoroastro.

Then suddenly, almost miraculously, Zoroastro seemed to come to his senses. "Leonardo, I'm sorry. . . ."

"For what?"

"For hurting you."

"Zoroastro, what has Ginevra to do with you and all this?" Leonardo asked, waving his hand to indicate the cradle in which his friend was imprisoned.

Zoroastro lowered his eyes and said, "I was in the employ of Luigi di Bernardo Nicolini."

"What?" Leonardo asked, shocked.

"I spied on you and Ginevra. I told him of your assignations. I kept him abreast of your intentions."

"You killed her, Zoroastro," Leonardo said, turning away in anger and disgust; he could not stand to look at his friend.

"Leonardo, I am certainly going to die. You must forgive me."

"Why did you help Nicolini take Ginevra away from me?" Leonardo asked. He shuddered, remembering how she had looked in her bed, her face bruised and swollen, her throat cut, her clothes torn from her. And he remembered. He remembered smashing and crushing the eyes of the thieves who had come to loot Nicolini's palace . . . who had raped and killed Ginevra. If Ginevra hadn't been the wife of a Pazzi sympathizer, she'd be alive today. "Why, Zoroastro? Why would you betray me?"

"I was in financial trouble. I was being threatened by thugs, my family was threatened."

"How could that happen? Certainly I paid you sufficiently."

Zoroastro shook his head. "It does not matter. But this does, Leonardo. As soon as I got free of my debts, I tried to help you with Nicolini. I tried to undo the harm I had caused. I never told him of your meeting with Ginevra at Simonetta's. I tried to help. I—"

Leonardo stepped back as if he were being pushed, as if he could not stand near the source of those words; and in his state of mind he imagined that the words, that every sound—every creak and grunt and susurration and whisper—were bombards, exploding, tearing Zoroastro's limbs from his torso, as if time itself had slowed to increase the pain of all the parties. Zoroastro looked directly at Leonardo, as if all his consciousness and pain were burning brightly, as if rays did indeed emanate from the eyes, the reservoir of the soul; and in that instant he burned Leonardo and consumed himself.

"So you have judged," Ka'it Bay said.

Before Leonardo could speak, the Caliph's men raised the cradle.

It lurched upward.

Zoroastro's cries of pain were but whispers.

"No!" Leonardo shouted, trying to stop the torturers, but he was too late, for the Caliph said, *"Yalla,"* which meant "Go on," and the cage fell, impaling Zoroastro on its iron spikes.

Kuan held Leonardo fast, for he had lunged toward the Caliph.

Sandro prayed. Years later, he would tell Leonardo that that was when he had decided to become a lay cleric; and that moment sealed his fate and doomed him in the future to follow the mad friar Savonarola.

But in that instant Leonardo was lost. Images of Ginevra being butchered in her home flickered and flashed against the darkness of memory.

His prayers were of blood and murder, yet he cried for Zoroastro, even as the frescoed angels smiled upon the machineries of fate working below.

———

Later that day, two dark-skinned slaves were lowering Zoroastro into the loamy-smelling earth. But the sudden retort of cannons frightened them, causing them to drop the rough-hewn bier and the muslin-shrouded corpse into the grave. Sandro, who had been praying for Zoroastro's eternal soul, was also startled. He shouted at the slaves in his own tongue; but they ignored him and began to methodically shovel the raw pile of stones and dirt into the grave.

"Little Bottle, they can't understand you," Leonardo said gently, almost in a whisper. The air was damp and cool here in the shadow of the castle curtain. The grass was high and the hillsides as precipitous as stone cliffs, hill upon hill breaking like waves against starch-white clouds; here and there were glistening streams snaking toward the heath-covered valleys below. The country was fragrant and warm, a place that might have reminded Zoroastro of his own country.

Another volley of cannons exploded, followed by others in quick succession.

"Finish your prayers," Leonardo said, although he had no tears for Zoroastro; he was dry as the sand he had crossed to get to the castle.

"I'm finished," Sandro said, gazing toward the castle.

There was another volley of cannons.

"We'd best get back to the castle," Sandro said, after crossing himself and taking a last look at the grave. "I would wager that the Caliph will be looking for you."

"Why would he look for me?" Leonardo asked.

"To show you off to his eunuchs."

Leonardo glanced at the younger of the grave diggers, who looked away from him, thus giving himself away. "Sandro, it seems that these . . . informants *do* understand you."

Sandro's face reddened, but when they were well away from the slaves, Leonardo asked why the Caliph would be looking for him.

"Because the cannon is of your design."

"So . . . ?"

"Do you think a red-blooded Mamluk could respect such a device? Only a castrate could love such engines. A real man wouldn't."

And in those words, Leonardo could feel his friend's anger.

"I'll go look after Amerigo," Sandro said. "Perhaps his fever has broken."

The room was dark; its tall glass and latticework windows were covered with heavy tapestries; and the air was heavy with the acrid smell of smoke and the thick, familiar scents of frankincense and coriander seed. The Caliph presided over a dozen high-ranking eunuch Mamluks sumptuously dressed in caftans of scarlet, green, and violet embroidered in silver and gold. They sat upon soft couches, leaned back against the cool stone walls, smoked tobacco from five foot pipes, and directed their attention to the Devatdar, who stood in the center of the room and held the open hand of a young boy who could not have been more than twelve. His face was painted like a prostitute and his fingers were hennaed.

Although the trappings were different, Leonardo recognized the performance; he had seen it before. This beautiful painted child would look into a magic pool of ink in his palm and peer into the supernatural world to question all available angels, devils, Jinns, and saints. Leonardo thought it all superstition, of course, although he remembered that his young apprentice Tista had seen the fire that had almost consumed Leonardo in Ginevra's bedroom.

Now Tista was dead, fallen like Icarus because of Leonardo's flying machine.

And Leonardo remembered: Tista had seen his own death, had pulled himself away from the Devatdar, who was holding his hand, and shouted, "I'm falling, help me."

The Devatdar called for his genii, his familiar spirits, and whereas Leonardo could not understand his Arabic incantations the first time he had heard them—in Toscanelli's *palazzo* in Florence—now he could.

Tarshun and Taryooshun, come down, Jinn.
Come down and be present, for whither are gone
the prince and his troops? Where are El-Ahmar
the prince and his troops? Be present
servants of these names.

This is the removal. And we have removed the veil
from thee, and today thy sight pierces.

Charcoal and aromatic herbs burned in the chafing dish beside the boy, and Leonardo felt his lungs expand, felt a chill burning throughout his chest, felt heady and then as focused as the single sliver of light that poured through a break between the tapestries on the west wall. He looked to Kuan, who had brought him here, but Kuan averted his eyes, as if to dismiss him.

The boy stared intently into his palm, as if he were experienced in searching for the gods and saints that inhered in all pools of ink, and said, "I see a Caliph and his army."

"Who is this Caliph and what of his army?" the Devatdar asked.

"It is the army of God."

"And the Caliph."

The boy shrugged and said, "The Caliph of God."

"Will the Caliph answer a question?" Ka'it Bay asked.

Again the boy shrugged.

"Where is the Grand Turk concentrating his army? In the mountains of Taurus, or to the west? Does he imagine himself marching south upon Halab? Does he presume to take Damascus, or even Cairo? Where will I—where *can* I meet and devour his armies . . . ?"

"Master, it is difficult enough to convince the Jinn to answer one question," the Devatdar said. "Would you confuse these creatures of fire with many questions?"

The boy dropped his hand, spilling the ink in his palm, which he then wiped upon his white robe, and said, "The Caliph is gone, they are all gone."

"Did he speak to you?" asked the Devatdar.

"He quoted the Kur-án," the boy said.

"Yes . . . ?"

" 'When the earth breaks and crashes, then you will ask what it means.' "

Ka'it Bay smiled grimly, for the child had quoted a line from the *surah Al-Zalzalah:* "The Earthquake."

The experiment had been a failure.

The Devatdar apologized to the Caliph and pulled the tapestries away from the windows himself, flooding the room with pale late-after-noon light. The boy, who seemed comfortable among these eunuch emirs of the highest rank, sat down on the couch of a large and formidable old man who wore a turban decorated with ostrich plumes. This eunuch had a wide, flat face and stroked the boy's neck as he gazed curiously at Leonardo.

Leonardo felt an odd pressure and turned to meet the eunuch's eyes. The eunuch smiled and nodded to him, and in that instant he, Leonardo, seemed to take in the entire room, as if he could see in every direction, into every heart. These men were not feminine, nor lifeless; they were soft in body and face, yet they exuded hardness and strength. Their eyes were lively, yet Leonardo could not help fearing these castrati who spoke in soft, high-pitched voices. The younger ones could model as angels for Sandro's paintings; the older one looked like an eastern patriarch. Yet if these were angels, they were angels of death, of that Leonardo was certain; and these were the creatures with whom Ka'it Bay was most comfortable. He had invited Leonardo to his inner sanctum to meet his familiars, and now—sitting here breathing in warm sunshine and the pungent odors of tobacco and heady herbs—Leonardo imagined that the Caliph had castrated him, just as surely as he had the boy who spoke with Jinn.

"Well, Maestro," asked the emir who was stroking the boy, "what do *you* make of Mithqāl's recitation?"

Mithqāl was the boy.

The Caliph, who had seated himself comfortably beside the old eunuch, watched Leonardo, as if impatient for an answer. He too stroked the boy.

"I'm sure I don't know," Leonardo said, surprised. "It would not be for me to say—"

"You were asked," the Caliph said. "Speak your mind."

"I have no idea. Surely someone who is intimate with the Kur-án should interpret what the boy said. I must confess that I do not believe in such necromancies."

"Do you mean the Kur-án?" asked the eunuch.

"Forgive me," Leonardo said cautiously. "I spoke out of turn, but I only meant magick."

"But *if* you were to choose . . . ?" asked the Devatdar, who stood in the center of the room where he had performed.

"I would guess that the Turk would push down from the west, depending, of course, upon what information he might have of your armies, King of Worlds," Leonardo said, addressing the Caliph.

"Why would the Turk do that?" asked the eunuch.

"Because the Persians are massing in the mountains, are they not?" When no one responded, Leonardo said, "Why should the Turk face two armies?"

"How can you be sure he would face two armies in the mountains?" the Caliph asked.

"If the man you tortured told you the truth, then A'isheh is being held in the mountains. Is not this war to be fought over her?"

The eunuch laughed at that. "So Mehmed would use A'isheh to lure us away from his armies."

"He certainly is making a good show of waging war in the mountains," said another emir, a beardless man who looked to be in his middle thirties—but, then, all of these men were beardless.

"Yes, Fāris, I understand he has carried fire and sword throughout the country," the Devatdar said. "He passed through Arsenga and Tocat, burning every town in his path, cutting every child and man and woman to pieces. He took Carle. The Persians can't stop him."

"It's his son, Mustafà," the eldest eunuch said. He sat beside the Caliph, but did not turn to look at him. "It is he who should be called the Red Jinn," and then he patted the Caliph on the shoulder as if he were a child. "But it is clear that the Turk can hold his own in the mountains where a few men can be as formidable as an army. Such warfare might appeal to the Turks and Persians, but not to you, dear Ka'it Bay. Although I am your intimate, the Grand Turk is your enemy; and sometimes enemies know us as well as those who love us." He smiled at the Caliph; there was gentle mocking in his expression.

It suddenly became clear to Leonardo that Ka'it Bay considered these emirs his family; they treated him with respect, but only the respect of one sibling to another, except for the elder emir, whom the Caliph called Hilāl. He seemed to function as a parent, and the Caliph as a child. Embarrassed to watch this freakish interaction, Leonardo gazed down at the carpet, which depicted Paradise: a garden woven with channels, pools filled with fish, and shrubs, flowers, ducks, and various birds in the undergrowth.

"Do you find the carpet so interesting?" asked Hilāl. "Sit down, Maestro. There, beside Kuan." One of the other emirs passed the old man a thick book bound in vellum, and as he leafed through the pages, Hilāl said, "Our master has been kind enough to show us your work, and we are all very impressed, especially with your prescription for gunpowder. Your proportions of charcoal, sulfur, and saltpeter make a more powerful discharge than ours. But your cannons, dear lad, it is there that you shine. Did you see our demonstration?"

"I heard the explosions while I was burying my friend," Leonardo said.

"Ah, yes, the traitor. A shame." Hilāl paused. "There will be more men buried today, I'm afraid. Your bomb was very effective."

"What do you mean?"

"We fired one of your explosive shells, and the projectiles it contained fell upon our own soldiers, who had drawn too close to the target. Their own fault, of course, but nevertheless . . ."

"I am sorry," Leonardo said.

Hilāl watched Leonardo. "It served as an effective demonstration, although I would be careful where I walked, Maestro." Leonardo looked perplexed, and the old man continued. "The other Emirs of a Thousand will surely not be disposed toward you."

"Because of their slain men."

Hilāl smiled. "Ostensibly, yes, but they hate you for your association with us."

"With you?"

"We understand the importance of artillery and firearms. Certainly our enemies do too, for they have been buying cannons from your countrymen for years. But the lusty men outside this room know nothing but horse-manship and the tactics of open warfare. They shit and fuck and compose poetry upon their horses. Your weapons will take them off their horses—for good, for one cannot ride against the Turk's battle laagers. And they know that."

Leonardo had heard that the Turks created portable fortifications by tying heavy wagons together and reinforcing them with cannons and arque-buses. He was curious to see those.

"They've also seen your poetry," the old man continued. "You should not have signed your field pieces, Maestro."

"What do you mean?" Leonardo asked, turning to Kuan.

"The field pieces had inscriptions on the barrel," Kuan said. "Courtesy of your friend Zoroastro. However, I do believe he meant to aggrandize you rather than hurt you."

"What did he write?" Leonardo asked, insistent.

" 'I am Dragon, the spirit of smoke and fire, the scorpion who desires to drive off our enemies with thunder and lead,' " Kuan recited, as if read-ing the words in the air. " 'Leonardus Vincius, Master of Engines and Cap-tain of Engineers, made me on time in 1479.' " Kuan paused and said, "He gave each cannon a different name."

"Every instrument needs a name," Hilāl said. "But the men are calling the engines by your name instead of their proper names." He shrugged and smiled. "Perhaps your friend has given you immortality."

"I have decided," the Caliph said, interrupting the conversation. "We shall fight in Anatolia, in the mountains. All of my informants tell me that Mehmed is in the mountains, and where he is, so will be his main army."

"Then you would leave the way open to Damascus?" asked Hilāl.

"I would do no such thing," Ka'it Bay said. "If he were going to make such a move, we would intercept him. Our intelligence on such matters has been excellent. We will burn him out of the mountains, for there we will have the support of our friend Ussun Cassano. The Grand Turk has brought A'isheh to bargain. Perhaps we can smash his fortress before he can send forth his delegation to us."

"However, negotiation would ensure your cousin's safety," Hilāl said.

"We must take her back."

"They might harm her."

"And that would throw every one of my soldiers into a frenzy. *Then* they would fight. I don't think even Mehmed would be that shortsighted."

"Mehmed is anything but shortsighted, Master," Hilāl said.

Ka'it Bay did not seem offended by the eunuch, but neither would he change his mind. "We shall give full play to his inventions," he said—and by that he meant Leonardo's inventions. "They have never seen anything like your siege engines," he said, directing himself to Leonardo. "And they will have never seen anything like them in pitched battle. We will surprise them, tear them to pieces and poison them with your exploding shells, route them with your armored carts and scythes." He glanced at Hilāl and said, "*If* the terrain permits their movement." He looked at Kuan. "And we will drop bombs upon them from *your* machines that float in the sky." He meant Kuan's balloons.

"Ah, yes," Hilāl said, a gentle mocking evident in his voice. "They will think you are a Jinn who flies through the air. We have heard the stories."

The Caliph bowed slightly and said, "Kuan has created these legends by dressing as if he were me."

"I do see the resemblance," Hilāl said.

The Caliph did not seem amused. "The effect of these inventions will be miraculous, and I will prove it to you, to all of you."

"Master, you do not need to convince us of the importance of artillery engines," Hilāl said.

"Fear will rout Mehmed's men. Come, I have a demonstration for you." He bowed to Kuan and said, "It's my turn to play the *thaumaturgus*. First a lesson in . . . awe. You should enjoy this, Hilāl, seeing that you have such antipathy for all those with testicles."

"Not *all*, Master."

The Caliph nodded to the hennaed boy, who ran out of the room, and he handed the vellum-bound book to Leonardo. "This is yours, Maestro." With that he left in the company of the eunuchs.

Leonardo leafed through the book. Each page contained a perfectly detailed drawing. He looked at a carefully drawn machine for making cannon barrels too large to forge; all the various angles of the gearing mechanisms were meticulously laid out. Another page: details of a conical combat tank, which was labeled "turtle"; hooked ladders for assaulting fortresses; platforms on wheeled pillars higher than citadel battlements; a giant rapid-firing crossbow on a carriage with inclined wheels. Every page was a revelation: breech-loading bombards, steam cannons, screws for elevating cannons, giant catapults with counterweight loading devices, doublesprung catapults, various ballistae, caltrops, scythed cars, missile-throwing machines, muskets and mounts, various explosive projectiles, pointed projectiles with fins like fish, details of incendiary cannonballs, shrapnel bombs, and mounted cannons; devices for defending battlemented walls and casemates, devices for knocking down assault ladders, various temporary bridges, architectural designs for fortifications and weapons of defense; and lastly, and perhaps the most beautiful: a design for a new flying machine. This contraption looked as fragile as a pond-flyer, those stick-figure insects that seem to hover above the surface of the water. It was a monoplane, its single wing—which was strung with gut as if a huge spider had spun her thread from edge to edge—was slightly arched, its tail fixed. The pilot would hang from the glider, as if he were wearing it: legs dangling below, head and torso above.

The next page was filled with detailed instructions for controlling the contraption.

"Kuan, this is much better than anything I had conceived," Leonardo said, marveling as he looked at the drawing of the glider. He paused, leafing through the pages, as if he could read them as quickly as they fell. "He's completely reworked my original drawings, and some of them are entirely his own. I had no idea he had such talent. He seemed such an . . . imitator, nothing more."

"Even I underestimated him," Kuan said. "I would not have wagered that he would have tried to make commerce with the Turk while he was in the Caliph's house. After all, he managed to set himself up as the master inventor and maker of bombards and cannons."

"But he wished to be captain of engineers."

"For all intents and purposes, he was."

"Then why was I given the title?" Leonardo asked, feeling his face suddenly become hot with humiliation.

"The Caliph wanted the fruits of your imagination, Maestro, but he also wanted you under his eye. You do have a reputation for not completing commissions."

"This was no commission."

"I think Zoroastro had the Caliph's ear . . . for a time," Kuan said, "and he painted you as the creative, but impractical, one."

"And himself as . . ." Leonardo did not need to complete the sentence; Kuan nodded in agreement.

"But these designs are wonderful," Leonardo said. "And he had maneuvered himself into a position of power. Why would he risk all that he'd gained to work for the Turks?"

"Perhaps for the same reason that he improved your designs."

"Yes?"

"His guilt?" Kuan said, although his voice lifted as if asking a question.

Leonardo felt homesick and wished in that instant that he could be back in Florence, wished for the lightness of youth that could be counted back in months. In that instant he could see the expression on Zoroastro's face when he, Leonardo, had humiliated him in front of Benedetto Dei. He felt remorse as if it were warm water washing over him and yearned to talk to Benedetto once again.

"Well, perhaps it was jealousy," Kuan continued.

"Jealousy?"

"If he was in Mehmed's employ, he could test his mettle against you, prove that he was the better man."

Leonardo was not aware that he nodded; but, indeed, Kuan was right. How could he have been blind to it before? Zoroastro would not have betrayed Leonardo again for money. It was to best him, to assuage Zoroastro's burning heart.

"What of Benedetto?" Leonardo asked.

Kuan smiled. "If the Caliph thought Benedetto was involved with Zoroastro's scheme, he would be in . . . Paradise with Zoroastro. And you would have buried him today."

"Sandro is sick with worry about him, as I am."

"Well, you needn't worry," Kuan said. "He's safe."

"In Damascus?"

"No, Leonardo. He's here. But I think the Caliph intends to surprise you . . . so you must not let on that you know."

"He's *here*?" After a pause Leonardo said, "He was tortured along with Zoroastro, wasn't he?"

"No, Maestro, he wasn't. There was no need. Zoroastro confessed. Believe me, the rack is an instrument of truth."

"A man will say anything to avoid torture."

"You give us little credit," Kuan said. "Zoroastro was questioned about Benedetto after he confessed about himself. You can be sure that he told the truth." Kuan took Leonardo's arm. "We must not dawdle, lest we keep the Caliph waiting."

As they climbed stone stairs to reach the bulwark of the highest tower, Kuan said, "The book of Zoroastro's that the Caliph gave to you—it was taken from a Turkish spy."

"Poor Zoroastro," Leonardo mumbled.

"What did you say?" asked Kuan as they reached the Caliph and his eunuch emirs, who stood together on the wide bulwark, their clothes snapping in the wind.

"Nothing," Leonardo said.

The boy Mithqāl stood precariously on the southern rampart, which was but an extension of a sheer cliff. He wore Zoroastro's version of Leonardo's flying machine as if it were some fantastical costume designed for one of Lorenzo de' Medici's fabulous tourneys or festivals. It seemed to be hardly more than a construction of translucent gauze wings, and the boy looked like an awkward angel with paste wings held in place with struts of wood and cords of twine. Indeed, the glider was as white as heaven, and

Mithqāl was dressed in a sheer white robe. Unable to keep in place, for the winds were gusting, he ran along the rampart and took advantage of the wind to jump from the battlements into the void. Leonardo could hear the snap as the air struck the underside of the wings, straining the struts and connecting cords.

He fell, and Leonardo remembered Tista.

The emirs who crowded to the edge of the rampart shouted in distress as Mithqāl fell, drifting sideways through the air for an instant and then down, like a leaf falling from a tree. Leonardo could not watch, and so he did not see the instant that the boy caught an updraft; but when the emirs shouted praises to God, he turned to see him soaring heavenward. The boy sailed over the castle like a bird swooping above a chimney. It was as if wings and flesh had fused into one to form an angel whose hennaed hands and painted face were known only to those who crowded about the Caliph— those who, without balls, were themselves closest to angels.

Leonardo followed the Caliph and his retainers, who rushed along the rampart to keep Mithqāl in sight, but the boy soared away from the castle, flew over the hills and fields, flew far beyond the fortifications and outworks as if he were heading into the sun; and Leonardo watched fascinated as the soldiers below fell to the ground in fright or awe, and prayed. An army of twenty thousand was camped in the countryside, and to a man, they were unnerved, turned into awed, frightened children. The boy seemed to take pleasure in swooping down upon them and shouting phrases from the Kur-án.

Thus did the Mamluk troops glimpse a miracle.

The heavens had opened to give them a sign, just as they had for the Hebrews at Sinai.

But there would be more to come, to surprise even the Caliph, for as Mithqāl flew over an encampment bordered by sharp reefs of stone, he dropped a single fragile shell that exploded on impact, burning grass and shrub and shooting shrapnel into the air. Soldiers ran in panic, horses stampeded, and the Caliph swore.

"Do not worry, Master," said Hilāl, who leaned precariously forward; Leonardo feared that the stone might collapse under his weight. "No one seems to be hurt."

"Did you know he had planned this?" the Caliph demanded.

The emirs shook their heads and swore they had not known. Finally Hilāl said, "I must confess that I knew, Ruler of Worlds."

Mithqāl was flying toward the castle, showing off; but he underestimated the capriciousness of the winds and suddenly fell, as if dropped, into the gorge on the southern side of the fortifications. He shifted weight and swung his hips, trying desperately to recover; but God's eyes seemed to be upon him, for an updraft picked him up like a dust devil, and he soared skyward on heavenly breaths of warm air.

More cautious now, he navigated toward the safer grounds to the west.

"Get some men to meet him where he lands and have him brought to me," Ka'it Bay told Hilāl. "Cover the men with cannon fire if you have to." He looked at the soldiers that covered the field like ants and said, "They'll tear the boy apart."

Hilāl took several of the other emirs and disappeared down a stairway. Kuan remained with the Caliph, who kept his distance from the other emirs, and walked along the rampart toward the western side of the castle. Then he shouted down to his soldiers. He caught the attention of a young soldier, and in moments a thousand other soldiers were looking up at him in silent awe, waiting for him to speak. "If the angel descends, which he will, turn away from him, lest you die," Ka'it Bay shouted. He paused to allow his words to be repeated by soldiers below so that all would be certain to hear. "Form yourselves over . . . there"—and he pointed to a field on the other side of the castle.

There was a gabble and garble of voices, and then the Mamluk emirs—not the castrate elite, but the general commanders—took control and marched their men to the far field. The whores were also marched out of harm's way.

Leonardo, Kuan, and the Caliph watched Hilāl's men as they met the boy where he landed, quickly removed him from his harness of wings, and escorted him into a secret entrance of the castle. "I will go down and talk to the soldiers," Ka'it Bay said. "Like Moses. After all, they have witnessed a miracle." He turned to Kuan. "But I have slighted you by using the maestro's machine."

"Master, I—"

But the Caliph interrupted him. "Even though Hilāl has tried to make a point with this demonstration of dropping fireballs upon my army, I still think much of your invention. Your machines that float can carry a heavier load of death to drop upon our enemies."

Leonardo was about to tell the Caliph that the wings of the glider could be made larger to carry more weight, but held his tongue.

"But it is difficult to navigate my machines, Master," Kuan said. "One is too much at the mercy of the winds; it is not the same with Leonardo's invention."

"Zoroastro's invention," Leonardo said.

"Ah, so you credit the traitor," Ka'it Bay said. "It is reassuring to see that you respect the dead."

Leonardo ignored the Caliph's remark. "Kuan's machines could easily be tethered to the ground. Thus, from the heavens, we could watch every movement of the Grand Turk's troops. Navigation would not be a factor."

"A good idea," the Caliph said.

"It wasn't my idea, Master. The credit must be given to Kuan."

Kuan looked at Leonardo sharply, for, of course, it was Leonardo's idea; but he accepted the Caliph's compliments.

"So, Maestro," the Caliph asked, taking Leonardo's arm, "do you love me or hate me for taking the life of your friend the traitor?"

Kuan said nothing, but Leonardo felt the tension in the air.

"Well, do you love me or hate me?" the Caliph asked, insistent.

"Both," Leonardo said after a beat; and the Caliph seemed pleased, for he did not loosen his grip on Leonardo.

And Leonardo could have sworn that Kuan sighed in relief.

—◆—

That night Ka'it Bay was awakened to receive a messenger sent by Ussun Cassano himself. The Persians had been soundly defeated near the Euphrates below Erzican, but they had fallen back and were still fighting Mehmed's army, which according to the messenger was "like fighting the sea itself."

Hours later, preparations were under way for a forced march that would take the Mamluk army past the northern borders of Egypt, past Cilicia and Greater Armenia, and into Persia.

••
••
••
••
••
••
••
••
••
••
••
••
••
••
••
••

Fortune is blind.

—Cicero

Hence those tears.

—Terrence

Oh, strange events such as never happened before in
the world.

—Niccolò Machiavelli

Portrait of Machiavelli

Part Four

Fortuna

Head of Leonardo's Father

26

For the Eyes

of . . . Ginevra

Like as from polished and transparent glass,
Or as from water clear and luminous,
Whose shallows leave the bottom
shadowless,

The image of a face comes back to us . . .
—Dante Alighieri

For this (that is for remembering the places of
Hell) the ingenious invention of Dante will help
us much. That is for distinguishing the
punishments according to the nature of the sins.
Exactly.
—Johannes Romberch

The days passed without rest.

As the army marched, the call to arms went out throughout the country. The Caliph's Mamluks grew from one column of twenty thousand men to five columns. Thirty thousand were the flower of his nation, his heavy cavalry commanded by his emirs of a thousand, who wore large turbans decorated with ostrich plumes instead of helmets. These seasoned soldiers carried lances and bows and damascened sabers, and their doublets were so thickly quilted that they could repel arrows shot at far range. Forty thousand men made up the feudal cavalry, ragtag tribesmen who carried fifteen-foot lances, small hide shields, and slings that were wrapped around their heads like turbans until needed for battle; all the other men, wearing red caps in their turbans, marched on foot, fifty thousand of them, not counting slaves, hungry and angry and anxious for booty—it was no easy task to keep them from raping and burning every farm and village and town and city they passed.

Even Leonardo was caught up in the excitement, for this was more than an army; it seemed like a city on the move, as if Cairo or Florence were mobile. Eighty thousand tents could be counted, and so many fires that they might be reflections of the stars in the clear sky. It had been impossible to tell how the army had grown with the addition of new columns, for men were chin to cheek everywhere, farting, swearing, and sweating; fucking the whores and gambling at night, complaining or shouting ecstatically as they marched, praying when the muezzin called them down to their knees: a great rapacious swarm that darkened the countryside like the seasonal migrations of locusts. To a man they seemed to burn with the hot fever of religious mission. It was as if they all understood some difficult philosophical question that was beyond Leonardo and his friends: that A'isheh was a trinity of God, sex, and state. They worshiped the idea of A'isheh, and as they marched, they called her in one voice that needed no inhalation, a constant ululation of *Mun shan ayoon A'isheh.*

For the eyes of A'isheh. . . .

Great beauty, eyes of God, breath of Kur-án, essence of spirit.

The army marched without sleep, marched in darkness like a nocturnal herd; and they pressed on during the day, as if gaining new strength from sunlight, from the hills and valleys and white sand; the army crawled north, through thistled fields, through precipitous passes and ravines slippery with moisture, across streams and pastures and hazy mountains that smelled as damp as a wolf's coat, past Ammān, Ajlūn, to Eski Sham, which was a caravansary, a center for spice caravans. Eski Sham was also holy, for it was there that the monk Bahira prophesied to Mohammed; there that the Prophet learned that his mission for God would be successful.

It was there that Ka'it Bay's volunteer cavalry—brigands who received only booty as payment and knew only how to burn, plunder, and slaughter—cut a holy man to pieces in a mosque as he was studying the Book. Ka'it Bay stopped them before they could torch the town, and he cut off the hands of the leaders and hung them around their necks. He prayed and fasted in the mosque, paid the imam a huge sum of money, and left every citizen of the town rich.

Nevertheless, it was a bad omen.

Leonardo cauterized the wounds of the men who had lost their hands, for Ka'it Bay's physicians refused to administer them any aid. Kuan would not help the men either. No matter what Leonardo did, they would die, if not by fever, then by a Muslim's knife. Indeed, they died within hours, and as Leonardo rode with the eunuch Hilāl and Benedetto—Benedetto, who was now a different person, a stranger—he nodded, falling asleep for seconds or minutes; but falling instantly, deeply into a dream that recurred with every sleepy slipping away, a dream that was as real as the hot night air and the farting, sweating minions around him.

He would awaken to find himself in his memory cathedral, and there before him on the polished floor would be the severed hands of the boy who had desecrated the statue of Our Lady in the Duomo; but Leonardo knew with a desperate certainty that these were Niccolò's hands, that Niccolò had been the boy who'd been scourged by the mob; and trembling, Leonardo would pick up the hands and wrap them in a handkerchief; he could feel them under the fabric, warm and gently pulsing; then he would feel the pressure of staring eyes, hot eyes, the eyes of his father when he was accused of *sodomia;* and when he turned around, it would be there, a three-headed demiurge coming toward him, blocking his way, as he knew it would—

"Leonardo . . . wake up, son." Hilāl smiled at him, his face smooth as the tiles in Leonardo's memory cathedral. He rode a huge white horse, as did Leonardo: gifts from the Caliph, his finest. Benedetto rode beside Leonardo, and he stared straight ahead, as if absorbed in his own thoughts, as if Leonardo were not there . . . had never existed. Behind and beside them were a hundred cannons and siege guns on wagons and carts linked together with chains; the lighter guns were fastened to their own wheeled carriages. A few of these cannons were of Leonardo's design, and there were also rapid-firing guns, all initialed "Vincius." There were also several of Leonardo's scythed cars, and an array of bombards, mortars, ballistae; the most modern of weapons rolled side by side with the most primitive: cannons that fired crossbow bolts when touched with hot iron, launching engines that had been in use since Roman times.

"I have just spoken with the Caliph," Hilāl continued. "We are to ride on ahead to Damascus."

"Yes?" Leonardo said. Benedetto turned to Hilāl, obviously interested.

"We will meet the Caliph north of the city. He will not allow his men near habitation, not after what happened at Eski Sham."

"But I planned to stay. The Caliph agreed that I could work on—"

"Would you disobey the Caliph?" Hilāl asked quietly, threatening. "Whatever is finished, is finished. There is no time for invention. We will carry off whatever cannons and engines we can, but it is the Caliph's wish that you join him. You are his engineer." He smiled. "So it seems that your dead brother will have the last word, after all."

He was referring to Zoroastro.

—————

Leonardo rode with Hilāl, who took only two regiments of his own Royal Mamluks, reputed to be the Caliph's best guards and riders, and his artillery men. They were all mounted, for speed was critical: two thousand men, mostly light cavalry. Ka'it Bay had changed his mind; they would now meet at Ussun Cassano's camp, for even if Hilāl arrived before his master, Leonardo's engines might give the Persian king the advantage over the Turk. Beside Hilāl rode the boy Mithqāl, who reminded Leonardo of a young Niccolò, although of obviously oriental cast. He was life and energy itself, constantly tugging on Hilāl's robes to point out this bower or that mountain or watercourse or flower. The mountains were alight with scarlet anemone and asphodel; the clear streams were like molten mirrors falling and coursing though volcanic ravines. They rode through passes where a handful of men could have stood against Hilāl's two thousand; they followed ancient routes across waste country of purple shadows and bright rock. This was a country of light or darkness; only at dawn and dusk did the world slip softly out of focus, the clear air growing soft and diaphanous like that of Florence—Florence, which from Leonardo's perspective was nothing more than a dream.

But Benedetto Dei also rode with them, a grim and silent reminder that Leonardo had once had a life before he came to this place.

Sandro, Amerigo, and Kuan remained with the Caliph, as did the Devatdar. Kuan had given his word to Leonardo that he would watch over Sandro. Leonardo did not worry for Amerigo, who he was certain had become Kuan's lover; but Kuan disliked Sandro, probably because Sandro was as mercurial and loose-jawed as Zoroastro. But whereas Zoroastro had always been devious and selfish, Sandro was an innocent who constantly excoriated himself for being weak . . . who believed that he was a poor conduit for the pure religious spirit that he poured into his paintings.

It was only when they reached the olive and orange orchards of Katana, a village near the great city, that Benedetto finally began to talk. Sunset, and ahead, over dusky plain, were the gardens of Damascus. Plain that had been rough and rocky and barren gave way to fields. In moments, the purple and orange swellings of sunset turned gray, and then all was darkness and shadow, as heavy as the odors of olive, pomegranate, plum, apricot, walnut, and orange that mingled with the foul and fusty scents of soldiers riding behind them: an army whispering, groaning, complaining, coughing, swearing, expectorating, and wheezing.

Benedetto appeared beside Leonardo like a specter and rode along with him. Leonardo knew better than to initiate conversation, for he had tried that before and failed. Now he waited. This specter didn't even look like the Benedetto Leonardo knew: his sleepy eyes were hard and alert, his full face had become thin as a ferret's, and his sun-dark skin and the definition of his high cheekbones allowed him to pass easily as an Arab. Only his yellow-blond shock of hair remained the same, but he kept it hidden, as a woman hides her face under veils.

" 'If Paradise be on this earth, Damascus it is and none but she,' " Benedetto said.

"So I have heard," Leonardo said.

"I quote a follower of the poet Abu'l-Hasan Ibn Jubair." Benedetto shrugged. "But his name is lost, just as Zoroastro's name will be lost, for all of his inventions bear your name."

Leonardo responded carefully. "I never realized he had such talents, and I only discovered a few days ago that he had signed my name to every engine."

"Well, Leonardo, in fairness, they were your ideas. Zoroastro was an elaborator, nothing more."

There was a long, uncomfortable silence, magnified by the darkness and the searching, clomping of hooves upon twig and stone. Finally Leonardo said, "But he was a brilliant elaborator."

Benedetto laughed and said, "Yes, indeed he was." Another pause. "Leonardo?" Benedetto asked.

"Yes?"

"Why did you kill him?"

"Sandro told you that?" Leonardo asked.

"Yes, he did."

"What else did he tell you?"

"He told me everything: how the Caliph called you both to see Zoroastro in the torture chamber. He told me what Zoroastro said, how he begged for your forgiveness, how—"

"Yes?"

"How you turned away when the Caliph ordered his executioner to raise and let fall the cradle of death."

"I ... I turned away when he told me of his treachery, it is true," Leonardo said, "but I tried to stop the Caliph from murdering him."

"No, *Sandro* tried to stop him. You waited until it was too late, until the cradle was lifted, until the Caliph gave the signal to ... kill him."

"That's not true," Leonardo insisted, trying desperately to remember, but the event seemed somehow vague; it was as if he were trying to remember a dream.

But what if it were true? What if he had allowed the Caliph to go ahead and kill his friend? What if he had tried to stop the Caliph only when he knew it would be too late? Thus could he assuage his guilt and take his revenge.

"So you aren't sure, are you?" Benedetto asked softly, the hard edge of anger gone from his voice.

Leonardo did not answer, could not answer. The darkness itself seemed to be the stuff of dreams; and he had the idea, irrational as it was, that if he nudged his horse to turn away from the caravan, he could simply ride back into the past and find the world unchanged. He would find Ginevra and Niccolò and Zoroastro and Simonetta ... and A'isheh. Sweet A'isheh, who had taken Niccolò from him.

"Leonardo, are you so lost in thought or do you not wish to answer my question?" Benedetto asked.

"I'm sorry, what did you ask?"

"I asked if you loved A'isheh."

Enough, Leonardo thought, suddenly feeling anger burning in his chest like hot liquid. "That is enough, Benedetto. Perhaps it is just another of my faults, but I do not enjoy your taunting and humiliation. I cannot change what you think ... or what Sandro thinks. You can both believe what you like of me, but leave me alone," and with that he rode ahead, pacing the boy Mithqāl and his master Hilāl; but he could not ride with them either, for his eyes were watering and he kept choking like a child who had been slapped in public.

He would shut them all out.

Yes, Zoroastro, I killed you. I would not forgive you; and yet, perversely, even as he prayed for Zoroastro's forgiveness—a hollow, shallow gesture—his thoughts turned to A'isheh, as if the thought of killing Zoroastro had kindled his need. He remembered how he had thwarted all her seductions, for he had been obsessed with Ginevra, yet when there was a chance that he might wrest Ginevra away from her husband, when she wrote him that her heart was his, Leonardo had taken A'isheh, taken her violently. But she had fought him, even as they sweated their way to orgasm, even as he called for Ginevra, even as he imagined that she was the Impruneta, the Madonna herself lying open to him, vulnerable, blessed, and then suddenly distant, as distant as the stars, for A'isheh had taken him. She knew he was dreaming of Ginevra. But right now, in this physical and emotional darkness, he wanted her; she would be Ginevra; she would be Simonetta; and he would kneel before her and beg for surcease, for death. He thought of her hennaed hands, her kohl-lined eyes, the bluish circles delicately tattooed between her pink-nippled breasts, and he could hear her calling to him with Niccolò's voice; he could just make out her outline swaying before him in the darkness.

But he did not love her.

Ahead was Damascus, its thousands of lamps charging the atmosphere, illuminating the surrounds, as if encompassing fields and gardens in a cloud of soft light. And Leonardo and his army were moving from the darkness toward the light, which was in itself a grail.

"The poem is true," Benedetto said; he had come up beside Leonardo like an apparition, no more than a shadow. Except for the sour smell of horseflesh, Leonardo could have believed him a ghost. "What you see ahead is Paradise, even with its filthy streets and sewage. 'Fair city and forgiving Lord . . . enjoy her—swift the hours will flee.' "

"If it can turn you into a poet, Benedetto, then perhaps it is all you say."

"It transformed Zoroastro into an inventor."

Leonardo pulled away from Benedetto to be alone and take his own counsel, but Mithqāl caught up to him and chattered away about Damascus and flying machines and himself. He told Leonardo that he was chosen by God for the battle that must come.

Leonardo smiled, thinking of Christoforo Columbus. "Yes, I knew someone else who thought he was chosen by God for a divine mission."

"But I truly *am,*" Mithqāl insisted.

"Ah, yes, and so was he." When he saw that Mithqāl was not to be put off, Leonardo asked, "And how do you know that God himself chose you, little soldier?"

That seemed to please Mithqāl. "Hilāl, my benefactor, told me."

"Ah . . ."

"He bought me from a place where they castrate black slaves."

"But you're not black, young soldier," Leonardo said.

"Hilāl found me there, nevertheless. You see, the ruler was Christian and would not allow those with black skin to be castrated. But there is a filthy town called Washalaw, peopled by savages who do not worship the true God. They do such illegal operations there, but those whom they cut usually die."

"Why?" Leonardo asked.

"Because those who practice the medical arts in that place are ignorant," Hilāl said, coming up to ride beside Leonardo. "Every child castrated in Washalaw has to be carried to another town where there are monks who know a technique to open the penis canal and drain away the pus. Nevertheless, all the slaves we purchased in Washalaw either died on the way or soon after the second operation, all except Mithqāl. I told him it was God's proof of his destiny that he was white, that he came to be carried to Washalaw, and that only he survived."

Leonardo nodded politely.

"And Mithqāl will soon serve God," Hilāl said. "The traitor Zoroastro trained Mithqāl himself, and Mithqāl trained others to fly your machines, Maestro."

"Children?"

"We prefer to call them young soldiers," Hilāl said. "Would you put a man of two hundred pounds into your contraption when you have the like of Mithqāl, who can make up the difference in weight with bombs?"

"We are prepared, you know," Mithqāl said. "We have many flying machines."

"And how many of *you* are there?" Leonardo asked.

"Almost a troop," Mithqāl said.

"Nay," Hilāl said, "there are but twenty of you."

"And you have twenty flying machines?" Leonardo asked.

"Yes," Mithqāl said. "And I am captain." Hilāl smiled at him as one would smile at a child.

Indeed, Mithqāl was a captain, a captain of angels who would surely die . . . if they could even get themselves into the air; and for that instant, Leonardo was lost in memory, memory as present and palpable as the child riding beside him.

Leonardo remembered Tista.

An angel shouting as he fell. . . .

———

Zoroastro's armory was situated in a khan with a roof of nine domes; it was close to the bazaars so that whatever goods might be needed could be easily purchased; and it was near the Citadel and protected by its soldiers. The bazaars were a city of covered streets filled with fellahs and bedouins, a twilight maze in the day pierced by swords of sunlight streaming in through roof apertures and a flickering circus of lamp and candle in the night. They smelled of soap and perfume and tobacco, of baked bread, coffee, piss, and offal; everything could be bought in these walled and ceilinged streets: metals, jewels, fabrics, spices, munitions, swords, and armor finer than any other in the world, books that had never been seen in the West, chemicals, amulets, whores, slaves, and all manner of magical goods. While Hilāl was occupied with billeting his men in and around the Citadel for the few hours that they would be able to rest, Benedetto took Leonardo to Zoroastro's *bottega*.

The *bottega* was guarded by a small army.

Zoroastro had taken a palace for himself: its gateways and interior courts were sculpted marble; even its fountains were roofed with domes. A stream bubbled through a lamp-lit court, and beautifully kept trees, which Leonardo had imagined could exist only in paintings or in Paradise, formed their own separate sculptured parks. From the outside it looked like a house of pleasure, as sumptuous and stately a building as might be found in the East; on the lintel to the ornamented door of the palace itself were inscribed the words of an old Arab proverb: *"El mà, wa el khòdra, wa el widj el hàssan."*

"Water, verdure, and a beautiful face are three things that delight the heart."

Leonardo followed Benedetto through narrow passages and across floors of marble mosaic, through rooms with niches in the walls as in a Florentine church, rooms with divans covered in silk and filled with ornaments and mirrors, until they came to the actual *bottega,* which was connected to the house. Its upper reaches were windowed, but it was walled like a fortress, and dark as a cave. It contained other rooms, for Leonardo could hear the muffled pounding and tapping and bustling of men working.

When the servants and soldiers lit the lamps in Zoroastro's studio, Leonardo looked around this narrow but high-ceilinged room in wonder. Machines or models for machines were everywhere; even the ceiling was utilized, for flying machines hung on wires attached to hooks, as did models of Leonardo's designs for *galleggiante,* the floating rafts of Kuan's invention. There were balloons shaped like sausages with ribbed frameworks and propellers; there were balloons with sails and rudders like ships. In fact, all of Leonardo's various designs could be seen in the models that hung from the ceiling, as if they were actually floating in a dark heaven: here, and everywhere else in this room, could be seen the very process of Leonardo's thought, as if his mind contained objects and these objects were laid bare, joyously, recklessly laid out as delicacies on a banquet table for all to see.

But it was Leonardo who was surprised. Surprised at the gliders, the same design as that which Mithqāl had flown, the one-winged apparatus that turned boys into angels. Had Leonardo invented these? No, but they were his nevertheless. It was as if this was Leonardo's *bottega.* Papers were scattered on the floor, on tables, books remained opened or were piled together, as if they were as cheap and plentiful as linen in Florence.

Benedetto crossed the room and opened a door that led into a stone corridor. The noise from the workshops became loud, and Leonardo could hear the hissing and soughing of a forge. "There's much to attend to," Benedetto said. "Hilāl will be here shortly to see how things are proceeding."

"Will there be time to return . . . here?" Leonardo asked.

"Yes, you can stay the night, if you wish."

"Benedetto, what is *that*?" Leonardo gestured toward a contraption beside a model of a long-barreled steam cannon derived from one of Leonardo's sketches.

It was, in fact, a vehicle with two wheels, pedals, a handlebar, and a complex gearing mechanism.

"You wish to take in the world in a moment," Benedetto said.

"It is . . . my world, Benedetto," Leonardo said, surprised at himself even as he said it, for, indeed, it was becoming obvious that it wasn't.

"It *was* Zoroastro's." Benedetto waited for Leonardo to take the bait, but he didn't. "He called it a horse," Benedetto said. "It was a contraption to propel his flying machines. That's how it began. But it didn't work."

And suddenly Leonardo understood that Zoroastro must have conceived of connecting the gearing mechanism to a propeller, as if it were a whirlybird toy; and when that failed, he had connected it to two eight-spoked wheels to create this wooden "horse." "Why didn't it work?" Leonardo asked.

Benedetto shrugged. "You ride it like a horse, yet it's a cart. If the ground is smooth, it works quite well. It's fast."

Leonardo could not help himself. He straddled the two-wheeled vehicle, tested the handlebars and the pedals, and pushed off. For a few seconds he moved forward, but before he was able to work the pedals, he lost his balance and fell sideways.

"It takes practice to stay on top of it," Benedetto said, smiling at Leonardo. "But once you get the hang of it, it's quite simple. Now I'll leave you to . . . your world," and Benedetto turned and walked into the hall. He was accompanied by guards; half of the unit remained with Leonardo, who stared at Zoroastro's wheeled horse and tried to remember Zoroastro's last few moments in the torture chamber. But it was a dream, and each time Leonardo tried to remember, the dream changed.

In one dream he killed Zoroastro.

In another he didn't.

He rose to follow Benedetto, and in turn, the soldiers followed him.

Again he was a prisoner.

And so, he imagined, was Benedetto.

———

Leonardo toured the *artilleries,* passing through foundry courts—which even now were all men and motion and hot metal—and ordnance-storage rooms, where Leonardo's explosive shells, wheel locks, incendiary cannonballs, shrapnel bombs, bombards, and multiple-barreled cannons were piled high along walls and in tightly spaced rows. This was a factory that produced and stored cannons and shells and wheel-lock culverins; each cannon the same as that piled above it; each bombard and shell as the next.

Leonardo tried to engage the master of ordnance in conversation, but the tight-faced, heavy Mamluk eunuch, who wore his finery even in the hot and steamy foundries, would not acknowledge him.

"Leonardo, this is Abd al-Latif," Benedetto said in Arabic. They walked through a storage room that opened out on forges and foundries; slaves and soldiers strained at the levers of several huge cranes, while wrights and masters oversaw the lifting of the heavy, squat bombards and multiple-barreled guns onto wheeled gun carriages that were then pushed into a central courtyard under heavy guard. "Abd al-Latif is not an especially trusting man," Benedetto said to Leonardo in Italian. "But he knows who you are."

"And what does he know of me?" Leonardo asked.

"He knows you as an associate of Zoroastro's."

"You mean an apprentice, don't you?" Leonardo asked, unable to keep the sarcasm out of his voice.

"I could not say, but he told me he considers you both traitors and that it was good that Zoroastro died by torture, although he will miss him. He's quite sentimental."

"Like you?"

"Oh, more so, Leonardo."

Leonardo turned away from Benedetto. "Master of Engines, why are there so few types of cannons and guns?" he asked the eunuch in Arabic.

"Is there not enough here to satisfy you?"

"I was in Maestro Zoroastro's workshop, and I saw many machines which would be most effective against the enemies of the Caliph."

"What we have made cannot be constructed in the field," the master said. "The wrights will make the bridges and siege works, and the masters of cannons will mix the powder."

"We will carry the scythes, which will be attached to carts, if needed," Benedetto said. "Everything else can be constructed as we need it."

"Was all of this Zoroastro's idea?" Leonardo asked.

"No," Abd al-Latif said. "It was my own, and the Emir Hilāl's. Strength lies in simplicity. Most of Zoroastro's inventions were . . . unwise."

"And these?" Leonardo asked, indicating the cannons being mounted by winches onto carts.

"Maestro Zoroastro didn't invent these," Abd al-Latif said. "I did."

———•———

The ordnance would be loaded by dawn, which was when Hilāl's regiments were to leave Damascus and travel north into Persia.

As there was nothing for him to do in the *artilleries,* Leonardo rummaged through Zoroastro's studio. He read Zoroastro's notes, examined his models and full-scale machines. Within minutes Leonardo knew his way around the studio, as if it were his own, which, in a sense, it was. Zoroastro had tried to become Leonardo and had almost succeeded, for Leonardo was hard put to separate Zoroastro's ideas from his own. Zoroastro had developed his own ideas for catapults and mangonels and pointed projectiles; he had designed rock-throwing machines and multiple-spring crossbows; but what fascinated Leonardo was a full-sized self-propelled cart, which was hidden in a closet that Leonardo discovered only by accident. This was entirely Zoroastro's own conception, but the gearing of the differential transmission was as familiar to Leonardo as if he had designed it himself.

Zoroastro had, indeed, come into his own here, and only now did Leonardo understand his friend. He had lost a kindred soul; the sketches and inventions in this room were not the work of an imitator. It was as if Leonardo had turned away and allowed his own murder; and as he—overly fatigued and musing as if he were dreaming—visualized his friend and remembered various incidents, he found himself turning his critical gaze upon himself.

It was like being watched by his father's burning eyes.

As ugly as Zoroastro was, so was Leonardo beautiful. But Zoroastro was a mirror of Leonardo's soul. What Leonardo saw as devious and self-serving in his friend was what he now saw in himself. As he knelt before Zoroastro's machine, surrounded by the wooden and iron icons, as if by various statues of the Holy Virgin herself, he fell asleep.

And as he dreamed, he heard the sound of the spiked metal cradle as it fell, puncturing Zoroastro's lungs and heart.

———•———

He awoke to find himself in Zoroastro's room, in Zoroastro's bed. The guards must have led him here on orders from Benedetto. Candles guttered in sconces, and there was a tapping outside the bedroom door, probably the guard's pike. Leonardo fell back asleep and dreamed.

Perhaps the tapping of the pike gave shape to the dream, for the door opened, and Ginevra entered the room. She disrobed before the bed and slid between the silk covers beside Leonardo. But when she slid into the bed, smelling of roses and sweat, Leonardo awakened.

"Ginevra?" Leonardo pulled back, in disbelief and fright, for he did not believe in ghosts, spirits, or Jinn, yet here in the flesh was Ginevra. He reached out and touched her face. She was real enough, yet as Leonardo gazed at her in the inconstant candlelight, he could see that she wasn't Ginevra. Her face was somehow softer, the lips narrower, less voluptuous, and the eyes black instead of green; yet the frame of her face, the set of the eyes in proportion to her nose and mouth, was Ginevra's. Actually, the features were very different, and her hair, although hennaed, was brown; yet upon first glance, she was Ginevra. Even now, with discovery, knowing that she was a poor counterfeit, Leonardo's heart pounded so hard that he imagined he could hear its echoes in his ears.

"Maestro Zoroastro thought I resembled this woman," she said in Arabic, as if she were answering a question Leonardo had actually asked.

"His woman?" Leonardo asked.

"Ah, I know she loved you; he told me that. He told me everything, the terrible thing he did to both of you. But he loved her, too. That's what he told me, yet I think perhaps he loved me, as well."

"I'm certain he did," Leonardo said sarcastically.

"Are you saying that in cruelty or honesty?" she asked.

Leonardo noticed that she was trembling. "Why are you afraid?" he asked.

She watched him, her eyes steady, but did not speak.

"Did Benedetto send you to me?"

She nodded.

"And did he love you, too?"

She looked away.

"Why did Benedetto send you to me?"

"To answer your questions."

"About Zoroastro?"

She shrugged. "Benedetto said that you will not see each other again, unless it is in Florence."

"Why . . . ?"

"He has completed his obligation."

"Obligation to whom?" Leonardo asked.

"To the Emir Kuan, who saved his life."

"Does Benedetto know how to make his way home?"

"Yes, Maestro," she said. "Would you wish to go with him?"

"You may tell your master that I have responsibilities here."

"He is not my master," she said. "You are," and she moved close to him, lowering her face into the crook of Leonardo's arm like a child, the curve of her back and long neck revealed, the nubs of her spine shadowed against pale skin. "Will you take me with you?"

"Do you know where I'm going?"

"Yes," she said, raising her head so she could look directly at him. She caressed his chest and stomach with hennaed fingers; perhaps Zoroastro found the color arousing.

"If you know that, then why would you wish to leave this palace?"

She ignored the question.

"Are you in danger here?" he asked.

"I have been the slave of a traitor."

"But you would be my slave?"

She nodded.

"I too am considered a traitor, am I not? There would be no safety with me."

"Will you take me?"

"Yes," Leonardo said, for without Zoroastro, without Benedetto, she probably would be in danger. He would see to it that she was taken care of; perhaps Hilāl would protect her. She caressed him, arousing him, and finally mounting him, as if she were Leonardo and he Ginevra, as if she had the same need that Leonardo had had for Ginevra; but that seemed so many years ago in a distant past that had no relevance in this place. He inhaled her odors; the sweetness of her perfumes combined with her pungent sweat, turning to musk, as if she had been running hard through fields of flowers. Her coarse hair brushed his face, and he looked into her kohl-stained eyes, searching. He could not—would not—pretend that she was Ginevra. As she balanced her weight above him, for her arms were strong, he took her breasts in his hands, gently pulling her toward him, burying his face in their spongy softness and feeling the rough texture of her erect nipples as she rocked above him. She was oblivion, succor, hidden memories of milk and caress: memory inverted. He was new again, a tabula rasa, and he felt clean and wet, as if he were dissolving in a stream of cool water, and he came in that same dream, feeling the fleshiness of her buttocks and thighs, pulling them to him as his penis became numb with pleasure; then, exhausted, he fell asleep. It was as if Ginevra was a dream, that this Ginevra was a dream, and he passed into other dreams, falling, numbed, paralyzed; and he

Walked through the carnage in the field after Ussun Cassano's son was murdered.

Moaned as his scythed carts mutilated flesh and cut through bone.

And he counted the cannons with Abd al-Latif, the master of engines . . . all the cannons piled side by side, all engraved with his name and covered with blood and feces and gore.

And Zoroastro falling inside his cradle.

He had murdered him, just as he had murdered Ginevra and cut to parts the Persian soldiers with his scythes.

Then Ginevra was kneeling before him in Simonetta's studio, flushed with desire for him; she was inside him, just as Simonetta had been inside Sandro; just as . . . and then the dreams hardened, became curtains, curtains as solid and textured as those Verrocchio used to dip in plaster as studies for his apprentices to paint.

As Leonardo came awake with a jolt, he remembered that his slave had called Zoroastro's name when she finally gave herself up to ecstasy; and as he lay in the darkness that would soon give way to dawn, he wondered what her name was.

27

Breaking

the Center

Oh, son of a whore, what an ocean!
—Ussun Cassano

Force I define as a spiritual power, incorporeal and invisible, which with brief life is produced in those bodies which as the result of accidental violence are brought out of their natural state and condition.
—Leonardo da Vinci

They had passed the places where ancient kings and gods born of women had enthroned themselves upon the tops of mountains; they had passed great Persian cities; they were now in a desolated land that Odysseus would surely have recognized, a land bereft of life, burned and charred, a country where only shades moved about. The land was flat, a mud plain. The villages were razed, some still smoking. Even color had been drained from this place. Everything was dust or mud: clotted rivers of mud, hills and houses and villages . . . and beyond sight probably entire cities of mud. The air was a miasma, as if the mud had been transformed into a gas, a mist. Leonardo often imagined he saw movement in the dead villages, and he felt the pressure of eyes watching him everywhere, felt the heat of those stares on the back of his neck, imagined ghosts flickering in the ether between life and death. Distance and size became mirage: a heron standing still as a stick looked enormous, and when it moved, it seemed to resize the very ground it walked on. The gray mass of the Taurus Mountains in the distance looked like immovable clouds, clouds softened by distance and limned with brown streaks. It was as if armies had burned and pillaged and ravaged this land a thousand years ago; and since then time had become inert, had dried out like a corpse, had become the stuff and matter of the land itself.

But that was all delusion, for Leonardo heard the faint sounds of drums and *naccare,* then a soft booming followed by the muffled sound of crowds cheering. The booming was faraway cannon; the cheering was the shouts of men charging into battle, of men lunging and stabbing and dying.

The soldiers around Leonardo began talking nervously, excitedly. The slave who rode beside Leonardo—the woman who resembled Ginevra—remained calm. She looked at Leonardo, then looked away, as if she had completed an entire conversation in a glance. Her name was Gutne. She didn't know her Christian name, for she had been a baby when she was captured by Ka'it Bay's soldiers.

Leonardo rode ahead to find Hilāl, who shrugged and said, "Perhaps we're too late to help your Persian friend."

"My Persian friend?" Leonardo asked.

"My master, may he be twice blessed, told me that you and the Persian king have a special bond."

Leonardo waited, hoping Hilāl would give himself away.

"The Persians are a strange race," Hilāl continued. "How a man could love another man who killed his son. Even though by his command." Hilāl spoke softly, as if musing, as if distracted.

"How do you know it is Ussun Cassano?" Leonardo asked. "It could be—"

"If I know the mind of the Grand Turk, it will be to strike at the king himself. Once his head is firmly set on a lance and held up to heaven, panic will seize his troops. The Persians will be routed with the swing of a single ax, for when the head is severed, the body dies."

"And if, God forbid, your master were killed, would *your* troops panic?" Leonardo asked.

"We are not Persians," Hilāl said, his fat, unwrinkled face as hard as ivory. "If you doubt it, watch how men without balls can fight."

Mithqāl had been riding behind them and obviously listening, for he came between Hilāl and Leonardo and said in a peevish voice, "Better than you, Master Leonardo, better than you."

Hilāl laughed and ordered the boy to fall behind and mind his business. "Well, Master of Engines and Captain of Engineers, what would you decide to do? Should we wait for our Caliph or risk danger or annihilation to aid the Persians?"

"We were sent to help the Persians," Leonardo said. "Why would you disobey your master's command?"

"I have an obligation to prevent our precious cargo from falling into the hands of the enemy. I will allow *you* to choose."

Leonardo shook his head. "There is no choice. The Caliph ordered us to engage the Turks."

"Spoken like a soldier."

"What would you have expected me to say? That we remain here? If I said that, would you have—" Leonardo hesitated.

"Would I have obeyed you?" asked Hilāl. "I would obey you if it suits me, or I wouldn't. I obey only God. Not even my son."

"Your son?"

"Yes, Master of Engines and Captain of Engineers. The Caliph."

— · —

They could smell the battle before they could see it.

Before them was a wall of smoke: dust billowing like clouds. There were the smells of blood and offal, the clanging of sword upon sword, the *phut-phut* of arrows, the ratcheting sounds of crossbows, the harsh shrieks of men being struck and men exulting from their kills, officers shouting commands, and the splashing of . . . water. Leonardo could feel the pounding in his throat like a small bird trapped and fighting to escape. His eyes stung from the dust, yet he could not help himself: he yearned to see what was happening, to push through the dust-cloud veil, as if to find life and color and reality, for just now he was a soldier, a warrior drawn to the melee just as a dog is aroused by a bitch in heat.

It was repellent, yet it swallowed him.

Mithqāl called to Leonardo and motioned him forward; the boy rode beside Hilāl. A contingent of Hilāl's best men was riding off to reconnoiter. Leonardo asked one of the men to look after Gutne, and then he rode with the eunuchs into battle. As he galloped into the dust cloud, he thought of the sweetish, metallic taste in his mouth and wondered if that, indeed, was the taste for combat: curious thoughts for such a moment.

A veil had parted, and suddenly he was swinging his saber for his life. A janissary cavalry officer lunged for him, swinging an ax, his reinforced mail armor jingling like cheap bells. His uniform was of course blue cloth, as were those of all the other Turkish soldiers, to show that they served but one man: Mehmed the Conqueror. But unlike the other Turks, the janissaries shaved their heads and faces, except for their huge mustaches. This janissary was no different: he was almost as big as Ussun Cassano; he was violence itself. He wore a white felt sleeve-cap decorated with a bird-of-paradise plume; and in that instant Leonardo took it all in, seeing—as it is said—like a dying man.

Leonardo ducked and swung his sword hard. The blade rang against the janissary's breastplate, almost knocking him out of his saddle; but the Turk reined in his horse and turned, coming after Leonardo, who knew him now as one animal knows another: from his sweat, his smell.

It was as if the Turk was in a frenzy to cut Leonardo to pieces, for he bore down upon him again, slicing. Leonardo again swung his sword, this time lunging for the Turk's armpit, which was not protected by armor. He felt the soft penetration into muscle, and then—

His horse fell away beneath him; and Leonardo fell backward, striking the ground beside his great white mare, which was in its death throes. The Turk had severed its head with the stroke meant for Leonardo, and blood spurted from its neck. Covered with gore, Leonardo focused on the Turk who had—impossibly—come about once more to cleave Leonardo in two. Leonardo's sword protruded from between his arm and chest, as if it had not been thrust deeply into his flesh, but as if he were holding it there by his own will.

Leonardo stood up, slipping on viscera as he did so, and looked around quickly for a weapon. In that instant he took in the details of the battle around him, as if indeed time had stopped, as if Leonardo were omniscient, above all the death and pain and fear: thousands of soldiers were engaged in hand-to-hand combat, opposing phalanxes skewering each other with twelve-foot lances, cutting each other to pieces with axes and scimitars, while cavalrymen clashed and trampled upon the infantry, upon friend and foe alike as lords and nobles sought out their own to scourge and kill, and arrows as neutral and deadly as the Black Death flew like hail in a high wind.

The officer was almost upon him.

It was as if the jannisary's entire life had been but a preparation to kill Leonardo. Leonardo ran a few paces, wrested a sword from a wounded Turk, killing him with a stroke, and then raised his sword to cut down the horse that carried the janissary. He felt a flush of warmth and strength, and then numbness; again time froze, and although he wished to slip into the cool darkness of his memory cathedral, for surely death was upon him, he braced for contact.

Hilāl suddenly came up beside the Turk and drove his scimitar expertly into his neck, then tore off the Turk's helmet and decapitated him. He threw the head toward Leonardo, who jumped away.

Hilāl caught the reins of the Turk's horse and said, "Maestro, you should take better care of the Caliph's gifts." He referred to Leonardo's dead mare. "Take this as a lesser gift. Hurry." Mithqāl appeared beside his master and looked down at Leonardo, grinning.

Humiliated, Leonardo mounted the Turk's horse, which was smaller than his own, yet marvelously responsive. He followed Hilāl, and as if they were cutting their way through brush, they cut a path through the pikemen, who jabbed at them; they killed and maimed anyone in their way; it was as if the blood and gore had been transformed into something ordinary and neutral; it was as if Leonardo was inhabiting one of his drawings of machines of war; and Mithqāl, small and young as he was, was a better fighter than most men, which he now proved. He wielded a double-pointed spear, which he expertly thrust into the faces of those on horse and those trying to unhorse him.

Ahead was the river, which was divided into streams by banks of mud. The Turks were crossing the river in great numbers, unchecked now; for rather than take down the enemy where it was most vulnerable, the archers were preoccupied with saving their own lives. Squadron after squadron of cavalrymen and foot soldiers crossed the river, their legs and waists crusted with the thick mud, as if it were part of their uniform. Upon seeing them, Leonardo wished only to retreat, for they were a great crush of screaming, rushing flesh intent on destroying him; it was as if they were charging at him alone. The Persians fought them in the river, for they had been pushed back from the bank where they had taken down thousands of Turks with twice as many arrows. The arrows still flew, landing ahead of Leonardo, sounding like a great buzzing of insects, but these arrows were released by the Turks. Persians fell, and as Turks came across the banks and over the river streams, the Persian center began to cave in.

The Persians were being massacred; the ground was covered with corpses, one atop the other, corpses trampled by men and horses, covered with mud and gore, quickly becoming part of the lay of the land, now featureless in themselves, their blood and gristle and intestines part of the earth like fossils in stone.

"Hilāl, where are you leading me?" Leonardo shouted, panicked, for there was not a second when he did not have to watch and wield his sword. His arms ached, the ear-ringing, blood-pounding passion of first battle encounter was replaced with fear. He wished only to run, for he felt as if suddenly luck had run out, that he was vulnerable to every man and boy with sword or spear.

"To Ussun Cassano, unless you wish to fall back and fight with the women," Hilāl said. Indeed, Persian women were in the fray, fighting alongside their men, but they had been pushed back, replaced by men who would protect them or take the sword point first. "There he is." Hilāl pulled his horse away from attack, allowing young Mithqāl to rush the Tartar who was bearing on him in his stead; Mithqāl speared the Tartar straight through the eye. Then he looked at Leonardo and grinned, as if this were nothing more than a game.

Leonardo could see Ussun Cassano ahead. He was riding a large horse and was trying to spur his men on, riding ahead of his guards, out of their protection, to show by example that the Turks could be pushed back into the river. He pushed his horse into the fray as if it were a beast of metal rather than flesh; and he cut and cleaved at the enemy, killing them one and two at a time: a giant killing men, a great red-haired Olympian tasting the blood of mortals. He held a sword in his left hand and an ax in his right, which he swung in an odd arc, from his left shoulder outward. He was directing and encouraging his army from the front, and, indeed, to slay him would be to rout the Persians. His special guards clung to him, forming a curtain around him. When he saw Leonardo and Hilāl, he stopped, then drove his horse toward them.

"Your master, where is he?" he asked Hilāl in a hoarse voice. The Persian king was covered with blood and mud. His face was almost black, and his lips looked like dead flesh in contrast. He wore a heavy-quilted doublet that could repel arrows and finely worked mail; but he carried neither shield nor bow, although he did have an empty quiver hanging from his shoulder. Leonardo remembered him on the bier in Ka'it Bay's camp, his face painted by his concubine, as he awaited his son. Now he looked even more like an angel of death.

"We're to meet him here," Hilāl said.

"How many men do you have?"

"Two thousand, Great King."

"Two thousand? That is all your Caliph could send?"

"He is bringing an army of more than a hundred thousand men. But we have cannons, and the multiple-barreled guns of Leonardo's invention. Our master hoped that if by chance we arrived first, our machines might be of use. That's why he ordered us to go forward at great risk—"

"Yes, yes," Ussun Cassano said. "The Master of Worlds was, as always, correct. When do you expect him to arrive?"

Hilāl shook his hand, indicating that he did not know. "I would hope by tomorrow, or the next day, or—"

"As you can see, Emir of Ten Thousand Men, our center is giving way," Ussun Cassano said, the impatience evident in his voice. "If we lose here, my men on the wings will panic and flee. All will be lost. You must aim all your cannons to strike in the center, here. And fire everything you have in a great burst."

"But, Great King, your own men will be killed," Hilāl said.

"They will be killed anyway. I have already lost an army." He looked at Leonardo bitterly. "But aim only at the center. Can you do this now?"

"In moments," Hilāl said.

Leonardo turned to Hilāl, surprised.

"Leonardo, would you care to ride with me?" Ussun Cassano asked. "Here's your chance to fulfill your obligation by keeping the Turkish blades from my neck." Then he looked at Hilāl. "Unless, of course, his talents would be better employed with you, Emir."

"Our task is but a matter of our cannoneers taking aim, Great King."

"Well, then?" Ussun Cassano asked, turning to Leonardo.

———

Leonardo decided to ride with Ussun Cassano into battle, staying beside him, keeping to his right, for the king had told his guards that Leonardo would take the position of honor. Actually, it was also relatively safe, for Leonardo was inside the ring of Ussun Cassano's bodyguards. But the king was not easy to pace. He rode hard through his lines of heavy infantry, ordering his ranks to flee the center, but to be ready to advance and attack; and he gathered around him his horsemen, who followed him west in retreat.

Seeing this, the Turks rushed across the river in pursuit, thinking the Persians were in full retreat; and, indeed, Ussun Cassano had given up many of his men to Turkish swords, for he could not be everywhere and there was no time for his commands to be communicated through all the lines. Many panicked, routed by the Turks; others were slaughtered by Turkish cavalry trying to get to Ussun Cassano.

The king could only watch, his face tight, as if he were in physical pain.

But the Persians were already rushing into the center.

The bombardment began, as shells filled with powder and shrapnel exploded, filling the air with thunder and fire and deadly fragments. It was a crashing, deafening, terrible music: a crash of thunder that not only shook the ground, but smashed into the very air like rocks through glass; then there was an unnatural flash of light, as if in this odious world of dung and death and entrails one would hear the thunder of the storm before being struck by lightning. As the shells exploded, men fell in groups, some losing limbs—hands, feet, arms, legs—or painlessly, as if cut by gut-cord, a finger or an ear; some were cleaved in two; while others were hit directly and turned into the human mash they had stood upon an instant before. One explosion followed another, and the multiple-barreled guns fired, mowing down ranks of men, as if indeed they were nothing but corn being threshed, Turk and Persian alike.

The Turks, who took the most casualties, were terrified, as were their horses, which bolted in all directions, and were, in turn, cut down by the deadly seeds of metal flying through the air.

Yet only seconds had passed, or perhaps moments . . . Leonardo could not tell, for even time was fouled; and Ussun Cassano could wait no more. Even while the cannons thundered and pounded the center, he gave the signal to advance. Several battalions of his heavy infantry attacked the extreme left of the Turkish line, which had not been bombarded.

Suddenly the cannons stopped.

The janissary commander had apparently gathered whatever cavalry he could to meet the attack of the Persian infantry upon his flank. While units of archers formed by Ussun Cassano fired upon the Turkish infantry, the Persian king led his cavalry across the front of the battle lines—skirting the Turkish cavalry just as Alexander the Great had done when he defeated the Persian army at the Battle of Granicus—and slaughtered the Turks on the left of the Turkish line, which was weakened. He was followed by light and heavy infantrymen.

Leonardo had all he could do to protect Ussun Cassano, who rode as if he had no fear and, by his courage, encouraged his men. They were routing the Turks, beating and slicing, pushing them into the river, which was now dyed darker than mud; all was shouting and commotion and bloodlust; all had been lost—now, miraculously, all could be gained; and the Persian king could not be mortal, could not be flesh and blood, could not be harmed; no, he was the eye of the storm, the wind upon a horse, even when his horse was cut from under him. Then Leonardo gave up his Turkish mare; but it was only for an instant, for Ussun Cassano himself brought him another.

There was no time for thought. The Turks were all around Leonardo, trying even now—especially now—to kill Ussun Cassano, who refused to leave the thick of the fighting, refused to rest and watch his enemy retreat, for he was past reason, past being human; he was caught in the dream of combat where there is no sense of time, and the only cause and effect are thrust and ride.

Perhaps it was like the Devatdar's hashish, permeating the air, for Leonardo had become part of Ussun Cassano's dream, was beyond thought and reason; all was the sounds and sights and terrible joy of slashing and killing and drinking up life. Here was the place of light described by Kuan's little book of Chinese wisdom; here was the foundation of thought and memory, the place without thought, the soil soaking up life, which could be apprehended only through the eyes of death; and Leonardo rode through this light, watching flesh turning into spirit and enjoying the terrible neutrality of it all.

Everything here was alive with light, alive and tangible: souls and spirits, men, horses, air, water, wood, and metal, all the same stuff; and Leonardo's function was simply to cleave and cut. He was death, he was possessed, he was asleep and yet completely awake, and the light grew brighter with every soul released, grew brighter with every cry and every susurrating breath, brighter and brighter with the suffusing light of a lamp in a fog, light become bright as the sun, clarifying, dispersing, until—

———

"It has been a precept of both valor and strategy that one should pave the roads with gold and make bridges out of silver for a fleeing enemy," Hilāl said to Ussun Cassano.

Those were the first words that Leonardo heard upon awakening. Disoriented, he asked where he was. His head and right arm pounded with pain. He lay upon a blanket, his head supported by pillows, and Gutne hovered over him, nursing him. It was dark and cool here, and for an instant Leonardo wondered when Ussun Cassano's son would arrive, when he would have to kill him. When it became darker, he thought, answering his question.

"You're in my tent, Leonardo," Ussun Cassano said. "After making a brave show about protecting me—and you saved my life perhaps once, twice, thrice, who could count?—then you—"

"Yes?" Leonardo asked, fully conscious now. He tried to lean on his elbow, but it was too painful, and he had to settle for lying flat and turning his head toward the king. His face and arms and chest were cut and bruised, as was his right knee. There was noise—the screams of men, shouting, yelling, even singing; all of it sounded unbearably close. But, of course, the water would magnify sound as a curved mirror magnifies sight.

The shouting came closer; men were crying for Ussun Cassano, chanting his name.

"You were thrown from your horse," Ussun Cassano said, ignoring them. "You fight like no Christian I've ever seen. You can fight like a Persian, but you certainly can't ride like one." Humiliated, Leonardo averted his eyes; and Ussun Cassano made for the tent opening.

"Will you not wait for the Caliph?" Hilāl asked.

"One would think *you* were the Caliph," Ussun Cassano replied; but there was humor in his voice.

"It is but a question, Great King," Hilāl said softly.

"Listen to them, Emir. Would *you* go out there and tell my officers we will not pursue the enemy? How long do you think I could remain... alive?"

"You are the king," Hilāl said.

"Perhaps in a few hours, or a day, but not now." He paused. "I will stop them as soon as I can."

"You will simply push them into the arms of Mehmed," Hilāl said.

"Perhaps when we're finished, there will not be so many to push."

"And Mehmed, how many men does he have left?"

Ussun Cassano seemed to sigh, and for an instant looked vulnerable. "Could you count the drops in an ocean? I look forward to seeing you soon, with your master. We will wait for you in the hills. Then we shall free the Caliph's cousin together." He looked at Leonardo. "And perhaps free your friend, too."

"Is he there?" Leonardo asked, desperation evident in his voice. "Do you have information?"

"Maybe a little," Ussun Cassano said, "but, then, who can trust a Turk, even under torture?" There was a great cheering outside as the king left the tent, and Leonardo was about to stand and follow him when he

Awoke again. His arm still ached, but his head felt clear. The headache was gone; in fact, he felt light-headed. It was quiet, yet the tent seemed suffused with flickering red light. Leonardo recognized the sound of machinery: soldiers were cranking gears to work the pestles on the mill wagon. They were grinding gunpowder.

"What is the light?" he asked Gutne, who was beside him.

"They are burning the dead."

"More like they are burning everything."

"So it would seem," she said.

Leonardo could make out Gutne's features in the light from the tent opening. Just now he did not think of her as a poor reflection of Ginevra; though perhaps as a sister; no, more likely a cousin, a cousin who bore the family features, but in gross, indelicate form. He felt desire, felt a throbbing heat in his groin, yet something was wrong. . . .

"I can smell the stink," Leonardo said, as if to himself. "And the gunpowder. Isn't it dangerous to be combing the ingredients for gunpowder when—"

"I don't think the emir would allow anything to be done if it wasn't necessary," Gutne said.

"So you know him?"

"He is respected. . . ."

"Even though he is a eunuch."

"Yes," Gutne said. She kept her eyes lowered, as if afraid to look at Leonardo.

"Why?" Leonardo asked. "Because of his relationship to the Caliph?"

"I know the Caliph tells all that Hilāl is his father. Perhaps that is why . . . because he has the favor of the Caliph. But one cannot order respect. It must be freely given. You, Master, have been given respect."

"Yes?"

"By the Persian king," Gutne said. "He left you his tent."

"A sop for my humiliation."

"I think not," Gutne said, and Leonardo pulled her toward him. Yet he hesitated, even as she was willingly pressed against him; he held her back, then pressed her so close that she could hardly breathe. In that moment he did not see Ginevra or Simonetta or even Gutne. He felt a burning, numbing, consuming need; and he knew that it was the killing and wounding of other men that aroused his desire. He felt brutalized and brutal, as one who is about to do something he will regret, yet is powerless to stop himself. If Gutne were not willing, he would have raped her, would have treated her little differently from the men he killed reflexively, as mechanically and automatically as the workings of ratchets and gears; and she closed her eyes as he combed his fingers through her pubic hair, as he entered her with his index finger, testing her, for desire had not lubricated her. She knew . . . knew, and he felt anger, as if she were pulling away from him. His desire took the form of heat radiating into his legs, his stomach, and his penis was numb, and as he tried to enter her, he realized that he was flaccid. His desire had not abated; he was an animal in rut; he felt consumed by it, yet try as Gutne might to help him, he was dead . . . neutral . . . as distant as the fire burning the battleground along the river.

He pushed her away, gently now, as if coming to his senses, and stood up. He dressed himself mechanically. She tried to coax him back. He told her to sleep, assured her that he would return, that he would not abandon her; and he felt calm now as he left the tent and walked past the wide, protective ring of close-set cannons and mortars and carts toward the fires and ash and charring flesh.

He understood now what he had lost to violence, to the bloodlust that still hung in the air like the ash and burning pieces of clothing wafting upward like burning souls to disappear before ascending into the heavens. Twenty thousand bodies burned like a great unending shout; and as Leonardo remembered, remembered viscerally the feel of blade penetrating flesh; he understood . . . and he slipped into the marble darkness of his memory cathedral to hide.

But the flaming, glowing bits of flesh and soul floated even here, ascending; turning into gray ash, turning cold and falling back, floating like leaves, to one side, then another; and Leonardo felt himself on fire, felt himself rising, rising into the empty, impotent, resounding blackness.

28

Heads

I entered into the city of Calindra, near to our frontiers. This city is situated at the base of that part of the Taurus Mountains which is divided from the Euphrates and looks toward the peaks of the great Mount Taurus to the West. These peaks are of such a height that they seem to touch the sky, and in all the world there is not part of the earth higher than its summit.

—Leonardo da Vinci

Child, I am lost now. Can I bear my life after the death of suffering your death?

—Homer's *Iliad*

They found Ussun Cassano desolate in a city of corpses and severed heads displayed on pikes. They found him in a small mosque, his army decimated. The stink of putrefying flesh was overwhelming; not even the fires roaring in what had been the town's marketplace could consume the bitter, nauseating smell. Whores and soldiers, Persian women who had fought beside their husbands, children and town burghers, all had become smoke. The town had been torched, yet it was impossible to determine who had burned and stabbed and carved and raped and looted: Persian or Turk?

Ka'it Bay had immediately ordered that all the remaining heads be removed from the stakes and given proper burial. To accomplish this, the men had to kill the dogs that snapped at them for the maggoty prizes. It was midday; the air was heavy with ash, turning the sun smeary, magnifying the heat. Air that was difficult to breathe ... air that turned everything into soft mirages, as if this place were merely a phantasm, a nightmarish apparition dreamed by a thirsty, dying soldier in the desert.

But even as the army settled down around the town, Persian lords and overseers accompanied farmers and Persians from neighboring towns that had not been sacked and burned to set up markets to sell their produce and make Ka'it Bay welcome. Already sutlers, butchers, bakers, cooks, and new regiments of whores were trafficking to make a profit—thus were merchants made rich, for Ka'it Bay's army had swollen to a hundred thirty thousand.

"The king asks for you," Kuan told Leonardo, who was with Hilāl and Mithqāl, drawing a great circle of cannons and artillery around the camp that enclosed even the soldiers waiting nervously in the hills. The Mamluks, who had been riding and marching, in phalanxes not so different from those of ancient Greece or Macedonia, who were ripe and yearning for battle, who had been praying joyously to Allah, the One God, the True God, and invoking His Name, who were calling to the goddess: the goddess of war, the goddess of life and death and sex and psalm—*"Mun shan ayoon A'isheh"*—were now shocked and subdued by the true and recent faces of death that surrounded them.

Leonardo nodded, and accompanied Kuan through the camp and into the heart of Calindra.

"I have heard about the bad blood between you and your friends," Kuan said.

"How is Amerigo?" Leonardo asked.

"He camps with me. You have had ample opportunity to see him, but you seem to prefer the company of eunuchs."

"Does Amerigo . . . agree with Sandro?" Leonardo did not want to be explicit, still did not want to give form to the possibility that he had indeed been responsible for the death of Zoroastro.

"You need to talk to both of them. Sandro is not sure of what he saw."

"Not sure?"

"He is not as fortunate as we . . . he has no system for remembrance."

Leonardo laughed, the bitterness evident. "No system serves at such times." Even to discuss these things seemed like a desecration; here, with the air choked with the stuff of souls and the ashen remains of what had once been living flesh, they were talking of petty grievances; in the face of the eternal, they were discussing the most base of the ephemeral . . . and yet it *was* important, for the fragile linkage of love and friendship balanced even all the death and butchery that was so familiar here as to become, for seconds, minutes, and hours, invisible. "Do you know how this happened?" Leonardo asked.

"It is as the Persian soldiers say. They were overwhelmed at night, most killed in their tents."

"It doesn't make sense. The king would never have been so lax as to—"

"Yes, Maestro," Kuan said. "There are times when every man falls asleep."

"You know what I mean," Leonardo said, irritated.

Kuan looked away from Leonardo and smiled, but it was an ironical smile. "He was also outnumbered and up against Mustafà's best janissaries."

"Mustafà . . . ?"

"The Turk's favorite son. He is most like his father, just as Zeinel was most like Ussun Cassano. They hid in the hills."

"Then the king underestimated him."

Kuan shrugged as they passed an open grave. Garments rent, skull bleeding where he had torn out his hair, a man knelt before the opening and screamed and cried; he shook uncontrollably, as if in convulsions. A woman stood behind him, alternately crying and wailing in a high-pitched voice. Although Leonardo knew better than to look down into the grave, he couldn't help himself. All the corpses were women and children.

Leonardo and Kuan walked past both Persian and Mamluk guards and into the mosque. It was cool and dim in the great room. Ornate prayer rugs were spread all over the mosaic floor, and light pierced into the columned room from high, narrow windows. Ussun Cassano sat near the center. His hair was greasy; his quilted doublet and green turban were blood splattered and filthy, as were his hands. Leonardo noticed his silver carnelian ring, the same ring he had looked upon for all those hours when he was waiting in the tent with the king; somehow, incongruously, he equated the ring with prayer. There was a glass flagon on the floor before him.

It contained the severed head of his son Zeinel.

"Where is the Caliph?" Leonardo whispered to Kuan, suddenly afraid to be alone with the king, but Kuan had turned heel.

There was nothing for Leonardo to do but to continue, for Ussun Cassano met his gaze. The king's eyes were wide and bloodshot, as if those eyes could see into hell, as if their internal fires had illuminated the rent in the world and shown him his own death. "Master of Worlds . . . ," Leonardo said, trying not to focus on the flagon before the king; but in a glance, he had taken in every detail: the young, unblemished face, eyes cold and blue as glass—which, indeed, they were, thick red hair tied in a tight knot behind the head, lips full yet closed tight, high cheekbones and slightly cleft chin. Except for the skin, which was as yellowed as old parchment, the face was Ussun Cassano's—younger, smoother, but a mirror image. The effect was haunting. "Now you've seen two of my sons, Maestro."

"I've seen them all, Great King . . . at Unghermaumet's funeral."

"Ah, so you have," Ussun Cassano said, staring blankly at the flagon. "*Now* you have, for here is my son Zeinel, a gift from the Turk. I reciprocated by sending his ambassadors back to him in pieces." The king paused, musing, then said, "It seems he kept the head of my son for his amusement. As a decoration for his tent."

"Surely you knew that . . ."

"It has been less than a year," Ussun Cassano said. "I prayed that he was alive. I had thought he was being held hostage by the Turk, for when I sent ambassadors to his capital, Mehmed did not deny it." Ussun Cassano laughed. Then in a voice barely audible he asked Leonardo, "Do you remember what I said to you when I killed my own son?" For a moment he stared ahead, as if listening to distant voices, to angels . . . or Jinn. "But I've killed two sons." He picked up the flagon and stared into Zeinel's glass eyes. "Now it is your turn to see, to witness." Then he looked toward Leonardo, as if impatient for his answer.

"No, Master, I cannot remember," Leonardo said.

"Search your memory cathedral, then, and don't lie to me."

"You said, 'One last humiliation' before you carried Unghermaumet out of the funeral tent."

"There, you see?"

There was nothing to say to that; Leonardo knelt beside Ussun Cassano, for it was disrespectful to stand higher than the king.

"I was wrong, very wrong, but now . . . I will tell you again, this will be the last, the very last humiliation . . . for me."

"What do you mean, Ruler of Worlds?" Leonardo asked nervously. He looked around the mosque. They were quite alone, although someone might—or should—be standing outside the carved entranceway.

Ussun Cassano ignored Leonardo's question and said, "So my only confidant is a *kâfir*, whom I saved from murdering my son. Did I not, Maestro?"

"Yes, Great King. You did."

"And to whom I gave my tent."

"That was most gracious," Leonardo said.

"I wish my son Calul to be king. He will not moan or mourn. He will fight. The armies will rally around him."

"But you are king."

"No, I am not. I told you that when I left our camp."

"You said, 'Perhaps in a few hours, or a day, but not now.' "

"So you do have a memory," Ussun Cassano said. "You must tell Calul my wishes."

"Why do you wish *me* to tell your son?"

"Because I trust you," and Ussun Cassano gave Leonardo a letter, closed with his royal seal. Then he produced his sword and placed it on the floor. "You owe me a killing. Do it now."

Leonardo stood up and took a step backward.

"I wish to be buried with my son, but no one must lay eyes upon him. He was my favorite, my most precious possession, my love, myself—if a father can possess a son."

"I cannot do this . . . *you* cannot do this, Great King. Your way is vengeance. Punish the Turks for what they've—"

"Don't presume to argue with me, or *you* will find yourself between swords."

"I will not murder you," Leonardo said. "I've paid my debt for failing you once." He turned and began walking away, fearing, wondering if at any second he would feel the cut of a blade or the point of an arrow for his disobedience. Instead he heard a moaning, a sighing; and when he turned around, he saw that Ussun Cassano had stabbed himself with a dagger below his navel and was trying to draw it upward.

For an instant they stared at each other: Leonardo shocked, Ussun Cassano squinting in agony; and then, without thought, Leonardo rushed back to the king, picked up the sword that lay upon the prayer rug, and as the king bent forward, decapitated him; and Leonardo heard himself praying, as if he—the disbeliever—could only find Him in blood and thrashing.

Then Ka'it Bay himself was standing beside Leonardo; he had been watching all along. "Now, Maestro, the debt is paid," and he took Leonardo's letter and led him out of the mosque. "He was already dead, before he stuck himself with the knife, before you helped him into heaven. He loved you, as I do."

And the Caliph explained everything to Leonardo, who was like a son to him . . . a slave who might command the privileges of an emir.

Leonardo, who an instant before had found God . . . for an instant . . . now felt the hot tickle of tears on his cheeks, and he cried in silence for this barbarian king, who had turned Leonardo into a murderer, who had turned him into . . . himself.

The image was Leonardo's own.

Just as Simonetta had looked into the eyes of angels, so had Leonardo glimpsed his own soul.

———

When the Persian prince Calul arrived, Ka'it Bay showed him the headless body of his father and, lying, said that the Turks had taken it as a prize. Then he led the grotesquely tall, balding, fair-skinned man to the funeral ground.

Calul stood between the Caliph and Leonardo, clutching his father's letter in his fist, and staring into the loamy grave as if it were a problem to be calculated. The prince seemed to be all intensity and cold anger; his narrowed blue eyes set deeply in dark frames of eyebrow and shadow were bright, as if proof that they were the mirrors of the soul. Behind him, and mostly unseen, his army of ten thousand waited nervously, as if unsure whether to call the Caliph and his troops ally or enemy.

"And what else did my father say?" Calul asked Leonardo.

"I've told you all."

"And you knew nothing of my brother Zeinel, that the Turk had—"

"I know only what I saw," Leonardo lied. He was uncomfortable, but he looked directly into the prince's eyes.

"You found my father with his sword in his hand?"

"I didn't find him, but he was on the battlefield," Leonardo said. "Do you think I would lie to you?"

"Of course not, Maestro Leonardo. But one of my officers believes he saw my father alive in the mosque."

Leonardo shrugged. "You must take your own council, then, Master."

"My father trusted you." Calul gave him the letter, which Leonardo read, even though he had read it before, when Ka'it Bay had opened it and then closed it with the king's own seal. How he hated this! He was not a good liar, but he had no choice.

He was part of the Caliph's plan.

Young Niccolò would have told Leonardo that it was for the best, that even Ussun Cassano would have approved of the Caliph's ruse; for if the Persians discovered that their king had committed suicide, they would be too demoralized to fight effectively. To that end did Ka'it Bay order the execution of any Persian who might have suspected anything.

Evidently, Hilāl—or Hilāl's henchman—had not been thorough enough.

––––––––

The Persian armies rallied around Calul, who had the height of his father, yet bore it on a slender frame. He was bookish and had none of the pure physical energy and beauty of his father; his spirit was narrow, focused as a ray of light cutting through cathedral darkness, and so strong that it seemed to cause his hands to shake. His lieutenants were afraid of him, yet his hatred of the Turks seemed to be the flame that drew his people to him.

Persian and Arab armies marched together, engaging the enemy wherever it could be found, slaughtering and burning through the high and wild regions as if all of this land was Turkish rather than Persian. Cutting deeper into the mountains, following signs and signals, following the trail of Mustafà's thousands, entering valleys below ravines that looked like windowed cathedrals in dawn's pale-yellowish light, following paths that wound and branched dangerously through mountains, fighting with men and cannons at passes, smashing rocks with projectiles as if the Caliph could create lightning and thunder to rival nature's anger, they neared the battlegrounds where Mehmed's massive army waited. The Turks had scourged this land for food. It was a deadland, even though the blue mountains, pine forests, glens, narrow valleys, and plains looked pristine, as if naiads and satyrs, centaurs and nymphs, dwelled here in natural shelters and feared only the gods who drew back the nights and closed the days. But they passed enough towns and villages burned and stinking of rotting flesh, to dispel any bucolic illusions.

Leonardo could see eagles wheeling around their nests in caverned vaults above him, as if they were waiting to sweep down upon laggards and carry them off for some Promethean repast.

As Leonardo rode with Hilāl and Mithqāl, Sandro joined him. He rode quietly beside his old friend, as if nothing had come between them; but he could not seem to get enough of Gutne, who rode behind Leonardo. Occasionally he would fall back to ride beside her and talk for short periods. During those times he would constantly glance at Leonardo, as if to make sure his friend was not angry or jealous . . . as if he, Sandro, were doing something wrong.

Sandro had become even leaner. Although he constantly complained of being unhappy, he looked robust. Hell seemed to agree with him. He had made friends with Ussun Cassano's imam, who was teaching him Koranic philosophy. It would not surprise Leonardo if his friend, for all that he was homesick, remained in these lands, a seer who would no longer be able to capture his visions and religious hallucinations with paint and canvas. But what would that matter to him? Prayer would be his bread.

They did not discuss Zoroastro.

They did not speak of Florence.

They simply rode together, as if constantly on the verge of breaking through their silence, which clung to their sporadic small talk and chatter like mist in heavy air, until they camped in a glen by a stream and natural fountain.

There Ka'it Bay received four of Mehmed's ambassadors. He received them in the open, in the drizzle that had been falling for hours. Calul, the Persian king, stood beside him and watched the proceeding impassively.

The Turks were dressed sumptuously in silks, as befitted members of the Caliph's elite guard; these men, armed with maces and axes, were Peyks: messengers. But they looked frightened, not at all like officers. They had the dulled look of line soldiers who had seen too much carnage; it was as if Mehmed had sent out peasants to meet the Caliph, as if their very faces were to be an insult to the King of Worlds, the Master of all Arabs.

The Turks bowed. Three of them carried gifts. The spokesman opened a letter sealed with the blue stamp of the Grand Turk and read; he seemed to have trouble catching his breath, and his voice choked, as if he could not inhale, only exhale. His hands shook.

They were all, of course, certain that they would be killed or at best mutilated after they completed their task.

"Mehmed Çelebi, great sovereign of the Turks, sends to you, Ka'it Bay, these gifts quite equal to your greatness, as they are worth as much as your kingdom." The spokesman flinched as he said that and did not look up. On cue, two of the Peyks laid a gold baton, a saddle, and a jewel-encrusted sword on the ground before the Caliph. "If you are a brave man," the spokesman continued, "keep these gifts well, for I will soon take them from you. I will take everything you possess against all right, for it is against the natural order that the bastards of peasants should rule over such a kingdom as you do."

Ka'it Bay drew his sword, his face coloring with rage and humiliation. Calul stepped away from the Caliph to give him room.

But the Turk continued, hands shaking, voice trembling; the others stared at the ground before them, as if they could wish themselves away, as if they could burn their own coffins with the heat of their gaze. "Mehmed Çelebi, great sovereign of the Turks, sends to you, Ka'it Bay, another gift, this of a personal nature, but for all to see. Just as we give this to you, so will Mehmed Çelebi, with his own hand, take yours for his entertainment and satisfaction." Then the third messenger put something covered in purple cloth before the Caliph. As he pulled away the cloth, the other messengers fell to the ground, on their knees, their faces in the dirt, their rumps raised in the air. Then the spokesman fell to his knees, expecting death.

It was a flagon exactly like the one that had contained Zeinel's severed head.

This one contained A'isheh's head.

The eyes gazing out, blue as porcelain; the face calm, mouth sewn shut, hair cropped and tied behind her head like Zeinel's; the skin brown and smooth, as if polished.

Ka'it Bay gasped and stepped away from it, but then regained himself and picked it up, holding it high for everyone to see. "You see," he shouted. "This is what they've done. Look now and remember. Remember."

The Mamluks began to shout *"Mun shan ayoon A'isheh."* The women all began a high-pitched wailing; the men shouted, rent their clothes as if they had seen their own sisters, wives, or daughters mutilated and exposed. The troops threatened to become a mob—this happening as quickly as a thunderstorm when just seconds before the sky was clear and blue. Leonardo could feel their surging, hysterical energy, and he stood beside Hilāl and Sandro and absorbed everything around him.

He was cold and dead; his thoughts were clear, but alien, as if they belonged to someone else, someone who was a witness or a scribe, who functioned merely to record; and without realizing it, Leonardo looked about, saw the shock on Sandro's face—his lips pursed, his eyebrows arched; saw Gutne calmly watching, for she, too, was an observer; and he memorized the faces of those around him, as if they were caught in the instant forever, a painting without brush or pigment; this, this was the moment of art, the choking second before pain and grief, the vibrating, shimmering opening up, as if one could see from every angle, every perspective, through every eye; and Leonardo heard himself moaning, heard it as a lowing in his ears, then as some kind of internal thunder; and he remembered A'isheh, remembered her in detail, remembered mundane moments spent with her, remembered her touch, remembered her *cassone*, remembered the hatred in her eyes when she took Niccolò with her on the ship.

Felt hot tears burning his face.

Yet his face was dry.

Now he would never know . . . never know if he loved her, for he was stone itself, as he was when he found Ginevra.

But he did not really know A'isheh.

She had loved him and turned him to stone.

Leonardo repeated her name to himself, or rather it seemed to repeat itself in his mind, and he saw Ginevra, Ginevra . . . but, no, she was Gutne,

Gutne lying mutilated, bloody, and white-fleshed in her room while he, Leonardo, eviscerated and cut and crushed. Everyone gone. Everyone dead. Everyone but Niccolò. Leonardo gasped at the thought of Niccolò.

What had happened to him? Had he met the same fate as A'isheh?

Then everything gave way to one thought. He had to find out if Niccolò was alive. He had to. If he knew nothing else, he knew that he loved the boy.

The Caliph's Mamluks pushed closer, and Ka'it Bay motioned them to stop. They did as he commanded, and he walked back and forth in front of the cowering Peyks, holding the head of his cousin, his tears mingling with the rain that shone like grease on his face. "You," he said to the Peyks' spokesman. "Rise and look at me." When the Peyk stood up and gained the courage to look into his eyes, Ka'it Bay continued. "I will exchange your life for a traitor's." He handed the vessel he was holding to Kuan, who took it and motioned his guards to stand around him, to hide A'isheh from the soldiers on the verge of hysteria. But the Caliph seemed to know what he was doing, for everyone was silent; they all watched him. "Surely, I am not so naive that I would believe that Mehmed does not have a spy in our midst. Give him to me, and I'll give you your life . . . and perhaps the lives of your companions. Do you owe Mehmed your lives? To be cut limb from limb? Surely, you know that's why he chose you. Surely, not out of love, for he knows what I will do, doesn't he?" Ka'it Bay looked directly at the spokesman, who was tall and gangly.

Leonardo noticed that he had a pimple on his neck; it was inflamed and infected, and it defined the messenger, as if it were a proper name. He saw everything as if with tunnel vision now, as if he were removed from it all and watching from a great distance, from the mountain heights where the air was as crisp and cold as rational thought. Pain and emotions were part of the fabric of dream, and he had finally awakened. He felt a tingling numbness; there, he could even feel the pressure in his fingers, as if his body had caught the same chill as his soul.

But he would find Niccolò. . . .

He would not consider that he might be . . .

No. He *would* find him.

"Well?" asked the Caliph.

The Peyk nodded and looked about the perimeter of soldiers, careful not to get too close, lest one of them disembowel him. They spat at him, slapped him, and he stumbled along; several of Ka'it Bay's guards accompanied him, pushing the soldiers back as he walked among them. He stopped before Hilāl, Sandro, and Leonardo.

He stared at Sandro, as if he recognized him, then stepped backward and pointed.

The Caliph came up behind him. "So you have chosen yourself a Florentine artist."

The Turk bowed his head, afraid to look around. Sandro seemed rooted in place.

"How do you know it is he?" asked Ka'it Bay.

"I have seen him."

"Ah, and where have you seen him?"

But the Caliph did not wait for an answer. He raised his sword; and as Sandro fell backward, praying, most likely thinking these would be his last words on earth, the Caliph brought his sword down on the Turk's head and literally cut the man in two.

Leonardo was covered with blood and viscera, as was Hilāl.

The soldiers went wild, cheering and chanting A'isheh's name, calling for the heads of the other three Turks. Ka'it Bay ordered the other Peyks to their feet, and they stood before him, ready to die. The Caliph walked back to them, stood before them and asked, "Is there a traitor in my midst?"

The Turks stood stiffly.

"Well?"

"Yes," whispered one of them, a short, barrel-chested man with a missing front tooth; his other teeth were black near the gums, as if painted.

"Then will *you* point out the traitor to me?"

The Turk looked down at his feet, and Ka'it Bay laughed. "Ah, do you think you will meet the same fate as your brother? Well, answer me!"

"I would not question the decision of a king."

"Then point out your man," Ka'it Bay said.

"I cannot. He—they—are unknown to me."

"So there are more than one?"

"I do not know, Master. Only that—"

"Yes?"

"That we would be watched, and if we failed, we would be killed."

"And you?" Ka'it Bay asked the other Peyk.

"It is exactly as my companion tells you." This man was the youngest, not more than twenty by the looks of him.

"Why did the Ruler of Turks choose you?"

"As a test."

"Why would he test *you*?"

"I bragged that I—"

"Continue."

"That I could stare into your eyes without . . ."

The Caliph began to laugh, his voice high-pitched, overwrought, but he quickly brought himself into control. "Without what, young snap?"

"Without shaking, Master."

"But you are shaking—and lying—aren't you?"

"No, no—"

"Didn't you brag that you would take *my* head?" The Caliph swung his sword from side to side, as if practicing.

The young Turk hesitated, then said, "Yes." Resigned, he bent his head and closed his eyes.

"Well, it won't be me who'll take your head, young soldier," Ka'it Bay said. "But your own master might when you present him with my gifts, and thanks." With that he picked up the jewel-encrusted sword from the ground and motioned for his guards to remove the baton and saddle. He whispered to Hilāl, who, in turn, spoke with one of his lieutenants; a moment later several men appeared dragging large sacks behind them. The smell of putrefaction was overwhelming, even here in the open.

"Show our guests our gift for the greatest of Turks," Ka'it Bay said.

The guards opened the sacks and jerked them back: heads rolled out. The heads of Turks. The soldiers cheered; one pushed past the guards and kicked a head into the crowd; the guards threw another one into the ranks, and another, until there were more then twenty arcing through the air. There was shouting and swearing, but no laughing; the troops would not lose their deadly temper . . . would not forget A'isheh, their Madonna— would, in fact, carry her with them as a holy offering of death.

As if her unseeing eyes could show them the way.

"Tell your illustrious sovereign that I shall soon have more gifts such as these to present to him. I shall multiply them a thousandfold and crown them with his own." The Caliph paused, then spoke to the youngest of the Peyks. "You'd best remember to be brave, young soldier, for if you or your companions lose your nerve—or my gifts—I shall have your heads, too. Do you think only Mehmed has spies?"

Ka'it Bay dismissed them, and watched them walk the gauntlet through angry Mamluks and Persian troops. Then he sent his best scouts to follow them and gain intelligence on the whereabouts and deployment of Mustafà's . . . and Mehmed's . . . troops.

Two days later the scouts were found near a rocky pass that led into a long, narrow valley. All twenty of them were naked and impaled on posts.

Their heads, of course, were missing.

———

This was difficult country for Ka'it Bay; his army was vulnerable because of its very size, and now the Turks began attacking in earnest, guerrilla tactics, skirmishing, biting into the army's flanks, then disappearing into the hills and mountains and forests, threatening to turn the Caliph's march of conquest into one of attrition. Regiments fanned out, following the

Turks—and more often than not, getting massacred; Hilāl's artillery was a burden for an army on the move, and useless against the Turk's strategy of sudden attack and disappearance. It seemed that the country itself was against the Caliph: the mountain trails, the sheer cliffs, the narrow passes where fifty men could hold up ten thousand. Calul, for his part, sent messengers out with a call to arms, and his army swelled, until Persians and Arabs, Mamluk and tribesman, Gholaum and Parthian, Georgian and Tartar, moved across the land in separate regiments and companies like the great shadows cast by mountains at sunset.

But soldiers and animals alike were hungry, for corn and barley had come into short supply. The Turks burned everything in their wake, and unless Ka'it Bay could cut through their lines that seemed to shift and dissolve like mud in water, his army would be routed by hunger before the Turks came forward to humiliate Egyptian and Persian with sword and pike.

The Turks mounted a night attack and were pushed into surrounding forest. Five thousand Arabs were killed, twice that wounded; the Mamluks took a heavy toll on Mustafà's troops, but flesh was cheap, and the son of the Grand Turk disappeared, leaving his own behind. He would strike again. But when?

As Caesar divided and conquered, Mustafà divided, hid, became part of the land, bit, and ran.

Angry, nervous, hungry, exhausted, the army marched, day after day, and well into the nights.

They no longer shouted A'isheh's name. They no longer screamed for Turkish blood. They were vigilant, dangerous, and as they were frustrated beyond limit, they turned on the Caliph; his feudal cavalry, those who had murdered the holy man in his own mosque, demanded double rations and pay and threatened to return home. Others joined him, although the Caliph's Mamluks remained aloof, thereby demonstrating that their sentiments were with the tribesmen mutineers.

The mutineers loosed arrows and threw their lances at Ka'it Bay's tent; they managed to get hold of a cannon and fired it in the Caliph's direction. That electrified his guards into action, but Ka'it Bay held them back. He mounted his horse and rode through the ranks, his sword in hand, allowing himself to be vulnerable to his men, haranguing them, carrying the head of A'isheh in the Turk's glass vessel. He humiliated them, shouting, "The cowards are free to return to their homes. I don't want cowards by my side. I will take revenge on the Turks if I have to take them all on myself. Alone!"

And then he rode off, making the most dramatic of exits.

Shouting, tumult, sporadic fighting between Mamluk and tribal cavalrymen followed. About a hundred tribesmen were put to the sword; others were blown to bits by the same cannon they had fired on Ka'it Bay. Then trumpets sounded, and there was a great surging forward: slaves, the red-capped bowmen and pikemen, seasoned bedouin soldiers, Mamluks, the wounded, even the women, rushed to follow their king, rushed to follow A'isheh, as if slaughtering their traitorous countrymen had healed them, helped them regain their taste for blood and revenge.

Leonardo was quick to take to his horse, lest he be accused of cowardice; he rode with Hilāl and his thousand guards.

The Caliph rode as if nothing had happened; in time, his own guards took their proper places, and behind him, to either side of him, his phalanxes marched and his Mamluks rode, a great sweating procession bent on killing.

"Leonardo."

Sandro was beside him with Gutne, who fell behind to allow them to talk.

"I've noticed that you have more than a passing fondness for my slave," Leonardo said.

"If you wish, I will keep my distance from her. But you left her behind."

Leonardo smiled, but it was a smile of resignation. "No, I trusted that you would care for her."

"Don't you . . . care for her?"

"Of course," Leonardo said. "Why? Are you asking for her hand?" Sandro blushed; Leonardo's gibe caught him, for he, Sandro, was obviously infatuated with her. "Your friend Mirandola is not here to exorcise you," Leonardo continued. "So I would be careful with my affections."

"I am sorry about A'isheh," Sandro said. He looked straight ahead as he talked to hide his discomfort. When Leonardo didn't answer, he continued. "I had no idea that you loved her."

"So now you have the ability to read minds, Little Bottle?"

"I can read yours, Leonardo."

Again, Leonardo smiled. "Ah, then surely you knew the Caliph would cleave the Turk in half. Is that why you fell backward, about to faint?"

That caught Sandro, who blushed and made the sign of the cross. "Leonardo, I—"

"Were you reading my mind, then, when you told Benedetto that I killed Zoroastro?" Leonardo continued.

Sandro was silent for a beat, then said, "Yes, I told him that, and I was wrong."

"Wrong?"

"When you walked away, I thought—" Sandro seemed to be measuring his words, considering what he could say, unsure of himself. "I turned it over in my mind a thousand times, Leonardo. I was angry when you turned away from him, and anger blinded me. I was wrong to accuse you."

"You might have been right," Leonardo said. "I too have turned it over and over. Perhaps I did kill him."

"No," Sandro said. "You did not."

"Why didn't you come to me earlier?"

"I tried, but you were so . . . cold, so distant. I thought you had changed, that all that had happened . . ."

"And have I?"

"I don't know," Sandro said. "But my heart went out to you when the Turk messengers revealed A'isheh. I've seen that same look on your face once before."

Leonardo turned to him. The path they rode upon would soon give way to a deep glen. Pine forest stretched away to his right, rising hundreds of feet; and as they descended to lower ground, the dark forest and craggy mountains seemed to envelop them in twilight, yet above, the sky was bright and clear as a shiny ribbon.

"What look was that?" Leonardo asked.

"When you stood in Ginevra's room looking out the window. Before you jumped to escape the fire. When you looked down at us, you had the same expression."

"I remember that I thought I saw Tista standing beside you and Niccolò. But Tista was dead. Poor Tista."

"I'm sorry, Leonardo."

Leonardo nodded to Sandro, squeezed his arm, then—without turning around—said, "But it seems that we have an audience." He spoke loudly for Gutne, who was riding close behind them. They slowed slightly so she could catch up. As her face was veiled, it was impossible to tell if she was embarrassed.

"It is not for A'isheh that my master grieves," said Gutne. She spoke to Sandro as if he were already her master . . . or as if she were his equal . . . or perhaps one who would have no master.

"Then for whom?" Sandro asked.

"For your friend . . . Naleeko," Gutne said, addressing Leonardo.

"Niccolò?"

"Yes, Neekolo."

"And how would you know that?" Leonardo asked, shaken.

"I have heard your dreams. . . ."

"My dreams?"

"You speak of him in your sleep, Maestro."

In that instant, Leonardo glimpsed Niccolò's face, saw it absolutely, even if in his mind's eye, saw it with the authentic clarity of sight rather than memory.

With the clarity of dream.

And he wondered, grieving, if he had looked beyond death.

———

Later, in his misery, he sought out Mithqāl; and they talked as they always did, as they rode. That gave him pleasure, solace, for Mithqāl was as voracious for knowledge and experience as Niccolò. And so Leonardo spoke of his memory cathedral and Pliny's history; he taught the boy algebra, the attributes of sight, and Guido d'Arezzo's sol-fa musical system.

He taught Mithqāl, just as he had taught Niccolò. . . .

But Mithqāl was obsessed with Valturio and Alexander the Great, was obsessed with war and its theory, for Mithqāl was a deceiver.

Unlike Niccolò, he only looked like a child.

29

Ruse

of Angels

I saw the aungellys mounte into huen on hye.
—Charles Caxton

. . . and the air full of screams, of sobs, and sighs.
—Niccolò Machiavelli

*M*ustafà's armies attacked again and again, like ferrets taking down flocks of geese; and Ka'it Bay pressed his armies as if they were in retreat. But the Caliph was determined to engage Mehmed, who was encamped on the northeast edge of a great plain at the end of a corridor of long, narrow valleys. It was in the heights above that plain, in a captured fortress in the black mountains, that A'isheh had been imprisoned.

Perhaps Niccolò was there even now . . . if he was alive.

Or perhaps the king of the Turks had sold him to one of his lieutenants: Basaraba, who led twelve thousand Wallachians, or Beglerbeg, who led sixty thousand Roumanians, or the chief of the Acangi, who no doubt would have put Nicco right in front of Persian or Arab arrows and pikes.

The Caliph called Leonardo to his tent at dawn. It was crisp, as if autumn, and the center of the sky was still star specked. Leonardo was bone-tired, for he had been up all night with Hilāl. The Turks had attacked once again at night, without torches, their only warning a deadly hail of arrows. Artillery was useless, for one could fire only at shadows, at woods, at the movement of branches in the wind. But this time the Turks had attacked the artillerymen, and were pulling Leonardo's repeating cannons away on their battle carriages: a fair gift for Mustafà; but Ka'it Bay's Mamluk cavalry took them down to a man.

Everyone knew they would attack again, in the morning, or afternoon, or in the middle of the night. These guerrilla fighters were conquering the Caliph's soldiers before they could reach the battlegrounds. They were not always greedy; sometimes they would kill and run. Those soldiers who manned the flanks of the columns knew they would die, as surely as if the Caliph were to cleave them in two. In their minds, the Turk was not a soldier—a fleshy mortal—but Jinn, created out of fire and smoke. Lack of sleep and the nightmare of sudden death had sapped the fiber of even the most battle-hardened soldiers. Ka'it Bay would not allow his men to foray out on raids, not even his volunteer cavalry—killers all, lest he find more of them skewered on stakes in neat rows.

Hilāl had been right: this was not the Caliph's kind of war.

"With all of your inventions, Maestro, with all your cannon and scythed carts, with all your engines of war, I am still helpless." Ka'it Bay sat in the shadows, which had a blue cast, as if it were twilight rather than morning; and he sipped coffee and puffed on a pipe as if it were noon. Kuan stood beside Leonardo, and beside the Caliph sat Hilāl with several eunuch ministers and chosen Mamluk generals. The air was close in here, as if saturated with a miasma of hatred and bile, for these men hated each other, just as they probably hated their master, Ka'it Bay, who had called them together.

"I am sorry that my engines could not be of more use, Master of Worlds," Leonardo said.

"Well, what do you plan to do about it?" asked the Caliph.

"Maestro Leonardo is a master of strategy, as well as master of engineers," Hilāl said; he looked directly at Kuan.

"Indeed, the great emir is correct," Kuan said.

Hilāl looked relieved.

"Ah, so my father and my brother—my two advisers—are in agreement at last." Ka'it Bay looked at Hilāl, then at Kuan, who were, of course, his slaves. "It seems that their love for you, Leonardo, is greater than their hatred for each other."

"So it seems," Leonardo said, wondering what they were up to.

"I have heard you tell stories of the exploits of Alexander the Macedonian to Mithqāl, whom I think of as my own child," Hilāl said. "Didn't you tell him that you knew what Alexander would do if he were in the position of our Caliph?"

"I was only entertaining the child," Leonardo said. "I did not realize that my musings and fabrications held such fascination for eavesdroppers."

"Tell us all what the great Alexander would do," Ka'it Bay said.

"Alexander used a ruse to conquer the Illyrian king, Cleitus, who was in revolt," Leonardo said. "Another Illyrian tribe was attacking Alexander as he marched, just as Mustafà has been attacking us. Alexander had to advance by forced marches to reach the fortress that Cleitus occupied. Even the terrain was similar, Master of Worlds, for Alexander had to trek through valleys and plains bordered by mountains. But, you see, Alexander's supplies were almost exhausted, and he was constantly being attacked by the Illyrians from high ground. Unless he could draw his enemy into the plain, where he could use his phalanxes and superior discipline, he would never reach Cleitus's fortress."

"Which is what *we* must do," Ka'it Bay said. "We must draw them down where we can fight them." He paused, then asked, "What, then, was Alexander's tactic?"

"He mounted a spectacle for them, a parade battle drill; and the Illyrian soldiers gathered to watch Alexander's phalanxes wheeling and turning and marching. They rushed down the mountainside to view Alexander's display; they gathered on the lower slopes of the foothills, for they were enthralled with the discipline and smartness of Alexander's maneuvers. Alexander had seduced them to gather on ground that favored his attack, and when he ordered the attack, they took the Illyrians completely by surprise. He had the Illyrians slaughtered with both pikes and engines of war."

"Would you have us put on a parade for Mustafà?" Ka'it Bay asked sarcastically.

"No, Master of Worlds."

"Then what does Alexander's spirit suggest we do?"

Leonardo could feel the Caliph's impatience, but he played it out, as if he were once again playing to Lorenzo's court, as if he were once again creating a soul out of a pig's intestine, for Ka'it Bay also delighted in the dramatic. Why else would he have brought Leonardo to visit Zoroastro in the torture chambers? "Alexander would have gathered the angels in heaven to descend upon his enemies," Leonardo said.

The Caliph smiled and nodded. "We have already had one such demonstration of angels descending upon our armies, haven't we?" He looked at Hilāl, who had staged Mithqāl's flight in Leonardo's flying machine at the Caliph's castle. "And now Mustafà shall have another."

———

"Congratulations," Kuan said as he and Leonardo left the Caliph's tent together.

"For what?" Leonardo asked, bitterness in his tone of voice. "For consigning children to die by falling upon the spears of the Turks?"

"You gave the Caliph advice, and he took it. That is no small thing."

"He has enough advisers," Leonardo said.

Kuan smiled. "Yes, more than enough, but that's only his way of being . . . gracious. He keeps his own counsel."

"What about Hilāl, and you?"

"Sometimes the Caliph listens to one, sometimes the other."

"But this time he listened to both of you."

"He listened to *you*, Maestro," Kuan said.

Leonardo forced a laugh. "Was the Caliph correct, Kuan? Do you hate Hilāl?"

"The Caliph, by definition, cannot be wrong," Kuan said.

"Of course," Leonardo said.

"Let's just say that I distrust him with intensity."

"You trusted him enough today."

"We had no choice. Would you see us lose to the Turk?"

"I will not let Mithqāl and the other children fly my machines alone," Leonardo said, musing. "I will lead them."

"I'm afraid that's not possible, Leonardo," Kuan said.

"And why not?"

"The Caliph values you."

"I *will* go."

"No, Leonardo. You will not, I promise you. If the children die serving their master, their reward will be Paradise. Hilāl would not allow you to diminish their destiny by trying to save them. Rather, you would get in their way. They are trained, you are not." He smiled sadly, as if enjoying a joke before telling it and said, "Paradise is not for you, Leonardo, for one cannot reason to get there. But don't worry, Maestro, there will be enough death to keep you and all the rest of us busy."

The armies didn't march that day. The trap was being set.

Ka'it Bay even agreed to Leonardo's idea of staging a display in the manner of Alexander's to arouse the curiosity of Turks and draw them near. Leonardo was in his element, for this was like a festival, a circus, or a jousting day. If, indeed, children were destined to die today, so were Turks. Leonardo was determined to make sure of it. To Leonardo's mind every Turk was the embodiment of his nemesis, Nicolini . . . Nicolini, who took Ginevra, captured her as cruelly as Mehmed had captured A'isheh. It was as if Leonardo needed to manufacture hatred to distract himself, as if this almost conscious ruse would serve to eradicate memory and guilt. If only he had not been obsessed with birds and flight and the mechanics of war. Why did he need to discover God's secrets and best the ideas and machines of the ancients? Why couldn't he have been more like Pietro Perugino, who had no other ambition but to be a painter and live in a fine house? Death would not weigh upon Pietro, only florins.

For Leonardo, there could only be the narcotic distractions of anger and activity.

The Turks would surely kill the children, the deadly cherubim who would drop fire upon them; and Leonardo would make certain that they paid, for A'isheh, for Ginevra, for . . .

For Niccolò.

Somehow, it was as if the children were *already* dead.

While the cannons were positioned and camouflaged to create cross fire upon probable Turkish positions, Leonardo created billowing pavilions out of masts and the brightly colored fabric of Kuan's hot-air balloon. A feast was prepared, which depleted the army's supplies. High poles were erected in conspicuous places and gold and silver apples placed atop each one. By noon Mamluks dressed in parade finery were riding their horses at breakneck speed and trying to knock down as many apples as they could with their arrows.

The Turks took the bait and came down the hills for a better view, until they could be easily seen by those in the Caliph's camp. They even cheered the heroes who could loose twenty arrows at full gallop and knock down twenty gold and silver apples. These were the perfect games, for they were of Turkish origin; and the smell of roasting meat alone was enough to drive Mustafà's army to attack.

Every man—Arab and Persian—knew that blood would soon pour; even the animals seemed to sense it, for they were skittish, as if just before a storm. But Leonardo could only watch the games and wait. He had tried to follow the children to the cliff where the flying machines were to be launched, but Hilāl's guards stopped him before he even got out of the camp. They summoned Hilāl, who seemed infuriated with him, as if Leonardo had given the order to send these children to their deaths.

Sandro and Amerigo approached Leonardo. They both looked lean, dark, and tired, like bedouins.

"Leonardo, the Caliph wishes you to be with him," Amerigo said.

"And he sent *you* to tell me that?" Leonardo asked. "Somehow I can't believe that. You, and the Little Bottle?"

"Kuan sent me," Amerigo said.

"Then who sent Sandro?"

"You're making this very difficult," Sandro said. "Your anger should be directed at me, not at Amerigo."

"I'm sorry. I'm not angry with either of you. What does the Caliph want with me?"

They spoke in Tuscan, falling naturally into it, as if everything they might say was secret. "It's about to begin," Amerigo said.

Leonardo laughed. "Every whore and slave knows that. They're all excited about the 'miracles' to come, never mind that it will probably be their blood that will soak the soil."

"And the Caliph wishes you to be in his company and protect him if you must," Amerigo said, as if completing a sentence that Leonardo had interrupted. "We wanted to be together before—"

"Why now?" asked Leonardo.

Amerigo looked embarrassed. "I tried to speak to you before, but you ignored me."

"I would not have done that."

"Why, you walked right past me this morning."

"I don't remember ever..." Leonardo caught himself, sighed, and said, "I've missed you, Amerigo."

"And I you. Like Sandro, I—" He just shook his head, as if he could not begin to find words to describe how he felt.

"We've let all this come between us," Sandro said. "Even after we talked. Why?"

"Perhaps because we feel differently than we'd wish," Leonardo said.

"I dreamed that I would never see you again, Leonardo," Amerigo said. He looked awkward, as he often did in public. "I believe it was a warning."

"I don't believe in dreams, but I'm glad you had this dream, if it brings us together," Leonardo said, and he embraced Amerigo and then Sandro. "You will fight alongside Kuan, I presume."

"I will," Amerigo said. "But Sandro will protect the women. That will insure that at least one of us will survive."

The women were safely hidden near the cannons and protected by cavalry.

"I will attend the cannons," Sandro said, his neck and cheeks red with embarrassment. "I thought to be with you, until the Caliph ordered you to attend him."

"Well, you can still come along," Leonardo said.

Sandro shook his head. "Kuan told me that the Caliph believed the Turk who accused me of being a spy."

"Then why did he kill the Turk?" Leonardo asked.

"To appease his troops," Amerigo said. "He had to take the Turk's life."

"If the Caliph believed that, Sandro would not be alive now," Leonardo said.

"Kuan said that Sandro's life was a gift to you from the Caliph," Amerigo said, but then he turned toward the eastern hills, as did everyone, as if pushed and directed by the susurration all around them. It was as if every man had drawn a sharp breath; then there was a great rolling wave of whispers and low voices that was palpable as wind, as touch.

The very sounds of awe, followed by explosions.

Mithqāl and the other children had jumped from a western cliff, where they would have the most cover from the Turks, then flew in a wide arc to reach the Turks on the eastern side from behind. Ka'it Bay's troops saw them, it seemed, before the Turks; but the Turks took notice when the first of Leonardo's shells exploded in their midst, shearing heads and arms and legs with shrapnel and setting men ablaze.

"It's too early!" Leonardo shouted, and he, Sandro, and Amerigo parted company, each running to his assigned post; but the others watched, mesmerized, even when the cavalrymen came down among them to make them ready.

Who could not watch the miracle playing itself out? The children circling like hawks above Mustafà's troops, their ribbed wings as white as their robes. Surely they could only be angels floating on the updrafts, one after the other. Surely this was proof that Allah was with Ka'it Bay, not the Turk. Who could not watch the angels swoop down upon the Turks and drop terrible gifts of fire and metal?

The rear ranks of the Turks panicked first, for they caught the first shells. A few dropped to their knees in prayer and were probably saved; for their comrades rushed forward toward the main body of troops, tearing into them as if they were the enemy; and the angels expertly dropped more bombs, driving the Turks forward, rank upon panicking rank, as if they were heavenly shepherds driving their sheep, until the Turks were in headlong flight down the hills and onto the plain.

Leonardo found Ka'it Bay near his tent. He had not yet mounted his horse, which was held for him by one of his guards. Beside him stood Hilāl and the Devatdar.

"You remember my Devatdar," the Caliph said to Leonardo.

Leonardo nodded, although he had seen little of him since the Devatdar had joined Ka'it Bay in the field. Hilāl had intimated that he had fallen out of favor; and, indeed, he had not been present at the Caliph's meetings. But who could trust Hilāl? He seemed to hate everyone but Mithqāl and his own guards.

"Shall I give the signal now, Master?" asked the Devatdar.

Ka'it Bay watched the Turks spilling onto the plain, a great massing of men, out of control. "Yes, now."

The Devatdar merely turned his head, and a guard rode away at full tilt. A moment later cannons were firing upon the Turks. A constant thunder, and the Caliph's cavalry and his phalanxes of foot soldiers appeared en masse on the eastern edge of the plain; they moved forward and were cheek to jowl with Leonardo, the Devatdar, and the Caliph. The Caliph had but to get on his horse and ride forward to lead his men to a victory of slaughter.

But this was only a portion of his troops; the others would converge from north and south and overwhelm Mustafà's men with their sheer numbers.

Ka'it Bay mounted his horse. Leonardo followed suit; the Caliph's slave had Leonardo's own horse ready. When the Caliph raised his sword, the cannons ceased firing and a great shouting seemed to propel him forward. Leonardo stayed close to him. The Caliph rode hard, directly at the enemy. His face was impassive, he was intent, and Leonardo worried that the king would be the first to be pierced by arrow or pike. Leonardo was not worried about himself, although his heart was pounding. He had found that fear transformed itself into a heightened consciousness; and he heard only the rushing of air in his ears and tasted dry metal in his mouth. In moments, he would enter death's realm. There was no place in battle for time and memory. Only the dance of combat, of exhaustion and exultation; the susurrating music of those sighing and pleading; the hymns of screaming and slashing and breaking bone and sinew.

It was a bloodbath, and it lasted until dark.

After the scythed cars had leveled the field, after heads were collected, after Mamluks fell exhausted to nap in the soaking blood and gore, after the Turk's supplies and foodstuffs had been gathered, the Caliph still pressed his men. He was determined that none of Mustafà's Turks should reach Mehmed. He was determined to take Mehmed Mustafà's head.

But Mustafà could not be found.

———

In the mountain-shadowed, blood-squelching, starry darkness, Leonardo found his friends. "You see, Amerigo, your dream was wrong," Leonardo said.

"And you," Sandro said to Leonardo, "you thought the children would die in your contraptions. Yet they are alive, all of them."

"Yes . . . they are alive," and then Leonardo lapsed into a numbed silence that was like a fever. He didn't recover until he sighted the castle in which Niccolò might be imprisoned.

30

The Black Mountain

So high above the world and so mighty, this little castle is impregnable to all but the gaze of the Almighty. . . ."
—Meister Eckhart

And every kind of thing flying through the air fell upon us; finally a great fire broke out, not brought by the wind, but carried, it would seem, by ten thousand devils . . .
—Leonardo da Vinci

The very mountains seemed to move as they marched, the vibrations of distant earthquakes that could be barely felt, yet it was as if the earth itself had lost its balance and would break apart and fall into the fires and icy plains of hell. As if in pain, the earth groaned; and, indeed, rocks fell from cliffs to explode like Leonardo's bombs. It grew hot at night, and dark, for a ceiling of clouds hid the stars and planets. Even Gutne, who seemed to lack fear or care, prayed to the one true God, while Sandro prayed to Mary and the saints to intercede with the God of his fathers. Gutne was now Sandro's . . . she might be his woman, that was all. She slept in his tent. Sandro kept close to Leonardo now, as if he understood that the time of binding—or rending—was near. Even Amerigo took his leave from his lover Kuan to be with Leonardo, as if he was not sure that *his* dream of rending would yet come true.

The world was on fire . . . and the Caliph was splendid.

He explained all the terrible signs and auguries as if they were commandments written across the gray, thunder-cloud sky, until his soldiers believed that the ground and mountains were shaking with impatience for Arab and Persians to reach the Turks and slaughter them. He promised that those who fell would be delivered immediately into Paradise, a paradise of the flesh without its agonies, a garden of physical ecstasy and spiritual joy; there exquisite houris would await them, a thousand A'isheh's awaiting a thousand brave souls suddenly severed from life's fleshy cord. Exhausted, filthy, and consciously putting one leg before the other on forced march, one could easily believe that death was desirable. Paradise bought for an instant—a pneumatic flash—of agony. Even Leonardo could visualize it, and that numinal image, lit from both inside and out, would become a room in Leonardo's memory cathedral.

Ka'it Bay had A'isheh's head raised upon a high standard so that every soldier could see it.

She led the way, and they followed.

The earth rumbled and the rain came down in sheets when they finally encamped in sight of the Turk's armies.

Before them on the western edge of the plain was the high, fortified castle that crowned a precipitous, five-hundred-foot limestone crag: the black mountain. The fortress was in a strategic location to control the flowering plain and wooded environs below.

But all was quiet, as if both sides realized that death would hold sway on enough in the shadow of the mountain.

The Turks had set a trap.

Leonardo realized it when he climbed the cliffs to the west with Hilāl and Mithqāl to get a better view of the castle. They had begun climbing at dawn, and although there was still a bite to the air, they were sweaty when they reached the crest of a crag that overlooked the only access to the castle: a saddle-shaped isthmus of rock. Beyond the rock, a narrow path that led to a village razed by the Turks disappeared around the curve of a hill. Hilāl was gasping for breath; Mithqāl wasn't winded at all. Strong gusts of wind slapped at them, as Leonardo looked through a beautifully engraved silver telescope that the sultan had presented to him. Actually, it was Leonardo's own invention.

Leonardo adjusted the tube until the castle seemed an arm's length away. He felt hopeless, for this was like no castle that he had ever seen. Its fortifications had surely been recently rebuilt. High, rectangular towers had been replaced by massive, squat bastions of stone that were no higher than the curtains and gave the huge cannons clear lines of fire. Cliffs and high sloping banks acted as moats to protect the castle's curtains. Although it looked as natural as the mountain itself, the fortress was a geometric perfection. Circles of fortification within circles; the cliffs carved into scarp and ditch and rampart.

"Leonardo, what do you see?" Mithqāl asked.

"More than enough, and not enough."

"Let me see," Hilāl said, and Leonardo passed him the telescope.

"I have never seen cannons that large."

"Nor I," Leonardo said. Just as he could detect the subtle movements of birds' wings in flight, so could Leonardo see details of the fortifications without the lenses. "We must tell the Caliph that the camp must be moved. It is within range of the Turk's cannons, of that I'm certain."

"But they could have fired on us before," Mithqāl said.

"It's much better to allow the chickens to build their own coop and settle down for the night," Leonardo said.

"We cannot simply retreat," Hilāl said. "The Caliph wouldn't hear of it. We must do something . . . here."

Leonardo gazed out at the road that led to the castle; it would be impossible to bring artillery along that route, for it was completely exposed. To pull cannons up the other side of the mountain might be possible, but it would take weeks . . . unless . . . He made a quick sketch of a novel tackle-and-pulley system that could lift the cannons up the great height of the closest cliff in stages.

"What do you think, Leonardo?" asked Hilāl.

"We must hurry . . . we must move our cannons out of harm's way, or there will be no chance," Leonardo said. "If we move our lines back, Mehmed will have to come to us. The castle can only ensure that his retreat would be safe. With time, we can break the castle."

"I know what to do," Mithqāl said.

His intensity was such that Leonardo could not but soften. "Yes, I'm sure you do. And it may well be correct."

"But I haven't told you yet."

"You didn't need to," Leonardo said, looking from Mithqāl to the castle, as if he could penetrate its very walls with the fire of his gaze and find Niccolò.

But perhaps he would find only another of Mehmed's gifts: Niccolò's head displayed in crystal, magnified all out of proportion.

His olive skin as white as chalk.

His lips as dark and mottled as the stone crags of this desolate place.

Before they could reach the camp, cannons began to fire from the castle and from the field, accompanied by the silent but deadly trebuchets and mangonels—siege engines that threw rocks as heavy as three hundred pounds into Ka'it Bay's compound. Leonardo felt the percussion as shocks. A dugout containing barrels of gunpowder was hit, and it exploded, throwing men into the air as if they were bits and pieces of clothing. At first it was simply slaughter, for Ka'it Bay's army was taken by such surprise that men didn't know where to run; it was as if the ground itself were boiling, a hail of hot stone and metal falling from the sky. Hilāl looked on, horrified, and Leonardo could hear him praying, intoning the words as if he wasn't aware that he was speaking.

From their vantage high on the cliffs, they could see everything as if they were watching from the air; there was a sense of distance mingled with the horror of what they saw, as if the men scattering and falling and dying were not real; it was more like watching a festival: the bombs and shot could only be fireworks exploding in harmless showers of sparks.

They watched the fascines, baggage chariots, and tents explode and catch fire, saw the Caliph riding through the chaos, rallying his men to retreat to safe ground.

But then the Turks were in the field.

Leonardo saw them before Ka'it Bay did; the Caliph would momentarily see their plumes and helmets rising, as if out of the earth, for Mehmed's cavalry came from behind a rill where they could not be seen. They rode in battle formation. Elite spahis riders from Asia Minor and cavalrymen from Europe flanked the phalanxes of Mehmed's marching janissary soldiers.

Fifty thousand more jannisaries marched inside a square formation of carts, and in the center of the four lines of soldiers and horsemen—a huge phalanx that spread across the entire field—were the battle laagers: three hundred cannons chained together. A hundred fifty thousand men marched, moving like a shadow across the empty field; and with the aid of his glasses Leonardo could see Mehmed and Mustafà, dressed like birds in colorful plumage, safe in the bosom of their troops.

But there was no need for heroics. Might was mass, and the Grand Turk had obviously planned for a full day of massacre.

"The cannons," Hilāl said. "And my men. Look, down there, the Turks will destroy them all," and as if he were running to save his own children, he clambered down the cliff; the overweight eunuch was more agile than Leonardo would have thought. But it seemed to take hours to reach the plain, and as they made their way down, they could see less and less of what was going on, for dust had risen into the air like a cloud, veiling everything. Surely, the Turk's cavalry would attack, for Mehmed would not constrain the flower of his army, the Akindjis and Kurds who would try to capture the Caliph's artillery, as if to rip the teeth from Ka'it Bay's mouth.

Hilāl was right about that.

Leonardo wished he was with Sandro and Amerigo; he concentrated to rein in his thoughts, for they crawled with fear; and he imagined the most terrible deaths befalling his friends, imagined them exploding, being torn apart, impaled upon sword or pike, imagined them begging for life while he looked on, helpless to save them. Once they reached the base of the crag, they rushed together toward their own artillery. But then, as if Leonardo's imagination had colored reality, just as his paint had colored canvas, a cannon projectile exploded before them, spreading shot and killing a soldier who ran right into the shrapnel. In an instant he was torn to bits, into gobbets, and his soul was explosively transformed into red mist as he became part of the miasma of battle.

He could have been Sandro or Amerigo or Mithqāl.

Safe behind an overturned baggage chariot, Leonardo let out his breath and squeezed Mithqāl's arm as if it were Niccolò's.

Hilāl's lieutenants had the presence of mind to move the cannons back and then around the Mamluk and Persian cavalry and foot-soldier phalanxes; in effect, flanking them, so they could fire into the mass of the Turks, fire upon the laagers and destroy them. The tactic was only partly successful, for the Turks had scattered their artillery throughout their ranks and were slaughtering Persians and Arabs; but their artillery was no match for Leonardo's cannons and repeating guns, which brought down Turks in great numbers until the plain was soaked with blood and covered with bodies and limbs: a great tapestry woven without design or straight-edge perimeter. The Turks tried to take the cannons with a cavalry charge, but Ka'it Bay's cavalry met and defeated them. Leonardo stayed with Hilāl, directing his own guns and cannons, and as he watched the explosions of metal and wood and flesh as men rode at one another, within arm's reach of Leonardo, breaking sword and pike against metal, felling each other in frenzy, he could not retreat into the numbing, adrenaline-pumping euphoria of hand-to-hand combat. He was alone, isolated, and completely, almost supernaturally, aware of the slaughter around him; and with every death, with every bursting of flesh and transformation into the stuff of the soul, he felt heavier, as if every loss was his terrible gain, until he felt that he too was falling; but the eye of guilt could not be closed, and he watched himself—fascinated and terrified—as he moved from cannon to cannon, helping when necessary, directing the noise and death as if he were the Red Jinn, heavy as Hilāl, emasculated, and implacable as the stone gods of Ka'it Bay's ancestors. But this battle could not be won by cannons or repeating guns, for Persians and Arabs met the Turks pike to pike, sword to sword; and like lovers, they became as one. To fire at the Turks would kill as many Persians and Arabs; so after firing at the last ranks of Turks, Hilāl ordered his eunuch Mamluks to retreat to safety with the artillery. Around Leonardo and the guns were the stomping, dust-pounding hooves of the cavalry mares, a wall of sweating horseflesh.

Beyond and before them, like a great cresting wave, cavalry met cavalry, clashing; and as all the screaming and moaning became one roaring waterfall crashing, Ka'it Bay's troops fell back toward the Arab lines, for although his troops were fighting bravely—as were the Persian's—they were still in retreat. Armies covered the plain, as if one great phalanx, or spiny beast bristling with pikes. As they retreated, Leonardo shouted to Hilāl above the din, "Where are the women being kept?"

Hilāl shrugged.

Leonardo worried about Sandro, and wondered if he was, indeed, with the women, wherever they might be. Odds were that they were hiding somewhere in the hills above; Leonardo, Hilāl, and Mithqāl could have passed right by them on their descent from the cliffs.

"And Mithqāl?" asked Leonardo. "He was here a moment ago."

Hilāl looked around, worried. "I can't imagine—"

"I can," Leonardo said. "Where are the other angels?"

"They would be in the mountains."

"Would they join the battle on their own?" Leonardo asked.

"Not without orders."

"Would they obey Mithqāl?"

"Of course, he leads them," Hilāl said.

With that, Leonardo left Hilāl's protection. A few steps and he was in the melee of battle. He found a sword and pried it out of a dead Mamluk's hand, and he took the man's horse, a dappled mare, which stood obediently over the Arab, as if the man had simply decided to take a nap and would expect the small, intelligent creature to be there waiting for him.

The angels would be encamped on the cliffs; he knew that. But where?

He rode through the battle. Only once did a pikeman almost knock him from his horse, and Leonardo let him go, for his objective was to find Mithqāl, which he did.

The boy was on foot, backing away from a Turk who had the advantage of size and a weapon. Mithqāl had somehow lost his, and he looked this way and that, terrified, suddenly a child; but below him was only blood-wet grass and mud and around him were men fighting, grunting, killing, oblivious to the boy looking for a weapon, too distracted with their own opponents to run him through for good measure.

Leonardo hacked off the Turk's head, swinging once hard, and as he looked at Mithqāl, he felt a sudden revulsion for what he had done, even though he had just saved the boy's life. It was as if he were caught, found out, revealed. For an instant, he remembered the judge high on his dais scolding him for *sodomia*.

He extended his hand to Mithqāl, who leaped upon the horse, holding on to Leonardo as if he were a child, breathing in gasps; and Leonardo tried to reach the southern perimeter of the battle, the edge of his own lines, where they would be safe. But he would be back in the fray soon after, for if he were ever to see Niccolò again, he had to find Ka'it Bay, had to maintain his confidence, had to tell him of his plan.

"Leonardo."

"Not yet," Leonardo said. "We're not safe yet."

"But I don't care about that," Mithqāl said.

"Shall I put you down here, then?"

Mithqāl didn't answer, but he tightened his hold around Leonardo. Even here, in the rear ranks, where Calul's Persian soldiers and Mamluks alike were fighting Turks, the clanging of swords, the shouting of men and women, the shooting whistling of arrows and crack of arquebus were so loud and immediate that they could be felt. Yet the clouds of dust gave the battlefield an unreal quality; indeed, perhaps Dante's conception of hell came from experiences such as this. Leonardo inhaled smoke and gagged on the sour, acrid odors of burning flesh . . . and saw Ginevra riding a Persian mare like a man, swinging a sword as if she had trained for it, hacking and killing with the determination of the other men and women around her. Persian women fought like men, perhaps better, for they had carried in their wombs the children they were fighting to protect.

But, of course, it was Gutne, who had been Ginevra, who had been Leonardo's slave for a few breaths before she found Sandro.

She saw Leonardo and rode toward him; together they left the pounding heart of battle and, as if passing through a veil, came through the dust clouds onto clear, open ground. Relieved to be out of immediate danger, even if for a few moments, Leonardo led them to the safety of a copse of trees. Behind them were striated cliffs. Mithqāl immediately dismounted, as if remaining on Leonardo's horse would signify humiliation. Her face streaked with dirt like tears, her arms and clothes filthy and wet with blood, Gutne watched Leonardo. She was not wearing a veil, nor a headdress; her hair, dyed bright red, as when she had first come to him, was pulled back from her face. She was Medusa, her hair coiled tight as coral snakes, and she radiated a passive hatred as naturally as heat.

"Why aren't you with the other women?" Leonardo asked. "And why—"

She laughed, interrupting, and asked, "Do you think only Persian women can fight? We have not all spent our lives in *hareems*."

Surprised at her aggressiveness, he said, "I meant no disrespect."

"But *I* have been disrespectful." She lowered her eyes, and as if suddenly realizing that her head was uncovered, she pulled up her painted muslin kerchief. She smiled at him, as if slipping into another guise, and said, "So that's how you recognized me." She paused. "But I recognized you, Master, as if God were pointing at you Himself."

"Did Sandro ask you to dye your hair like . . ."

"Like Ginevra?" she asked. "No, but it was she who gave me the idea to do so again."

"What do you mean?"

"I wanted Calul."

"Ussun Cassano's son?"

She nodded. "I dyed my hair and found him. He saw me and saw himself. Now I am his." She paused, looking surprised. "Do you object? Since you gave me to Sandro, I . . ." She allowed her voice to trail off, but she looked at him carefully, as if trying to detect whether he wanted her back.

"What about Sandro?" he asked.

"He told me that he could not remain in these lands."

It was Leonardo's turn to be surprised.

"He told me he loved me," Gutne continued, "but he could not make love to me. He told me he would carry my image in his heart. Do you know what he means by that?"

Leonardo knew only too well, but said nothing.

"He told me he has consecrated himself to God. He made provisions for me, but I refused. When he found out about Calul, he became angry."

"Where is he now?" Leonardo asked, worried.

"I don't know. He would not tell me."

"Where are the women being kept?"

"Is he with them?" she asked.

"I think so," Leonardo said.

"I don't know. No one knows, but those who are protecting them," and with that she mounted her horse, then turned back. "Do you really care about him?"

Leonardo could only look at her.

"I think you care for no one but Neekolo. And he is probably dead." Then she rode back into the battle, back to Calul's soldiers, disappearing into the dust cloud as if she were made of smoke.

"She hates you, doesn't she, Master," Mithqāl asked, but it was really a statement. After a pause he said, "I know where the women are, Master."

———

Leonardo found the Caliph conferring on horseback with Kuan, the Devatdar, and other high officers, all Emirs of a Thousand. They huddled together, their Mamluk guards around them, at the edge of the fray. When the Caliph saw Leonardo, he nodded to him and motioned to his soldiers to open their ranks and let him pass through.

"I see that at least you live," Ka'it Bay said, "while the rest of my men are slaughtered."

"More Turks are dead than Arabs or even Persians, Ruler of Worlds," Leonardo said.

"Thanks to your engines, Maestro. But what good are they now?"

"Your army was perhaps too eager for battle."

Kuan looked worried, for the Caliph was exhausted, physically and emotionally; but Ka'it Bay said to Leonardo, "Soldiers can stand still to die only so long. Do you imagine you could have held the line longer?"

"No, Master, of course not."

"What do you think, then? Are we victors, or the Turk?" He smiled, for they stood as if in a charnel house; the smell of death was stronger than perfume. "Well . . . ?" There was a dangerous edge now to his voice.

"We cannot win until we have the castle," Leonardo said. "Mustafà's troops will be safe in the umbra of its protection."

"We could starve them out," the Caliph said.

Leonardo glanced around at the other men. None would speak. "Would you remain here the winter?" he asked. "And possibly starve along with the enemy?"

"We will crush them, even if we perish to a man."

"I have a plan, Master of Worlds," Leonardo said. "Would you like—"

"Perhaps *you* are my herald, Maestro." The Caliph ignored what Leonardo had just said.

"I'm afraid I don't understand what you mean."

"If we are not all dead, I will call you later, Maestro," the Caliph said, dismissing him. "Your duty is to stand with your machines, if they have not all been smashed by the Turk's cannons. We will bury Hilāl later. With honor."

Hilāl dead?

Leonardo bowed and took his leave, certain that the Caliph had detected his surprise and dismay.

———

"Mithqāl, can you keep a secret?" Leonardo asked.

"Of course, Master. Have I not proved myself to you?"

"If you could destroy the Turk and gain yourself glory by trickery and sleight of hand, would you do it?"

Mithqāl looked uncertain. "It would depend, Master."

"On what?" asked Leonardo, baiting him.

"I don't know, but I would never betray my Caliph," Mithqāl said warily.

"I would never ask you to betray your king. But would you lie to your superiors to help me?"

"Yes."

"Why?" Leonardo asked, surprised that the boy didn't hesitate.

"Because you saved my life."

And so Leonardo told the precocious angel of death his plan.

31
The Plan

Night shall speak, night give its counsel,
Night shall bring thee victory.

—Plutarch

Wait, thou bird of blackness;
There thou shalt find a plenty of human flesh.

—Plutarch

K a'it Bay finally summoned Leonardo to his tent, which had taken thirty soldiers to erect. A slave gave Leonardo a pipe and coffee; the smells of strong coffee and tobacco were delicious, and it was then that he realized how tired and hungry he was.

"Do you interpret dreams?" the Caliph asked him.

"No, Master."

"No . . . ? My Devatdar does."

Leonardo nodded to the Devatdar, who looked most uncomfortable as he sat on a couch opposite the Caliph and beside Kuan.

"I had a frightful dream just before dawn," the Caliph continued. "I called my imam and my Devatdar. But it seems that one cannot answer, and the other gives me an answer I cannot accept." He gazed at the Devatdar, and his imam; the holy man looked nearly eighty and was stooped and shrunken and enfolded in his clothes as if he were hiding in them, but his eyes were direct and somehow menacing.

Then the Caliph turned to Leonardo.

"I dreamed that a huge snake was coiling around me. It reached my neck and began to choke me, but as it stared at me with eyes that looked like jewels, it suddenly transformed itself into an eagle. It spread its wings and lifted me into the air, and carried me in its talons for a long distance, until I saw a staff glowing like embers on desert sand below. It was a herald's staff. Then the eagle set me gently down beside the staff. When I touched it, I felt free from terror and doubt." After a pause he said, "Tell me your interpretation, Maestro Leonardo."

"I don't believe in necromancy," Leonardo said, trying not to expose his excitement. Indeed, if Leonardo had believed in superstition, the Caliph's dream would be a gift from the gods.

"That doesn't matter. Neither does Kuan."

Kuan lowered his eyes. "My slave and brother agrees with my Devatdar's interpretation," Ka'it Bay said. Then he motioned to the Devatdar. "Tell him."

"The snake represents defeat," the Devatdar said. "But we are not defeated. We are victorious."

"One knows when he is victorious," Ka'it Bay said. "I may tell my troops we are the victors; but victory is decisive. I'm sure Mehmed is telling his armies that *they* are the victors."

"Then even if we are defeated," continued the Devatdar, "we can only be utterly destroyed if we stay. For the snake is the Turk, and he will strangle us."

"He will strangle *me,*" Ka'it Bay said. "That was how it was in my dream."

"A dream is not literal, Master."

"Perhaps it is, perhaps it is not. But continue."

"If you pull back now, with honor—and by that I mean the honor of the greatest of generals—your nation will be safe. If you obey the dictates of your dream, then defeat will become victory—the eagle—and carry you home, to Egypt. If you do this, you will be free of terror and doubt. That is the gift of the herald."

"And who is this herald?"

"It is you, Great King," the Devatdar said.

"You see?" the Caliph said to Leonardo.

"Surely you don't doubt the intentions and bravery of these men," Leonardo said.

"Hate each other though they might, they would fight beside me until death."

"Great King, we are brothers," the Devatdar said. "There is no enmity between us."

"Master, although their interpretation fits perfectly, I disagree with that interpretation," Leonardo said.

"Then why do you disagree?" asked the Caliph.

"Because I don't believe you should leave this land without conquering it, and I have a plan."

Ka'it Bay laughed and nodded. "At least you are honest. But before I listen to your plan, I will listen to your interpretation of my dream."

"They are one and the same, Caliph. You dreamed my plan." Leonardo paused for dramatic effect, then continued. "Your able counselors were indeed correct to tell you that the snake in your dream represents defeat. But your dream told you that you can turn defeat into absolute victory."

"How is that?"

"You have eagles, Master of Worlds. You have flying machines at your disposal. They can open the castle to you . . . tonight."

"Tonight?"

"Would you wait for the enemy to attack?" Leonardo asked.

"I would let my men have a few hours' rest," the Caliph said. "Have you lost faith in your engines and cannons?"

"Master, we are all prepared . . . for a long siege. Is that what you wish?

Mehmed would never expect an attack tonight, but even now we have little time."

"And the staff, Leonardo?" Ka'it Bay asked.

"Master?"

"In my dream . . ."

"You were right to think that I was the herald," Leonardo said. "I am giving you the staff." He held out his hand to the Caliph, who nodded but made no move to grasp it.

"Why should we use the angels and your flying machines, Maestro?" Ka'it Bay asked. "Kuan, why can't we float your ships over the enemy and drop fire upon them? Would that not roast their flesh and break their ranks, just as Leonardo's machines did when the children flew over their ranks and dropped fire and iron?"

Before Kuan could speak, Leonardo said, "We cannot be sure that would work again, Master. Mustafà has no doubt warned his father and his armies. . . ."

"We lost all but one of the floating ships in the fighting," Kuan said. "The baggage carts that contained the linen were struck by cannons and caught fire."

"Besides that, Master of Worlds, the floating ships are utterly dependent on the winds," Leonardo said. "And even if the Turks' cannons had not destroyed them, we could not control—"

"Maestro, you do not have to protect Kuan from me," the Caliph said. "Better look to yourself and to your friend Sandro, who has been accused by the Turk."

"If you mean to follow your dream exactly, Master," Leonardo said, ignoring the Caliph's threat, "you could watch the engagement from Kuan's ship, which would be tethered to the ground. You could watch—"

"What preparations have you made on your own hook?"

"The flying machines and your angels are safe, high in the cliffs."

"With the women?" the Caliph asked.

There was nothing for Leonardo to do but be honest. "Yes." Then he said, "And I must also take responsibility for moving a portion of the cannons to a position where they can fire effectively upon the castle."

"How did you do that?" the Devatdar asked.

"We devised a tackle-and-pulley system to pull the cannons up the cliffs."

"We?" asked the Caliph.

"I did, Master."

"And Hilāl knew of this?"

"No."

"You removed siege engines from the battlefield?"

"Yes, Ruler of Worlds, for they could be of no use then, but they can be now." Leonardo was prepared for the fury of the Caliph.

"You must have had help in such an endeavor," Ka'it Bay said. "Who would take such initiative without my permission?"

Leonardo bowed his head, but did not reply.

"What is your plan?" the Caliph whispered.

"Angels will land on the northern ramparts of the castle, for they will not be heavily guarded."

"You would use children to do men's work?" asked the Devatdar.

"Once they shed their wings, they would not likely be noticed by the Turks," Leonardo said. "After all, they are . . . children."

"But these children fight like men," Kuan said. "I have seen for myself how quick and deadly they are . . . like the Persian women who fight beside their men."

"We will make our way to the gateway and open it to your soldiers," Leonardo said to the Caliph.

"We?"

"Yes, I will go to—"

"You will *not*," the Caliph said. After a beat he said, "Now, continue."

Leonardo regained his composure and said, "Once the gateway is open, our troops will take the castle. When we fire the Turks' own cannons on Mehmed's camp, that will be the signal for your army to attack."

"It is pitch-dark," Ka'it Bay said. "There is no moon to guide us. Do you think those who follow Allah are cats?"

"Lanterns have been prepared," Leonardo said. "The scythed cars will advance first, while my guns and cannons lay down a barrage ahead of them. The explosions of my missiles will give enough light to guide the carts and men. When you are upon them, then you can light the lanterns, for if we do not have control of the cannons in the castle, the Turks would not fire down on their king. But either way, Mehmed's troops will be in a cross fire of cannon, Master of Worlds. The Grand Turk will taste the same surprise he gave us this morning."

"What do you mean . . . 'either way'?" asked Ka'it Bay. "If you do not succeed in taking the castle, there will be no signal, and no reason for us to charge into their cannon fire."

"If the children are not successful, we will barrage their fortifications to destroy their cannons," Leonardo said. "From our new vantage, I believe we can destroy most of the cannons, for my machines can be aimed precisely. And we also have artillery in place to fire upon the Turks' camp below. The range will be limited, but deadly, I assure you."

"If you cannot get in by stealth and gain their fortifications, I will not risk my army."

"Would you not risk them now when you can surprise the enemy and vanquish them?" asked Leonardo. "You would be honored like Alexander; you would be the king who conquered the Turk."

"Kuan, did you know about Leonardo's plan?" the Caliph asked.

"No, Master, he did not ask my counsel." Yet after he spoke, he looked at Leonardo calmly, as if, indeed, he did know.

"And you?" he asked his Devatdar.

"Certainly not, Great King."

"What do you think of it?"

"Foolhardy," the Devatdar said. "Would you stake your army on the success of a few children flying his contraptions? And if the children failed, which they surely would, Leonardo would then immediately lay siege to the castle and have us invade their camp. In my experience a siege could take months, yet our brilliant and illustrious Florentine would tell you that he can take this heavily fortified castle in a night."

Leonardo was about to respond when the Caliph turned to Kuan. "And you, my counselor, do you agree with my Devatdar?"

"Yes," Kuan said. "My head tells me to agree with our astute counselor, but my heart yearns to follow Leonardo's course. It is so daring that it might end the war in a day. If such a plan succeeded, they would sing your praise for a thousand years. It would demonstrate your power, for what country would dare go against you? A king who flies through the air and routs his enemies in a day."

"Would you doubt that they would sing my praises without Leonardo's plan?"

Kuan bowed his head and said, "Of course not, Master."

The Caliph smiled. "If the plan failed, Kuan, would you be willing to die with your guards?"

"I would always be willing to die . . . for you, Master."

"You have not answered my question."

"No, Ruler of Worlds."

"Would you be willing to make sure that Leonardo meets the same fate as my soldiers if *he* fails?"

Kuan glanced at Leonardo and said to the Caliph, "If that is your wish, Master."

"Well, have you found words yet?" the Caliph asked the holy man.

"Allah planted your dream in your sleep. Follow it."

"That is no answer," Ka'it Bay said angrily.

"That is all Allah gives us." And the imam gave Leonardo a toothless

---

A regiment of a thousand of Kuan's best soldiers left the camp as surreptitiously as possible for an army on the move; they left in units of forty men before sunset. Kuan had taught his men to move as if they were invisible, as if they were without weight. They dressed in black to greet the oncoming night and covered their faces with mud, and Leonardo could smell the earthy blood of the battlefield on the soldiers, as if they were perspiring death itself.

The sky had turned gray and the very air seemed bluish, especially in the distance; soon the sky would turn dark blue, then shadow-black. They had to climb the precipitous rock crags and shelves and get into position while they could still see well. They took advantage of a steep stairway cut into the rocks on the far western side, but the stairs were badly damaged. Once, the stairs had extended around the crags, and villagers could climb them to reach the castle; but most of the stone treads and risers had been demolished by the Turks, who had no need to make the way easy for the villagers.

Kuan's army settled near the south side of the fortress, where they waited.

Above them were rock and castle; gauzy light emanated from the balistraria and from the ramparts of the fortress, and the starry heavens were so clear that one might imagine it was a winter night. To the west were ravines and rivers and wooded hills, but now it was dark country, bereft of contrast and demarcation. Below, in the Turks' camp, were ten thousand fires.

The darkness was not so dark; there was enough light—enough to see, and so the hours slowly passed.

The earth itself was asleep. The ragings of distant earthquakes and discomforts had subsided.

"You should not be here," Leonardo said to Sandro. He sat on a projecting crag between two of his cannons and looked down with his telescope at the Turks' camp. His cannons had clear lines of fire upon one portion of Mehmed's troops; if the cliffs had not been so sheer, Leonardo's cannons could have been positioned to devastate Mehmed's entire camp. His exploding shells could turn it into a bonfire. Enough cannons were also pointed at the fortress, which was but a little higher than Leonardo's cannon emplacements. The castle would burn. Please God that Niccolò would not be hit.

Please God that he is alive. . . .

"Would you have me be with the women every minute?" Sandro asked.

"They are too far away for you to reach them easily."

"They are more than well protected, I assure you. And why would you care?"

Leonardo shrugged.

"You are not with the troops. Are you going to man the cannons?"

"No, I will enter the castle with Kuan," Leonardo said.

"And Amerigo?"

"He is with the Caliph's guard."

Sandro seemed surprised. "I would have thought he would be with Kuan."

"I imagine Kuan is guaranteeing his safety," Leonardo said. "Amerigo will be well protected by the guards."

"Amerigo once bragged to me that lovers fighting together make the best fighters." Sandro paused, musing. "Something is not right."

"I think you are overly nervous," Leonardo said.

"Perhaps I am," Sandro said. "Are we still in agreement?"

"Only if I find Niccolò."

"If he were dead, Leonardo, would you still remain in this heathen place?"

"It was not so long ago that you seemed quite taken with the teachings of Allah, Little Bottle."

"I was in error. The Madonna called me home."

"Indeed," Leonardo said. "The Madonna?"

"In a dream that was as real as"—he waved his arm—"this, she sat beside me as I slept until I awakened . . . in my dream. She looks so very different than either of us imagined, Leonardo. She . . ." Sandro paused, as if he had said too much about her appearance. "She asked me if I intended on remaining an apostate, and she told me that my destiny was in Florence. She said that her own friar would find me there and teach me to do her will."

"I put little faith in dreams," Leonardo said. "It seems that you and the Caliph have quite a bit in common. He, too, allows his dreams to rule his life."

"And you have not dreamed, Leonardo? Didn't you see Tista, didn't you hear him calling you away from the flames in poor Ginevra's room?"

Leonardo did not answer. But Kuan, who had obviously been listening, stepped out of the darkness and said, "All you Florentines are dreamers. Even my own Amerigo."

Surprised and wary, Leonardo asked for Amerigo.

"He was upset that he could not embrace you, Leonardo," Kuan said.

"As was I," Leonardo said. "I looked for him, but . . ." Leonardo indicate there had been no time, that he couldn't find him.

"He asked me to give you this," Kuan said, smiling, which he did rarely; and he kissed Leonardo hard on the lips. "Amerigo told me of your plan." When neither Leonardo or Sandro responded, Kuan continued. "I know of your plan to escape."

"He gave me his solemn word," Sandro said in a whisper, as if he had blurted out their secret himself.

Leonardo felt a chill of fear, as if a cold drop of perspiration had run down his back. So Amerigo would be their undoing. But it didn't make sense for Kuan to tell them this now, unless . . .

"Ah, you think I would betray you?" Kuan asked.

"What do you want?" Leonardo asked. "You would not have waited this long—nor let us live this long—unless you had something to gain."

"You are correct, Leonardo," Kuan said, "but you have become far too cynical." He handed Leonardo a letter. Leonardo could feel the silky waxen seal. "This letter bears the Caliph's seal. It will ensure you safe passage through any of our lines, across any of our lands."

"The Caliph signed this?" Leonardo asked, dumbfounded.

"I signed it for him," Kuan said. "You should also be safe in the territories of the Turk." He looked at Sandro. "Isn't that right?"

Sandro did not reply.

"He retained a letter from Mehmed," Kuan said. "You see, Leonardo, he is not the idiot he would have us believe."

"I never believed him an idiot," Leonardo said, regaining his composure. "But why are you helping us?"

"Are you so sure yet that I am?"

Leonardo could make out Kuan's smile.

"My floating ship is hidden in a field below. The cliff that resembles a horseshoe points directly to it; you need only walk a straight line, although it is a considerable distance," Kuan said. Leonardo knew the cliff he referred to. "When you are ready, so will it be."

"I think we would be safer making our way on foot or by horse," Sandro said, obviously frightened at the idea of floating above the earth.

"I have to agree with Sandro," Leonardo said, bemused that Kuan had even suggested such an idea. "As I told the Caliph, we would be at the mercy of the winds; and we would become a spectacle. That is not the way to effect an escape."

"Dreams seem to have gained power these last few nights," Kuan said. "Even the Caliph's imam revealed a dream to the Caliph. He told him that if the Caliph was victorious, God would appear as fire in the sky, just as he had made the earth quake and growl. But if we are victorious and the sign fails to appear, then that will be an omen of death for the Caliph and Egypt."

"And the Caliph believed this?" Leonardo asked.

"Of course, Maestro, but he also understood that the omen could be effected by launching the floating ship. He even considered overcoming his fear." Kuan laughed. "But you could make a tether of iron and connect it to the ground and the Caliph would not sit in that machine. Not even if Mohammed appeared and told him to, which perhaps He did in the imam's dream." He paused. "So the Caliph expects to see the sign."

"Who does he expect will navigate this ship?" Leonardo asked.

Kuan smiled. "Either one or both of us, Maestro. But slaughtering the Turks is, of course, the first order of business. The Caliph is not so superstitious that he would take me away from my duties to fulfill an omen. So I delegate the job to you."

"The Caliph would allow me to navigate your machine, yet refuse to allow me to fly my own invention?"

"Even though he would not go near it himself, he considers *my* invention to be perfectly safe," Kuan said.

"Why are you doing this?" Sandro asked.

"Is it not obvious?"

"Is that why Amerigo is not with you now?" Leonardo asked.

"He begged me to help you, even at my own risk," Kuan said. "As is right, for one should love one's oldest friends the best. But I would not put temptation in his way, for he is homesick."

"Then he has traded his freedom for ours," Leonardo said.

"No, he is free to do as he wishes," Kuan said. "He made his decision to stay with me. But don't look so glum, my friends, for this will not be the last time you see either of us. We will make our way back to your lands, and then—who knows?—perhaps *I* will live there."

Leonardo and Sandro were silent. The wind whistled and rushed past the rocks like an army of men out of breath, and one could hear the faint susurration of thousands of voices, a faraway storm of sound, its tongues mixing into the language of Babel, a soft stirring, as if war and raised voices could not be made in the thickness of the night.

"It's time," Kuan said. "I will send the message to the angels."

"I will do it," Leonardo said.

"You are to watch for them with your magnifying tube, so we will know when they take flight."

Leonardo gave the telescope to Kuan.

"The Caliph told you that you were to remain with me," Kuan said. "You are not to fly in their contraptions."

Leonardo could not mistake the irony in Kuan's voice.

"And did the Caliph also tell you to write his letter and affix his seal?" Leonardo asked.

Leonardo found Mithqāl and five young eunuchs waiting nervously
for the messenger. They were dressed in Turkish garb, so they would not be
noticed once they were inside the fortress. A few guards sat listlessly waiting;
they would rejoin Kuan's army below after the planes were launched. Six
gliders were covered and tethered to the rocks, lest they be carried off or broken by the wind.

"What are you doing here, Leonardo?" asked Mithqāl.

Pleased to see the boy, Leonardo bowed and said, "I am your messenger. It is time." Hearing that, the guards and the angels began uncovering the
gliders, which had been rubbed with kohl or some similar substance until
they were black as the sky. Leonardo helped the eunuchs get the gliders
ready and then told one of them he would fly in his stead. The boy looked to
be thirteen or fourteen; he was gangly and surly and had the smooth, delicate face of a beautiful woman. He looked at Mithqāl and said, "I am to fly."

Mithqāl was still arguing when the boy drew his knife and rushed toward Leonardo. Leonardo was already in harness and fighting the wind
pulling upon the wings, for he thought he would be the first to jump from
the rocks. He pushed himself backward and one of the guards intercepted
the boy, flinging him over the cliff. Two other guards held on to Leonardo's
glider, so that it would not be carried away by the wind. The young eunuchs
chosen for this mission watched the death of their comrade with horror, and
one of the angels left his machine untethered and drew his knife, as if he
were the equal of the husky, battle-hardened guard. Leonardo was about to
intercede when Mithqāl said, "Leave him be." He looked at the guard as he
spoke. "We will kill him later. Do you doubt that?" The guard was smirk-
ing. "Do you doubt that we're your equals?"

"The wind is right," Leonardo said. "Mithqāl, will you take command
or shall I?" Leonardo would make sure that the guard was taken care of
later.

Mithqāl nodded to the angel farthest along on the cliff. With the help
of two guards he stepped into the glider, which he wore like a carapace, although in the air he would actually hang from it. Then he leaped into the
wind, descended quickly, and then arced away, as if a falling leaf had been
transformed into a bird. At long intervals the others jumped, each one to fly
to a different rampart of the fortress that stood like an empty shadow behind
them.

When only Mithqāl and Leonardo were left, Mithqāl nodded to
Leonardo. It was Leonardo's cue to jump. The guards stepped back to give
him room, but he said, "No, I will be last." He would not give the guards a
chance at Mithqāl, who had humiliated them.

Mithqāl jumped.

Leonardo followed, keeping the boy in sight.

He pushed himself into the darkness, his heart drubbing like a fist clenching his throat, and the wind felt wet on his face as it shrilled in his ears, and he fell, as he had fallen when Lorenzo the Magnificent and his father and all the people of Vinci had watched him—if he could only be there now, in the arms of his mother, if he could only feel the strong embrace of Achattabrigha, if he could only see the familiar towers and streets and bridges of Florence just once more—and he caught the updraft and sailed upward behind Mithqāl, close to the forbidding and dangerous cliff face, pulled upward toward the stars as if by God's inhalation; and he glided around the cliffs, allowed himself to fly a wide arc, higher than he should, but as he looked below, at the fires and shadows upon shadows, he felt suddenly ripped free and wanted to stop himself in midair and fall faster than thought.

Below him was Mithqāl, a bat flying through a cave roofed with stars.

Here was freedom, blessed freedom for an instant before death, which was the fortress walls below. He circled, following Mithqāl in his spiral toward the northwest bastion. The plan was for the boys to reach the southern barbican. Leonardo suspected that there were two portcullises with pulley chains behind the timber platform drawbridge, which he had seen extended for Turkish troops. The boys would have to be as good as their reputation with knives and stealth, for they had been taught by Kuan, who had in turn been taught by Hilāl.

The black air, it seemed, was full of ghosts.

The stone ramparts hurtled upward at Leonardo as he tried to land. He had great difficulty, as did Mithqāl, for the air was like breakers crashing around the castle, pushing and pulling like undertow, like riptides, and he slid along the stone, tearing the skin on his arms and legs, but he unfastened himself from the glider, slipped through it, and kicked it over the exterior edge: like a great bird it swooped, then crashed silently deep in the cliff crevasses below.

"Are you hurt?" Mithqāl asked in a whisper. He had been certainly more adept at landing than Leonardo; he, too, had pushed his wings over the edge, for they could not be allowed to fall into the hands of the Turks, who would then be alerted.

"No, I'm fine," Leonardo said, even as he tied a piece of cloth tightly around his leg, which was bleeding heavily. "Come on, we can take those stairs." They were part of the rampart itself. The sections of the walls were independent and connected by wooden bridges, which could be removed. Thus the enemy would be forced to expose themselves and take the stairs. "Where are the others?" Leonardo whispered.

Mithqāl shrugged. "Probably at the gateway already."

Leonardo had not seen them; nor had he seen their gliders. There were encampments and fires on the grounds of the inner ward; this place was larger than Leonardo had imagined. Smoke from the fires burned his eyes; there were many below, and several on the parapets. Light poured from windows and loopholes, and shadows skittered like animals. The cannon emplacements were well guarded, and curious as Leonardo was, he did not pause on the stairway near them, but kept low and crept without a breath past them. Rather than kill him, they waited for a Turk to move from the stairs where he seemed to be doing nothing more than pondering the heavens. Below them, soldiers clustered in groups; they drank and laughed and told dirty stories, the eternal fare of the warrior.

Leonardo and Mithqāl made their way to the southwest barbican, keeping to the shadows with Mithqāl on the outside, for, dressed as he was, he would be less noticeable than Leonardo. They passed the lime-washed stone walls of the great hall, which bordered on apartments: these were opposite the soldiers' barracks. Leonardo wished to stop as they passed an ancient tower that had not been rebuilt. It was the chapel tower, and if Niccolò was alive, if Niccolò was here, he would be in that tower, in the dungeon below ground. Ahead was the gatehouse, its arches black and deep in shadow. But the iron-capped portcullis was up and the iron-strapped wooden doors were open and Kuan's troops were pouring in like black smoke. Although he could not see any corpses in the shadowed darkness, Leonardo could smell the feces of freshly killed men. They had done it. The children, these eunuch assassins, these babies, had sneaked and cut and talked their way through; and now Kuan's guards stormed the walls from the inside and set fire to the barracks, killing every Turk they could find in a silent bloodlust that Leonardo found more terrible than any fighting and killing and slaughter that he had yet witnessed.

Leonardo saw Kuan, who invited him to join the artillerymen already deployed on the ramparts. When Leonardo refused, Kuan ordered his own guards to protect him as he searched for Niccolò; and Mithqāl insisted on staying with him. They found their way into the tower, and the guards rushed ahead, slashing at every shadow, cutting down anyone in their way, men and women alike.

The castle trembled with the first boom of cannons firing on the Turks' encampment, and even here in the damp darkness, cut only by torchlight, Leonardo could imagine his scythed cars moving across the field . . . Ka'it Bay's army in the darkness behind them. In his mind's eye he could see them lighting their lanterns and surrounding Mehmed's camp, which was exploding as if the very ground had opened up to swallow all Turks. Every time one of the Turks' cannons was fired, Leonardo felt it as well as heard it, as if he were exploding with every shot.

They followed steps to the basement, where they found a trapdoor in the floor. They climbed down into the dungeon, which was lit by narrow openings in the thick walls near the ceiling. Gray swords of light cut into the blackness ahead of them as they walked through empty dirt-floored rooms the size of corridors. Curiously, all the doors were open. As they walked deeper into the dungeons—the guards walking ahead with torches snapping and cracking as if the flames themselves were angry—Leonardo smelled rotting flesh. He gagged as they approached the last room, which was little more than a large hole into which bodies in various states of deterioration were thrown. The acrid odor of lime, which had been thrown upon the corpses like dirt, burned his nose.

The guards mumbled incantations and turned heel in fear.

"Leave us a torch," Leonardo said. He spoke in hardly more than a whisper, for he had lost hope. He was certain that here was where Niccolò's life had ended, in a trash bin of rotting flesh.

The guards gave Leonardo and Mithqāl torches and disappeared.

"Ach, why didn't the Turks burn them?" Mithqāl said, holding his torch high and looking at the corpses.

"I suspect these were to be gifts for the Caliph," Leonardo said. "Do you recognize any of them?"

Mithqāl shook his head.

Leonardo forced himself to search through the corpses for Niccolò.

"Master, you will die if you touch them," Mithqāl said. "Disease . . . plague."

"Then I will die, little soldier," Leonardo said.

To his great relief, he did not find Niccolò in the ruins of bone and flesh.

Nor did he find him anywhere else in the castle. . . .

32

The Path of Remembrance

By ascending through the airs, man changes truly.

—Ludolph von Sudheim

Behold now the hope and desire of going back to one's own country or returning to primal chaos, like that of the moth to the light . . .

—Leonardo da Vinci

eonardo looked over the battlements at the battlefield below. The lanterns and torches seemed to cast a spell, as if the dim lowing of battle—the cries and grunts and deathgasps—was the faraway cheering of crowds at festival. Sky and land blended in darkness, punctuated by stars above and lantern below. The slaughter was complete. The cannons had stopped firing. Men were fighting hand to hand. Mehmed's defeat was absolute. Dawn would reveal the truth: a hundred thousand men dead . . . too much rot for all the carrion birds in Persia, and Niccolò was not here.

But if he was on the battlefield with Mehmed or Mustafà, and surely he was, then he was dead—dead and buried under an autumn leaf-fall of Turks, soon to be burned as anonymously as any beggar who fell by the way. Leonardo felt rooted to the spot, frozen, as if caught in a lucid dream in which he could play out different consequences; and he saw himself making his way down the cliff in less time than it would take in reality, somehow crushing time to make it work for him this one time, this one and only time, but . . .

He would go down, he would face it, he had faced it, he had death all over him, had dug through those men and women and children in the dungeon; and as he thought about it, he should have burned them, let their souls mingle with the fire, let the Jinn take them up through the chimney, for there was a chimney, but he couldn't, just as he couldn't move now; of course, he could jump, and for an instant, an eternity, he would float in the darkness, in air, as if he had wings, as if he were his own flying machine, then to descend, the wind whistling in his ears, the songs of children, the songs of . . .

And then he was running across ramparts and bulwarks, down stairs, under the arches of the gatehouse, through one portcullis, then another, and over the timber platform of the drawbridge onto the ramp carved into cliff, over the stepped path, which would lead him down, dangerously in the darkness, to the pit of the horseshoe-shaped cliff, where Sandro would be waiting.

"Wait," shouted Mithqāl in a voice that sounded to Leonardo like his own thoughts, like dreambabble running, running, "Waitwaitwaitwait" in Arabic *"Wakkaf . . . afafafafaf,"* music without lyric, thought without reason, and then Mithqāl pulled on Leonardo's arm, and as if jolted out of sleep, he took notice of the boy. "Where are you going, Maestro?" Mithqāl asked. "I looked everywhere for you, and then when I find you . . . you walk and then run away."

"Kuan will take care of you," Leonardo said. "Find him, he will protect you."

"I don't need his protection," Mithqāl said. "Leonardo, you are sick, I told you not to touch those corpses."

"Find Kuan," Leonardo said softly, then felt his way down the cut stairs, careful of his footing but slipping nevertheless. "He will be with the Caliph."

"I wish to be with you."

"Your friend wished to fly his machine and was thrown over. Is *that* what you wish?" Leonardo asked.

"If you would do that, then that is what I wish."

"I cannot take you to where I'm going."

"Are you leaving this place?"

"Yes . . . no."

"Are you looking for Niccolò?"

"No," Leonardo said, and that caught him, as if his own words could teach him what his soul was seeking. But he *was* looking for Niccolò.

"Then why can't I come?"

"Would you leave this land? Would you leave your Caliph?"

"My master Hilāl is dead," the boy said. "It will go badly for the others like me, of that I'm sure. Yes, Maestro, I would leave this place . . . forever."

"Well, I am not leaving," Leonardo said.

"Then I will stay, too."

What did it matter now? Leonardo thought as he climbed down, nearing the foot of the cliff where he would find Sandro, where he would

Leave or tell him good-bye?

But Sandro was not there.

———•———

Leonardo saw the glow of a fire in the distance. This place was indeed isolated, for when he reached the field, which was concealed by trees on all sides, a natural *palazzo* of soil and bole and holly, he saw the fire raging. Beside it were the accoutrements for the balloon and the balloon itself, a field of dyed linen within the field of wild olive and laurustinus. Slaves loitered, waiting for the command to raise the balloon. And there, standing together a distance from the slaves, were Sandro and three other men.

One of them was Amerigo. The other was an older man Leonardo had never seen before, yet he wore the clothes and hat of an Italian merchant.

And beside them was Niccolò Machiavelli.

Flames lit their faces, made their features dance, as if substance were smoke and all men were Jinn.

"Leonardo," Amerigo said, running to greet him. "Look who we have found."

Leonardo embraced Niccolò, who seemed taller, older, and certainly more reserved . . . as he had been a year ago when Leonardo had first taken responsibility for him. When Leonardo released him, he bowed and said, "Maestro, I would like you to meet Messer Giovan Maria Angiolello, ambassador from Venice to the empire of the Turks."

Leonardo bowed politely, then turned to Niccolò and asked, "And how did you come to be here, Nicco?"

"Niccolò," he said, correcting Leonardo.

"Your son saved my life," said the ambassador to Leonardo. The Venetian was a dark, handsome man. "The Grand Turk rode away without us, leaving us without even a horse, leaving us to face"—and he shuddered when he said it—"the Mamluks, who were butchering everyone in their path."

"Niccolò talked one of the Caliph's officers into bringing them to the Caliph himself," Amerigo said. "Kuan intercepted them and brought them to me. I brought them both here, for Niccolò would not leave his friend."

"We were going to take a chance and submit to the Caliph's generosity," Niccolò said. "Perhaps he would have given us our lives, perhaps not. Perhaps he would have tortured Messer Giovan. Perhaps not. But once we found Amerigo, I could not take the chance to leave him, and Kuan was most generous."

Leonardo could only stand and listen . . . and feel the numbing shock of seeing the object of his desire and discovering a stranger. As if the earth itself were but an extension of Leonardo, the ground shivered slightly but nauseatingly, and a distant rumbling could be heard.

———

And so they floated upward from darkness into dawn, Leonardo, Sandro, Niccolò and his friend, and Mithqāl, all standing on the wicker base, each one away from the other for balance. Leonardo fed the brazier, and they rose into the still, humid air, into the grayness above the cliffs, above the castle, and he looked at the battlefield, at the pyramids and avenues of corpses, at the still-smoking entrenchments, and he looked at Niccolò, who was polite and distant and empty. Indeed, Niccolò had learned well from kings and ambassadors, but most of all from Leonardo, and in a terrible revelation, Leonardo imagined that he and Niccolò were now one and the same, able to speak to each other but no longer to communicate. Yes, he had taught Niccolò, taught him by losing him. The boy had become a man, and the man was dead.

As dead as those below.

Leonardo felt for his notepad, which hung against his leg. He should fling it over the edge, fling it into the mountains, but he held it tight nevertheless, for he could not yet part with it.

Even if the carnage below was his fault alone.

Surely he, and not Mithqāl, was the angel of death, for wasn't everyone dead around him? Weren't the piles of corpses created with his cannons and exploding shells and guns and scythes as surely as with his pen?

Had he not created Niccolò, who now examined everything without the passion of a child?

Mithqāl took his hand, as Niccolò once had—Mithqāl, who understood death and killing and emptiness.

Death reaching out to death, to Leonardo, who gazed inward, into his memory, into the great edifice that was his memory cathedral, which seemed to hang weightless and transparent in the air before him like the very constellations. And Leonardo remembered . . . he remembered what St. Augustine called the three times: the present of things past, the present of things present, and the present of things future: all were rooms and galleries, a labyrinth of chapels and apsidals, the stuff of memory.

As he had so many times before, Leonardo entered the cathedral.

Once again he stood before the three-headed demiurge, the bronzen statue that was his father, Toscanelli, and Ginevra; but Ginevra's head turned away from him, lest he become overwhelmed with grief. Her heavy-lidded eyes were closed, as if in death; but the heads of Toscanelli and his father gazed at him, and Toscanelli smiled, as if to welcome him. Then the demiurge stood aside and gestured toward the distant dark rooms and galleries and shadowy corridors of the future, which now seemed to glow as if illuminated through stained glass. Toscanelli nodded, giving him leave, and Leonardo did not pause as he passed the well-lit rooms of his recent past, through the rooms of caliphs and kings, through love and fear, through the agonies of thousands; and he knew better than to pause just now in Florence, where Ginevra lived untouched in memory. He followed her example and averted his eyes, lest he peer into her bedroom, where she was killed, and become caught—Toscanelli had warned him of the dangers of the past. He passed murders and conspiracies; he passed musings and paintings and frescoes, inventions and enthusiasms; and he felt the stabbings of loss and loneliness as he passed Simonetta, who once again mistook him for an angel as she gazed past his face and into the perfect rose of heaven.

He passed through aisles divided into vaulted squares . . . he passed through bronze doors that led into baptisteries of Vinci, where he glimpsed his mother, Caterina, and his stepfather, Achattabrigha. He could feel the rough working hands of Achattabrigha, smell the perfumes of garlic and stew that suffused his mother's clothes, see and feel and smell the grottoes and woods he had discovered as a child. But he moved quickly now through darkening squares and corridors and chapels and choirs, and then into the stained-glass illumination of St. Augustine's present of things future. Here in the gentle, suffusing light of contemplation he looked into a room with whitewashed walls streaked with soot; wan light filtered through high, narrow windows, refracted through the bull's-eye center panes as if they were poorly constructed prisms. Books and papers and rolled sheets were stacked along the walls and on long desks; and scattered on the tables and on the floor as well were maps and papers and instruments and lenses.

An old man sat before a small fire and dropped the pages of one of his most precious notebooks into the orange-streaked flames. The fire sizzled as the green, unseasoned wood perspired drops that evaporated in the heat with a snap; and the pages curled like flowers closing, then blackened as they burst into flame.

As Leonardo looked away from the shadow that would one day be himself, darkness began to fill the empty rooms and corridors and galleries of his memory cathedral.

And as the Caliph's portent rose toward the twisting dawn-colored clouds and moved miraculously to the west, as distant earthquakes destroyed distant towns; and the earth shivered as if with cold, Leonardo realized that all of this—all that had happened in these foreign lands—must be relegated to dream and nightmare. He was content to lock these doors to the world, as if these adventures had never happened. Although he still held tightly to his notebook, he knew it would someday be consigned to the flames. But he could be content for the moment, for he had glimpsed his greatest work, created out of love and pleasure and agony, out of guilt and loneliness and genius and darkness.

He had glimpsed his memory cathedral entire.

He had seen the three times.

He could lock the doors to the world.

Afterword

Leonardo exists as a legend, a myth, a puzzle, with various historians and schools of historians claiming one piece or another. Yet we don't really have a coherent picture of him. History, especially the history of great personages, is a kind of collective mythmaking, an extrapolation of the known into narrative. I set my story between the cracks of known history to explore Leonardo's character and the moral ramifications of his brilliant ideas and inventions.

I began with Leonardo's own science and invention to create a fictive dream in which he eventually accomplishes his goal of flight. We know that Leonardo invented workable submarines, machine guns, grenades, parachutes, and even tanks. (Much of this is explicitly detailed in the famous letter he wrote to Ludovico Sforza, ruler of Milan.) We know that Leonardo was fascinated with flight from the time he was a child, as witnessed by his dream of the Great Bird. Leonardo was an acute and astute observer, and he studied birds for some twenty-five years (we have his notes in Manuscript B, begun in 1488, and his manuscript "On the Flight of Birds," written sometime around 1505). It was said that he would buy caged birds from vendors in the street only to let them fly, to give them their freedom. Actually, it was to study them. Leonardo wrote that "the genius of man may make various inventions, encompassing with various instruments one and the same end; but it will never discover a more beautiful, a more economical, or a more direct one than nature's, since in her inventions nothing is wanting and nothing is superfluous."

It is because of this reasoning—and a few other errors of observation—that he was loath to look for another mode of flight, to consider the fixed-wing. He literally wanted to fly like a bird, and he was fascinated with the concept of ornithopters until his last years (although, of course, he did make drawings of a machine that is the forerunner of the helicopter). But he had, in fact, done a series of sketches, which can be found in the *Codex Atlanticus,* that experts agree to be the first European conception of gliding flight.

So he could have gone in the direction of fixed-wing flight to create a workable glider, as Lawrence Hargrave and others did in later years. Yet it should be noted that making that imaginative leap to the idea of a fixed wing was as difficult for Lawrence Hargrave in 1890 as it was for Leonardo da Vinci in my fictional universe of fifteenth-century Florence.

To bring my vision to life, I nudged history a bit. By extrapolating, by using what Leonardo and his contemporaries knew, I had him come naturally to the idea of the fixed-wing aircraft.

I also nudged history by aging Niccolò Machiavelli a bit and making him Leonardo's apprentice (in later years they did really know each other). I have no doubt that many readers will have discovered other historical "nudges."

I took a compelling minority view concerning Leonardo's sexuality. The popular belief that Leonardo was a homosexual is heavily influenced by Sigmund Freud's work on his psychosexuality, specifically *Leonardo da Vinci and a Memory of His Childhood.* In that work, Freud was projecting his own mind-set upon Leonardo. The book begins with Leonardo's famous dream of the great bird, in which a hawk swoops out of the sky and slaps him upon the face with its tail. (There is, of course, the obvious connection of this, his first remembered dream, and his lifelong fascination and preoccupation with flight.) But Freud read Leonardo's notes in translation, not a very good translation that confused the word "kite" (i.e., a hawk) with vulture. Freud went on to detail how the vulture stood for Mut, the Egyptian mother goddess, a feminine symbol, and the tail was symbolic of the nipple, but in fact kite, *nibbio* in Italian, was a masculine symbol, like a hawk or an eagle. Furthermore, Freud did not have access to Leonardo's *Codex Trivulzianus,* which contains copious word lists that illuminate some of the dark country of Da Vinci's unconscious.

Raymond S. Stites, author of a psychoanalytic study, *The Sublimations of Leonardo da Vinci,* writes that "Leonardo had availed himself of the technique Freud himself had developed for revealing unhealthy complexes, and his [Freud's] diagnosis lacking this important evidence, is obviously faulty." After a rigorous examination of Leonardo's Codex Trivulzianus, Stites concludes that "Leonardo, from all the evidence, was a full-blooded man with normal heterosexual desires."